The
MX Book
of
New
Sherlock
Holmes
Stories

Part XLVII
Occupants of the
Canonical Realm
(1890-1898)

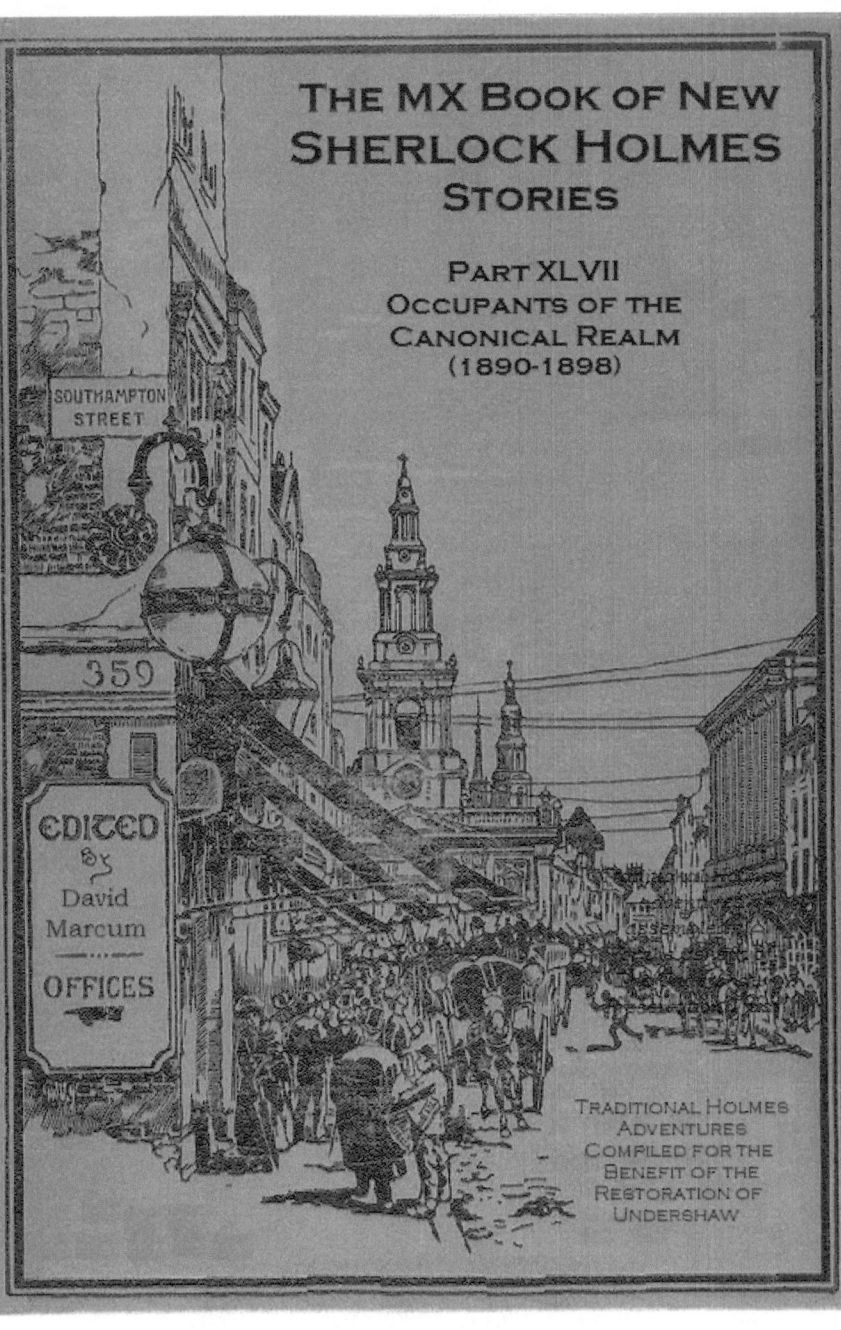

THE MX BOOK OF NEW SHERLOCK HOLMES STORIES

PART XLVII
OCCUPANTS OF THE CANONICAL REALM
(1890-1898)

SOUTHAMPTON STREET

359

EDITED BY
David
Marcum

OFFICES

TRADITIONAL HOLMES
ADVENTURES
COMPILED FOR THE
BENEFIT OF THE
RESTORATION OF
UNDERSHAW

ISBN Hardback 978-1-80424-563-7
ISBN Paperback 978-1-80424-564-4
AUK ePub ISBN 978-1-80424-565-1
AUK PDF ISBN 978-1-80424-566-8

Published in the UK by
MX Publishing
335 Princess Park Manor, Royal Drive,
London, N11 3GX
www.mxpublishing.co.uk

David Marcum can be reached at:
thepapersofsherlockholmes@gmail.com

Cover design by Brian Belanger
www.belangerbooks.com and *www.redbubble.com/people/zhahadun*

Internal Illustrations by Sidney Paget

CONTENTS

Forewords

Adventures

(Continued on the next page . . .)

(Continued on the next page . . .)

(Continued on the next page . . .)

**These additional Sherlock Holmes adventures
can be found in the previous volumes of**
The MX Book of New Sherlock Holmes Stories

(Continued on the next page . . . .)

(Continued on the next page . . . .)

PART V – Christmas Adventures

(Continued on the next page . . . .)

PART VI – 2017 Annual

(Continued on the next page . . . .)

The Unwelcome Client – Keith Hann
The Tempest of Lyme – David Ruffle
The Problem of the Holy Oil – David Marcum
A Scandal in Serbia – Thomas A. Turley
The Curious Case of Mr. Marconi – Jan Edwards
Mr. Holmes and Dr. Watson Learn to Fly – C. Edward Davis
Die Weisse Frau – Tim Symonds
A Case of Mistaken Identity – Daniel D. Victor

PART VII – Eliminate the Impossible: 1880-1891
Foreword – Lee Child
Foreword – Rand B. Lee
Foreword – Michael Cox
Foreword – Roger Johnson
Foreword – Melissa Farnham
Foreword – David Marcum
No Ghosts Need Apply (A Poem) – Jacquelynn Morris
The Melancholy Methodist – Mark Mower
The Curious Case of the Sweated Horse – Jan Edwards
The Adventure of the Second William Wilson – Daniel D. Victor
The Adventure of the Marchindale Stiletto – James Lovegrove
The Case of the Cursed Clock – Gayle Lange Puhl
The Tranquility of the Morning – Mike Hogan
A Ghost from Christmas Past – Thomas A. Turley
The Blank Photograph – James Moffett
The Adventure of A Rat. – Adrian Middleton
The Adventure of Vanaprastha – Hugh Ashton
The Ghost of Lincoln – Geri Schear
The Manor House Ghost – S. Subramanian
The Case of the Unquiet Grave – John Hall
The Adventure of the Mortal Combat – Jayantika Ganguly
The Last Encore of Quentin Carol – S.F. Bennett
The Case of the Petty Curses – Steven Philip Jones
The Tuttman Gallery – Jim French
The Second Life of Jabez Salt – John Linwood Grant
The Mystery of the Scarab Earrings – Thomas Fortenberry
The Adventure of the Haunted Room – Mike Chinn
The Pharaoh's Curse – Robert V. Stapleton
The Vampire of the Lyceum – Charles Veley and Anna Elliott
The Adventure of the Mind's Eye – Shane Simmons

PART VIII – Eliminate the Impossible: 1892-1905
Foreword – Lee Child
Foreword – Rand B. Lee
Foreword – Michael Cox
Foreword – Roger Johnson
Foreword – Melissa Farnham

(Continued on the next page . . . .)

Part IX – 2018 Annual (1879-1895)

(Continued on the next page . . . .)

(Continued on the next page . . . .)

(Continued on the next page . . . .)

PART XIV: 2019 Annual (1891 -1897)

(Continued on the next page . . . .)

The Poisoned Regiment – Carl Heifetz
The Case of the Persecuted Poacher – Gayle Lange Puhl
It's Time – Harry DeMaio
The Case of the Fourpenny Coffin – I.A. Watson
The Horror in King Street – Thomas A. Burns, Jr.

PART XV: 2019 Annual (1898-1917)

Foreword – Will Thomas
Foreword – Roger Johnson
Foreword – Melissa Grigsby
Foreword – Steve Emecz
Foreword – David Marcum
Two Poems – Christopher James
The Whitechapel Butcher – Mark Mower
The Incomparable Miss Incognita – Thomas Fortenberry
The Adventure of the Twofold Purpose – Robert Perret
The Adventure of the Green Gifts – Tracy J. Revels
The Turk's Head – Robert Stapleton
A Ghost in the Mirror – Peter Coe Verbica
The Mysterious Mr. Rim – Maurice Barkley
The Adventure of the Fatal Jewel-Box – Edwin A. Enstrom
Mass Murder – William Todd
The Notable Musician – Roger Riccard
The Devil's Painting – Kelvin I. Jones
The Adventure of the Silent Sister – Arthur Hall
A Skeleton's Sorry Story – Jack Grochot
An Actor and a Rare One – David Marcum
The Silver Bullet – Dick Gillman
The Adventure at Throne of Gilt – Will Murray
"The Boy Who Would Be King – Dick Gillman
The Case of the Seventeenth Monk – Tim Symonds
Alas, Poor Will – Mike Hogan
The Case of the Haunted Chateau – Leslie Charteris and Denis Green
          (Introduction by Ian Dickerson)
The Adventure of the Weeping Stone – Nick Cardillo
The Adventure of the Three Telegrams – Darryl Webber

Part XVI – Whatever Remains . . . Must Be the Truth (1881-1890)

Foreword – Kareem Abdul-Jabbar
Foreword – Roger Johnson
Foreword – Steve Emecz
Foreword – David Marcum
The Hound of the Baskervilles (Retold) (*A Poem*) – Josh Pachter
The Wylington Lake Monster – Derrick Belanger
The *Juju* Men of Richmond – Mark Sohn

(Continued on the next page . . . .)

Part XVII – Whatever Remains . . . Must Be the Truth (1891-1898)

Part XVIII – Whatever Remains . . . Must Be the Truth (1899-1925)

(Continued on the next page . . . .)

Part XIX: 2020 Annual (1882-1890)

(Continued on the next page . . . .)

The Adventure of the Matched Set – Peter Coe Verbica
When the Prince First Dined at the Diogenes Club – Sean M. Wright
The Sweetenbury Safe Affair – Tim Gambrell

Part XX: 2020 Annual (1891-1897)
Foreword – John Lescroart
Foreword – Roger Johnson
Foreword – Lizzy Butler
Foreword – Steve Emecz
Foreword – David Marcum
The Sibling (*A Poem*) – Jacquelynn Morris
Blood and Gunpowder – Thomas A. Burns, Jr.
The Atelier of Death – Harry DeMaio
The Adventure of the Beauty Trap – Tracy Revels
A Case of Unfinished Business – Steven Philip Jones
The Case of the S.S. Bokhara – Mark Mower
The Adventure of the American Opera Singer – Deanna Baran
The Keadby Cross – David Marcum
The Adventure at Dead Man's Hole – Stephen Herczeg
The Elusive Mr. Chester – Arthur Hall
The Adventure of Old Black Duffel – Will Murray
The Blood-Spattered Bridge – Gayle Lange Puhl
The Tomorrow Man – S.F. Bennett
The Sweet Science of Bruising – Kevin P. Thornton
The Mystery of Sherlock Holmes – Christopher Todd
The Elusive Mr. Phillimore – Matthew J. Elliott
The Murders in the Maharajah's Railway Carriage – Charles Veley and Anna Elliott
The Ransomed Miracle – I.A. Watson
The Adventure of the Unkind Turn – Robert Perret
The Perplexing X'ing – Sonia Fetherston
The Case of the Short-Sighted Clown – Susan Knight

Part XXI: 2020 Annual (1898-1923)
Foreword – John Lescroart
Foreword – Roger Johnson
Foreword – Lizzy Butler
Foreword – Steve Emecz
Foreword – David Marcum
The Case of the Missing Rhyme (*A Poem*) – Joseph W. Svec III
The Problem of the St. Francis Parish Robbery – R.K. Radek
The Adventure of the Grand Vizier – Arthur Hall
The Mummy's Curse – DJ Tyrer
The Fractured Freemason of Fitzrovia – David L. Leal
The Bleeding Heart – Paula Hammond
The Secret Admirer – Jayantika Ganguly

(Continued on the next page . . . .)

Part XXII: Some More Untold Cases (1877-1887)

(Continued on the next page . . . .)

(Continued on the next page . . . .)

Part XXV: 2021 Annual (1881-1888)

(Continued on the next page . . . .)

(Continued on the next page . . . .)

Part XXVIII: More Christmas Adventures (1869-1888)

(Continued on the next page . . . .)

Part XXIX: More Christmas Adventures (1889-1896)

Part XXX: More Christmas Adventures (1897-1928)

(Continued on the next page . . . .)

The Adventure of the Chained Phantom – J.S. Rowlinson
Santa's Little Elves – Kevin Thornton
The Case of the Holly-Sprig Pudding – Naching T. Kassa
The Canterbury Manifesto – David Marcum
The Case of the Disappearing Beaune – J. Lawrence Matthews
A Price Above Rubies – Jane Rubino
The Intrigue of the Red Christmas – Shane Simmons
The Bitter Gravestones – Chris Chan
The Midnight Mass Murder – Paul Hiscock

Part XXXI: 2022 Annual (1875-1887)
Foreword – Jeffrey Hatcher
Foreword – Roger Johnson
Foreword – Steve Emecz
Foreword – Emma West
Foreword – David Marcum
The Nemesis of Sherlock Holmes (A Poem) – Kelvin I. Jones
The Unsettling Incident of the History Professor's Wife – Sean M. Wright
The Princess Alice Tragedy – John Lawrence
The Adventure of the Amorous Balloonist – I.A. Watson
The Pilkington Case – Kevin Patrick McCann
The Adventure of the Disappointed Lover – Arthur Hall
The Case of the Impressionist Painting – Tim Symonds
The Adventure of the Old Explorer – Tracy J. Revels
Dr. Watson's Dilemma – Susan Knight
The Colonial Exhibition – Hal Glatzer
The Adventure of the Drunken Teetotaler – Thomas A. Burns, Jr.
The Curse of Hollyhock House – Geri Schear
The Sethian Messiah – David Marcum
Dead Man's Hand – Robert Stapleton
The Case of the Wary Maid – Gordon Linzner
The Adventure of the Alexandrian Scroll – David MacGregor
The Case of the Woman at Margate – Terry Golledge
A Question of Innocence – DJ Tyrer
The Grosvenor Square Furniture Van – Terry Golledge
The Adventure of the Veiled Man – Tracy J. Revels
The Disappearance of Dr. Markey – Stephen Herczeg
The Case of the Irish Demonstration – Dan Rowley

Part XXXII: 2022 Annual (1888-1895)
Foreword – Jeffrey Hatcher
Foreword – Roger Johnson
Foreword – Steve Emecz

(Continued on the next page . . . .)

Part XXXIII: 2022 Annual (1896-1919)

(Continued on the next page . . . .)

(Continued on the next page . . . .)

Part XXXVI: "However Improbable . . . ." (1897-1919)

(Continued on the next page . . . .)

(Continued on the next page . . . .)

(Continued on the next page . . . .)

Part XLI: Further Untold Cases (1877-1892)

Part XLII: Further Untold Cases (1894-1922)

(Continued on the next page . . . .)

Part XLIII: 2024 Annual (1874-1888)

(Continued on the next page . . . .)

(Continued on the next page . . . .)

The following contributors appear in these companion volumes:
Part XLVI – Occupants of the Canonical Realm (1861-1889)
Part XLVIII – Occupants of the Canonical Realm (1899-1924)

The MX Book of New Sherlock Holmes Stories
Occupants of the Canonical Realm
Parts XLVI, XLVII, and XLVIII

are dedicated to

Kelvin Jones *and* David Stuart Davies

Both of these long-time Friends of the MX Anthologies
passed as these volumes were being prepared.
The world – Sherlockian and otherwise – will miss them both greatly.

R.I.P.

Editor's Foreword:

More are Still in the Works
by David Marcum

In his essay, "Who Shall Ever Forget?", * Ellery Queen related his first encounter with Sherlock Holmes. At age twelve – in 1917, since Ellery was born in 1905 – the young future Great Detective was in bed with his annual earache and, as a distraction, his grandmother brought him a copy of *The Adventures of Sherlock Holmes* The first story wasn't too inspiring for a lad of that age – "A Scandal in Bohemia", with an illustration labeled "*The gentleman in the pew handed it up to her . . .*" – but the other tales fired his imagination. He wrote that he finished the book that day, passed the night without any sleep while thinking of Holmes – "*All the Queen's horses and all the Queen's men couldn't put Ellery together again.*" – and early the next morning, before the city had arisen, he bundled himself up, a wad of stained cotton protruding from his ear, and set forth to visit the public library, where he expected to find shelves upon shelves – entire rooms and wings – devoted to further adventures of Mr. Sherlock Holmes.

Alas, after waiting hours for the place to open, sitting huddled on the cold stone front steps, he discovered that such was not the case. In the entire library, he found just three previous volumes, *A Study in Scarlet*, *The Memoirs of Sherlock Holmes*, and *The Hound of the Baskervilles*. I was about that age, a couple of full generations later, when I discovered Sherlock Holmes, and I completely shared his disappointment – because even though there were a few more Holmes adventures available by then, there weren't shelves upon shelves and entire rooms and wings of them.

I was ten in 1975 when I first picked up an abridged copy of *The Adventures*, and then *The Return* – unknowingly skipping "The Final Problem" and reading "The Empty House" first, thus (*Spoiler alert!*) learning that Holmes didn't die at Reichenbach, and how he survived. (NOTE: *Always always always* read chronologically if possible.) I quickly devoured the rest of The Canon, acquiring the remaining books in the form of Berkeley paperbacks with excellent cover paintings by Guy Deel, and then I purchased the flawed Doubleday edition (with the wrong versions of "The Resident Patient" and "The Cardboard Box") – my first great Sherlockian purchase, setting me back a whole ten dollars! (My dad gave me a big months-ahead advance on my fifty-cent-per-week allowance, and then he even drove me to the bookstore that night after supper. I remember riding home with that big book perched carefully on my lap, almost afraid to start reading it because it was so new and perfect. It was the first major monetary loan of my life, and very much worth it.)

As I was reading the Canonical sixty stories, I was unknowingly treading closer and closer to that Great Grimpen Mire where all new Sherlockians eventually find themselves: *I've read them all! Now what?*

Of course, I re-read the Canonical stories. And I was very grateful a few months later when my parents, ordering from a catalog of remaindered books that regularly arrived at our house, bought three Holmes-related volumes as a Christmas gift: *Holmes of the Movies* by David Stuart Davies, *The Sherlock Holmes Scrapbook* as edited by Peter Haining, and a true game-changer, *Sherlock Holmes of Baker Street* by William S. Baring-Gould.

I actually read Baring-Gould's brilliant biography before I'd finished all of the Canonical stories. I don't remember feeling that any of the narratives were spoiled by meeting them early that way. Instead, it presented Holmes from a different perspective that raised him in my mind to an even higher level. At that young age, I observed and understood that Holmes and Watson were historical figures existing in a fixed place in time. I saw them both young and old, and not presented and locked into some fixed middle age. I was exposed to the idea of *chronology*, wherein the adventures occurred at specific times, influencing and being influenced by what came before and after. And I saw that there was more to the *entire lives* of Holmes and Watson than the pitifully few sixty Canonical tales.

The Holmes Canon references approximately 140 *Untold Cases* besides the published adventures – from the famed Giant Rat of Sumatra to the oft-forgotten case where Holmes caught a coiner by the zinc and copper filings in the seam of his cuff. But even these Canonical hints of other cases weren't enough. Fortunately, I was primed and hungry for more post-Canonical adventures when I picked Nicholas Meyer's *The Seven-Per-Cent Solution* (1974) at a school Reading-is-Fundamental (RIF) event, and not long after, when I bought the next related volume, *The West End Horror* (1976). *The Seven-Per-Cent Solution* touched the flame to ignite the current modern Sherlockian Golden Age that we all enjoy now, and the fire has only burned hotter and hotter over the subsequent decades . . . but it wasn't an inferno at first.

The Seven-Per-Cent Solution showed that, for members of the starving public – Like me! – additional Watsonian manuscripts were out there in the world, waiting to be found and shared, beyond those too-few "official" titles that had crossed the First Literary Agent's desk. One simply had to put forth enough effort to excavate these adventures and publish them. They initially appeared in dribs and drabs – *Enter the Lion* (1979) by Sean Wright and Michael Hodel, for instance, and *Hellbirds* and

2

The Earthquake Machine by Nick Utechen and Austin Mitchelson – but at least they did appear. And I was lucky enough and diligent enough to find them, grabbing them as they were published because, even at that early age, I understood that I'd better get them and hold on to them when I could, because finding them later would be either expensive or time-consuming pesterments, or both.

The New Sherlockian Golden Age began in 1974 and has never ended, but it still took a few decades for Sherlockian adventure addicts like me to start to feel satisfied. If it was up to the traditional publishing dinosaurs to lumber into motion and recognize the need, we'd all still be waiting with great yearning disappointment. Thank heavens for MX Books, and later Belanger Books, which spun into motion from MX's initial efforts. With these two defining Sherlockian publishers now in place, so many more of Watson's discovered manuscripts can finally reach a desperately hungry public.

With the availability of so many more Holmes adventures, there is room to revisit all aspects of that world – including the other occupants of the Canonical realm. The World of Sherlock Holmes is wide and deep, and it has many Canonical individuals besides Our Heroes and the regular stalwarts like Mycrft and Mrs. Hudson, and Lestrade and Gregson. The theme of this set of MX anthologies was simple: To include a Canonical character – possibly in a large role, or sometimes just in passing. All of the contributing authors did a wonderful job, and now the game is afoot for the readers to spot some of those in some stories who are less well known.

When Ellery Queen went to the library as a boy in 1917, the entire Canon wasn't yet in existence. When I was about the same age as that, in the mid-1970's, the amount of available tales – Canonical and post-Canonical – was just about as slim. Now, thank Heavens, we finally have thousands of traditional Canonical adventures, set in the correct time period, and featuring the *True* Sherlock Holmes – not a modernized sociopathic murderer or continent-shifted tattoo-covered prostitute-paying drug addict, or a Van Helsing substitute or an anachronistic era-hopping Time Lord. I'm very proud that this latest set of MX anthologies brings us to almost 1,000 of these new True Holmes adventures – and as of this writing, more are still in the works. Stay tuned . . . .

* * * * *

"Of course, I could only stammer out my thanks."
– *The unhappy John Hector McFarlane,* "The Norwood Builder"

As always when one of these sets is finished, I want to first thank with all my heart my incredible wonderful wife of over thirty-six years,

3

Rebecca, and our amazing son and my friend, Dan. I love you both, and you are everything to me!

I can never express enough gratitude for all of the contributors who have donated their time and royalties to this ongoing project. I'm constantly amazed at the incredible stories that you send, and I'm so glad to have gotten to know so many of you through this process. It's an undeniable fact that Sherlock Holmes authors are the *best* people!

The contributors of these stories have donated their royalties for this project to support the Stepping Stones School for special needs children, located at Undershaw, one of Sir Arthur Conan Doyle's former homes. As of this writing, and as mentioned above, these MX anthologies have raised over $125,000 for the school, with no end in sight, and of even more importance, they have helped raise awareness about the school all over the world. These books are making a real difference to the school, and the participation of both contributors and purchasers is most appreciated.

I also want to particularly thank the following:

- *Dan Andriacco* – I first met Dan in 2011 at the third *From Gillette to Brett* conference, where he was in the Dealer's Room selling his books. I saw him again the next year at *A Gathering of Southern Sherlockians* in Chattanooga. From there, we began to correspond, and run into each other on occasion at various Sherlockian events – which attends a lot, and me quite a bit less.

  Over the years, he's risen from success to success in the Sherlockian World. He's written a number of Holmes novels, and additionally the ever-growning McCabe and Cody series, which I dearly love. They are Golden Age-type mysteries, heavily influenced by Nero Wolfe and Archie Goodwin, and with all kinds of Sherlockian aspects. In addition to all the other rich deep characters in the books, the setting of Erin, Ohio is a character too. I look forward to each new volume. And after all this, Dan took over as the editor of *The Baker Street Journal.*

  I've been trying to recruit him for years to contribute a story these books – and I'm still trying! – and with his foreword, I'm glad that he's now part of the MX Anthology family.

  Thank you, Dan!

- *Roger Johnson* – I'm more grateful than I can say that I know Roger. His Sherlockian knowledge is exceptional, as is the work that he does to further the cause of The Master. But even more than that, both Roger and his wonderful wife, Jean Upton, are simply the finest and best kind of people, and I'm very lucky to know both of them – and I was lucky enough to see them in June 2024, during my fourth Holmes Pilgrimage to England and Scotland. I can't thank you enough, and I can't imagine these books without you.

☐ *Steve Emecz* – When I first emailed Steve from out of the blue back in late 2012 and early 2013, I was interested in MX republishing my previously published first book. Even then, as a guy who works to accumulate *all* traditional Sherlockian pastiches, I could see that MX (under Steve's leadership) was *the* fast-rising superstar of the Sherlockian publishing world.

The publication of that first book with MX was an amazing life-changing event for me, leading to writing and then editing more books, unexpected Holmes Pilgrimages to England, and these incredible anthologies. When I had the idea for these books in early 2015, I thought that it might, with any luck, be one small volume of perhaps a dozen stories. Since then they've grown and grown, and by way of them I've been able to make some incredible Sherlockian friends and play in the Holmesian Sandbox in ways that I'd never before dreamed possible.

All through it, Steve has been one of the most positive and supportive people I've ever known, letting me explore various Sherlockian projects and opening up my own personal possibilities in ways that otherwise would have never been possible. Thank you Steve for every opportunity!

☐ *Brian Belanger* – Brian is one of the nicest and most talented of people. His gifts are amazing, and his skills improve and grow from project to project. He's amazingly great to work with, and once again I thank him for another incredible contribution.

And finally, last but certainly *not* least, thanks to **Sir Arthur Conan Doyle**: Author, doctor, adventurer, and the Founder of the Sherlockian Feast. Honored, and present in spirit.

As I always note when putting together an anthology of Holmes stories, the effort has been a labor of love. These adventures are just more tiny threads woven into the ongoing Great Holmes Tapestry, continuing to grow and grow, for there can *never* be enough stories about the man whom Watson described as *"the best and wisest . . . whom I have ever known."*

David Marcum
September 25th, 2024
The 136th Anniversary of
the first day of
The Hound of the Baskervilles

Questions, comments, or story submissions
may be addressed to David Marcum at
thepapersofsherlockholmes@gmail.com

NOTE

*   Ellery Queen's essay regarding his first meeting with Sherlock Holmes has appeared in at least three different versions. The best and most succinct is his foreword to the 1975 Ballantine edition of *The Adventures of Sherlock Holmes.* Versions also appear in *In the Queen's Parlor* (1969, as "Who Shall Ever Forget?") and also – much reduced – as "Who Shall Ever Forget?" in *The Golden Summer* (1953, by "Daniel Nathan").

Foreword
by Dan Andriacco

"*And so, reader, farewell to Sherlock Holmes!*" Arthur Conan Doyle wrote in the Preface to *The Case Book of Sherlock Holmes*. The exclamation point is telling. Conan Doyle was excited to be finished at last with that annoying consulting detective.

But the world was not.

The author's efforts to shed himself of his most famous creation are well known to all Sherlockians. He wanted to stop writing about Holmes after the sixth of the *Adventures*, and then after the twelfth, and then believed that he had finally done with deed with the ominously named "The Final Problem" at the end of what became *The Memoirs*. Many of us can recite most of the opening words of that story by heart: "*It is with heavy heart that I take up my pen to write these last words in which I ever record the singular gifts by which my friend Mr. Sherlock Holmes was distinguished.*"

The author was wrong, of course. One of my favorite cartoons related to Sherlock Holmes is by Jeff Decker (reprinted in the Summer 2023 *Baker Street Journal*) showing Conan Doyle at his desk, pipe in hand and a startled look on his face as a dripping Sherlock Holmes stands at the open-door yelling, "*Nice try, Doyle!*"

Two novels and thirty-two short stories would follow before the Canon was complete at sixty stories. One of the later tales, my favorite, is called "His Last Bow." But it wasn't.

Why is that man so hard to get rid of? Even the death of the canonical author couldn't stop the flow of new adventures of Sherlock Holmes. (I have been guilty of a few myself.) The reason is elementary economics: Supply meets demand. As long as there are legions of us around the world who want to go back again and again to Baker Street – which is likely to be forever – new stories will be produced.

It is not entirely about Holmes, however. The world of The Canon is also peopled with dozens of other characters worth spending more time with as well. And you will find many of these occupants of the Canonical realm within the pages of these volumes – Parts XLVI, XLVII, and XVLIII of *The MX Book of New Sherlock Holmes Stories*. Some surprises await!

Dan Andriacco
Editor – *The Baker Street Journal*
July 2024

"In the Old Rooms in Baker Street"
by Roger Johnson

The Festival of Britain in 1951 was intended as "a tonic to the nation" in the austere years after the Second World War, and every local authority was expected to make its own contribution to the festival. The Borough of St. Marylebone chose to mount a Sherlock Holmes Exhibition, with a re-creation of Holmes and Watson's sitting room as its centrepiece, and the Abbey National Building Society offered space in its headquarters, located in what had been, until 1930, Upper Baker Street. Abbey House, completed in 1932, occupied a site that had briefly included the only house that ever legitimately bore the address *221 Baker Street*, and for nearly twenty years a member of the staff had acted as Sherlock Holmes's secretary, to answer the many letters that arrived addressed to Mr. Holmes or Dr. Watson. *

The exhibition was a great success, attracting more than fifty-thousand visitors before it closed, and during that five-month period the little group of volunteers and professionals who created it had founded *The Sherlock Holmes Society of London*. Eventually the various exhibits that had been loaned were returned to their owners, and many of those that remained, including the sitting room, were bought by Whitbread, the brewers, and installed in a handsome old public house called the *Northumberland Arms*, in Northumberland Street, near Charing Cross Station. In December 1957, it was formally opened as the *Sherlock Holmes*. The sitting room is approximately one-third of its original size, but all the important landmarks are present. Diners in the restaurant can view it through the plate glass window that replaces the fourth wall of the room. There are also viewing windows in the door and corridor alongside the room and in the patio area.

In early 1992, my wife Jean Upton was having lunch at the pub and noticed that the sitting room looked very shabby. The managers told her that they had only recently taken over, and were faced with several problems, including water damage from a washing machine that had overflowed in the room above the sitting room. Jean offered to help with cleaning and restoring the items in the sitting room, and as she clearly knew a good deal about Sherlock Holmes, her offer was gratefully accepted.

8

That was the start of our direct involvement. We discovered that some items had been damaged, and some had disappeared, so we have done our best to repair, restore, and replace. It took nearly a year to find an affordable pair of brown leather boxing gloves to replace the missing originals, but other items have proved less elusive — suitable oil lamps, a handsome mantel clock in working order, a tea service that looks very much like the one Jeremy Brett and his two Watsons used in the Granada Television series . . . The deerstalker and cape now hanging behind the door were given by the director of a television programme for which I was interviewed at the pub.

Among the many things we have added are the *Legend of the Hound of the Baskervilles* — the manuscript read aloud by Dr. Mortimer to Holmes and Watson, the plans of the Bruce-Partington submarine, Watson's commission as an army surgeon, various letters and other documents. These are items that we have made ourselves. Many years ago I bought a swordstick as a theatre prop. It now has a place in the sitting room at the pub, because it is identical to the stick carried by Jude Law in *Sherlock Holmes* and *Sherlock Holmes: A Game of Shadows*.

We do our best to make sure that the room looks as if it really exists in the late 1890's. We cannot disguise the smoke alarm on the ceiling, but we were able to provide a pinboard, with appropriate documents attached, to hide a modern electric socket on the wall beside the chemistry table.

During our three decades as curators of the sitting room, the *Sherlock Holmes* has undergone two changes of ownership, several changes of management, and at least two extensive refurbishments. It is an honour for us to maintain the long relationship between *The Sherlock Holmes Society of London* and the *Sherlock Holmes* pub. Just to be able to enter the sitting -room is exciting. To be trusted with ensuring that it always looks authentic is a great privilege and a great pleasure.

The side door of the pub opens on to Craven Passage. Look to your left at the building opposite and you'll see three formidable wooden doors, above which are attractive oriental arches and decorative blue-and-white tiles. This is all that remains of the Turkish Baths where we find Holmes and Watson at the beginning of "The Illustrious Client".

Now, bear with me, please. You may remember that Neville St. Clair – alias Hugh Boone, the Man with the Twisted Lip – lived at a house called The Cedars, near Lee in Kent. Remarkably, The Cedars is a real house: It stands on Belmont Hill in Blackheath, very close to the neighbouring town of Lee, and until his death in 1878 it was the home of one John Penn, whose widow was apparently still living there in 1907.

John Penn was an English marine engineer whose innovations in engine and propeller systems led to his company becoming the major supplier to the Royal Navy as it made the transition from sail to steam power. By the time of his death, Penn's firm had built engines for 735 ships, ranging from river ferries to battleships. He was elected a Fellow of the Royal Society in 1859, and the following year he was a founder-member of the Royal Institution of Naval Architects.

Back in Northumberland Street, next door to the *Sherlock Holmes* pub, we find – Guess what! – the Royal Institution of Naval Architects.

As Mycroft Holmes remarked at his first meeting with Dr. Watson, *"I hear of Sherlock everywhere . . . ."*

Roger Johnson, BSI, ASH
Editor: *The Sherlock Holmes Journal*
August 2024

NOTE

* That rôle ceased in 2005, when the building society sold Abbey House and departed from Baker Street.

An Ongoing Legacy
for Sherlock Holmes
by Steve Emecz

Undershaw
Circa 1900

As we head into the autumn of 2024, we're delighted to have some more volumes of *The MX Book of New Sherlock Holmes Stories*, which continues to support the wonderful school at Undershaw. It's one of several projects we work with that you can read about on our website:

https://mxpublishing.com/pages/about-us

We continue to release dozens of new titles every year, and are entering our seventh year providing cases for the mystery subscription series *Dear Holmes*, which has now had over 50,000 aspiring detectives take part.

We look forward to another busy season with a variety of books from authors old and new.

Steve Emecz
August 2024

The Doyle Room at Undershaw
Partially funded through royalties from
The MX Book of New Sherlock Holmes Stories

A Word from Undershaw
by Emma West

Undershaw
September 9, 2016
Grand Opening of the Stepping Stones School
(Now *Undershaw*)
(Photograph courtesy of Roger Johnson)

It is always a pleasure to share the latest news from Undershaw, especially on such a momentous occasion. This year, we are not only celebrating the 20th anniversary of our school's founding, but also the 8th year of being housed in the historic and inspiring building of Undershaw, the former home of Sir Arthur Conan Doyle. Moving into this incredible space in 2016 marked the beginning of a new chapter for our school, and in 2021, we renamed the school to honour its legacy, recognising its deep connection to one of literature's most beloved creators, the mind behind Sherlock Holmes.

The journey we've taken as a school has been filled with milestones, and we have been fortunate to be supported by many, but none more so than MX Publishing. The interest, encouragement, and partnership we have received from MX Publishing has helped shape our community into what it is today. Just as Sir Arthur Conan Doyle enriched the world with his stories, MX Publishing has enriched our journey, and we are deeply grateful for their friendship and support.

As we reflect on our growth, we also celebrate being shortlisted for the prestigious "Outstanding Impact" award by the National Association of Special Schools. Out of more than four-hundred schools, being in the top three finalists is a testament to the dedication of our staff and the incredible impact of the Undershaw Diploma. Designed to develop the skills young people need to succeed in life, this diploma reflects our mission to tackle the challenging statistic that only 4.8% of adults with learning needs are in full-time employment. Through our accredited program, we are equipping students with the essential skills to ensure their futures are filled with opportunity and that they can be socially and economically engaged.

In addition to these achievements, we were honoured to receive the Gold-standard Anti-Bullying Charter Mark from Surrey County Council, a recognition that speaks volumes about the culture we nurture at Undershaw. The assessment team were impressed by the ethos of our school and the positive experiences shared by students, staff, and parents alike. We take pride in creating a school environment where every student feels valued and safe, as one student beautifully expressed: "Undershaw is like a second home."

We look ahead with excitement to what the future holds. As we continue to grow, we remain committed to the legacy of Sir Arthur Conan Doyle, using the skills of creativity, resilience, and curiosity that he embodied. And as we celebrate our twenty years of transformation and success, we extend our deepest thanks to MX Publishing for their unwavering support and their role in helping us thrive.

Undershaw is more than a school. It's a community, a home, and a place where young people are empowered to become the best versions of themselves. We are proud of all we have achieved so far and excited for the road ahead.

Until next time . . . .

Emma West
Headteacher
September 2024

"Undershaw", Hindhead. Conan Doyle's House.

Editor's *Caveats*

When these anthologies first began back in 2015, I noted that the authors were from all over the world – and thus, there would be British spelling and American spelling. As I explained then, I didn't want to take the responsibility of changing American spelling to British and vice-versa. I would undoubtedly miss something, leading to inconsistencies, or I'd change something incorrectly.

Some readers are bothered by this, made nervous and irate when encountering American spelling as written by Watson, and in stories set in England. However, here in America, the versions of The Canon that we read have long-ago has their spelling Americanized, so it isn't quite as shocking for us.

Additionally, I offer my apologies up front for any typographical errors that have slipped through. As a print-on-demand publisher, MX does not have squadrons of editors as some readers believe. The business consists of three part-time people who also have busy lives elsewhere – Steve Emecz, Sharon Emecz, and Timi Emecz – so the editing effort largely falls on the contributors. Some readers and consumers out there in the world are unhappy with this – apparently forgetting about all of those self-produced Holmes stories and volumes from decades ago (typed and Xeroxed) with awkward self-published formatting and loads of errors that are now prized as very expensive collector's items.

I'm personally mortified when errors slip through – ironically, there will probably be errors in these *caveats* – and I apologize now, but without a regiment of professional full-time editors looking over my shoulder, this is as good as it gets. Real life is more important than writing and editing – even in such a good cause as promoting the True and Traditional Canonical Holmes – and only so much time can be spent preparing these books before they're released into the wild. I hope that you can look past any errors, small or huge, and simply enjoy these stories, and appreciate the efforts of everyone involved, and the sincere desire to add to The Great Holmes Tapestry.

And in spite of any errors here, there are more Sherlock Holmes stories in the world than there were before, and that's a good thing.

David Marcum
Editor

Sherlock Holmes (1854-1957) was born in Yorkshire, England, on 6 January, 1854. In the mid-1870's, he moved to 24 Montague Street, London, where he established himself as the world's first Consulting Detective. After meeting Dr. John H. Watson in early 1881, he and Watson moved to rooms at 221b Baker Street, where his reputation as the world's greatest detective grew for several decades. He was presumed to have died battling noted criminal Professor James Moriarty on 4 May, 1891, but he returned to London on 5 April, 1894, resuming his consulting practice in Baker Street. Retiring to the Sussex coast near Beachy Head in October 1903, he continued to be associated in various private and government investigations while giving the impression of being a reclusive apiarist. He was very involved in the events encompassing World War I, and to a lesser degree those of World War II. He passed away peacefully upon the cliffs above his Sussex home on his 103rd birthday, 6 January, 1957.

Dr. John Hamish Watson (1852-1929) was born in Stranraer, Scotland on 7 August, 1852. In 1878, he took his Doctor of Medicine Degree from the University of London, and later joined the army as a surgeon. Wounded at the Battle of Maiwand in Afghanistan (27 July, 1880), he returned to London late that same year. On New Year's Day, 1881, he was introduced to Sherlock Holmes in the chemical laboratory at Barts. Agreeing to share rooms with Holmes in Baker Street, Watson became invaluable to Holmes's consulting detective practice. Watson was married and widowed three times, and from the late 1880's onward, in addition to his participation in Holmes's investigations and his medical practice, he chronicled Holmes's adventures, with the assistance of his literary agent, Sir Arthur Conan Doyle, in a series of popular narratives, most of which were first published in *The Strand* magazine. Watson's later years were spent preparing a vast number of his notes of Holmes's cases for future publication. Following a final important investigation with Holmes, Watson contracted pneumonia and passed away on 24 July, 1929.

Photos of Sherlock Holmes and Dr. John H. Watson courtesy of Roger Johnson

The
MX Book
of
New

Sherlock Holmes Stories

Part XLVII
Occupants of the
Canonical Realm
(1890-1898)

Mission
(Some Sort of Sonnet)
by Anon.

Observe what those around you do not see.
Assist the folk who climb the stairs to plea.
At times the case can be solved from your chair,
but you like best to move around out there.

Opine when Scotland Yard misses a fact.
Your role is fixed to make up what they lack.
Over time they learn what you have long shown,
Watson smiles – before the rest he has known.

Index random facts that seem quite *outrè*.
Plain and dull then, shining with light today.
It's your mission to see what they all miss.
Finding the truth has always been your liss.

Since a lad you have known your direction:
Mastering *The Whole Art of Detection*.

The Neckinger Mills Mystery
by DJ Tyrer

It was one morning in the June of 1890 when I was in the middle of enjoying a hearty breakfast that the doorbell rang and my wife rose from the table to see who had called. As a medical doctor, it was not unusual for me to be disturbed at unsociable hours to come to the aid of the sick and injured. What I wasn't expecting was for my good friend Sherlock Holmes to enter in place of my wife.

"No time to waste, Watson," he declared. "Put on your hat and coat and come with me, I have a cab waiting."

I swallowed my mouthful of toast and asked whatever was the matter that had put him in such an agitated state.

"You remember Inspector Bradstreet?" he said.

"Yes," I replied, pausing only to finish my cup of tea. We had worked with the inspector on some cases the previous summer. "Why?"

"He's injured."

"What!" I leapt from my chair at the words.

"Oh, he'll live. Don't worry. He has no need of your medical ministrations. It is our investigative nous that is required."

"If you say so."

I followed him out into the hallway and retrieved my hat and coat from the rack and put them on, bidding farewell to my wife as I did so, before joining Holmes outside in the waiting cab.

He gave the driver an address and we were soon at our destination, which proved to be the small flat which Inspector Bradstreet called home.

We were let inside by a woman whom I presumed to be the inspector's wife and directed into a bedroom, where Bradstreet lay atop the bedclothes, a battered example of humanity. The tall, stoutly-built man had his left leg in plaster and his face was discoloured with bruises and marred where the skin had split. He appeared a ghost of his former powerful self.

Bradstreet awkwardly began to push himself up into a sitting position and I swiftly moved to assist him.

"Thank you," he said, gruffly, clearly frustrated at his infirmity. I recalled my own frustrations as I recovered from the wound I received in Afghanistan and felt a surge of sympathy for him and anger towards whoever had inflicted such wounds.

31

I began, out of habit, to look him over, but he waved me away from him.

"I have received what I am assured is the finest medical treatment," he said. "Cuts and bruises in the main. I shall look a fright for a bit. Worse is this," he tapped the plaster encasing his leg. "It will be a while before I'm mobile once more, and I shall surely have a limp."

"But what happened," I blurted like a fool. "I mean, who would do such a thing?"

He snorted. "I have many enemies, but most of them are north of the river."

"But," said I, "we are north of the river."

Bradstreet managed a faint laugh at my confusion.

"I was attacked in Southwark," he said.

"Southwark? Whatever were you doing there? That is M Division, is it not?"

He nodded. "Yes."

When last we had worked with Bradstreet, he had been at the B Division and, before that, E Division. As he didn't appear to be the kind of man to cause mischief with his peers, it seemed that the reason for his having served in at least three different divisions of the Metropolitan Police in little more than a year wasn't due to animosity. Although nothing specific had been said, I took the respect Holmes seemed to hold for the man to indicate that he had the role of some sort of expert for the police, being sent wherever there was a particular problem that required his attention.

"You had best explain," said Holmes, who had been silently observing.

We had, I realised, not come on the whim of my friend upon hearing of the inspector's injuries, but rather, had been summoned by Bradstreet himself.

"I was sent to Southwark to investigate what we believe is a gold-smuggling ring. Oh, we are wasting time – they may panic and shut down their operation."

"Rest easy," said Holmes. "If they panicked after assaulting you, then they are already gone and agitation on your part will not speed our pursuit of them. If, on the other hand, they believe you have been dealt with, then they are going nowhere, and a clear account will allow us to apprehend them before they make a move. Now, start from the beginning and leave nothing out."

Bradstreet nodded, winced a little at the movement, and then began his account.

"We had evidence of gold coming out of Southwark without legal provenance, a small but steady flow. It hadn't been assayed as there was no hallmark, and tests showed that the gold was adulterated, indicating that it was either of foreign origin or was being reduced in quality in order to defraud purchasers. As we had detected no upsurge in gold being stolen, nor had there been any major robberies, we suspected that it was being brought into the country from abroad, perhaps as a means of disposing of items stolen overseas or purchased legally, and then smuggled into England to avoid paying taxes.

"But even though we were certain that the gold must be entering the country through St. Saviour's dock or a wharf nearby, we have been unable to detect its arrival, nor have we been able to ascertain exactly how it's leaving Southwark for the rest of the country. I – "

He gave a groan and slumped back into his pillows.

"Careful, man," said I, leaning closer to check he was all right. "Try not to overexert yourself."

"Take it slowly," said Holmes, "and let us tease out what is of import."

Bradstreet gave a weak nod and paused to sip from a tumbler of water, then resumed his explanation.

"I was directed to M Division to take charge of the investigation. There was a concern that some of the officers there might be in league with the smugglers."

"I see," said Holmes. "Which explains why you have summoned us, rather than entrusting the investigation to your fellow officers."

"That's correct. Oh, there will be an investigation, of course, but will it be thorough? Timely? I wish I could say for certain that it would, for we have a reputation that such doubts tarnish."

"Doubts we shall keep in confidence," said Holmes.

"Thank you."

"What more can you tell us of your investigation?"

"Not as much as I would wish," said Bradstreet. "I must admit my luck with the case had been minimal, although I clearly got close enough to worry them. I had narrowed the search down to an area of Southwark where the primary industry is leatherwork. The owners of Neckinger Mills, Bevingtons and Sons, produce light leather for shoes and fancy goods and, as you can imagine, there is a constant flow of rawhides into their property to be processed into leather, and finished goods out. Now, I approached them, discreetly, and received permission to carry out checks on both deliveries of untanned hide and the shipment out of finished goods.

"Nothing going in," he said, "and though I randomly checked the shipments out, I discovered nothing."

"And," I prompted, "St. Saviour's Dock . . . ?"

"Nothing. I have searched the vessels moored there, to no success. There was a rowboat that I spotted entering the dock for which I had high hopes of being involved in the smuggling – after all, gold is heavy, but doesn't necessarily take up much space – yet, they happily complied when I called for them to heave to for me to search it and I found nothing."

Bradstreet shook his head, then winced a little at the movement.

"I'm certain I have the right area, yet I have had absolutely no success."

Holmes steepled his fingers and looked off into space for a moment, then said, "It would appear that you have correctly narrowed the field of your investigation. It is also evident that they were aware of this. Just a little more information would, doubtless, allow us to pinpoint their location and plans."

He looked intently at Bradstreet. "Tell us now of their attack."

"What is there to say? I had been looking around the dock, to no avail, and was on my way back to the station when I was set upon by three men. None of them was anything but scrawny and, I am certain, I could have easily handled one or two of them, but three was enough that I couldn't fend off the blows of their sticks, and I was overwhelmed and beaten to the ground, receiving the injuries you see before you."

"Sticks, you say? Walking sticks?"

"Yes, or canes. I didn't get a good look."

Holmes gave a nod.

"What is it?" I asked, perplexed at the apparent importance of the fact.

"Walking sticks would imply that the ruffians sought to be taken for ordinary folk out for a stroll and not thugs on a mission of violence."

"Naturally," said Bradstreet. "Street thugs seldom brandish pistols or swords or anything that would see them immediately identified as criminals."

"Yes," said Holmes, "but this was in a leatherworking district . . . An awl, a shoemaker's knife, a pair of scissors – all could have been wielded with deadly intent, while staying in character as law-abiding workers.

"Thus, we can infer that our villains aren't amongst the workforce employed by Bevingtons and Sons, despite their proximity to them."

Bradstreet gave a slow nod and I had to concur.

"But," said I, after a moment, "if they aren't workers at the mill, how are they getting the gold into the shipments leaving the workshops there?"

"That," admitted Holmes, "remains a mystery to me, for now, although it could be as simple as just one or two workers assisting the smugglers – assuming our assumption of the means isn't incorrect.

"Right," he asked Bradstreet. "Was there any more?"

"No, I believe that covers the pertinent facts of my investigation. As I said, I had little luck with it, and whatever caused them to attack me remains unknown to me."

Holmes nodded. "Now, we must turn to your clothes. Where are they?"

"You must ask my wife," said Bradstreet. "The doctor cut me out of my trousers and my shirt and jacket were in quite a mess, stained by blood. I daresay nothing is salvageable."

"Watson, please speak to Mrs. Bradstreet," said Holmes, and I did as he bade.

Returning moments later, all I had to offer was the inspector's jacket.

"The trousers were completely ruined and went in the bin, as did the shirt, and the dustman has already been."

Holmes snorted. "I abhor efficiency in those trades that impact my ability to collect evidence. But it appears that you have with you the jacket . . . ?"

"Yes. It seems Mrs. Bradstreet has some hope of restoring it to something approaching its prior condition, so here it is."

I handed it to him. A button was missing from it, lost in the struggle, and there was a tear in one sleeve, and blood stained the collar and elsewhere, but not so deeply that it would be impossible to remove.

Holmes looked it over. "Hmm . . . See here, Watson, Bradstreet." We peered closely. "There is something here, a chemical residue." He looked at the inspector. "Had you come in contact with any chemicals?"

"Not that I'm aware of – though, of course, with all the work going on, it isn't impossible that I did."

"Not impossible, but perhaps improbable. Yes, see here, it is layered above a splash of blood, meaning it must have been transferred to your jacket either during or after your fight."

"What does that tell us?" I asked.

"At this point, Watson, absolutely nothing. I must examine it and ascertain what it is. It may be that it is of no consequence, just some discarded splash that Bradstreet happened to fall into when he was struck, but, from the way it is smeared, I would suggest it was delivered either by one of the canes that struck him or else was smudged onto his jacket from the clothing of one of his attackers when they pressed in close to him."

"Which means," I slowly said, "that if it can be linked to a specific part of the process by which the leather goods are created, it might just lead us to which part of Neckinger Mills is of interest to us."

Holmes nodded. "Certainly."

35

He looked down at Bradstreet. "Don't worry, sir, for Watson and I shall locate and detain these dastards for you."

The inspector managed a weak smile and thanked us and we left.

Upon our return to Baker Street, Holmes immediately began testing the chemical he had found on Bradstreet's jacket, while leaving me to look up the area around Neckinger Mills.

Poring over maps and directories, I ascertained that it was in the vicinity of what had once been one of London's most vile and notorious rookeries, Jacob's Island, until it had been cleared some decades before to make way for industry and warehouses. Neckinger Mills itself stood on land that had once belonged to Bermondsey Abbey. But, though Jacob's Island would have been the perfect place to find the sort of criminals we were seeking, it seemed that nothing in the history of the area, nor anything I could learn about Bevingtons and Sons or the modern usage to which the remainder of the district was put to, nor any information concerning crime in the area, offered any useful clues, and I had to admit I had nothing much to present when my friend announced he had completed his tests.

"Phosphor," said Holmes. "Mixed with not a little organic muck."

"Phosphor?" said I, bemused. "Is that used in tanning leather?"

Holmes shook his head. "Not that I am aware of. It can give off a glow and is used in the manufacture of matchsticks, but it is neither used to produce leather, nor is it a by-product of the process."

"Which would seem to suggest it could tell us where the gang of smugglers are located, only my researches have yielded nothing." I gave a vague gesture to the directories I had been perusing. "It is possible that matches are stored in a warehouse, but I found no information to help us."

"Indeed," said Holmes, "it is possible it is a false clue – given the material it was mixed with, Bradstreet might have got it on his jacket when he fell during the struggle.

"No, it seems that success in this endeavour will require our presence at Neckinger Mills, and observation."

The proud supports of what would soon be a new bridge across the Thames were visible as we crossed to Southwark to begin our investigation. Even though the June of 1890 wasn't a particularly warm one, there was an unpleasant miasma over the district, emanating from the fish shops and butchers, the sluggish waters of the Thames, and, worse, from the sewer gratings, all topped off by the especial smell of the tanneries at Neckinger Mills.

"If ever there was a place suitable for wickedness," I said to Holmes as we approached the road in which Bradstreet had been ambushed, "this is it. Surely, the very pits of Hell can smell little worse."

My friend chuckled at my words. "I concern myself only with the evils of this world, Watson, but the air certainly does have a diabolical smell to it. A-ha! I do believe we are here."

There had been no attempt to clean the splash of blood that besmirched the cobbles where the inspector had been struck down. Holmes and I conducted a close examination of the street, but it yielded nothing of any use, although Holmes did spot the button that had been torn from the cuff of Bradstreet's jacket during the struggle.

"He fell here," he pronounced, "and his attackers doubtless came from that alley there. A dead-end, so they were lying in wait for him, not in pursuit."

"They knew where he was headed . . . ."

"Yes. That might indicate his fears of a traitor on the Force are correct, or it might be no more than guesswork on their part." Holmes snorted. "Suggestions, but no solid facts. Come, let us see what we can discover."

Despite Holmes's confident stride as he led the way down the street towards Neckinger Mills, it seemed that the answer to his words was "nothing", for though we applied a keen eye to the area and spoke to anyone we saw, none of our efforts brought us any information concerning either the smuggling or the assault upon Inspector Bradstreet. Nobody would admit to having seen anything, and there was nothing to explain either the phosphor that Holmes had found on the inspector's jacket, nor how the gang were moving gold into and out of the area.

We had been on the case for several fruitless hours when a police constable approached us. I glanced at Holmes, wondering what this boded, but he maintained an air of indifference, nodding casually to him as the man neared us.

"Hello," called the constable with a cheeriness quite at odds with our previous experiences with the local population. "You must be colleagues of Inspector Bradstreet."

"Must we?" I asked, a little tersely, recalling what the inspector had told us of his suspicions.

"You must, if you're the two fellows who've been going about asking questions. My name's Constable Hinchley. I was helping Inspector Bradstreet with his investigation. I was sorry to hear he got himself into a scrape and was injured."

"A scrape?" asked Holmes.

"Yes. A bit of a silly mess, as I heard it told. Apparently, he popped into a public house for a few pints to relax after a long day traipsing about the area – I mean, you can hardly blame him, can you? Place stinks to High Heaven and we'd had no luck at all – and what transpires? He gets himself into a bit of a donnybrook. A drink was jostled, no doubt, and, well, he came off the worst. Shame. I do hope he is recovering well . . . ."

Holmes gave a curt nod. "He'll live, Constable, but he will be off the case for some weeks. Not, it seems, that there is much of a case. If there was a gang here, it seems likely they have left the area. All we're interested in is catching the miscreants with whom he brawled last night. Assaulting a police officer, even a drunken one, is a serious offence.

"Not," Holmes added, "that we've had any luck. If anyone knows who they were, they aren't talking."

"Yes, they are like that when it comes to scions of the law," said Constable Hinchley. "Of course, the lads responsible may well have disappeared from the district – many of the workers are casual labourers – so I wouldn't waste too much effort in trying to track them down, as much as you would want to. Still, if I hear a dickie bird, I'll let you know."

"Thank you. Pass the word via your superiors, for it seems unlikely we shall be investing any further days on the case in person."

The constable gave an understanding nod. "Give my regards to the inspector, should you see him."

"Oh, I shall," said Holmes, as Hinchley strolled casually away.

"What nonsense!" said I, once he was out of earshot. "Even if Bradstreet hasn't relayed the full details of what happened to him, surely that fool doesn't believe he was injured in a bar-room brawl!"

"I agree. Oh, it's possible that is one of the rumours doing the rounds, but if this Hinchley had really worked closely with Bradstreet, I doubt he would give it much credit. It may not be that he is actively involved with the smugglers, but I wouldn't be surprised if he were receiving a payoff from the gang, or perhaps has some other little swindle going on that he would prefer nobody look too closely at.

"Hopefully, I managed to convince him we know nothing, and will not be busy here for long."

"We really don't know anything," I said with a sigh, "and even if we return every day for a month, I fear we have little chance of uncovering the gang."

Holmes shook his head. "We aren't done yet."

Indeed, there were more doors to knock upon and more workers to question, but none produced any leads and, after a while, I turned to Holmes and said, "It's getting late, and we appear to be wasting our time. Should we draw the ire of the gang with our questions and they attack us, it shall prove as needless an assault as the one they launched upon Bradstreet."

Holmes smiled, darkly. "If they did choose to make their presence known, I, for one, would be pleased. It would save a great deal of effort in searching them out and, unlike our colleague, we would be ready for them."

"Of course," said I, "it's possible Bradstreet was right about them panicking and there is now nothing to find."

"That may be true. But even if they're gone, there may yet be clues to point us in pursuit. Come, Watson, here's another warehouse. Perhaps it contains matches . . . ."

He walked up to the warehouse doors and rapped smartly upon them with his cane.

After a very brief wait, there was a sound of shuffling from within, and then a small door set in the main one opened and an elderly man looked out at us from the shadows within, a look of annoyance upon his poorly-shaven face.

"Yes?"

Holmes introduced us as a pair of detectives, allowing an inference of officialdom to be incorrectly drawn, and the man continued to look upon us with annoyance. It was perhaps naive on my part, but I suspected that a criminal would either be more belligerent or worried than annoyed to discover detectives at his door, or else would effect *insouciance*. To my mind, annoyance was the genuine emotion of a caretaker roused from his rest.

"We are investigating criminal activity in the area," my friend continued, adopting the semi-imperious, somewhat-bored tone so common amongst policemen. "Have you seen or heard anything suspicious?"

The man gave a sharp laugh. "Nah, I don't see much shut in here."

"What do you store inside?" I asked.

"Nothing." He laughed, this time with more humour. "Best job in the world, this! Paid to watch over nothing. Nobody wants to steal nothing, so I don't get bothered. As long as the place don't burn down or nothing like that, I'm fine. Why Harry ditched his job, I'll never know. Probably the ghosts."

He laughed again.

"Harry?" I said, bemused. "Ghosts?"

The man nodded as if my repetition had given clarity to what he had said.

"Who was Harry?" asked Holmes.

"Caretaker here, before me."

"And, he left the position?"

"Left? Nah, up and vanished, he did."

"Vanished?" probed Holmes.

"Yeah. One day, he weren't here – or so the gossip goes. The bosses were quite fed up with him. Some said he fell into his drink. Others that the ghosts scared him."

"Ghosts?" said Holmes with a quizzical eyebrow.

"Yeah. Never seen nothing like that, meself, but they say old Harry said he'd seen glowing figures. Probably the drink, either way," he added with a chuckle.

"Quite," said Holmes, glancing at me. "Well," my friend said after a moment, "we must be pressing on."

The man closed the door as we walked away.

After we had gone a short distance, Holmes stopped and turned to me and said, "What do you make of that?"

"Ghosts? I think he was right and that Harry fellow was in his cups."

"Oh dear, you are failing to connect the threads of this case."

"I'm not sure I follow."

"Smugglers. Glowing ghosts. Phosphor . . . ."

"Oh." The realisation made me feel like a fool.

"It is hardly original," Holmes said, "but I suppose ghost stories do work well to dampen the curiosity of a certain class of people."

"You think these smugglers are pretending to be ghosts to scare away anyone who might see them moving their gold about?"

"I have no doubt. It is the only thing, so far, that makes sense of the phosphor on Bradstreet's jacket, doubtless deposited upon him from the clothing of one of his attackers who, at some earlier point, had been playing the part of a ghoul."

"That still doesn't answer the question of *how* they are getting the gold in and out undetected," I had to point out. "I mean, a glowing ghost is rather more obvious than a stealthy figure, and there hasn't been a rash of ghost sightings in the district. Only one: Harry's." I considered. "Could they be based in the warehouse? No. Even with the previous watchman gone, his replacement is surely an impediment to their free movement." I shook my head. "No, I remain stumped."

"Do you know," asked Holmes, "why they call the works here 'Neckinger Mills'?"

The *non sequitur* threw me. "I have no idea."

"Around here," said Holmes, "quite probably following the course of this very street, there once flowed a river called the Neckinger, which discharged into the Thames. Indeed, it still does, only now it is wholly subterranean and little more than a sewer.

40

"The Neckinger flowed alongside what was then Jacob's Island and entered the Thames at St. Saviour's Dock, and was once navigable as far as Bermondsey Abbey."

"Fascinating," said I, a little caustically, "but I fail to see the relevance."

Ignoring me, Holmes went on to note that "Neckinger" likely derived from "neckerchief", and probably referred to a cant phrase "the Devil's neckerchief", meaning a hangman's noose.

"Because," he concluded, "pirates were once hanged near here."

"Are you saying the gang are pirates?" I asked, bemused at his monologue, as interesting as it admittedly was.

"No, although I suspect there is a buried treasure involved. What I believe is that the rowboat which Bradstreet stopped was indeed that of the gang he was seeking."

"He searched it and there was no gold."

"Correct, but that was because he was looking in the wrong direction. You see, he was looking for someone smuggling gold *into* Southwark, so when he found no gold aboard the rowboat, he assumed the men in it were innocent of involvement and ignored them from then on, although they were sufficiently spooked by his actions to plot an ambush. But there was no gold because they never were smuggling any gold into Southwark, only *out*."

"Sorry?"

"Connect the evidence, Watson. We know there is gold coming from Southwark, although there is no evidence of any arriving. The gold isn't of a standard quality. The phosphor on Bradstreet's jacket was mixed with organic muck. Bermondsey Abbey? Neckinger Mills – ?"

"The river!" I exclaimed, although I still wasn't entirely certain what that actually meant.

"Yes, Watson, the river. Still there, beneath our feet. I suspect that our so-called smugglers discovered a trove of gold, perhaps hidden when King Henry dissolved the monasteries, and have been smuggling it via the sewer that the river Neckinger has been reduced to."

"Hence the . . . muck," I supplied.

"Yes. And, out via St. Saviour's Dock in the rowboat. Had Bradstreet but stopped it going in the other direction . . . but he wasn't to know."

"If they're still in the area, they are most likely beneath our feet."

I looked to the pavement.

"Correct. How do you feel about going underground?"

Night was stretching its dark cloak over the city as we climbed down from the quayside at St. Saviour's Dock to where an archway allowed the egress of the foetid waters of the Neckinger, but I didn't light my bullseye lantern until we were inside, not knowing if any observers were hidden amongst the warehouses and alleyways.

I must admit that I wasn't too keen to make the journey, especially as I wasn't entirely convinced by my friend's conjecture about hidden abbey gold, despite the presence of a rowboat tied up just inside the tunnel entrance, for the former river stank terribly and rats scurried with impunity about our feet . . . but make it we did.

A little way in, Holmes paused and drew my attention to the brick wall of the tunnel.

"See here," he said. "Phosphor."

It seemed he was right about the connection between the Neckinger and the thugs who had assaulted Bradstreet.

We continued on into the darkness, the lantern beam seeming inadequate to the task of lighting our way, until we reached a point where a section of brickwork had been removed.

In a quiet voice, Holmes bade me douse our lantern, which I did. We were not, as might be expected, dropped into utter blackness, for a glow of candlelight escaped through that breach into the tunnel.

Placing his lips close to my ear, Holmes said, "I believe this is our destination. Let us go inside, carefully, and see what we may learn. But remember, these blackguards are desperate and violent men, so be ready to defend yourself."

I followed him through the gap in the brickwork, drawing my revolver as I went.

Through the gap was a stone vault that doubtless, as Holmes had conjectured, belonged to the long-since demolished abbey. It was lit by candles and lanterns, and men were busy at work clearing rubble and decaying coffins from a side chamber. The detritus of their work had been piled to once side of the vault and, amongst the stones and bricks and scattered bones and pieces of splintered casket, there lay, half-buried, the body of an old man, whose death clearly long post-dated the sealing of the chamber. It seemed that we had discovered the sad fate of Harry, the missing watchman.

Holmes and I ducked down behind the pile and observed the scene and, as we did so, I leaned close to him and whispered that even if the attack on Bradstreet and theft of treasure trove weren't enough to seal the criminals' fates, the murder certainly would.

There were three men, all of whom might be described as scrawny, busy at work clearing the rubble. There were surely the trio who had attacked the inspector. A fourth man, one of prodigious girth and clearly the leader of the gang, was seated upon a wooden chair that creaked

42

alarmingly with his every movement,. He was constantly issuing instructions to the men who were digging. A table was set beside him with a half-eaten pork pie upon a plate.

I had to agree with Bradstreet's assessment of the men who had attacked him: That it was only their number that had made them any threat, and as for the fat man, I doubted he was much of a danger. Even outnumbered two-to-one, I was certain that Holmes and I could apprehend them without undue effort.

But then, before we could act, we heard footsteps in the tunnel behind us.

We sank into the darkness of a corner of the vault and watched to see the new arrival.

"Hinchley!" I couldn't help but exclaim, but my voice was muffled by sounds of the shovelling of rock and earth.

He strolled in casually, as if this weren't a hidden vault off a stinking lost river.

Despite wearing the uniform of a representative of the law, there was no doubt that the constable was in league with the villains, for he greeted them like old friends, taking off his helmet and dropping it onto the table beside the pie, and, moving to stand beside the seated man, slapped him upon the shoulder.

"Trouble?" the man asked him.

Hinchley shook his head. "No. Bradstreet is off the case, and the streets, and the two detectives they sent to look into his injuries have made no headway. They bought my story about a bar-room brawl and casual labourers. Nobody is looking in our direction now."

He laughed, but the echoing sound was cut off in mid-guffaw as Holmes rose and stepped forward and struck him a mighty blow with his stick.

The constable went down without a further sound, clutching at his head, dazed, and there was a moment of silence before the uproar when the fat man shouted to his associates and they turned, shovels in hand, ready for violence.

As Holmes moved to meet the three men, revolver raised, I was surprised to see the fourth man lunge from his seat towards him with an alacrity that belied his size. I barely had a moment to raise my revolver and fire and save my friend from his attack.

Although my shot went wide, it caused him to turn to face me.

A second shot echoed about me, fired by Holmes, but I couldn't see what had happened, for the big man was coming at me.

I went to fire again, but he grabbed his chair and threw it at me, knocking the revolver from my hand, sending it flying off into the shadows. So disarmed, I switched to my walking stick and leapt at him.

Although I slammed into the man, he didn't go down, and he began to grapple with me. In his grip, I was unable to make effective use of my walking stick and found myself being overpowered by his weight and strength. We knocked into the table and sent it and the items upon it flying.

On the edge of my vision, I saw that Holmes too appeared to have lost his gun, though he had shot one of the three men, who was on the floor clutching at his leg. There was blood on his face from where he'd been struck, but he was vigorously defending himself against the vicious swings the remaining two delivered with their shovels.

For a moment, forced down as I was onto the floor, I was certain that I had failed Holmes, that he would be overwhelmed as I found myself being overwhelmed, but then, the fat man was pulled off of me and beaten into submission by my friend who, somehow, had managed to deal with his two opponents.

"You're hurt," I said, gasping.

"Merely a cut to the scalp," he replied, taking my hand.

I felt a fool as Holmes helped me to my feet, having so grievously underestimated my opponent, but any recriminatory thoughts and concern for my friend were swept aside by the realisation that the constable was no longer laying in a daze upon the floor.

"Holmes – Hinchley!" I cried, gesturing vaguely.

"He's making a run for it, Watson. He didn't come past me, so he must be in the tunnel. There should be some stairs somewhere nearby, a way up into the warehouse . . . Find the caretaker and have him summon the police for this lot. I'll go after Hinchley."

I hated to leave him to pursue the villain alone, but I knew he was right and that, the longer we delayed, the greater the chance of the other gang members recovering and making their own escapes. I grabbed a lantern and made my way in search of the warehouse's cellar, while Holmes ran off into the tunnel and towards the dock.

The caretaker was startled to see me appear inside his warehouse and not a little incredulous as I told him, in simple terms, what had happened, but he listened and did as I commanded him and went to fetch a policeman. I could only hope that Hinchley was the only corrupt officer in the division.

Then I returned to the vault and followed the tunnel back to the dock.

I was too late to see the chase that had ensued as Holmes pursued Hinchley, but was there for the conclusion.

The constable had climbed up onto a crane that jutted out from a warehouse over the quayside and my friend was just behind him. With nowhere left to go, Hinchley drew his truncheon and turned to face Holmes.

The fight was brief, Holmes fending off a clumsy blow, and then striking Hinchley twice in the knee, causing him to buckle and stumble, then fall.

Holmes reached for him, but it was too late.

Hinchley smashed into the stone of the quay and lay still. I didn't need my medical training to tell that he was dead.

The police arrived at the dock a few minutes later and, though we had quite some explaining to do, we were the heroes of the hour and the dead constable the target of opprobrium when they learned of his involvement in assault and murder.

When we were finally done giving our statements, Holmes and I immediately headed to Bradstreet's flat to wake him and his wife with a vigorous knocking upon their door. I felt a great sense of pride as Holmes told him that the men that caused him both vexation and injury were now either in custody or dead, and amusement to see the expression on the inspector's face as Holmes explained the true source of the gold for which he had been hunting.

But as much as he may have been bemused by my friend's explanation, Bradstreet had the look of a man who had shed a great weight from his shoulders by the time Holmes was done.

"Thank you," he said, shaking our hands.

His wife echoed the sentiment and placed a kiss upon our cheeks. I was certain that as she did so, I saw a momentary smile of satisfaction twitch across my friend's lips, though it might be that I was just seeing what I myself felt.

The Debt to Jabez Wilson
by David Marcum

"If you could stop by and see the poor man, Doctor, it would be a comfort – to him, and to me as well."

Mrs. Hudson looked expectantly at me, and how could I say no?

She had arrived at my Paddington doorstep just five minutes earlier with her request, explaining that she had business in the neighborhood, and that a chance to stop by and say hello was more welcome than taking time to explain the whole business in a note. I agreed and asked if she would stay longer, and have some tea. I still had several patients to see, but I would make them wait a moment or two for a chance to visit with my former landlady. She declined, however, reminding me to be in Baker Street at nine o'clock the next morning. Then, stating that she would pop in and say hello to Mary on her way out, she left my consulting room, and I fell into a brown study, staring at the card that Mrs. Hudson had pressed into my hand.

I had first met the man two years earlier, nearly to the day, when I'd stopped in Baker Street to visit my friend, Sherlock Holmes, and found him engaged with a new client. A series of quick deductions about the fellow had led to the sharing of his apparently comical story, and Holmes and I had burst out laughing. The humor had faded, however, when Holmes heard enough to suspect that there was villainy afoot, hidden behind the man's curious tale. Before we were finished, a notable criminal had been captured, and a bold plot to steal a fortune from the cellar vaults of a bank had been prevented. It had been an interesting case, and I had recorded it in my notes and then used it the following year when publishing a series of sketches about Holmes in a rather new periodical. But as to the original fellow who had first brought the unique problem to Holmes's attention – ? Why, I confess that I hadn't given him a moment's thought since, assuming that he'd settled back into his old life.

What new problem, I wondered, *has Jabez Wilson gotten himself into?*

The next morning was overcast, and several times on my walk to Baker Street, a cold October wind whipped a hint of rain into my face. Depending upon the direction of the streets I traversed, the wind seemed to be intensified, as if it found a path that it preferred, allowing it to speed ahead unimpeded. It was a stark contrast to the pleasant weather I'd enjoyed just the day before, with a sky so pure and blue that it looked like that of Scotland in my boyhood – the same blue as on the Scottish Saltire, but with an additional glow from the autumn sun.

Sherlock Holmes was dead. It hit me yet again, as it always did throughout every day since early May of the previous year when he'd fallen in combat at the Reichenbach Falls. This time, I was reminded as I crossed the intersection of York Street and Upper Montague. I felt that if I looked just right, I could see the time back in '88 when Holmes and I had been cornered there by four toughs, sent by Lord ----- when he felt that we were getting a bit too close to identifying one of the Rippers. A proud Mason when required, and a wastrel always, Lord ----- had been tasked with shutting our mouths, but he sent the wrong men to do the job. I wondered if I could still find any of the biggest one's teeth if I looked in the nearby gutter. He'd certainly left that night without any of them still in his mouth. The second had lingered for a week before peritonitis took him. I'd seen the third a year later, when I'd had reason to visit Newgate Prison, sitting on a little cart in the yard because his legs no longer functioned. The fourth was a craven coward, and his testimony helped to definitively send Lord ----- to the gallows. Holmes and I were there that day, and the man refused a hood, staring at my friend as he dropped into his eternal punishment. I wish that he'd spared a glance for me as well. There were dark thoughts that I wished to convey to him before he departed.

It seemed that over the last few years, some of these dark thoughts found their way into my head far too easily. The events of the investigation and destruction of the Rippers cabal were some of the darkest that I've ever witnessed, and I found myself rather changed afterwards, as my belief in the innate goodness of mankind was cracked. That was in the dark autumn of 1888, and not long after, Holmes's investigation into the terrible web of Professor Moriarty had accelerated. I believe that Holmes's defeat of The Rippers – evil men at all levels of society, from the cess-pool bottoms to the highest seats of power – was his finest hour, even greater than when he ended Moriarty's reign. The latter might have been even more worthy and far-reaching, but I couldn't completely say it was a victory, for it ended with my friend's death.

Now, in October 1892, I was faced with further opportunities for despair as my dear wife, Mary, seemed to be sliding deeper into ill health, and I didn't know what to do to prevent it.

I threw myself into my work during the day, and otherwise made sure to save time for my beloved wife. I'd been through too many previous losses, and I'd learned my painful lessons about wasted opportunities. I still maintained my interest in the detection of crime – How could I not? – and Mary often encouraged me to wade a little deeper, making myself

47

available to my friends at Scotland Yard when they came calling. (And it was fortunate that I did, because it cemented my friendship with them, and they lifted me up when I could not otherwise be lifted the following spring, when Mary passed.)

During this time, I occasionally visited Baker Street, usually to see Mrs. Hudson, but sometimes when it was necessary that I retrieve some item from the abandoned sitting room. Curiously, it was maintained nearly as it was before Holmes died, looking much as it had when he and I had departed London on 25 April, 1891 – with only one of us to return a couple of weeks later. The only differences in the room from the way it had been before, likely noticeable only to Mrs. Hudson and myself, was where Mycroft Holmes had paid to have it restored following the fire of 24 April, the night before we left, when Moriarty had a fire set and tried to burn Holmes out. Some of the items and papers lost that night were now gone forever, but otherwise, the room looked as if Holmes could return at any minute. (If he did, he'd be dismayed to find that Mrs. Hudson was dusting it regularly in his absence. He always set a great store of value upon the levels of unremoved dust.)

I had seen Mycroft Holmes on a number of occasions since Holmes's death, some sombre, and others quite dry and businesslike, but I'd never had the courage to ask him why he paid to maintain his brother's rooms, as if it were some museum that only the landlady and I could see. Mrs. Hudson once told me that Mycroft never visited the place, so he wasn't keeping it as his own effort to find connection with his late brother. Perhaps I didn't ask because I didn't want to force Mycroft into admitting he had a soft and sentimental side. I liked to think of him, in those days when my thoughts were often too dark, as the cold blunt edge of the British Government, using his agents to deal with any problems that arose.

Soon, I would find myself in that same position, to a lesser degree, directing my own agents to right a wrong.

I arrived just at nine, even as a hansom cab discharged its fare. I paused on the doorstep, the key I still possessed out to open the door, and waited for Mr. Jabez Wilson to join me.

He had aged terribly in the two years since we'd last met. Then, he'd been elderly and florid-faced, but now he was pale, as if his heart was giving him trouble. His once bright-red hair seemed dull and rusty, and there was a great deal of white around his ears and in his weepers and streaked up and across through the rest of the mass – now also a bit thinner than before. He had been stout. Now he looked to be down at least two stone. His previously shabby clothing looked to be even more so. He still had the curious square Chinese coin upon his watch chain, but his Masonic tie-pin was gone.

48

"Dr. Watson?" he said, peering up at me as he approached. I confirmed it, and he shook my hand. Then, noticing my up-and-down examination, he frankly stated, "I've come down a bit in the world since we last met." He shook his head and passed a hand up and down to display it, as if to say, "Look upon me and despair!"

At that moment, the cold wind pressed us, and I urged him to come inside, ringing the bell as I unlocked and opened the door. As we entered, Mrs. Hudson came from within her ground-floor demesne and helped take and hang our coats. Then, I indicated that Wilson should proceed me up the stairs. He did so, wearily, two and three steps at a time, and pausing at the turn of the landing to catch his breath.

At the top, he stepped aside so that I could lead him into the sitting room. Before I could do so, however, he spoke with a small laugh.

"It really is seventeen steps," he said, causing me to turn my head curiously.

"Eh?"

"Seventeen steps," he explained. "You and Mr. Holmes remarked on it in one of your stories – the one about the German king."

"Bohemian," I corrected. "A nobleman from one of the moribund houses."

He nodded, but he wasn't really listening. "Do you report everything that happens? Are you completely accurate?"

Leery of which way this seemed to be drifting, I answered with a cautious, "Yes."

He nodded again. "Umm-hmm. Umm-hmm. And the story about snake? Was the wicked doctor's name really 'Royal'?"

"Well, it was 'Roylott'," I corrected.

"So you changed it for the magazine!" He said it with vigor, and not as a question.

"No, you misunderstand. His name was 'Roylott', and that's how it was reported in *The Strand*."

He seemed a big deflated then. "Oh. I'd hoped to find that you – at least sometimes – made changes when you prepared Mr. Holmes's cases for publication. After all, you stated that my pawnshop was in Saxe-Coburg Square, when it's actually Charterhouse Square, near Barbicon, and when describing where the interviews for the League took place, you called it 'Pope's Court' instead of Mitre Square."

In fact, I did sometimes make minimal changes, and I had altered these place names as he indicated – not willingly, but upon the advice of my literary agent, who felt that identifying the real locations might serve to irritate the other residents of those spots. I sometimes altered a name as well, but in this case, hadn't felt that it was necessary. But for the purposes of this conversation, to keep things simple, I merely replied, "Mr. Holmes wouldn't have appreciated if I fictionalized important details. He always argued for a scientific presentation of his work."

Wilson frowned, and a pair of vertical lines formed below the corners of his mouth. I didn't recall them from when he'd been heavier – even when vexed by the machinations of the Red Headed League.

"I am disappointed to hear it," he said. "I'd hoped to bring action against you – No offense, sir! – for being willing to change details when relating some people's misfortunes, but choosing to reveal every accurate aspect of my little problem for the world to see and ridicule. I saw you glance to my missing Masonic tie pin." I nodded. "It was taken from me – the Masons kicked he out for being a fool – which they discovered by reading your story!

"I spoke to an attorney – Although one can't buy much advice for what I can afford these days! – and he said that I have no case, but I thought that I would try anyway. Not knowing how to reach you – The offices of *The Strand* magazine are singularly tight-lipped! – I attempted to see Mr. Holmes here in Baker Street, but the housekeeper – "

"The landlady," I interrupted. "Mrs. Hudson owns the lease on the building. Mr. Holmes – and I before my marriage – were tenants."

He nodded and went on, politely waiting until I was done, but not listening. "The housekeeper told me that Mr. Holmes was unavailable. I returned several times to the same story, and finally she suggested that she could get a message to you – which was what I wanted all along, but never quite thought to convey. My mind is all over these last few months, you see, and I'd hoped that, by bringing a lawsuit for defamation against you – No office intended, sir, I assure you! Nothing personal – Just a matter of business! – that I might gain enough coin to get out of my unfortunate situation and move along. I've considered it anyway – simply walking away from the shop and never looking back – but I'm too old to start over somewhere else, and they would know what I was planning should I start to sell things in order to raise capital."

I raised a placating hand. "Hold up, Mr. Wilson. I'm interested in your story, but you must tell it in order." We had been standing near the doorway, and I gestured toward the fireplace and the familiar chairs grouped there. "Would you care to have a seat and share the details?"

He suddenly looked wary, as if suspecting a trap. "And see it told in next month's *Strand*? No thank you, sir!" Then, as if hearing himself, he sagged a bit, stating, "I apologize, Doctor. Two years ago, you and Mr. Holmes came to my aid – even though I didn't suspect how much I required it – and you couldn't have known what it would lead to. And your story: I know that you were simply relating one of Mr. Holmes's more interesting cases. It probably never occurred to you how it made me appear to my neighbors and customers – just a gullible old fool, easy to bring to a disadvantage. Not the most optimal position for a pawnbroker!"

By then I'd led him to the basket chair. There was a cheery fire going, and the room was already warm and cozy, courtesy of Mrs. Hudson. I stepped to the open landing door, called down for tea, and then seated myself in my old chair to Wilson's immediate left.

Under no circumstances would I have instead chosen Holmes's armchair. I still half-expected to look over and see him sitting there again someday.

"You allude to unpleasant circumstances," I prompted. "May I ask you to elaborate?"

He sat up straighter – he had been abjectly slumped – and looked around. "Where is Mr. Holmes? No offense, sir, but I'd prefer to wait and just tell it just once."

I let a silence fall as I considered my response. Over the past year-and-a-half, I'd had to explain more times than I could count that Holmes was dead. It had been reported in the press at the time, but one must remember that while he was widely known in certain circles – those he'd helped and those he'd defeated, the good and the bad, the police and the criminals – many others hadn't yet heard of him, and whatever appeared in the press was likely ignored. So many people still came looking for him, having heard his name and reputation, and they had to be convinced that he was no longer available to look into their varied problems.

Clearly, Jabez Wilson was one of those people.

"Mr. Holmes is no longer with us," I said, my mouth stumbling as usual to find a more gentle euphemism for *dead*. "Early May of last year. It happened while he was investigating a complex case on the Continent."

Wilson chewed on that for a moment, and was still silent until after Mrs. Hudson had come and gone. He held his quite-sugared tea for a number of long moments before raising it, giving the cup a couple of gusty cooling puffs, and then drank it all down. Licking his lips, he set the cup aside and made to rise.

"Well, then," he said, clearing his throat, "if there's no help to be had here, I'd best be returning to my shop."

I rose as well. "Hold, Mr. Wilson! At least tell me your story. Perhaps I can suggest something."

He gave me a suspicious look, as if still believing that I was seeking more fodder for my magazine narratives. Then, with a shrug, as if to say that he had nothing better to do, he sat back down, put his hands on knees, rocked forward and back a couple of times, and told me of his life since October 1890.

51

"In some ways, the morning that I visited here, and told my curious story to you and Mr. Holmes, [1] was my last easy moment. Before then, I was able to fool myself that all was well. Oh, I don't blame you. If my young assistant, Vincent Spaulding – I mean *John Clay* – had been able to successfully rob the nearby bank, then the tunnel back to my shop would have been found, and there would have been so many questions, and suspicions that I was also involved, even though I hadn't fled. It would have been assumed that I knew about the tunnel, and gave permission for it. And no one would have believed that farrago concerning the League. In hind-sight, I can barely believe it myself.

"Afterwards, I had no assistant, and seemed to have no luck finding another. The girl that had worked for me left as well. I suspect she – let us say that she had a . . . a *fascination* with John Clay. My wife having died years ago, I was alone, and thus could only open the shop in a limited capacity. On top of that, the City and Suburban Bank slapped a bill on me for repairs caused by the tunnel intruding into their cellar! That ate up the last of my savings, and I was forced to take a small loan besides, which I could barely repay.

"And then last Christmas, I had a visit from Fraser Guy."

He said it and then paused, as if waiting to see my reaction, but I had none, for I'd never before heard the name. *Perhaps Holmes knows of him,* I thought, glancing without thought to my friend's chair. But he wasn't there.

When I didn't react, Wilson continued. "He is a dangerous fellow in those parts, there on the edge of the East End and only a mile from where the Ripper roamed, and he'd smelled my weakness and came to take advantage of it. 'Ho, Mr. Wilson!' he said that first visit as if were friends. 'I hear that your days have been dark of late. I'm here to change that – to throw you a life-line, you see.' He took a look around, stepping here and there and prodding my meager wares as if he were poking a finger into a refuse pile. 'What you need is a *partner*, and I'm that fellow! Congratulations, Mr. Wilson!'

"Then he rubbed his big hands together briskly and proceeded to explain what this 'partnership' actually meant. You look as if you don't know him, Dr. Watson. I envy you that safety. He is a notorious fence, and he rightly perceived that setting up in such a shop as mine – nearly destitute and empty, and ridiculed to boot – would make it the perfectly anonymous place he needed to carry out his activities. 'And I even hear that you can provide me with a tunnel into the bank on the next street," he said, and laughed and laughed. I was too despondent to offer any correction, or truly any resistance at all. This seemed to be the natural progression of my sad life since that day I'd dropped by here, sitting in this very chair, to ask about the sudden cessation of the Red Headed League. Oh, for those carefree days!" And he threw up his hands dramatically. If he'd been a minister, the sincerity of the action might have been enough to win over a soul, but instead I was simply left with an uneasiness, feeling somehow responsible for this mess.

"This 'Fraser Guy'," I said. "He's still there?"

"Oh yes," was Wilson's emphatic reply. "He's infested my cellars like the filth in King Augeas' stables. It would take a Hercules to force him out, but – " And he now glanced toward my old friend's empty chair. " – as you say, the only Hercules that I've ever met is gone." He then shook his head and stared at his feet. "No offense, sir."

I chewed my lip, wondering if I was about to bite off something too big to swallow. Then, "Mr. Wilson, are you still residing in the building?"

"I am. Guy lets me keep a room upstairs. 'Wouldn't do,' he says, 'if someone comes knocking, not to be able to show them the owner.' But no one has ever asked. Either they don't know or care, or they're afraid of Fraser Guy and will never come knocking."

I stood and he looked up, my sudden motion leaving him rather confused. "I will help you," I said. "I don't quite know how, yet, but I will." I gave him my card. "This is my home and practice. A message there will reach me. In the meantime, just return to the normality of your days, such as they are, and I'll set some plans in motion. I'll . . . I'll come up with a plan."

He stood then as well, peering up at me. He seemed to see something that he could accept, for he stuck out his hand and shook mine firmly. Then he turned and, without a backward glance, opened the door, stepped onto the landing, went down the stairs – seventeen of them, as I re-confirmed from counting his solid descending footsteps – and so out the front door and back into the passing masses.

"Well," I said aloud while sighing heavily and glancing again at Holmes's chair. Once again I was amazed at how nothing is ever truly finished. Wilson's brush with the Red Headed League had been two years earlier, and now it was back. Holmes had died on the fourth of May, 1891, and still his affairs reached out to involve me.

And perhaps Mr. Fraser Guy had also had previous involvement with Sherlock Holmes – and now he'd learn that the connection wasn't severed for him either.

I found an entry for Guy in Holmes's scrapbooks. It had taken me a while to decipher his system, but by the time of his passing, I'd become fairly comfortable with locating what I needed. I lamented that the volumes hadn't been updated since he left England, but they were still a valuable resource, and I wondered that Mycroft, in preserving the rooms, hadn't at least seen about donating them to the Yard. Some there wouldn't have known what to do with them – but others would appreciate their value.

Guy was forty-four years old, a transplant to London from Manchester. As of early 1891, he was unmarried, but had four sons ranging from twenty-eight to thirteen by three different mothers. This was attributed to his unexplained animal magnetism over some types of women, and his aggressive abuse of others. All four sons served as his lieutenants. He was a big man, and his sons nearly as large, even the youngest, and they, along with four or five other men of the lowest character, made up his gang, which was fancifully called "The Stepney Saints". (Holmes had once wasted some time in tracking down the origins of the names of different London criminal gangs, thinking that as he perceived a pattern, it might reveal some truth that he could record in a monograph, but he lost interest when it appeared that names were randomly generated for irrelevent reasons.) As Wilson had mentioned, Guy's specialty was fencing stolen goods. A spot in Wilson's stagnated pawn shop would make a perfect location for such work.

"Doctor," said Inspector Lestrade, apparently on his way out, but willing to stop and talk when I unexpectedly arrived at his office door. "You were right – when Wilkins went back to where Harbolt's body was found, the grass was dead, indicating that he'd been there for several days longer than we thought. It must have been Trigiani that stabbed him, since his alibi – now proven false – was the only thing keeping us from arresting him."

"That's good news," I said, "but I'm actually here about something else."

"Oh?" He shifted his focus away from the Harbolt murder and invited me to a chair, which he uncovered by moving a foot-tall mound of leaning files. "How can I help you?" he asked, shutting the door.

Since Holmes's passing, I'd formed closer friendships with a number of the Yard's inspectors. For quite some time I'd worked with them, and I'd always had a great deal more patience toward them than the late detective. Also, I felt something of a kinship with them, possibly due to my military days, as they themselves had the same respectful camaraderie, despite their rivalries, that one found in the service. "*We few, we happy few, we band of brothers . . . .*" Sadly, it took Holmes's passing and removal from the equation for my connection with the inspectors to truly grow and solidify, for he was always like the gravitational pull of great celestial body whose transit affected all the other smaller objects around it.

"What can you tell me," I asked, "of the Stepney Saints?"

Lestrade leaned back and eyed me speculatively, saying "They aren't a bunch that you should be messing with." He declared it without need for consideration. "In the last year, Fraser Guy has proven himself to be a master at the art of fencing, and since he's also demonstrated that he's a master at the art of murder, he's eliminated his competition. He's smart enough to do it without leaving any evidence that ties him to what we can prove, and he's become the leader in his field, one might say."

"And how has this been allowed to happen?" I asked. "If he's so well known, then why not arrest and prosecute him?"

Lestrade shook his head, apparently at my *naïveté*. "Knowing and stopping – or arresting and prosecuting, as you say – are two different things. One reason – and this is not something we're proud of – is that the villain you know about is easier to deal with than the one you don't. We've rather let Guy run the table – for a while – so that he's a monopoly unto himself. That way, when we are ready, we only have to take him down and not worry about the concurrent small fry – because just then, there aren't any small fry left. He's eliminated them for us. Of course, taking him out of the game means that there's a new vacuum to fill, and a new set of criminals inevitably arise to fill it. That's how Guy found his place: When Professor Moriarty's organization was destroyed, all of the little fish that were left, as well as the organizations from elsewhere that were slavering to get into London, having previously been kept away, now had an opportunity. We let them thin the herd, in a Darwin-like way, to see just who we'd be facing at the end of the day. That was Fraser Guy. He's had his year. Now it sounds like he's ripe enough to pluck – that is, if you have something for me that we can use."

"I don't know," I said. "I met with someone today – one of Holmes's old clients – whose business has been unwillingly subsumed into Guy's enterprise, and he seemed rather hopeless – enough so that I said I'd help. Afterwards, however, I realized that my skills in this type of fight are limited." I then told him of Jabez Wilson, reminding him of the events of October 1890, and relating what had occurred to the poor fellow since then. "I cannot disguise myself and go loitering about the East End as Holmes would have done, putting in my hand at just the right spot and plucking out the one person with the one fact that can unlock the puzzle. However, I have some ideas of who to approach – and you and the Yard were at the top of the list."

Lestrade nodded. "Rightly so." He stood. "Let me go find Peter Jones. That red-headed business was his case, and Fraser Guy falls squarely in his bailiwick."

With a promise that he'd return in a moment, he stepped out, leaving the door open. I sat quietly in my chair, my mind wandering from meeting Jabez Wilson that morning, and back two years to the first time I'd seen him. It was easy from there to drift into other memories, good and bad. The laughter Holmes and I had shared when first hearing Jabez Wilson's curious story, and his understandable embarrassment and anger. The subsequent visit to Wilson's shop in the southeast corner of Charterhouse Square. The discussion the previous year with my literary agent about renaming that location for the published story, as someone nearby tenant might have objections (without either of us ever considering renaming Jabez Wilson).

I thought of the branch bank on Aldersgate Street, just behind Wilson's shop, which had been the location of a second robbery attempt just three months later – partly because, Holmes thought, its weaknesses had been identified during John Clay's defeated attempt. Holmes had been consulted on that affair as well, quickly resolving it to the manager's complete satisfaction. Then there was the matter of the street drain a quarter-mile far west, in the intersection of Charterhouse Street and Farringdon Road, opening downward into the lost River Fleet. I would never forget when Holmes and I had tracked the Smithfield Market Skinner, that terrible murderer who mutilated his victims to steal as much as he could of their largest bodily organ. When cornered, he had fled under the street to the lost Fleet, and we had followed down and through the darkness, finding his lair in a dank chamber far back and below Fetter Lane, where the horrors we'd seen before that day were only a precursor. Holmes had pushed me aside when the Skinner came for him, and if I hadn't found my service revolver in the darkness and pulled the trigger when I did . . . .

A constable leaned in abruptly, interrupting my reminiscences. "Seen the inspector?" he asked. I didn't know him, but he seemed to recognize me. I said that Lestrade should be back shortly, and he nodded. "Big break in the Molesey case," he said before vanishing back the way he'd come.

Lestrade rejoined me just a moment later, bringing with him Inspector Peter Jones, a fellow that I didn't know as well as some of the Yarders, but whom I very much respected nonetheless.

"A constable was looking for you," I said. "He said there's been a break in the Molesey case."

"Ah!" A smile lit his face. "Big doings. A pity you're tied up with this Fraser Guy business. Fancy a side-trip down to Molesley? You've never seen a victim done up quite like what we found in nearby Hampton Court Palace."

56

"Perhaps I'd better not," I said. "I'll forego it his time. My regular duties are where my efforts must lie."

"Don't be too sure," Lestrade responded. "Your surgeon work is much more trusted that of Fernard. I'm still not going to be satisfied until you're working for us full-time." He turned to Peter Jones. "Fill me in when you have a plan. I want to go with you." Then back to me: "Feel free to use my office. Now I must hurry to Waterloo. Good luck to both of you. Fraser Guy is a villain whose time has come."

Then he was gone, and Peter Jones was saying, "Fraser Guy, eh? What can I do to help?"

I hadn't seen Jones for some time, as his duties had gradually altered since the arrest of John Clay. Saving the French gold – albeit with Holmes's guidance – had been quite the feather in his cap, but Clay's capture had also been something of a burden, as the fellow was one of Professor Moriarty's mid-level creatures, and therefore, Jones was indirectly drawn into the escalating multi-front investigations into the Professor's affairs. As such, Jones, who had previously shown an aptitude for the tedious work required when chasing down obscure and twisted financial records, was shunted onto an administrative path that meant more responsibility and prestige within the Yard, but a disconnection with his previous police duties – something that I felt did not entirely please him.

When I began, mentioning Jabez Wilson, Jones shook his head.

"Poor fellow," he said. "His pawn shop was barely squeaking by. If Clay hadn't worked there practically for free, it would have already closed before the robbery ever occurred. How does Fraser Guy enter the picture?"

I finished relating Wilson's story, and then Jones excused himself for a moment. When he returned, he explained. "I telephoned the station that's responsible for the area around Barbican, Smithfield Market, Charterhouse Square, and so on, and spoke to one of the constables. He stated that Wilson's shop is doing a steady business, but he sees nothing suspicious – just the usual pawn-broking trade going in and out, and the store is filled with more items than it's had in years."

"So does this mean that Wilson simply spun a story for me, for some reason of his own? Perhaps related to the publication of his indirect involvement in the gold robbery?"

Jones shook his head. "Not at all. This is exactly the type of thing that Fraser Guy would set up, and if he's using the pawn shop as a cover for his fencing operation, then he'd want the shop to appear somewhat successful, to cover when people on his business go in and out. If the shop was nearly dead, the neighbors might pay more attention when Guy's people show up." He tapped his lip and said, "I take it that the point of this is to get poor Mr. Wilson out from under."

"It is, but that's only half of it. I also want to make sure that he still has a good business left when Fraser Guy has been excised from his life. I have an idea about that, separate from what the Yard can accomplish."

Jones nodded. "Give me a day or two, and I think we can come up with something that you'll like."

I took a moment to explain what I was thinking and, as it would serve to pull in tandem with what Jones had planned, we shook hands, and I left the building and turned east along the Embankment, seeking a Wiggins.

After meeting with Jabez Wilson that morning in Baker Street, I had arranged to have my practice covered for the rest of the day by my obliging neighbor. It was something that he'd done quite regularly just a few years before, when it was typical for Holmes to request my presence, either at the Baker Street rooms for some appointment, or when stopping by my Paddington home and practice unannounced to pick me up as we set out for what might be a couple of hours or a couple of days.

Although I was nearly certain that Holmes wouldn't – without prior warning – commit me to weeks away from London after I was married, as he had during my bachelor days in Baker Street, there was always the shred of worry that he *might*. He'd had no compunction about volunteering my extended services in the fall of 1888 during the Dartmoor expedition, or the time in '84 when I learned on the morning of my departure that I was to spend nearly two weeks in Bath, watching for the passage of a one-eyed man along the north side of the Abbey. My time was wasted – the fellow never even went to Bath – but Holmes did acknowledge that my efforts weren't mispent and that his case was bolstered ten-fold when I was able to report that a beautiful woman was there every day, waiting with ever-increasing disappointment for the same man who never arrived.

My journey was nearly two miles, and a cab would have been quicker, but I wanted time to think. Since Holmes's death, I hadn't remained entirely unconnected to the world of investigation. Knowing my long association with my late friend, his acquaintances were occasionally desperate enough to seek my help when they found themselves in situations beyond their control. In most cases, relying on my own intelligence guided by experience, I was able to assist them. Sometimes these same people recommended me to strangers, and I did what I could. More often, the inspectors at Scotland Yard sought to include me. We had become friends, and also they were often frustrated with the police surgeons that they were forced to use, like Doctor Fernard, so they asked for my outside opinion. I was flattered, and did my best, but there was never an instance where at some point, I didn't ask myself, "*What would Sherlock Holmes do?*"

Because of this, I used my time walking from Scotland Yard to Gray's Inn to consider Wilson's story, and what I recalled of the area of London where his shop was located. But my observations were of limited value. I needed something better.

I followed the Embankment to Waterloo Bridge, and then turned north and east alongside Somerset House, working my way toward High Holborn, and thence into Gray's Inn, and the chambers of my attorney, Marchmont. He was glad to see me and asked what I needed, and I pointed to one of his clerks. "Can I borrow him for half-an-hour? I need to talk something over with him."

Marchmont, always a fine fellow, readily agreed, and the clerk followed me out and down to the passage leading to Gate Street, just northwest of Lincoln's Inn Fields, and thence into The Ship, where we found a quiet corner for a talk.

Michael Wiggins was looking prosperous and happy, and I was glad. I'd always worried that he was too thin, but he now looked fit and healthy. I congratulated him upon noticing the wedding ring on his left hand, recalling that he'd been married just the year before, and he proudly told me that he was to be a father in the spring.

I had first met him sometime in the early eighties, when he was one of the ever-changing group of lads (and occasional lasses) that made up Holmes's unofficial Irregulars, a band of street children ranging across various ages whom he had recruited to serve as his eyes and ears, seeing and hearing what others could not. He'd already had this organization in place when I met him in 1881, having formed them up several years earlier during the time he was establishing his practice while living in Montague Street.

One of his first Irregulars was a lad named Wiggins, who had quickly demonstrated his quality and settled in as the leader of the bunch. Holmes had performed a service for the Wiggins family – namely, saving their mother from a charge of murder [2] – and afterwards, a firm bond had formed between them and the detective. As the Irregulars grew, older members departed while younger took their place – many of them members of the extended Wiggins family, and usually with a Wiggins in charge. Michael Wiggins, while never a leader, had been an important and effective member of the troop nearly ten years before. Then, when he reached adulthood, Holmes found him a position as one of Marchmont's clerks.

One aspect of Holmes's use of the Irregulars that is often forgotten was that he didn't simply pay them the random shilling for following someone or confirming some obscure fact. He made sure that they were clothed and fed and schooled, and then he found places for them – jobs, or even careers for the ones who were willing to work hard and study and pay their dues. London was full of former Irregulars who owed their success to Sherlock Holmes, and his death the previous year hadn't negated that. When I explained why I was there and what I wanted – namely, for a report on Wilson's situation from an Irregular perspective – Wiggins understood immediately, and knew exactly who to involve and what to do.

Finishing our drinks, I walked Wiggins back to Marchmont's office and then continued east, three-quarters of a mile or so to Barts, to confer with The Sphinx.

Passing through the Henry VIII Gate on Giltspur Street, I wound through the dark passage and then right across the hospital's inner court to the modest side-door, opening into a wing of the great hospital. From there I went up the bleak stone staircase and the down a corridor, and so into the chemical laboratory.

The Sphinx was Henry Barth, a chap who worked as a laboratory assistant, alongside the student physicians, to clean up their messes and help set up experiments as needed. Due to a congenital handicap – the poor fellow had been born with a hunched back – he'd had difficulties all his life, but his steady work ethic and bright intelligence had led him to a position in which he seemed most satisfied. He'd already been at Barts for quite some time when I was a student, and he was still there now.

The origin of his nickname, "The Sphinx", was much debated when I was a student, and that likely hadn't changed amongst the current crop. Some said it was due to his physical shape, somewhat similar to the Great Sphinx of Giza. (Having been there and having seen The Sphinx, I didn't see the resemblance.) Others claimed it was because of his round-about way of answering questions that could grow tedious, as they resembled riddles more than definitive responses. Whatever the case, there was one thing about him that I required that day: His knowledge of local criminals in that area.

I believe that I'm the only person that Henry ever told about his secret. He was a model hospital employee in every way – except that sometimes he stole inconsequential medical supplies. Nothing more than small amounts of bandages, for instance, or needles and suture for sewing up wounds. The only way I knew is that once he'd needed help for a procedure that was more than his informally acquired skills could conclude. It was then that I learned about Henry's informal clinic, where he provided care for those in society who would not receive it otherwise, either because of their lowest stations, or their fear of approaching anyone in authority, even a doctor.

60

Henry had a brother, Albert, and both had been born within a mile of Barts. That was their world. While Henry had displayed the gumption to work hard and find a position, using his intelligence to overcome his difficulty, Albert had become a petty criminal, and not a very good one. He got by through his loose attachment to local gangs. He never made many ripples, except for once, when he was shot by being in the wrong place at the wrong time. Henry tried to treat him, could not, and recruited me. That was when I learned his secret. I recognized the stolen materials, and Henry confessed. I kept the knowledge to myself, knowing that Henry Barth was too good a man to lose over such small potatoes, and that Albert Barth was harmless and helpless, and didn't need to be thrown into the indifferent arms of the Law. For this Henry was ever grateful.

Now I wanted to ask him a question – unrelated to the information that Wiggins was assembling, and something that could be best obtained by a long-time resident, since this was Henry's part of London, and he could locate the answers I sought.

I explained why I was there and what I needed, and why I needed it, not worrying that Henry would betray me, or the fact that Jabez Wilson was seeking to escape from someone as dangerous as Fraser Guy. Henry frowned and nodded, understanding the implications.

"What would happen to the man who bites the hand that feeds him?" he vaguely asked, from which I assumed he referred to Wilson and Guy, should the latter find out that the former had looked for help from a friend of the late Sherlock Holmes. "Will all who seek answers be satisfied, or will the only response be the monotonous sigh of the unchecked and indifferent winds?" A moment's consideration led me to think that possibly he meant that I might or might not be content with whatever he learned.

I nodded as if that was it, told him I'd be back to see what he'd found in a couple of days, and left – glancing, as I always did whenever visiting here, over to the old chemical table where I'd first met Holmes on that New Year's Day over a decade before. How often does one realize that he or she is in a moment that will change life's direction forever? On battlefields, of course, and when attending births or deaths, or at terrible accidents where lives are lost or ruined. But what about the quiet moments, such as when I was first introduced to Sherlock Holmes at that table? I had no intimation then of that moment's importance. I'd awakened that morning, worried about my finances and ill-tempered. I'd met an old friend and we'd gone to lunch. He'd mentioned someone who was seeking to share lodgings – which was exactly what I *needed*, even if it wasn't what I *wanted*. I'd been doing fine by myself in a hotel off the Strand – except for the small qualification that my expenditures were running ahead of my limited income. I'd gone along to Barts to meet a possible future co-lodger, not realizing the precipice that I approached, or that I was stepping beyond the edge and jumping headlong into a different life.

That old table had been used hundreds – nay, thousands – of times since I was introduced there to Sherlock Holmes. It was just a table, and it was in just a room, but it was where I'd taken a momentous step, and I could never see it without remembering all that happened after.

I had one more stop that day. I wanted to see Jabez Wilson's old pawn shop.

Upon exiting the hospital, with St. Paul's in view just to the south, I worked my way through a couple of passages to the east, whereupon I set my steps on Aldersgate Street toward the Underground Station. Just a short walk past it, I turned left toward Charterhouse Street, and almost immediately reached Charterhouse Square.

It was much as I remembered it from two years earlier. When I'd published the narrative related to Wilson's curious experience, I'd described it as *"a poky, little, shabby-genteel place, where four lines of dingy two-storied brick houses looked out into a small railed-in enclosure, where a lawn of weedy grass and a few clumps of faded laurel-bushes made a hard fight against a smoke-laden and uncongenial atmosphere."* There was nothing royal-looking about it, and I had to wonder at the obscure reasoning behind my literary agent's insistence that I change the location name from *Charterhouse Square* to the royally associated *Saxe-Coburg Square*. But he had lots of strange and curious "fancies", as he called them when our disagreements over his editorial notions became heated, and he often sullenly retreated by insisting that his "fancies must be consulted, Watson. They must be consulted."

Wilson's pawnshop, No. 42, was at the southeast corner. The woodwork was painted black, and three gilt balls beside a brown board lettered *Jabez Wilson* marked the place from its neighbors. Two years earlier, I had wondered how such a business might thrive in this dull little pocket, with no cross-traffic from the nearby busy road besides the residents, and no reason to come here – it wasn't even a square, but rather a pentagon – unless some historian wished to gaze upon the enclosed grassy garden, which had once been a fourteenth-century plague pit.

Wilson's shop seemed more prosperous than before, and now I understood why. I considered going inside – I could ask for a quote to pawn my brother's old pocket-watch before deciding to keep it after all – but I realized that seeing the inside of the building would add nothing to my limited knowledge. Fraser Guy was almost certainly not there, and I might encounter someone that I had met before, which would jeopardize whatever scheme we were trying to assemble. Perhaps even coming to the Square had been a mistake – but I had inexplicably felt the need to see the place once more. Perhaps it was because I knew that Sherlock Holmes would have wanted to survey the field before the battle, as he had that day in October 1890 when we'd stood there and faced John Clay, while Holmes sought indications of a tunnel.

Having taken my look, I retraced my steps to the station and had a noisy unpleasant ride back to Paddington.

For two days, I went about my usual affairs – seeing patients at my practice and in their homes, helping at the nearby St. Mary's Hospital, and most of all, spending time with Mary, worrying to myself at her worsening health while staying cheerful and positive to hide my fears.

And I also made and kept one appointment with a banker of my acquaintance that might do some good, or might be a waste of time, depending on how the campaign against Fraser Guy progressed.

It had been a Tuesday when I met with Jabez Wilson in Baker Street, and on Friday, I attended a conference at Scotland Yard. Lestrade was there, and Inspectors Gregson and Bradstreet as well. Athelney Jones had invited himself, and I appreciated it, for what he lacked in intelligence was more than balanced by his exceptional character and thirst for justice. He was speaking with Michael Wiggins, who seemed completely at ease, even laughing at one of the inspector's asides – something about how young Michael had once vexed him, but now "All water under the bridge, lad!" Peter Jones opened the meeting, speaking for just a moment before turning over the reins to his colleague, Inspector Patterson.

"After your visit the other day, Doctor," Peter Jones explained, "the first thing I did was seek out Patterson. He has an encyclopedic knowledge on the criminal classes, and I knew we'd want him involved, now that it's Fraser Guy's turn to walk the plank." He nodded to Patterson and sat down.

There were many who dismissed Inspector Patterson as an "odd duck" – though less since the destruction of Professor Moriarty's gang than before. Upon joining the Yard, he'd been an introverted and often absent officer, and when one did encounter him, it was an awkward event. The man wasn't eloquent or loquacious by any means, and he preferred being out in the shadows to spending time in the office.

Holmes had spotted Patterson's talents immediately – his ability to disguise himself, and then insinuate whatever identity he'd assumed into the criminal element. As this was also one of Holmes's gifts, he had found a kindred spirit. It was during this time that the confrontation with Professor Moriarty was escalating, and Patterson was an early and eager recruit to Holmes's specialized little army, filled with only those that he could truly trust. After Moriarty's defeat, one might have thought that Patterson's major work was done, but he'd stayed busy, using the same methods he'd perfected over the previous years.

Unlike Jones, Patterson remained seated when he spoke. His tone was low but clear, and everyone in the room held to his words.

"Like most of them when they get so successful, Fraser Guy has gotten arrogant and careless," Patterson explained succinctly. "He doesn't try to hide anything anymore, and we have more than enough witnesses – solid witnesses – to charge him with everything from receiving stolen goods, smuggling, intimidation, beatings, theft, and murder. For a time, he's useful to us, as watching the comings-and-goings of his foot soldiers, and those doing business with him, has let us keep accumulating evidence while seeing which further trails to follow. It was a method that Mr. Holmes and I worked out a few years ago. It was successful when boxing in the Professor, it was foolproof against Guy.

"Now is the time to remove him, because his successor is already positioning to make a play, and we'll be happy to see him fill the empty spot when Guy is gone: Sidney Fulworth – 'The Blade' he likes to call himself, playing up a knife fight he had when he was young, winning only because his opponent slipped in Sidney's blood. But he's a fool, and even as he seizes control, he'll mismanage everything as if it's a music hall comedy.

"I believe that the warrants are prepared?" Patterson glanced at Peter Jones, who nodded. Then Patterson leaned forward to see Michael Wiggins. "And you can tell us where to find everyone?"

Wiggins nodded, sitting up straighter on the edge of his chair. "After Dr. Watson visited the other day, I found some of the other lads – grown now, like me, but still interested in helping. We spread out and asked questions. We can tell you where everyone you're seeking can be found – lead you right to them."

"Good, good," said Patterson, leaning back satisfied. "Best to take them completely unawares, with nary a shot fired."

I had again arranged for my accommodating neighbor to watch my practice – "Just like the old days!" he'd chortled. "Will you tell me about it when you're done?" – and I went with the inspectors to arrest Fraser Guy – for all of them wanted to be there when the evil man was taken.

While a small army of constables, sergeants, and other inspectors spread out over London, each led by one of the former Irregulars to where Guy's various lieutenants would be found, I rode in a growler with Lestrade, Gregson, and Wiggins, while the other inspectors followed in another. There had been some cursory concern about including Wiggins in our group – "You never know who might start shooting," Lestrade had declared. – but in the end, I felt that the young man had earned his spot. Additionally, I knew that Marchmont dabbled enough in criminal matters that it wouldn't hurt for his rising clerk to have some additional experience associating with the police, and seeing an arrest of this importance first-hand was invaluable.

Fraser Guy's abode was in the first-floor rooms above a Cecil Court bookshop. Following Moriarty's organizational arrangement, he was only accessible to a few trusted lieutenants. In turn, the next level down in this unlawful hierarchy reported to the lieutenants, and so on. In this way, there was never a constant and suspicious trooping of numerous shady characters along the narrow street. Instead, the five men who reported immediately to Guy were the only ones who visited his lair, and they were always taken for bookstore employees or customers.

Police officers stoppered both ends of the narrow passage, and surrounded the back as well. There were even constables on the roofs of adjoining buildings, should Guy try to escape by going up, and Patterson had researched the cellars as well, making sure that there were no forgotten entryways into the city sewers. ("I learned that lesson when Mr. Holmes and I nearly missed taking Constance Riddick," he explained to me in a soft tone as we took our positions at one end of the court. "She was a snake, that one, and would have escaped clean had not Mr. Holmes been willing to go down after her. Nearly took a stab wound for his trouble, but it all worked out. They say that slipping on the soap was what broke her neck, and no loss it was, but I know that it was the other prisoners that done it. They never could abide a child killer among them.")

Then the signal was given and the officers charged forward, in overwhelming numbers that could not be answered or denied. I'd wanted to join the scrum, but Lestrade forbid it, and he was correct. I had other responsibilities.

I hadn't known what to expect when Fraser Guy was dragged into the light, and at first I had difficulty believing this soft fat man was any sort of danger. He seemed comical and rather foppish. But when the constables holding his arms stood him up in the street, and I was able to walk closer and take a look into his eyes. I could see that he was something else indeed, a wolf that had been left free for too long to grow fat among the sheep. His eyes even had a wolfish cast to them, with a wild feral aspect to their shape, and an inhuman yellowish cast to both the irises and the surrounding *sclera*. He had a small pursed mouth, now pulled back to expose similarly yellowish teeth, each just a bit too pointed, and a very red tongue that darted around like a skinned rodent trying to break free from its toothy cage. The corners of his mouth were flecked with foam, because he was

65

ranting like a madman, threatening death to whoever fell within his gaze. I don't know how, but he knew my name along with everyone else's, and he promised to flay me alive, and my wife as well. I was more relieved than I would admit that Patterson had done so well to build an airtight capital case against this monster. I was in attendance when he was hanged later that year, and I freely confess my relief that he was gone.

Jabez Wilson had stood no chance against one such as him, and he probably had no idea how close to the edge he had skated, should have made any kind of open resistance. Fraser Guy was not the sort to tolerate opposition.

Following Guy's arrest, I had one other bit of business to conduct on Jabez Wilson's behalf. Michael Wiggins joined me, this time as a representative of Marchmont's legal firm.

We obtained a hansom and headed east. We took a moment to find a post office, where I could send three telegrams, and then we rode to Threadneedle Street, specifically to the offices of Holder and Stevenson, the second largest private banking concern in the City of London. Upon identifying myself, we were led deeply into the building where we were received by Alexander Holder, Senior Partner.

I had arranged to meet with him two days before, on Wednesday, and was shocked to see how he had aged so considerably since early 1888, when he'd first shown up in Baker Street, acting as a madman. [3] His expression then had been of overwhelming grief and despair, and he had swayed and mumbled and pulled at his hair before unexpectedly rising and beating his head upon our wall. We had calmed him enough to get his story – a valuable Royal heirloom that was deposited with his bank as collateral for a loan had been stolen from his home, and he feared that his reputation, and all that he'd worked for, was gone in an instant. Holmes had recovered the stolen coronet fairly easily – although it had been damaged during the theft – but Holder's grief was deeper than before when he learned that it had been stolen by a trusted family member – his niece – who had fled with the true villain before being confronted.

Holder welcomed Wiggins and me into his spacious office quite graciously, asking if we wished for refreshments, which we declined. I thanked him for his time, as I had two days earlier when he'd agreed to see me. I'd traded on his debt to Holmes, seeking the appointment and then a favor, and he'd been most willing to oblige.

I was pleased to see that my telegrams had all served their purpose. Besides alerting Holder to our impending arrival following the successful arrest of Fraser Guy, they had also successfully summoned Jabez Wilson, puzzled and confused but present as I'd previously asked him to be. With him was The Sphinx, Henry Barth.

"The villain?" asked Holder when we were seated. "He is in custody?"

"He is," I confirmed, before providing a few bare details. Wilson's eyes widened, and he shook his head as if disagreeing that it was so easy, but he didn't offer any comment.

I turned to Barth. "What did you discover?"

He settled into the chair as best he could, his short legs dangling above the floor, and said, as if the pawn-broker wasn't sitting there beside him, listening, "Mr. Jabez Wilson has the highest reputation in that part of London. Time was when his shop was the by-word for honest dealing." His countenance turned a shade sad. "His business suffered some – Well, in truth, quite a bit – when his wife passed ten years ago. It's like the heart just went out of him. But even as his prosperity declined, and the shop dried up, and even after that criminal took advantage of him to dig the tunnel into the adjacent bank, his own personal reputation never declined. No one blamed him or thought him criminally involved. People simply understood that, for him, times weren't what they had once been."

Throughout these comments, Jabez Wilson had been becoming more and more focused, taking in what was being said and working to understand its relevance. I felt that it was time to explain.

"Mr. Wilson, you have been the victim of a series of unfortunate events: The death of your wife. Taken advantage of by the criminal, John Clay – and then worse, by Fraser Guy. But your reputation is still excellent, and I have no doubt that you can rebuild your business. That's where Mr. Alexander Holder here comes in.

"Several years ago, Mr. Holder needed help from Sherlock Holmes to retrieve a stolen object."

Wilson nodded. "I read of it in *The Strand*."

"Holmes found that the thief had already sold it to a receiver – a most dishonest pawn-broker – from whom he was obliged to buy it back at a most inflated price. When I recalled this aspect of the affair to Mr. Holder last Wednesday, he agreed that there is a place – a *necessity* – for someone honest and discreet in your line of work for his type of client – not like the broker who bought and sold the jewels from the Coronet – and he's interested in becoming your partner. That is, if you are willing to work hard to rebuild your business. I think that you are. After all, your name is on the sign, painted in large white letters, and it's your reputation that needs to be restored. What do you say?"

When Wilson appeared to be overwhelmed by the sudden unexpected opportunity, and found that he could not speak, Holder prompted him.

"What say you, Wilson? Don't turn it down. I've made my own investigation and heard nothing but good things. You've just had some deuced bad luck, that's all – and I certainly understand that. Say yes, and then let's get to work."

He stood, walked from behind his great desk, and offered his hand. Wilson looked from it to Holder's beaming face, then stood himself, and shook, sealing the deal.

It was a profitable undertaking. Within a year, Wilson's business had been restored, and more. Soon, with Holder's support, he pivoted to specializing in antiques – specifically furniture – and it wasn't so many years after that when the small pawnshop metamorphosed into *Wilson and Holder*, whose sterling reputation needs no explanation.

But perhaps most of all, the two old widowers became the best of friends – a most unexpected result to the long chain of events that began several years earlier, when the criminal John Clay spotted the interesting juxtaposition between red-headed Wilson's dying pawn shop and a nearby bank that had been chosen to temporarily hold a fortune in French gold, and plotted how to connect the two by way of a tunnel and the creation of a clever but bogus Red Headed League.

"Life is infinitely stranger than anything which the mind of man could invent," Holmes had once told me. "We would not dare to conceive the things which are really mere commonplaces of existence. If we could fly out of that window hand in hand, hover over this great city, gently remove the roofs, and peep in at the queer things which are going on, the strange coincidences, the plannings, the cross-purposes, the wonderful chains of events, working through generations, and leading to the most *outrè* results, it would make all fiction with its conventionalities and foreseen conclusions most stale and unprofitable."

He was correct, of course, and I wished very much that I could have shared with him just how well this particular chain of events had turned out.

NOTES

1. See "The Adventure of the Red-Headed League", occurring on 25 October, 1890, and originally published in *The Strand* in August 1891.
2. See "The Adventure of the Gower Street Murder" in *Sherlock Holmes: Tangled Skeins* and *The Collected Papers of Sherlock Holmes – Volume II: Records*.
3. This was described in "The Beryl Coronet", 3-4 February, 1888, and published in *The Strand* in May 1892.

Behind the Wells of Light
by Marcia Wilson

It started in small steps.

Watson hadn't realized how his thinking had been affected by the worst of his experiences until he looked back and read his own words. *Why had he given Gregson an impression of bloated paleness? Why had he all but implied Lestrade was untrustworthy?*

His natural instincts were to find the answer, but even as he tried, he knew he already knew the truth, and it was an ugly one.

In the weeks of their new friendship, he had been bitter about Holmes's ability to maneuver throughout the city. While he had been trapped with his lingering illness, forced to experience London through the glass, Holmes had been free to come and go as he pleased. He of course had no inclination to hold back his own profession to coddle a sick veteran from the most disgraceful of wars – so disgraceful that in his worst nightmares he imagined the survivors lined up and humiliated before The Crown for failure to bring about the victory needed.

In a way, he had punished himself. Rather than return home in his shame, he had chosen London. That was an exile in itself, a city to be lost in, to be buried beneath the sheer numbers. To become one of the millions hiding beneath a curtain of London fog. The greasy London fog swirled its yellow path of contagion through the streets. It twirled with silent menace into every crevice of the city . . . and hours would pass as he watched the oily patterns slide down on the glass. It caught on the imperfections of the glazing, and piled up in the tiny ledges of the panes. Never had he known a dirtier city . . . and in a way it was fitting, for he belonged in such a place. The cool, rocky forests and bracing sea-waves of his boyhood belonged to the firm in body, mind, and spirit.

It was like watching a contagion coil upon a single organism. He envied the constitution and the will of those who could be out in those sunless streets, moving with impunity against a force that would attack his weakened constitution.

Logic and emotion. Head and heart. His head had understood Holmes had a reason for leaving their rooms. Who wouldn't if he had the power? But his heart had tentatively grown to encompass the strange, magnetic man in friendship . . . and in his absence, the loneliness of his lost family, lost friendships, and the lost camaraderie of his soldiers swelled up hundredfold.

Watson tried burying himself in words. He did his best to renew his interest in language and even took a stab at writing, but he felt flat and dull, and the paper stayed blank on his desk, mocking him to make something with it.

He had been an athlete once. He had played for Blackheath. He had excelled in sports. He had been a good shot before the military. He had passed his exams and his training with honors . . . honors he had worked for, burning midnight oil and sacrificing his own sleep in the knowledge one never gained back a lost day. He'd sworn fealty to whatever gods had favored accomplishment, and now he was so unworthy he could not even light a candle on their altars. The paper mocked him in that, too.

Holmes was everything he'd warned as a lodger, and more. But in the same light, he was a blessing. No ordinary man would have taken his attention so thoroughly. Being infuriating, maddening, and compelling was an unexpected benefit, for it undeniably captured the attention and created a distraction from himself.

Holmes was a peculiar man. He had peculiar habits. He seemed to need the rigid order of a set schedule – of sorts. His habits were peculiar, but he could not live without them. And gradually, his new lodger became one of his habits, as surely as he needed a particular hour in which to rise, and a particular pipe to express his moods.

He learned by degrees that the oldest objects were the ones Holmes needed the most. It was his tattered mouse-colored dressing-gown that he wore when a new one hung clean in the closet. It was the ugliest, oldest, and worst-looking pipe of the lot that he chose when he was feeling good. And his violin, as old as any Strad, was his most precious and well-loved possession.

But despite all the milestones of understanding between them, there was one about Holmes that loomed between them like a chasm: The dull, stupid spells of inaction, where he appeared paralyzed by his own mind, or worse, crushed by it. A distraction was usually the only thing that could heal this massive travail.

A part of Watson grew as resentful of these periods as much as they concerned him. After all, he had the wish to be out in the world, but his body would not let him. Holmes had the reverse problem, and for all his mental gifts, appeared to be ruled by his mind, not the other way around.

Surely his mind could be urged along to a better state of health between mind and spirit. Surely it only needed some encouragement.

And it was something to do.

And when Gregson asked him to come, Holmes reacted just as he feared: To give up, mock, and flip it all aside, giving up before he even started. The frozen black mood that stymied his own efforts in his career.

What must it be like, to know what you want to do with your life so absolutely, to make a career with your gifts . . . only to have another piece of yourself attack you with lassitude and bitterness when you cannot fight it off?

"But he begs you to help him!"

A milestone only to those who knew Holmes – and not a milestone that occurred to Watson just yet. Persuasion was a wily thing, with few results on the detective.

But persuasion from Watson's mouth . . . *worked*.

It must have been the honesty in his fiber. To not be able to do something when asked was unthinkable.

And so, on Holmes's capitulation, Watson entered London again . . . and for the very first time. It was a London all men suspected, but few truly encountered.

His journey was on Holmes's ticket. Perhaps even then he was chafing at the bit at the same time he wallowed in his new freedom. But the colors were sharper, the beauties greater . . . the horrors matchless. For a man who was hungry to live again, he had been sequestered far too long. Every human flaw magnified in his absence from the masses. The police were dull and stupid as Holmes said. The emotions were tangled and erratic, infuriating and wasteful. Then the further the case sunk into humanity, the more absorbing it grew for them both. Holmes made the most basic of errors right after scolding a policeman for his.

Another milestone: That Holmes confided his flaws to him, but not to the police. They were closer after that point . . . and by just another notch, Watson felt himself drawn deeper into Holmes's private world.

It would never be his to achieve. Holmes's mind was too glittering, too strong, too . . . *much*. But Watson could explore what he could and enjoy the experience, the way a man is proud of swimming above sea-waters too deep to dive.

Holmes was far worth the venture. His mind was as restless as the coils of fog against the glass . . . but nowhere near as slow. No study of his thoughts were predictable, and too many times his mind moved with the speed of a turbine. Watson thought of him as the Flying Scotsman barreling through the night, lamps a-blaze, piercing the night and the fog with a scream of triumph to its destination – the conclusion of a case wrapped in the fog of mystery and crime. Holmes's eyes, grey and alive, were wells of light, and shone all the brighter for what lay behind those wells could be as dark and distant as a London Night. It was a fitting analogy, for Holmes's eyes were his intellect, shining in the dark of London the way the lamps illuminated the swallowing fog of the city. *Illuminated*. A word for light, epiphany, civilization . . . *Intelligence* . . .

and *enlightenment*. There was no better word for what Sherlock Holmes was and what he did.

But it was the fog-times that Watson dreaded. When Holmes lay upon the couch with all the lifelessness of a corpse, and the thick shag smoke coiled and curled into the atmosphere. Watson would watch as the smoke stroked against their side of the window-glass, and on the other, the sinister yellow fog tried to reach in misty friendship. It worried him like nothing else – for something intangible rested in the air on these nights, unspoken with a promise of suffering.

He would open the window to let the shag out . . . when he had to. But it was a struggle to breach the fortress he was working to create of warmth, and light, and civilization and sanity. The chill damp of the fog would rush in, briefly, but air came with it, and when there was enough he would shut the window against it all, and the fog would recoil, its broken fingers left behind in the sitting room. Something between his shoulders would un-knot at those times, as if he'd watched something fail to happen.

He did not like the fog that Holmes so loved, for Holmes appeared to commune and bond to the phenomena with the understanding a dying man has of disease . . . if that wasn't putting it too baldly. He sulked when mortal man fled the creeping damp. He pouted when no one used the simple cover like they ought to in committing crimes worthy of his notice. That it was unhealthy to be out . . . Well, how could a man so skilled at ignoring his own body be expected to lower his mind to baser planes?

Forgiveness came with understanding. And Holmes required a great deal of understanding, for he was simply so complex.

Over time, they each shifted and grew into mutual understandings. The least expected one was the mechanism that freed Holmes's mind from its prison: A small grain-packet of cocaine mixed twice or thrice daily in pure solution. At first Watson witnessed the realization in deep disbelief: Holmes was so clean, cleaner than most human beings even in the hospitals, that the notion that he was polluting himself with an outside substance was for the alienists.

There was no denying the facts. With the weak solution, Holmes was finally free from the pull of his couch and able to focus on his cases. Cajoling and begging were no longer needed, and something echoed under the surface of Watson's epiphany, that a simple chemical from South America had replaced his personal, hard-worked efforts to see Holmes's potential bloom.

He was jealous of the drug. He was jealous of the drug for the same reason why he was jealous of Gregson and Lestrade. They belonged to a world Holmes skirted, danced with, and visited with a confidence to be envied. Watson did not claim such skill. His life had been spent being upright and honest. His life had been clear light, warm fires, the comfort of hot food and steaming tea within a sheltering box of patterned wallpaper and carpet and shining brass fixtures. The straight and narrow world of honesty and integrity was built along those lines, and boxed-in from the outside with wall and window glass.

They were on the other side of that glass, another aspect of the slow-swirling, menacing fog that promised threats and obscured the light of day. They walked in it. Holmes out of his natural needs and compulsions, for his Art meant everything, and that meant living in the criminal world. The inspectors walked in it for different reasons: It was their career, their chosen life, and they plodded through those dark streets of cobblestone and weeping blue brick. Holmes did it to seek out crime. These plain-clothed men did it because, in order to help, help must first be there. They were little different from the slow, plodding constables who walked miles in badly-fitting shoes, with a single bull's-eye lantern to stand up against the pitiful hiss of the gaslights that danced against the fog like light made of white water. On occasion, they paused at the red lamp of a private practitioner, and the emblem of healing cast the colour of blood into the fog, until a great red wound seeped throughout the night.

His own anger shamed him, but shame does not dissolve rage. It mixes badly, like morphine into cocaine. He never took the shame of drugs. It was not worth the candle, nor was it something he could risk. His body was broken and only half-familiar to himself. He watched London from the inside of his rooms, but at the same time, he watched London from the outside, and from afar. He was distant and remote in long tracts of existence as his illness coiled within his soul. Not that life felt any less real to him – but his own importance faltered.

All his life he'd been of use to someone . . . and now, he was barely of use to himself. A stranger peered back at him in the translucent mirror of window and fog. A stranger devoured by illness phantoms while another, chill spectre swirled inches away from his fingertips. Himself. John H. Watson was changed, and who was he becoming now?

A man is worthless if he is not of use. What is a man if he does not have his own place among his fellow men, if he cannot contribute in some way?

He had the good sense not to write that down with the rest of his thoughts at night. But surely Holmes, with his mental powers, would be able to read it anyway? With the depth of the ink and pencil into the paper, or the regularity of angry underscores of words that could be seen as revealing?

Holmes was the only lifeline he had to re-learning his sense of self.

74

It started out in small steps. Something to do, something constructive and worthwhile to take his mind away from his body while his body healed. That Holmes was in need of his own form of help made it simple – even logical.

But brilliance cannot be met with a lesser intellect. It can only be complemented by another quality. Watson was slow to learn his own talents within that area. Slowest to realize he might have a gift as strange and marvelous to Holmes as Holmes was to himself.

Patience was required. For both of them.

And over time, in small steps, like a policeman stepping through the fogged night with his tiny lantern . . . Watson began to see through the shrouded streets. A stone through mist. His gaze grew more developed. His constitution rallied by degrees.

But his inevitable growth went alongside change. It was while he was at the threshold of his own recovery that he learned of Holmes's first experimentation with the cocaine. At first it was nothing to be alarmed at. All physicians practiced self-experimentation upon themselves – the scrupulous ones did, at any rate. How better to know the effects of a drug upon the people who trusted them for aid?

But the tiny flicker of concern upon seeing the bill from the chemist was stifled carefully. Holmes was not a man of medicine. He was a man of chemistry – organic chemistry. His fascination with all poisons and alkaloids and altering substances ensured this new addition to the chemistry table by the window was not out of character, or a step out of pattern.

It was years before the enforced vacation at Cornwall, and not long before he would start searching for poor Whitney in the opium dens, but still something made Watson avoid both magnets. He read the advertisements as well as the next man of letters, but that something, that intangible quality that was the amusement and puzzlement of Holmes . . . that something stayed his hand from self-experimentation. If he was in pain, it never quite occurred to him to take something past a mild powder of salicylic acid – barely stronger than the willow-bark tea of his ancestors that led to the distillation.

He was a remarkable man, Mr. Sherlock Holmes of 221b Baker Street. A man of intellect so high that he never completely understood how high he was against the masses. That lack of understanding led to his worst qualities: His impatience, depression, cynicism. His occasional anger, annoyance, and contempt. So sure of his methods, Holmes never understood why so few people could follow him, or believe in him blindly over the conventional, plodding methods that "made do" for so long. "Elementary," he explained it all away. "Very simple." "A child could do it." "Simplicity itself." "Hardly worthwhile." And the phrases, initially calculated in a strange form of reassurance, had the opposite affect by driving away those who came to him for help, for no man has limitless humility, and is content with being condescended to as part of the price for asking for help.

And it was the policemen Watson initially resented, Fat-handed Gregson and sly, shifty-faced Lestrade, who continued to consult when no one else would. If Holmes likened them to a pair of jealous beauty queens, but Holmes was the diva of London: A soothsayer who told you the future even as he scolded you for not knowing it himself. And slowly, Watson came to see how these visits were important to all of them – even himself.

He was a remarkable man, Dr. John H. Watson of 221b Baker Street. A man of intuition and impressions that operated on a barely human plane of existence, a man who could use logic to the extent that once he understood the cogs that operated behind a man, he could withstand the risks of their company despite the emotional gunfire. He was a man who could see the ordinary within the remarkable, and also take the remarkable and render it into words a common mind could read. He was a translator of the amazing, and it remained amazing with his telling. His strength was so past the lines of normality that while he wrote away the evenings of cases present and past, he never knew that the same level of awe was directed his way.

The steps stretched down the streets, through the London Fog, and from Baker Street the steps passed into weeks, months, and years. The fog in his soul dissipated. In contrast, the streets of London grew less wholly dangerous. Watson felt the city was less a morass rendered callous by its sheer numbers, and more like a living, thriving organism carrying its own form of intelligence. The streets were the pathways of the organism, as vital as the blood vessels were his. Here each man was a molecule, carrying some task, some function to the whole.

All roads led to Rome. All streets led to London, and all worried steps led to Holmes. It was a way of the world, the way of a new, exciting era where crime was a science to be taken apart and put back together clean. Cases were solved, held up as examples . . . and delighted in. The sunlight pierced the fog-bank with the return of Watson's practice, and the rising reputation of Holmes's work. Watson noted that some members of the force did not come often to Baker Street, if at all, but the rising number of the wealthier clients who had problems that did not precisely require a policeman's badge or arrest warrant . . . those were becoming more common, and they were far more lucrative.

More sunlight came to earth and split into the hundreds of candles that lit the wedding ceremony between himself and Mary Morstan. For a moment in time, Paradise itself was borrowed for the occasion, for Holmes attended voluntarily, and the gleam in those grey eyes was for once lacking in ulterior thought. He was regarding his friend as though he had never quite realized the pleasantness of the activity.

The streets opened between home and hearth, practice, friendships, and duties. The streets walked into years, and Holmes was a familiar habit, one he knew was there . . . one who visited rarely because he had always been a very busy man, and only twice did Watson recall Holmes ever "visiting" someone just to see them. Their streets diverged now – their lives were more separate, yet the ties between were still there, tugging every now and then as if to remind them they had once lived in a way that created a single unit. An organism that created sum totals of success against misery.

And Holmes was busier than ever. His name rose and fell with the seasons, and when the rooms stood empty in the night, Watson knew it was because he was out and away on a case. It was strange to look from the street into the window he'd once peered out of, and from the cobblestones it was a very different feeling indeed. Now he could see how so much brighter the lights glowed. How sharp and strong against a weak, chill and slow-moving fog.

There were nights when the silhouette moved back and forth, and cases were read of in the papers. A royal affair. A request from one government or another. The gratitude of a shipping line. The request of a country . . . or a missing child found hale and hearty. Other times the papers revealed all by not saying things in particular, but there were too many times when Holmes paced before the window, or was absent, coinciding with peculiar news-items such as the strange return of a stolen jewel, or a noble afflicted with amnesia and mysteriously discovered within a mile of his own home. Holmes would wear affections of his clients upon his cuffs or his throat. He used a snuffbox that was a gift. He grew comfortable in his possessions, and Watson was content and happy enough with his own life that he made the mistake of thinking Holmes had come into his being the same way he had with his medicine and wife. Work meant so much to his friend. It would seem that he had come into a place in life where he could live contentedly within a sphere of his own making.

A happy man forgets sorrow, and a secure man forgets fears. And Watson had never completely suffered the depths of self-imprisonment the way Holmes had suffered. He had risen above the new and permanent restrictions upon the body he had once been so proud of . . . but Holmes had never been concerned so much about the body – his organism was the brain. And the brain was a hard thing to master.

The physical comforts given to him by grateful clients had never meant quite so much to him, except what they symbolized: The recognition of his efforts and his successes. For Holmes could be vain, but that vanity was rooted in the lack of recognition and gratitude in the past. Too late, Watson realized the bitterness of those lean years could return on his friend, just like the bitterness of his wounds and the death of his first dream of a military career came back to face him.

The cocaine grew in frequency.

The cocaine grew within him.

Moriarty happened.

Despite the pain that split his heart, Watson had to remember that Holmes had died the way he had chosen: Just as he had lived his life. And the clinical physician within him sought comfort in facts, and the quiet, cool whisper in his mind pointed out the slight signs of psychosis and increasingly irrational behavior when Holmes was not on a case. In the road-map that was London the organism, a defender of the body against the fog could not stand fast forever. And Holmes had been alone for too long. It was miracle enough that Watson had been with him up until the last half-hour of his life.

Where were the thanks of kings and queens, when no one of import appeared at the small chapel? Where were the affectations and labels? Very busy men and women they were, managing affairs of the state, that they could not remember the work of a man they themselves admitted, "saved their names", their reputations, their children.

It was the police who met him at the train, packed the church, and drowned the memorial stone in flowers. Police still filthy from duty, eyes tired and full of soot and dust. Two of them had a bad cough they tried to stifle in their sleeves, and out of honor he took them aside later with a cough syrup. One constable showed up with his arm still in a sling, his eyes bright from pain-killers. He nodded off several times, and his friends wordlessly propped him between their bodies. Watson never learned the man's name . . . or what had happened . . . or most of all, why had Holmes been so important to this lowly constable that he had crawled out of a hospital to attend his funeral?

It was almost enough to let him forget the true nature of the fog: What it lacked in physical power, it made up for in sheer size. It was all over London. It *was* London. Mary died. The fog killed her, because it hid the disease, and the coughing, and the blood . . . and the candles in his life guttered to near-extinction. He had forgotten how the fog had outnumbered those small, strong lights. It swirled in his soul now, with no recognition between day or night.

He kept to his practice. He kept to his streets out of rote, for to die or allow himself neglect would insult the two people who loved him best. And the fog crept against the glass of his empty house, waiting to enter the rest of the way. He ignored it. He drew the curtains against its weeping chill and turned his back to the way it dripped yellow slime down to the sill and spread damp as far as it could under the thin cracks. He was a doctor. He still had purpose – in the eyes of others if not in himself. But he became a changed man. He kept his hours along his private practice, but his hours at the hospital were moved completely to the night.

What he was trying to learn, or prove, or come to terms with . . . he didn't know. It was a strange sort of peace to be walking along by himself with only his revolver for a companion, and the click of his shoes upon the pavement was soothing in a way he had not expected. He found he preferred to walk away from the bleeding red halos of the surgeries. He passed through the softly hissing islets of the gas-lamps while the Thames whispered almost as gently. The organism was half-asleep on these walks. London dozed, its dramas lowered and saved for the light of day.

He came upon Lestrade then, at the accumulation of twelve years' acquaintance. No motion had been made to his foot-falls, no reaction as the small man watched the fog play at the string of lamps wreathed like a hissing necklace around the lines of St. Bartholomew's. Like lamps his eyes burned, fueled from lack of sleep.

For the first time in Watson's experience, Lestrade ignored his appearance. His coat was battered and rumpled. A disturbing stain rested at his shoulder that the doctor and soldier could identify in his sleep. His hat hung in his hands as his dark eyes stared into London and nothing else. Watson knew grief and anguish when he saw it – felt its echo for its own.

"I'm sure he'll be all right, Lestrade." He said it gently enough, but when those eyes looked up, it was like staring into pools of misery.

"It was bound to happen eventually," the little man said brokenly, and his smile was warped. Trying to put on a brave front, which touched Watson all the more because this was his rival fighting for his life in a hospital that had just been attacked by the government for its lack of cleanliness. "He was getting too close to Saffron Hill. It's dangerous for any copper over there . . . especially now."

There wasn't much room, but Watson found enough for them to share the space. "Gregson's a stubborn man, you know that. He'll pull through."

"He will or he won't." Lestrade stared blankly into the fog again. "We're not getting any younger . . . and . . . it's all changing again. A man can't change with the times every time . . . Sooner or later he gets out-moded . . . or obsolete."

"You sound like you're machines, not men!" Watson tried to chivvy his spirits with a low laugh. "When have you ever given up, Lestrade? Holmes himself swore you were incapable."

"Giving up? No." The little detective let his head swing from side to side. "But there comes a time when you know the sands are running out of the glass. That's when you have to be extra careful . . . Can't die before you're ready . . . That's the plan, anyway. We know not the hour nor the day." He sighed. "A doctor can always practice, so long as he's able. A copper can't say the same. Look at Gregson. He's one of the last of us . . . If he gets pulled . . . or dies . . . that's one less of the old guard out there. And you can't replace that sort of experience . . . " He stopped to rub at his eyes. "His cases will probably go to Hopkins." Was the mutter. "If Hopkins can read his awful hand . . . ."

And Watson had nothing he could say. For a man who treasured words like food and drink . . . there were too many times when only silence could speak. Holmes had said that was a rare gift. Watson still didn't know what that meant. So he did what he knew, and waited in the darkness.

"It's always quiet this time of night." Lestrade said so quietly, and yet so unexpectedly, Watson almost jumped inside his coat. He followed the little man's gaze. It was on the slow-dancing fog again. "We started out at night . . . That's how they know if you've got what it takes. A lot of us were killed in the first five years. The fog killed us."

"I . . . I didn't know that." Watson thought he meant the diseases of the lung that came with the fog.

"They'd hide in the fog, you know." Lestrade spoke casually, his conversation so calm and matter of fact that Watson could feel each hair stand up, one by one, on the nape of his neck. "It was easy to lie in wait against the river. Our lanterns told them where we were . . . where we were going . . . and that close to a lantern, you can't really see much past the glare. They could hear our boots, too. A lot of us didn't have the whistles. Those silly rattles didn't carry a call for help for any decent distance, I can tell you that."

He toyed with the hat in his hands without being aware of it. His whole awareness was focused on the fog. "You'd trip over the corpse before you even knew it was there. Or smell it. Even in the winter, you'd smell someone drowned in the gin. How could you not contaminate the location of the crime?" He shrugged as if to himself. "There'd be times when we wouldn't see the sun for months on end. The fog was in the way. By the time we met you, I think we were becoming a part of the fog . . . I was yellow as sulphur . . . and Gregson was white as a mushroom."

"Has it not gotten better for you, Inspector?" Watson whispered.

"Better?" Lestrade didn't understand. He blinked several times and glanced twice at Watson. "We have a better system now . . . if that's what you mean."

"I mean . . . are you not safer now than you were back then?"

"Oh," was the quiet answer. "I see." He hesitated, but the honesty had been cracked, and there was nothing but to let it all out. "We're not safer, no. Suicides are up again among the Force. It's one thing to walk the beat or risk one's reputation on a murder no one wants to touch, you know. We're only human. Sometimes a man can't take the pressure of doing his job, and coming into the station for another round of abuse from the chiefs. That's what causes most of the self-murders, you know. Just the way we're treated by our own people . . . ."

"I'm sorry." Watson has no idea what else he could say. "But you have a reputation, Lestrade. You and Gregson are the best of the lot."

"You're only saying that because Mr. Holmes said that."

"And he said it because it's true."

But Lestrade only smiled wearily and shook his head again. The fog swirled away from him briefly, before re-settling about them.

"Might have been true to him, but that doesn't make it true to the Home Office."

"Lestrade . . . If the Office didn't believe in you, why did they give you permission to carry a gun? Hardly any policeman has that honor."

"Honor?" The small man repeated, as if surprised again. He slowly fell into silence again. The fog took their attention as it shifted among the lights.

"You met Mr. Holmes after the Threadneedle Murders."

"I don't recall Holmes ever mentioning it."

"Ugly case." Lestrade glanced down at his fingernails, which were clean. "Man killed his rival by arranging his promotion in the local bank. Poor boy was a sensitive, worried sort. The responsibility of his new post crushed him like an ant. Nothing we could ever really prove." He shrugged. "A policeman permitted to bear arms is a stick of dynamite waiting to go off."

"Forgive me, but you haven't . . . 'gone off' thus far."

"Certainly not. How could I let Gregson win the post as best by default?" Lestrade stood up then, too cheerful against the watery lamps. "With that in mind, I ought to remind him he's not getting out of that so easily. Are you working tonight, Doctor?"

Watson stood too. He had known Lestrade for twelve years, but he wasn't certain if he had actually *known* any policeman until now. "Yes." It was his answer to many questions. "It just so happens, I am."

"Silly question, actually." Lestrade said, almost to himself as he picked up his walking stick. He struck it against the pavement and the sound made a low, cracking sound – a declaration of defiance, or of war to the things that used the fog to hide in. "This is London. When are we ever not working?"

"When . . . indeed . . . ." Watson murmured.

They walked through the smoky curtain together, and like it always did, the fog parted ways before them. It was larger than they were, and ultimately more powerful, but it had no substance on its own. It needed man for that, Watson thought as they reached the entrance to Barts and he held open the door.

The Voice in the Night
by Arthur Hall

It will be recalled that when the nature of a problem presented to him suggested it, my friend, the consulting detective Mr. Sherlock Holmes, was quick to deny the possibility of a supernatural explanation. During the years when I was privileged to accompany, and on occasion to assist, in his investigations, his view regarding the fantastical never altered. Yet from time to time, situations that at first appeared to contradict his conviction arose. Sometimes these would amuse him briefly, while the less-obvious falsehoods roused his interest when he found himself between enquiries of greater interest. The following account is of one such case.

The years of Holmes's absence from the capital, during which my beloved Mary had passed from this earth, had come to a close. I had resumed my shared occupation of the rooms at 221b Baker Street, and of assisting my friend with such of his enquiries as he saw fit. It wasn't long after the defeat of the infamous Colonel Sebastian Moran, that I returned from an early morning call to discover that the breakfast things had been cleared away and Holmes had acquired a new client. I made to apologise for my intrusion and withdraw, intending to descend to the kitchen and prevail upon our landlady to provide me with something of my missed breakfast, but he would have none of it.

"Ah, Watson! Do come in, dear fellow, and meet Mr. Parker Osmond. He arrived only minutes ago, so you have missed nothing of the tale he has to tell." He turned to his client. "Doctor Watson has been of considerable assistance to me with many of my past enquiries, and I can assure you that he is he soul of discretion."

The stranger indicated his assent to my presence. When I had divested myself of my hat and coat, I crossed the room and shook hands with him, a cheerful sort of about forty years of age. He was short and heavily built with a moustache that stretched almost from ear to ear, and I regret to recall that I detected a faint aroma of fish about him. His apparel, I noticed, was of good quality, if a little well-worn.

Mr. Osmond was installed in the basket chair, while I took my usual seat, my notebook at the ready.

"You will have deduced that our client is a fishmonger," my friend began. His method of defining this passed apparently unrealised by Mr.

Osmond, or he chose to ignore it. "He has just revealed to me that he has consulted me previously, but I have no memory of such an occasion. Have you any recollection of it?"

"None at all," I replied after a moment's thought. "When was this, sir?" I asked.

"A few years ago," the fishmonger said pleasantly. "I didn't actually visit these premises then, but made a request by letter for an appointment. I received no reply, but realised later that you were busy with the affair of Lord St. Simon, according to the newspaper accounts, and the circumstances about which I wrote to you happily resolved themselves shortly after."

"I am delighted to hear it," Holmes answered. "But now, Mr. Osmond, as you have declined tea, perhaps you will tell us the nature of your present difficulty."

"It isn't me who is in trouble," the little man said quickly, "but my cousin, Miss Helen Melhuish. She is at her wits' end."

"Then why does she not accompany you, or attend alone?"

"She resides far away, in Minehead. On the fringes of Exmoor, in Somerset."

Holmes nodded. "And what is it that torments her?"

Mr. Osmond leaned forward in his seat, as if to be sure that we heard all that he had to impart. "She has recently been plagued by a series of distressing events. Her parents died some months ago when their coach left the road and fell from the summit of a cliff. She was flung from the carriage to the ground, sustaining minor injuries from which she has since recovered, before the horses broke free and the coach plummeted. She is a girl of delicate disposition who loved her parents, and she has blamed herself for their deaths ever since."

"For what reason?" I interjected. "If she was with her parents in the coach, how can she be seen to be responsible?"

Our client shook his head in an exasperated gesture. "So I, and others, have impressed upon her, for her conclusion of guilt is quite ridiculous. She maintains that, because it was she who insisted on them accompanying her on the journey – it was to Taunton for some secret special treat that she had devised for them – their lives were lost. For days after, she wailed repeatedly that they would be alive today, had she not made the arrangements."

"I have known similar instances," Holmes said then. "It isn't uncommon for those of a certain turn of mind to needlessly assume blame where none exists. Usually reason prevails after a short time, and the sufferer dismisses the notion, but sometimes medical help in the form of sedatives is found to be necessary."

"In my experience," said I, "I also have met this condition several times over the years."

"This is a most unfortunate situation, Mr. Osmond, and I am indeed sorry to hear of it," Holmes assured him, "but how do you think I would be able to help?"

"That's what I am coming to, Mr. Holmes. You see, the thing that is continually terrifying my cousin, preventing her from healing from her grief, which I believe will drive her to madness if it continues, is her mother's voice. It speaks to her in the night, and blaming her for the deaths of both her mother and father. I confess to believing her letters about this as fanciful at first, but she is so insistent that I feel it can no longer be dismissed."

Holmes had rested his chin on his steepled fingers as he listened, but now he sat straight in his chair. "Has anyone else heard the voice? Has Miss Melhuish attempted to prove the authenticity of her claim?"

"She slept with her maid, Miss Alice Tanders, in her room as a witness, one night. The voice came again, causing my cousin to tremble, but the maid claimed to have heard nothing. It took hours for her to calm my cousin afterwards. She was on the edge of hysteria."

My friend said nothing for several minutes, then addressed our client again. "Mr. Osmond, you presumably know of your cousin's disposition from past experience. What do you, yourself, conclude from what you've told us? Is Miss Melhuish given to hallucinations, imagined experiences, and the like due to her somewhat nervous disposition, or is the hand of someone who wishes her harm for some reason as yet undefined present here?"

"I have said that she is of a delicate nature," Osmond reminded us, "but never before has she acted in this way. Her parents' death was a catastrophe, of course, but in the past there have been other tragedies from which she has emerged strong. No, I cannot believe that her mind is sick."

"Then I'll take your case, but allow me to make it clear at once that I will not consider that the answer lies in the realms of the supernatural, for I have yet to find a genuine example of such."

"We are in your hands, Mr. Holmes."

"Excellent." My friend rose to indicate that the interview was at an end. "Doctor Watson and myself will travel with you to Minehead, on the morning train tomorrow."

Mr. Osmond paused before replying. "Thank you. Unfortunately, I will be able to stay there overnight only. I have left my wife and eldest son in charge of the shop, which isn't an ideal situation."

"In that case, be so good as to furnish the Good Doctor with all details and inform Miss Meluish by telegraph of our intended arrival, and there will be no need to accompany us. When some progress has been made, you'll hear from us."

Our client was effusive in his thanks to us both, and I recorded the necessary information in my notebook before he took his leave.

"What do you make of this?" Holmes asked as he returned to his chair.

"He seems a genuine-enough fellow. His concern for his cousin is evident."

"So it would appear. I must say though, that I'm becoming somewhat weary of these affairs where the supernatural is falsely employed. I sometimes find it hard to believe that so much superstition remains, in this day and age."

"The current fashion among the rich of holding séances encourages it."

"Quite so. I recall, Watson, that you have more patients to see today. As for myself, I have to visit Gregson at Scotland Yard in order to deliver my observations on the Brierley murder. He should be able to apprehend Tom Sparker without difficulty afterwards, providing that distasteful fellow has not yet made his way to the coast."

It was late evening of the following day before Holmes and I found ourselves approaching the residence of Miss Helen Meluish, Cliff Top House. In the failing light I saw that the upper storey was in ruins, and the building was in a condition that suggested years of neglect. It appeared to be constructed of the local stone, as were many others in the district, visibly crumbling in places. In the silence, which was broken by the crashing of the sea, it looked a gloomy place, and the approaching storm added to the dreary atmosphere that was at once apparent.

We had arrived in Taunton to find no carriage waiting. At first, I had expected that we would need to seek a local hotel for overnight accommodation, but Holmes engaged the station master in conversation with the result that the man's brother, a carter, was summoned to transport us across the twelve miles of countryside to Minehead. The steep ascent from the road, along a tree-lined track barely wide enough for two coaches to pass, provided us with spectacular views of the darkening coastline and the white-topped waves that advanced with gathering force beneath.

Our scant luggage was handed down to us as soon as we alighted in the somewhat neglected courtyard. I paid the carter more than he asked and received a grateful acknowledgement. The man politely bid us farewell and set the horse to a fast trot. We looked up at the house, dark against the impending storm, until all sounds of the animal's departure had ceased.

It was clear from my friend's expression that he had formed the same impression of the place as I, but he said nothing. We picked up our bags and walked across a grassy patch that could have once been a lawn until we found ourselves before a massive door with tarnished hinges and long in need of a coat of wood preservative or paint. Holmes rapped upon it loudly with his stick, and was about to do so again, when it swung open to reveal a man who I judged to be of about sixty years with a magnificent head of grey hair. His butler's attire was immaculate, and he bowed in welcome.

"Mr. Sherlock Holmes and Doctor Watson, I presume," he said in quiet tones. "Good evening, sirs. We are of course expecting you. I am Daniels."

He took our luggage and we preceded him into the hall, which was tidy but had clearly seen better days. The passage before us had doors on either side, but no sound issued from them. Before we had progressed halfway along, the butler paused and turned to us.

"Shall I tell cook that you gentlemen require dinner?"

Holmes, I believe, would have foregone food, but the journey had left me with an appetite.

"If you would be so kind," I said quickly.

The butler assented, and Holmes asked him. "Will Miss Melhuish be joining us?"

"I believe she has retired, sir. She complained earlier of feeling unwell." He glanced towards a tall window as the storm delivered its first rain. "I will show you to your rooms, so that you can refresh yourselves while your food is being prepared."

At that moment, a loud thunderclap was followed by lightning, and a door at the end of the dimly-lit corridor slammed open. We heard a scream, and the butler dropped our bags to the floor as a young women clad in a long nightdress burst from the room. Her hair stood out in wild disarray, and her face appeared deathly pale as she staggered uncertainly towards us.

"Miss Helen!" Daniels cried. "What is it?"

At once I moved to meet her, but she avoided me to confront my friend.

"Mr. Holmes? Are you Mr. Holmes, sir? Yes, it must be you. Parker promised he would send you if you would come."

I asked the butler to get her a brandy and he left, leaving us alone with his mistress.

"I am indeed Sherlock Holmes, Miss Melhuish," he hastily assured her. "Your cousin has told us of your plight. Try to calm yourself and tell us what has occurred, but first let us adjourn to a sitting room where it will be warmer. Daniels will bring you a brandy in a moment."

In a dream-like manner, she led us into one of the other rooms, which proved to be furnished in good taste and to be well heated by a roaring fire. A gas chandelier provided sufficient illumination. She half-fell upon a long sofa while Holmes and I divested ourselves of our outer clothing and then occupied surrounding armchairs. She was still in a state of great excitement, and seized the glass from the butler's hand to down it in a single swallow.

When her anxiety seemed to have lessened, and she had come to herself, Daniels asked her, "Is there anything more I can do for you, Miss Helen?"

"Just stay with me, while I talk to these gentlemen."

"Very good, Miss Helen."

"When you're ready," Holmes said soothingly, "pray describe to us, as best you can, what has frightened you so."

She looked away from Daniels, who remained by her side, standing in readiness, and swept an unknowing glance across my friend and myself. Her eyes, I noticed, appeared glazed, and there was a long pause before she answered.

"The voice." Her words came to us as if from a great distance. "I heard it, as before."

"The voice of your departed mother?"

"It was. But of course, Parker will have told you of it. I killed my mother and my father with my foolishness, so it is of no surprise that she has returned to taunt me."

Holmes leaned towards her. "Miss Meluish, I can assure you with absolute confidence that the voice you heard was not that of your mother. About that you can immediately set your mind at rest. Doctor Watson and I have conducted many enquiries where a supernatural agency was suspected, but none where a normal explanation wasn't eventually discovered."

"But I heard her! She told me that I caused their deaths, and that I will suffer for it."

"Clearly, someone wishes you to believe this. If you ask yourself whether your mother would wish to punish you for an accident that was beyond your control, you will surely begin to see the impossibility of it."

"She was not a cruel or vengeful woman."

"Then already you begin to see the deception here. Tell me, does this voice always speak to you in the same room?"

"My bedroom. Yes."

"And for how long has this been occurring?"

88

She considered briefly, her eyes clearer now. "It began about a month ago. At first it was every three or four nights, but it grew more frequent. Now it is almost every night."

"Has it changed in any way since the beginning?"

"Sometimes it sounds nearer – perhaps louder."

"Very well. If I could see your bedroom, I may learn something. There is no need for you to go with us, Daniels will show us the way."

"It is the room from which you saw me emerge."

We both rose and the butler accompanied us from the room. Miss Melhuish sat unmoving, staring blankly before her. She seemed oblivious to the raging storm without.

Daniels showed us into a spacious bedroom with a high ceiling. I noticed that the sounds of our movements had an extraordinary quality, wherein slight noises seemed to be amplified. He lit two oil lamps, which cast grotesque shadows around us, before turning to Holmes.

"Will you be requiring me further, sir? I am concerned for Miss Helen."

My friend shook his head. "Pray return to her. Doctor Watson and I can manage."

When we were alone, Holmes cast his eyes around us. His gaze took in the dishevelled bed, the nightgown hung on the door, and the Bible on the bedside table. After a while he moved to a corner and tapped the wall as he listened carefully, slowly progressing until he stood where he had begun. He inspected the floor, particularly the thick and slightly worn carpet, then murmured something to himself, not loud enough for me to catch, before regarding me with a mildly perplexed expression.

"At least the walls seem solid enough. Come, Watson, we will return to Miss Melhuish."

The lady appeared somewhat recovered, and I revised my former intention to administer a sedative. Daniels had doubtless been offering encouragement and support.

"Have you discovered anything, Mr. Holmes?" she asked in a way that was almost a plea.

"Only inasmuch as I have disproved one possibility. Tell me, Miss Melhuish: Does this voice occur repeatedly during the night?"

"Not as yet," she replied in a stronger voice. "I hear it about an hour before midnight – slightly later than tonight."

"Then if you have no further fears for now, I suggest we all avail ourselves of a night's sleep."

He paused, remembering something. "Oh yes. Tell me, pray, what is above your bedroom?"

"Little more than the open sky. The entire upper storey of the house was destroyed by a fire, many years ago. At the time we were unable to meet the expense of repairs, and so what was left of the floor above was sealed and subsequently forgotten about as we became accustomed to no longer having access to it."

"Thank you. Could Daniels now conduct us to our rooms? I will consider this further in the morning when we have refreshed ourselves."

After assuring his mistress that he would return soon, the butler showed us to two adjacent rooms with views of the neglected garden in another part of the house,. His fatherly interest in her was clear to see, and he left us immediately. Our dinner appeared to have been forgotten, and as I made to wish my friend good night he put a hand on my arm and spoke in whispers.

"There is more to this, Watson. That bedroom has an acoustic quality that would cause the voice that Miss Melhuish claims to have heard to be altered and magnified considerably. Yet the maid, while sleeping there also, heard nothing. I will interview her, and the other members of staff, in the morning."

With that, we parted. Before I slept, I listened to the storm, which had as yet lost little of its ferocity. Between the thunderclaps were brief periods of quiet, and when I fancied that I heard my friend pacing as he does when some aspect of a problem has eluded him. Then rain beat against the window with renewed force, and all other sound was lost to me as I slept.

Breakfast was taken in a room resplendent with the history of the Melhuish family. Swords and shields, halberds and daggers were displayed at intervals above us around the dark-panelled walls, and faded portraits of later ancestors who stared at us grimly were much in evidence.

Daniels served us with a hearty breakfast at a long banqueting table, but neither Holmes or Miss Melhuish ate to any extent. Given our surroundings, I had expected him to engage her in conversation about her family's long and varied history, but instead he talked lightly of general things, and I participated occasionally.

When our coffee cups were empty, our hostess enquired if she should call for more, and we both declined. On being asked if she objected to strong tobacco, she replied that she was well used to it, since her father had always smoked. We lit our pipes, and after a moment Miss Melhuish spoke in a voice that I was pleased to hear had lost much of its fear and uncertainty.

"You will need to question me before you begin your investigation, Mr. Holmes. This morning I feel restored, because your reassurance has dismissed my conviction that I was losing my mind. I pray that you will unravel this affair as you did the others of which you spoke, and I am at your disposal to assist in any way that I can."

Holmes blew out a final stream of fragrant smoke and put his pipe aside. "Thank you, Miss Melhuish. Doctor Watson and I are delighted to learn that you are somewhat recovered, and that you have realised that whoever is responsible for your torment is as human as you and I."

"Ask me then anything that is relevant."

"First: How many staff do you employ?"

"Danvers you have met. The others are Alice Tanders, my maid, Benton the groom, and Mrs. Waldron, a local widow – the cook."

"May I ask how long they have served you?"

She considered for a moment. "Daniels has been here since my father's time. I was a child when he came. Mrs. Waldron also was engaged by my father, shortly before – " Her words stumbled here. " – the accident. I understand that, with her husband recently deceased, she could no longer afford the rent on her home. My father, being a kindly man and already acquainted with her, bade her take one of the empty rooms and employed her to prepare our meals."

"Do all your staff live on the premises?" I enquired.

"They do, Doctor. Each has always seemed pleased with the arrangement."

"Excellent," said Holmes. "Were the remaining two engaged later?"

"Benton and Alice began here at about the same time, I think. That would be scarcely six months ago. My parents had just died and our old groom had retired. Elizabeth, my previous maid, had passed away suddenly."

Holmes looked up at once. "In what circumstances, pray?"

Miss Melhuish surprised us both by smiling faintly. "Oh, it was nothing sinister. The poor girl slipped on the steep steps as she emerged from the wash-house at the rear of the property. I understand she carried a heavy bundle of wet clothes or bed linen. It was an icy morning and very cold. Luke got to her first, but nothing could be done, as she had already expired."

"Luke?" I queried. "Another member of staff, perhaps?"

"Heavens, no. Luke Mulderne is the man I am to marry, on his return from South Africa. There are interests of his father's there that have to be settled. He is Lord Endworth, the eldest son of Lord Mulderne of Argyll."

"Are you, then, to live in Scotland after your marriage?" Holmes asked.

"I would have welcomed that, but Luke will not hear of it. He and his father quarrel often, and he has had enough of it. We will be living here and, hopefully, he will be happier."

91

He nodded. "Let us return to this voice that plagues you. Does it resemble that of your mother?"

"To some extent, but it is indistinct. Nevertheless, I have found the constant accusations and references to the past most distressing."

"Understandably. Why do you suppose that your maid failed to hear it?"

Miss Melhuish frowned. "Alice has since admitted to some deafness, but at the time I began to believe that I was indeed on the verge of madness. On that occasion, the voice seemed to me to be in the room with us, as opposed to further away as at other times."

"And you're certain that no one else has heard it?"

"I asked, and all denied having done so."

"You have mentioned that the rooms above were destroyed by fire," Holmes enquired after a brief silence. "But what of the rooms beneath? Is there a cellar?"

"There may be, but I have never ventured there. My father forbade it. He once told me that part of it had collapsed, and is filled with earth. I think that occurred even before the fire."

"So," I ventured, "for many years, your family have lived in the part of the house that still stands?"

"Fortunately, a good portion remains."

"We'll begin interviewing the staff shortly," Holmes said, "but first, we must inspect the outside of the house. After that, we will begin with the maid."

Miss Melhuish nodded. "I will tell everyone to hold themselves in readiness."

We retrieved our hats and coats and set out to circumvent the house. I wasn't surprised when Holmes paused at every door and window to examine it and the surrounding ground. The storm had passed by now, leaving many nearby trees bent over and almost leafless. As my friend worked, I glanced beyond the cliff to where the dark sea writhed under heavy clouds. The horizon was invisible, hidden by a distant mist. The wind had abated somewhat, but blew bitterly cold.

"There are no marks from a forced entry anywhere," he concluded as we returned to the front of the building, "but the storm has destroyed any footprints that there might have been."

"Miss Melhuish's tormenter doesn't gain entry from without," I ventured, "leaving only those already in the house."

"Precisely. This I had already suspected, but it's always as well to eliminate other possibilities."

As we turned to approach the main entrance, we were hailed by a thick-set, rather brutish-looking fellow who appeared from the other side of the building.

"You'd be the detectives from London," he said as he confronted us.

"And you would be Mr. Benton, the groom," Holmes replied.

"Aye, I am that. Are you here to look into that poor girl's death of some time ago? The one who fell from the steps?"

Holmes raised an eyebrow. "Was there some mystery in that?"

"No, but it was a shock to the rest of us." He scratched his unshaven chin. "Any mystery would be with the man who found her."

"Lord Endworth?"

"That's him. Some say he killed her, like the girl before."

"Perhaps you could tell us more."

"Indeed," said I. "Explain yourself, sir."

"I wouldn't want this getting back to Miss Helen. I'm not sure she knows, but she wouldn't like it if she found out."

"We are interested only in seeing that all is well. Otherwise, our lips are sealed."

Mr. Benton hesitated and looked at us both in turn. "I suppose that's all right, then. The fact is, gentlemen, that someone in the village – You wouldn't know it, being strangers, but that's Warrens Croft. – has relatives in Scotland who know of Lord Mulderne's son. It seems he's been betrothed before now, to a local girl called Martha Jukes, and it ended badly."

"Kindly elaborate," said Holmes.

"Well, it was like this, sirs: Mr. Luke had a reputation as a ladies' man, if you know what I mean, and the girl was very much the jealous kind. One day, she saw him talking to a woman in the street, a neighbour's wife as it turned out, and did no more than enter the local butcher's shop and snatch up a cleaver. She attacked them both with it, and Mr. Luke barely took it out of her hand in time. Luckily, no one was harmed, but the other lady was badly shaken."

I anticipated my friend's next question. "What became of Miss Jukes?"

"She was eventually sent to an asylum, but that's where the mystery is, you see. Some say she died there, but others swear she escaped about two years ago. Yet, while on a visit to Glasgow, one of our villager's relatives says he saw her in the flesh." The telling of his tale had excited him, but now he became calmer. "At least, that's what he claimed afterwards. I'm told he was a man who liked his drink, so who knows?"

This didn't seem to me to be directly connected to our enquiries, since Lord Mulderne's son was at present in South Africa, but Holmes appeared quite interested. He gave the man a half-sovereign for his trouble.

"One more thing, sirs." Mr. Benton paused before walking on. "Please be especially careful in allowing what I have told you to go no further. I was once a prisoner, you see. I did a stretch in Taunton Gaol for robbing a house. After that, I resolved never to get on the wrong side of the law again. Miss Helen knew of it when she gave me a chance, but if she found out I've been spreading gossip, she might send me packing."

"I have said that our lips are sealed," Holmes reminded him. "You may take that as definite."

"Thank you, sir." With that, Mr. Benton touched his cap and walked away, in the direction of the stables.

"A sorry story indeed," I remarked, "but with no relevance to our enquiries, I would think. He misunderstands our purpose here."

"Don't dismiss his words so quickly, Watson. Mr. Benton's information may yet prove to be a piece in our developing puzzle."

We were admitted by Daniels, who took our outer garments and informed us that the maid, Alice Tanders, awaited us in the sitting room. This was where we had spoken to Miss Helen after her unnerving encounter of the previous evening.

The fire had warmed the room well, a relief after the outside chill. Near the mantelpiece stood a thin girl of average height with red hair worn in a bun. Her uniform appeared well-starched, and her features hung loosely, as if she had recently recovered from a serious illness.

"Miss Tanders," Holmes began when we were seated. "My name is Sherlock Holmes, and this is my friend and colleague, Doctor John Watson. Doubtless Miss Melhuish has told you of our purpose here."

"The mistress has said that you are detectives from London, sir," she replied respectfully, "here to find out about the voice she hears at night."

"Quite so. I understand that you were with your mistress on one occasion when this occurred."

She nodded hesitantly. "I was, sir. Miss Helen had asked me to sleep in her room in order to hear this voice also."

"But you heard nothing?"

"I saw that she became concerned, and acted as if there was someone else present. She was listening carefully and with some distress, so I strained my ears to see what ailed her. I heard only the sighing of the wind from the sea. Otherwise there was silence."

Holmes turned in his chair so as to face her more directly. "From that incident, what do you conclude?"

94

"It isn't my place to have opinions about my betters, sir."

"Did it cross your mind that your mistress could be ill?"

"No, sir, because I am not qualified to make such a judgement." She paused, apparently searching for a way to express herself. "This is an old house, and since I began working here I have heard many unusual sounds and creaks within it. I assumed that, if Miss Helen had heard anything, it could have been something of that sort."

"Indeed, Doctor Watson and I have often found ourselves in such places," my friend confirmed. "I take it, then, that since your employment commenced here, you have witnessed nothing that could be termed as strange or unusual?"

Her eyes narrowed for an instant, but Holmes didn't miss it.

"Come now, Miss Tanders – Any small thing might assist us. Pray have no fear as to being disbelieved or mocked."

She avoided our eyes, fixing her gaze on the carpet. "I have seen the White Lady, sir. It was no more than a flash in the darkness, gone in an instant. I have heard no one else mention such a sight, and so have kept it to myself, but I did wonder if she is connected to the mistress' troubles."

"How did this apparition appear to you?" I enquired, watching her face,

"It was several days ago – I cannot remember exactly when. Darkness was falling as I drew the curtains in the windows at the back of the house, where the view is of the cliff and the sea. Before I had closed them completely, I saw what I first thought was a white sheet, adrift and floating in the wind. It was blown nearer, just for a moment, and I could then make out that it was a woman. Her hair was bedraggled, and she was dressed in a long white garment and held her arms out to me, as if appealing for something. Then she was gone, and there was only the wind and the darkness." She looked up with a tearful glance that embraced us both. "Please, sirs, don't tell the mistress or anyone else of this. I would be thought mad and taken away."

"You need have no fears," Holmes assured her. "But tell me: Do you believe this woman to be Miss Helen's mother?"

"I didn't know the lady, but because of what happened to her, I thought this must be so."

"Don't distress yourself, for I can promise you that there is nothing to fear from this."

"Yes, sir." After a moment of silence: "Is there anything more, sir?"

My friend shook his head. "Not for the present. You may return to your duties now."

"Thank you, sir." She curtsied politely and turned to leave us.

As she reached the door, Holmes called in a low voice. "Ah yes, there is one more point on which I wish to be clear, Miss Tanders."

At once she turned again to face us. "Yes, Mr. Holmes?"

"As I understand it, this apparition didn't speak to you."

"No, sir. She was gone from my sight in an instant."

"Thank you. That is all."

Our luncheon was suddenly disturbed.

Miss Meluish, Holmes, and I were seated and finishing bowls of a thick mushroom soup when Daniels entered the room and approached her quickly. He leaned towards her and whispered something to which she responded with a shocked expression.

"Take the dog-cart and go to Warrens Croft immediately," she said nervously. "We must inform the local police at once."

The butler acknowledged the order and left, and our hostess saw our curiosity and explained.

"Gentlemen, I have to tell you that Daniels has just taken food to Benton, and discovered him dead in the stable."

Holmes stood up at once. "Miss Melhuish, pray excuse us. I must make an examination of the body. No, don't get up. It is essential to our enquiry that Doctor Watson and I reach the stable before the official force arrive. Please bear with us."

The lady didn't object to our sudden withdrawal. We set off in the direction that the groom had taken subsequent to our earlier conversation, and soon came upon a long low structure from which sounds of disturbed animals reached our ears. We entered, closing the door behind us, to see a fine black stallion careening before three other stalls as their occupants looked on anxiously. At the sight of us, the escaped horse appeared wary at first, but was soon still and allowed us to guide him back to his open stall. Only when he was settled did we approach the body of the groom, which lay sprawled in a corner nearby, with a bloody head wound.

Holmes inspected the corpse at length before glancing around the straw-scattered floor. He appeared satisfied after a while, and transferred his attention to the stallion. When he had calmed the animal further, he examined its hooves, murmuring to himself as did so. Leaving the stall, he latched it securely, and I assumed his attention was at an end, but on emerging from the stable he proceeded to walk in ever-widening circles around it for several minutes.

"It appears that the horse was alarmed," I concluded as my friend rejoined me, "and kicked Benton as he sought to take it out for exercise."

"That is one possible explanation."

"Have you formed a different theory?"

"I have identified three other possibilities. Now I suppose we must await the arrival of the official force."

On returning to the house, we spent some little time with Miss Melhuish.

"What happened out there, Mr. Holmes?" she asked as we took our seats. "Daniels said that it appeared that one of the horses had kicked Benton. Is that your opinion also?"

"That is how it seems, but let us await the observations of your local man before drawing firm conclusions. Why, by the way, did you send for him if the situation is most likely accidental? Wouldn't a physician have been more appropriate, to pronounce the poor fellow as having expired?"

"We were notified, some weeks ago, of several burglaries in the area. A constable asked us to report unusual events of any kind. I believe the local force to be anxious for any clue to aid them in this."

Holmes nodded, and we all turned to the window at the sound of the dog-cart returning. Daniels tethered the horse and led a short man, whose movements were quick and sudden, into the house by the main door. Moments later they entered the room.

The stranger removed his hat. "Inspector Quince," he announced. "I understand that there has been an unexplained death here. May I see the place where the body was discovered, Miss Melhuish?"

The lady showed no sign of recognition of the inspector, so I presumed him to be unknown to her. By his lack of greeting, he struck me as rather blunt.

"Thank you, Inspector," she replied coolly. "Daniels will show you to the stable."

"If you have no objection, Miss Melhuish, Watson and I will undertake that," my friend interjected. "As we have already visited the scene, it may the quickest way to resolve the matter."

The inspector turned to us at once. "Ah, of course, Mr. Sherlock Holmes. We have heard of your triumphs, even in this part of the country. I don't know that I approve of you getting to the scene before me, but I suppose it can do no harm to have you and the other gentleman accompany me. Two – " He glanced at me. " – or even three pairs of eyes might see more, after all."

"You are most kind," Holmes acknowledged with a hint of sarcasm or irony which went entirely unnoticed. "Perhaps we could adjourn to the stable now."

During the short walk, I was pleasantly surprised when the inspector mentioned several of my friend's recent cases with approval. I judged his age to be nearing fifty, but from his remarks, it was apparent that he hadn't held his position for long. Thus, was explained the lack of resentment to

Holmes's presence that we had so often encountered, for it was likely he needed my friend's aid.

The horses shifted uncomfortably as we entered the stable. Both men knelt by Benton's body while I looked on.

"The butler said that he thought one of the horses had kicked this fellow," the inspector remembered. "I must say, I see nothing to contradict that."

"Let us look a little more closely. My suspicions were aroused when I saw the position of the body. One would have expected such a kick to be delivered as the groom took the horse from the stall, yet he lies at least six feet away in the corner."

"Possibly, but surely that isn't conclusive?"

"No, but when you consider that the blow was to the back of the head, rather than when he confronted the animal, does it not raise doubts?"

Inspector Quince fingered his moustache. "Then you believe this was murder?"

"I know it. There is no blood on the hooves of the horse that was deliberately released from its stall to give the impression that it had run amok."

"Then there should be a weapon, yet there is none."

"That I will show you in a moment."

"But why was this man killed? Was the intention to steal a horse, before the groom disturbed the thief?"

"Perhaps. I've heard that there have been other robberies not far away."

"Indeed, there have. We get little crime here, but recently one or two of the old manor houses on the other side of Warrens Croft have been broken into. This looks to me as if it could be the work of the same gang, if that is what we are faced with here."

"I wish you luck with your enquiries in that direction," Holmes said with sincerity. "Am I to take it that you will arrange for the unfortunate groom's removal?"

"I'll issue instructions when I return to the station. For now, I am curious to see the weapon you mentioned."

We left the stable and I closed the door behind us. Immediately Holmes led us to a patch of earth and stones a few yards away. After inspecting it he indicated a large rock in the midst of the turf and apart from the others.

"You can see the blood from here, Inspector. I found it earlier. It's undisturbed, I assure you, for there was no need."

"So the murderer took this stone into the stable and struck the groom, then discarded it on leaving?"

"That is my conclusion."

"And so premeditation is proved at once, since the weapon was adopted in advance."

"Precisely."

He smiled suddenly. "Thank you, Mr. Holmes, for your insight. I will consider it as part of my investigation, of course. The sooner we can get whoever is responsible for this behind bars, the sooner people hereabouts can sleep easier in their beds again."

"Indeed."

Shortly afterwards we returned to the house, where the inspector explained to Miss Melhuish that the body would be collected later for further examination. He assured her that no effort would be spared in the apprehension of the intruder whose presence he had detected, but made no mention of the murder. He left soon after.

"He reminds me of Lestrade, as we knew him years ago," I remarked to Holmes when we were alone again.

My friend smiled. "Inspector Quince is a good man, but he is anxious because his promotion has come a little late in his life. He fears he will go no further, and feels the need to grasp every opportunity to win the approval of his superiors. We have seen it before."

"Could it be that the groom may have been observed earlier, in conversation with us? If the murderer believes that the man still had information that could be dangerous to him, might that not have been the reason for the killing?"

"That had occurred to me. The timing of the murder was unlikely, otherwise. And, as I'm sure you were about to conclude, Watson, this means that the murderer can only be someone in Cliff Top House."

I nodded. "And we have yet to interview the cook and the butler."

Holmes inclined his head, listening. "Ah, but I hear the gong summoning us to dinner. I'll conduct both interviews afterwards. Come along. Let us notify Miss Melhuish."

During a meal of well-cooked partridge, he advised our hostess, who still appeared rather pale after the events of the afternoon, of his intention. After some little thought, she informed Daniels when he served dessert. Before he withdrew, he mentioned that some local men had already arrived to remove Mr. Benton's body.

"Both Daniels and the cook will be available to you this evening, Mr. Holmes," she informed us then. "They will not be returning to their quarters until you no longer require them."

"Thank you, Miss Melhuish. Pray be so kind as to tell us where you will be."

"I have some papers to attend to, in the library. Afterwards, I will remain there to read until I retire."

"Capital." Holmes pushed away his empty coffee cup. "With your permission, Doctor Watson and I will immediately adjourn to the sitting room."

The cook, Mrs. Waldron, didn't match my preconceived impression. I had expected a small, round woman, who would tell us that, in her opinion, the voice that her mistress heard was imaginary. She who awaited us in the sitting room was quite different. I judged her to be well over five feet, and of slim build. Her glance was piercing and her expression grave, but it was easy to see that she had been attractive in the years of her youth.

Curiously, Holmes specified that the door of the room should be left ajar. In answer to my query, he said it was to allow some ventilation.

As we hadn't seen the lady before, my friend spent a few moments putting her at her ease, although I hadn't thought that to be necessary. The evening had grown cool, and he indicated that we should settle ourselves near the fire.

"You are aware," he began, "that we are here to attempt to explain the voice which disturbs your mistress' sleep?"

"Indeed, sir." Her expression didn't change. "She fears it is that of her mother."

"Tell us, pray, have you, yourself, heard this, or have any explanation of your own?"

She didn't hesitate. "I haven't heard this myself, sir. Nevertheless, I have reason to believe that there are curious goings-on here."

"Kindly explain."

"I was referring to the strange sounds that I have heard in the evenings. They were like hollow echoes. I was puzzled, but felt that an enquiry to Miss Meluish might be seen as an impertinence, so I took other steps."

"What form did they take?" I asked.

"As this is a house with some history, and the upper storey is unusable, I realised that the sounds must originate in a vault below, or a cellar. The local priest is a kindly man, and I was able to persuade him to allow me to examine the parish records of many years past. I soon discovered that there is indeed an extensive cellar beneath the property, noted because it collapsed long ago and was partially destroyed. However, the part that had at one time served as a priest hole is, as far as is known, almost intact, so it could be that the mistress is the victim of someone who wishes her harm from concealment there. Although," she shook her head in a hopeless gesture, "I cannot imagine why. Of course, I could be quite in error. The sounds could also be a natural occurrence, such as strong wind passing through a tunnel."

Holmes looked at her with admiration. "I congratulate you on your astuteness and perseverance." He held his head to one side for a moment as if listening, before a faint smile of satisfaction crossed his face. "In fact, Watson and myself have resolved to inspect the cellar this very night, so perhaps we might clear things up."

"I do hope so, sir."

"I understand," he continued, "that it was Miss Melhuish's father who proposed that you should adopt your present position?"

"That is so. He was a most kind and thoughtful man."

"Because you were recently widowed and without support?"

"Yes, sir." But both her expression and her voice had changed noticeably, and that Holmes had seen this was apparent at once.

"Were there unusual circumstances involved? I regret asking you this, but I must pursue every avenue of enquiry."

"But those happenings aren't connected with the events in this house," she said in a suddenly subdued tone.

He smiled sympathetically. "To cause you distress isn't my intention."

"Very well, sir." Mrs. Waldron looked down at the carpet. "When my husband passed on, there were rumours in the village that it was my doing. Some were saying that I had poisoned him. The place has several gossip-mongers who delight in the ruin of innocent folks' reputations. It was said that even Miss Melhuish had come to believe this tale, but it was her father who rescued me from these hateful lies."

"Has your mistress mentioned her opinion, since you began your employment here?"

"It is never spoken of."

"So you have no means of knowing whether she ever truly held such a view?"

"None, sir. I assumed that everyone was satisfied when the local police exonerated me."

"Were there frequent quarrels between your husband and yourself?"

"No more than with anyone else. We had our ups and downs.

Holmes stole a sly glance in the direction of the door. "Quite so. I think we need nothing more for now. Again, my apologies for any discomfort which I may have caused you."

"Thank you, sir." She left with much of her previous disposition restored, so that I wondered as to her real self.

"It is a vile cruelty," I said then, "to poison the minds of others against someone whose guilt is no more than assumed."

"It is indeed," he replied absently. "But now I see that it is growing late, and the butler still awaits us. Perhaps you would summon him for me."

I rose and left the room. Daniels must have been watching for the cook to reappear, for I met him on his way to join us. He showed no irritation at the delay of the interview, and preceded me into the sitting room with a wistful expression.

"My apologies for the wait you've had this evening," Holmes said at once. "Pray be seated."

"If you don't object, sir, I will remain standing."

"As you wish. I don't expect this to take long."

I resumed my seat, noting that the butler's countenance was set and that his grey hair was slightly dishevelled.

"How can I be of service, sir?" he asked.

Holmes regarded him thoughtfully. "I merely wish to know if you have any knowledge of this voice that has disturbed your mistress so, several times recently."

I was surprised to see the relief on Daniels' face. "I have heard no such thing myself sir, but after seeing the effect upon my mistress, I cannot fail to believe that it is genuine."

"But you have experienced nothing out of the ordinary, such as unusual sounds or sightings of strangers in the grounds?"

"No, sir."

Holmes studied him carefully. "I'm curious as to the cause of the stains on your fingers, though I perceive that they are old. What, pray, occurred that resulted in these?"

"Why, sir, you're the first person in all the years since to notice them." He spoke casually, but we both saw wariness creep into the butler's face, and there was now a tenseness about him.

"It is my business to notice such things."

"Of course." He now appeared, I thought, to be experiencing some sort of internal struggle. After a moment he seemed to decide, as had many before him, that it is impossible to keep important facts from Holmes. "They are acid stains. Many years ago, before I took up my position here, I worked for the Royal Mint. I was involved with the design and production of gold sovereigns, a position of trust and requiring some skill. All went well until my wife was abducted by a gang of coiners, who informed me that I would never see her again if I failed to comply with their instructions."

"What did they demand of you?" I enquired with some astonishment.

"I was forced to falsify illness, so as to be absent from my employment, while actually producing counterfeit sovereigns for the gang

102

in a place they had prepared. I was blindfolded during every journey to and from there, and so had no way of identifying the route."

"Was this ever discovered?" My friend asked.

"Never, although my employers found out that my illness was fictitious. I was subsequently discharged, and had no means of support until Miss Helen's father hired me."

"He appears to have been a kindly soul," Holmes observed.

"Indeed, sir, but he was unaware of my past."

"What of your wife?" I asked then.

Daniels' face grew grave. "The coiners, who were never caught, were at least as good as their word for she was returned to me unharmed. However, the experience had been too much for her delicate nature to sustain, and she died soon after."

"Pray accept our condolences," Holmes offered. "I think there is nothing more that we need to discuss for now. You may return to Miss Melhuish, or perhaps your bed."

After entreating us not to divulge his history, the butler departed, and I closed the door after him. Holmes sat smoking in silence.

"You will have realised," I began, interrupting his reverie, "that each of Miss Melhuish's employees has something to hide. Even the departed groom."

"That fact had not escaped me," he confirmed, blowing out a cloud of fragrant smoke. "However, the situation is now clearer, and I expect to be able to offer an explanation before long." He knocked out his pipe in the hearth and consulted his pocket-watch, before getting to his feet. "But for now, Watson, sleep beckons. We will see what tomorrow brings. Let us return to our rooms."

"But you mentioned that we are to keep a vigil in the cellar!"

"Unless I'm mistaken, Miss Melhuish's tormentor now believes this and will therefore commit no mischief tonight. Our presence would be a waste of time, I think."

The following morning, I breakfasted alone. Daniels served grilled kidneys with bacon and informed me that Holmes had eaten early before leaving in the dog-cart, indicating that he would be absent until late afternoon at least.

I had finished my second cup of coffee when Miss Melhuish appeared. Her tired and drawn countenance was not, she told me, due to the voice that haunted her, but simply from difficulties in sleeping. My offer to prescribe something was declined. I noted that Holmes had been correct in his prediction that the voice wouldn't be heard the previous night. Our hostess asked about the progress of our enquiries, and I

103

informed her that Holmes was close to concluding them and had left for Warrens Croft to do so. She seemed satisfied, but ordered only coffee when Daniels came to serve her. When he brought it, he seemed hesitant to withdraw.

She was aware of it at once. "Is something amiss, Daniels?"

"It is Algernon, Miss Melhuish." The butler bowed his head, avoiding her eyes as he spoke.

"Is he ill, again?"

"He is dying, Miss."

"Very well. Inform the maid that she must assume your duties for a day or two, and you may leave immediately. Take one of the traps to the station and arrange for it to be returned. Kindly notify me by telegraph when you intend to re-join us."

Daniels bowed and thanked her, and was about to take his leave when a thought occurred to me.

"One moment, pray!" I called. "With your permission, Miss Melhuish."

"Of course." She appeared surprised at my sudden exclamation, but allowed me to continue.

"How have you learned of this man's condition?" I asked him.

"I received a telegram, sir."

I indicated the tall window. "I've been watching for such a delivery myself, for I feel sure that Holmes will send me certain notifications soon, but I saw none."

"It arrived early, sir. Before first light."

I nodded. "I see. Thank you, Daniels."

He acknowledged politely and left us.

"You surely don't suspect him?" Miss Melhuish asked me in an incredulous tone. "Why, Daniels has been with us for many years."

"I have assisted Sherlock Holmes with many investigations, Miss Melhuish, and one thing I have learned from him is never to draw either favourable or unfavourable conclusions prematurely. We'll know before long who is your tormentor. I am curious, though, as to who is 'Algernon'."

"He is Daniels' nephew," she explained. "His only living relative, whose health has always been poor. This isn't the first time that Daniels has had to rush to his side."

I said nothing more, although I would dearly have liked to delay the butler's departure until Holmes's return. I hoped that I hadn't failed my friend.

"You are right, I am sure, to be suspicious of everyone." Miss Melhuish said in a tired voice.

Shortly after the maid had cleared away the breakfast things, our hostess complained of a sudden and severe headache and retired to her chamber once more. I spent the morning in the library, where I was delighted to discover a volume dealing with ancient medical practices. She didn't reappear for luncheon, which the maid served on the stroke of midday, and I resolved to take an afternoon walk around the grounds. The weather was now much improved, and the early flowers delightful. All was quiet so that I nearly fell asleep on a bench in the midst of the garden. The time passed swiftly, and just after I'd awakened and returned to the house, Holmes returned earlier than his promise.

"My dear fellow," he said when greetings and a few words had been exchanged, "I have much to tell you. Where is our hostess?"

I was about to answer when the lady appeared suddenly in the doorway of the sitting room.

"Are you quite well now, Miss Melhuish?" I asked.

"My head has cleared. Thank you, Doctor. I heard Mr. Holmes's arrival and came at once." She paused. "But I am forgetting my manners. Have you eaten, Mr. Holmes?"

My friend shook his head. "There has been no time, for I've been exceedingly busy. Although dinner is but an hour from now, I would welcome a pot of strong coffee. Watson tells me that Daniels has been called away, so perhaps the maid could bring it."

There was something in his tone that alerted me at once, and Miss Melhuish gave him a curious look.

We sat near the fireplace. Miss Melhuish frowned and summoned Alice Tanders who, I noticed, avoided Holmes's eyes. She acknowledged her mistress' instructions, curtsied, and left.

"I fear," said Holmes, "that we are likely to have a long wait for that beverage."

"Whatever can you mean, Mr. Holmes?" the lady asked curiously.

I turned to my friend. "Is the maid responsible for the outrages here," I enquired.

"Unless I'm greatly mistaken, all will become clear very soon." I caught the glint of triumph in his grey eyes as he glanced towards the doorway.

He was quickly proven correct. A silence fell upon us, so that we heard the closing of the door at the main entrance clearly, although the intention had doubtless been to conceal it. Moments later, the noise of the door reopening came to us, followed by the entrance of Inspector Quince and a constable into the room. Between them they held the restrained Alice Tander who, having changed from her maid's uniform, continued to struggle violently.

"We caught her fleeing the house!" the official detective cried on seeing Holmes. "Just as you said we would, sir!"

Miss Melhuish rose at once. "Inspector, what is the meaning of this?"

"Mr. Holmes will explain fully, Miss Melhuish." The two men forced the maid onto a straight-backed chair where she was held securely. The inspector was left breathless. "By God, this girl has the strength of ten men."

"That isn't unusual among those possessed by criminal madness," Holmes remarked, "as Watson will confirm."

"Indeed," I confirmed, "but – "

"Pray have patience, and I'll relate to you the activities of the inspector and myself this day. I would have returned earlier, had I not been obliged to await the answer to several enquiries by telegraph."

Miss Tanders then gave forth to a stream of obscenities and oaths, such as I have seldom heard from other than men of the lowest classes, and Inspector Quince threatened to scour her mouth with soap if she didn't desist immediately. Wisely, she contented herself with hostile glares at each of us.

When calm had returned, Holmes began his explanation.

"I suspected the maid almost from the beginning when, after claiming deafness to her mistress, she had no difficulty in responding to my question put to her in a deliberately quiet tone from a short distance away. What puzzled me for a while was the apparent lack of any cause for her actions."

Miss Tanders squirmed in her seat and the constable tightened his grip.

"Do feel free to correct any inaccuracies in my explanation, if you see fit." Holmes told her as he continued. "Although I'm confident as to the truth of it all."

"I see already that I have been blind." Miss Melhuish shifted in her chair uncomfortably. "Alice, are you really responsible for the anguish that I have suffered? Yes, I see that you don't regret it. How could you?"

"You took what is mine!" the maid snarled.

Our hostess' expression was one of total incomprehension, until my friend resumed his revelation.

"This woman isn't Alice Tanders, for no such person exists. Her true name is Martha Jukes, and she is the former fiancee of the man you are to marry, Lord Luke Endworth."

"Oh, no!" Miss Melhuish covered her mouth with her hand, severely shocked. "But I was told that she was afflicted with madness, and placed in an asylum."

"And so she was, until her subsequent escape during which a nurse was badly injured. Since then, according to the received answers to our

106

telegrams to Scotland, it has been discovered that she was befriended by a retired actor some time before journeying to Somerset, on what she saw as a mission of revenge upon you for assuming her place as Lord Luke's intended wife. I recall, Miss Melhuish, that you stated that the voice that tormented you was of a different quality on the night when the maid shared your room. That was because Miss Tanders, as we then thought, produced it by means of ventriloquism, a technique taught to her by the old thespian that she lived with for a while. At other times, to enhance the convenient acoustic features of your bedroom, I suspect she used some sort of device to disguise her voice. Doubtless, this will be found among her possessions."

"Did she murder Brenton, the groom?" I asked.

Holmes nodded. "She feared that he would confide to us information about her former life. She may have accidentally mentioned something in previous conversation with him that she couldn't risk he might divulge. There is, however, one aspect of this that I am uncertain of." He confronted the prisoner. "Miss Jukes, you must see that it is all up with you now, so it can avail you nothing to conceal anything more." He hesitated, watching her face. "Did you murder Elizabeth, the maid whose position you assumed?"

She continued to glare at him in silence.

"Come on, girl!" Inspector Quince shook her impatiently. "Speak!"

"She was in my way," was the sullen reply. "What else should I have done?"

"You were responsible for Elizabeth's death?" The colour had drained from our hostess' face. "And that of Brenton? Oh, dear God!"

I recognised a hint of hysteria in her voice, and recalled that our client had described her as being of a delicate nature. However, as I attempted to be of assistance, she seemed to draw on some inner strength to restore her composure. A glance from Holmes told me to allow the lady to calm herself.

"And then we come to the so-called 'White Lady' you claim to have seen," he continued to Miss Jukes. "I imagine that was nothing more than an attempt to persuade me that the voice was of supernatural origin."

"Why else would I make up such a story?" she spat.

"Mr. Holmes," Inspector Quince began, "I can understand how you came to suspect the maid, but how did you first come to realise who she actually is?"

"I observed the looseness of the skin of her face, then realised that her limbs also had this, and her body appeared the same. Then I noticed that the roots of her hair were of a different shade. Why else would a young woman starve herself to quickly become much slimmer, as well as colouring her hair with henna or some such preparation, if not to disguise her appearance? Why would she need to do this? The answer of course is that if Lord Endworth were to appear unexpectedly, he would immediately recognise her otherwise. Further confirmation will be the photographic portrait of Miss Jukes, which will be arriving in a day or two. Last night, I knew that Miss Melhuish wouldn't be troubled, since I stated that Watson and myself would be guarding the cellar. I said this, without intention of actually doing so, when I was certain that Miss Jukes was eavesdropping on our conversation. Clearly, her campaign against Miss Melhuish, who she had never set eyes upon until she began her employment here, was planned well in advance."

"My thanks to you, sir," the inspector said at length, before speaking reassuringly to Miss Melhuish and, with the assistance of the constable, half-dragging Miss Martha Jukes from the room as they took their leave.

When their conveyance had gone from the courtyard our hostess, now apparently fully recovered, thanked Holmes and me heartily.

"I fear," my friend observed, "that you now require replacements for the positions of both groom and maid. That is to be regretted, but hopefully you will again employ a full staff soon. For now, perhaps Mrs. Waldron would not be averse to feeding us. Both Watson and I will be taking the early train to the capital tomorrow, for I must be back in Baker Street by mid-day."

A Penny for the Guy
by Brenda Seabrooke

It was a raw day in early November, and Holmes and I had just finished a delicious breakfast. Not long after, the downstairs doorbell rang. In a moment, we heard our landlady climbing the steps.

"There's a person to see you, Mr. Holmes," Mrs. Hudson said from the doorway, "a Mrs. Ivy Dove. She says you'll remember her son. Shall I send her up?"

"I can't recall a Mrs. Dove, or anyone by that name." Holmes steepled his fingers and closed his eyes as if thinking deeply.

"Her son's name is Simpson."

"The only Simpson I know was that boy who ran with the Irregulars for a time," I said. "A sturdy little fellow and very good at his tasks. Haven't seen him in a while."

"Simpson. Yes, yes. Send her up, if you please, Mrs. Hudson."

"He must be about fourteen or fifteen now," I said.

"Fourteen," Holmes said.

I wondered what had happened to him as Mrs. Hudson announced from the doorway, "Mrs. Ivy Dove."

A small woman peered around the doorjamb, as if she weren't sure where she was supposed to go.

"Come in, please," Holmes said. I rose to bring her to the basket chair close to the fire while introducing myself.

Ivy Dove almost tiptoed into the room and sat carefully in the chair, which didn't creak much with her slight frame. "Dr. Watson, sure I 'member you 'elping Mr. 'Olmes."

"Cup of tea?" I asked, already lifting the pot which held sufficient for another cup. I poured, added cream and two sugars, and then a third one.

She accepted the cup and sipped the tea before trying to speak. She possessed sharp brown eyes, a nose reddened by the wind, and chestnut hair in a bun showing under a squashed-down navy-blue straw hat with a brave daisy stuck in the band. Her black cape seemed to be fashioned by several draped on her or sewn together, the same color but different materials. She gulped down half the tea and held the saucer on her lap.

"You remember my boy? Simpson? 'E worked for you sometimes when 'e was littler?"

"Yes, indeed," Holmes said. "He performed his tasks excellently."

I nodded and waited for her to go on. She finished her tea and looked for a place to put the cup. I took it from her. "What can we do for you, Mrs. Dove?"

"'E's in trouble. 'E's in jail. E's a good boy, you know 'e is, Mr. 'Olmes." The words pleaded for us to agree with her.

"Tell us what he's accused of," Holmes said.

She rummaged in a bag and pulled out a handkerchief. I thought she was about to dab at tears, but she handed it to Holmes. "Hit's all I got now, but I'll get more."

Holmes took the coins knotted in the handkerchief and placed them on the table beside him. "Tell us," he said again.

"It's murder," she whispered. "They said 'e did murder."

"Who was murdered?" I asked.

"Simpson got a job delivering for a hapothecary – it was the owner who died. Hit was most three year ago, an' I couldn't keep 'im, an 'e got to go to a Ragged School. 'E learnt to read 'n' write 'n' figger. 'Bout a month ago, a man come to the school and looked over all the boys. 'E chose my Simpson and took 'im to work at the shop, and we moved back to the old place."

"What was this man's name? This man who chose Simpson for the job?"

"'E said hit was Mr. Rookwood.

Holmes looked at me, but I was already pulling out my pencil and notebook.

"Mr. Rookwood took him to the apothecary shop," Holmes confirmed. "Was he the chemist?"

"No, that were Mr. Keyes. 'E owned the shop. It were 'im that was killed – 'it over the head, and then the shop set on fire. The fire didn't amount to much, and Simpson found 'im when 'e went to work yesterday morning."

"What sort was Mr. Keyes?"

"A good fellow. 'E was teaching Simpson a great deal."

"And what about this Mr. Rookwood? Did Simpson tell you anything about him? Was he tall or short. Fair or swarthy? How was he dressed? Did he speak like a Londoner?"

Her eyes almost closed with concentration. "'E were tallish, dark 'air 'n' eyes. 'E dressed like a gent. Simpson was taken with 'is dress. 'E talked a little funny, though, like 'e might've come from someplace else."

I leaned forward. "Some place in England or Scotland perhaps?"

"No, 'e spoke furrin-like."

I was sure a Scot would sound foreign to Mrs. Dove. I said a few words to her.

She shook her head. "Not like that, sir."

I tried it with a Welsh accent and an Irish one, but she shook her head at both. "Hit were furriner than that."

"From the Continent then," I said.

Her eyebrows drew together as if she were thinking harder.

"Did you think of something?" I urged her.

"'E were quite in awe of 'im, Simpson were."

"Very well, Mrs. Dove," said Holmes, "we shall take the case. I gather Simpson is being held at Scotland Yard."

"Yessir."

"Watson, please see Mrs. Dove out and get us a cab."

When our hansom stopped in front of the turreted red-brick building that housed Scotland Yard, a group of urchins bearing a garish concoction meant to represent Guy Fawkes, one of the men who tried to blow up Parliament in 1605, descended upon us shouting, "A penny for the guy! A penny for the guy!"

Every November, these homemade "guys" were wheeled around England and Scotland to collect money for fireworks to set off on the fifth, when the guy effigies would be burned to celebrate the failure of the plot. I dug in my pocket and came up with a coin. "Will a ha'penny do?"

The closest boy grabbed it and gave me a cherubic smile. Holmes gave them a tuppence.

A policeman exiting the building admonished them. "Off with you! This be police business here."

The boys ran away, giggling with their coins and shaking the flimsy guy. "Did you ever make a guy?" Holmes asked me as we walked to the entrance.

"I did. It was great fun to run the streets begging for money for Bonfire Night – somewhat akin to the American Halloween. Did you?"

We were at the door then and he only smiled briefly. My conclusion was that he had once done it, if only to observe the behavior of others

Holmes gave his name to the desk constable and stated our purpose.

"Yes, sir." He beckoned over an older policeman to take us to Simpson's cell. I had difficulty reconciling my memory of the boy with that of a murderer.

Jakes the constable had the cell door opened for us and crowded in with us.

"Thank you, Officer. I will need to confer with my client in private," Holmes said. My attention was on the lad. He sat hunched over, shivering, his arms hugging his legs on the bench.

"Simpson," Holmes said, "we're here to help you."

Simpson Dove had grown taller since last we saw him. His sandy hair had darkened, but the same cowlick kicked up at the crown and his eyes were still blue. "Mr. 'Olmes, sir, thank you for coming. Mum said she would talk to you, but I didn't know if you were too busy to see 'er. We don't 'ave no money to pay you – "

Holmes waved that away. "I've made arrangements with your mother. Tell me about yesterday."

Simpson sniffed and shoved his hands into the pocket of his too-short coat. The cell was cold and dank. How much worse it must seem to those detained in here. "What time did you arrive at the shop?" I prompted.

"I di'nt look at a timepiece, but I 'eard the church bells ring the 'our as I reached the shop. That were seven sharp."

"Was Mr. Keyes usually there when you arrived?"

"'E often arrived just behind me. I reckon that 'e'd go somewhere to get 'is breakfast and then take 'is constitutional."

"That would be his morning walk."

"Yes, sir. 'E'd walk down to the docks and back most every day. 'E lives – " He gulped. " – *lived* over the shop, an' 'e liked to walk early to get his blood flowing, 'e said."

I nodded. "Was he a healthy man?"

"Dunno, sir. I never saw 'im sick."

"So on a normal day, he would open the shop and the two of you would enter," Holmes said to move the interview along. "What is the first thing you usually did?"

"I always sweep the floor. I always do that before I leave for the night, too, but the night before . . . before I found 'im, I 'ad a late delivery and Mr. Keyes told me to go 'ome from there, so I did."

Holmes nodded at the aberration in routine, though it might not hold any significance. "The morning before you found Mr. Keyes – tell me what happened. Leave out nothing, no matter how small."

"Well sir, 'e 'ad me 'elp 'im move a late delivery from the day before to the back room."

"Do you know what this was?"

"Yessir. I logged them in as we moved them. It were lots of barrels of saltpeter, 'n' sulphur, 'n' some charcoal, 'n' a crate of lemons, a pound of rose petals from the Canary Islands, 'n' packets of 'erbs – lavender, burdock, chamomile, 'n' such like."

"How can you remember all of those?" I asked him.

"I wrote them all down, and once I do that, I never forgets. I learnt to read 'n' write at the Ragged School before me mum and me moved back to St. Giles."

"What else did he have in the back room?" Holmes asked.

"'E 'as – 'ad – a distillery back there where 'e made 'is own vinegar and wines and spirits fer 'is concoctions."

"Did he ever teach you to make any of his concoctions?"

"Sometimes, if somethin' needed a lot of grinding, 'e'd tell me to do it, but mostly I kept the shop tidy and made deliveries. 'E said 'e would be teaching me when I'd been there long enough."

"You helped Mr. Keyes stow away the deliveries. That must have taken up a lot of the morning."

"Yessir, it did. Then 'e 'ad me go to a shop and buy his lunch fer 'im. 'E wanted a pork pie, but they was all sold out, so I 'ad to go to other shops 'til I found one. Then all afternoon I made deliveries and 'elped people in between what come in the shop to buy things."

"Things such as – ?" Holmes asked.

"Toothbrushes, 'eadache powders, feathers for singing when somebody faints. Tussy-mussies. Them things went out of style a long time ago, Mr. Keyes said, but older people still come in wanting them.

"'Bout duskfall, 'e sent me to make a last delivery not far from St. Giles, an' 'e told me to go on 'ome fer my supper. Said I'd earned it, an' give me my wages an' something extra to buy something fer me mum. I did, an' then the next morning I come to work and found the shop 'alf-burned up, and Mr. Keyes dead . . . ."

His eyes filled with tears. Keyes didn't sound like a man anybody would warm up to, but this boy had seen a lot of hardship in his short life. Losing his job was an enormous blow, and now he stood accused of killing a man.

"I'm interested in how you got the job at the apothecary shop. Tell us how that happened."

"Well, sir, I was in me class, an' the 'ead of the school come to me class an' sez this gentleman has 'a offer of employment for you'.

"You coulda knocked me over with a feather. I never thought that woulda 'appened to me. Mr. Meltton taken me to meet this man waiting at the front door. 'E said to the man 'Will this boy do?'"

"The man looked at me and asked me some questions. I answered best I could, an' 'e said I would do."

"What was his speech like? Toff English, or some other kind?"

"Oh, it were toff enough, but sounded a little bit furrin' ta me."

"Foreign like a Frenchman or a Spaniard?"

"No, it were more gruff-like."

"Possibly German. Can you describe him for me?"

"'E were tall and strong-looking. Big feet, I 'member noticing. And 'is face were red-like."

"Hair color?"

"Black or dark brown. 'E 'ad a beard, an' it were black. An' 'e wore a pinky ring – a big gold one with blue stone in it."

Holmes nodded.

We left him then with assurances that Holmes would take his case. Although it was against the rules, I gave him my muffler, an old one which seemed to ease his shivering, and we left him feeling hopeful.

Inspector Lestrade waited for us in the hall. "Not a good one to take, Mr. Holmes," he said, his narrow ferret face confident that he'd got his man. "The boy did it."

"Murder is a violent act," Holmes said. "Why would he do that?"

"Robbery, most likely, or maybe Keyes gave him a hiding for breaking something." He rocked on his feet. "The victim, William Keyes, had been hit from behind by a hammer, still lying beside the body. He's in the morgue now, should you care to examine him, but the fatal wound most certainly came from the hammer . . . ."

Holmes shook his head, and Lestrade continued. "After striking the man and seeing what he'd done, Simpson Dove must have lit the Bunsen burner to destroy the evidence. The fire was finally noticed in the early morning hours – it must have taken a while to get established. It did a lot of damage, and burned through to some of the other floors and the cellar, but the sandbags placed in the shop to prevent the spread of fires kept it from being worse. The boy didn't know that would happen, and he must have believed that the body would be burned up, and the evidence destroyed."

"We shall see," Holmes replied. "We'll be looking at the apothecary on our way back to Baker Street. I trust you have no objections."

"None. Gates, take Mr. Holmes and Dr. Watson to Keyes Apothecary and let them look as long as they wish."

The game was afoot, but in this case the life of a boy was in danger.

Gates drove us to the apothecary in a police vehicle. It was a silent ride. He seemed awed to be escorting the renowned consulting detective.

The apothecary shop was on the shabby end of a street just short of Whitechapel. A crowd was gathered around, being kept away by a pair of officers. The blue paint peeled, though whether from age or fire, I could not tell. The murky window, not broken by the heat of the blaze, looked like it might have originally come from an early greenhouse when it was believed that sun's rays could damage plants. No doubt such rays could alter chemicals in the shop as well.

Gates led us through the door and into a small dark room. Toward the back, the walls were blackened. The stench of ashes and chemicals and something sweet and lemony was overpowering as we surveyed the

114

broken vials, bottles, jars, and clay pots, as well as broken shelving, niches, and countertop. A tussy-mussy would indeed be of use here.

Gates pointed to the back of the shop behind the counter. "There, sir. That's where the fire started, and the body was found here." He indicated an area half in the back and half in the front area. "The bags of sand kept on each floor burned, allowing the sand to pour out. It stopped the fire from spreading to the front, sir."

"How was he lying?" Holmes asked. "On his back or front?"

"Back, sir."

"Face toward the fire?" I asked.

"Yes, sir."

Holmes nodded. "What was down in the cellar?"

We peered at the area where the fire had burnt most of the flooring away.

"Big glass jars of chemicals, sir. Mostly broken. A crock of vinegar. Wooden boxes. Nothing of any importance."

"No barrels or kegs of anything?" Holmes asked.

"No, sir."

The cellar stairs were ruined, but those leading to the living quarters upstairs were in good shape. We climbed them to find a Spartan room with a bed, chairs, a table, and a washroom, plus several small empty rooms.

We rummaged, but found nothing that told us why the apothecary lay dead in the morgue and the shop damaged by fire. The thought in my mind – and probably in Holmes's – was why would a boy so happy to do well in his job cause this ruination and murder?

"He wouldn't and he didn't," Holmes said, apparently reading my mind as he opened a drawer to find a stack of what looked like bills. He leafed through them. "Haberdashery. A ticket for a new coat, two pairs of trousers, and a morning coat. A gold pocket-watch. An umbrella from James Smith and Sons.

Holmes pocketed the bills and we rejoined the constable at the door. "Thank you, Gates. We'll find our own way home."

"But, sir, the inspector will want to know why you wouldn't let me take you!"

Holmes smiled briefly. Gates didn't want any black marks on his record, such as Sherlock Holmes refusing to let me drive him home. "No worry. I'll put in a good word for you at the Yard."

"Thank you, sir."

"Did you have a reason for turning down the ride?" I asked as Gates drove away. Carriages and dogcarts alike tended to give a wide berth to police vehicles on the crowded London streets, thus shortening travel time.

"I want to question the neighbors to find out what they might have seen or heard."

Holmes crossed the street and left me to investigate a drapers shop, a butcher's, a watch repair shop, and one for sewing supplies. No one had seen or heard anything. They worked long hard hours and slept soundly all night until the arrival of the fire brigade in early morning when the flames were spotted. The proprietor of the sewing shop did report noises like thunder sometime after midnight. She couldn't pinpoint the time, but thought it was after one o'clock.

Holmes fared no better across the street. Two thought they heard a cart about midnight, but remembered nothing else. Directly across from the apothecary, the cobbler's shop was closed. "That was a waste of it," I said as we returned to Baker Street in a hansom.

"On the contrary, it was most informative."

I turned to look at him to see if he was joking. He wasn't. "I beg to differ. Random street noises heard by people who didn't even know the time can hardly add anything to the case."

"And that's why you're a doctor and I'm a detective."

"Same thing, really. I look for clues in the human body, and you look at the location of a crime."

"Our methods are similar. You wouldn't ignore a patient presenting with palpitations and ignore swollen ankles."

"Certainly not."

"The symptoms are also present in this case."

I mulled this until we arrived in Baker Street to find that Mrs. Hudson had ready for us a supper of stew loaded with vegetables and a basket of scones, followed by a treacle pudding. Afterwards, I poured brandy into my remaining coffee and lit a cigar. I noticed Holmes packing his pipe. "A two-pipe problem or three?"

"Undoubtedly three, but I may stop at two."

He lit the bowl and settled down to stare at the flames from the small fire in the grate. I picked up a medical journal and soon nodded off over diseases of the chest. Not long after, I rose and didn't even say good night. He didn't like to be interrupted. His eyes were closed as he took an occasional long pull at his pipe.

If I thought about the case, I didn't remember it because sleep was almost upon me before I removed my shoes. Under the covers, I went over the comments from the shopkeepers. They were just ordinary sounds. What had street noises to do with the case?

Morning street traffic thinned by the time we reached the Ragged School that Simpson had attended. These schools were started about fifty years earlier, with the first one being located in Spitalfields. They were meant to improve the lives of the poor by giving them education, deportment, meals, religion, and donated clothing. The school that Simpson attended was in the charge of a Mr. Hurlbert Meltton III. That was how he presented himself.

Holmes introduced us. "We are inquiring into the background of Simpson Dove, who attended this school up to about a month ago."

Mr. Meltton consulted a ledger whose wide pages were filled with names written in spidery brown ink. I didn't see a single blot.

"Simpson Dove." Holmes repeated the name.

"A promising lad. He came to us three years ago, eager to learn. He was a quick study. I had no qualms recommending him to Mr. Rookwood."

"Could you describe Mr. Rookwood for us?" Holmes asked.

"A tall, well-made man, finely dressed. Pink waistcoat, gold watch. He wore a black beard and had dark hair. And he had a florid complexion, as if he rode a great deal in the weather."

"Had you had previous dealings with Mr. Rookwood before he came to the school?"

"None, but he came highly recommended with letters of introduction – even one from Lord Percival himself."

I tried to look suitably impressed. Holmes merely said, "Indeed. Did he ask for Simpson by name?"

"No. He asked to see the boys about fourteen years of age, and I had six of them brought to my office. He questioned all of them in turn – just routine questions: Who were their parents? Where had they lived before? What were their goals in life? Simpson was the only one who said he wanted to earn money to help his mother. 'An admirable ambition,' Mr. Rookwood said. 'This is the lad I choose for employment at the apothecary shop.' They left straightaway. I've heard naught of Simpson since that day. I trust he hasn't done anything to besmirch the name of the school."

I started to say he was in gaol accused of murder by Scotland Yard, but Holmes replied quickly, "No, he's done nothing. Thank you for your time."

I didn't ask why he didn't tell Mr. Meltton why we were inquiring. We walked until we found a cab. By now, it was past lunchtime and teatime approached. I suggested we seek sustenance, but Holmes would have none of it. "Scotland Yard," Holmes told the driver, who headed in the direction of the Strand.

"The Yard? Whatever for? Do you think Simpson has something to add to his recitation?"

"I think he knows something that he doesn't know he knows."

"No doubt we all do, but how will you get it out of him?"

He gave me an enigmatic glance and pulled a folded newspaper from his pocket. I wished that I'd had the forethought to bring reading material or a biscuit. Traffic in the streets was heavy this time of day, but eventually we walked through the gates of the Yard.

Inspector Lestrade was out, but he'd left word to allow us to see Simpson again, should we stop by. "Just rap on the door, sir, when you wants to come out," Constable Brown said.

Simpson was curled on the slab that passed for a bed and appeared to be asleep, muffler wound around his neck and his hands wrapped in the ends. With his fair hair tousled, he looked younger than his fourteen years – indeed more like the child we'd known years earlier. He perked up considerably when he saw who his visitors were and sat on the edge of the slab. "'Ave you found the murderer, Mr. 'Olmes?"

"Not yet, but we're closing in. I have a task for you.

"Anythin'."

"As I recall, you are somewhat artistic. I need you to draw what you remember Mr. Rookwood looked like." From his prodigious pockets, he pulled out a few sheets of paper, a book, and a box of colored chalks, and I wondered if he might have a sandwich in there as well. My stomach was beginning to complain, as it was hours since breakfast, and luncheon was over now too.

Simpson took the proffered materials. He laid the paper across the cover of the book. I couldn't see the title – something scientific, no doubt. He opened the box of chalks, selected a black one, and began to outline a man. Soon the man took shape, wearing fine clothing with a violet crimson vest. With the black chalk he laid a scrolled pattern over the waistcoat. He added a watch chain and a yellow stick. With the red and white and some yellow chalk, he rubbed the colors together to create a ruddy complexion, and finally, he added a squiggle above the beard line on the left cheek. He colored the hair and beard black, with eyes dark brown embedded in sinister lids that put me in mind of a cobra I'd seen in India.

I was mightily impressed with the lad's unexpected artistic talent.

As he started to fill in the black of the figure's trousers, Holmes reached out and pointed to the squiggle. "What is that?"

Simpson brought it closer to his face. "I don't know. I just remember it being there."

"Do you know what it is, Watson?"

"Indeed. I've seen many scars from the time of infliction to the scabbing over and the raised healed flesh."

"What would you say caused this scar?"

"A sharp blade."

"Indeed. The scar extends downward under the beard."

118

"It does. And hair cannot grow in scars because scar tissue lacks follicles. Therefore, this man is wearing a false beard."

"Excellent, Watson. Simpson, you have solved the case. We shall soon have you out of here, but first we have work to do."

We left the constable locking the cell door as Holmes rushed along the corridor and I hurried after him.

"You know this Rookwood," I said. "You seemed interested in him from when we were visited by Mrs. Dove."

"I didn't know if it was him or not then," said Holmes, "but I've had my eye on someone named Rookwood for some time – and it seems as if this is the same man."

"Where are we going?"

"To see the Prime Minister."

"On a murder case?"

"This is not simply a murder case. Well, it is, but a small cog in the machinery of events about to take place."

I gaped at him as he hailed a hansom. "Come, Watson, you must not dally."

I scrambled into the cab and he slammed the half-door.

"Where to, Guv?" the driver asked.

"10 Downing Street, and hurry!"

The driver blinked in surprise, but turned the horse and wove in and out of traffic as we made our way to the blackened brick façade of Downing Street. I turned over what Holmes had just told me: *The murder of a seedy apothecary and burning of the shop to hide the crime merits an audience with the Prime Minister?*

Holmes bounded out of the cab almost before it stopped while I, as was often the case, paid the fare, and wondered just what was afoot.

"Good luck, Guv," the driver called down to us.

I joined Holmes on the stoop. "What the devil is going on?"

"I hope he's in," was all he said as he lifted the black iron lion's head knocker on the stout black-painted oak door. It was opened immediately by an impeccably dressed man I knew to be the butler.

"Sherlock Holmes and Dr. John Watson to see the Prime Minister on a serious and urgent matter of national security."

The butler didn't look surprised. He spoke to a page who then hurried down a hall and turned back to us. "Please come in," he said, and we stepped onto the black-and-white chequered floor of the entry. We were then ushered through a series of halls and rooms to a small antechamber lit by a cheerful fire which kept the day's chill at bay.

We waited over half-an-hour before Archibald Philip Primrose, the Earl of Roseberry and the Prime Minister himself, entered and bade us sit.

119

He looked like a graven image of a man carrying the weight of the Empire on his shoulders. Long lines carved runnels on each side of his mouth while wrinkles encircled his eyes. He took a seat on a tufted dark-green sofa across from us and nodded. "Mr. Holmes, good to see you again. Dr. Watson: I enjoy reading your tales. To what do I owe your visit?"

Holmes went straight for it. "Prime Minister, do you know what today is?"

Gladstone blinked. "November the fifth. Bonfire Night. '*Remember remember, the Fifth of November,*'" he recited. "It's the anniversary of the Gunpowder Plot. One of the conspirators, Guy Fawkes, was caught bringing explosives into Parliament to blow it up the next day when Queen Anne and all the dignitaries of the realm would be present for the opening ceremony. We are fortunate our gracious Queen will not be opening Parliament tomorrow."

"We are indeed," Holmes acknowledged, "but today will be the date of another attempted explosion in an effort to subvert the government of the Empire and throw it into chaos."

Primrose sat up straight sat up. "This is a serious allegation. What evidence do you have?"

Holmes pulled out the drawing Simpson had done. "This is the perpetrator of today's scheme. He calls himself – "

"Edmund Rookwood. Yes, I have met him. A good likeness. What has he done?"

Holmes explained that a boy who once worked for Holmes carrying messages and other jobs –

Again the Prime Minister interrupted, "Yes, one of your 'Irregulars'."

Holmes didn't look surprised, but I did. He really had read my stories. "Simpson. He attended one of the Ragged Schools and recently was offered a job as a delivery boy at Keyes Apothecary Shop. Two nights ago, Simpson made a late delivery and didn't return to the shop before closing because he was close to his rooms where he lives with his widowed mother, and Keyes told him to just go on home. The next morning when he reported for work, he found the proprietor dead from a blow on the head and the shop burned inside. The police arrested him for the crime, and his mother, Mrs. Dove, came to me for help because she knows Simpson didn't do it. I concur."

Primrose drew his brows together in puzzlement. "And this pertains to the Guy Fawkes Day danger how?"

"Simpson reported deliveries of barrels to the apothecary. Normally this wasn't unusual, but there were a lot of them, and they were filled with the necessary ingredients to make gunpowder – enough to successfully pull off what the original cabal could not, albeit in other venues than the

120

original. Simpson saw the bills of lading. When the fire cooled, none of these barrels were found, and indeed – if they had been there we would already know it. The barrels were in the cellar when Simpson left the shop. After the murder they were missing. It is my belief that the boy was meant to be a scapegoat for the perpetrators of this Gunpowder Plot to remove the chemist so he couldn't lead the police to Rookwood and his cohorts. According to his bills, the apothecary, Keyes, has become something of a dandy and was spending a lot of money." He pulled the bills he'd found in Keyes' rooms from out of his pocket.

"Supposing their plans were carried out," asked the Prime Minister, "why would the police suspect the apothecary? Why would it need to be burned, or a scapegoat arranged?"

I didn't know the answer, but I assumed Holmes did, and I was correct. "Most likely Keyes demanded more money for his part in the plot. Remember the names of the conspirators in the Gunpowder Plot: Robert and Thomas Wintour, Robert Catesby, John and Christopher Wright, Thomas Percy, Thomas Bates, John Grant, Sir Everard Digby, and Frances Tresham, Ambrose *Rookwood*, and Robert *Keyes*. The owner of the apothecary shop is William Keyes. Edmund *Rookwood* is similar to Ambrose Rookwood. Possibly the other conspirators have similarly connected names to those of the original traitors."

"Could they all be descendants of the original conspirators?" the Prime Minister asked.

"No, not necessarily, though some could be. This may be a smokescreen for something even more sinister."

"Do you mean foreign intervention?"

"I do," Holmes said. "I believe Rookwood found men bearing some, if not all, of these names, so that the crime will be laid at the doors of home-grown traitors, and not a foreign country."

"Devilishly clever," The Prime Minister said, almost to himself. "Count von Caprivi would like to throw us into chaos so Germany can move on Nigeria, and he needs something big to consolidate his position following in Bismarck's formidable shoes. Kaiser Willy with his militarism and vacillating policies would be thrilled to seize South Africa." Looking up at us, he asked, "Where do you think they will strike?"

"A celebration tonight with the most ministers and government officials. The one you are attending, most certainly."

Primrose stood abruptly and left the room.

I turned to Holmes. "I never suspected. What put you on to the plot? The gunpowder ingredients?"

Holmes nodded. "We weren't meant to know about those, and we wouldn't have – nor would the police – if Mrs. Dove hadn't come to us, and if Simpson hadn't been a noticing boy."

The Prime Minister returned, followed by several aides. He handed Holmes a list. "I presume you'll want this."

I looked over Holmes's shoulder to see a list of various Gunpowder celebrations planned for that night. Three were listed, two in Mayfair and one in Belgravia. "Do you have the guest lists?" I asked.

"We need to know where the most important government leaders will be tonight," Holmes added.

"Tyndale?" the Prime Minister said, turning to a man beside him.

"At Lord Percival's – the ninth Earl of d'Aubigny, in Mayfair. You are expected to put in an appearance at all three, Prime Minister, but d'Aubigny's is where most of the Government will be."

We were interrupted by a noise in the hall as Lestrade and two other officials from the Yard strode into the room. "What's this about an attack?" Lestrade demanded.

"I alerted Scotland Yard," the Prime Minister explained. "Thank you for arriving so quickly, Inspector. We believe that this man is the leader." He showed Lestrade the sketch that Simpson had made.

"He calls himself Edmund Rookwood, but that may not be his real name," Holmes said. "A man named Rookwood was one of the original Gunpowder Plot conspirators. This Rookwood has been moving in high circles. The Prime Minister has met him." He then explained his conclusions to Lestrade. "It's possible all three celebrations will be under attack, based on the number of barrels of gunpowder ingredients that Simpson counted. The sound of the explosions will be lost in the noise of the fireworks, but I'm certain the most important one will be at d'Aubigny's. And that's where Watson and I will be." He turned to go.

"Wait," the Prime Minister said. "I want the two of you with me as my guests."

"Prime Minister," I said, "we aren't attired for a reception."

"Then attire yourselves," he said, already looking beyond us at the events to come.

Holmes sent me to gather the necessary articles of clothing suitable for the celebration. "Don't forget those two special articles." He gave me a meaningful look and I nodded.

With Mrs. Hudson's help I managed it, changing into my evening clothes and returning barely an hour later. Holmes donned his evening attire in record time, and we followed the Prime Minister outside to his carriage. The police vehicle ahead of us cleared traffic through the crowds that were gathered on the streets to enjoy the bonfires and fireworks, while others were congregating in the parks. Explosions burst all around the City as we crossed it in route to Mayfair.

In the carriage, the Prime Minister turned to Holmes and said quietly, "Do you think Lord Percival is involved?"

Holmes answered immediately. "It's possible, but unless one of the conspirators turns on him, I doubt it will be provable."

Scotland Yard sent men to the other two parties in Belgravia and Mayfair. They decided that the Prime Minister shouldn't attend those, but instead go straight to d'Aubigny's. We were betting that was where Rookwood would be to make sure of his demise. The Queen's Guard was alerted, and liaisons were sent to Buckingham Palace in case the conspirators also had plans for the Sovereign.

As we neared the elegant d'Aubigny townhouse, glittering in the smoky night, a wagon passed us to turn at the corner.

"Holmes," I said quietly.

"I saw. They're going around to the cellar entrance. Come, Watson." We left the Prime Minister to enter at the front while we slid through the maze of shadows. The night was punctuated by more explosions as the acrid smell of smoke filled the air. Around the corner, we entered the mews as the wagon turned into the rear of Lord Percival's house. It stopped at the cellar steps. Two policemen disguised as footmen addressed the wagon.

"Identify yourselves!" one of them ordered, more like a policeman than a footman.

"I'm Bates," said the wagon's driver, a burly man with his cap pulled low. " This here's Grant. D'livery for the Earl."

"Champagne 'n' some kegs of ale," Grant said.

"We'll need to inspect your load," the other disguised policeman said. "Stay where you are." He walked around to the back of the wagon, pulled up the covering, and looked over the kegs and wooden boxes, presumably filled with champagne bottles. The footman turned the spigot on the first keg and the odor of ale wafted through the night air, which already had an ashen cast from all the bonfires. The ale splashed on the stones. He reached over to the back of the wagon and turned the tap on another keg. Black powder spilled out just as Bates lashed the horses and Grant turned with a gun in his right hand, aimed at the footman behind the wagon. He hadn't seen us, and thought he could shoot his way out.

Holmes and I had just whipped our revolvers out when a shot came from somewhere else. Grant's head snapped around in the direction of the sound and he took aim at the shadows. I didn't dare fire from this side, lest my shot hit one of the men in the shadows. Instead, I put a bullet into a spoke of the wagon's back wheel at the same time Holmes fired at the stones under the wagon. Thoroughly confused now, Grant began shooting wildly, and for a moment I was back at the Battle of Maiwand, with Jezail bullets flying all around me. My pulse quickened and my palms broke out in sweat.

Bates attempted to turn the confused and frightened horses, but the two policemen used all their weight to stop them. Men jumped out from the shadows and caught the horses' bridles, preventing them from completing the turn and escaping out of the mews. That couldn't happen as more men, some in uniform, blocked the entrance.

"It's over," Holmes said.

Grant aimed at Holmes. "It's never over." He pulled the trigger, but his gun was out of bullets.

Someone lit a torch and Grant saw he was surrounded. He dropped his arm. I snatched the pistol while Holmes continued to point his at Grant.

"I'll take it from here," Lestrade said from the shadows.

Holmes put his revolver away and I did the same as the two men were led to the waiting police wagon. Two policemen drove the wagon filled with kegs to Scotland Yard.

"What about Rookwood?" I asked.

"I'm going after him now," Lestrade said, and he walked around to the front entrance of d'Aubigny's.

"Should we follow?" I asked.

"I think we should wait here."

The mews was quiet as celebrations silenced momentarily before resuming, with several guys nearby set alight and firecrackers exploding like gunshots.

Holmes stationed himself on one side of the cellar door. I thought we should go to the front entrance and seek Rookwood, but followed Holmes's lead and moved to the other side.

We didn't have long to wait. The cellar door opened noiselessly. Was Lestrade returning? Had Rookwood escaped through the front door?

A tall figure poked his head from the cellar and scanned the darkness before leaping up the steps with a fencer's agility. I had time to see a black goatee before Holmes said, "Halt!" in a quiet, deadly tone.

Rookwood lashed out with something he'd picked up in the cellar, perhaps a bat or a cudgel. Holmes leaped aside and raised his revolver. Rookwood raised his weapon again, but I had gained the steps and stuck my Adams between his shoulder blades. "Drop it!"

I may have yelled it. Holmes later said I bellowed it, but that was all right because it was effective. Rookwood dropped the weapon and we marched him back into the house at the point of two revolvers. We crossed

124

the dimly-lit cellar and entered the kitchen, where all was in chaos as the staff rushed to serve the party above stairs.

"Excuse us," Holmes said, shoving Rookwood toward the backstairs. I stayed close and held onto his coat. Holmes pushed the baize door opened and we entered the realm of the party. The Prime Minister saw us first. "Ah, Rookwood. They found you, I see."

"Anyone here from Scotland Yard?" Holmes asked.

"Inspector Lestrade."

At the sound of his name, Lestrade joined us, looking embarrassed because he hadn't found Rookwood first. "He don't look at all like the picture that Simpson drew," he muttered as he put manacles on Rookwood.

"Rookwood is adept at disguises. Take a good look. One thing gives him away: The tip of the scar on his cheek." He reached out and pulled at the dark side whiskers, styled differently than when the man had visited the Ragged School. They came off in his hand, revealing the telltale scar.

Four policemen marched Rookwood out to a waiting vehicle that would take him to Scotland Yard.

"You'll release the boy now," Holmes said as Lestrade prepared to leave.

"No," Lestrade said.

"No?" I asked. "Tonight's events prove him innocent."

"I admit he gave good information trying to clear himself, but there's still no evidence that he didn't kill the apothecary," Lestrade replied. "It's just as likely Rookwood found him dead and then set the building on fire to cover up the removal of the gunpowder."

Lord Percival, looking somewhat dazed at the night's events, invited us to enjoy some libation after the night's successful work. He didn't appear worried at being accused of treason, either because he was a lord or because he wasn't involved.

Holmes declined and we left the celebration, stepping into the night and finding a waiting cab.

"Where to, Guv?"

Holmes gave the address of the apothecary shop.

"Do you know what time it is?" I asked him.

"I will not rest until that boy is released from prison."

I'd only had a quick bite when I went for our clothing, and I tried not to think of the delectable dishes we were leaving behind at Lord Percival's townhouse.

Holmes directed the cab to pull over directly across the street from the apothecary, at the cobbler's shop. Holmes bounded out, and I asked the driver to wait for us as Holmes knocked on the cobbler's door.

"I'm coming, I'm coming!" a man's voice yelled within. "Who needs shoes in the middle of the night? Your feet should be tucked up in bed."

The door opened. A rotund man stood there in nightshirt and a nightcap, feet thrust into shoes without socks or lacings. His hair was gray and his eyes were brown in a rounded face. He goggled at Holmes. "I guess you don't need shoes. What's so important it can't wait 'til morning?"

"Are you the proprietor of this shop?" Holmes asked.

"I am. Sylvester Siddons. Now what is this about?"

"I have a very important question for you."

"And who are ye that I should have to answer questions to?"

"I am Sherlock Holmes."

The man stared at Holmes. "Well, bless my soul, so you are! I've seen ye picture in the newspapers."

"Did you see the apothecary's delivery boy leave the shop on the night of the fire?"

"The night of the fire? I did. He had parcels to deliver."

"Do you remember the time?"

"It were earlier than usual, but I reckoned he had more deliveries than usual."

"Did you see Mr. Keyes after that?"

"That I did. He closed up the shop about half-hour later and went down to the pub for his supper."

"Get dressed."

Mr. Siddons was bemused to be driving through the night to Scotland Yard. "I never been there," he marveled.

"The first time is always the most exciting," I said.

The night had quieted from the ear-splitting earlier celebrations. A few groups of late revelers were about, but all the burnt guys lay in ashy heaps about the streets, and the fireworks were spent.

Scotland Yard was a bustling hive compared to the streets. Lestrade was on hand and we hurried to his office.

"Mr. Holmes, Doctor Watson – To what do I owe the pleasure of this visit? Couldn't it have waited until morning? We caught four more marauders at the other two houses. Not the whole group, but enough to remove their threat. I wager the others are on the Channel by now, headed for Germany – unless they're home-grown and gone to ground. Who is this?"

"Mr. Sylvester Siddons. He owns the shop across the street from Keyes Apothecary. He has some information for you."

Siddons related to the inspector what he'd told us earlier. He saw the boy leave and later Keyes went in search of supper.

Lestrade scowled, but he couldn't refute the man's testimony. He released the boy and we took him home. He was still wearing my muffler. He started to remove it, but I told him to keep it.

At Simpson's knock, Mrs. Dove opened the door and burst into tears of joy as she hugged her son. "I knew you could do it, Mr. 'Olmes. Thank you, thank you, Dr. Watson!" she said over and over, shaking all our hands while tears ran down her cheeks. "Thank you!"

Mr. Siddons, who was still with us, was crying, too.

We dropped him at his shop where candlelight light flickered in the window. "Me wife's waiting up," he explained.

We thanked him for speaking with Lestrade.

"That were better than a play," he said. "Thank ye for letting me partake. Any time I can help, wake me up."

Holmes laughed. "Indeed. I wish all cases ended as well as this one."

"It's been a long and exciting night," I said as the driver turned the hansom toward Baker Street.

"What will happen now to young Simpson? He lost his job. I guess he could return to Ragged School or to running with the Irregulars, but I suspect he's past all that now."

"No doubt he'll be offered places at a number of businesses. His problem will be to decide which one. By morning, he'll be famous as the boy who foiled the second Gunpowder Plot and saved the Government, not to mention a lot of lives."

I nodded. I could see it all happening. "What about Lord Percival? Was he guilty of anything?"

Holmes shook his head. "He had no idea that his guest was a foreign agent. He was as shocked and horrified as anybody. Even if the other conspirators try to drag him into it, there's no proof, and nobody would believe he would want to blow up his own house."

Death of a Sails Man
by Roger Riccard

Chapter I

It was 7 February, 1895 – a Thursday as I recall. London was blanketed in snow and I was returning home from an early morning call on a patient near Regent's Park. I arrived back at 221b Baker Street around nine o'clock. Holmes had not yet risen when I went out, and, before I went up, I enquired of our landlady, Mrs. Hudson, if he had breakfasted yet.

"Aye, Doctor," she said. "And he's got a young man up there now. I believe you know him. You go on up and I'll bring you up a nice hot cup of tea."

I proceeded up the steps and quietly entered the sitting room. I was pleased to see the fellow who sat in the spot Holmes preferred for visitors. He was flaxen-haired and handsome in his youthful way. His blue eyes registered initial surprise at my appearance, but then a welcoming smile came to his clean-shaven face when he recognized me. It had only been six months since last we saw him.

Holmes practically bellowed upon my appearance, "Watson! Come in! You remember John Hector McFarlane, of course?"

I entered and extended my hand to the gentleman. McFarlane was the client in the case I have chronicled as "The Norwood Builder". That had occurred just the previous August, and Holmes had set Inspector Lestrade and Scotland Yard aright in proving that the supposed victim, Jonas Oldacre, was not only still alive, but guilty of attempting to frame the young solicitor for his murder.

"You are just in time," Holmes continued, as I took a seat on the sofa. "Mr. McFarlane was just informing me of a possible murder that has come his way that he believes the police have mistakenly declared to be death by natural causes. Please go on, sir."

McFarlane leaned back to better have both Holmes and me in his line of sight, then proceeded with his tale. "My client, Cornelius Andrew Seaward, recently died, and I am the Executor of his Will. In my due diligence, working with the police reports and verifying the identities of beneficiaries, I've come across some information that, to me at least, seems suspicious. Plus, the fact that his own doctor refused to sign off on a cause of death as he could not be certain it was natural causes due to some discolouraton of the fingernails. He insisted on an autopsy by the police. That appears of have been rushed through and signed off without much due diligence."

Mrs. Hudson arrived at that moment with a tea tray and cups for all of us, to which my friend responded in exasperation, "Mrs. Hudson, your efficiency has put you terribly in the way. Please leave us."

McFarlane, shocked at the detective's poor manners, thanked the landlady and I, used to Holmes's lack of social skills by this point, exchanged looks with her that conveyed my thanks and my sympathy as she *Harumphed* her way out.

"Go on, sir," encouraged Holmes. "Go on, and leave out no detail."

McFarlane cleared his throat and proceeded. "Well, then, Mr. Seaward is the owner of a sail-making factory. He started out as a sailmaker in his youth and became quite adept at it. He served on several merchant ships, until he decided he no longer cared to risk his life repairing sails torn by storms or pirate canons while the ship was in distress and could pitch him into the sea at any moment. So, at the age of thirty, he took a job ashore with one of the large sail-making firms that supplied the major shipbuilders. His work ethic, skills, and inventiveness allowed him to rise up and eventually take over the business. Of course, with the advent of steam vessels, the demand for sails has slacked off considerably, and his company is one of the last survivors of the major manufacturers.

"Naturally, there are still plenty of uses for canvas and, with some re-tooling, the company could conceivably switch over to making tents, tarps, canvas bags, backpacks, clothing, or any number of goods for either the marketplace or the government. His heirs won't be stuck with an obsolete business."

"And who are his heirs?" enquired Holmes

"His wife, Penelope, twin boys, Peter and Paul, a married daughter, Christie Broderson, and his twin brother, Cornwallis."

"Have you any reason to suspect foul play on the part of any of them?"

"Certainly not his wife," replied McFarlane. "They were a devoted couple. I was well-acquainted with them, and saw nothing but complete admiration for each other between them.

"The sons are both in their mid-twenties and had gone to work for their father when they finished their schooling. Peter, the eldest by some seven minutes, is quite adamant about expanding the business into those other areas I mentioned as soon as possible, before the demand for sails decreases even further. He sees great opportunities for profits, whereas his father was a tried-and-true sails man, with no desire to step out of what he was comfortable doing."

Holmes interrupted. "How does the younger son feel about that?"

"Paul has always lived in his brother's shadow. They have the usual brotherly squabbles, but in this matter, they are in agreement. Paul is just less vocal about it."

"What of the sister and her husband?"

"Christie's inheritance is a mere five-hundred pounds – roughly thrice what her husband, Sidney, makes in one year as one of the supervisors at the factory."

I spoke up at that, "So the supervisor married his employer's daughter. Could he have been expecting a greater reward than what she received?"

Our client tilted his head in thought. "It could be. They do have a daughter, Sarah Joy, so he may have been expecting more on her account as the only grandchild. I've had little social contact with them since the marriage, as I generally dealt with Cornelius at his home, where only his wife and sons were present until Peter moved out on his own."

"And your client's brother?" asked Holmes.

"I've only met the man once. At Christie's wedding, as a matter of fact. Unlike my client, Cornwallis remains a seafaring man, never married, and is rarely home for very long, as he works on trade ships to the Far East. He stays with his brother when he's in port. The house is on Manor Road in Tilbury. I discovered that Cornwallis was between voyages and in town at the time of his brother's death, and is still residing there."

Chapter II

"Very good," replied Holmes. "Now tell us: Just what was the date, time, and manner of Cornelius Seaward's death?"

"It was just this past Monday, Mr. Holmes. Mr. Seaward was found shortly after lunch in his office at the factory by his younger son, Paul. He was slumped over at his desk. There were the remains of a beef sandwich wrapped in paper on a napkin to one side of him, and a flagon of cold water tipped over on the blotter to his left. There were papers directly in front of him which he had apparently been reading while eating. In spite of the family doctor's concerns, the police surgeon has ruled it death by heart attack."

Holmes continued to question the manner of death. "I presume there were no signs of foul play. No wounds on the body, or ligature marks of strangulation?"

"None, Mr. Holmes. Just the slight discolouration of the fingernails."

"Who was the inspector assigned to your case?

"Tobias Gregson."

Holmes nodded. "And why do you doubt his findings?"

Before McFarlane answered, I added a question of my own. "What was your client's age?"

"He was fifty-six, Doctor, but he was in the peak of health. He had just taken out a ten-year term life insurance policy when he turned fifty-five last year, and was required to take a physical due to the unusually large amount of ten-thousand pounds. He was found to be in excellent shape as he had stopped smoking years ago, only drank moderately, and was not overweight. That is the reason for my suspicion. That, and the fact that the police report came back unusually fast. I think they rushed to an easy conclusion instead of being thorough – such as what happened in my case, as you recall."

Holmes nodded. Inspector Lestrade had jumped to the easy conclusions that were planted by Oldacre and arrested McFarlane without digging deeper into the victim's life. Had Holmes and I not done so, the lad now before us may have been hanged on circumstantial evidence.

"Why the large amount?" asked the detective.

"It was to ensure that there would be enough money to keep the company solvent while they went through the change of leadership."

"Who is the beneficiary of the life insurance?" asked Holmes.

"His wife gets four-thousand pounds. His daughter and brother get five-hundred each, and the other five-thousand goes into the company."

"Who takes over as head of the company?"

"That will be Peter. He is awarded fifty-five-percent ownership, and Paul forty-five percent, with the stipulation that their mother receive ten-percent of the profits for the remainder of her life."

"Well, there are certainly people with motive," said Holmes. "Is there anyone you suspect more than the others?"

McFarlane hesitated. Now that the question had been put to him so bluntly, he realized what his opinion might mean. He held his palms in front of his lips as if in prayers while he thought, then folded them into this lap and said, "I've already stated that Penelope is above reproach. I've only met the brother once, and do not know his life circumstances or what needs he might have for money. I haven't seen Christie or Sidney since their wedding three years ago. Peter and Paul seemed devoted to their father, even when they disagreed with him. I cannot imagine either of them would stoop to patricide."

He took a breath, "I suppose, Mr. Holmes, I would start by looking at Cornwallis or Sidney."

The detective nodded. "I shall take your concerns and suspicions under advisement, Mr. McFarlane. Can you arrange for me to examine the scene of Seaward's death as soon as possible?"

"I shall try to schedule it for this afternoon, Mr. Holmes. I'll stop by the factory and speak with Peter and then send you word."

"I would advise you not to mention my name or to voice your suspicions. Tell him that the insurance company wants to send an examiner to get the details for their report before they approve the payout."

"Very good, Mr. Holmes."

"Exactly where is this factory located?"

"The factory is adjacent to the Tilbury Docks on St. Andrews Road," replied our client, giving us the street address.

We then bid him good morning and Holmes turned to me, "Watson, I suggest you go to the kitchen and ask Mrs. Hudson for some morsel to tide you over until lunch. We must be off to see Inspector Gregson as quickly as we can."

Chapter III

Despite the streets being wet with slush, our cab driver made good time to Scotland Yard, and we found Inspector Gregson tucked away in the warmth of his small but neat office. He looked up with a surprised but friendly face as Holmes and I entered.

"Mr. Holmes, Dr. Watson. Come in, sit down. Whatever brings you out in this abominable weather?"

Gregson is tall and fair-haired. Holmes once referred to him as the smartest of the police detective force. But while he has overlooked Holmes's occasional bending of the law, he confines himself to its limits, which curtails him from finding clues and other data that Holmes takes advantage of. He held out his big, square hand in greeting and waved us toward the old but sturdy wooden chairs in front of his desk.

Holmes got right to the point. "We have been solicited by Mr. John McFarlane to take a closer look at the death of Cornelius Seaward."

Gregson frowned, "The factory owner who just died of a heart attack? Who is John McFarlane, and why is he involved?"

"McFarlane is the family solicitor. In preparation for the disposition of the Will, he has some suspicion that Seaward's death wasn't from natural causes."

Gregson pursed his lips, "The police surgeon's report was fairly clear on the matter. I saw no reason to dispute his findings."

"McFarlane doesn't share your confidence. He has had poor experience with police rushing to judgment, and believes that to be the case here."

"What experience?" asked the inspector, his eyes narrowing in suspicion.

132

"You recall the Oldacre case last summer?"

"The one where Lestrade arrested the wrong man and you had to set him straight? Indeed I do. Served him right, the little cock-o-doodle."

Holmes smiled and replied, "McFarlane was the man he arrested."

Gregson sighed in acknowledgment. "Ah, I see. Well, I can certainly understand his attitude. But what is it about this case that has raised his hackles?"

Holmes went on to explain the life insurance policy and the healthy condition and lifestyle of the victim. Then asked, "What was the process of your investigation?"

"Well, after the concerns expressed by the family physician, Oh, we did the usual, Mr. Holmes. We interviewed witnesses. The food he ate was tested for poison. I collected evidence from the desk where he sat. The room showed no sign of any visitors, and was in sight of several workers who could have seen anyone entering or leaving. There was no possible entrance from the outside. In short, he was alone and there was no indication of suicide. The surgeon's examination of his heart indicated a – What is it called? Myocardiac infraction?"

"Myocardial *infarction*," I automatically corrected him.

"Yes, that's it. None of his family expressed any concern about murder, so we chose not to dispute the police surgeon's findings and went with our initial assessment."

"Well, we should like to take a closer look before any evidence grows colder," said Holmes. "Would you please write out a note for the police surgeon who handled this case, asking him to provide us with his cooperation?"

Gregson shrugged and reached for a pen and paper, "I can do that. This was handled by one of Dr. Fox's assistants, as it seemed fairly open-and-shut."

He handed the permission order across to Holmes and added, "You will keep me posted, of course, so that I may take any official steps necessary?"

"Naturally," stated Holmes, but as we turned to leave, he gave me a wink that told me he was going to do whatever it took, and not worry about following Gregson's restrictive rules.

At the police surgeon's facility, we were introduced to one of the assistant physicians, Dr. Linville. He was a young man, likely just out of medical school. He had a square face with a weak chin and thin lips. He hardly presented a presence of confidence, and quivered with intimidation when Holmes announced our names.

Fortunately, Dr. Sylvester Fox, who had replaced the retired Dr. Drake, with whom Holmes had shared many cases in his early career and

133

had learned much, was standing by and stepped in to assist with the investigation.

"I need to see whatever evidence you have retained in the case of Mr. Cornelius Seaward," said Holmes.

"Seaward?" said Linville in a quivering voice. "That was just the other day." He nervously led us to another room, where he pulled out a box and the file of the examination.

"What is it, Holmes?" Fox asked. "Has some new evidence come to fore?"

Holmes tilted his head and shrugged his shoulders non-committedly, "Nothing concrete. Just speculation by the victim's solicitor. He believes Seaward was in too good of health to have suffered a heart attack, and he has suggested people with possible motives for murder."

Fox snatched up the file and queried his assistant as he read. "There are no results here of running the bowels, or checking the stomach contents, or the lungs!"

Linville tried and failed to answer with confidence, "There was no need, sir. The food checked out, and the heart indicated all signs of a heart attack. Without evidence of poison, there was no reason to look further."

"Young man," stated Fox as sternly as I had ever heard him speak, "every case is required to have *all* tests run – especially when another physician has noted this discolouration of the fingernails." He pointed to the notation. "I once had an 'accidental' decapitation, which should have been the obvious cause of death, used as a cover-up for a poisonous injection into the jugular vein."

He handed the file to Holmes, who read through it and said, "This shows you tested the food, but not the water."

By now the assistant had wrapped his arms around himself and was looking downcast. He tilted his head and tried to defend his decision, "There was no water to test, sir. The flagon was empty. I was told it had all spilled out onto the desk."

Holmes handed the report to me and, while I read through it, my companion opened the box of items Gregson had collected from the scene after the initial concerns were reported by the family physician. He was looking for one thing in particular and found it quickly. Retrieving it from the box, he made a point of bypassing Linville and handing it directly to Dr. Fox.

"Doctor, would you please run a chemical analysis of the water stain on this blotter and check it for poisons, and please include exotic and tropical possibilities?"

"Right away, Holmes," he said. Turning to his assistant he ordered, "Come with me and learn something!"

Chapter IV

Knowing it would take time to run these tests, Holmes and I chose to take our investigation to the factory and the scene of Seaward's death. We sent word to McFarlane, and he met us there and introduced us to Peter Seaward, the elder son. Peter was a broad-shouldered fellow in his mid-twenties. An active life of heavy labour in the factory had given him a muscular build, and he used his physical appearance to attempt intimidation when he felt it necessary.

While my friend, Holmes, is not so bulky, his height often stands him in good stead, and his ability to look down upon this younger man worked to his advantage. When Peter protested this intrusion to McFarlane, Holmes stepped up to face him down and added the veiled threat, "Mr. Seaward, I empathize with you regarding the death of your father. I sincerely do. But if you stand in the way of our investigation, I cannot sign off on the payment of the life insurance claim to your family. Do you really wish to put your mother through that, on top of all else she is suffering right now?"

Seaward, forced to look up several inches into those steel-grey eyes, grudgingly stepped aside and waved toward his father's office. "All right, go ahead. But I'm telling you, there is nothing to find. This is a waste of time."

Once we were in the office, Peter stood by the doorway. Holmes sat in Cornelius Seaward's chair and spoke out the chain of events to give clarity to the situation and ensure the facts were reported correctly.

"So, I am your father. I have some paperwork in front of me, but it is lunch time, and I am hungry. I take the sandwich from my briefcase which my wife has packed for me. I also remove the flagon. Why a flagon? Why not a flask? And why bring water at all? Water is available to all the workers in the factory by way of several sinks."

"My father used his flagon," Peter answered, "because it held more water than a normal flask. He also preferred his water as cold as possible. Mother kept his flagon filled and in the ice box at home all through the night before. She would even shave slivers of ice off the block and place them into his water."

"Unfortunate," stated Holmes. "The shape of the flagon allowed all of the water to spill out, whereas the neck of a flask would have kept some water within, unless it was completely turned upside down."

"What does that matter?" asked the son.

"We could have more easily tested the water for poison if some had remained. Now we have to see what Dr. Fox can retrieve from the stain on the blotter."

A look of surprise came across Peter's face. "He can do that?"

Holmes gave the lad a look and replied, "It will depend upon the poison, but there is a possibility, yes."

"But who would poison my father?" demanded Peter. "We all loved him, and even his employees held him in great regard. He had no enemies. No, this must have been a heart attack, like they said."

Holmes sat back, thought a moment, then asked, "Has the company ever been sued?"

McFarlane straightened up with a jolt. "Why, yes. Two years ago, there was a lawsuit against the company, claiming a sail had failed a yacht caught in a storm and resulted in the boat capsizing. There was some loss of life as I recall, but the investigation proved that it was faulty rigging, and the sails were in perfect condition."

"I remember that," said Peter. "Some rich lord – Hammersmith, was the name I believe – thought he could handle the craft with just his family aboard and no crew. When a squall came up suddenly, it caught him off guard and his incompetence caused the lines to foul and the rigging to fail. He sent his wife and daughter below, but kept his teenage son on deck to help him try to weather the storm. The boy was thrown overboard and lost at sea when the boat capsized. The rest of the family managed to swim to the lifeboat which had broken free and survived until the Coast Guard came. It was a tragedy, but not due to our sails. The court found us non-culpable and dismissed the suit."

At that moment, Paul Seaward approached and asked what was going on. While his facial features were identical to his brother's, he wore his hair differently and had a moustache and short beard, whereas Peter was clean-shaven. His physique was also not quite as imposing as he was the more sedentary of the two, being an accountant in the office while Peter did the more-physical labour on the shop floor.

McFarlane gave him the insurance investigation story and, rather than protest as his brother had done, he merely asked, "How long will this investigation take?"

"It should only be a matter of a few days at most," stated Holmes. Then he added, "Why do you ask?"

"I have arrangements to make. Once I am officially forty-five-percent owner, I intend to pursue a career in another field. I'll hire a clerk to do the daily accounting entries, and then just audit the books once per week."

"You aren't really going through with that?" Peter protested.

Paul glowered at his brother, "I'm not going to sit here in your shadow performing menial work for the rest of my life! I have grander plans than that. Without Father holding me back, I intend to live my own life, rather than the one he pigeon-holed me into."

136

"What," said Holmes, "if I may ask, do you plan to do?"

Paul stood tall with some pride and said, "A friend from my school days says he can get me on board at his stock brokerage firm. I intend to use my mathematical talents to make my fortune, rather than count somebody else's money."

Peter slapped the doorframe in frustration, but Holmes nodded. "Hopefully, we can wrap this investigation up quickly and send you on your way. I imagine we'll be able to finish up no later than next week."

The younger brother nodded. "I can assure you that Peter is right. Father didn't commit suicide. It had to be a heart attack. So please, do your due diligence quickly for all our sakes – especially Mother's."

While both brothers were present, Holmes asked, "What papers were your father looking at when the incident occurred?"

"Just the sales reports from the week before," answered Paul. "I had given them to him that morning. We'd had a good week, and there was certainly nothing in them that would cause him distress to commit suicide."

Holmes nodded, but added, "But then, there should also have been nothing distressing to cause a heart attack either. Doctor, did you have questions for either of these gentlemen?"

As we had planned, I asked the brothers questions regarding their father's recent behaviour, and especially his appearance that particular morning. Nothing they noted indicated any signs of depression, or impending suicide, nor of an on-coming heart attack, for that matter.

I turned to my companions and said, "That's all I need to know for now. The police surgeon's report should tell us the rest."

Chapter V

In the silence that followed that statement, Holmes stood and announced, "That's all I need to see here. Mr. McFarlane, I believe we have one more stop."

As we began to leave, Peter asked, "Did you learn anything one way or the other?"

Holmes responded, "As yet, nothing seems to discount the 'natural causes' diagnosis, but there is still more for us to do. As I said, I should have an answer for you in the next few days."

Our next stop was the Seaward residence. Upon arrival, McFarlane introduced us to Mrs. Seaward, again as investigators for the insurance company, and advised her that we would need access to the home to look for any indicators of suicide.

Penelope Seaward was quite comely for a woman approaching fifty. She was full-figured, but had not succumbed to the typical overweight condition brought on by the aging process. Her complexion was youthful, and her hair was long and chestnut brown with no sign of grey. Her honey-brown eyes were bright, and her manner bespoke intelligence despite her grief.

"Gentlemen," she said. "I understand you have a job to do, but I can assure you that it is impossible that Cornelius committed suicide. He was in good health, our marriage was perfectly happy, and business was going well. He had no reason to kill himself."

I noted that she gave a slight gasp at the end of this statement, as though reiterating the fact of her husband's death out loud was a painful recognition of the unpleasant fact.

Holmes, rising to the occasion of the role he was playing, bowed to her and in a conciliatory tone replied, "I understand, Mrs. Seaward, and I sympathize. It is an unfortunate matter of business that we are required to conduct these investigations, especially when so large a sum is involved. I promise you that we shall be as quick as possible so that your claim may be settled at all due speed."

"Very well," she replied, sitting down in a nearby chair. "Do what you must."

I was a bit surprised that she chose to remain where she was rather than accompany us. But I also surmised from this that she had nothing to hide, or she would have come along to steer us away from any possible evidence.

Holmes started in the kitchen where he searched cupboards and drawers, then did the same in the pantry. The only agent found there was a box of arsenical rat poison, but as that was a common household item, it wasn't particularly damning evidence, and arsenic poisoning generally works over time, and does not cause a sudden heart attack.

We then proceeded upstairs. Before doing so, we ascertained which rooms were whose. The master bedroom was at one end of the upper hallway, then the upstairs water closet, Peter's old room, Paul's room, and finally a guest room, currently being used by the visiting Cornwallis Seaward, who wasn't home at the moment. Peter no longer lived at home, so his room had been turned into a storage space.

In keeping with the roles we were playing, Holmes began with the master bedroom, ostensibly to search for any chemicals or drugs that could have been used for suicide by the sailmaker. Then he searched the medicine cabinet in the water closet where there was a prescription for Mrs. Seaward, but there was nothing that could cause a heart attack. No other drugs were found. He skipped over Peter's old room for now and moved on to Paul's. The young man seemed anxious to get out from under his father's rule, but I didn't think his frustration had achieved the level of murder as a solution.

However, Holmes did find an unlabeled brown bottle containing a reddish liquid with an odd smell. He held it out to me, but even my medical training couldn't identify the peculiar odor. "It seems to have an alcoholic scent. It may be laudanum with some spirits added, but it's unlike any liquor or medicine I know of."

He poured some into one of the corked vials he carried with him, along with envelopes he used to collect evidence, and slipped it into his pocket to take home and run a chemical analysis on. Nothing else about the room seemed suspicious, so we moved on to the guest room.

Cornwallis Seaward's trunk was at the foot of the bed and Holmes made quick work of the lock. It held the usual trappings of a well-traveled seaman, including some contraband which he likely didn't pay the duty tax on. Yet there was a jar containing a green substance that, from the smell, may have been some type of Oriental spice. It looked like crushed or chopped leaves, similar to basil or oregano. Holmes put some into one of his envelopes to test as well. He locked the trunk and we had made our way to search the closet when loud voices emanated from the ground floor, followed by the pounding of heavy boots upon the staircase.

Cornwallis Seaward appeared in the bedroom doorway, nearly filling the space with his large frame. Decades at sea had turned him into a muscular specimen, and his long hair and full beard added to his look of barely controlled anger indicated by the balled fists at his sides and the roar of his voice.

"What do you think you're doing? Get out of my room! You've no right to be in here!"

McFarlane, despite being a much younger man and of a slight build, stepped forward as the legal authority and explained our purpose.

"I don't care!" bellowed the mariner. This outburst was accompanied by a rough cough from the exertion he had put behind it, but he continued, "You've no right to search my room without a warrant!"

Holmes and I stepped up to flank McFarlane, and frankly to protect him should this fellow become violent. The solicitor replied, "Under the law, we don't need a warrant if we have the homeowner's permission, which Mrs. Seaward granted to us."

Then Holmes spoke up. "What is it that concerns you so, Mr. Seaward? We are merely trying to ascertain if your brother committed suicide and hid the chemicals in here so they wouldn't be found in his own room."

"My brother had a heart attack!" Seaward growled. "Serves him right for settling down to a life without exercise. Don't get me wrong, gentleman. I loved him, but the sea has been in our blood since the family took up its name centuries ago. It was unnatural for him to abandon his roots. That's what killed him!"

Holmes nodded and asked one last question. "You may quite possibly be correct. We just need to make sure." He looked to the trunk and back to Cornwallis, "Did your brother have access to your trunk?"

The big man crossed his arms and said in a low menacing voice, "No, and I keep the key with me at all times, so no one could have put anything in there, and you will *not* search it!"

Holmes smiled indulgently and replied, "If he couldn't get in it, there's no need. We shall be on our way."

Chapter VI

From Tilbury, we took the train back to central London. McFarlane returned to his office, and we to Baker Street, where Holmes would conduct analyses of the items he had found at the Seaward residence.

It was now late afternoon and fortunately, Mrs. Hudson had tea and biscuits prepared, as I was famished from not having lunch, which was quite often the case when Holmes was hot on a scent.

I partook of the refreshments while Holmes immediately took to his makeshift laboratory and began preparing chemicals for the tests he would perform. First, he concentrated on the liquid from Paul's room. "Based on the colour, I suspect you are correct about a laudanum derivative, though I also have never come across a mixture with that smell before."

"It would explain why it wasn't labeled," I responded. "And, if it contains a strong enough concentration, it could cause a heart attack."

Holmes mixed drops of the substance with some other chemicals and awaited the reaction. While he did so, a messenger arrived with a telegram. I accepted it and advised Holmes it was from Dr. Fox.

"Please read it," he asked, keeping his eyes on the chemicals in the test tube.

I did so. When finished, I added, "Well, there's our answer."

"It would appear so," he replied. "This result," he said, indicating the vial in front of him, "is consistent with that. But let us test the substance from Cornwallis' trunk, just to be sure."

Within a half-hour, he was satisfied with his findings. "Well, now we know *who*. The question, however, remains *why*."

"If I may make a suggestion?"

He looked at me with anticipation and said, "By all means. I am always ready to hear your opinion."

When I made my case, my friend looked at me. "Oh, my poor Watson! How your years of association with me and exposure to the seedier side of human society have corrupted your soul. Confess it. Fourteen years ago, that thought wouldn't have entered your mind."

"I suppose not," I agreed. "But do you believe I am right?"

He nodded gravely, "I do, for I had reached the same conclusion. I also don't believe Mrs. Seaward is aware of the deep emotions that precipitated the act."

"What is your plan?"

"In my opinion, there's more to it than the motive we have identified. I'm going to spend tomorrow exploring various avenues to see what I may turn up that caused this action to be taken at this time. I shall wire Gregson and McFarlane tonight to keep them apprised and hopefully, by tomorrow afternoon, we can agree on our plan to expose the truth."

The next day, Holmes was already off when I awakened for breakfast, so I enjoyed a hearty meal and time with the morning newspapers. It was nearly noon when he returned. He greeted me cheerily, tossed his hat and coat onto the rack, dropped his umbrella into the stand, and strode over to the fireplace where he stuffed his pipe with tobacco from the Persian slipper which hung from the mantel. He then sat with smoke drifting above his head, a look of satisfaction upon his features.

I gazed at him from my seat on the sofa across from him and declared, "You look like Lewis Carrol's Cheshire Cat! What have you discovered?"

Something about my comment drew a chuckle from my friend, which amazed me, for Holmes's exhibiting humour was a rare occurrence. When the moment had passed, he said, "Forgive me. It was just that your analogy is so apropos when I think of the fact that this case resolves around characters similar to Tweedledee and Tweedledum."

"The twins?" I replied.

"Indeed. Two men who both want the same thing, but one is blocked by the presence of Mr. Cornelius Seaward, and can only gain his desire by that man's elimination."

"Where have you been and what did you learn?"

"I spent some of the morning in the neighborhood of Tilbury, and have just now come from a certain banking institution that owed me a favour – one which Inspector Gregson would undoubtedly frown upon, for he would require a warrant, whereas I have less-legalistic means of gaining information. Again, he gave me that wink of an eye.

"As we arranged, McFarlane and Gregson will meet us here this afternoon so that I may lay out my proofs and we may make our plans. I

141

suspect Gregson will want to move immediately, but I am going to suggest that tomorrow morning will work just as well for our purposes. Are you free?"

"I rarely schedule patients for a Saturday, unless there is something critical. You can count on me."

"Excellent! Ah, Mrs. Hudson, thank you."

This last addressed to the landlady, who had brought up some hot tea to stave off the chill of Holmes's morning excursions. Despite his bouts of rudeness, she still maintained her decorum and gracious manners.

"By the way, we shall be having guests at two o'clock," stated Holmes. "Inspector Gregson and Mr. McFarlane. If you would please send them up when they arrive. No need to stand on ceremony."

She nodded and enquired when we would like lunch. We answered as soon as convenient, and then she departed to her kitchen. Once she was gone, I turned back to Holmes. "So what is it you have discovered that has allowed you to determine the motive of the man whom you have already proven is the killer?"

"I've discovered the gentleman's whereabouts as to how he obtained the poison, the fact that he has a serious health condition, and a cache of money which would allow him to pursue his plans once Cornelius was dead."

"Where did the money come from?"

"That is what lifts this case beyond the commonplace. The poison was already in his possession, while he waited for his moral compass to decide whether to cross the line or not. The influx of money was what tipped him over to do the deed."

He would give me no further details, saying he would reveal all when Gregson and McFarlane arrived. At precisely two o'clock McFarlane came through our door, anxious to hear what Holmes had to say. He was forestalled by my friend, however, who insisted upon waiting for the Scotland Yard Inspector. Gregson arrived about ten minutes late, apologizing for his tardiness, "Sorry, gentlemen, but I do have other cases demanding my attention besides this one. Now, Mr. Holmes, Dr. Fox has told me of his findings proving murder instead of natural causes. You say you know who and why?"

"Yes, Inspector. Pray, take a seat, and let me give you the facts which we can now prove."

Step by step, my friend laid out the course of action that led up to the murder of Cornelius Seaward. McFarlane verified the fact of the evidence Holmes had found at the house, and Holmes showed Gregson documentation from the bank where the money had been deposited and where it had come from.

Gregson read over the papers and shook his head slowly. "It looks like we have two arrests to make. You are sure of this, Mr. Holmes? You trust your source?"

"This came directly from the bank director, who owed me a favour for solving an embezzlement case for him in the past. You can be certain of its veracity."

"Well, then I should return to the Yard immediately and obtain arrest warrants so we can take these culprits tonight."

"By all means, obtain your warrants, Inspector," replied Holmes. "But I should like to propose an option to make the arrests in the morning with a method which will ensure everyone will be home when we arrive."

Chapter VII

Saturday morning at seven o'clock, Gregson and McFarlane met us at Baker Street Station, and shortly after eight, we were gathered outside the Seaward residence. A telegram McFarlane had sent the day before per Holmes's instructions advised all the family members to meet at the house, where they would be advised of the insurance company's findings and be able to have their inheritance verified.

Out of sight of the windows, Gregson had arranged a Black Maria van from the Tilbury Police Station to be standing by to transport our culprit to the train station, where constables would take him to Scotland Yard for incarceration.

When we were admitted to the house, the entire family was seated around the dining room table, the only room sufficient for the number in this gathering. We stood at the end where the foot of the table was. When all had settled, Peter demanded, "Well, McFarlane, are you satisfied that Father didn't commit suicide? Can we get this insurance matter settled so we can move on?"

McFarland folded his arms across his chest and announced, "I have a confession to make. I was the one who initiated the investigation. These gentlemen aren't from the insurance company. This is Mr. Sherlock Holmes and Dr. John Watson. And this," he said indicating, Gregson, "is Inspector Gregson of Scotland Yard."

Murmurs and mutterings arose, but Holmes stepped forward and addressed the elder brother. "You are correct, Mr. Seaward. Your Father didn't commit suicide."

A sigh of relief came from Penelope Seaward, and Holmes turned his attention toward her, "I am afraid though, Madam, it wasn't a natural heart attack."

Looks of confusion arose around the family seated at the table. "What do you mean?" asked Paul Seaward.

Looking back to the younger brother, Holmes replied, "He was murdered."

"What!" cried the two brothers and their sister simultaneously.

"Yes, gentleman. And it was done by the person who now sits in your father's chair at the head of this table – a position he hoped to make permanent."

All eyes shifted toward Cornwallis Seaward who stood and menacingly glared at Holmes. "How dare you, sir! I – "

"You," interrupted Holmes, "obtained leaves of the Bintaro tree on your travels to the Orient. It bears a fruit that yields a powerful poison that has been used for both suicide and homicide, as it causes fatal heart attacks. Hence it is also called the 'Indian suicide tree'. We discovered a jar of its crushed leaves in your trunk the other day, and the police surgeon's report confirmed its presence in the water stain left on the blotter from your brother's desk where his flagon had spilled."

"That doesn't prove – "

Again, Holmes interrupted, "I have verified with your shipmates that your health has been declining, and none of them expected you would make another voyage. We also have the bank records indicating that you were paid the sum of five-thousand pounds by Lord Hammersmith to take out his revenge upon your brother. You saw it as an opportunity to obtain what you coveted most, your brother's life and his wife."

At this pronouncement, Penelope jumped up and dashed into the arms of her oldest son, who was also standing at this point. Her body was trembling and tears were flowing. Her daughter also rose and stood by her side to add comfort.

Paul, asked, "But how did he poison the water?"

"He knew the ways of the house," my companion replied. "He knew your mother would prepare your father's flagon of water and place it in the ice box the night before. He merely had to slip into the kitchen in the middle of the night and drop some of the poison into the flagon. He became the poisonous water bearer."

Cornwallis tried to plead his case to Penelope, saying he loved her and that his brother took her for granted and was unworthy of her, but she was hearing none of it and screamed at Gregson, "Take him away! Get him out of my house!" Then she collapsed again in tears into her son's shoulder.

Cornwallis resisted Gregson's attempt to handcuff him, but Holmes brought him down with one of his Baritsu wrestling moves and, once he

144

was on the floor, he was easily manacled and led off to the waiting police van.

An hour later, Holmes and I accompanied the inspector to Lord Hammersmith's manor and assisted in his arrest for the crime of murder for hire. Hammersmith insisted it was Cornwallis' idea and that he had come to him. The brother had known of the lawsuit's failure and offered to get the rich man's revenge for a price.

Cornwallis' share of the insurance payout was given over to Penelope Seaward, who in turn gave it to her granddaughter, Sarah. Paul followed through on his plans, and, while he isn't yet a rich man, is still a successful stockbroker and was able to break the laudanum habit he had formed while being depressed working for his father.

Peter successfully converted half of the factory from sail-making to producing other canvas products. He became a military contractor during the Boer War, and subsequently Seaward's Canvas Products became one of the primary suppliers to Britain's armed services during the Great War.

John Hector McFarlane was recognized for his diligence by his employer and was promoted to a supervisory position in the firm. I am pleased to report that it wouldn't be the last case where we would be called in to assist him.

Dinner at St. Luke's
by Alan Dimes

My readers will perhaps recall that in 1895, Holmes and I visited one of our great university towns, where my friend carried out researches into early English charters. These researches were interrupted by the case which I have related in "The Three Students", but we were presented shortly after with another problem, the details of which I have refrained from making public. This was at the explicit request of Mr. Hilton Soames, who was still in a state of nervous agitation after the successful conclusion of the affair.

Despite the fact that Holmes's investigations entirely exonerated the College of St. Luke's and all its academic staff from any involvement in the death of Marcus Cullingford, lecturer in Ancient History, there was still gossip in the town concerning the nature of his demise. I assured Soames that if I chose to record either of the events which we had investigated, I would change the names of all those involved, and omit any details which would enable the reader to identify the college. He consented to my telling the tale of Bannister and Gilchrist, but baulked at the idea that I should turn Cullingford's death into a story for public consumption.

Now, however, many years have passed, and as I am maintaining the incognito of the college and its members, I feel that there is nothing to be achieved by suppressing the facts any longer.

Holmes returned to his researches in the university libraries on the day following the business of the unseen translation, while I took a morning walk through the town, had a pleasant lunch in a little pub by the river, and then returned to our lodgings to resume reading a yellow-backed novel I had brought with me.

At three o'clock there was a knock on my door, and I opened it to see before me the tall, spare figure of Hilton Soames.

"My dear Dr. Watson," he exclaimed with a smile. "It's all prepared. All settled. I have spoken to the other dons, and they are all agreed."

"One moment, sir. What is prepared? What is settled? And what have the dons agreed to?"

"Why, that in consideration of the service you and Mr. Holmes have done the whole college in averting a scandal, we should like you to come to dinner at the High Table tomorrow evening. I assure you, our head cook is a virtuoso and the wines will be of the finest vintage."

"I will inform Mr. Holmes of your invitation."

"Splendid. We shall expect you at seven-thirty."

Holmes came back at a little after four, in a remarkably good mood. He strode into my room without knocking, a sheaf of notes clutched in one hand.

"I've done it, Watson!" he exclaimed. "I've established beyond question that the charter supposedly granting land to the Bishopric of Athelney in 705 was in fact a forgery, made a hundred years later. Don't you see what that means?"

"I'm afraid I don't."

"Why, man, it means that all the rents and land taxes imposed by successive Bishops over the intervening centuries were essentially illegal. It makes the land common property. The Church may even have to reimburse the current tenants for the rents they've paid."

"That sounds as if it's going to have some serious consequences."

"Justice sometimes does, but it is justice, nevertheless."

He brandished the handful of papers.

"It's all here, and cannot be denied. I confess, Doctor, I feel like celebrating. A good meal and a bottle or two of fine wine, I think. What say you?"

The mention of food and drink reminded, me of the invitation to the High Table, so I informed Holmes of Soames" visit.

"You didn't accept?" he said with a groan. "You know how I feel about social gatherings of that kind."

"No, I merely said I would tell you that we had been invited. But I have to say, I think it would be churlish of you to refuse."

"Oh, you do?"

"Yes, Holmes, I do. You have done these fellows a great favour. Allow them to thank you in the best way they know how. If you don't, they will feel dishonoured."

Holmes gave a deep sigh.

"Very well. I suppose it is a small price to pay for the interesting little problem with which Soames presented us."

The following evening found us in St. Luke's dining hall at the designated hour. We were greeted effusively by the company and, when the first glasses of wine were poured, Hilton Soames led a toast in our honour. As he had promised, the food and the wine were both excellent. The first course was pea-and-ham soup, followed by crab flakes in a shrimp sauce with mayonnaise and Dijon mustard. The main part of the meal consisted of shoulder of mutton in gravy accompanied by boiled new potatoes, green beans, and broccoli. The dessert was hot apple pie with

Devonshire clotted cream. All this was washed down with a fine Bordeaux.

I confess that I do not remember the names of those at table as well as I recall the repast. Whatever they might be like when encountered individually, collectively their demeanour had that combination of the schoolboy and the monk which frequently marks those men who have had no significant contact with women of their own class since leaving their mothers to go to one of the public schools. Their conversation consisted mainly of gossip about academics from the other colleges, little jokes at each others' expense, and observations related to their own individual disciplines. One man who did stand out, however, was Marcus Cullingford, and this was not solely because this was fated to be the last night of his life. To judge from the greetings he received when he took his seat – "Didn't expect to see you here, Cullingford" and "Finally decided to dine with us, eh?" and the like – I assumed that his presence at such gatherings was a rare event. Another thing which made him worthy of note was that he was the youngest of the company, with a full head of dark hair in contrast to the bald pates or white hair of the majority of the dons. He said little, but consumed rather more wine than the others.

Holmes had also remained largely silent throughout the meal, which he had clearly enjoyed, but was subject to a little ragging when brandy and cigars were served.

"University man, Holmes?"

"Yes, though not, I regret to say, at this estimable establishment."

"Detective, eh? Bit of a rum sort of profession, what? Sneaking around and digging out people's secrets."

"It provides me with my bread and cheese and, as Watson here can tell you, once or twice we've been able to serve our country by 'sneaking around and digging out people's secrets'."

"Is that so?"

"Please remember that Mr. Holmes and Dr. Watson are our guests of honour," interjected Hilton Soames.

"Perhaps you could tell us a little about some of your other exploits," suggested another of the dons.

"Ah, storytelling is Watson's department," said Holmes.

I then regaled the company with the case of the Bogus Laundry, which had the advantages of being relatively short and easy to relate, while demonstrating both Holmes's powers and his patriotism.

"You didn't do much in that, Watson," observed Cullingford, who was now beginning to look somewhat inebriated.

"My friend is a modest fellow," said Holmes, "and he continually underplays those personal characteristics which make him the perfect

148

companion and helpmeet. And in a dangerous situation, there is no one I would rather have at my side."

"That's told you, Cullers!" chuckled a short, tubby don whose head was completely bald, apart from a circle of fluffy white hair at the back.

Cullingford did not reply, but gave the man a venomous look which seemed wildly out of proportion in response to that mild piece of badinage.

Holmes and I returned to our lodgings at about eleven o'clock.

"Admit it, Holmes," I said as we climbed the stairs. "You enjoyed the meal."

"Yes."

"Even if the company was a little lacking."

"The most interesting one was Cullingford. There's something eating away at that man, though as it is unlikely to be criminal, it does not come within our purview."

His words proved slightly prophetic, for an hour or so after we had our breakfast the following morning, there was a frantic knocking at the door of our lodgings. The landlady opened it to reveal the presence of Hilton Soames, who looked straight past her to Holmes, just coming into the hall, and about to head off for another day's research at the university library.

"Mr. Holmes! Mr. Holmes! You've got to help us!"

His voice was high with anxiety and a cold sweat was forming on his pale, broad forehead.

"Good Heavens, man! What is it?"

By this time I had heard the commotion and came to see what it portended.

"It's Marcus Cullingford! He's been murdered!"

"Murdered? How?"

"Has the university doctor been consulted?" I asked.

"Yes, and he thinks it's poison, though without an autopsy he can't say what kind."

"The police will have to be called in," said Holmes.

"That's why I'm here. I want you to take a look at him. Perhaps you can sort this out without informing them."

Holmes gave the agitated academic a stern gaze.

"We will, as you say, take a look at him, but the police will have to be told eventually. And if we come to the conclusion that someone who was at table with him, or one of the catering staff, was responsible, we will not withhold that information from the constabulary. Is that understood?"

"Yes, yes. I have a cab waiting."

149

As we were driven through the historic mediaeval streets, Holmes asked, "Did the university doctor decide on a time of death?"

"Some time in between two and three this morning, he said," replied Soames.

"That might well suggest that the poison was administered during the dinner. Who discovered the body?"

"Cullingford's scout. He came into the bedroom to wake him, as usual, at about 8:30. It was obvious from the terrible expression on his face that he was dead, and had died in agony. The scout came to fetch me, and I went to summon Dr. Cartwright."

"Did Cartwright carry out the examination *in situ*?"

"Yes. Nothing has been moved, as I decided to ask you in almost immediately."

Soames hesitated.

"Before we reach Cullingford's rooms, there is something I must tell you. You must have gleaned from some of the remarks made when he sat down that Cullingford had not attended the dinners in some time. I learned from Dr. Cartwright that Cullingford came to him some time ago suffering from stomach cramps. He believed that someone was slowly poisoning him, but the doctor assured him that the cramps were caused by overwork and nervous tension. Cullingford apparently did not take the medication Cartwright prescribed in case it was the doctor who was trying to kill him. This obsession grew until Cullingford ate all his meals in town and refused to socialize with the other dons. But now . . . ."

"You think his suspicions may have been justified."

"Yes."

"Did he have any enemies?"

"Dons have rivalries, not enemies – at least, that is usually the case. I can't think of anyone who disliked him enough to murder him."

We arrived at an ivy-covered court very similar to the one occupied by Soames, which was arranged on virtually the same pattern. Cullingford's rooms were on the ground floor. A porter admitted us, and Holmes turned to Soames.

"We will come to your office as soon as we have anything to report."

"Thank you."

As the don hurried across the court, I remarked, "You were rather harsh with him."

"I only agreed to this because Soames was obviously distressed. There is little we can do here. The police must know, and soon. A lengthy investigation will probably ensue, and we have no time for that. We are due to return to Baker Street tomorrow."

We entered Cullingford's suite of rooms. The late lecturer in Ancient History lay on his back in bed, and his mouth was contorted into a truly horrific rictus. Dr. Cartwright had not closed the dead man's eyes, and their pupils had rolled upwards to the limit of their orbit. I concurred with the university doctor's diagnosis that poison was the probable cause of death.

"Let us see if the other room can afford us any useful data," said Holmes. That room was dominated by books and papers, the shelves being crowded almost to the point of collapse with teetering towers comprised of further volumes in front of them. There were two piles of essay papers, presumably marked and unmarked. There was also a locked cupboard, but Holmes drew my attention to an escritoire in the corner of the room which was entirely free of clutter, there being only one sheet of paper on it.

"Presumably this paper was of some importance, since Cullingford appears to have made a point of keeping it separate, so that it would be to hand when needed. Let us see what is on it."

He looked at it for about half a minute. Then, handing the paper to me, said, "How's your Latin, Watson?"

"A little rusty."

I read:

Nobilissimum autem est Mithridatis, quod cottidie sumendo rex ille dicitur adversus venenorum pericula tutum corpus suum reddidisse. In quo haec sunt: costi P 1.66acroi P.V 20; hyperici, cummi, sagapeni, acaciae suci, iridis Illyricae, cardamomi, singulorum P.8 II; anesi P.12 III; nardi Gallici, gentianae eradj, aridorum rosae foliorum, singulorum P.16 IIII; papaveris lacrimae, petroselini, singulorum P.17 IIII casiae, silis, lolii, piperis longi, singulorum 20. 66 V styracis P.21 V castorei, turis hypocistidis suci, murrae, opopanacis, floris iunci rotundi, resinae terebenthinae, galbani, dauci Cretici seminis, singulorum P.24.66 VI nardi, opobalsami, singulorum P.25 VI thlaspis P.25 VI radicis Ponticae P.28 VII; croci, zingiberis,cinnamomi, singulorum P.29 VII Haec contrita melle excipiuntur, et adversus venenum, quod magnitudinem nucis Graecae impleat, ex vino datur. In ceteris autem adfectibus corporis pro modo eorum vel quod Aegyptiae fabae vel quod ervi magnitudinem impleat, satis est.

I endeavoured to translate what I could.

"*Rosae foliorum* – rose leaves. *Cardamomi* and *cinnamoni* are almost the same in English. *Anesi* is anise, *terebenthinae* is turpentine, and *zingiberis* is ginger, and *croci is* saffron. Is this some sort of recipe?"

"In a way, yes. I believe this lists the ingredients of a *mitridate*, named after an ancient king of Pontus, who is mentioned in the first line. Have you heard of it?"

"As a doctor, of course I have. It is a concoction supposed to act as a universal antidote against any form of poison. But surely, it's entirely mythical."

"Well, whoever wrote this clearly didn't believe so, and neither did Cullingford. As a professor of ancient history, he would have heard of Mithridates, who wished to avoid the fate of his father, who was assassinated when Mithradates was twelve. According to one version, he took different kinds of poisons in small doses to build up immunity against them, but others say he developed this universal antidote, and after his death at a ripe old age there were several attempts to recreate it, of which this, I fancy, is one – probably from Celsus' *De Medicina*. Some of the ingredients here would have been very difficult and expensive to get in those days, so its efficacy probably wasn't often put to the test, but there would be little difficulty obtaining them now. Do you begin to see how this explains Cullingford's behaviour?"

"He didn't attend the meals because he thought someone was trying to poison him, but he put the mitridate together and took it before the dinner. Believing himself immune, he ate and drank freely. But the mitridate didn't work, and he succumbed to whatever poison was administered to him."

"Possibly," said Holmes, "but I believe there is a simpler answer, and if I am not mistaken, the answer may be found in this locked cupboard. Fortunately, it is my reprehensible habit to carry my lock picks wherever I go."

He worked at the doors for a few seconds, then threw them open. Inside were three shelves, on which stood a number of large bottles of the type found in chemists' shops.

"The ingredients, I believe. In large amounts, because the effect of each individual dose would not be permanent – assuming one believes it would work at all."

"Did he eat all those things?"

"No. According to the paper they have to be dried and then ground, so there's probably a mortar and pestle here somewhere. Yes, here at the back. So they were dried and ground and mixed with honey, then formed into a pellet which was swallowed."

Holmes unscrewed the lids and examined the contents one by one, until, on opening the seventh, he gave a small "Ah!" of satisfaction.

"You have found the answer?"

"Yes. Let us go and inform friend Soames of the news.

"Come!" yelled Soames in answer to Holmes's knock.

"Good news, Mr. Soames," said Holmes. "You may safely report this matter to the police without an ensuing scandal or investigation. Marcus Cullingford was the author of his own demise, as the police autopsy will confirm."

"Suicide?"

"No, no. An accident, the unfortunate result of a misinterpretation of a Latin text. Mr. Cullingford must have been slightly less proficient at Latin than he imagined, and he certainly had no knowledge of toxicology."

"Please explain."

Holmes gave Soames a brief description of what we had found, and the significance of the paper bearing the Latin text, which he had brought with him.

"The formula contains rhubarb. Cullingford must have interpreted this to mean rhubarb *leaves*, of which he had a large supply, rather than rhubarb *stalks*. Now, while rhubarb stalks are harmless, the leaves contain a high concentration of oxalic acid, which can cause failure of some of the vital organs. Drying and grinding them probably concentrated it further.

"Normally that would produce great pain, so I can only surmise that one or more of the other ingredients in the mithridate acted as an analgesic while it did its work, enabling him to attend the dinner with no signs of the ill effects. No doubt the autopsy will also reveal the truth of that."

"Thank you, thank you, Mr. Holmes. And you, Dr. Watson."

"You're welcome, Mr. Soames. And now, Watson – Baker Street calls."

An UnChristian Act
by Paula Hammond

"So much for *The Daily Chronicle*," Holmes said, dropping the paper on the floor with a sigh.

May 1895 had started warm and breezy, with a promise of a glorious summer ahead. Alas, it seemed that Mother Nature had other plans. By Thursday the sixteenth, thick smoky fog had moved in. A flurry of snow fell overnight, turning day into night and the streets outside into an ice-rink.

So it was that Holmes and I found ourselves gloomily wrapped-up against the weather, when we'd much rather have been wrapped in sheets, enjoying the dry heat of our favourite Turkish bath.

I sat in silence for some minutes, weighing up the effort of retrieving the newspaper against moving from my warm spot beside the fire.

The Chronicle was one of the better dailies, with a reputation for fair and factual reporting. I had no doubt, however, that the main reason Holmes read it was for the extensive personal advertisements it carried.

"Any insights?" I asked languidly, secretly longing for some excitement to shake me out of the morning's funk.

"Let me see," Holmes replied with a yawn, "*CAD* is utterly brokenhearted, promises that all can be made right. *BUNCLE* demands inviolable secrecy. *IPR* offers proof of good intentions with a letter to *CG*, in Paris."

Knowing my friend's knack for unpicking these opaque missives, I knew he wouldn't miss the opportunity of demonstrating his skills. "Oh?" I prompted.

"*CAD*, as the lady no doubt playfully dubbed him, is Charles Arnold Delabole. Once heir to the Delabole slate fortune, now down on his luck, and linked to the rich widow, Lady Farriers. This, despite being engaged to the very beautiful but penniless *chartreuse*, Marianne LaBrea. *CAD* indeed!

"*BUNCLE* is a Scot's dialect corruption of Bonkyll – referring to Bonkyll Castle in Berwickshire – ancestral home to our dear Queen's current *aide-de-camp*. A visit to the old homestead is unlikely to require inviolable secrecy. Nor, indeed, a personal ad. I'd warrant, then, that Her Majesty is planning a trip to the Scottish Isles.

"*IPR* is clearly my dear rival, Ignatius Paul Pollaky. How curious. Old Paddington Pollaky, as he's known, used to specialize in intelligence on aliens living in Britain. I understood he'd retired. I wonder what's tempted him away from the comforts of Brighton domesticity?

"Still, there's nothing of especial interest to us here, although maybe the mail will offer more inspiration?"

I'd often thought there was something preternatural about Holmes. He could see, hear, and smell things that were simply invisible to mere mortals like myself. But that morning, his abilities appeared all the more remarkable for the seeming lack of effort required to employ them.

True to his prediction, Mrs. Hudson appeared in short order, carrying the morning's mail on a silver tray, with the promise of hot cocoa to follow.

It wasn't unusual for Holmes to receive upwards of a dozen letters daily. As for myself – I rarely received correspondence. My life was in London. I had no family, and friends did not need to write, for they saw me often enough to dispense with the effort.

Holmes worked his way through the little pile of mail with a series of *Hmm*'s and *Ha*'s. I watched as he picked over the contents of each letter before they were crumpled into balls and tossed into the fire.

"Missing dogs, errant husbands, wayward sons . . . *comme d'habitude*! At least there are none those unwelcome social summonses which call upon a man to lie and invent some prior commitment. If you were hoping for an excuse to escape Baker Street today, my dear Watson, then I'm afraid there's nothing . . . Ho, hold on! What's this?"

There was something about his tone that set my heart pumping.

"For you," he said throwing me the last letter on the tray. "Don't dally now. I swear my mind has been so starved of late that I can almost taste a mystery here. Look, now – have you ever seen an address written with such force? The nib has gone through the envelope at the end of each line, and the ink has pooled so much on the last line that he's likely to have snapped the nib entirely. Your well-connected friend in Dorset must have had quite the shock to have been at his desk before dawn, and for it to have arrived by then in London."

I looked at the envelope and saw that it was postmarked at half-past-seven – Whoever had written it must have been awake very early – or very late – to catch the first post of the day.

I opened the envelope, feeling the heavyweight paper which had given Holmes the clue to its sender's social status. By the time I had unfolded the message within, my hands were shaking with anticipation. Holmes was right – there *was* a mystery here!

"Good Lord!" I cried in surprise. "It's Tadpole Phelps – you remember, Holmes? That Foreign Office affair with the missing papers, some four or five years ago?"

155

Holmes shot me one of his keen, questioning glances. "Indeed! Go on."

I read the letter aloud before passing it to Holmes, knowing that he would be able to squeeze every ounce of meaning from the remarkable letter that Phelps had written.

Watson, [it began]

It has been some time since we spoke, and I hope that life has been as good to you as has to me. You'll recall my maternal uncle, Lord Holdhurst, whose preference for me was always the subject of so much teasing in school? Well, the poor fellow died two years ago, and I was left his sole heir. I'm now firmly ensconced in the family pile, a Member for South Dorset, and Justice of the Peace to boot – if you can imagine that.

I confess that the 'Tadpole' you knew at school would have laughed at the thought of so much responsibility falling on his bookish head, but I am determined to prove my worth and show the naysayers that my uncle's faith in me was not misplaced.

This evening, however, has tested me sorely and, as JP, people are looking to me for reassurance and answers.

There has been a murder, Watson! And one so strange and shocking that I worry how the town will respond once all is known. For the sake of our old friendship, I write to ask that you and Mr. Holmes come as soon as you receive this letter which, by my reckoning, will be first post.

I will instruct a carriage to wait at Swanage Station and check every train, so that you can be brought to Studland without delay. As I write, the boy is waiting to catch the post, so I will save details for our meeting.

Please do not fail me.

Your old school-fellow,
Tadpole Phelps

I glanced at Holmes and saw that familiar look of suppressed excitement being kindled. "Excellent!" he said. "Excellent! Just what the doctor ordered. Now, where's that *Bradshaw's*?"

Studland is a sleepy sort of place, nestled between Poole Harbour and Studland Bay. To the south lie the Purbeck Hills – a hog's-back of a ridge, half-a-mountain high, and beautiful in its windswept desolation.

To the north are the mossy carpets of the Bagshot Beds. Follow the sloping heathland down towards the sea, and the curious traveller will eventually reach the ever-busy harbor, where fishing boats jostle for elbow-room with steam-packets, wooden dingys, and pocket cruisers.

Studland village lies in the southern curve of the bay and is the only sizable settlement in these parts. It's a pretty village comprising rows of heavily thatched cottages, lined up along pressed-dirt lanes, which wouldn't have looked out of place in the time of Shakespeare. Within the village, there are few buildings of any note or distinction besides the manor house and the Church.

The house was built as a villa and much enlarged by Lord Holdhurst's parents to create a rambling sort of place whose charm lies in its apparent unplanned confusion. Part one-story, part two-story, part gabled, part hipped, with a mess of turrets and chimney stacks, diamond-pattern windows peek from beneath the slate roofs, like tired eyes. Untamed gardens festooned with wild flowers add to the picture-book quality of the whole.

In contrast, the church of St. Nicholas – to the east of the village – has that square solidness of design that characterizes early Norman architecture. The building is fortress-like in appearance, reflecting the violent past of this now sleepy headland where raiders from the sea were once frequent visitors.

From Waterloo to Swanage took us six hours. At Wareham, a new branch line wound its way across towards the coast before reaching a delightful stone-built station, which looked more like a cozy cottage than a busy seaside terminus. It amused me to note that the word "*Swanage.*" on the running board had a large full stop at the end, as though to dissuade any arguments to the contrary. Or perhaps it was to indicate to travelers that, here, modern comforts ended. For, to progress any further, we would have to endure the bumps and bruises that are part of the package when one travels by carriage on country roads.

On the platform, we were greeted by a gentleman sporting a fulsome Mexican mustache and a hat a size too big, and chosen, presumably, to accommodate his prodigious ears.

Charteris, as the macrotia-blessed individual proved to be, chatted amiably as he escorted us to the carriage. We settled in while he telephoned Phelps, grateful to find that blankets had been provided to insure us against the cold.

157

When our driver returned, he refused to be drawn on the events of the previous evening, saying only that he had instructions to take us directly to Studland where Phelps would be joining us.

We were delighted to discover that old Tadpole had also provided a hamper, which we attacked with the eagerness of two men who had missed a much-anticipated breakfast.

Inside the hamper we found a veritable *smorgasbord* of sandwiches – beef and curry-butter, egg and chutney, celery cream, cod's roe – along with bottles of fiery ginger beer.

We also found a copy of the morning newspaper, with a report circled in pencil and a note scribbled in the margin, declaring:

> *The local news hounds have beaten you to the chase. But be assured that the scene is secure. I await you arrival.*
>
> *Phelps*

"Good grief!" Holmes cried. "Look at this, Watson – " And he handed me the newspaper.

> *Considerable sensation has been evoked in the town of Studland, Dorset in consequence of a body found on top of the Agglestone at the southern end of Studland Bay. Disturbing reports link the death to the discovery of a number of foot-tracks of a most mysterious description.*
>
> *On Thursday night, there was a very heavy fall of snow in the neighborhood. The following morning, inhabitants were surprised at discovering the tracks of what they took to be someone running barefoot towards the cliff tops that lead to Handfast Point and Old Harry's Rocks. The prints were to be seen in all kinds of inaccessible places, including the tops of houses, and inside walled gardens. The tracks progressed in a series of long strides or hops, and it was upon following them that the local vicar discovered the body of a yet-unidentified young woman.*
>
> *That great excitement has been produced among all classes may be judged by the fact that the victim was found on top of a stone long associated with pagan sacrifices and unChristian acts. The Justice of the Peace, Mr. Percy Phelps, MP, has assured residents that investigators from London have been called, and will be attending within the day.*

"'*Pagan sacrifices*'?" I said, digesting the article along with the remainder of my sandwich.

"Well, as I've often said, the vilest alleys in London are less terrible than the isolated beauty of the countryside. Give me an honest East End villain over a sequestered community any day!"

"Surely not!" I said, suddenly feeling protective of Tadpole's little slice of England.

"I'm in deadly earnest. Look around. What do you see?"

I wiped a circle in the condensation on the carriage window and peered out. "Why, nothing but wild spaces and nature."

"Exactly," Holmes said. "No one is ever really alone in a city. There are eyes everywhere. Not all of them are friendly, to be sure, but most are. Even the direst rookeries contain good people, willing to do the right thing. But here? A body could lie undiscovered forever, with no one to claim it. And while in a city the weight of public opinion can be mobilized to fight for justice, in places like this, the law is often little more than some Baskerville-esque tyrant."

"You can't mean that!" I spluttered. "Besides, Percy is hardly some tyrannical lord of the manor."

"Oh?" Holmes said, a whisper of a smile growing across his face. "Well, perhaps we'll make an exception for Phelps on account of his good taste in friends. But I warn you: Should we end up being sacrificed to some pagan god, then I'll hold you personally responsible."

I chuckled along good-heartedly but as the coach rattled along the narrow lanes, I could see the news report begin to work its own peculiar magic on Holmes. Soon, he had adopted that far-away look, and all conversation was lost.

I, too, could not help but dwell on the newspaper article. We were racing towards a new century – and such superstitions belonged in the past. But then, the growth of spiritualism in recent years had proved that, no matter how sophisticated our world had become, there are always those who find comfort in the unknown. If man can evolve, then, so too, can he devolve.

Thus occupied by our thoughts, it seemed no time at all before we arrived in Studland. The carriage had barely stopped when the door was thrown open – and there was Phelps himself, his pinched, pale-face looking eerie in the glow of the carriage lantern.

"My dear fellow!" he cried, pumping my hand like a thirsty man pumping for water. "You came? What am I saying? Of, course, you would, of course you would!" He turned then to Holmes and said, in the same excitable tones, "Mr. Holmes, thank goodness! Come, come, the crowds have been growing by the hour, and more snow is expected. You must see it. The full horror of it, before busy feet and the weather obliterates everything."

The particular stress that he laid on the word "horror" made my stomach lurch. I could see that Holmes, too, was alarmed by the urgency of Percy's speech.

Despite the cold and the snow, which still lay thick from the previous evening, it seemed that the whole village had come out to witness the events had befallen this tiny community. People stood in the doorways of barns and cottages, small groups huddled together under mighty oaks, and a few eyed Holmes and me with a curiosity bordering on hostility. But for the most, their attention was focused on the thin line of armed men who stood by, guarding the church.

The militia that Phelps had employed to keep the "scene", as he put it, clear of interference had certainly done their job well.

At this time of year, it wouldn't be dark for few hours yet, and the footprints mentioned in the newspaper were still perfectly visible.

Indeed, it would have been impossible to miss them. The tracks were small enough to have been made by a child. In some places, only the barest imprint of toes could be seen, as though the girl had been running, pell-mell on tiptoes. In other places, one could see the imprint of the whole foot, buried deep in snow – sometimes one foot, sometimes two – so that it seemed she'd been playing hop-scotch. No human child, however, ever could ever have left such footprints behind. They appeared and disappeared with huge gaps between each step. Prints appeared halfway up walls, on the side of houses, and most remarkably, over the ridge of the church nave.

Phelps led us through the line of militia towards the church. Holmes had yet to say a word, and Percy quickly gave up his desultory attempts at conversation.

We could see the vicar and another man nervously poised in the arched porch of St. Nicholas's, awaiting our approach.

Finally Holmes broke his silence. "Well done, Mr. Phelps," he said warmly. "You've done a splendid job here."

"I did what I could," my old school friend replied, in that quiet, nervous tone he had. "I'm afraid I couldn't stop the whole village from going about their business, but the vicar was willing to keep the church closed up until you had the chance to examine the prints. They run through village, across the boundary wall, over the church roof, through the churchyard, then on, towards the heath. I've more men posted along Heath Green Road and at the Agglestone itself, where the body still lies."

Holmes nodded. "And when were the prints discovered?"

"Around eleven o'clock yesterday evening by Mr. Bastin. Here he is now. The portly chap beside him is our vicar, Reverent Merchant."

"Portly? Whose portly?" A round, smiling face emerged from the shadow of the stone archway that covered the door.

Introductions made, we quickly retreated inside the vestibule, but not before Holmes's keen eyes had spotted something of interest.

"Ah, you've noticed our corbels, have you?" the vicar said, waving a pair of chubby hands to indicate something presumably running under the exterior roofline. "Everyone does. Those medieval stone masons were a scandalous lot. The ladies they carved must have been contortionists! Of course, our parishioners get in quite a stew about them, but, it's just ancient history."

"Pagan?" Holmes asked.

"Some believe so," the genial gentleman replied, blinking furiously. "The old beliefs hung on longer than many like to believe. And some of them seem to be older than the current building, suggesting they've been imported from some more-ancient structure. But I'd say they're playful rather than pagan."

"Not everyone agrees?"

"Oh," Merchant's smile broadened, "I'm forever having to stop irate mothers from knocking lumps off them. Mrs. Eggins – she's my housekeeper – keeps sewing valances to cover them up. Thankfully the wind here is more persistent that she is. They never last the night!"

Holmes glanced back towards the churchyard, where neat little headstones were crowded up against stubby trees, which had been bent by the wind into curious shapes. "Interesting," he said, although I wasn't at all sure he meant the valances.

A tall man stood beside the vicar looking like someone who'd who wasn't used to so much scrutiny. "'Now, then Mr. Bastin," Holmes began, "what can you tell us?"

Phelps gave the vicar a nod, as if to free him from any injunctions that had been laid on him. The vicar responded by giving Bastin a gentle tap on the shoulder and, as he did so, I noticed how, despite his calm tone, his hand trembled.

Bastin reacted like a racehorse at the starting whistle – galloping through the events of the previous night as though he'd explode if he didn't tell everything he knew immediately.

"It were around eleven," he said in that lilting accent Devon folk have. "I'd spent the evening in the Bankes Arms. It were busy, and we'd all stayed longer than intended, on account of the weather. The snow came in around nine. Then the wind, which were already strong, whipped up sumut awful. About ten, I heard this strange sound, like sumut being

161

dragged down the street. Now, this area has a reputation. They say piskies dance on the rooftops come nightfall and, true or not, no one wanted to go out and see what the matter were."

"Piskies?" I interrupted.

Bastin looked at the vicar and licked his lips uncertainly.

"What Tom means are the fey. This area is full of legends – the Agglestone, on the hill, was said to have been thrown here by a giant. And the hill itself is named after Old Nick. But piskeys are the souls of children who died without being baptized. I'm afraid that the early Church had no shame at all. They used all sorts of underhand tactics to convert people to Christianity!"

"I see!," Holmes said in a low, excited whisper. "Please, go on, Tom."

"It were near eleven when we finally trooped out. I started up the road. There were plenty of cloud, but they were movin' fast, and the moon were cumin into its last quarter – big an' bright – so, I saw 'em straight away. Footprints. Toe prints really, as though from dainty little feet.

"In some places, the snow were all smudged, and I had a fancy that whoever made 'em had been twirling around, like doing a jig.

"About 'alfway up the lane, the prints vanished and I backtracked to the inn, to see if maybe they'd gone another direction, but there'd been so many comings and goings, there were no way to tell.

"I headed back the way I came – my farm is just past the church, see – and sure enough, the footprints started up again. I'll be honest, Mr. 'Olmes, I'd had a few, and at that moment, I quite fancied catching myself a piskey or two. They might not be Christian, but fairy ladies are said to be mighty pretty. But then I saw those footprints up high, on the church wall, and then on the roof, and I lost my nerve. Ran hell-for-leather into the church, where the vicar found me, and thankfully let me sleep off my drunk. Felt right foolish, too, until I heard about the body and figured I'd done right to stay on Holy Ground!

"You were there when they found the body?" Holmes asked, turning his attention towards Merchant.

"Why, yes," the vicar answered, "but how did you know?" He refused to meet Holmes's steady gaze, instead fussing over his his cassock, as though plucking off imaginary lint.

"Forgive me, but you've the air of a man who's had a terrible shock," Holmes said gently.

In reply, Merchant gave the ruddy-faced farmer another tap on the shoulder. "Tom," he said, "I think if Mr. Holmes is agreeable, you can go back home now."

I was sure that Bastin would rather have stayed on Holy Ground, but he shrugged manfully and headed out of the church. No sooner had he left than the vicar visibly deflated, that odd, forced cheerfulness, quite vanishing.

"You're right Mr. Holmes, it's been terrible! But Tom and most of the villagers only know the barest details, and Percy has been keen to keep it that way. I know you'll want to view the body before the weather closes in, but we've a few hours yet, and if you'll come through to the sacristy, there's a kettle on the fire. What I have to tell needs at a good strong cup of Ceylon.

"There aren't many youngsters in these parts," Merchant stated. "The girls get sent into service, and the lads to the factories or the boats. Those who have no offers or money to move away quickly get into trouble. That's why I've started to use the sacristy in the evenings. I can keep an eye on the church better from here.

"I was here last night, reading beside the fire, when I heard a hellish commotion. It started suddenly – a low, desperate wail, followed by the clatter of hobnails on stone.

"I expected to find youngsters riffling the poor box, or breaking up the pews for firewood. Instead, I found Tom, flat on his face, eyes wide, mouth opening and closing, but no sound coming out, save for pitiful whelps.

"I helped him up, dusted him down, and filled him with tea. But it wasn't until the second cup that he dared tell what had spooked him so.

"In all honesty, I thought he was seeing shapes in the shadows. But I'd heard a noise myself, earlier, over the rooftop, so I thought it best to go investigate.

"I saw the prints instantly. But it was a curious thing: My lantern flicked and gutted, and the clouds overhead did the same, so that in that juddering light, it appeared that the footprints were actually moving.

"That fairly froze the blood in my veins, I can tell you! But I reminded myself that even if piskies turned out to be real, a portly man of the cloth was unlikely to be of any interest to them.

"I followed the tracks out of the churchyard. On reaching open ground, you cross into a lane which leads to a winding track, then a forested area. I was certain our night-time visitors must have returned to whatever woodland glen they hailed from because I lost the trail there. Still, some instinct told me to press on.

"I crossed the footbridge, which takes you to a narrow path that skirts the woods, and ultimately leads out, onto the heath.

"The path itself is treacherous, with patches of boggy furze and hidden hollows that will break your ankle if you aren't careful. My progress was painfully slow, but I picked up the tracks again at the point where the heath starts to curve up, towards the Agglestone.

"The rock is a giant wedge, shaped much like an anvil, and rises from the centre of an amphitheater of bog, dotted with clumps of cotton grass, crisscrossed by rivulets.

"Its name comes from the Anglo Saxon '*alig*', meaning '*holy*' – suggestive of an ancient pagan site, which time has turned into something ominous. I had always dismissed tales of human sacrifice, of blood rites, and evil – until that very moment.

"First I saw that mass of prints in the snow, just in front of the stone – caused, I believe, by some frantic last minute struggle. Then, I saw *her*.

"That poor child, laid on top of that dreadful slab, dressed in sacrificial gowns. Her ankles and wrists were bruised, where she had been tied down. Her head was twisted, her eyes staring, and there was that wicked, raw, red gash across her throat, where some fiend had bled her dry."

So affected was I by the vicar's speech that I could think of nothing to say, but Holmes was never one to stand on ceremony.

"There was blood at the scene? You saw that?"

"No, but I assumed the snow had covered it."

"Was the girl covered in snow?"

"Why, no, no . . . ." Merchant said, stammering now. "But the wind could have blown the snow off."

"Her throat was definitely cut, though?" Holmes insisted. "You saw that?"

"Not then. But Percy had ladders taken up later, and that's what it looked like."

"Mmm. So, you went straight to Phelps to report what you'd seen?"

"That's right," Percy said, his voice heavy with anxiety. "Knocked me up around one. I called the local constable, and we three went up. It was the constable who arranged for men from the neighboring villages to be brought in as guards, until you'd had a chance to see everything."

"No doctor?"

Phelps shook his head.

Holmes looked at me. His face was a mask, but in the firelight of that little stone room, his eyes looked like they were ablaze.

The evening was bright, crisp, and clear. The snow lay on the heath, as thick as goose-down. Everywhere, blue marsh flowers and white asphodel glowed as our lamps glinted off the hoar frost that lay on the blossoms.

I recalled how Homer had described the Greek Meadow of Death as covered in asphodels, and found myself shuddering.

Holmes walked beside me, his head bowed, his eyes fixed on the those pitiful little footprints.

As we reached the dip that led to the Agglestone and our own meadow of death, the winds rose, making our little cortege stumble in the boggy earth.

Just as Merchant had described, the tracks ended before we reached the rock itself, but it seemed to me that, rather than a struggle, what we were seeing was some strange dance. What was it Bastin said? Like someone doing a jig. "What do you make of it?" I asked Holmes.

"Interesting! And did you notice how the trees here-abouts have been bent by the dominant easterly winds? Yet, as we get closer to the Point, the winds start to plunge over the cliffs, creating swirling back-eddies."

"Is that important?" I asked.

"Watson, it's the key to everything. But a look at this poor, dear girl will fill in the details we're so sorely lacking."

Made of sandstone, the Agglestone must have been at least thirty feet high, and several hundred tonnes in weight. Yet its entire bulk was balanced, unfeasibly, on one small point and, stretched out on its flat surface, lay the body of a young girl, dressed in white, her skin as pale as the surrounding snow. Never had I seen a more mournful nor uncanny sight.

The ladders that Phelps had brought up to the stone were still in place. Holmes and I gingerly claimed one apiece, and began to examine the child.

"No blood," Holmes noted.

"No – none. What Merchant took for the mark of a knife seems to be the imprint of a rope of some kind."

"Strangled?"

"Garroted would be a more accurate description, given the deep neck abrasions and the hemorrhages on her skin. It's hard to be sure without a more thorough examination, but her neck may be broken. But look, here, Holmes! Look at the way she's lying, the position of her body. It's almost like she's been dropped from some higher point. Unless you believe in giants, that's hardly likely. Could she have climbed up herself?"

"The footprints we followed are undoubtedly hers. But the last visible tracks are at least four foot away from the base of the stone. She couldn't have been carried and placed here, because there are no other prints. She certainly couldn't have jumped up. How indeed? But see here," Holmes continued, distractedly motioning to the abrasions around the girl's legs and feet. "There are no marks on the skin to imply she was held or tied down. No indentations from fingers, or trace fibers. But, given these bruises on her feet, I can see why Phelps might have thought that.

"So what do we have? The bruises curve over the dorsum. I hate to speculate, but given that we're working in straitened circumstances, I'd say they're from shoes. Not the usual ankle boots that a girl might wear for every day. Something showy and fashionable, with a high tongue, like evening pumps. That would account for shape of the bruises. Especially if they were too small, and chaffed at her feet. Perhaps she borrowed them from a friend because they matched her dress? Then there are the smaller cuts and abrasions on her legs, arms, and face, almost as if she'd been walking through thick undergrowth . . . ."

"But there *are* rope marks on her wrists," I said.

"Yes, but given that we need these very long ladders to even view the body – Who could have tied her down? And there's nothing to tie her to. I'd suggest she was holding onto something, rather than tied to something. Or tangled in something Yes! That's the ticket!" Holmes added in a sudden, excited rush. "Yes, yes! You were absolutely right!

"Now, look at her clothes. These aren't sacrificial robes. This is the lady's Sunday best. See the ribbons in her hair? Made from lengths of serge – offcuts – in navy blue. The exact blue, and the exact material, used by the British Navy. And the Royal Navy Base at Nothe Fort is almost exactly due east. We have it, Watson, we have it!"

It took Holmes two hours, waiting for replies to telephone calls and telegrams to confirm the details – and what a sad story it was.

On the morning of Thursday the sixteenth, fourteen year old Mary Williams, dressed in her only good dress, with navy ribbons tied in her hair, and a pair of striking blue velvet pumps borrowed from her young cousin, climbed onto a trapeze bar strung beneath a giant kite, outside Nothe Fort, Weymouth, Dorset.

The Fort had been built as a coastal defense in the 1860's to protect the Royal Navy Base at Portland and the kite's inventor, Jennings Wilcott, hoped his demonstration would help sell his "war kite" to the navy.

Wilcott's idea was that "spotters" could be sent aloft, and trained to identify enemy troops to warn of an impending attack.

On the day of the demonstration, thousands of people gathered to watch the ascent and descent. "A companion and I stood on the harbor," said the reporter from *The Weymouth Telegram*, who was just finishing the story for publication when Holmes telephoned. "We had a fine view of both the kite and of the girl. The kite was a large contraption, constructed of a series of rectangular boxes, stung four in a line, and

166

attached to a winch on the ground with a long rope. The girl, Mary Williams, was in comparison tiny – seeming like a doll besides the kite.

"She was a local girl and, indeed, had many friends in the crowd who spoke glowingly about her pluck. It was said she'd recently lost her position and was hoping the flight would make her fortune, and many were there to cheer her along.

"The wind had been high all day. The kite rose quickly, and the spectators thrilled to see the girl lifted so high above the Fort. Then, suddenly the wind dropped, the kite fell, and we feared she would be unseated.

"But she stayed up, and a great roar went around the crowd. This seemed to encourage the man on the winch, who let out more rope, allowing the kite to climb even higher than before.

"By now the wind was coming in stronger, and there were cries for her to be pulled back in. We could see the girl was struggling to remain on her seat, but the man – Mr. Jennings Wilcott – shouted up to her to not be afraid.

"However, the crowd was getting restless. It was wrong, people said, to take advantage when she was so young. Others said that she was always headstrong, and if things went bad, she only had herself to blame. Thankfully there were more for her than against her, and once again, the cry went up to bring her down. And, once again, Wilcott remained unmoved.

"The girl had been up almost ten minutes when there was a terrible noise, as of tearing cloth and before our eyes the top portion of the kite disintegrated, like wet paper.

"Wilcott panicked and in his rush to reach the winch, he knocked the bar which locked the remaining cable in place. All we could do was watch, in horror, as the rest of the rope unspooled, setting the kite to fly free.

"The girl did indeed have remarkable pluck. While the women on the quayside cried and howled, she remained calm. We could see that she seemed to be working her arms and feet, as if trying to steer the thing out to sea. If she could have landed in the water, then she would have been safe. And it seemed she would have her way. But then, at the last minute, the wind took her – and she could not resist.

"The kite bucked and shook, and for one horrible moment, it looked like it would break apart entirely.

"The wind eased off again, and the crowd gave another cheer, but it was quickly seen that something was wrong. In her attempt to maneuver herself away from land, she had become entangled in the kite strings. 'Oh Lord, she's dead!' said someone in the crowd, but by then the kite had been carried over the Fort and quickly vanished."

167

A week later, Holmes and I were sitting in the drying room of our favourite Turkish bath on Northumberland Avenue. It was over a smoke, lying on a couches, that I spotted the coroners' report on the front page of the morning's newspaper.

The inquest on Mary Williams had concluded the previous day, and had ruled that the deceased had "*accidentally died, when the strings of the kite which was carrying her wrapped itself around her neck. It appears,*" the coroner was quoted as saying, "*that Mary Williams's body was dragged some thirty miles across country, before the bobbing kite was caught in crosswinds. As the ropes that she was caught in untangled, her body was deposited on top of the Agglestone rock in Studland. It is assumed that the remains of the kite was carried out to sea.*"

In his summing up, the coroner added, "*We wish to censor Mr. Jennings Wilcott, showman and inventor, in that he showed great carelessness and disregard for the safety of such a young girl by allowing her to attempt the ascent without proper forethought or training. It is recommended that Mr. Wilcott be prohibited from carrying out further demonstrations until suitable reparations are made to Miss Williams's family.*"

Thinking about how cruelly the girl had met her end, it was a small comfort know that we had, at least, been able to ensure that the truth about her death was known.

"No, Watson, it's no comfort at all," Holmes said, sadly, reaching for the pouch of tobacco secreted in the inside pocket of his coat, "Mary Williams is still just as dead. You may call me a fool, but when it comes to murder, give me an honest cutthroat any day, for it seems infinitely more horrible to die at the behest of someone looking, as our American cousins would say, to get rich quick, than at the hands of some unthinking hothead."

"How is a cutthroat any better?"

"He isn't. But while the cutthroat goes to the gallows, accepting the penalty for his crime, Wilcott gets to go to dinner parties and plan his next escapade, in the full knowledge that there will always be someone desperate enough to take the risks while he takes the glory."

NOTES

☐ According to the Meteorological Office's weekly reports, 16th-17th May did indeed see a sudden cold snap that brought snow and thundery storms.

☐ *The Daily Chronicle* was considered a liberal newspaper, carrying regular features on striking workers, Irish home rule, and what it called "Greater Britain Day by Day" with news from the Colonies. It was one of the first papers to popularize small personal adverts, which were often written in coded language.

☐ In the late Eighteenth Century, ownership of Bunkle Castle passed to the Earls of Home, meaning that the aide-de-camp Holmes mentions would be the 12th Earl, Charles Alexander Douglas-Home.

☐ Ignatius Paul Pollaky (1828-1918) was a contemporary of Holmes. His offices were at 13 Paddington Green – hence the nickname. He retired in 1882 but, if Holmes is right, then it seems that he remained active in the business – at least unofficially.

☐ In Victorian London, postal deliveries were made at least twelve times a day in most cities. The first delivery was at 7:30 a.m., the last one at 7:30 p.m.

☐ The Foreign Office affair that Watson mentions was in 1889 – six years, not four or five years earlier.

☐ *Bradshaw's Railway Companion* was a timetable book that became an indispensable item for regular travelers – so much so that *Bradshaw's* became a household name.

☐ Studland Manor House is as quirky as Watson describes. It is now a National Trust property.

☐ Period photos show the Swanage Station running board does indeed have a full stop, which was strange enough for Watson to note.

☐ The end of the Nineteenth Century saw a growth in spiritualism. Secret societies, such as The Hermetic Order of the Golden Dawn, promoted occultism and magic, blended with esoteric eastern philosophies. This was seen as a reaction to Darwinism, and the search for "meaning" and spiritual certainty. Max Nordu was a doctor and social critic who argued that such spiritualism was proof of the degeneration of the species. His book *Degeneration* was published 1882-1883, so Watson was certainly keeping up with his reading.

☐ The corbels of St. Nicholas's Church are famously pornographic, including several *sheela na gigs*, and some very acrobatic couples!

☐ The Agglestone fell onto one end and side in 1970 and is no longer the distinctive anvil shape Watson describes.

☐ The use of kites in warfare dates back to ancient China. Victorian interest in aeronautics, and its practical applications for warfare, revived the idea. In the 1820's, British inventor George Pocock developed the first modern "man-lifting" kite, using his own children in his experiments. Expositions in which inventors would demonstrate balloons or kites became hugely popular, and often involved hoisting young girls into the air – the ladies being both lightweight and offering a certain glamour to the proceedings.

☐ Aeronauts continued to use young girls in their displays. Just a year after Watson's account, another fourteen-year-old girl, Louisa Maud Evans, died when the balloon she was in went out of control. She did have a parachute, which she used to jump to safety, but she fell into the Bristol Channel and was dragged under the water by the weight of the chute. Until the invention of airplanes, parachutes were generally only used by acrobats, who performed stunts on a trapeze bar suspended from a descending chute.

☐ The type of kite that the journalist describes seems to have been based on the box kite invented by Lawrence Hargrave in 1885. His design used four box kites tethered together, and it could lift an adult man. The American, Samuel Cody, and Captain Baden Fletcher Smyth Baden-Powell (brother of the Scout leader) also developed their own kites for aerial observation. Cody's "Man-lifter War Kite" was adopted by the War Office Balloon Companies of the Royal Engineers in 1906.

The Adventure of the
Illustrious Author
by Tracy J. Revels

"The lady is either a captive or a specter, Mr. Holmes! If the second, you may write me up as an ass. But if she is a prisoner, it is my duty to liberate her."

My friend Mr. Sherlock Holmes considered the young man who had arrived at Baker Street that lovely summer afternoon. Mr. Jonas Clark was a sturdy specimen of English manhood: Tall, barrel-chested, bright-eyed, and squared faced with a chiseled jaw and dark brown hair smoothed flat with pomade. His whole being, from his boots to his checkered jacket to his hound-headed cane, spoke of the hearty country life, and it was easy to imagine him as the eldest son of the village squire, a youth blessed with fine health, handsome features, and a modest fortune. He was clearly a person of substance and grand expectations in his small, rural world.

"I do not waste my time with phantoms," Holmes replied. "However, if a woman is confined against her will, you are correct that you have an obligation to aid her. But first tell me more about yourself, Mr. Clark – for besides the fact that you studied at Camford, have recently lost your mother, and earlier today endured the indignity of being struck about the head by an enraged female, I know nothing about you."

Our guest's jaw dropped. His eyes bulged. I made a quick glance but spotted only one clue.

"The tie?" I asked.

"Yes. The school colours are familiar to me," Holmes said. "I assure you it is no great trick, Mr. Clark. Your neckwear revealed your alliance to your *alma mater*. The loss of your mother is made clear by the antique lady's ring which you wear upon the smallest finger of your right hand, in place of a more masculine signet. As the delicate band has not been battered or misshapen, I suspect your bereavement occurred earlier in the year – but not in the last few weeks, since you are without an armband or a black ribbon on your hat. As for the assault – " Here Holmes rose and deftly plucked two fluffs of feathers from just behind the youth's right ear. " – unless you were set upon by an ostrich on your way to the station, or somewhere along the thoroughfares of London, I fear you have angered a specimen of humanity's 'gentle sex',"

At this, our client broke into chagrinned chuckles. "No wonder they say you are a wizard, Mr. Holmes. Even in sleepy Chadworth, we know your name. And it is the God's truth, sir, all of it. My sainted mother passed away at Christmas, and as for the attack, it helps to explain why I am in need of your wisdom."

"Very well. Let us have your story."

"Chadworth, as you know, is three hours from London, but it might as well be perched off on some distant isle, it is so far removed from the excitement of the great city. There are no more than six-hundred residents of the village, and we all go about our lives in a quiet and orderly fashion. Therefore, you can imagine the excitement when, just two months ago, Willow Hall, a great old Georgian pile that has stood empty since the last owner shot himself over gambling debts back in 1810, was finally rented. We were all interested to see who would take up residence. The poor folk hoped for a benevolent patron, while the sporting lads wished for a new companion in the hunt. As it happened, only the ladies were not disappointed."

Clark paused. His face slowly took on more color, glowing with a rosy hue that matched the passion of his words.

"You are older than I, Mr. Holmes. I am certain that you understand women."

My friend gave a sharp laugh. "The fair sex is Dr. Watson's department," he replied. "My friend has the benefit of an adventure in matrimony as well as – " Here he could not resist a hint of a grin. " – vast experience in the field of romance. Is it three continents or four where the ladies sing your praises, Doctor?"

Clark shook his head. "Even so, sir – don't you think women should be satisfied with what they have, and not go chasing after what they can't have? Chadworth might not be London or Paris, but there's nothing amiss with the local fellows. Why should a girl who has the eternal love of a fine British man feel the need to – "

"What is the young lady's name?" Holmes interrupted. Clark's already pink face turned scarlet with embarrassment.

"Miss Tabitha Bailey. I've known her since we were both toddlers, there's no prettier girl in all of England, and I thought – I hoped – I believed – we had an understanding, if not exactly an engagement. And then *he* came," Clark grumbled.

Holmes arched a brow and nodded for the young man to continue.

"Willow Hall was taken by an elderly American man and his son. They arrived with two servants, a husband and wife. The old man's name is Silas Duncan, and he is a foolish drunkard. That is unkind, I know, but the description fits. He was some type of manufacturer of buttons or coats

172

or boots – I'll be hanged if I can remember which he said – during the Great Rebellion in America. He made a tidy fortune from that tragedy and has spent the remainder of his life swizzling away his money. He is blind as a bat, but every day his servants bring him to The Pig and Piper, where he drinks himself into a stupor and regales the village loafers with stories of his adventures. He claims to have been a great soldier, says he fought Indians and Mexicans and would have thrashed the Johnny Rebs single-handedly, had he not lost his sight smiting evil doers in some place he calls 'Bleeding Kansas'. He's a braggart and a buffoon, though entertaining enough. Had it only been the old gentleman, there would have been no trouble."

"But the son?" I prompted.

"Yes. He is the problem. You wouldn't think it when you first look at him. He is tall and thin, perhaps thirty or so years of age, wears heavy spectacles, and has the appearance of a man who has never taken exercise in the fresh country air, as God intended. He smells of expensive cologne, not good honest sweat. The first time I met him was when he arrived at The Pig and Piper to fetch his father home, about two weeks after they took up residence. McNally – he's our local bully – decided he didn't like the gent's fancy looks and threw a punch at him. I thought Duncan's face would be smashed, but in the twinkling of an eye Duncan seized McNally's arm, rolled the lout over his shoulder, and slammed him across a table, which broke all to pieces. Duncan calmly brushed himself off, gave the publican two quid for the damage to the furniture, collected his father, and departed."

"A memorable display," Holmes said.

"Indeed, sir. But how I wish I had never witnessed it, for it caused all my problems. That very evening, I paid a call upon Tabby, and thought I would amuse her with a recounting of the affair. If only I had kept my mouth shut!"

"'What is the young man's Christian name?' she asked.

"'It's some kind of a bird – I heard his father call it. Let me think. Ah, I know, it is *Lark*.'

"'Lark Duncan?'

"'Yes.'"

"And at that, Mr. Holmes, Tabby's eyes got bright, and she let out a squeal. The next thing I knew, she'd bolted for her room, and when she returned, it was with her arms filled with books.

"'He is a *writer*!' she proclaimed. 'My favorite writer of all time! He's very famous.'

"'Then how have I never heard of him?' I asked.

173

"'Because you read nothing but boring old mysteries!'" Our client looked suddenly abashed. "I hope you'll excuse her comments, sirs."

"Both of us have heard worse," Holmes assured him. "Do continue."

"I looked over the books. The name '*Lark Duncan*' appeared on every cover. But they were all *romances* – those trite, vapid stories women are so fond of: Shop-girls marrying lords, princesses pretending to be diary maids, that kind of nonsense.

"'Oh, I can't wait to tell my friends!' Tabby said, clapping her hands and dancing around like a child. 'And you must introduce us to him. How thrilling, that someone so illustrious should come to live in Chadworth!'"

"Of course, I would do anything for my dear girl, so the next day I went to pay a social call upon our new arrival. He received me politely enough in his library, but I could tell that he was annoyed to be interrupted at work.

"'It is always gratifying to know that ladies have enjoyed my tales,' he said. 'I fear, however, that I am not a very outgoing individual. I mean no disrespect, and I would not wish to disappoint anyone, but I make a habit of declining all social invitations, to maintain my focus on my writing. And, as you have seen, my father is not a gentlemen fit for polite company.'"

"I found it very strange: What sane man, residing in one of the most beautiful parishes in all of England, would want to sit at a desk and scribble all day when he had the wealth to avoid labor entirely? But I knew that should I fail in my quest, Tabby would never forgive me, and I would rather face a wild boar unarmed than my dear girl's wrath! So I badgered Duncan until, at last, I got him to agree to give a reading of his work at Willow Hall the following Saturday. When I told Tabby, you would have thought I had slain a dragon and laid it at her feet.

"The event was a success. Every lady in the village attended, all of them clad in their greatest finery, glittering by candlelight. My Tabby sat on the front row, immediately before the little podium. Duncan appeared in formal attire and gave a dramatic reading from two of his novels. Afterward, he answered the audience's questions about his heroines and their 'sentiments', whatever that might mean. I must confess, Mr. Holmes, I have never spent a more tedious evening!

"Tabby, however, was enamored of the man, and all her friends were equally smitten. Even some of the married ladies, matrons of fifty years or more, acted like schoolgirls swooning over a handsome teacher! For weeks, all the Chadworth men have heard is prattle about the talented Mr. Duncan, his wealth, and how he must want a wife to complete his happiness."

174

"The Chadworth ladies are well up on their Austen," Holmes observed.

"Really? Who might he be?"

Holmes shot me a wry look. "Do continue, Mr. Clark."

The big man leaned forward, one fist grinding into the palm of the opposite hand. "At least Duncan gives them no encouragement. I have seen him in the village only twice, though he attends church faithfully. He slips into a back pew just moments before the service begins and flees the instant the organ starts to play the concluding hymn. I'm sure he croaks like a frog when he sings and is too embarrassed to raise his voice."

"Where is the imprisoned lady in all of this?' Holmes inquired.

"I'm just getting to her. Last Thursday, Duncan agreed to give another reading at Willow Hall. This time, Tabby went with her sister, and I knew nothing of the event until the next day when I met Tabby for luncheon. When I questioned why I was not summoned as an escort, she dismissed my feelings with a wave of her hand."

"'Oh, you would have ruined the fun, sitting there with a glower on your face. You are a good man, Jonas, but you don't have a spark of chivalry or romance in your soul. I could listen to Mr. Duncan read for hours. His words transport me! But . . . do you know, I happened to drop my favorite fan at Willow Hall last night, so I will go over and retrieve it.'

"I told her she most certainly would not. The very idea of her calling at an unmarried gentleman's house, all alone! She said she would take her sister, but Imogene is equally smitten. The dastard might try and seduce both girls! Instead, I resolved I would get her fan back that very afternoon.

"I walked the two miles to Willow Hall and, on the way, I encountered the old man and his servants in a cart, headed into the village. I tipped my hat but did not state my intentions. When I reached the Hall, I knocked several times but received no answer. It occurred to me that Lark Duncan might be away, perhaps gone to London to visit his agent. My trip had been for naught."

"Then a foolish thought struck me. Tabby had accused me of lacking chivalry. I recalled that the latest novel she'd read – and regaled me with, when I had no interest in a summary – was a story about a noble burglar. I decided on the spot that I would imitate this fictional fellow, break into the house, and rescue her fan. You are right to smile, Mr. Holmes. It was a silly thing to do, and if I had not consumed two glasses of wine at lunch with Tabby, the absurd idea would never have come to me.

"The front door was locked, and windows looked too sturdy to force open, but the back of the house is surrounded by a high wall of bricks in an ornate honeycomb pattern, with a gate at the very rear. Surely I could find a way to unlatch it, or scale the wall, and the kitchen door would be handily unlocked.

"As I strolled around the Hall, I was aware of a hauntingly beautiful voice, softly singing an unfamiliar tune. I paused and listened, but could make out only something about 'all quiet' and 'Potomac'. I crept further along, peeped through the holes in the wall, and beheld, to my astonishment, a woman sitting on the grass beneath a tree. It was she who was singing. Now, as I watched, she hunched forward and began to weep.

"I stood frozen in shock, for while I could not see her face, I could see her clothing. Mr. Holmes, she was clad in a yellow, ragged dress, a frock so thin, old, and tattered that it was almost indecent. Her hat was an old-style poke bonnet, one like my grandmother wore in her portrait, and it too was stained and broken in spots, tied on with a moldy ribbon, obscuring the girl's face. Her appearance was so bizarre that I must have given an audible gasp, loud enough to be heard, for the next moment the apparition leapt from the ground and darted back into the house. I noted her feet were bare and dirty, and she ran in a clumsy manner, almost tripping over her skirts. I stood in place for the longest time, wondering what exactly I had witnessed."

"Perhaps she is the daughter of the younger gentleman," I suggested. "Or the child of a servant?"

"Impossible," Clark muttered. "The servants are both Asian in their features, and from her bare arms and throat, it was clear this was a white woman. And she was a woman, not a young girl or child . . . forgive me for my bluntness, but her attire was so threadbare there was no mystery in that regard, even though I never saw her face."

"What did you do next?" Holmes inquired. I sensed he was intrigued by the tale.

"I returned home and had another glass of wine – no, brandy! But the next morning, I woke up determined to learn the truth. I waited until the late afternoon, when I was certain the old gent was in his cups at the pub and returned to Willow Hall. I spotted the Duncans' servants in the market as I departed from the village, so I knew I should not be disturbed in my investigation. This time I did not knock but went straight to the spot where I had stood on the previous day. Mr. Holmes, to my amazement, the same woman, in the same ragged dressed, was seated in the very same spot! Once again, her song turned into weeping. Now, I gave a loud shout, calling to her, demanding her name. And once again, without a backward glance, she fled into the dwelling, though this time she moved with such fluidity I was not sure that she was human. Yet I mastered my nerves, climbed the wall, and ran to the door at the rear of the house, banging

176

loudly and demanding to be admitted. No one answered and, after a fruitless hour, I went home.

"The next day was Sunday. I waited in the churchyard, concealing myself behind a high tombstone. Lark Duncan arrived in a dogcart, just as the worshippers began singing the first hymn. I bolted from my hiding place and confronted him on the chapel steps.

"'See here,' I said. 'Who is that woman at your home, the one you force to wear old rags, who sits in the garden and weeps? I have seen her twice and her treatment is a disgrace to humanity. Be straight with me, or I shall go to the authorities!'"

"He favored me with a cold, forbidding stare. When he spoke, his words were low and filled with menace.

"'You have seen the ghost of Willow Hall,' he said. 'When I took the house, I was told the legend of its last lady, who grieved herself to death. I have looked for her daily and never encountered her. Perhaps she only shows herself to locals.'"

"This last word was spat out almost as a curse. I was tempted to give Duncan a taste of my fists for his impertinence, but it would be undignified to squabble before the house of God. He returned to his vehicle and took something from the seat. It was Tabby's fan."

"'You had only to knock and ask for its return,' he said. 'If you did so, and I did not hear you, it is because my work is all-consuming. I am in another world when I write. Please understand I have no interest in your lady or anyone else's. If you insist upon this persecution, or accuse me of some misdeed, I shall depart this village immediately.'"

"And with that he walked back, took up the reins, and drove away, without ever attending the service. I went to the graveyard and sat down to think things over. I am not a superstitious man, but the more I considered it, I felt I remembered the story of the Weeping Lady of Willow Hall, a ghost who continuously mourned because her husband squandered the family wealth and forced her to go about in tattered clothes. But would such a phantom appear in the broad daylight? The creature I'd beheld seemed more flesh than spirit. Duncan's coldness suggested he was capable of cruelty, but if I erred and he made good on his threat to leave – and Tabby learned of my part in it – surely our engagement – I mean our *understanding* – would be no more.

"This morning, after three days of debate, I decided to lay my case and my suspicions before my beloved. It seemed safer and wiser to tell her all before I acted. I did so – and was bashed over the head with her feathered fan for my pains!" The young man slumped on our divan, clearly exhausted by his tale. "My only chance for redemption is to have the matter cleared up beyond all debate. If you can prove what I witnessed is

177

a supernatural vapor, or free an innocent lady from Duncan's imprisonment, perhaps Tabby will love me again. If not, Mr. Holmes, all is lost!"

A silence fell upon the room. Holmes considered his guest with amused compassion.

"Yours is a most unusual predicament, Mr. Clark. Give me a day to indulge in some research. Today is Thursday, and I shall travel to the scenic village of Chadworth on Saturday. I will send you a message when all is in order."

"You do not perceive any danger?"

"None presently. Return home and make amends with your sweetheart. Some flowers and chocolates might be in order – perhaps Dr. Watson can advise you on a florist and a confectioner."

Clark departed with a firm handshake and a hearty thanks. Holmes lit his pipe and turned to me with a chuckle.

"Are you familiar with Lark Duncan, your brother author, Watson?"

"Only by literary reputation. His novels, despite Clark's low opinion of them, have received good reviews. I haven't read them, of course, but the critics deem them far superior to most of their genre." I shook my head. "In truth, I assumed Lark Duncan was a woman."

"Why? Come, Watson, have I not taught you the dangers of making deductions when you do not possess the facts?"

I bristled. "It is a perfectly natural assumption – women write romances, for only women read them!"

Holmes waved his pipe around. "Since when is literature the possession of one sex or the other? I would speculate that a fair number of ladies consume your tales of my adventures, which are decidedly masculine in nature. And even a male writer may use feminine expressions, crafting his prose into fancy swirls and delicate flourishes. How many times have I chided you to remove the poetry and romance from your scribblings?"

"There is no need to be insulting."

Holmes raised a hand. "I am being prickly only to prove a point, my friend. Words and stories belong to everyone. The pen is neither male nor female, yet it is only recently that talented women have been able to write and enjoy success under their own names. Even the Brontë sisters were first published under male pseudonyms. But let us dine rather than squabble! A savory supper will provide the fuel for a good day's work tomorrow."

By chance, the following day found me busy with patients. When I returned to Baker Street late that evening, I found a note from Holmes requesting my presence the next morning, upon the ten-thirty train from Victoria to Chadworth, as well as a startling and confusing assignment I was to undertake before meeting him.

"Ah, right on time," Holmes said the next day, as I hurried across the station platform. "Your punctuality is a great virtue, Watson."

"Your task almost made me miss the train entirely!" I grumbled, looking down at the wicker basket on my arm. "Where have you been? Do you have any idea how hard this exact one was to find? What on earth do you need with a – "

The whistle blew and we hurried for our compartment. As we settled in, Holmes fiddled with the item in the basket, then finally began to address my confusion.

"It would be best not to smoke, so let us talk instead. I have spent the last day in conversations with many members of the literary community, and in sending telegrams to my discreet colleagues in America. I have learned several items of interest about our client's nemesis."

"Such as?"

"Let me begin with Silas Duncan. He was indeed, as he boasted, an American manufacturer of leather goods who made an enviable fortune during the late Civil War. He was also, in his younger days, a military hero, a fighter of Indians and a captain of volunteers in the American conflict with Mexico. He chased down a party of men known as 'border ruffians' in Kansas, an area of the United States that suffered mightily in the 1850's, when battles for ballots were fought with guns and machetes. It was in this action that he was nearly blinded, and afterward turned from military affairs to entrepreneurial ones, to the benefit of his purse, if not his reputation.

"It was left to Lark Duncan to carry his father's banner, and he did so with great aplomb. The family resided in Pennsylvania, and the young man, who was twenty at the outbreak of hostilities – "

"But Holmes," I interrupted, "we were told that Duncan appears to be thirty years of age. Someone who was twenty in 1861 – "

Holmes nodded. "All will be revealed in due time, Watson. To continue: In 1861, twenty-year-old Lark Duncan enlisted with a Union company. He rose in the ranks, becoming a Colonel and winning numerous commendations and accolades for his boldness on the field. It is said that during the Battle of Gettysburg, a lone Confederate assassin somehow penetrated the Union camp, with the intention of murdering General Meade, and young Colonel Lark pounced upon the wretch, pummeling him into submission and saving the general's life. Lark Duncan is a name all Americans should remember."

"And now he writes ladies' romances," I sneered.

179

"Only if he writes them from the spirit plane," Holmes countered. "Colonel Lark Duncan was hit by an explosive shell at Sailor's Creek, three days before General Robert E. Lee's surrender at Appomattox Court House. The lad's body was, in the words of his commander, blown to bloody pieces."

"Then who is the gentleman who bears his name?"

"That is our central question. I was only able to trace Silas Duncan for a year following the war, when he sold his company and departed for California. I am hopeful that our new friend may help us learn the rest of the story."

I glanced at the basket. "But how?"

Holmes yawned. "I spent many hours last night reading Lark Duncan's ornate prose. I could use a nap. Wake me when we reach Chadworth Station, please."

And with that, Holmes drew his cloth cap over his eyes and dropped instantly to sleep, leaving me, as usual, rather perplexed.

A few hours later, we disembarked, and Holmes asked for directions to The Pig and Piper. We paused within long enough to consume a sandwich. Holmes nodded toward a stout gentleman in dark glasses who was slumped at a far table.

"Silas Duncan – His clothes mark him as an American, as does his speech," Holmes said, as the man bellowed for service. "Let us hope his stories are entertaining to the publican, who must endure his odious presence. Ah . . . What have we here?"

An elderly couple had entered and joined Duncan. The pair were of an Asian race, the man small and lithe, the woman wrapped in a heavy, bell-sleeved robe despite the warmth of the weather. Holmes tapped my shoulder and drained his glass.

"Let us go now, while the proverbial coast is clear. It is best this interview be conducted in private."

We left the pub and were fortunate to spot a farmer with a cart, who permitted us to ride in its rear, saving us many steps down the narrow country lane. The farmer's hound was clearly intrigued by the contents of the basket, but Holmes kept the dog occupied, tossing a single stick which the canine was delighted to retrieve, no matter how far Holmes threw it. We bid our driver farewell at the entrance to Willow Hall, then climbed the somewhat stained and broken stairs, knocking boldly on the door.

"If Duncan does not answer?" I whispered.

"Oh, I have every reason to believe he will," Holmes said, taking the basket onto his arm. "He dares not provoke any more mysteries for his inquisitive neighbor to solve. Ah, here is the man himself!"

Mr. Lark Duncan was almost as tall as Holmes, slender and elegant, clean shaven, perhaps thirty to thirty-five years of age. His sharp face was framed by tight waves of light brown hair and spectacles magnified his blue eyes. The author had clearly been engaged in his work, for while he had tugged on a jacket, his long fingers and parts of his cuffs were ink stained.

"Mr. Lark Duncan?" Holmes asked, breathlessly, with the obsequious tone of one who is awe-struck in the presence of celebrity.

"I am."

"Excellent! My name is Poe, and my friend is Mr. Hawthorne. We have been charged with delivering a tribute from one of your most ardent admirers." Holmes motioned to the basket. Duncan gave a low, barely audible groan, the sound of a man who has no patience for distractions but is continually forced to endure them. He reached for the basket, but Holmes took a half-step backward.

"Do forgive me, sir, but the certain gracious lady who entrusted us with the delivery has insisted we accompany you inside your domicile and witness your reception of the token. She will be in terrible distress if we cannot provide an accurate accounting of your response."

"Very well, but only if you will leave immediately upon the competition of your task."

"Of course, Mr. Duncan. Might we take this to your library? Our patron would be most gratified to learn all about the place where you work."

He signaled for us to follow. I noticed how sparsely furnished the home seemed, as if its residents had never settled in, or had no intention of remaining there with any permanence. Holmes, meanwhile, kept up a steady stream of annoying chatter.

"The noble lady bid me to tell you that her favorite book is *The Lonely Princess*, and her second favorite is *The Soldier's Daughter*. Or was it *The Scandalous King*? No, no I am certain it was *The Royal Cousin* – I can imagine why she has a certain fondness for that one! What are you working on now? Her Majes – I mean, our lady is most curious to know."

"She may read it when it is published, just like the rest of the world," Duncan snapped, his voice growing shrill with annoyance. He recovered himself and gestured for us to take the pair of seats opposite his desk. His library was the only room in the manor that seemed filled, In fact, it was over-stuffed with books, maps, newspapers, magazines, and other articles that spoke to a love of research. "Forgive me, gentlemen – I did not intend to be so rude, but you have come at an inopportune moment. My father and I will be departing our residence shortly, and I must finish this manuscript before we go. If I may have the gift, I will compose a suitable thanks for you to bear to your employer."

Holmes nodded and placed the basket on the writer's desk, amid his messy pile of papers.

The basket wiggled.

For a long moment, Duncan sat frozen. Then, very gently, he lifted the lid.

He gasped in astonishment. His face – so tense and gruff – seemed to melt, to reconfigure and rearrange itself. He reached with trembling hands and drew out the contents of the basket.

A small, very fluffy white kitten, with eyes as blue as Duncan's own, gave a small meow. Duncan brought the animal to his cheek, reveling in its softness and scent.

"You will find a message attached to its collar," Holmes said. The writer shifted the kitten into the crook of his left elbow and unfolded the paper tucked within the velvet band.

"I . . . Yes, it is pointless to . . . how did you know?"

"Rest assured that I have not come to meddle or to persecute. But there is clearly no ghost in Willow Hall, and as I have often said, the reality of life is much stranger than any fiction man could invent. I would very much like to hear your story, Miss Duncan."

"Lark died three days before the war ended," the lady said. "And because he was killed, I was forced to take his place."

"Your father lost his only son."

The lady nodded. "My father was a great military hero, but when the Civil War broke out, he was too old and blind to fight, and turned all his attention to his business. Lark was my half-brother. I was born to Father's second wife in 1860. My poor mother perished while giving birth to me, and my raising was relegated to our Irish maid. I have no clear memory of my much-older brother, though I recall Father's overwhelming pride in all of Lark's accomplishments, how he would boast and brag. I do, however, vividly remember the day the terrible news came to us of Lark's death, and that his body had been so blasted by a shell he was lost to us forever. We were denied even the comfort of a funeral.

"Father was never the same. The house was hung in black, and Father spent a month locked in his room, wailing. I stood at the door and heard him curse Heaven for taking his 'hero son' and leaving him only a 'worthless girl'.

"At last, Father called me into his room. He took a pair of scissors and cut away my curls, then tore apart my dress and pinafore. He put me into a rough shirt, a pair of trousers, and a little cap. He even tied hard boots upon my feet. The maid came inside and gave a shriek when she saw what Father had done. She called him a lunatic. He sacked her upon the spot. I cried as she ran away, for Maggie was my only friend. Father slapped me and told me that from now on I was a boy, and my name was Lark."

"What was your name before?" Holmes asked. The lady shook her head.

"In truth, I do not remember." She looked about the room, as if seeing it for the first time, her hands slowly stroking the little feline now dozing on the desk. "Father sold his business and we travelled west. Father dedicated himself to making me into his 'little man' – teaching me how to walk, sit, speak, and even hold my fork in a different manner. He made me do exercises to build up muscles, and worst of all, he beat me until I no longer had tears to shed.

"We settled in San Francisco, and Father hired a couple, Haruto and Akiko Tanaka, immigrants from Japan, as our only servants. For my entire youth, I was confined to a house on Russian Hill, permitted no playmates except the occasional street ruffian Father would bring home to 'test my mettle' in a fight. If I lost, I would be punished, deprived of food or sleep, and sternly lectured about how the real Lark would never have been so weak.

"There was one thing that Father did not deprive me of, and that was books. In them, I found escape and comfort. I could imagine myself inside the stories, and when I did, I was filled with happiness. Within the pages of marvelous adventures, it did not matter if I was a girl, a boy, or somehow *both*! Soon I was inspired to write stories of my own.

"Our servants were recent converts to Christianity, and it is from them that I drew my deep faith. Had I asked them to, they would have reported my treatment to someone, perhaps a priest or a policeman. But I knew Mr. Tanaka was blamed for a man's accidental death in Edo, and there was a warrant for his arrest in his native country. My father – a war hero, a rich man, a *white* man – could surely have him deported, so we all maintained our silence.

"The Tanakas were kind to me, and they gave me priceless gifts. Mrs. Tanaka helped me understand how I could hide the feminine aspects of my body. And Mr. Tanaka is a master of *jujitsu*. He taught me new ways to fight, strategies to employ against physically stronger opponents. When I was eighteen and Father lashed out at me, I threw him across a room. Afterward, he ceased to strike me, though vile and hateful comments never stopped spewing from his lips.

"When I was twenty-two, I discovered, to my horror, that very little of Father's fortune remained for us to live on. I had often amused myself by writing stories for magazines, sending them out under pen names, and collecting a few dollars of my own. I decided to try a romance and was startled by how well it was received. The publisher demanded more. By this time, Father was a hopeless drunkard, and my one act of revenge was to publish my romances as Lark Duncan, which would have offended Father if he had retained the ability to remain sober for more than an hour. As Lark Duncan, author of ladies' books, I became the family provider."

"Why did you not leave your cruel father?" I asked.

"I suppose it is because I imbibed my Christianity in tandem with a Japanese sense of duty and reverence for ancestors. The one way I might truly honor my late brother was by caring for our shared father. I confess that more than once I considered fleeing from Father with the Tanakas, but I feared that if I did so, he would set the police upon them. They are my true parents, in spirit if not in blood, and I love them deeply. I would rather die than have anyone mistreat them.

"What are your plans now?" Holmes asked.

"I must leave this village. I did something foolish – Clearly, you know what it was."

Holmes inclined his head. "When you took possession of this house, you found a trunk or wardrobe containing women's antique clothing. You were overcome with the desire to wear a dress when no one was around."

"Exactly. When I pulled out that Regency gown, even though it was old and threadbare, I loved it. Denied female finery for my entire life, I was curious as to how I would look in it, but I dared not don it until I was certain of being alone. Finally, on a day when father and the Tanakas were out, I put on the gown and went into the garden, enjoying the warmth upon my neck and arms. I was careful to add the bonnet, for I did not wish to be sunburned on my face. I sang a bit of an old war song, but then I turned sad, thinking how I would have to put the dress away before anyone returned. I suppose I began crying, but when I heard a sound, which made me aware of my foolish risk, I bolted and nearly tripped over my skirts, since I did not instinctively gather them into my hands as I ran to hide."

"And the second day?"

"Father and the Tanakas were gone again, and I convinced myself that it was only my nerves that had sent me indoors. But this time the man – his name is Clark, I think – called out to me and I barely evaded him. He confronted me the next morning with some nonsense about how I was holding a woman captive. I bluffed as best I could with a ghost story created on the spot, but I knew it would be safer for us to move again. We have done so many times in the past, and Father cares not where we go, provided a public house, tavern, or saloon is near."

"Whatever brought you all the way to England?" I asked, still quite astonished by her tale.

"I wished to be closer to my publisher. I . . . I rather fell in love with him through the mail. It is a silly infatuation since I dare not act upon it."

"Your father will not live forever," Holmes said. "What will you do then?"

"I shall start my life anew, sir. And I will not wish Father dead, for that is uncharitable, but oh . . . how much I long to be myself, at last."

A soft mew interrupted our conversation. Miss Duncan laughed and picked up the kitten, cuddling it like a baby.

"I have spent my entire life like one of Shakespeare's ladies, hiding within a masculine role. Never once have I given myself away, and yet you knew the trap to bait for me. I adore kittens, especially white ones. Did you just assume no woman could resist such a darling creature?"

"Watson will tell you that I am no admirer of assumptions," Holmes said, with a wink in my direction. "But I had the advantage of having a conversation with a lady librarian yesterday. She is an admirer of your work and could quote long passages verbatim. It was she who observed that in every story, the heroine somehow acquired a white kitten with blue eyes. It occurred to me the kitten might be more than a convenient plot device, but rather a symbol of some deeper longing."

Miss Duncan sighed. "Sir, will you keep my secret?"

"I will. Watson?"

"Of course!"

"And I will speak with Mr. Clark. I think can convince him that you are a good neighbor."

"Thank you, sir. And this kitten . . . ."

"Please, it is a gift . . . from a most dedicated admirer."

We returned to the village. Holmes sought out Mr. Clark and informed him that Willow Hall had neither a ghost nor a prisoner for him to be concerned about, and he should allow Mr. Duncan to live in peace.

"You have my word that Lark Duncan has no designs upon your lady. He is merely a recluse who should be given the privacy he requires, so the world may continue to enjoy his literary gifts. What say you, Watson?"

"I concur. And, a bit of advice, Mr. Clark. If you show more attention to Miss Tabitha and less to Mr. Duncan, you will certainly win back your intended's affections."

The youth looked properly corrected. "You are both wise gentlemen. I will do as you say."

We strolled back to the station, where there was a half-hour's wait for our train. As we sat, a question occurred to me.

185

"Duncan claimed to have made up the story of the 'Weeping Lady' on the spot – yet Clark claimed it was one he recalled hearing in childhood!"

Holmes nodded and rattled the newspaper he was reading. "The power of suggestion is perhaps an author's greatest gift – a fact you know well, my friend! And have you ever visited an English village that lacked a ghost story? Duncan had only a toss out a seed, and Clark's imagination grew the tree."

Six weeks after our visit to Chadworth, Silas Duncan, the cruel father, collapsed at The Pig and Piper, dying before the village physician could be summoned to aid him. Mr. Lark Duncan and his servants departed the village shortly after his father's funeral. At Christmas, Mr. Jonas Clark and Miss Tabitha Bailey travelled down the aisle and began a very happy marriage which, by last count, has produced five daughters.

It was Mrs. Hudson who provided the final act in the drama. I was in the kitchen at Baker Street, asking her to prepare a feast in celebration of Holmes's latest deductive triumph, when I noticed a novel upon the table. The cover read *The Detective's Lady*, and the author was Lark Duncan.

"Why, I met this fellow once," I said.

"Ah, then consider yourself lucky," Mrs. Hudson replied. "He was a talented writer."

"Was?" I asked, with some alarm.

"Why yes – that's his final book. He died just after he wrote it." Our good landlady never looked up from the potatoes she was peeling. "But they say his sister, Dove Duncan, is equally talented. I have her first novel on order at the bookseller's – it's called *The Doctor's Mistress*. I will read both and tell you how they compare."

The Georgian Dragon
by Tim Newton Anderson

Holmes and I were in our sitting room, having consumed one of Mrs. Hudson's excellent lunches, when she ushered up a client. Holmes stood from his chair by the fire and walked over to shake the hand of the nervous gentleman who had entered the room.

"Welcome to our lodgings, Lord Ridgeway," my friend said. "I assume you wish to consult me on a matter that is both urgent and sensitive?"

"How did you know who I was?" the gentleman asked. He was of middling height with pepper-and-salt hair and a ginger beard stained around the moustache from the smoking of cigarettes. He wore an expensive tweed jacket and plus-fours, which must have been excessively warm in the August heat.

"I sometimes jest with my colleague, Dr. Watson, about his inability to observe the details of appearance which give away a man's profession and mental state," Holmes said. "However, even he couldn't fail to recognise the Coat of Arms on your carriage which sits in the street below us, or avoid noticing your state of agitation. The perspiration on your brow could have been due to the summer sunshine, but your agitation can only be the result of nervous anticipation. I can also see your tremulous grip on the leather briefcase in your hand, which suggests its contents are of considerable concern to you."

Lord Ridgeway collapsed into one of the armchairs by the fireplace, glancing anxiously around at the state of the room. His eyes flicked past the *V.R.* which my friend had inscribed with bullets above the mantelpiece, and the Persian slipper full of tobacco that sat by his clay pipe, and travelled to the table full of scientific apparatus where Holmes had been testing the properties of different types of dried blood for his latest monograph. He had recently solved a case where pig's blood had been used to soak a victim of poisoning to make the murder look like a hunting accident, and he wished to devise a quick test to differentiate human blood from those of animals.

"Although the matter on which you wish to consult me is one you feel is of a delicate nature, please have no hesitation in discussing it in front of my colleague," said Holmes. "I would trust Watson's bravery and discretion with my life, and indeed have done so on many occasions. His

187

insight has often proved invaluable in helping me when solving a case, even if his conclusions haven't always matched mine."

"I'll take your word for it," said Lord Ridgeway, "but what I have to tell you must go no further than this room, or I am ruined, as is the reputation of my family."

"I'm aware of the importance of your support for the Prime Minister in the House of Lords given his current Parliamentary problems, but your words indicate to me that this is a more personal matter."

"You have deduced correctly," said Ridgeway. "An item has been stolen that my family has guarded for generations. If its loss is discovered, it would mean I have failed to maintain a proud tradition, as well as losing one of the nation's great treasures."

"Whatever has been taken?" I asked. "Some family heirloom?"

"Worse than that," said Lord Ridgeway. "That would merely be a sad loss from which we could recover. The item that has been taken has more than sentimental or financial value. It is an un-replaceable piece of history."

"You had best tell us the whole story," said Holmes. "Beginning with the nature of the item."

"At the time the country was recovering from the Jacobite Rebellion, King George the First acquired a statue. It was a golden dragon – twelve inches high and studded with precious stones," said Ridgeway. "He was aware from the recent uprising that many opposed a Hanoverian sovereign and would prefer a relative of the late King – a Catholic rather than a protestant monarch. By referencing our patron saint – George – he felt he could rally patriotism around his name and reduce religious tension. The statue was sent on a tour around the nation, and attracted large crowds wherever it was displayed. The rumour that attached to the statue was that it had been created by the Templars during the Crusades but had been captured by the Moors, from whom it had been rescued or ransomed by King George. In fact, it is far more likely he simply commissioned it from some discreet jeweller."

"And how did the statue come into the ownership of your family?" Holmes asked.

"My ancestors have always been prominent in public life, and were key supporters of the Hanoverian monarchs," said Ridgeway. "I am sure you are aware of the reputation of the last King George for profligacy – especially in the years in which he was the Prince Regent during his father's illness. However large the allowance given him by Parliament, his spending exceeded it, and it caused great tension between him and his Prime Ministers. He approached my ancestors with a request for a loan, and offered the Golden Dragon as a guarantee. The loan was never repaid, and my family have held it on behalf of the Royal Family ever since. I suspect it had been forgotten by them, as it was never redeemed."

"And did your family never think of simply returning it to The Crown?" I asked. "Your family is wealthy, and could surely have afforded to."

"Alas, we were in no position to do so for many years," said Ridgeway. "I'm afraid to say the loan to the King had strained the family's resources to such an extent that we had to take out our own loan, again against the Dragon. What would have happened if we had defaulted, I dread to think, but fortunately some sound investments were made in shipping and manufacturing, and that loan was paid back. We would then have been able to return the statue, but my grandfather decided that since it had been created to save the monarchy in a time of crisis, unless they asked for it we would save it until they faced another time of great trouble before producing it. So far, thankfully, that has not happened. But unless it is found and returned to us, that will be impossible."

"Have the police made no progress in apprehending the culprit?" Holmes asked.

"I haven't involved them," said Lord Ridgeway. "The matter would be sure to get into the newspapers, which would be almost as bad for the family's reputation as failing to recover it. That's why I have approached you, Mr. Holmes. I read Dr. Watson's account of your work in the case of the Beryl Coronet, and wondered if you would be able to act on my behalf to get the statue back. As Dr. Watson rightly said, my family is wealthy, and we would be able to defray any costs involved."

"Are you not curious about the identity of the thief?" asked Holmes.

"Of course," replied Ridgeway, "but the recovery of the Golden Dragon is my first concern. I would be delighted if you could bring the thief to justice, but please bring the treasure back to my family's safekeeping."

He lifted his case to his knee and brought out a photograph.

"This is the sculpture," he said. "I had a photograph taken for insurance purposes, although it is, of course, priceless."

"I think you had better tell us more about the circumstances of the theft," requested Holmes.

Lord Ridgeway had relaxed considerably since relating his tale, and as Mrs. Hudson entered with some tea, gratefully raised his cup to his lips.

"I keep the statue in my safe in the library at Ridgeway Hall," he said. "It is a combination lock whose combination is known only to myself and our family lawyer. I gave him the details in case some accident befallsme"

"I only open the safe once a week or so, as I have a separate cash box for general spending and most of our money is kept in the bank. There are a few important papers in there – my will, the deeds to the hall, and suchlike – as well as some jewellery which is of no use since the death of my wife. I passed ownership to my daughter, but Claudia is something of a Bohemian – a sculptor. She told me she would never wear any of it. A shame, because if she would agree to dress in a more ladylike fashion, she might have a better chance to attract a suitable husband. I would be happy to see my daughter marry well. That is, of course, hardly relevant."

"One can never be certain what is or isn't relevant to a case of this nature," said Holmes. "You shouldn't omit the smallest detail."

"Certainly," said Ridgeway. "Anyway, I can only tell you that the dragon was stolen sometime between Monday last week and yesterday, when I opened the safe and found it was missing. Nothing else had been taken – the jewellery was still *in situ*. I believe the thief, whoever he is, knew exactly what he was looking for."

"Are the jewels of any value?" I asked.

"Some few hundred pounds," said Lord Ridgeway. "Certainly worth stealing if the thief was simply after money."

"And far easier to dispose of," said Holmes.

"That is a large part of my concern," said Ridgeway. "The statue is a unique piece which can never be sold on the open market. To melt it down would be a tragedy I scarcely dare imagine."

"Were there any clues as to how the theft had taken place?" asked Holmes.

"None," said Lord Ridgeway. "The servants and I made a thorough search of the house and the grounds, but not only was there no sign of the statue, there was none of forced entry. I questioned all of the staff who said there had been no strangers on the estate since I had last opened the safe. Neither had any of them left, and each stood testimony for at least one other that they had remained within the house and grounds. The gardeners and gamekeeper could have left unnoticed, of course, but none of them had been inside the house during this period, as they live in three cottages side by side in the grounds. Again, they stated they hadn't noticed any of the others being absent for any significant period. It's quite some distance from the nearest town – we are largely self-sufficient in terms of produce from our farm. The nearest railway station is even further away, and would require a round journey of three hours.

"I know our servants as well as I know my own family, as they have served us for generations. I cannot believe that any of them would be responsible for this. In any case, the existence of the Dragon is a secret only known to my family and has never been shared with anyone, including them."

"I wish to examine the scene for myself," said Holmes. "I have some business to conclude first, but there is a train that arrives at King's Lynn at noon tomorrow, so I would be grateful if you could arrange a carriage ride for Watson and myself to your home."

"I will attend to it as soon as I arrive back at Ridgeway Hall," Lord Ridgeway said. "I hope you're able to bring this matter to a speedy conclusion."

"I already have some thoughts about how the matter was accomplished," said Holmes. "However, I wish to check some details before I can say definitively. You may rest assured that I am confident of assuring the return of the statue. In the meantime, keep searching any departing vehicles."

As soon as Lord Ridgeway had departed, I questioned Holmes as to his thoughts.

"All in good time, Watson," he said. "First you must put on some old clothes and accompany me to Spitalfields. I would be grateful if you would bring your service revolver, but keep it well concealed about your person."

"Are we going in disguise?" I asked.

"I'm sure the person I am visiting employs people who are trained to see through any disguise," he said. "However, he operates from a dangerous part of the City, and it would be unfortunate if we were attacked en route by some criminal scenting a quick profit from some West End toffs."

After we had changed clothes, with Holmes in an outfit from his extensive collection of disguises, we set off for the East End. As soon as we entered the district, there was a dramatic change in both the houses and inhabitants. Instead of the large buildings of central London, we were surrounded by run-down tenements, often sub-divided into single rooms which would house generations of the same family, or a dozen young men or women combining their meagre wages to meet the rent.

I had put on my oldest clothes, but they could have some from Saville Row compared to the worn-out rags covering the passersby – most bent by poverty and hard manual work. I knew from past visits that some of those we passed supplemented any honest income by theft and prostitution, and their appearance belied their physical age due to the dilatory effects of drink and drugs, as well as physical hardship. When I'd had my own practice, I had sometimes donated my time and expertise to assist the sick of the borough.

The cab let us off at Spitalfields Market, unwilling to risk the side streets where they could be waylaid by opportunist thieves. Holmes led me through a maze of back alleys and courts where I'm not ashamed to admit I was somewhat nervous of our safety. My army revolver was in my greatcoat pocket, and I gripped it tightly.

At the end of one alley was a thick wooden door. The paint that covered it was flaking, but the wood underneath looked solid, and the dull sound created when Holmes knocked upon it showed it was also thick. There was a wooden window at face height which opened to expose the darkness inside. Whoever had spied outwards was obviously satisfied with our identities, and the door slowly opened to admit us to a dark corridor. The large figure behind the door stood to one side to let us enter, and followed us along its length until we reached another door which was opened to expose a large room illuminated by gaslight from sconces spread around its walls.

"Welcome again to my humble enterprise," said a man behind the large table in the centre of the room. It held two sets of scales and a number of eyepieces and magnifying glasses. Two cloth bags were also on the table, but they had been closed to hide their contents.

"Joseph Grizzard once more at your service, Mr. Holmes," the man said. "Those beryls you purchased from me were satisfactory, I trust, to bring you back to my business premises."

In contrast to the other, poorly dressed, denizens of the room, Gizzard was clad in an expensive grey suit, and looked as if he had wandered in by accident on his way to a city bank or the Inns of Court. In his mid-thirties, he was about my own height with wavy black hair and expensive cologne, which fought with the smell of his large Havana cigar. Looking round the room again, I could see that despite its initial run-down appearance, it was clean and reasonably well maintained.

"'Ere, Kemmy, is this cove Sherlock Holmes?" said one of the two large ruffians who flanked Grizzard. "Do you want me to do for 'im?"

"Mr. Holmes is here on business, Ozzy," Grizzard said. "If he was here to arrest me, he would have brought more assistance than Dr. Watson and his service revolver. Is that not right, Mr. Holmes?"

"I am merely here to ask some questions?" Holmes said. "At present your activities are none of my concern, although I should warn you that if you move from disposing of stolen goods to commissioning their robbery, we may very well find ourselves at odds."

"Duly noted," said Grizzard. "While the interest of the police force is something I can deal with as a normal hazard in my line of business, I wouldn't relish attracting your attention. Our last meeting was profitable to us both, according to the Doctor's published account, and I trust this will be too."

His voice had a faint hint of a Germanic accent under the carefully cultivated tones. I suspected his parents were émigrés.

"Have you heard of the Georgian Dragon?" Holmes asked. My friend showed no sign of nervousness in this criminal den. Indeed, he seemed to be relishing the prospect of a verbal duel with the fence.

"May have," said Grizzard. "One hears all sorts of things in my line of business. Why do you ask?"

"It is a matter of some academic interest," said Holmes.

"What you mean is, do I have it?" said Grizzard. "I can tell you for free that I don't, although if you require more information there will be, shall we say, a small fee for helping you with your inquiries."

"You have already told me all I need to know," said Holmes. He glanced at the table. "Thank you for your hospitality. The diamonds in those bags are from the Hatton Garden robbery, I presume. You should know that Mr. Welstead's accomplice is already in police custody, and Mr. Welstead will almost certainly be arrested as soon as he's back on the streets. That information is also free, and what you do with it is up to you."

Grizzard gave an angry look to the man on the other side of the table, who I presumed was Welstead. Holmes smiled, nodded to Grizzard, and took my elbow to usher me back to the street. Once there, I asked him about the meeting.

"What did you mean when you told him he had told you everything?" I asked. "All he said was that he didn't have the statue. Surely you cannot believe what he said?"

"It was not *what* he said, but the *way* he said it," Holmes said. "Grizzard is one of the premier fences in the City, and he has achieved that position by keeping calm in the face of questioning. However, there was no disguising the glint of excitement in his eyes when I mentioned the Dragon, which means he doesn't have it, but wishes he did. I'm sure he will be sending his men out to try and locate it as soon as he has sent Welstead packing with his stolen goods. Welstead's partner is, in fact, actually still at large, but I had heard a rumour he was behind the Hatton Gardens robbery, so I took a calculated risk. Hopefully the police will now be able to arrest him before he finds someone else to dispose of the jewels."

"If you're correct, Grizzard doesn't have the stature, but surely there are other dealers in stolen goods who may have it in their possession," I said.

"Grizzard has told us that isn't the case by what he didn't say," said Holmes. "There is no love lost between him and his rivals, and if he knew one of them had it, he would have told us. As far as he is concerned, the fewer competitors he has, the better. I believe whoever took the statue still has it in his possession. From Lord Ridgeway's description, it isn't something that can easily be sold, and there aren't many people with

Grizzard's connections who would be able to find a discreet private buyer able to pay something approaching its true value. If there was a buyer behind the theft, Grizzard would have been approached. We know the motive was not simple robbery – Ridgeway told us the jewellery was still *in situ* – so we can discount an opportunist who has melted the statue down. I will make reservations on the next train to Ridgeway Hall, and we'll set off first thing tomorrow."

Holmes and I arrived at King's Cross Station at nine the next morning and we boarded the train. As per his instructions, I had packed an overnight bag, but he had assured me we wouldn't need to be armed. When we gained our carriage, he opened his own bag and pulled out a large bundle of newspaper cuttings which he read in silence. I questioned him on his thoughts, but he brushed off the question, saying he was confident all would become clear to me when we arrived at our destination.

"I have been reading about Lord Ridgeway's daughter," he said. "A fascinating young lady. She was due to attend the usual round of coming-out balls a few years ago, but publically denounced them as nothing more than a flesh market. Since then, she has also denounced the peerage, the government, and male domination of the professional world in general. In fact, she's as well known for espousing the cause of female emancipation as she is for the excellence of her sculptures and paintings. I'm very much looking forward to meeting her."

"She sounds like a bit of a dragon, herself," I suggested.

As Lord Ridgeway had promised, a pony and trap was waiting for us at the station, and the smiling servant placed our bags in the back of the vehicle and set off towards the manor house.

"Are all of the family and servants present at the house?" Holmes asked the man, whose name was Abel Baker.

"Yes, sir," he replied. "His Lordship insisted. We have had some deliveries of supplies, but his Lordship has checked them all in and made sure the baskets and carriers' carts were empty when they left."

"Good," said Holmes. "I had suggested as such to his Lordship."

Ridgeway House was an impressive sight as we commenced the long drive up the tree-lined entranceway. Originally a Tudor Mansion, it had been extensively remodelled during the Georgian period when the family's finances were at their peak, before their loan left them in more straightened circumstances. It wasn't the grandest stately home I had visited with Holmes, but it was certainly one of the most imposing.

We were greeted at the front door by Lord Ridgeway's butler, Wilson. His suit was jet black, rather than the family colours of grey and red, and I momentarily wondered if he were in mourning for the loss of the family treasure. He placed our bags in the dark oak-lined hallway and ushered us through to the drawing room, where Lord Ridgeway was pacing in anticipation of Holmes arrival.

"Do you have any news for me?" he asked. "Is it recovered?"

"Not yet, but I would ask you to have faith," my companion answered. "I believe I'll be able to bring this matter to a speedy and satisfactory conclusion."

I couldn't see how Holmes could make such a bold assertion on the basis of what I had witnessed of his inquiries so far, but I knew from experience not to doubt his expertise. I nodded in assent to give the client further reassurance.

"May I see the location of the crime?" Holmes asked. "There are a few matters I wish to clarify before I can share my conclusions."

Lord Ridgeway was about to usher us into the library when a young woman of striking appearance entered the drawing room. Dressed in a floaty purple dress, and with red hair bound in black ribbons, she wore a paint-splattered apron over the front of her clothes. I should describe her features as handsome rather than beautiful, and the resemblance to Lord Ridgeway was easy to ascertain.

"This will be your famous detective," she said. "I have read of your exploits, Mr. Holmes, and find them entertaining, but sadly behind the times in many of your attitudes. The only woman who is represented as being in any way independent is Irene Adler, and though you profess to admire her, she is still written in a way that questions her choices in dealing with a world where men have all the power."

"My daughter, Claudia," said Lord Ridgeway, "believes women should have the vote."

"And be able to accede to titles and sit in the House of Lords," she said. "My father is disappointed I will not be able to carry on the family name."

"You may criticise my opinion of the female sex," said Holmes, "but in fact I believe many women are as capable of voting intelligently as most men. I have been engaged in a number of cases where our current laws relating to women's ability to have control over their own property have tempted men to treat them badly to take their estates."

"Surely you must approve of our Queen," I said to the girl, "who has presided over a golden age while holding the highest office in the land."

"And what has she done with her privilege to help other women?" Claudia Ridgeway countered.

"I'm sure Mr. Holmes and Dr. Watson can argue politics later, Daughter," said Lord Ridgeway. "First, he must solve the theft of the Dragon. I'm taking him to see the safe in the library."

"Then I'll return to my art and leave you *men* to it," she responded, striding out of the room.

"Fascinating," said Holmes. "Exactly as I would have imagined her from the newspaper clippings describing her work in art and politics. A formidable personality."

The library had the same dark oak panels and beams as the rest of the house, along with many floor-to-ceiling bookcases filled with leather-bound volumes. As most were in uniform editions, I believe they had been purchased for decoration rather than to read. The exceptions were well-worn law journals near a large desk and chair at one end of the room. Lord Ridgeway and many of his ancestors had pursued the legal profession.

"The safe is behind here," he said. "The key is kept locked in a drawer in my desk, and the key to that is always on my person – hanging from my watch chain."

Holmes walked first to the windows and tried to pull one open without success.

"I'm afraid they have been warped shut for many years," said Lord Ridgeway. "My father and then myself never saw any reason to fix them, as the thick walls keep those room at an even temperature throughout the year."

Holmes then continued to the safe, which was built into the wall behind the desk.

"I assume you also saw no reason to replace this with a more-modern version," he said. "While solid, this safe would be child's play for any competent cracksman to open."

"I keep little cash and few items of jewellery in the house," explained Lord Ridgeway.

"Only a precious national heirloom," replied Holmes. He had taken out his magnifying glass and was closely examining the safe and the carpet around it. He gave a smile of satisfaction.

"But it is as I said," said Ridgeway, "no one outside the family and servants know of it, and a common burglar would also have taken the cash and jewels."

"Can we assume from your statements about your daughter's lack of interest in the jewels and papers that she does not visit the safe regularly?" Holmes asked.

"I cannot recall her ever doing so," said Ridgeway.

"Then we must visit your daughter's studio," said Holmes.

"But surely you don't suspect her?" his Lordship expostulated. "She has no need for money. Why, aside from the family wealth, she is a successful artist whose paintings and sculpture sell for hundreds of pounds."

196

"Nevertheless," said Holmes, "would you be so good as to take me to her?"

Lord Ridgeway didn't look happy about any suggestion that his daughter might be involved, but reluctantly led us from the study to the rear of the house, where we found his daughter in a converted orangery.

I am no connoisseur of art, but could see that she had considerable talent. Canvases lay against walls to dry, and there were a number of bronze and marble statuettes on the floor. She was clearly influenced by the Pre-Raphaelites, as her art featured myths and legends as their subjects. I recognised that most featured female gods and strong women from literature and history. In a large table in the centre of the room was a phoenix arising from a base of flame, it had been created in plaster of Paris prior to being moulded and cast in bronze. It was magnificent as it arose reborn, and seemed to climb into the air as if alive.

Claudia Ridgeway herself was busy adding details to the sculpture with a knife – feathers and flames. Her strong jaw was clenched in concentration. She had donned an artist's smock to protect her dress from paint or plaster.

"A splendid creation," said Holmes. "I know little of art, but can see the inspiration and skill in the work. You should be proud of your daughter, Lord Ridgeway."

"People tell me she has a great talent," he said. "But it takes too much of her time. There is an estate to run, and a proud family to continue."

Holmes walked around the table, admiring the statue from all angles.

"Am I right in assuming you were planning to return the Dragon to The Crown on the occasion of the Diamond Jubilee in two years' time?" Holmes asked.

"How the devil did you know?" asked Ridgeway.

"An elementary assumption," said Holmes. "You are no longer in need of the return of the loan, and I'm aware of your continuing political ambitions – Lord Chancellor perhaps. Such a public and magnanimous gesture would do much to further that."

"I make no secret of my hopes," Lord Ridgeway said.

"I'm sure your daughter in particular is aware of them," Holmes said.

He walked across to the unlit stove that warmed the room in winter and picked up a large iron poker. Striding back to the table, he struck the phoenix a heavy blow and shattered it.

"Vandal!" screamed Claudia Ridgeway. "What are you doing?"

Holmes dropped the poker and swept away the broken plaster. Underneath was a splendid golden statue covered in precious stones: The Dragon.

197

"I agree it is a shame to destroy such a splendid work," said Holmes, "but I'm sure a person of your talent can recreate it. I believe this is what you have been looking for, Lord Ridgeway."

"Claudia!" he gasped. "Why? How?"

"Because this family cares more for status and power than for the people of this country," she said. "This statue was created to shore up a monarchy that did little for those it was supposed to serve. Our ancestors did the same injustice by helping a monarch who was ruining the nation with his profligacy, and if you achieve office, you will be content to continue the *status quo*, rather than helping the women and who are unjustly deprived of the right to say who runs Britain. You believe my only role should be to provide you with grandchildren, despite my talents and you would have all women tied to the hearth."

"But why steal it?" Lord Ridgway asked.

"Steal it?" said Claudia. "I merely moved it to another place of safekeeping. I had a thought I might offer it to the Queen myself in return for support for women's suffrage. She may only rule in name, but adding her voice to the cause may have some positive effect."

"I presume you have no wish to get the police involved in this matter?" said Holmes. "Lady Claudia is correct in stating that no actual crime has been committed. I would also think twice about taking any other punitive action. As you said, she is more than capable of making her own way in the world, and the return of the dragon would be a poor exchange for the loss of a daughter."

Lord Ridgeway *harrumphed* and stormed out of the orangery.

"How did you know, Mr. Holmes," asked Claudia Ridgeway.

"I knew from my inquiries that it was extremely unlikely that a professional or amateur thief had taken the statue," he said. "My examination of the library confirmed that there had been no forced entry. Therefore, someone inside the property had taken the statue. Lord Ridgeway told me that you never used the safe, yet there was plaster of Paris on the floor next to it – I assume you wore your smock. It was therefore a matter of finding the statue's hiding place. I assumed you were mixing plaster before you did the deed, and the statue seemed a perfect size to conceal the Dragon. It would have been a shame to destroy such a splendid creation had I been in error, but I was secure in my deduction."

"I am uncertain whether my father will ever forgive me," she said.

"And I am sure he will return when he calms down," I said. "Holmes is an excellent judge of character, and I believe he is correct in stating your father loves you in his own way."

"I am also sure you are correct," said Claudia Ridgeway. "I'm afraid I thought up my plan to get him to take me seriously as a person, rather

198

than a poor substitute for the son he hoped would carry on the name. It may take him some time to see that, but he will come around in the end. He may be stubborn, but he is a good man."

Indeed, when Holmes and I left the orangery and walked back towards the front door, Lord Ridgeway met us and thrust a cheque into my friend's hand.

"I don't share my daughter's beliefs, but I acknowledge her actions stemmed from genuine convictions," he said. "I am grateful to you for resolving this situation without bringing embarrassment on the family."

"Your daughter is an impressive woman," said Holmes. "You would do well to take her seriously, or risk losing a great asset to your family."

On the train back to London, I asked Holmes if Claudia Ridgeway would now join Irene Adler in the small list of women he admired.

"It isn't a matter of admiration or respect," said Holmes. "I extend those to all who use their talents to the full to improve the world, man or woman. I expect great things from Lady Ridgeway and look forward to her career with interest. However, for me there is only one woman who has bested me so far, and for that she will always be '*The Woman*'."

"'Why, dash it all!' said he, 'I've let them go at six-hundred for the three!' I soon managed to get the address of the receiver who had them, on promising him that there would be no prosecution. Off I set to him, and after much chaffering I got our stones at £1,000 apiece.
"The Beryl Coronet"

The Adventure of the Stradivarius
by Steven Connelly

"You should, Watson," said Holmes, "tell your readers about the Stradivarius matter, as it really does have certain aspects to it that lend itself towards your literary habits of embellishment . . . ."

He returned to scratching on his own violin tunelessly. I turned to pen and paper and reached into my dispatch box for some notes I had made on the case he mentioned . . . .

For those regular readers of Sherlock Holmes's cases, one might believe that every narrative began with someone bursting into our rooms at 221b Baker Street with a perplexing story to tell or problem needing unraveling, but this wasn't always the case.

I recall that it was a glorious summer evening in early August 1895. We had spent the day at the Old Bailey, with myself as an observer and Holmes as a witness in the case against Patrick Cairns in the sensational murder of Peter Carey. As we nodded our heads goodbye to Carey's wife and daughter, Holmes and I decided on a gentle stroll back down Fleet Street. We watched the masses bustling in and out of the offices like worker bees at a hive, churning out the stories that were like nectar to Holmes and his unquenching thirst for criminal misdeeds.

And so onwards we walked, buying some tobacco and, having worked up quite an appetite, we decided to stop at Simpsons in the Strand for a spot of dinner. We sat in the upper room, and it was over the courses of julienne soup, *filet de soles*, spring chicken, and a dessert of Charlotte Russe, all the while Holmes perused a copy of *The London Evening Standard* as I gazed outside at the pedestrians, cabs, and coaches that filled the early evening air with that familiar cacophony of the city, that I looked up I could see a glint in my friend's eyes.

"What is it?" I asked.

He looked towards me. "I believe that crime sometimes creeps in like the tide, slowly and inevitably towards us. There are currently crimes happening many miles away that, mark my words, within a few months will be knocking on our door." He enigmatically refused to elaborate any further on the matter, and I quickly forgot as Holmes told me of his plans to at least provide poor Patrick Cairns with some degree of comfort, with

200

plans to send him a regular supply of tobacco and rum while he awaited his execution at Newgate Prison.

Two months later found us both in our Baker Street rooms. Holmes was deep in a chemical analysis, while I was writing up notes on the recent cases that had involved us, including the peculiar incident of the Colchester corpse, and the mysterious Hatton Garden jewelry thefts, which Holmes solved without much effort and to the extreme embarrassment of Inspector Lestrade, who had incorrectly arrested a worker in one of the shops.

The smells of cooking were wafting up the stairs, and I was just considering what culinary delights Mrs. Hudson would soon be bustling through our sitting room door, when we heard a loud peal from the front doorbell.

Soon a dapper stocky little man of around fifty with a prominent mustache presented himself. He was carrying a violin case. He looked at both of us in turn and spoke in excellent English, with a hint of an accent.

"Mr. Holmes?" Not looking up, my friend bid the gentleman to sit while he finished his experiment.

I introduced myself, offered him a chair, and then we sat in silence for a few minutes until Holmes finally, with an exasperated sigh, set down a test tube and looked up and around at our guest.

He then gave a slight smile and said the most astonishing words to this man, clearly unknown to both myself or him. "I can see you were born in France, you have lived in England most of your life, you own a restaurant, and have recently purchased a fake violin from a very fat man for an exorbitant price."

The man and I both looked astonished, but he finally found his voice and exclaimed, "It is all true! But how can you know all of this?"

Holmes shrugged off the question and in reply stated, "All I still need to know from you is your name, and what restaurant you own."

"I am Monsieur Jacques Jonquet, the proprietor of The Cafe Bordeaux in Piccadilly."

"Please hand me the violin for examination while you tell us your no-doubt interesting tale."

I poured the little man a brandy, lit his cigarette, and bid him to commence his story. Meanwhile, Holmes picked up a magnifying glass and prepared to examine the violin case.

"It was a busy evening service," explained Jonquet, "when a very fat man came and ate by himself. He had with him this violin case."

Holmes interrupted him. "Please describe him and his clothing precisely."

Monsieur Jonquet complied. "He was in his mid-thirties, about five-feet-six-inches, very fat, with sandy-coloured hair that had started to thin at the temples, and a well-spoken English accent. He wore a slightly tight-fitting but once-fashionable black suit. When he finished his meal, the waiter presented him with the bill, and I could see the two having a conversation. The waiter then beckoned me to come over, which I did. The man, who explained that his name was Mr. Smith, said he had left his billfold in his nearby hotel. He asked if he would be excused to collect it, and offered to leave his violin as guarantee. He said it probably had no great value, but it had been left to him in his uncle's will, that he'd just collected it, and that he was probably going to sell it, but that it certainly had a value more than commensurable to the meal."

The little man, who had paused to look over at Holmes, then continued. "His appearance and speech were that of a respectable Englishman, and I saw the violin inside was certainly worth more than the price of the meal, so I agreed to await his return."

Holmes looked up from his minute examination of the violin and said, "And then you met the tall thin man?"

Jonquet again looked startled. "How could you – " he started. "Were you there?"

Holmes merely smiled, looked back to at the violin, and said, "Pray, don't let me interrupt your most illuminating story."

Jonquet took a moment or two to regain his composure. I offered to top up his brandy.

"It was just as you say," he began. "Some fifteen minutes after Mr. Smith had gone to collect his billfold from his hotel, a tall thin man came into the restaurant, enquiring about my best table for a party of six that forthcoming Saturday. I replied that – "

"Description please" interjected Holmes, without looking up.

"He was a respectable well-spoken gentleman, just over six-feet tall, and very thin, with short brown neat hair. He was beautifully dressed in a well-tailored dark-blue Savile Row suit. My first impressions were that he was some sort of diplomat, very charismatic and used to getting his way in life."

Jonquet paused and took a long drink of his brandy before continuing. "At this point, for the first time, the tall man seemed to perceive the violin case placed behind my station. He picked it up and opened it, saying, 'Oh my, is that what I think it is?'

"I can honestly tell you that I had no idea what he was talking about. He then opened the case, turned the violin over, and murmured appreciatively. 'Do you know what you have here, my good man?' he asked me.

"'No,' I replied.

"'This is a Stradivarius. It is quite rare, and – ' He lowered his voice. 'Needless to say, quite valuable. Would you be willing to sell it?' He then presented a card to me, which read – "

Holmes reached out a long thin arm for the card, taking and examining it underneath his magnifying glass. "Best quality paper," he said. "No other distinguishing features."

He then handed it to me. I read aloud: "'*Percy Hill, Expert in Antiques and Restoration, 12 Bruton Street, WC*'."

Holmes went back to the violin, turning it to examine the inside through the *f*-holes.

I urged Monsieur Jonquet to continue his extraordinary narrative, and he looked at both me and Holmes before continuing, "I explained to him that I would gladly sell it to him, but it wasn't mine to sell. I then explained to him about Mr. Smith and how it had been left in his uncle's will. Mr. Hill then told me that he would have waited to buy the violin, but he had an urgent appointment and was already running late, with none other than a minor royal who wished to purchase a diamond brooch he owned. He then asked me to give Mr. Smith his card and told me to tell him to bring it around to his shop.

"He went on to explain that he hadn't had time to examine the Stradivarius in detail, but it was most likely the prized Molitor Stradivarius, once owned by none other than Napoleon Bonaparte, and if substantiated, he would offer the owner four-thousand pounds for it. He then confirmed his table booking and rushed from the shop."

Jonquet then stopped, as Holmes had finished studying the violin and was staring at him intently.

"Was that when you first started having thoughts of greed?" Holmes asked.

Jonquet looked sheepish. "Yes. I admit that I thought if I could get what Mr. Smith thought of as an instrument of low value for a relatively small price and sell it to Mr. Hill, then I could open a second restaurant sooner than I had expected. I do admit a certain guilt which continued until I saw Mr. Smith return about twenty minutes later to pay his bill. I assuaged my guilt by thinking that he would welcome a very good price on something he had received for free and didn't value. I also surmised that he would probably only sell it to someone who would recognise it for what it was and offer a fraction of what I would."

Droplets of sweat had appeared on his forehead, and I again re-poured his drink, whereupon he swallowed half in one gulp before continuing.

"I asked Mr. Smith back into my office and told him that I had my granddaughter's birthday coming up, and that I wished her to take up an instrument. I explained that his visit had been fortunate, and perhaps he wished to sell the instrument? He admitted he had no use for the violin, but to his untrained eye it looked old and he wouldn't accept less than three-hundred pounds. He had looked at me with such a look of hope, longing, and cunning that I would accept such a ridiculously high sum that it led me to negotiate with him for form's sake. We agreed upon the price of two-hundred-seventy-five and, with an exasperated sigh, I relented, stating that my granddaughter must have it.

"Then I went to my safe, withdrew the money, and wrote a receipt. When we had it witnessed, we concluded the purchase. He looked delighted, as though he had completed a wonderful transaction, and quickly left before I could change my mind. For my own part, I couldn't tell you how delighted I was with myself – so much so that I took the violin home and spent the next few hours in front of the fire just staring at this thing of beauty, probably once owned by France's greatest hero. I couldn't wait to go to Mr. Hill's shop the next day, determined that I wouldn't settle for just four-thousand pounds, or accept his first offer. Oh, Mr. Holmes, I can't tell you the excitement I felt that evening!"

My friend chuckled. "And then when you went to the address in Brunton Street to find that the business wasn't there."

"Yes! How did you know?"

"It's my business to have an exact knowledge of London," Holmes replied, "and I know all of the shops in the West End, certainly enough to know that there is no antiques shop under the ownership of a Mr. Percy Hill."

Jonquet looked dismayed. "Then what am I to do now?"

My friend looked at him sternly. "You have learned a valuable life lesson about greed. If something appears too good to be true, then it is. As for your money, it is gone. We'll eventually catch the men that duped you, and when we do our fee will be a dinner at your fine restaurant at your expense. You, however, will at least have the pleasure of knowing these men face jail time, and you will appear as a witness to their trial."

"I agree," the little man said, "but one thing I cannot see is how you knew why I'm here, and about the violin, and about those men."

I agreed with Jonquet, *but* having known my friend for many years, I knew if he explained how he knew it would seem to be simplicity itself, and the illusion of magic would dissipate. How Holmes could see what others didn't never ceased to work its wonder on me. For people seeing it for the first time, it appeared to be witchcraft.

"Don't worry how I knew," Holmes replied. "The important thing for you is that I do." And with those words, Holmes swiftly ushered Jonquet out of the room and downstairs.

I had many questions I wanted to ask, but I knew Holmes's habits of old. When he resumed his chair, he tucked his legs beneath him and silently proceeded to pack his pipe, a sure sign that he meant to meditate silently and reach a solution to a case, the beginning of which I couldn't even grasp.

To keep my mind from dwelling on the matter, I reached for a favourite Clark Russell novel and quickly became absorbed in it. I must have fallen asleep, as when I awoke, Holmes was gone, and I saw that Mrs. Hudson had left a plate of cold meats for me on the dining table.

I didn't see Holmes for the next three days, as he was involved on a number of other cases, but breakfast on the fourth morning brought to Baker Street both Holmes and a welcome visitor in the shape of our friend, the rising figure at Scotland Yard, Inspector Stanley Hopkins, who was indebted to Holmes for helping to solve a few of his cases and, in turn, always keeping him abreast of any developments or interesting cases at the Yard.

I took the opportunity to congratulate Hopkins on his recent exploits in taking down Ezekiel Gotlieb and his young gang of pickpockets who had plagued the fashionable West End for many months, and whose capture I had read about in the newspapers.

"Thank you, Doctor," Hopkins replied, "but I couldn't have done it without a little additional assistance." As he said this, he had looked up at Holmes. I then turned inquiringly to my friend, but he merely smiled and changed the subject.

"Now, Hopkins, I require some assistance from the Yard. I would be most grateful if you could arrange for constables from each station – from Land's End to Dover – to call at each and every musical instrument maker and enquire if they have supplied an order of replica Stradivarius Violins to either a very fat or thin gentleman in the past six months. I myself have visited every maker in London these past three days, to no success."

"Of course," Hopkins said. "But to what end, Mr. Holmes? It's a big job."

Holmes went on to explain about Monsieur Jonquet's curious case, and I used this opportunity to finally ask, "By the way, how did you know one was fat and one thin?"

Holmes smiled and said, "You remember a few months ago, I said that crime was like a tide washing towards our shore? Well thanks to news agencies, I've found similar stories printed in far-flung places like Glasgow and Cardiff. I'd been reading of a series of similar crimes perpetrated by two con men along the seaside towns of the south coast, and I knew that when the summer season was over, we would see this pair spring up in London."

"You astound me. So you were expecting them?"

"Yes," my friend replied, "and they'll strike again soon while the iron is hot. But remember – these are clever men who will be on their guard, with the wariness senses of gazelles. However, our advantages are that they don't know we're on their trail, and also we know their *modus operandi* – that is, visiting French Restaurants."

"How will that help us?" asked Hopkins.

"We wait like spiders and – " Holmes raised an eyebrow. "No disrespect Hopkins, but I have my best men – well, boys – on the job."

"You mean the Irregulars?" I asked.

"Yes. As we speak, they've been sitting and watching for the past two days, across the road from all of the expensive French restaurants, each one selling newspapers and matches, and generally blending in invisibly as though they were bricks in the wall, collecting their usual daily fee and a Guinea reward for the successful Irregular who spots them. As soon as the fat man is located, they'll send a telegram to me here, and I plan to hasten there and follow him back to his lair. Also, if you look outside, you'll see Wiggins with his hansom, waiting at my call."

Wiggins was, by this point, a strong weather-beaten young man of four-and-twenty, tall and rugged, but with a quick wit and charm. He had outgrown the Irregulars, but as to how he could have afforded a hansom at such a young age I didn't know. I rather suspect my friend was behind it. Moreover, I also suspected that it was to the great benefit of Holmes having a driver that knew every street as well as he did, and also had access to every scrap of gossip and criminality that was happening within the city's streets. Wiggins was currently hired exclusively for Holmes as he went about his investigations.

I went to the window and saw him sitting upright at the driver's seat smoking a pipe. While observing this scene, I observed Mrs. Hudson taking him a mug of tea and a sandwich, for which he rewarded her with a huge grin. Mrs. Hudson had grown exceedingly fond of Wiggins after he had finally learned to remove his dirty boots before going up to see Holmes when still an Irregular. She was delighted to see him move up in the world, and never missed an opportunity to mother him in his not-infrequent Baker Street appearances.

After a pipe, Inspector Hopkins took his leave to return to Scotland Yard and send off instructions to the various South Coast police stations in the search for the violin maker. Holmes also asked him to keep a couple of strong constables free to assist when he had tracked down the two men's hideout.

At six o'clock, I was called to an urgent case from one of my nearby regular patients who was complaining of a recurring malady. By seven, I had reassured myself that it was a simple case, prescribed some medication, and returned to Baker Street to find both my friend and Wiggins gone.

My curiosity in the matter led to such a distraction that I found myself unable to concentrate on anything for more than a minute. I stood by the windows smoking more than I usually allowed myself in a day. I paced back and forth in the sitting room. I tried to read a medical journal, but barely took in a word. Would Holmes send for me? In a final effort to distract myself, I decided to take out and spend twenty minutes cleaning and oiling my trusty revolver that had certainly seen more action in London than it had ever had overseas

Darkness had descended into Baker Street when I felt someone gently shake me, and I awoke to find Holmes looking down on me.

"What time is it? What happened? Did you catch them?"

"Watson, one question at a time please. Move over by the fire while we light our pipes, and then I'll give you a full account of the matter."

We seated ourselves in our armchairs and I waited until we had our pipes alight. In a fug of smoke, Holmes began. "About twenty minutes after you had gone, I received a telegram from young Johnston, who had been observing L'Escargot in King William Street near the Monument, informing me that our fat man was seen to enter. Wiggins made excellent speed along the Euston Road and down The City Road, reaching our destination within forty-five minutes of receiving the message. We arrived just in time to be told by Johnston that the fat man had left about five minutes previously. I paid Johnston and told him to wait and follow the thin man when he departed.

"And you went in to wait for the thin man to show up?" I asked.

"Yes. I bid Wiggins to wait nearby and entered the restaurant. I sat at the nearest table I could find to the entrance and awaited the appearance of the thin man. There, within plain sight, was a familiar looking violin case. The thin man didn't disappoint either, and some ten minutes later he arrived, smartly dressed as Monsieur Jonquet described. His interaction took less than five minutes and off he scurried. Almost if upon a stage production, a quarter-of-an-hour later brought back the fat man. The owner now treated him like a long lost relative, and they went to a back office, doubtless to conclude a deal on the violin."

"He was soon back, and then he went straight outside. I knew they would probably be meeting together nearby. I followed with a plan of myself tackling the thin man and Wiggins the fat man. One thing that area doesn't lack is plenty of policemen on the beat, so I knew there would be help if required."

Holmes stopped his narrative and took a long puff of his pipe while staring into the fire. "And this is when the readers of your tales think I'm infallible."

"Why?" I asked. "What happened?"

"I told you these two had senses for danger like prey. We followed the fat man almost until we almost reached The Bank of England when he suddenly jumped into a cab. There was no sign of the thin man, and Wiggins and I had no time to return to his cab. I shouted for Wiggins to leave me and I dashed for the nearest available cab. By the time we commenced, the other cab was about two-hundred feet in front and making haste. We kept this distance down past St. Paul's, up past Barts, and beyond Smithfield. In Little Italy, however, my quarry discharged from his cab, slipped down an alleyway, and quickly became quite lost to me in the throng of people out in the evening London crowds. I curse my stupidity, and can only hope Johnston was more successful than me."

We had to wait about half-an-hour for our answer when there was a knock on the door and Mrs. Hudson came up the stairs. "Mr. Holmes, there's a young boy to see you, and he's quite a dreadful sight. I have him lying on my chaise lounge. Please bring your medical bag, Doctor." At this she scurried back down to her rooms, and we quickly followed.

Upon arrival, we found Johnston in quite the described state. He had a blackened eye and dried blood on his chin from a burst lip. Further examination thankfully showed nothing more serious than a missing incisor tooth and a few bruises from which he would soon recover.

"I'm sorry!" Johnston cried at the sight of Holmes. "I followed him to the end of the street, and he turned into an alleyway. I hurried down through the dark, and suddenly there he was behind me, and he grabbed me. He wanted to know why I was following him. I didn't answer and he bashed me proper, demanding answers. Luckily a workman came down the alley at that moment and he released his grasp on me. I took the opportunity and ran."

It was quite the disappointing end to what had promised to be a very interesting case.

As for the fat and thin men, they clearly knew someone was after them and simply vanished, no doubt leaving the Metropolis well behind. The next few days brought Inspector Hopkins with further bad news: The search for the violin maker had been unsuccessful.

I wrote up notes for the case and put it in my ever expanding folder of unsolved cases. "You really should reveal all those unsolved cases,

Watson," Holmes said while watching me write. "It would certainly burst that bubble of faultlessness you have built around my exploits."

Other cases came and went over the following year, including the St. James's Park kidnapping, and the Greenwich Naval Case, which I may one day be allowed to publish. He didn't mention them again, but I knew my friend keenly scoured the papers every day for any news of his elusive con men.

We were sitting by the cozy fireplace in our rooms in the late autumn of 1896, with the first wintery tendrils creeping across London, when we had a visitor bringing Holmes the most welcome news. This was Wiggins, and he burst into the rooms almost like the Wiggins of old. "Mr. Holmes, you'll never guess who I picked up in my cab at King's Cross Station this evening!"

"A very fat man," replied Holmes, "and also a very thin man."

I looked on, astounded, as I had almost forgotten that pair of rogues.

"Yes, and I have the address that I took them to," replied Wiggins. "In Dean Street, near Soho Square."

Holmes looked as delighted as I had ever seen him, "By Jove, what extraordinary luck! We cannot let them get away again. There is no time to lose. The game is afoot! "

With that, Holmes retired to his room and within ten minutes reappeared in front of us as a stock-and-trade British tradesman. "Now, Wiggins, take me to the address and we'll do some reconnaissance. Watson, my friend, sometimes your assistance is invaluable and other times a hindrance. In this case, it's the latter. You're far too conspicuous."

With a slight bow, both he and Wiggins departed.

For the next two days, Holmes didn't return, and I heard nothing from him. I kept myself busy with some medical cases and spent the evenings reading and writing while awaiting word from my friend.

On the third day I received a telegram from him, asking me to be available that evening at six o'clock and to bring both my medical bag, a change of clothing for him, and my revolver. This, I will admit, stirred my emotions, and 5:30 p.m. found me watching the road in anticipation.

When Wiggins arrived and we commenced our journey, I took the opportunity to grill him on the events since I had last seen Holmes.

Wiggins explained that Holmes had managed to rent a room on the opposite side of the street from the duo's address in Dean Street. From behind a curtain, he was able to observe the comings and goings of the pair, but due to his previous experiences, he didn't actively follow them.

He did, however, have the Irregulars placed outside every main junction and expensive restaurant in the West End.

Wiggins left me at Soho Square and, quite the medical man with bag in hand, I walked to the address indicated. The door deftly opened and Holmes guided me to a first-floor room, which was entirely in darkness. We stood by the window and watched the scene across the road. "They occupy the street-facing room on the first floor," Holmes said. "I've been watching their comings and goings." He produced a small telescope. He handed it to me and slightly moved the curtain, beckoning me to observe their lighted room. From here we could see a scene which could almost be myself and Holmes, except for the difference being that the bigger man was much bulkier than me. They were seated either side of a fireplace and both smoking cigars. The thin man was talking animatedly and gesticulating. The fat man was laughing at whatever was being said.

"They are quite set in their habits," Holmes explained. "They have lunch and dinner in a cafe in Old Compton Street, and will have a seemingly innocuous stroll thereafter. I know they have been casing high-class restaurants and, just this afternoon, I saw the thin man return to their room with what appeared to be small packages under his arm. My hypothesis is that these will be their means of extracting monies from the greedy restaurant owners."

I asked Holmes why he hadn't just arranged for the men to be picked up by Hopkins or Lestrade while dining at the café.

"Watson, dear fellow," he replied, "a medical man like yourself should know that the memory has a habit of forgetting, especially if time has passed. If we put either of these two men in a police lineup with other fat and thin men and show them to Monsieur Jonquet, do you think he will pick them out over a year later? No, we cannot take the risk. I want to catch these felons red-handed."

"What's the plan?" I asked.

"Again we wait. We wait, and when they attend any one of the expensive West End restaurants which fit their usual method, we'll be waiting.

When, at seven, we saw both of the men leave their room carrying a small wrapped-up parcel, Holmes sprang into action. "They have their prop. Now it's our chance to snare a couple of rabbits." He then stepped out to send a telegram message to Scotland Yard from a nearby post office. Within thirty minutes, we found ourselves in the presence of Inspector Hopkins and six strapping young constables.

"So," said Hopkins, "we are finally to catch our men."

"Yes," said my friend, "and I most certainly look forward to a conversation with that pair."

Holmes bid two policemen to stay by the windows in our room, and when the two men returned they should go across to guard the front door, thus blocking off their means of escape. Two further men were directed to the back yard, and the last two to remain on the other building's second floor landing.

Holmes, an expert locksmith, picked the door locks as easily as if he had used a key. Holmes, Hopkins, and I soon found our way to the pair's room and noiselessly entered. Holmes, after days of watching, was well versed with the layout, and our eyes quickly became accustomed to the darkness. We then began our wait, sitting in the chairs which only an hour earlier had held the men for whom we'd been long searching.

It was about nine o'clock, and in the silence I thought I heard the far-off chimes of Big Ben when we heard the front door open and the sound of voices as they walked noisily up the stairs and in exuberant spirits. Holmes and Hopkins took positions behind the door, and I behind the chair with my revolver in hand.

The door opened and the two men, one fat and one thin, walked into the room. As soon as the thin man had lit the lamp, both Holmes and Hopkins sprang into action. Holmes tackled the thin man to the ground, and Hopkins had only put his hands on the fat man, who immediately put both hands up in surrender. Hopkins blew a whistle, and suddenly the small room was full of Scotland Yard's finest. The two men were quickly put in cuffs.

"I told you we shouldn't have come back to London, Alfie!" said the fat one.

"Shut up, Sam!" said the man called Alfie. "Keep *schtum*! They don't have anything on us."

Holmes bid Hopkins to seat the men, and then he looked at both in turn before addressing them. "Samuel Turner and Alfred Jones, you have certainly led me a merry dance, but I have to tell you that your time is up. I know all about your games along the South Coast, and can directly implicate you in five cases." With these words, he deftly reached inside Turner's jacket and took out a bundle of ten-pound Bank of England notes. "Well, let's call that six cases," he said with a smile.

Samuel Turner and Alfred Jones looked surprised. Then annoyed, and then dejected.

Holmes, who had only ever referred to them as the fat and thin man, surprised even me, who knew better than anyone my friends never-ending abilities to pull rabbits out of his hat.

"Men, the game is up," Holmes said next. "I have all the evidence to ensure you both serve long sentences. The only choice left to you is to give me a full account of your misdeeds, and Hopkins here will ensure you

211

serve your sentence together and in the same cell. Otherwise, he'll see to it that you're in different prisons, and neither of you will see your friend again."

Sam looked at his accomplice and said, "The job's up, Alfie. We might as well tell him everything, and at least we get to stay together."

A crestfallen Alfie looked at Sam, and then Holmes before nodding. Holmes told him to begin from when they first met.

While Hopkins took out his notepad, Holmes poured the men a large whisky from a decanter before Alfie began his story.

"I was born into a bad family in Stepney, with my father and uncles always in trouble. By the time I was sixteen, I was well known to the local police, and knew that if I stuck around, I would end up in the same place as my relatives. I moved to Brighton and got a job as a waiter in a good restaurant. It was here I met Sam, and as by this time we both learned manners and had a talent for accents. We lost our jobs when some money went missing from a guest's room. As Sam and I were such pals, we were both sacked, even though they didn't have any proof."

He sat back in his chair and asked if the handcuffs could be loosened slightly. Hopkins nodded and allowed a constable to do this. Alfie then continued. "Me and Sam played the three-card monte circuit for a while around London. We were good at it, so much so that local gangs would continually look to take a cut of our earnings, no matter where we plied our trade. We were also caught a couple of times and given a month inside the nick. We decided it wasn't lucrative enough or worth the effort, and that during the summer season we would target the greed of south coast restaurant owners. That's exactly what we did."

"Yes," Holmes said. "I tracked your exploits – first in Plymouth, and then Exeter, Bournemouth, Southampton, and Portsmouth. You were clever by never staying in one place for too long. I knew that when the season ended, you would probably be in London and was expecting you."

"So it was you who was following me from the restaurant in Monument?" Sam asked. Holmes nodded in affirmation. Sam somberly nodded in reply.

"How is the boy?" Alfie asked. "I didn't mean to bash him up too much. I just wanted to find out who was following us."

Holmes replied that all was well with Johnston, and that he was the only Irregular not out in the streets that night for fear that he would be recognised by Alfie – but he would no doubt be delighted to hear of the capture.

I took the opportunity to ask, "What I don't know about is how you knew the names of these men?"

212

"Simplicity itself," answered my friend. "The day after I followed Samuel, I went to the Yard and went through their information until I found descriptions of a pair of criminals known as Alfred Jones and Samuel Turner."

"We quickly scarpered from London," Sam said, "and made for Manchester to lay low for a few months. We played a few turns in Liverpool, Newcastle, Glasgow, and Edinburgh, but then decided to get out of the game, and by that time we had almost enough to open our own restaurant. Alfie wanted to touch a couple more restaurants, and argued that the heat would have died down in London where the pickings were always bigger. I didn't want to, but we agreed on two last jobs, and then out."

"Where have you stored all of your ill-gotten gains?" asked Hopkins.

Alfie shook his head. "Sorry, Inspector. As we have no intentions to return to a life of crime once we finish our sentence, that money will be our nest egg, and we won't give it up. Threaten us as you may, but it's safely hidden away."

When further questioned, Alfie and Sam wouldn't elaborate on the identity of the man who supplied them with violins, stating that they didn't want to implicate an innocent man.

Holmes shrugged. "A mere trifle."

Alfie looked at Holmes and then Inspector Hopkins. "We have told you everything we can. I believe we have kept our side of the bargain. I hope you are both gentlemen of your word and ensure we stay together after our trial."

Holmes nodded his assent, and Hopkins made to escort the pair out to a waiting police van.

"Please," added Holmes, "just one final question: What was the painting for which you received the money this evening?"

"Oh, you're a cunning one, and no doubt!" Alfie cried. "Have a look for yourself." With that, they were led out.

Holmes reached for a small paper-wrapped parcel. He unwrapped it and softly whistled.

It was a very small painting of a young woman doing needlework. The work appeared of some age, and quite unknown to me. "What is it?" I asked .

"It is a copy of 'The Lacemaker' by the Dutch Master Johannes Vermeer," said my friend. "As you know, I have an artistic side to my family, and have a knowledge of the works of great artists. Indeed, I once saw this very painting exhibited in the Louvre when visiting Paris."

Holmes then chuckled to himself. "Alfie and Sam really are quite the most ingenious pair. I shall miss further pitting my wits against them."

When we got back to Baker Street, Holmes explained more about Vermeer. "Johannes Vermeer was a great Dutch artist of the seventeenth century – the Dutch Golden Age. He was virtually forgotten until art historians Gustavus Fredrich Waagen and Theophile Thore-Burgers published an essay detailing his works just thirty years ago. It reinvigorated an appetite for his paintings, which are now much valued and sought after."

At their trial just over a month later, Samuel Turner and Alfred Jones both received seven years each, and Hopkins was as good as his word, ensuring the pair served their time together at Pentonville Prison.

As for Holmes, he was quite taken by his little painting and hung it on the wall on his side of the fireplace. Moreover, when Inspector Lestrade would pay us a visit, I would always see him wince at the sight of it, as it served as a reminder to the adulation that had once again been poured upon Inspector Hopkins after the story of his capture of the con men, to which the story had become a newspaper sensation.

Sherlock Holmes's part in the case, as usual, had been kept as quiet as possible at his own request, and needless to say, Holmes and I enjoyed a fine belated meal at Monsieur Jonquet's restaurant.

The Disappearance of the Cutter *Alicia*
by Alan Dimes

One morning in June 1926, I was pleased to find, among my meagre correspondence, a letter postmarked from Sussex. I knew of only one person living in that particular county, and instantly recognized Holmes's handwriting, which, though he was a mere two years my junior, was as firm and clear as it had ever been in those far-off days when we had shared rooms together. I confess that I felt a thrill of the old excitement as I eagerly slit the envelope open.

> *My dear Doctor,*
>
> *I trust that you are in good health. You may wonder at my writing to you after so long a silence, but the enclosed papers, which are in the nature of a death-bed confession, finally provide the solution to a long-standing mystery. You went so far, in the introduction to one of your little fables, as to describe our participation in the case as "a complete failure". But now I find that my speculations, wild as they may have seemed at the time, had some basis in truth, though of course they went unsubstantiated. I refer to the affair of the cutter Alicia, which sailed into a patch of mist and disappeared, and whose crew were never heard of again.*

The sting of Holmes's few defeats had remained in my memory just as clearly as the elation of his many successes, and I laid the letter on the table and fell into a reverie.

That year saw Holmes at perhaps the peak of his powers and the greatest height of his international fame. The social status of any potential client was entirely irrelevant to him, and while he was far from indifferent to the state of his bank balance, he refused to examine many cases which would have brought him a princely fee in favour of those which offered him an intellectual challenge or appealed to his sense of justice.

It was, I recall, a fine morning in late spring. Holmes was looking through a pile of the letters and telegrams which were now arriving at our lodgings every morning. I confined myself to a close examination of the morning papers, for I knew that if he found nothing in the post to pique his interest, his next move would be to ask me if there was anything worth scrutinizing in the news.

"Well, well, " he said suddenly, "it seems that wonders will never cease."

He waved the thin paper of a telegram in my general direction.

"We are about to have a visitation from my brother, Mycroft. Now, as you will recall, he rarely leaves the fixed circle of his existence to visit these humble rooms unless it is to warn us away from a sensitive subject, or to engage our assistance with something he perceives as being of national importance."

"Well," I said, lowering the newspaper, "you must admit that he has been generally right about the latter. So which is it?"

I smiled as Holmes read out the telegram in a fair facsimile of his brother's somewhat deeper and more portentous tones.

"'*Sherlock – Drop whatever case in which you may be involved and expect me to call on you at eleven o'clock this morning on a matter of national security. Be sure to be in your rooms at that hour. Mycroft.*'"

Holmes tossed the telegram onto his desk and rubbed his bony hands together.

"To do him justice, every case he has brought to my attention has been of interest. Luckily, he calls when I have nothing on hand. You will recall that I sent a message to Gregson at Scotland Yard last night."

"Yes."

"It was the final piece of evidence that will secure the prosecution of Thomas Lansdown. And as for the Treharne matter, I am confident that there will be no new developments in the next few days. Was there anything in the papers that might be connected to Mycroft?"

"Not that I saw."

"Then perhaps the matter is still secret."

"We'll soon find out," I said, pulling my watch from my waistcoat pocket. "It's almost eleven now, and your brother has never been less than punctual."

Holmes rose, went over to the window, and gazed down into the street.

"His carriage is just arriving now, and he isn't on his own."

"Lestrade? Bradstreet?"

"No, I've never seen the man before."

There was a knock at the downstairs door, and shortly after we heard the heavy clump of Mycroft Holmes's ascent, accompanied by the sound of the footfalls of a somewhat lighter man.

The older Holmes brother entered, accompanied by a shorter man whom I took to be in his early fifties. His wavy brown hair and beard were sprinkled with grey, and his face was somewhat swarthy and creased with lines. He was wearing a black pea-jacket, dark canvas trousers, and a pair of heavy brown boots.

"This is my brother Sherlock, and this, his friend and colleague Dr. John Watson," Mycroft Holmes began, "and this, gentlemen, is Arthur Coppard, the – "

"Indulge me, Mycroft. Let me exercise such small powers as I possess."

"Oh, if you must."

Holmes took Coppard's hand and shook it vigorously.

"I am pleased to meet you, Mr. Coppard. You are a sea captain, though you have come up through the ranks from a private seaman, and haven't been in your present position for very long."

"That is true, sir, but how did you know it?" Coppard said, in an accent which smacked of the West Country.

"Mycroft, would you care to explain?"

"No doubt my brother observed you leaving my carriage and coming with me to the door. Though a short distance, it was enough for him to see that you have that distinctive gait which is the mark of one who has been long at sea. When you entered the room, he noted your air of authority, which indicated your position of command, but when he shook your hand he felt its hardness, and the callouses which come from the work with ropes and tackle which is the lot of the common seaman. Hence, you haven't long left the fo'c's'le for the captain's cabin."

"Well," said Coppard, "I hadn't thought there was one such a man in the world, let alone two!"

"Let us be seated, gentlemen," said Holmes, " and you can tell us the reason for your visit."

Mycroft gestured to Coppard that he should speak.

"I am Arthur Coppard, captain of the *Christabel*, a ship in the employment of the Liverpool Cotton Association. We transport raw cotton from the Americas. A week ago, we were making our way back to the port with a full cargo when I saw a cutter some five-hundred yards to the west of us. Apart from the fact that she was a little far out to sea for such a small vessel, she appeared to be in distress, for she was moving erratically, with the changes of wind and current. There seemed to be no one at the tiller. We shifted our course to go to her aid and, as we did so, she entered a patch of mist. We followed, but when the mist dissipated a few minutes later, the cutter had vanished. Into thin air, not a sign of her."

"Had the mist entirely dissipated when you noticed the cutter's disappearance?" asked Holmes.

"No, there was some left a few feet above the water, but it was clear that the ship had somehow vanished, so we turned our course to Liverpool, and I told the authorities what I had seen at the earliest opportunity."

"Thank you, Captain Coppard," said the elder Holmes. "I must ask you now to return to the carriage and await me there, for what I must now discuss with my brother is a case of national importance."

"As you wish, sir. Good day, gentlemen."

"Do you wish me to leave too?" I stood up as the sailor made his way downstairs.

"Stay where you are, Watson, " said Holmes. "My brother knows that it is both or neither where you and I are concerned."

Mycroft raised one broad, flat hand in a gesture of acquiescence.

"So, Sherlock," he said, "what do you know about smuggling?"

"I assume from Captain Coppard's story that you are referring to smuggling by sea, rather than across land borders. When I embarked on my examination of the various forms of criminality in this world, I studied the subject with some assiduity, but I confess that since fewer cases involving smuggling have come my way, my knowledge of it has somewhat atrophied. I'm aware that it still exists on the western coast of the United States, in China, and some parts of Africa. It used to be widely practised in the West Country, but surely that ceased at the beginning of this century."

"Well," said Mycroft, "not entirely. It still occurs from time to time in that part of the country, and all the coasts of the British Isles are still regularly patrolled to prevent it. That brings us to the relevance of Captain Coppard's experience. The majority of the boats performing that service are cutters. The only such vessel that hasn't returned to its designated berth is the *Alicia*, currently captained by one Albert Hutchinson. My suspicion is that the craft Coppard saw was the *Alicia*, and the reason that she was moving erratically, why there seemed to be no one at the tiller, was that the crew had been abducted. Now, if that is the case, our national safety is at risk."

"How so?" I asked.

Mycroft answered, slightly impatiently. "Of necessity, all the captains of the cutters employed by the government in this capacity are kept informed of all the movements of all the craft plying the coast, and this includes those patrolling the sea against the possible incursion of foreign vessels whose intent is, shall we say, not peaceful. If Captain Hutchinson has fallen into enemy hands, they may force him to reveal what he knows, enabling them to evade the security patrols and attack the

218

mainland. Now, thus far we have had no such events, but the situation must be resolved. Captain Coppard and his crew have been ordered on pain of prosecution to keep silent about the matter. Now, Sherlock, I am leaving this in your hands because I have more immediate business to deal with. A revolution in San Bartolo is imminent, which threatens our mineral interests in that country, and there is the possibility that the Korean *won* will be subject to inflation. Good day, gentlemen. Should you wish to contact me, you know where I am."

"A pretty mystery, is it not, Watson? And in his understandable eagerness to ensure the country's safety, Mycroft ignored the chief feature of the story: How did the *Alicia* vanish after sailing into that patch of mist, whether its crew was on board or not? It is a mystery which by its nature might seem to most who hear the story to be explicable only in supernatural terms. Was the *Alicia* the victim of some giant, undiscovered creature from the sea bottom which rose from the depths and dragged the cutter and its unfortunate crew down to destruction in a matter of moments? Or perhaps Captain Hutchinson was a sinner equal to the legendary Vanderdecken, and the Devil rendered the ship invisible and sentenced him and his crew to sail the seas until Judgement Day. Or if, like the mathematician Charles Howard Hinton, we wish to dress our speculations in a cloak of pseudo-science, then the ship may, in some inexplicable manner, have entered another dimension. There is, of course, a more simple and fully rational explanation."

"Which is?"

"You studied Latin and Roman history at your school, I imagine?"

"Yes, of course."

"Then you will no doubt remember that the notoriously debauched Emperor Nero was also a matricide."

"Yes, and when the assassins came for his mother, she pointed at her womb and said, "Strike me here," because it had been guilty of bearing such an unfilial son."

"Correct. But before that he tried another method."

"How is any of this connected to the fate of the *Alicia*?"

"Patience, my dear Doctor, patience."

He stood, went over to his bookshelves, and took down three volumes, opening each one after another and skimming through the pages until he found the passages for which he was searching.

"Here is Suetonius, from his *Twelve Caesars*," he said," passing me one of them. I read:

219

> *Nero's next stratagem was to construct a ship which could be easily shivered, in hopes of destroying her either by drowning, or by the deck above her cabin crushing her in its fall.*

"And Tacitus, from *The Annals*."

> *The vessel had not gone far, Agrippina having with her two of her intimate attendants, one of whom, Crepereius Gallus, stood near the helm, while Acerronia, reclining at Agrippina's feet as she reposed herself, spoke joyfully of her son's repentance and of the recovery of the mother's influence, when at a given signal the ceiling of the place, which was loaded with a quantity of lead, fell in, and Crepereius was crushed and instantly killed.*

"And lastly, Cassius Dio's *Roman History*."

> *Sabina, on hearing about this, began to persuade Nero to get rid of his mother in order to forestall her alleged plots against him. One day they saw in the theatre a ship that automatically separated in two, let out some beasts, and came together again so as to be once more seaworthy, and they at once had another one built like it.*

"Now, Watson, I am sure you will concede that if there were shipbuilders in the First Century who were capable of constructing such a vessel, it would present no problems to a modern builder who would have access to our century's superior techniques."

"The accounts don't exactly agree."

"True, although they all concur that Agrippina survived by swimming to shore. Suetonius is often accused of purveying malicious gossip, and while Tacitus has a somewhat better reputation, he is not without his critics. Dio was writing a little later, but still, most of our contemporary historians think the story essentially true. I think we can take the use of such a stratagem as a working hypothesis in the case of the *Alicia*. You may have noted that I asked the good captain if the mist had entirely dispersed. If he hadn't turned the *Christabel* and left before it was completely gone, I fancy he would have seen wreckage floating on the water. The presence of both the *Christabel* and the mist cannot have been planned, so the perpetrators presumably intended flotsam bearing the *Alicia*'s name to be found."

"But why was it done? And by whom?"

"Clearly, what our friend the captain saw wasn't the *Alicia* herself, but a collapsible replica, as I don't think it would be possible to alter an existing vessel to fall apart in that manner. This implies that the real *Alicia* is still in existence somewhere, and that there are those who gain an advantage from her being believed lost."

A thought suddenly occurred to me.

"Holmes! Supposing the *Alicia* has been captured by smugglers. In her, they might approach other Navy boats, which, perceiving her as friendly, would allow her to draw alongside. The smugglers could then swarm aboard and kill or capture the revenue men."

"That isn't impossible, but such a theory has an insurmountable flaw: If it had happened, would Mycroft not have informed us? He can be secretive, true, but he would gain nothing by concealing the fact."

"Who, then?"

"The only others who could carry it out would seem to be the crew themselves. They would be able to take her into a harbour where it could be duplicated. It must have been a long-term plan, since the construction of the false *Alicia* would take some time. I have no experience of such matters, so I don't know how long, but it must surely be measured in weeks."

"But why should they do such a thing? What advantage could they gain from it?"

"It would be believed that they were dead, drowned in the sinking of the vessel. To me that hints at some crime in which they were all complicit. Dead men are notoriously difficult to prosecute. Now, unless it can be proved that all combined to carry out some crime on land, which I consider unlikely, we must consider those crimes which are connected with the sea."

"Mutiny?"

"As I said before, the construction of the false *Alicia* must have taken some time, and mutiny is usually carried out spontaneously, or at least planned not long before the act. I am inclined to think that, as with so many misdeeds in this fallen world, monetary gain is at the heart of it. Who could they steal from with absolute impunity? The smugglers themselves. Let us say that they captured a smuggling vessel which had accumulated a large amount of loot. Tempted by greed, they take the money and dispose of the smuggling vessel's crew. But how are they to spend the money without arousing suspicion? Presumably there is enough, cutters' crews being small in number, for them to start new lives elsewhere, so they secrete the money in a safe place, using some of it to pay an unscrupulous shipbuilder to construct the false *Alicia*. They then sail away in the real one, after setting the replica adrift at sea. Will it serve?

"I'm sure you have hit on it. But there are problems."

"Indeed. How do we prove it, and even if we can, how do we bring the perpetrators to justice?"

I will not try the reader's patience with a lengthy description of the fruitless efforts we made over the ensuing weeks. The wives and families of the missing men were interviewed by Mycroft's agents, but they clearly knew nothing of the matter, and were given financial help on the basis that their menfolk appeared to have died while in the service of the government. The only shipbuilder with criminal antecedents who could be identified had left the country, which supported but didn't corroborate Holmes's hypothesis. In the end, he was forced to concede defeat. Mycroft Holmes was far from satisfied with this outcome, but his annoyance with his younger brother subsided when none of the dire predictions he had made that morning came true.

And there it had stood for many years. I turned my attention once more to Holmes's letter.

> *I received this communication from a gentleman in Australia who signs himself* P.J. Webb, *although from the internal evidence, assuming the tale is true and not some peculiar hoax, he would seem to be in truth Arthur Swinscomb, the youngest of the six crewmen of the* Alicia. *In any event, I am sure it will be of interest to you, as it was to me.*

> *Yours sincerely,*
> *Sherlock Holmes*

The enclosure read:

> *Dear Mr. Holmes,*

> *My doctor informs me that I have little time left in this world, and before I depart it altogether I would like to make my confession. I have never been a religious man, and have no conception of what, if anything, awaits me when I have quit this life. Word reached me that you were charged with the investigation into the disappearance of the cutter* Alicia.

[Next to this was a marginal note in Holmes's handwriting: *This suggests that despite Mycroft's precautions, Captain Coppard revealed that he had visited us, though how that information then reached Swinscomb is likely to remain a mystery.*]

     I would gain no solace from conversation with a priest, but as I know you came to no firm conclusion concerning its fate, [No doubt he had read that piece of sensational fiction you entitled "The Problem of Thor Bridge"!] *it would please me to finally enlighten you after the passage of so many years. I believe I am the last survivor of our little band of brothers, and so there is none other who can perform this service, and I now have no family to be adversely affected by my revelation. I was the youngest of us, but I was, nevertheless, a grown man, in full control of my destiny, so I cannot use my relative youth as mitigation for my misdeeds.*

     I was born in Whimple, in Devon, to honest God-fearing parents, and I swear it is no reflection on them that I turned out the way I did. I was as proud as a man might be when, at the age of twenty-three, I was assigned to the cutter Alicia, *with the responsibility of keeping a section of the west coast of our islands free from smugglers. In truth, we rarely encountered any, but we proudly put that down to our presence, and felt sure that had we not been there, the sea would have been rife with them. There were six of us, including the captain, Albert Hutchinson. He was a tall, imposing man with a great red beard. He was hard as nails and brooked no nonsense, but he was generous and fair, and we all respected him.*

     His mate, Thomas Groome, had served with him for several years, and when he was assigned to the Alicia, *it was only natural that Groome should join him. Groome was almost as tall as Hutchinson, but was slim and wiry, and could scramble up the rigging with the speed and surety of a monkey. Next came John Tremayne, at forty-seven the oldest of us all, fair-haired and golden-bearded, still fit and muscular though probably not fated to stay in the service for much longer. Then there was Simon Gascoyne, who had come from what was known as "a good family", but had joined the Navy after that family had been bankrupted by bad investments. A few years my senior, he too was taller than average, with a face that remained pale no matter how hard it was battered by the weather, slim with curling dark hair.*

223

Bob Roberson, my closest friend on the Alicia, *was, like me, of middling height, though we didn't resemble each other in any other respect. He was married and I was single. He was fair and I was dark. He was loud in his laughter while I was quiet and shy. He loved to gamble, drink and sing, while I kept a close hold on my money. But of all my comrades, he was perhaps the easiest to like.*

We all worked together as a smooth unit under Captain Hutchinson's steady eye and there were no complaints of our conduct by those in charge. What, then, caused our downfall? What led to one of us lying dead on the deck of the Alicia *and the others dispersed to the corners of the world?*

In a word, greed. The oldest trap in the world. The love of dead pieces of paper and metal that somehow becomes more powerful than the sense of duty and responsibility towards one's fellow-man. And in truth, though the money we took has assured me a comfortable life, it has also been a lonely one, with the shadow of my guilt hanging ever over me.

Enough. To my tale. If you were a man of the sea, and especially if you were also a native of the West Country, you would have heard of the legend of Black Bart's Treasure. Of all the smugglers of the eighteenth century, he had been the most successful, and the story was that he had secreted a vast hoard somewhere, in some cave on the Devon coast. His plan was to make one final smuggling voyage and then escape with his accumulated wealth to the New World, but on that last voyage he had quarrelled with his first mate and in the course of a bloody duel with cutlasses, each killed the other. A storm then hit the ship, and it went down to Davy Jones' Locker. One sailor escaped, clinging to a piece of wreckage, and after he was found on the shore he survived long enough to tell the story to his rescuers. So the legend grew up, and in time it was said that there was a curse on Black Bart's loot. Perhaps there was.

Like Black Bart's ship, the Alicia *was caught in a fearful storm. The night was falling fast, and there was no sign of a lighthouse. But unlike Black Bart, in the teeth of a storm we managed to make our way to safety in the form of a sheltered cove. We dropped anchor and prepared to spend the night, but there was no fresh water on board. Bob Roberson and I volunteered to go ashore and look for some. What we found, instead, was a cave. With typical bravado, Bob suggested that*

224

we go inside and look around, for who knew, maybe Black Bart's treasure was in there.

And yes, against all reason, and in keeping with a hoary, improbable tale, that was what we found. Some of it was in the form of paper money unusable in this day, but the majority of it was gold and silver coins, innumerable great piles of them. Like the two honest fellows we felt ourselves to be, we went back and told the others of our find. Soon all six of us were there, staring at more money than we could have hoped to see in a dozen lives. It was then that the great sickness of greed began to overtake us. I certainly knew in my heart that this wasn't ours, that we should notify the authorities to come and retrieve it, that such an injection of money would greatly benefit the county and even perhaps the country. Were we not bound to be given some reward, some honour, for the selfless act of handing it over? No doubt this went through all of our minds, but not one of us said anything to that effect.

We began instead to discuss how we might escape with it, how it could alter our lives so much for the better. Those of us who were married, Groome, Tremayne, and Roberson talked of how they couldn't bring any of it home to their wives and families without arousing suspicion. It was Groome who said that if we could make it seem that we had perished at sea, then our families would get compensation and we could take the hoard aboard the Alicia, drop anchor on a foreign coast and divide it. Then we could scuttle the ship and go our separate ways. From there the plan grew with the relentlessness of an avalanche. Gascoyne knew of a boat builder who could make a replica of the Alicia. When, just before our next scheduled voyage, we consulted him, he assured us that if nails made of beeswax were substituted for certain crucial iron nails, it would be possible for the ship to drift on the ocean until the heat of the sun and the action of the seawater melted them, at which point the false Alicia would collapse into wreckage. With luck, that wreckage would eventually be found and our loss confirmed.

The weeks during which we awaited the replica's completion were tense. None of us were able to speak of it, but then one day John Tremayne found his voice.

All six of us were on deck when he said, "I can't keep my peace any longer. What we are doing is wrong. You know what I'm saying. Abandoning our families, all for gold and

225

silver. Betraying the trust that's been placed in us. Dammit, in your hearts you all know it isn't right!"

"So what would you have us do, Johnny?" asked the captain. "Go back to our lives of toil and danger when there's a way out, a way to safety and a comfortable life? Is that what you want?"

"All right. If I can't move you, at least I can go."

"Then go," said Gascoyne, "and more for the five of us."

"How do we know you'll not betray us? asked Groome.

"We don't," said Gascoyne.

Suddenly there was a flash of smoke and the report of a gun, and to my horror I realised that Bob Roberson had shot Tremayne, who fell to the deck with a scream of pain. Moments later he was dead.

"That solves the problem," said Bob, and I stood aghast at the transformation of my best friend into a cold-blooded killer. In that moment, I knew that I was complicit, that as a participant in the whole scheme I shared in the guilt of Tremayne's death.

"Don't look so pale, boy," the captain said to me. "Help me throw his body overboard."

The rest you can no doubt deduce. Everything went according to plan. Where the others went, I cannot say. I used my share to carry myself to the other side of the world, as far as I could from England.

Signed this day, the 18th May, 1926, by

P.J. Webb

The Widow's Pique
by Victoria Weisfeld

One Friday evening in the time about which I write, the mid-1890's, I returned late to the lodgings Sherlock Holmes and I shared at 221b Baker Street. My tardiness was occasioned by the enthusiasm and persistent questions of my students at the School of Medicine for Women. To fill out its limited faculty, the school occasionally invited guest lecturers, and I was happy to oblige them, finding the female students generally more conscientious than their male counterparts.

Suffice it to say, I entered our chambers well into the dinner hour and found Holmes hunched over his microscope. A half-circle of stubby candles mounted on a horseshoe-shaped contraption surrounded the stage on which he'd placed his samples, an invention of his intended to improve lighting of the viewing area, while highly likely, I thought, to start a fire.

"Holmes, I'm sorry," I blustered. "I'm afraid I've delayed our dinner."

He didn't look up. "It's Mrs. Hudson you should apologize to. She's interrupted me three times to see whether you'd returned."

"I'll go down at once."

Presently I returned, carrying our dinner on a large silver tray, Mrs. Hudson behind me with a well-browned pie, the object of her concern. I set the tray down and began arranging the table, with another apologetic word of thanks.

She closed the door behind her, as Holmes continued peering into his instrument.

"Holmes, about Mrs. Hudson – "

"A-ha! I've got you now!"

"What on earth are you investigating? Your workbench looks like the sweepings of a dress shop. But about our dear landlady – " I began, before being cut off again.

"Exactly. I've been studying cotton cloth. I have samples from seven countries, and each has peculiarities that let me distinguish, for example, a scrap woven in England from one originating in India or China or Egypt. Or even America. Come look," he said.

I eyed my plate, with its steaming slice of roast beef, sighed, and joined him.

He showed me several cloth samples, each about two inches square, and even my most intense inspection revealed no differences among them.

All the samples were white or near to it, and no color or pattern provided a clue.

In some American samples, he explained, the weave was slightly looser, and in those from England, quite tight. The thread in the samples from Egypt was particularly fine and lustrous.

"I see," I said, though I suspect a note of doubt crept into my response.

"Here is evidence from something I'm looking into." He pushed another scrap onto the microscope stage. "What are its origins?"

I hesitated. "It looks to me most like the American samples."

"Quite right. Since cotton cloth is something England generally exports to America, not imports from it, this bit of cloth substantially increases the likelihood that the wearer either is an American or has visited there recently. The partial buttonhole indicates it is from some garment."

"Amazing! But please, Holmes – Mrs. Hudson. Did you not notice her red eyes and distraught expression?"

"You mean because of the illness of her cousin, Evelynne Turcott, who lives in the house Walthamstow once owned by their paternal grandparents?"

"Ah. Of course, you are ahead of me. I've just learned about it from Mrs. Turcott's physician – Dr. Ernest Charles – Do you know him? Tall? Blond? He's downstairs giving her a report. I fear the situation is grim."

"Mrs. Turcott's housekeeper found this scrap in her mistress's hand," he said, pointing to the bit of cloth we'd only just examined. "Evelynne Turcott appears to have torn it from someone's clothing in a struggle. She collapsed soon afterward – I say 'soon', because she was still clutching the scrap of cloth – and has been bedridden ever since. I'm told she's hardly eaten anything for the past fortnight. The housekeeper, a thrifty soul, saved the scrap, in case the torn garment appeared needing repair." He settled at our dining table.

"And that precipitated your interest in the manufacture of cotton cloth?" A rather slender investigative reed, I thought.

"Of course. This dinner is nearly cold." He flourished his napkin and began cutting his slice of roast. "The housekeeper gave it to me yesterday when I stopped by to give Mrs. Turcott some of Mrs. Hudson's pills."

"You did what?" I threw my napkin down in dismay. "What pills?"

"Nothing you are involved with. Pills a dispensing chemist gave her. They do her a world of good, she says. I suggested she share them."

"So you're practicing medicine now? The Royal Medical and Chirurgical Society won't be pleased."

"There's no use hoarding those pills when they might help her cousin."

"Indeed." I was too flabbergasted to enumerate everything that was wrong there.

As we ate, he told me the cousins had been very close as girls, spending much time together in their grandparents' home. The grandfather was a wealthy mill owner, specializing in the manufacture of cotton and linen fabrics. His oldest son, Evelynne's father, inherited the business and the house. When he died, the property went to his only child, married by then to a man named Turcott. Also by that time, Mrs. Hudson had a position of her own and could visit Walthamstow only occasionally.

"She told me her cousin's butler and cook – a married couple – have served the family for almost fifty years. A maid and housekeeper go in daily, except Sundays. A gardener works twice a week."

"You've learned a great deal about the household arrangements."

"As Dr. Charles no doubt explained, Mrs. Turcott's malady is rather mysterious. Her only problem is an inexplicably sudden and almost complete refusal to eat. Since she rarely goes out, I cannot eliminate the possibility that the cause somehow originates within her home."

"Hmm," I said, my mind grasping the several implications. "You believe it's deliberate? She's being drugged? Poisoned?"

"Possibly. Dr. Charles hasn't fully accepted the idea yet, but I believe he will arrive at the same conclusion."

A further thought came to mind. "Does Mrs. Turcott have children?"

"A daughter, Alice, living in town – now Mrs. Ambrose Higginbotham-Wells – and an estranged son, Alexander, who departed for America some years ago under pressure from the family. Evelynne said to Mrs. Hudson that 'the boy's skilamalink doings will be the death of me.'" Holmes looked thoughtful and crossed to his desk. "One moment, Watson." He riffled through a stack of newspapers, scanned a few pages, then rattled the paper in triumph. "I thought I recognized the name."

Higginbotham-Wells is rather a mouthful, I was about to say.

"Yes," he said. "No other Ambrose has crossed my path in a dozen years or more. Ambrose Higginbotham-Wells, though, has had a run of bad luck. According to this notice, he is selling off his business, lock, stock, and barrel."

"Short of funds then," I said, cutting into the pie.

"Precisely."

Promptly after breakfast the next day, we bundled into a cab to visit Mrs. Turcott. Mrs. Hudson stood in the doorway, her apron clutched in her hands, watching us leave.

"I hope we can relieve her mind," I said. "If her cousin is indeed being poisoned, perhaps we can put a stop to it."

Holmes grunted, staring out the window. A few moments passed in silence, and, to make conversation, as it was rather a long and tedious drive, I said, "Holmes, I wonder whether I could interest you in the lecture I gave at the medical school yesterday afternoon. My subject was the placebo effect. Do you know it?"

"Quack medicine."

"Not at all. The placebo effect can be very beneficial for certain mild conditions. Truthfully, all medicines work better when patients believe in them."

"There's no overstating the gullibility of the average Briton."

"Don't judge too quickly. A doctor in Edinburgh tells his patients outright that the pills he's giving them have no 'pharmaceutical properties'. Even knowing that, they say the pills make them feel better."

Holmes barked a laugh and knocked his walking stick against the roof of the cab. "We've arrived."

We entered the sickroom quietly and saw the good lady was half-asleep. I took her pulse, rapid and faint. On the bedside table huddled a number of pill bottles and tonics, and a small box with her name in Holmes's distinctive penmanship. While he busily examined items elsewhere in the room, I slipped the box into my coat pocket. He might not be worried about the consequences of handing out medicines willy-nilly, but I had to be.

I felt her forehead for fever and found none, although Mrs. Turcott certainly looked weak and drawn. Her speech was faint, and it seemed she didn't understand my simple questions. Because she repeatedly dozed off, we kept our visit short and proceeded downstairs to speak with the household staff. At the bottom of the steps, Holmes asked that I take the lead in questioning them.

"Me?" My surprise surely showed.

"Yes, Watson. Your easy manner will help them relax their guard. You can discuss inconsequential domestic matters much more easily than I. To me, such things are tiresome in the extreme."

What he meant, and in this he was correct, was that he had no gift for polite conversation and didn't see the need for it. I, however, believe it greases the social wheels.

Gathered around the kitchen table besides myself were: Mrs. Skelton, the cook, who poured our tea, Mr. Skelton, the butler, Mrs. Wright, the housekeeper, her daughter Jenny, the maid, and her teenaged son Bob, the part-time gardener, who also did household errands. Due to an insufficiency of chairs, Holmes took his tea to a bench by the window. He

230

hoped, I'd wager, they would be more forthcoming if they forgot that the detective was in the room, listening intently.

After a few compliments about the pleasant room, I asked, "Has Mrs. Turcott had any visitors these past several weeks?"

"Before her collapse?" Skelton asked. "No. And who would visit now, with her in such a state? Except for Mrs. Hudson. That woman is a saint." My sentiments exactly. "And of course, Alice, who comes as regular as rain and tries to be a cheerful influence on her mother."

"Has any unusual mail or delivery come into the house?" I was at my wits' end, trying to figure out what questions to ask. Holmes, gazing out the window, offered no help whatsoever.

"She doesn't receive many letters," said Mr. Skelton. "Nothing social. She's been a bit of a recluse in recent years."

"As her physician may have told you," I had to tread cautiously here, "it is difficult to treat her condition without knowing its cause. I spoke with Dr. Charles yesterday evening, and he says the case is far from clear." I couldn't reveal Holmes's suspicions, of course, because if someone were acting against her, the culprit might be sitting right alongside me.

I was getting nowhere and soon fell back upon predictable questions about their length of service, daily activities, and the like. They appeared uneasy, Jenny especially. She seemed bursting to say something. But if they had questions for me, they hesitated to broach them. Finally, Bob blurted, "Is Miz Turcott going to die on us?" Their reaction was a combination of horror and relief.

"I hope we get to the bottom of this long before that could happen, certainly. But if Mrs. Turcott were to leave us," I asked Mr. Skelton, in as kindly a tone as possible, "what would you do?"

"Mrs. Skelton and I have lived here so long it would be quite a wrench to leave, naturally. But we have savings and might buy a little place down in Kent. Near the sea would be nice."

"And you'll get a nice legacy," said Jenny.

"Hush," Mrs. Skelton said. "We don't know that."

Jenny nodded with youthful certainty. "She talked about it. With the ghost."

Holmes's attention sharpened, and I followed up. "Ghost?"

"Don't be daft, Jenny," her mother said. "These gentlemen will think we take stock in such fancies."

"I heard them. They had a regular quarrel about the legacies."

"Jenny!" Her mother chided her, and the girl sank back in her chair. "How could you even hear such a thing?"

"Remember, when Mrs. Turcott started to do poorly, I slept in the alcove one night? That's when I heard them, snapping at each other. 'Not a single penny!' she said, and then he said, 'You'd give it to strangers?' On and on, each one accusing the other of all kinds of frightful meanness. I would have peeped out, but then I figured Mrs. Turcott always slept so soundly and it didn't really sound like her – What if it was ghosts? – and I stayed right where I was."

"Then you dreamed it."

Jenny's face crumpled as if she might cry. "I did not!"

A change of subject seemed advisable. "What about you, Bob? What would you do?"

"Mam says I should get an apprenticeship. Mam says there's all sorts – carpenters, bootmakers, tailors."

"That world is changing," I said. "If the owners can get a machine to do something, they will, and what will the next generation do? In France, they're selling men's clothing ready-made! A death-knell for tailor shops, I fear."

After more desultory conversation, Holmes coughed, signaling we should take our leave, which we did, thanking the staff for their graciousness.

"Very instructive, Watson," Holmes said after we settled ourselves into a cab.

"It was? All I noticed was that Jenny is not much of a seamstress. Her right sleeve was sewn up most awkwardly."

"Yes, but her dress wasn't of the material we examined last night. That's merely inexperience."

Since it was clear Holmes wouldn't say more until he'd mulled over our visit and smoked several pipes doing so, I returned to my earlier topic. "The placebo effect is a fascinating new area of study," I said.

Holmes merely grunted.

"You must agree it at least fulfills medicine's fundamental precept: 'First, do no harm.'"

"Perhaps, but I find the opposite effect far more intriguing," he said.

"Opposite?"

"Yes, Watson. What if you give a man a substance or a treatment that is essentially harmless, but he believes it to be dangerous to his health or well-being? Could you induce illness? Even death?"

"Death? That's going a bit, don't you think?"

"A fainting spell, then, or a headache, just from the suggestion. Or, at the extreme, *angina pectoris*. In an exaggerated situation, you might have the perfect murder weapon."

The next morning, when Mrs. Hudson brought our breakfast, Holmes asked her to join us.

232

"It remains possible that another party is involved in Mrs. Turcott's illness, though we don't know this for certain, nor what the agent or mechanism might be. For now," he asked, "could you tell me whether Mrs. Turcott is well-off? Obviously, the house is grand, opulent even, but sometimes these long-held properties rest on weak financial footings."

"Her father's estate made Evelynne wealthy, and her late husband was a successful businessman. By the time he died, I understand her fortune had grown considerably. We rarely discuss financial affairs, though, as she is sensitive to the discrepancy in our circumstances." Mrs. Hudson stated this without any bitterness or apology.

"And there are the two children?" Holmes asked.

"Three, if you count her stepson, James, who has lived in India for many years. He has a prominent position and appears in the newspaper occasionally. Mr. Turcott was a widower when he married Evelynne, and James was about five years old then."

"What else do you know of him?" I asked.

Before Mrs. Hudson could reply, a tremendous knocking came at the front door.

"Goodness," she said, going out of the room.

In a moment she returned, announcing Inspector Lestrade, who blustered in, red as a boiled lobster.

"Tea?" she inquired.

He mightn't have heard her, because he launched right in. "Is Mrs. Evelynne Turcott your client?" he asked Holmes, more an accusation than a query.

"No, she has not engaged me," Holmes said.

I added, "As she is rather too ill to do so."

"Mr. Holmes and the Doctor visited Evelynne at my request, Inspector," Mrs. Hudson said. "She's my dear cousin."

"Then I regret to inform you," Lestrade said, somewhat more mildly, "there was a break-in at her home last night. A servant chased the intruder away, and his wife found Mrs. Turcott unconscious on the floor of her bedroom. Reported it this morning."

I jumped up to help Mrs. Hudson to a chair. Turning to Lestrade with some bewilderment, I said, "We visited her only yesterday. She looked too ill and weak to be climbing out of bed." My hand, looking for a place to fidget, found my coat pocket and the small box of pills Holmes had delivered to her.

"What do you know about all this?"

We proceeded to tell Inspector Lestrade everything. I recounted the symptoms that Dr. Charles and I had observed, as well as what we inferred from reports by the household staff.

In the cab on the way to the address in Walthamstow, Mrs. Hudson described the Turcott family and household for him.

Lestrade summarized. "We have Mrs. Turcott's two children, her daughter's husband in financial straits, and her stepson. Any of the four might be interested in hastening their inheritance. And then there's the five servants."

"I believe you can eliminate Mrs. Higginbotham-Wells and her husband," said Holmes. "It's true his business affairs have done poorly of late, but he is the heir to a substantial estate quite separate from any legacy his wife might receive."

"I've never known Alice to be anything but a loving and dutiful daughter," Mrs. Hudson said. "And the servants are impeccably loyal."

"Hmm," doubted Lestrade. "Does the patient have a will?"

"I don't know," Mrs. Hudson said. "Her solicitor is Alfred Babbitt in Oxford Street."

"I'll pay him a call early tomorrow morning," Lestrade said. "He should be aware there may be mischief afoot."

At the Turcott home, an anxious Mr. Skelton greeted us. He described being awakened in the early morning hours by a loud crash. He hurried down the back stairs to the hall and saw a faint flicker of candlelight as he reached Mrs. Turcott's room. Someone pushed past him, ran downstairs, and escaped through the front door. He couldn't describe the person, or even say if it was a man or woman. All he saw was a hat pulled low and a long dark cloak.

"Mrs. Turcott was on the bedroom floor, and Mrs. Skelton and I helped her back into bed. This morning, she seems even weaker, if that is possible."

Mrs. Hudson remained with the Skeltons while Holmes, Lestrade, and I climbed the stairs. As we stood around the bed, Holmes rubbed his chin and asked, "What do you notice?"

"There's no evidence of an attempt at strangulation or suffocation," I said. "The bruises on her arms do suggest someone held her down, and the bump on her forehead might have resulted from the fall."

"I see some of the dresser drawers are hanging open," Holmes said. "Is anything missing?"

"The maid, Jenny, believes not," said Lestrade.

Holmes was strangely quiet in the cab on the way home, content to let Mrs. Hudson and me do most of the talking – and, I admit, considerable speculating. I was sure he had some plan in mind, and, indeed, promptly after dinner, he disappeared.

234

I didn't see him again over the next two days, during which time Lestrade reported there indeed was a will, though Babbitt wouldn't reveal its contents. He confirmed the stepson was actively serving in his government post in India. "One suspect eliminated," was Lestrade's only comment. The whereabouts of the son, whether in England or still in America, were unknown.

During the time Holmes was away, Mrs. Hudson wanted to visit her cousin again, which is why, on Tuesday, I accompanied her. Quite a number of people were about: Women going to the shops, servants running errands and, to our surprise, being that the area was some distance from the industrial part of town, a fair number of men in dirty work clothes. Inevitably, a pair of beggars, or perhaps they were pickpockets, lounged about, eyeing the pedestrians.

Mr. Skelton opened the door to us, and Mrs. Skelton brought tea. Jenny accompanied Mrs. Hudson and me upstairs, where I observed her continuing slow deterioration. I left our landlady sitting with her cousin and speaking calmly of household affairs. While I waited for her return, Mrs. Higginbotham-Wells appeared, and I met this gentle lady at last. Her distress at her mother's condition seemed quite genuine.

As Mrs. Hudson and I proceeded down the walk toward the front gate, she said, "That Jenny is a bit of a flibbertigibbet. I hope she's reliable enough to watch over Evelynne." She caught sight of the more disreputable of the two filthy beggars hanging about and whispered, "My, he's a nasty-looking one."

The blackguard started to approach, and I positioned myself between them. "Away with you, man!" I raised my walking stick.

"Beg pardon. No offense." A voice that rough could emanate only from a man whose life had taken an uncountable number of wrong turns. The cackle of the other beggar followed us into the cab.

Tuesday evening, I took advantage of Holmes's continued absence to do some sleuthing of my own. The packet he'd delivered to Mrs. Turcott contained six round white pills, with a sheen that made them look as if they'd fallen from a pearl necklace. I'd noticed a jar of similar pills in the cabinet next to the downstairs washstand. Never one to pry into such personal matters, I hadn't asked Mrs. Hudson about them. Now that they might somehow figure in Mrs. Turcott's situation, I took one of the pills from her jar, as well as one from Holmes's packet, and halved them. Under the microscope, they looked identical, pure white and slightly crystalline inside. I touched a piece of each to my tongue and confirmed they were identical. Now I knew why these pills did Mrs. Hudson so much good.

Later that evening, Dr. Charles visited me in our rooms.

"I have to admit, Watson," he said, running a hand through his blonde hair, "I am rather disturbed by all this. Mrs. Turcott has a somewhat weakened heart, and unless she begins to eat properly, will undoubtedly injure herself." Dr. Charles shook his head sadly. "But I'm worried Inspector Lestrange – "

"Lestrade."

" – won't pay attention to *why* she's stopped eating, being so focused on the actions of this intruder."

Dr. Charles was a conscientious physician, and I strove to reassure him. "Lestrade is simply concentrating on the aspect of this situation – the break-in – that involves a crime. Mrs. Turcott isn't eating isn't really a police matter, is it? As far as we know."

On Wednesday morning, Mrs. Hudson had brought my breakfast upstairs when someone pounded on the front door. "Goodness, not Inspector Lestrade again! Bad news follows him like night follows day."

"I'll go down with you," I said, setting aside my newspaper and looking longingly at my rapidly cooling boiled egg.

A constable stood on our front step, gripping the greasy collar of the worse of the two Walthamstow beggars. "'E was about to enter your house, ma'am, when I nabbed 'im. Probably fixing to rob ye. We don't want the likes of 'im round 'ere." And in the man's ear, the constable said, "This be a respectable neighborhood."

"Watson, be so good as to tell this fellow that I live here." The voice was unmistakable.

"Holmes! We never would have recognized you." I took his arm, reassuring the constable that this scruffy individual was indeed a member of our household. Mrs. Hudson covered her mouth in surprise and, I think, to stifle a laugh.

While she prepared a second breakfast, Holmes removed the wig and blotchy dark make-up. By the time his egg and toast arrived, he looked himself, wrapped in a burgundy silk dressing gown.

He reported that his peculiar brand of research had produced excellent results. He had quickly realized his companion in beggary was Mrs. Turcott's missing son, Alexander, who intently watched the household's comings and goings. He'd hide his face when his sister Alice visited, afraid she might recognize him despite his disguise, and what appeared to be the ravages of hard living abroad.

When he got Turcott talking, the young man muttered a great deal about cotton mills and looms and thread and other such items associated with his family's business. He talked too about Lawrence, Massachusetts – an important mill town, Holmes said. Apparently, Alexander had spent

236

time there, and could get himself quite worked up about what he called his "exile".

When Holmes also observed him skulking around the offices of the solicitor, Alfred Babbitt, he alerted Lestrade, who increased the local constables' patrols.

"But, Mr. Holmes, where have you been sleeping?" asked Mrs. Hudson. The good lady had noticed the dark circles under his eyes hadn't disappeared, though the oily grime was gone.

"Another profitable use of time." He smiled, sipped his coffee, and said no more.

After breakfast, Lestrade paid us a call. Ushered in by Mrs. Hudson, he said, "Now what's this all about? I had that young derelict detained, based on your advice, but to hold him, I need the particulars."

"Your first question is rather easily answered. The young man in question is Mrs. Turcott's missing son, Alexander."

"But what has he done," I asked, "other than make a nuisance of himself?"

"I'm confident the Inspector will have questions for him. But, as the man has a habit of disappearing, I deemed it advisable to keep him where we know we can find him."

"True enough," Lestrade agreed.

"All right. As you know, he has been lurking near the Turcott house in his medicant's disguise to learn whatever he could. He can't have missed the doctor's daily visits, which would have told him her condition is precarious, and may have inspired a more diabolical scheme," Holmes said.

"And he was spying on Babbitt, as well," I said triumphantly, "hoping somehow to learn the contents of her will!"

"Then the young fool is not much acquainted with solicitors," Lestrade said. "Closed tight as oysters."

"Ordinarily," Holmes said, "one might believe that a son, even an estranged one, wouldn't think his mother would be so unforgiving and so untouched by remembered affection that she would deny him his inheritance. But I believe that's exactly what Mrs. Turcott said she intends. And her son knows it. He couldn't gain access to Babbitt's office to confirm his suspicions, so proceeded with his plan of nightly visits to the house."

"How does he get in?" Lestrade asked.

"With his key. Skelton says they've never changed the locks, though they are having it done today."

"My men can test that," Lestrade said.

"We have other tangible evidence, as well," Holmes said. "You'll recall that the night Mrs. Turcott collapsed, Mrs. Wright retrieved a scrap of linen cloth from her hand. If you examine Alexander Turcott's 'beggar's costume', you'll find his shirt has a missing piece." Waving a hand in the direction of his microscope, he said, "That piece lies there." He spoke in his usual phlegmatic way, sounding ready to dismiss the evidence altogether.

"The diabolical scheme?" I prompted.

"As you know, I was away from Baker Street three nights, as well as two days."

I nodded.

"With the Skeltons' assistance, I spent those nights in the sleeping alcove in Mrs. Turcott's bedroom. This idea originated with Jenny and her 'ghosts'. The first night was quiet, and I resolved to try again. The second night, I was wakened by soft footsteps and the creaking bedroom door. Through a slight gap in the curtains, I saw Turcott and heard him talking to his mother in a low voice. 'Poison, poison. They are poisoning you.' 'Everything you eat is tainted.' 'Everyone wants you dead,' and more in that vein. Regrettably, this sorry charade was repeated on the third night."

"But why?" asked Lestrade.

"We know he wants money, and when his mother refused him, he took this other tack. He approaches her in secret, when she is asleep or nearly so. It is a kind of hypnotism – one of the tricks of you doctors use." He glanced my way. "Under his malevolent influence, she has become too frightened to eat, for reasons she probably cannot explain, and has nearly stopped eating altogether."

"Well, yes, hypnotic suggestion can be powerful." I said. "But we should be able to release her from its grip rather easily."

"Then we must try to do so. Otherwise, the inspector will have a murderer on his hands."

Later, Mrs. Hudson, Mrs. Skelton, and I devised a strategy of taking our meals with Mrs. Turcott so that she could see they produced no ill effects. I brought in a French-trained medical man who used hypnotism to counteract her son's truly poisonous suggestions, and I also quietly returned Mrs. Hudson's pills to her bedside. In a week or so, thankfully, the restorative effects of our strategy became apparent.

Turcott was questioned, and while his actions were undoubtedly ill-intended, he had excuses. He had a key to the house, after all, so claimed he wasn't really breaking-and-entering. The servants wouldn't let him see his mother (nor did she welcome his visits), so he said he was forced to visit in the night. He said what Holmes overheard him say about poison merely expressed his fears and concerns for his mother, and wasn't a threat at all. The legal advice Lestrade received was that a prosecution stood a fair chance of failing. The inspector didn't like this assessment, but he agreed with it. The result was a persuasive conversation with Turcott advising him to return to America for good, which he did.

On a Friday soon after Alexander Turcott was arrested, I again taught my class at The School of Medicine for Women. Once more I arrived home a bit late and in high spirits.

Over dinner, I said, "You will recall, Holmes, that I have been discussing the placebo effect with my students."

"So you've said."

"Well, today, I asked them for examples from their own experience. A charming one came from a student whose aunt was run quite ragged by her five young children. Every hour, some tumble or scrape resulted in a fit of crying. The mother would snatch up the tearful child and offer 'a sip of water' from a pitcher on the kitchen table. It was plain water, but presented with such conviction as to its restorative powers that the crying instantly stopped. It's hard to conceive of a more vivid example of the placebo effect!"

"I concede the strategy might occasionally work with a small child. But really, Watson, I'm surprised you believe any rational adult could be so easily manipulated. You or I wouldn't be. And Mrs. Hudson is far too sensible."

My eyes strayed to the microscope where I'd examined the sugar pills Mrs. Hudson put so much confidence in, and I smiled. "Yes, she is."

The Case of the
Many Marshal Mendlers
by Ian Ableson

The first year after Sherlock Holmes returned from his apparent death plunging down the Reichenbach Falls caused a great many changes in my life. I have mentioned in a previous writing that during this time, Holmes asked that I sell my practice and return to both our quarters at Baker Street and my position as his unofficial partner and chronicler. I have also written that I found the practice astonishingly easy to sell. I was immediately approached by a young doctor by the name of Verner who made the purchase. Readers of exceptional memory may remember that in "The Norwood Building", I revealed another fact about the doctor that heavily factored into his purchase of my practice, though at the time I did not reveal how I had learned the truth. The facts (of which I will keep quiet for now, though all will be revealed by the end) were in fact made clear to me when Dr. Verner went from mere business acquaintance to client.

It was a relatively dreary Tuesday morning when the young doctor burst through the door. He took little time for introduction. He looked much the same to me as he had when I sold him my practice a year prior – a man full of directed energy. Every motion deliberate, every sentence punctuated with some movement of his hands, face, or feet, as though he were presenting himself on stage rather than speaking to a person in the same room. He had a rather pointed facial structure and had adorned his upper lip with a thin pencil moustache.

"They say that you," he said, indicating Holmes, who lounged in his chair, his violin balancing on this lap, "have one of the best minds in all of England for reducing mystery to fact. I must confess that I have need of it now, for when I bought the practice of fine Dr. Watson here, no one cared to inform me that the place was a magnet for strange and foolish men looking to deceive an upstanding medical professional!"

"Calm yourself, man," said Holmes. He stood and poured our unexpected guest a small glass of brandy and handed it to him. As for myself, I must admit that I was far too taken aback to respond, and I certainly had not been prepared for accusations regarding my old practice. I gathered myself and addressed the man as he took a swig from the glass.

"I assure you I know of no such strange behavior from any of my previous patients. Is this someone new?"

"More than one person, I'm afraid, Dr. Watson. Either I am the victim of some cruel prank that aims to discredit me and all that I do, or else it is the most unlikely contrivance imaginable, and fate itself has made me its play-thing."

"Perhaps you could provide us with a little more detail," said Holmes lightly. "Please, have a seat." Consistent readers will note that Holmes enjoyed revealing details that he'd deduced about clients upon first meeting, partially as a way to assure them of his own talents and partially (and sometimes, I suspected, primarily) for his own amusement. Perhaps the fact that he did not do so on this occasion should have been my first hint that he was already acquainted with the man. Dr. Verner sat heavily on the chair.

"Yes, perhaps I could. I might owe you an apology, Dr. Watson – I did not intend to sound accusatory. You are owed no blame in this. The strangeness, as it is, started not long after I bought the practice from you, although there was nothing strange about it at the time.

"As inevitably happens when there is a change in medical professionals, a few of the patients that had been under your care chose to go elsewhere once the practice was in my hands. While regrettable, I do not begrudge them for it – some people are uncomfortable with a younger, less-experienced doctor – and I quickly gathered a few of your patients had very few issues at all, and consistently visited the practice more for pleasant conversation than for diagnosis. Regardless, in the first few months of owning the practice, I was in the market for new patients and paid for an announcement in the newspaper advertising as such. This proved relatively fruitful. I am pleased to say that by this time, one year later, I am nearly at capacity, although I do still keep a few time slots open for new patients.

"Less than a week after I first posted in the paper, a new patient by the name of Marshal Mendler visited my practice. He had an aristocratic bearing to him – high arched cheekbones, thinning hair, a well-manicured beard hiding a round and well-fed chin, perhaps a few years younger than myself. Once I had him situated, he wasted little time with introductions. He had heard of my practice from an . . . acquaintance of his at the Diogenes Club who is familiar with me as well. Given the club's rules regarding socializing – rules that I know you're familiar with, Holmes – I haven't the slightest idea how the acquaintance in question had the opportunity to pass along my name. He told me that over the past few days, he'd been experiencing a whole host of symptoms – extreme fatigue was at the forefront, but he also listed a sore throat, a mild fever, and excessive sweating. The man claimed he could hardly use his bedsheets from one day to the next, so drenched were they every night. The symptoms he listed could be indicative of a few things, so I told him I would need to proceed with a physical examination."

I must confess, at this point the mindset of the doctor, a state of mind that is kept at bay during my time on a case but never truly disappears, came back with a vengeance, and I interrupted Dr. Verner. "Did you examine his lymph nodes? Check the roof of his mouth for *petechia*?"

In spite of himself, Dr. Verner laughed. "You can take the doctor away from his practice, but you can never truly take his practice away from him, hmm, Dr. Watson? Yes, I did, and I can tell that you've already figured out the diagnosis for yourself. I diagnosed him with glandular fever. It's a relatively newly described disease – first identified by German physicians in 1889. They refer to it as *Drusenfieber*, and it's generally spread through contact of bodily fluids with the infected – saliva appears to be the most common. Very rarely fatal, though a serious case can lay even the healthiest man low for months.

"I made my diagnosis, prescribed him some medicines for pain and fever reduction, advised him towards fluids and bedrest, and sent him on his way. He arranged his payment with my secretary and asked that I write a short note regarding my diagnosis on the paid and dated invoice, referring to him by name, as he said his employer would want to see that he was being truthful about his illness. I did so without question, for it's hardly the first time such a request has been made of me, and he went on his way. As the months went by, I rather forgot about Marshal Mendler. He never returned to my practice, so I assume he recovered in due time.

"He had all but faded from my mind, nothing but a one-page notation in my files with his name and diagnosis for the purposes of record-keeping, when I was struck by the most astonishing case of *deja vu*. A man visited my practice – another new patient – whose case was similar to Marshal Mendler's in every way. Extreme fatigue, sore throat, swollen lymph nodes – he was missing the *petechia*, but as you know, Dr. Watson, those only appear in approximately one-half of patients anyway – and to my mild amusement, his name was also *Marshal Mendler*. Certainly not the same man, as this fellow was a tall man, swarthy, with ruddy pockmarked cheeks and a hooked nose. I did not say anything to him. It was, in my mind, one of those strange little coincidences that life sometimes gives us to keep us on our toes. A relatively uncommon diagnosis and a relatively uncommon name. He paid for his visit, took his copy of the paid invoice with a note regarding his diagnosis on it, and went on his way.

"Now, this time I remembered the whole sequence of events well enough, as such a strange whim of chance is sure to make an impression on the mind. Still, it was little more than an anecdote to provoke a quiet chuckle from acquaintances, and I thought it of little consequence – until two months later, when I experienced it all over again.

"A *third* man arrived, completely unlike the first two, this one a skinny but handsome lad with a shock of wavy red hair and a mild Irish twinge to his accent. And once more, he came in with the aforementioned symptoms of glandular fever and introduced himself as *Marshal Mendler*. I must confess I was rather reeling through the revelation, and in truth I may have been a little remote in my examination of his symptoms, but I was so sure of my diagnosis that further examination felt unnecessary. Dr. Watson, just for the sake of collegial information sharing, this Marshal Mendler did have the *petechia*, and the distinctive rash on his back as well.

"I could keep my silence no longer. 'Mr. Mendler, I believe you have a case of glandular fever. I will give you a prescription and some advice shortly, but first, I must ask about your name. Is it terribly common in this part of London?'

"Mendler was rather slow to respond, and seemed a little hazy in his thoughts. You must remember, Mr. Holmes, that one of the most notable symptoms of the disease is extreme fatigue, and this Mendler seemed to be fighting through it more than most. He waded through whatever murk had covered his mind and gave me an odd glance.

"'Oh, no, not so common around this part of London. Truth be told, I've never met anyone else here who shares it. But it's common enough back in my country.'

"'Really?' I asked. 'I suppose Mendler is not an English surname, but it's not an Irish one either, is it?'

"At this point, the man's expression changed to one of confusion, but it cleared up quickly enough. 'Ah . . . It's not, no. I have an Irish mother, but a father from the Continent. Took on her looks more than his, if that weren't already clear.'

" I decided that whatever was going on here, I wasn't going to wrench it from this particular Marshal Mendler, and the poor man was nearly ready to collapse from exhaustion regardless. We finished up the visit, and he took the same invoice with a short note as the others. I was tempted to question him further, but so tired looked he that to interrogate him may have arguably violated the Hippocratic Oath, and I let him leave without further comment.

"I will tell you, Holmes, this mystery nearly ate me alive. But it was still, in my mind, in the statistical realm of possibility that this was coincidence. That three Marshal Mendlers came down with glandular fever during the same year, and all came to my practice for their diagnosis was nearly impossible to believe, but it was not yet out of the question. But I drew the line at *four*!

"I will admit with some shame that when the fourth Marshal Mendler introduced himself, I rather lost my temper. I had not even begun my examination, only heard the man's name and glanced at him long enough to see the fatigue wearing at his unlined face, the swollen lymph nodes, and the sweat-stained shirt, before I started yelling.

"'What is this?' I asked him, striding over towards the man. 'Is this some prank? Do I have some unseen enemy who would induce a state of paranoia in me? Who put you up to this? Name him, for I will not be haunted by Marshal Mendlers with glandular fever for my entire medical career!'

"Holmes, I will admit that it was not my finest moment, and in fact I rather think I overdid it. So startled was the man that he fled the office like a frightened rabbit, saying not a word to me, apart from his name. Afterwards, I asked my secretary to close the practice for an hour and came straight here. In retrospect, perhaps my actions were rash, but I am so utterly mystified that I couldn't dream of doing otherwise. You are the only person I know who I can imagine might be able to get to the bottom of such strangeness. On top of that . . . Forgive me for being blunt, but I do believe you owe me a favor, Holmes." At this point, the young man looked pointedly in my direction, although at the time I could not figure why that would be the case. Something else that the young doctor had said early prodded at me as well, but for now I allowed myself to sit back and listen to Holmes's familiar rhythm of follow-up questions.

"The four Marshal Mendlers – were they different in ways apart from appearance? Voice, mannerisms, height?"

"Yes. The third in particular was much shorter than the other three."

"And when you told the first Marshal Mendler your diagnosis, how did he take the news? Did he inquire more about the disease?"

"No, he seemed familiar with it. As to how he seemed . . . I suppose I hadn't thought about it. Not surprised, to be sure. Yes, now that you mention it, I remember thinking at the time that he may have expected it."

"And the others? How did they react?"

"The second seemed . . . satisfied, perhaps, through the layer of exhaustion. The third was somewhat guilty, if I had to put a word to it. The fourth fled my office so quickly that any emotion he may have shown was impossible to see."

"Interesting. Have you brought this up to any of your fellow medical professionals? Any of the other local physicians?"

"Why, no. I don't want any of them to think I'm going around the bend."

"I suppose if you were suspected of hallucinating Marshal Mendlers, it may have some effect on your reputation in the medical community. Go ahead and reopen your practice, Dr. Verner. We shall meet you back there when we have discovered anything of interest. Rest assured that based on the information you have provided me, I don't believe there is any risk to your well-being or place of business, but I will be sure to let you know if that changes."

Holmes chuckled a little to himself after Dr. Verner had left. "Well! This is an odd case. There are several possible solutions in my mind, but with a little legwork, we can effectively narrow it down. I believe a strategy of divide and conquer will be most effective. Watson, would you be willing to speak with some of your colleagues in the medical field? Best to start with – Oh, let's say any doctor working within five streets of your old practice."

"Certainly. I'm already familiar with many of them. What would you have me ask?"

"I would determine whether Dr. Verner's experience is unique to him, or being repeated at other practices."

"Sharing patient information is generally frowned upon, but many of the local doctors are aware of our partnership. If I tell them I'm on a case with you, most of them will likely be willing to help."

"Excellent. There are one or two other avenues I will pursue in the meantime. Let us go about the day separately, and we'll reconvene here in the evening."

It was with these marching orders that I spent a rather pleasant day. At first I attempted, through idle means of idle chit-chat, to determine whether my erstwhile colleagues had noticed anything unusual about the recent cases of glandular fever outbreak. When this proved fruitless, I brought up the name Marshal Mendler to see whether that might spark a response. No one reacted to the name or had any particular observations, but many of them promised to let me know if they heard anything. I also added one or two questions of my own devising to the list, but I do hope readers will forgive me if I play the "Holmes" once in my own story and leave that reveal for the end.

Around half-past-three o'clock, I strode into the office of one Dr. Levick, stationed in a small practice about four streets from my old haunt. His name was unfamiliar to me, but I had been directed to him by one of my colleagues, who mentioned that he had just opened his practice about a year and eight months earlier. By a stroke of luck, Dr. Levick had just seen his last patient for the day and was wrapping up some paperwork, and was happy to see me, as he'd heard my name before, and was apparently a devoted reader of my publications. Occasionally my very association with Holmes is a source of some minor advantage – something that I try not to rely upon during my personal life, but one that seems perfectly justifiable to make use of in the course of investigations such as this.

Dr. Levick was a large, jovial fellow with an open face, booming voice, and a greying beard. He shook my hand vigorously upon our introduction.

"Forgive me my lack of decorum, Dr. Watson. I am still becoming accustomed to the ways of the city. I have spent all of my career thus far as a rural doctor out in Glastonbury in the southwest – Have you ever been? Beautiful town, rich in legend. It's supposedly where King Arthur and Guinevere themselves were buried, if you're a man for folklore! But it's much smaller than London – the sort of place where a man will run into half of his patients while out doing the weekend errands. Ah, but my mother needs my care, and she's been a Londoner all her life. Couldn't convince her to move out to the fresh air with me, so I came here to take care of her. Besides, my wife has always had eyes for the city, and she ought to get a chance to experience life here, don't you think? But listen to me prattle on – What can I do for you, my dear Doctor Watson?"

"Nonsense," I said, rather charmed by this new doctor's affable and open demeanor. "It's good to know that the patients of Kensington are in good hands. But I will confess that today I come to you in my role as Sherlock Holmes's chronicler rather than as a medical professional. I shan't take up much of your time."

"Please, ask away. Happy to provide any assistance that I can."

"Have you noticed anything unusual about any cases of glandular fever that you've seen since opening your practice?"

"Hmm? Well, let me think . . . Nothing unusual about the symptoms, no. Certainly a little more common than I used to see in Glastonbury, but there's no surprise there, what with the density of people and fluids in this city, eh Doctor?" He laughed at his own crassness, and I will admit that I chuckled a little as well. "No, I think the disease itself has been largely the same. Although there was the strangest coincidence with two of the young lads who came in with it . . . ."

Expectant hope swelled in my breast. "Yes?" I prompted.

"It's nothing about the disease itself, but it did strike me as a little odd. Two lads, both young men but otherwise completely unlike each other, both with the exact same name and the exact same disease. Not an English name either. Something from the Continent. Alliterative too, both the first and last name started with an '*M*' . . . or maybe it was '*N*' . . . ?"

"Was it Marshal Mendler, by chance?"

"Why, yes! How did you know? Or was that the information you were searching for?"

"It was indeed. Thank you, Dr. Levick. After a day's fruitless search, you are the first positive result that I've found. Now, if you could tell me upon which days they visited, and whatever you remember of their appearance . . . ."

Dr. Levick happily checked his records, thrilled to be able to help with a case, and I left his practice feeling buoyed by the success. None of the other practices that I visited reported a similar experience, but I nonetheless returned to Baker Street looking forward to reporting my findings to Holmes.

Upon his return, Holmes was in a chipper mood, humming a tune that I'd heard him playing on the violin a few days before. I took this to mean that the day's search had produced results for him as well. I quickly explained Dr. Levick's experience to him and gave him my notes about the men's appearances and dates of illness. He laughed cheerily and clapped me on the shoulder.

"Well done, Watson! And this Dr. Levick – You say he is new to his practice? Much like Dr. Verner?"

"Yes, although he has been at it a little longer."

"But still in place less than two years. That is excellent work, and it eliminates a few possibilities, including the rather unsavory idea that Dr. Verner was indeed being personally targeted by some bizarre scheme. I'm sure he will be most relieved to hear it. Combining your findings with my own, I believe I have a good sense of what has so perplexed our dear Verner, but the reasoning behind this phenomenon is still a mystery to me. I have a few ideas, but as of yet no evidence to lead me in one direction or another."

"And I suppose you're unwilling to reveal your findings to me until your mind is made up?"

"Ah, you know me well, but I shall give you the hint that I did not find the most crucial piece of information on my own – it was found by one of the Irregulars. They are ever a useful set of eyes and ears along the streets of London, although I must say that the high rate of illiteracy among them makes certain tasks a little more difficult. Do you happen to know any good teachers of letters? They're bright lads, and it would make them substantially more useful . . . Ah, well, a discussion for another time. Now, Watson, I need you to tell me everything you know about glandular fever."

"Certainly. What would you like to hear?"

"Any piece of information that you deem important to know in order to convincingly falsify the symptoms of the disease. If my suspicions are correct, we will have this case wrapped up by tomorrow afternoon."

This was hardly Holmes's first time pretending to have an illness for a case, nor was it my first time assisting him in the deception. We had the distinct advantage that some of the symptoms of glandular fever – fatigue and a sore throat – were easily imitated through acting ability without the need for physical trickery. After some discussion we opted against imitating the *petechia*. Even though Holmes could come up with many concoctions that could imitate the color of the distinctive spots, I steadfastly refused to allow him to actually put any of them in his mouth.

We compromised by applying a hot water bottle to his forehead to give him the heat of the feverish. Finally, he asked me to forge a doctor's note stating that I had diagnosed him with the disease, something that I did with some reluctance. Even without my practice, I had never been one to willingly help a patient fake a diagnosis, and I suppose now that I am recording this story, I will have to make reparations in whatever manner the medical community deems fit.

At three o'clock in the afternoon, medical fakery accomplished and based on information Holmes had received, we made our way to a tavern in Kensington known as the The Glenburrough. It was a large and dignified establishment, finely decorated like a northern hunting lodge with all manner of taxidermy and polished weaponry set upon the walls. It was a fairly large place as well, with space on the first floor for tenants to rent rooms. The tavern keeper, a broad-shouldered man with a wispy tawny beard, hurried over to us as soon as we walked in and seated us at a large table by the fireplace.

"You look like the Thames itself chewed you up and spat you back out. Might I assume that you are here with a case of . . . What was it now? A disease of the glands?"

"Yes," said Holmes weakly. He swallowed a few times in the manner of one attempting to comfort a sore throat, then shook his head. "I read an advertisement on a bulletin . . . ."

"Say no more, man. You look as though every word is killing you. Who's this with you?"

"I brought my doctor to verify my condition." I resisted the urge to glare at Holmes for the half-truth.

"You hardly need the extra proof. Sit tight there. I'll let him know." He left us and disappeared up the stairs taking them two at a time.

"On your guard, Watson," Holmes murmured, the scratchiness miraculously vanished from his throat as he watched the top of the stairs like a hawk. "I know not what sort of man we are about to meet who stands at the crux of this odd little tale. I think it overall very likely that he will be harmless, but we should be vigilant all the same."

248

The man who descended the stairs behind the tavern owner was the very image of a certain type of aristocrat that can be found somewhere in every circle of nobility: A man who is determined to make an impression in any room where he happens to be found. Despite the setting around us more closely resembling a hunting lodge than a formal ball, he was dressed to the nines in a formal suit and bow tie, a gaudy shirt of bright eye-piercing purple, and rimless *pince-nez* glasses, topped off by an expensive golden watchchain peeking out from underneath his suitcoat. He was a young man, likely not yet twenty-five years old.

Beside me, Holmes relaxed. "Yes, rather harmless indeed, I should think," he murmured.

"Good evening, gentlemen!" the man cried out when he reached our table. Although his English was quite good, the German burr beneath his words was unmistakable. "Although not so good of an evening for you, I believe, eh, my friend? Ah, but as much as you are likely unhappy now, if you have answered my advertisement, then you know that I will compensate you generously for your participation in my little experiment."

"Thank you kindly, sir," said Holmes weakly. He punctuated his statement with a weak cough, which I felt may have been overplaying his hand. "The advertisement said that I needed 'proof of affliction', so I brought my doctor here with me."

At this point, the man looked over at me for the first time. He seemed a little uncomfortable. "Ah. It's wonderful to meet you, Doctor, but your presence is not required. Most people have been bringing a note. In fact, I think I may have to insist that you leave before we get into details. Medical propriety and all that. I'm sure you understand."

"Before my doctor goes," Holmes wheezed. "We should all be properly introduced."

"Ah, but of course! Where are my manners? My name is Marshal Mendler. A pleasure to meet you both."

"You can stay where you are, Watson," said Holmes. He sat straighter in his seat, the fatigue gone from his face and the gleam of triumph alight in his eye. "But you, Mr. Mendler, have a fair bit of explaining to do. You have been running a rather odd con out of this tavern, and while I feel confident that I understand your methodology, I would hear your reasoning in your own words before determining what manner of crime you've been committing. I advise that you be truthful. My name is Sherlock Holmes. I am not with the police, and as such am not bound by their rules of sentencing."

Many times now I have witnessed a man's disposition go from relaxation to alarm after a few sentences from Holmes, and Marshal Mendler was no exception. His composure cracked immediately. His face fell, his eyes darted towards the door, and he looked ready to spring away from the table at a moment's notice. But he deflated equally quickly when he saw us tense, ready to pursue should he choose to run. Instead, he slumped against his chair. He did not seem inclined to speak, however, and so Holmes pressed on.

"For quite some time now, you have been hiring men afflicted with glandular fever to pretend to be you, receive invoices or other notations from the doctors, and bring them back to you. You posted your advertisements publicly, claiming to be a medical researcher looking for patients diagnosed with the disease for some research project – a believable falsehood, given how recently the disease was described – and you've promised compensation. I have a copy of one of the advertisements myself, taken by my men in the field from a posting board on Gloucester Road.

"Now, I'm sure not all of the men you've met are willing to participate when they learn your actual purpose for seeking them out, but I imagine enough are enticed by the money to keep your scheme running. You've hand-selected some very small number of new doctors that you send the men to – likely because newer doctors are less likely to spread word to colleagues, or perhaps you thought they would be so desperate for new patients as to overlook the scheme entirely. I don't yet know what you've been doing with the doctor's excuses, or what sort of financial gain you've achieved."

"Financial gain?" The man repeated, seemingly bewildered and offended by the very suggestion. "I can assure you, Mr. Holmes, that I have gained no financial benefit from this little game. Quite the opposite, in fact: It has funneled wealth away from my own pockets and into those of the afflicted and their doctors. No one has been hurt by it, and I have treated all fairly in my dealings with them." Mendler passed a hand over his face, sighing deeply. "I suppose this was an inevitable eventuality. I knew when I started it that the whole plan was not going to be sustainable forever, but I'd hoped to have a little more time.

"Yes, I am the true Marshal Mendler. I have been in London for almost two years now, and I do not wish to leave. I am from a family of some prominence in Frankfurt, and my father has had my life laid out for me since the day I was born. He has had it set in his mind that I would graduate a good German university with a degree in financial matters, then take a position at his company. But I do not want to know nothing but Germany all my life! After much wheedling, I finally convinced him to make a single concession in his plan for me – one year in London after my graduation. I convinced him that in order to truly be successful in business, I must know more of the world. Boundaries of trade between countries are

250

a thing of the past, don't you think, Mr. Holmes? After I graduated, and with some reluctance, he gave me enough funds to last here a year, gave me a handful of names of business associates in the city, and sent me on my way.

"I obeyed some of his requests. I did not stay at the glamorous hotel he selected for me, but instead found this charming tavern and rented lodgings above. It has suited my needs nicely, and allowed me to stretch my funds besides. I met with his business associates once each, but in truth I had several university friends living in the city, and quickly found myself graciously accepted into their social circles. Still, always I have had the ticking clock hanging over my head – that constant reminder that all of this joy, all of this independence, has a time limit.

"In my last month – Indeed, within the last three weeks before I was meant to return home – I contracted a case of glandular fever. I will not tell you how, for I am here to besmirch no one's honor, my own included. But so ill was I that I could barely leave my bed. I owe much to the gracious tavern keeper, who kept me alive and brought me meals during that time, and eventually called a doctor to come see me. He diagnosed me with the aforementioned disease. Knowing that I would be in grave trouble if I didn't contact them, and being equally sure that my father would think I was inventing some excuse not to return, I sent them a letter with the doctor's diagnosis and invoice enclosed, to prove that I wasn't lying. Then I returned to bed.

"To my surprise, my parents not only sent a letter back encouraging me to rest and recover before I tried to travel, but included some additional funds to help purchase medications and pay for continued lodgings. Two weeks later, I was back on my feet and well enough to travel – but I had no wish to! Surely they'd never know if I waited one more week before packing my bags. So new is this disease, after all, that they would have no reason to doubt my words if I exaggerated the time to recovery just a little.

"Suffice to say, a week turned into two and then four. I could tell by the tone of my parents' letters that they were growing suspicious, so I hatched the plan you have so succinctly summarized. I post advertisements calling men who have the disease to meet me here and pay them a handsome sum to meet a relatively new doctor and bring back a letter with my name on it. Then, I send the enclosed diagnosis back to my parents. I claim to be improving, steadily but surely, so that they don't worry enough to come here themselves. I am lucky in that it is a disease that can occasionally have long-lasting effects, so the falsehood is believable. Besides, my father would never leave his business to come to me, and he would never let my mother travel alone. But it would seem my days living the lie are done. I will go upstairs and draft a letter to my parents, letting

251

them know that I will start my return home by the end of the week. No, that I will begin my journey on the morrow. I have tarried long enough, and to stretch out my goodbyes will only make leaving that much more difficult. I suppose you wish for some money for your silence?"

Holmes's eyes had softened somewhat over the course of Mendler's story. "Just as it seems that you are not the hardened criminal that I worried we might find at the end of this trail, so too am I not the blackmailer you expect. I would ask that you meet with the doctors who were involved in your scheme, explain to them what you have explained to me, and give them some compensation for the mental anguish that I know that you have caused at least one of them. While this was a foolish plan, Mr. Mendler, and certainly goes against one or two facets of the law, I believe you yourself to be relatively harmless. If you perform the tasks I have set before you, you can consider our business together to be complete."

"Meeting with all of the doctors will not be doable by the end of the day tomorrow, Mr. Holmes."

"I suppose it won't. You will have to plan on leaving by the end of the week, as you originally mentioned. Farewell, Mr. Mendler. I wish you the best of luck in your future endeavors."

It wasn't until Holmes and I had returned to Baker Street, humming cheerily in the post-case thrill that would carry him through the next few days, that I decided the time was ripe to reveal my own deductions.

"Well, Watson," said he cheerfully, "another case solved. And as is often the case, the truth is not the result of some grand conspiracy, but merely the result of one human being trying to repave the path upon which he or she walks through life."

"Indeed," said I, as neutrally as possible, "I'm sure your cousin will be most pleased to know that he was selected by chance, rather than any personal targeting."

Holmes stopped, and I knew by his smile that I had hit the mark. "Why, Watson!" he cried in delight. "You have been conducting your own deductions behind my back! Please, you must elucidate me as to how you learned of my relationship to the doctor."

"Even you make mistakes, my dear Holmes." I said. "Dr. Verner is not the first person to burst into our rooms without introducing himself, but he is the first who you have not sat down and forced the introductions upon afterwards. That meant that not only did you know the man, but you knew that I knew him as well. As I have only had one interaction with him, you had to know he was the one who bought my practice. This was curious, as I don't recall ever mentioning the purchaser by name, nor did I give enough description of him for you to know him by sight. Furthermore, he

252

mentioned that he knew you were aware of the rules of the Diogenes Club, which I could only imagine must mean he knows Mycroft and your relationship with him. Not many men know Mycroft – not nearly as many as know you – so this struck me as odd as well.

"When I went to interview the doctors of the city, I thought I would look into what they knew of Dr. Verner as well. For the sake of the case, of course, but also to see if I could determine, with a little digging, why you had chosen not to reveal your knowledge of him to me. As it turns out, it wasn't too difficult. An old colleague of mine, one whose word I would trust to the grave, told me that Dr. Verner had spoken to him about his purchase of my practice over a glass of strong brandy. He'd said that a relative had given him the funds to make the purchase – not to help Verner, but in order to help ease my transition out of my practice. There is only one man with such incentive to see my return to Baker Street."

Holmes was nearly giddy with glee. "Watson, after all these years, you have truly absorbed my methods. Well done! Yes, you are correct in all points. Verner is my second cousin, and a capable doctor besides. I gave him some funds as a gift to purchase your practice at full price. You see, I knew that you only returned to Baker Street at my request, and had you needed to compromise on the worth of your practice in order to do so, I would have felt quite guilty indeed. This seemed the easiest way to ensure a smooth transition – and help my cousin besides."

I shook my head. "The webs you weave are far too many to count, my friend. Even the weakest among them captures many flies at once."

"I hope you will forgive me my deception. I did not wish to wound your pride. But you have certainly had your revenge, for I am the one who has come out behind in this particular game. Come, Watson – I will buy you dinner to celebrate your victory."

NOTE

For the curious, the "glandular fever" that rests at the center of this tale now goes by a different name – *mononucleosis*, or *mono* for short. While the symptoms were first identified in 1889, the name mononucleosis did not appear until 1920. The underlying virus that causes the disease, the Epstein-Barr Virus, wasn't identified until 1964.

253

The Lilac Flame
by Marcia Wilson

"Mr. Holmes, *do not* approach the dead man."

Even as he said this most necessary thing, Inspector Lestrade wondered if it were his eternal fate to voice common sense and reason to men lacking both.

If he wasn't telling Holmes the obvious, he thought darkly, it was Gregson. Both were incapable of keeping their tempers where they should be, which was inside a stout box with many locks.

In some ways, this was almost a compliment. Quarreling was a distraction that could steal the results of his hard labours right from under his nose. (This had been accomplished, frequently, by Gregson back before Lestrade learned the skill of holding his breath and counting to ten because Gregson refused to believe he lacked the patience for even that.)

On the other hand, if his work should intersect with Sherlock Holmes's clients in any way (not unlike a cart paused across train-rails), he needed to make certain that the man's facts were correct. *He* wasn't a sworn Officer of the Law, and it was doubtful the man's large brain had room for *all* the regulations, policies, and updated procedures the police were duty-bound to follow.

Or, as Gregson once said, Sherlock Holmes could put "phalanx" in his testimony and the court would accept it, but should a policeman do the same – ? He'd be laughed out of the same court.

"Mr. Holmes, do you hear me? If Dr. Watson learns I didn't stop you from moving around with that broken ankle, my fate will be worse than anything *Punch* could write!"

The police feared *Punch* more than a foreign invasion.

Mr. Holmes grunted and hobbled back from the corpse as if he wasn't in agony and set his legs straight out and flat upon the floor, his skinny spine propped against one of the warehouse's filthy packing-crates. His newspaper splint crackled against the musty wooden planks.

Lestrade took a relieved breath. He would reserve his prayer of thanks once this night was done and he had the full list of gratitudes assembled. He didn't believe for one second that man was as hale as he was acting. His ankle was shattered, like glass hitting the most unfortunate combination of pressure and angle – the difference between a fist or a ball-peen hammer. His white face was damp with sweat, and he was pausing, holding his breath in at irregular times as he pretended he wasn't leaning on Lestrade's bull-oak walking stick. (*Just correcting his balance, I'm sure.*) Lestrade could spot the signs of an old beat copper pretending he wasn't injured and *Yes, sir. I'll be right as rain after a moment . . . .*

If he tries to walk again, so help me, I am . . . Lestrade clenched his teeth behind his lips. Oh, dear. It seemed that Mr. Holmes wasn't finished complaining . . . .

". . . are wasting time while your men go for Watson," the amateur finished. "Nor we have confirmed the body as Canary Wilson's."

Long experience kept Lestrade from voicing his dangerous thoughts, which were: "*Of course, because as you know there are* so many *men in London with a left leg a quarter-less the length of the right, and they* always *clad their clubfoot in a white boot with the other foot in a perfectly ordinary brown cowhide brogue.*" The dead man's feet (if nothing else) were clearly visible, even in the dark of the warehouse, the white orthopedic boot glowing like a bone in the dark nimbus of lamplight.

Sherlock Holmes was annoying, and he was right. The identity must be confirmed. The way Lestrade's luck was headed, Canary Wilson was a twin or triplet, and they *all* had that deformity.

"Wilson or not-Wilson, the dead man shall remain dead, Mr. Holmes, and if it should be Wilson, please remember he spent half his life in East End! You wouldn't prod a plague-rat, eh? There could be more traps in this warehouse, such as the one that just smashed your leg – and it's a wonder you've avoided breaking something this long – plus we both know that outside this blessed maze, the weather is sour and dangerous!" Splinting that break with scrounged-up copies of *The London Times* and packing-string had not been the highlight of the night for either man.

Lestrade was still shaky from their close call. The trap had been crude but effective – a tipping-over crate larger than a hall-clock and heavy as a boulder, meant to push its victim down the crumbling stairs and tumbling after to crush him like an eggshell – but Holmes's swift reflexes had saved his life. Looking back, Lestrade didn't know how he was still surprised. Holmes was a natural born bantamweight, lean and light and quick as a bird.

Holmes made another sound, more vinegar-y than before. A troubling sign of things to come – that man could sit with the patience of a frozen rock for his answers.

Clearly, something was troubling the man.

Something he hasn't told me, I'll be bound. Some "fact" that he'd say doesn't exist because he hasn't proven it yet . . . and yet he says his guesses are better than my facts. Isn't this a cheery addition to a cheery night!

Far overhead, thunder muttered. Dust and dry mould, fine as fernseed, snowed down from the ancient rafters. Lestrade sighed. His breath slithered grey in the chill. Canary's warehouse was an old gunpowder factory, so the walls were thick under a light roof. The rain wiggled snakelike down the tiles, the soft *pat-pat-pat* of the first drops hitting the floor below the roofing-holes. They were in for an unpleasant wait until the constables returned with Watson.

"We can at least confirm the identity." Holmes pressed. "For if this is not old Canary, we will have to redouble our manhunt."

"Very well. If you promise to write down what I recite, we can do something useful while we wait. Just hold on to your lantern and lift it up if I need the light." The little detective said this in a voice so calmly and evenly that no one could tell his own brain was screaming to stop and this foolishness and stay put like a man with half-a-teaspoon of common sense.

Holmes nodded, and something flickered in his gunmetal eyes. "If I tell you to jump, Lestrade, do not waste time and ask me where or how high."

Thank God. Some awareness at last. "Agreed!" Lestrade rose to his feet, feeling every dot of his age (*I can't believe he's only eleven years younger than me!*) as he held up his own lantern, the blind open. Before him yawed the confusion of Canary's warehouse: A cavern of age-blackened timbers (old blasting accidents) and sloppily-stacked crates and cartons with enough spiderwebs to please a nightmare. Some of the crates were polite enough to be written in languages he recognized. Others were just so much chop and gibberish.

He didn't trust the nice words he could read: *Inspected Pure* or *Dated Wares* and *Upright Only* could mean anything if you were wandering about in a warehouse owned by someone who would sell his own granny's teeth as easily as Marwood's rope.

The Lord must still believe in small mercies, however, because there were no signs of his "respectable" trade by day: The sad, peeping little blinded canaries had been found in the back of his pawnshop, and he devoutly hoped the charities would take in the poor things.

His son, Martin Lestrade, spoke of being a policeman someday as he nursed starved kittens to health and fed his one-legged hen seeds pilfered from the park. He didn't know why his father didn't want him to follow his footsteps.

How can I tell him man's cruelty to other men won't break your heart, but what's done to the dumb creatures beholden to our care will . . . ?

The path of light slipped over a row of knife-sharp edges of crate. Rough splinters stood up in the moment like jagged teeth. Overhead, a ship's chain shed flakes of bloody rust.

Lestrade loathed true blackness. It gave a false flatness of reality and played havoc with depth perception, like missing an eyeball.

"The odds are slim against there being more than one tripwire or trap, Lestrade."

"And how would you know that?" Lestrade knew he sounded peevish as an old aunt but couldn't help himself – How could Holmes bring the worst out of his temper so well?

"Because if I am correct, the dead man is Canary Wilson, and Morris was determined to kill him."

Yet you're almost desperate to confirm the identity. Lestrade grimaced. *What do you know?* "Are we trusting the word of a madman like Morris right now?"

Holmes sighed – Lestrade fancied he could hear the eye-rollings – as he made the unmistakable sounds of fixing up a cigarette. *Good. Might cool his blood a bit.* "Madmen are only strangers to reason, not integrity."

"I can't argue with that. Right." Lestrade had gotten as close to the body as needed, and cautiously lowered himself to one knee. He wished he didn't have to be close at all. The reek of death had settled the fluids in the corpse. Lantern oil sloshed as he set it to the side and opened the blinds. "I'm going to describe what I see in the hopes it will satisfy you on whether this is Wilson.

"Tall white man, thinning reddish-yellow hair, sideburns trimmed down to his jowls. His eyeglasses are all crushed up under his chin. They are widely-spaced, set in silver and . . . the lenses are shaped like very long ovals. That's an odd shape! Almost like sausage links!"

"He was light blind." Holmes explained Lestrade's puzzlement. "He rarely looked up. The lenses accommodate his left-to-right vision of the world. Continue."

"Ah, I see the leather case for his spectacles. It is large – almost as large as those flasks gentlemen use to keep their brandy-bottles. It is brown leather, tooled in a pattern: *GWR* – presumably for *Great Western Rail* on the side in fancy script, with a train puffing steam on the front. He is wearing a dustcoat over a working suit of dark brown sack, brown right shoe, left white orthopedic boot, brown kidskin gloves, brown rain-hat, and . . . brown belt and vest . . . Shirt is eggshell linen, the cheap kind you get in a Lambeth pawnshop . . . He is overweight, especially about the middle, at I estimate a good twenty pounds. There's . . . huh, a small nick out of the lobe of his left ear, like someone took a paper-puncher to it. He's got a book of train-tickets poking out of his pocket . . . and a flat, square leather eyeglasses-case with a clip-clasp, dark brown and pebbled like pigskin. *Hmmph.* Tickets look like he was planning to cross the Channel tomorrow morning."

"What of his fingers? Are there rings?"

257

"I'll have to take off the gloves first, if you don't mind . . . ." Lestrade grunted at the effort with the nearest hand. It was the dead man's left one and board-flat against the floor-planks. Finally, it came free.

"Large blue glass signet ring. Looks like gold-washed iron band . . . Oh, yes, a poison ring for certain. There's a tiny bit of white powder on the rim of the little hinge."

"Try not to touch it."

"Do you really take me for that much of a fool?" Lestrade snapped. "D'you know what? Forget I said anything." He took a deep breath. "No pocket-watch that I can see . . . ." Lestrade twisted his head around, back and forth. "I . . . don't see a watch at all – ?"

"Surprising."

Holmes was understating. A man's watch was his pride. To lack one demonstrated a vulgar nakedness. Even the poorest men kept one, even if it didn't work. They just kept shells or turned the face about. A poor watch was better than no watch.

A man simply didn't lack for a watch. They thought about this incongruent thing, this aberration, for a moment before Lestrade collected his wits.

"I'm about to roll him over to see the face."

It took effort. The man had collapsed on his front, his malformed leg bent halfway to his floating ribs and his good leg straight. Both arms were splayed out crooked and the face was completely flat, nose to the boards.

Lestrade pondered his few options for a moment, aware that every split-second was an eternity to Holmes's lightning-fast brain. "He's extremely dead, Mr. Holmes," he said at last. "There is a dried pool of vomit spread in a large area, about a foot in breadth. His face is black with congested blood and swollen. His tongue is out, and his eyes are frogged as far as they can go. The way he's clenched up under himself, it looks as though he had a heart attack and suddenly fell."

Holmes made a sound between derision and irony. "He was taking amyl nitrate for his heart. Possibly the least illegal thing he was paying Morris to mix."

Lestrade wondered if he was going to have a heart attack himself. Sherlock Holmes was speaking without facts based on the bimetallic? "Are you *really* going to say *Morris* killed him? He can't walk, has one good hand, and it tremors!"

"It would fit the facts." A plume of smoke rose over the crates, showing Holmes was staying put. "Morris was more than his angry assistant, as you know."

"Assistants always are," Lestrade sighed. "Look, Mr. Holmes, I know you're not telling me everything, and I understand your confidence with your clients. Very well. I can't force you to divulge, but I hope no other crimes or deaths will result from your silence, because then I shall have to arrest you."

"I would expect nothing less."

Holmes's casual acceptance of this fact somehow stung. Lestrade bristled. "Then do believe me when I say I've seen dead men! You're convinced Morris did this, but the vomit *could* mean accidental or purposeful poisoning – Suicide even! I can't look for other clues such as blue skin, or flushing. The blood's pooled too long in the body, and – Here, now!"

"What is it?" Holmes asked eagerly.

"I owe you an apology."

"I'd prefer information!"

"There's an empty bottle under him. It was so small I didn't see it at first." Lestrade growled. "Apple-green glass," he snarled. "I know what that means!"

"Not all chemists put their poisons in green glass bottles."

"They should!" Lestrade prized the glass tube out of the crack between the planks. "Thank God for the Arsenic Act," he muttered for possibly the sixth-hundredth time since becoming a copper. It made him queasy to think of the years before 1851, when poisons weren't registered by law. "Empty." He reported gloomily. "Just a smattering of silverly looking dust in the bottom and sides. Cork looks new."

"I would ask you to help me over there for my own examination, but Watson would know." Holmes complained.

"Yes, he would! If there's nothing else you need, I'm going to come back and have a sit."

The men settled themselves side-by-side for scant warmth. It was eerily quiet with no scurry of rats or flutter of pigeons – Possibly, Lestrade thought spitefully, because that little green bottle wasn't the only poison here. Rain continued to drip overhead.

"I'm honestly surprised we're in a dry spot," Lestrade said at last. He was trying to pull together his cigarette-case and had put his matches in another pocket somewhere.

Holmes huffed. "Watson would call it a fluke of physical science."

"He would indeed." Lestrade had gotten to know the doctor rather better in Holmes's years of absence – and the doctor had no self-doubts when it came to expressing the questionable delights of a long night vigil. "Mr. Holmes, if I may . . . How did you enter this case with Wilson? I mean, I am not at all surprised you're here – but Canary's – was – a dirty little eel, and he must have had half of London's worst beholden to him in some way."

Holmes wordlessly offered the tip of his cigarette. Lestrade gratefully pulled the flame into his own and they smoked appreciatively. The younger man's long, white fingers trembled suddenly, as if a shiver had attacked his constitution. It was the first tremor of delayed shock. Gregson always shook like that when his body lost too much heat. Lestrade pretended he saw nothing.

"Morris came to me under confidential circumstances. I can tell you that Morris is not his birth-name, for he was originally Morris Standlake."

"*Standlake*? There's an uncommon name. I've only heard of it through Standlake's Nutritious Fertilizers." At Holmes's twist of the mouth, Lestrade clarified hastily: "Best for the soil if you want to grow good crummocks, to hear old Bradstreet. He makes us eat it with bacon and lentils every Hogmanay." *And Easter, All-Saints, and any time he can find an excuse to cook it,* Lestrade mentally added.

"What a small world London can be. In fact, he was from that very same family that founded the company, albeit through an indirect line, and I am certain that is to the relief of his relatives. He began as a clerk and learned his tools of trade in organic and inorganic chemistry. I shouldn't under-estimate his intelligence. The problem is the workings of his mind, and a surprising degree of gullibility."

"Well, Canary was good at pulling in men like that." Lestrade muttered and picked at a splinter on his knuckle. It was black. Clea would make him scrub it out tonight, even if he had to clean to the bone.

"Ah, so his nickname came from his ability to persuade the courts of his innocence. I had thought it was because he was a canary trainer."

"Oh, he was singing to the Law *before* he was a canary trainer. He earned the nickname twice. Back in the old days he was a rat-catcher, helping himself to other people's safes and lock-boxes while clearing off their vermin. He'd drop the money and jewellry in the rat-bag, and no one in their right mind would want him to open it up to take a look!

"But the rat-catchers have their own honour, and a fire took his business. He moved to canaries and deliveries after that." Lestrade pretended to spit in the corner, a gesture of contempt. "I've never met more loathesome snakes than them who blind birds for a living." The injustice of it gnawed in his breast. It always had. "They *know* birds do not sing better in the darkness. Heavens forbid they let truth interfere with a sale."

Holmes made a peculiar sound, a soft, short exhale and wrapped his arms around his chest inside his overlarge dust-coat.

"We've got to find homes for those poor things," Lestrade added, because it had been preying on his conscience.

260

"Mrs. Hudson would take two, I am certain."

That would be cheerier than her little dog they watched put down for age and illness during the Jefferson Hope case. "Two down, six to go." He watched the motes of his breath dance in the hazy lamplight for a moment, remembered he had Constable Chary's tea-can, and offered Holmes the first sip. Chary had a strong hand with his leaves, and a stout black Assam could only help, correct? Lestrade bravely took his own portion of the strong brew. It was heavy with Lyle's Syrup.

Lestrade's entire body froze. Come to think of it, Holmes hadn't asked to see the little green bottle, nor had he grabbed it out of his pocket.

That was . . . not a good sign.

He glanced sideways at the younger man, but his eyes were closed, and smoke slipped, very slowly, through his lips. Were they turning blue? Was it from the cold? Or more shock? Or just the strength of the smoke?

"Couldn't be arsenic," Lestrade coughed, and spoke too loudly. "I can't see it all that well, but there's no soot in it, or indigo."

"That leaves a large field of possibilities." Holmes roused himself enough to show some of his old impatient self. "And we are discussing possibilities within a man's skills in a chemical factory."

"Here's the bottle. Can you make any sense of it?"

Holmes clutched it up, his pocket-glass in the other hand. "This is not powder," he announced. "It is residue. I should not say without tests, but amyl nitrate can look like this."

"You say this like you aren't convinced that it is what you see."

"I am not. The signs of death resemble potassium chloride."

"Potassium? Hmmph!" Lestrade snorted. "And people think poison is the murder women of woman."

"We should determine if it is."

Lestrade's mouth fell open to argue the painfully obvious. There was no point in pushing the hands of the clock forward until they reached a proper laboratory – but he heard his teeth slowly click shut as some part of him, the more intelligent part of him, realised a truth before his conscious thought.

Holmes normally had the patience of stone. But he was gravely injured, pinned to one spot and in great pain. He was going shocky. And he was proud as a girl, would not want to say he needed help.

The professional portion of the old copper's brain knew that for what it was. Any display of weakness could be picked apart later when the question of credulity came up. It was why all his men walked on broken bones and wrapped their joints and drank tea because they were too ill to eat and then pushed through the miles on the beat.

Watson might, just might possibly . . . restrain from boxing his teeth through his ears for what he was about to do, but needs must in these circumstances.

"Can we test it here?" He challenged, and put a proper whine to his voice, the tone that Watson swore was a screech married to a yelp. "Well? Can't we? Isn't there a way? You *are* a chemist, are you not?"

Lestrade could have sworn he heard their watches ticking in the sudden silence.

"Flame."

"Eh?"

Holmes's eyes were fully open and angry and sharp as his cheek-bones. "A flame test."

Lestrade read, in his precious free time, journals on crime that delved into a depressing number of cases where doctors went awry of their morals. He was not sure what a flame test required.

"Splinters. Wooden splinters if they are clean, but silver wire would be best." Holmes was saying between deep breaths. He was still plainly annoyed that Lestrade was goading him along, but that was good because it was keeping him awake.

"I don't see anything that could be used for clean splinters." Lestrade was putting it mildly. "What do you suggest?"

"We are surrounded by bits and bobs of his laboratory tools." Holmes fell into muttering the other man could not hear, his head twisting back and forth to see about in the gloom. "Should we find something proper to dip into the bottle, and set that residue on fire behind a screen, the colour of the flame would tell us if it is amyl nitrate or fatal potassium."

"All well and good, but I can't say we've got a lot of silver wire here! I'll look at these half-open crates. It looks like he was planning to muck about . . . ."

Lestrade told himself he was doing this despite being stiff, sore, tired, hungry, and cold because the alternative was to let Sherlock Holmes go on a treasure-hunt amongst the death scene. There was a very real possibility the dead man's silver eyeglasses would be petitioned for this make-do laboratory test in the field.

The time crept, slow and grudgingly. Lestrade could tell by the frequent scritch-scratch of sandpaper and puffs of fire that his partner was burning up his collection of cigarettes at an alarming rate.

Keeps him from crawling around the floor looking for things . . . .

An answer came in a tipped-over box of pasteboard. Long glass rods had been knocked aside by the dead man on his fall, and several had broken and rolled into a corner under a packing-crate table that had not the slightest speck of light underneath. The wounded glass reflected sea-green in his lamp. Lestrade scowled, baffled, and reported the finding.

"That will do once they are completely burnt off in the flame."

"Then there's our splinters – Glass splinters! Don't we have everything we need?" Lestrade's heart pounded. It was ridiculous, he thought. This wouldn't save them much work and it certainly wouldn't give him more sleep that night, but to know the answers. It was exhilarating!

"No."

The policeman paused. "No?"

Holmes scowled at nothing. "Did I not mention a screen? I am certain I did."

"W-well, you did, but you didn't say what sort of screen," Lestrade bluffed desperately.

"Potassium is a tricky element, Lestrade. If we were to suffer this flame test, it would still be inconclusive because it needs to be viewed through a cobalt lens. That screens out the spectrum and lets one see the true lilac flame."

Lestrade thought of a few words collected from patrolling on the east side that would apply to this situation and collapsed back at Holmes's side. He closed his eyes, admitting defeat.

Oh, well. I kept him awake and alert a bit longer.

He was so weary, and this miserable night wasn't over. Not by a long chalk. Regulations insisted he file his reports no matter how early or late the hour, and he was already composing the start in his head. Ultimately it wouldn't save him a jot of time, but it would keep his brain from running off –

. . . running off . . .

"Wait." Lestrade's eyes snapped open. "Did you say *cobalt glass?*"

Holmes frowned. "It is the only way to prove the presence of potassium under a flame test."

His voice was slurring. The pain was taking over. Oh, dear. Of all the times the man would be struggling to think.

"Mr. Holmes," Lestrade clutched at the man's sleeve and his fingers bit down, urgent with the need to keep him awake for Dr. Watson. "Mr. Holmes! *There was a railroad ticket in Canary's pocket!*"

"Yes, I know that." Holmes snarled.

Lestrade ignored him in the rush of thoughts swimming through his muddled brain. His spine locked upright as one frantic thought shifted into one gear, then the next. "He was planning to go to France at noon. That's when the sun is at his brightest . . . And you – *You said he was light-blind?*"

"Why are you asking me when you know I did say this?" Holmes's peevishness was on-target for a man in considerable pain and exposure.

And then, like a lightning-strike, Holmes's grey eyes swelled up like moonstones. "Yes, Lestrade! Look!"

Lestrade needed no encouragement. He hopped to his feet and threw the lantern in a circle about the warehouse.

"He had to have it on him . . ." he muttered out loud and scarce knew it. "But would they be smoked?"

"A man like Canary? Not likely!" Holmes said this with a confidence Lestrade found amazing, moreso as he didn't know what the man *meant*.

"Follow his arm." Broken ankle or not, Holmes was trying to stand in his excitement.

"Eh, what – *No!* By the Lord, sit you down!" Lestrade thought he was admirably calm, but later, Holmes told Watson he was screaming like an owl. "I know you haven't much love for detectives who sit in chairs all day and tell the police what to do – and thank you."

"The spectacles-case, Lestrade! Great Western Rail!"

Lestrade felt the fool. Canary's crumpled spectacles were small, narrow reading spectacles, and the leather case for his eyeglasses – the same case he'd picked up and put aside without opening it . . . that leather case was made for much larger eyewear.

The little detective stamped over to the dead man one last time and, with the protection of his gloves, prized open the leather case. There were glasses inside, and they shone cobalt blue, to protect the eyes of the dedicated train-traveller.

"Now, Lestrade," Holmes began to laugh. "Lift the blind on your lamp and let us see."

Oh, clever play on words. You already know what we're going to find, I'll be bound, but you haven't the proof and this was killing you, wasn't it?

"Very well, Mr. Holmes," Lestrade held out the lenses with a sarcastic bit of flourish. "Very well. I believe the honours are yours . . . ."

The Adventure of the Unfortunate Cardinal
by Alan Dimes

It was shortly before my friend Sherlock Holmes's retirement that we received the news that Pope Leo XIII had died. While neither Holmes nor I had any specific religious convictions, and the Pontiff's death hardly came as a surprise, as he was ninety-three years old and had been in poor health for some years, nevertheless, we heard the report of his passing with sadness. We had been of service to him on two separate occasions, the recovery of the Vatican cameos and the murder of Cardinal Tosca. While the first case received more publicity, Holmes was wont to dismiss it as "a little affair" because he had been able to solve it after a few hours' contemplation of the facts, without moving from his armchair. Needless to say, the Holy Father and his Cardinalate did not take the same view. The cameos dated back to the late fourth century and were said to have been created at the behest of St. Siricius, who had formulated many of the rules still adhered to by the priesthood. So, while they were not technically Holy Relics, they represented a link with the past whose absence would have been keenly felt.

As well as rewarding Holmes handsomely, Leo had been loud in his praise of the detective, and it cannot be doubted that this added to Holmes's growing international fame. Nor did it come as a surprise to us when, some years later, we were summoned to Rome to deal with the rather more delicate and potentially scandalous matter of the death of Cardinal Tosca.

The Cardinal had died, apparently from poisoning, not long after an unscheduled audience with the Pontiff. Holmes was uncomfortable if he had to leave his books and his scientific equipment, and the comforts of our life in Baker Street, for longer than a few days, so while the summons might have been expected, I was a little taken aback when he immediately dispatched a telegram agreeing to the trip. It transpired that, however complex or simple the case might prove to be, Holmes was eager to actually meet the Pope. I was happy to accompany him, for who could resist a journey to the Eternal City, even if the circumstances were unfortunate, and there was little likelihood that there would be time to view the full splendours of the ancient capital. Holmes informed Mrs. Hudson of our impending absence, and also sent a telegram to Inspector Lestrade to let him know that he would be unavailable for consultation until further notice. Then we were off, and we had ample opportunity to discuss the matter during the four days we spent on the Continental Express.

"What do you know of Cardinal Tosca?" Holmes asked me on the first evening after we had just finished a splendid meal and were partaking of brandy and cigars.

"Not very much, I'm afraid."

"Then let me enlighten you, as after we received the telegram I spent some time examining his career in my index, where I found him between a German music-hall performer and an American admiral. The name is Italian, but he was French, born in a little village in Provence in 1857."

"Young to be a Cardinal."

"Indeed. His family was poor, but he managed, on the basis of his ability, to get a place at the Sorbonne. He apparently came to the priesthood after a long spiritual struggle, which I understand isn't uncommon among intellectuals who embrace the Church, but once in, his talent guaranteed him a swift rise up the echelons. There were those who thought he would be a worthy successor to Peter's chair, even though he would have been the first non-Italian Pope in four-hundred years – since Adrian VI, that is, who was Dutch. Leo looked favourably upon him at first, doubtless seeing in him a man of potentially equal ability to himself."

"I take it that something caused a rift between them."

"Yes, indeed. In 1891, Leo issued an encyclical called *Rerum Novarum* – in English, *Rights and Duties of Capital and Labour*. It was an open letter, passed to all Catholic patriarchs, primates, archbishops and bishops, and in it Leo rejected both socialism and *laissez-faire* capitalism, and championed the right of workers to form trade unions. Despite coming from a humble background, Tosca was opposed to trade unions. He believed that if employers operated their businesses on Christian principles, as was their duty, then there would be no need for unions, and in any case, they were the thin edge of a wedge that inevitably led to communism and atheism."

"And you think Tosca's death may somehow be connected to this disagreement?"

"Well, it is certainly a possibility, but it would be a capital mistake to assume that it were so until we have had the opportunity to examine all the data."

At the end of our journey, we were met at the elegant Stazione Termini in Rome by Cardinal Salvatore Lombino, a vigorous man with iron-grey hair in his early sixties who spoke near-perfect English, having spent some years in London as a young man as a deacon in St. George's

Cathedral, Southwark. He was, duties permitting, to act as our interpreter throughout our stay. I had no Italian at all, and Holmes, characteristically, had little command of the language other than words connected with crime.

As a porter helped us load our luggage onto a smart little horse-drawn carriage, Lombino told us, "Accommodation has been arranged for you at the Hotel Emilio, which is in St. Peter's Square, within walking distance of the Apostolic Palace."

As it turned out, I would be glad of that last fact, for while that ride through the streets of Rome was a parade of magnificent buildings and places of historic interest, the surfaces of the roads were in bad need of refurbishment, which made for a jerky and uncomfortable journey, When we arrived at the Emilio, somewhat shaken up, Lombino gave us an hour or so to rest and refresh ourselves before taking us into the presence of the Pontiff. When we arrived at the Apostolic Palace, it transpired that unexpected business would delay the start of our audience, so Holmes took advantage of this waiting period to question Cardinal Lombino.

"Have you any idea why Tosca wanted to see the Pope?"

"That, of course, is a private matter between Cardinal Tosca and His Holiness, but it was clearly something urgent."

"Why do you think so?"

"Because a list is always prepared in advance of who the Pope will see and the order in which he will receive them. Tosca wasn't on the list. He simply arrived, sent in a note, and was admitted into the audience chamber on the Holy Father's order, before he saw anyone else."

"Do you have any idea why this was?"

"I can only speculate. Perhaps Tosca's faction had secretly grown, and he felt he had the power to urge the Pope to retract *Rerum Novarum*. But it seems equally possible that Tosca had come to assure His Holiness of his continuing loyalty, despite their disagreement and the growing number of his adherents. But – and this is the strange thing that seems to even further complicate the matter – there was another victim. He didn't die, but is seriously ill in hospital."

Holmes's eyes narrowed.

"Another victim? Who is he? Does he have any connection with Tosca, other than being high in the Church?"

"He is Michael Schwerzinger, the Bishop Emeritus of Sion in Switzerland. I think it doubtful that he and Tosca even knew each other, except perhaps by sight."

"Has Schwerzinger ever expressed any opinions about *Rerum Novarum*?"

"Not to my knowledge, no. In fact, Tosca was one of the few non-Italians who had strong feelings about it one way or the other. Nearly all his followers are Italian. Besides, my impression of Schwerzinger, from the little I know of him, is that he wants a quiet life in which he can enjoy the privileges of his position. I doubt that he would be drawn to factionalism of any kind."

"Has he been questioned?"

"No, the doctors have determined that at the present time he is too weak."

"Why was he visiting the Pope?"

"He isn't in Rome very often, so I imagine he was simply paying his respects."

"After we have seen Pope Leo, I would like to speak to the doctor who signed Tosca's death warrant."

"That is easily arranged. His name is Dr. Rizzio. Ah, I believe the Holy Father is ready for us."

To be in the simultaneous presence of Sherlock Holmes and Leo XIII was a remarkable experience. It need hardly be said that both were highly intellectual, but there was an immense contrast in the form that that intellect took in either man. It wasn't merely that the Pontiff was more than forty years older than the detective. Leo's faith had given him a serenity that underlay his sophisticated theological pronouncements. There was about him, above all, an impression that his very being was permeated with a sense of stillness.

In his most elevated moments, Holmes might attain a similar stillness – as when, for example, he was playing his beloved violin, or listening to a favourite piece of music. But his mercurial nature was such that this mood couldn't stay long in the ascendant. He might descend into near-despair when there was nothing of substance upon which he could exercise his formidable talents, or become voluble and excited when those same talents were being exercised to their highest degree, or, perhaps less forgivably, resort to sarcasm and mockery when dealing with the fumbling efforts of less-astute minds.

The Pope extended his hand for Holmes to kiss his ring but, despite the detective's respect for the Pontiff, he declined to do so, and I felt it incumbent upon me to follow suit.

Cardinal Lombino was horrified.

"You cannot insult the Holy Father in this manner!"

"We wish him no insult," said Holmes, "but we aren't of the faith."

When this was translated, the Pope looked severe, but nodded his head in deference to our principles.

"Let us continue," he said.

Having been given much of the information by Lombino, Holmes decided to keep the interview short in consideration of the Pontiff's advanced years.

"Do you still have the note given to you by Cardinal Tosca?"

"Yes."

"May we see it?"

"No, I am afraid not. Even though Tosca is with God now, the note, and our conversation, must remain confidential."

"Even though it might lead us to his murderer?"

"I assure you it would not."

"Then can you tell us what was said when Bishop Schwerzinger saw you?"

"It was simply a greeting, then an exchange about our health. Nothing more."

"One last thing: May we have the list of visitors for that day?"

"I will ask my secretary to make you a copy. The original must remain in the archives."

Lombino did not accompany us to see Dr. Rizzio in his office, as the doctor spoke excellent English, a legacy from a period at Barts in London.

Rizzio was a big man with grey hair and a neatly trimmed goatee. There was an air of professional expertise about him which inspired confidence. A brief conversation elicited the information that before he had been appointed the Pope's personal physician five years previously, he had worked in France and Spain, and, after he and his wife had decided to return to Italy to start a family, had done a fifteen-year stint as an examiner for the state police, followed by eight years in civil practice.

"I was called to the Hotel Emilio near St, Peter's – Do you know it? Visiting dignitaries are often lodged there."

"We are staying there."

"I see. Well, I often get called in if one of the Pontiff's guests falls ill, since they are mainly clerics of advanced years. When I arrived, Cardinal Tosca was in convulsions. My assessment was that these were caused by *Aqua Tofana*, probably in a highly concentrated form. Do you know of it?"

"A Sicilian poison," said Holmes, "odourless, tasteless, and colorless. First concocted in the seventeenth century and named after Giulia Tofana, who sold it to women who wanted to do away with their husbands."

"Quite so," said Rizzio. "I administered an antidote, but it was too late. The cardinal died twenty minutes after my arrival. He'd hardly passed away when I was summoned to the room of Bishop Schwerzinger, who was suffering the same symptoms, though not as severely. The antidote was successful, though he still needed to be hospitalised. I immediately asked the hotel staff if the two men had had the same breakfast, since if they had, there was the possibility that other guests might fall ill. But no, Tosca had had croissants and *cafe noir*, while Schwerzinger breakfasted on kipper with fried onions and oolong tea. I sent a message to the Holy Father's secretary to inform him of the situation, and was told not to bring the matter to the attention of the state police."

"Thank you, Dr. Rizzio."

We later dressed for dinner, then went down to the ground floor to the Emilioo's restaurant. But before we went in to dine, Holmes approached the reception desk and asked for the room number of Monsignor Noonan, the second name on the list given us by the Pope's secretary.

"He's in room 127," said the receptionist, in heavily-accented but near-perfect English, "but he's at table eighteen in the restaurant if you want to speak to him now."

The monsignor was a short, stocky Irish-American with a head of wispy greying hair. His nose and ears bore signs that he had boxed in his far-off youth. There was an aperitif glass before him, half-drained, so he must have been waiting to be served his meal.

"Monsignor Noonan?"

"That's me. Whom have I the pleasure of addressing?"

His accent could only be from New York.

"I am Sherlock Holmes, and this is my colleague, Dr. Watson."

"The detective? Then I guess you're here to investigate the death of poor Tosca."

"Yes. Did you know him?"

"A little. Can't say I agreed with him on everything. *Rerum Novarum* struck me as exactly the right stance for the Church to be taking. Still, Tosca was an upright sort of man, and I don't think anyone questioned his right to follow the dictates of his own conscience."

"May I ask you," said Holmes, "were you ill on the morning of the fourteenth?"

Noonan made an amused face at the oddness of the question, then said good-naturedly, "Well, since you ask, I was a little nauseous, and a bit dizzy, but I lay down for about half-an-hour, and then I was fine. How did you know?"

A waiter was approaching Noonan's table with a tray bearing a bowl of soup, a plate of vermicelli, and a glass of wine.

"I didn't. I was testing a theory. Thank you for corroborating it. And now we shall leave you to enjoy your meal in peace."

270

"Have you come to any conclusions?" I asked Holmes as we climbed the hotel stairs after finishing our own meals.

"Well, I think I know how it was done, but as to who, and why? That will take a little more investigation."

We had arrived at the adjacent doors to our rooms. I said, "It seems to me that all we have is that what the three have in common is that they all had an audience with the Pope. And for some reason, however the poison was administered, it was done in decreasing doses."

"What else did all three do in the audience chamber, besides talk to the Pope?"

I thought for a few seconds.

"Presumably they all sat down."

"True, but that wasn't it."

With that enigmatic statement, he entered his room and closed the door.

The following morning we stood once more before the Pope, but this time the role of translator was taken by the Papal Secretary, Lombino being occupied on some other business.

"Thank you for seeing us again," said Holmes. "We have only a few questions. First, does anyone have access to your bedroom at night, other than yourself?"

"Only my head of security, Mateo Bisch, and his deputy."

"Which one was on duty on the night in question?"

"Bisch."

"Would he have access to the following day's audience list?"

"Of course."

"Your Holiness, are you a heavy sleeper?"

"What is the possible relevance of such a question?" the Papal secretary demanded.

"It is relevant, I promise you. Please translate."

The Pope replied with a wry smile.

"Yes, I am. The burdens of office . . . ."

"And lastly, do you remove the Papal ring when you go to bed?"

"Always. When I am awake, I am Leo XIII, Pontifex Maximus, Head of the Roman Church, Christ's Vicar on Earth. In my nightshirt, without the ring, I am once more, for a few brief hours, only Gioacchino Pecci from Lazio."

"And you keep the ring by your bedside?"

"Yes."

"Thank you. And now, Sir Secretary, if you can arrange it, we will need a small room in which we can question Mateo Bisch, with a member of the Swiss Guard posted at the door."

Mateo Bisch was a tall, muscular man in his late thirties with a strong-jawed but sensitive face below close-cropped dark hair.

"Signor Bisch," Holmes began, "it is a tenet of your faith that confession is good for the soul, so I give you this opportunity to tell us freely how and why you brought about the death of Cardinal Tosca."

Bisch put his elbows on the table and said nothing.

"Very well, I shall tell you the how. You went into the Papal bedchamber once you were sure the Pope was asleep and you smeared his ring with concentrated *Aqua Tofana*. You did this because you knew that the first thing that happens in a Papal audience is that the visitor kisses the Pope's ring. Even that little contact would be enough to kill. But you overdid it. You killed the first man, but enough remained on the ring to make the next man gravely ill, and even then there was enough left to make a third person dizzy and nauseous. And then of course there is the fact that you killed the wrong man. Your target wasn't Cardinal Tosca. It was Bishop Michael Schwerzinger. You saw the list of audiences the previous evening and realised that at last your opportunity had come. You couldn't know that Tosca would arrive early the following morning and see the Pope before Schwerzinger. Am I right?"

Bisch's features writhed.

"Oh yes, you are right, you oh-so-clever Englishman, Mr. Sherlock Holmes."

"Why do you hate Schwerzinger enough to want to kill him?" I asked.

Bisch stood up.

"You ask me why? Why? I'll tell you why! Because he is a foul, disgusting creature! Because he killed my brother, as surely as if he had put a bullet through his head. I had to make my own justice. Where was justice for Alesio, if I didn't make it? I swear, I would go into that hospital and squeeze the life out of him now with my bare hands if I could."

Bisch fell back in his chair, put his head into his hands, and burst into passionate sobbing.

Holmes and I fell silent. At length, Bisch wiped the tears from his face with the back of one large hand.

"All my life, I have been a devout son of the Church. All I ever wanted was to serve it in some capacity. I wasn't academic enough, or unworldly enough, to join the priesthood, but I was tall and strong and vigorous, so I applied to join the Swiss Guard, and was accepted. When I

272

was deemed too old for the Guard, I sought a job in the Vatican security service, and again was accepted, and rose to be the chief.

"I was born in Basle of a good family, the oldest of eight children. We have all served our church or our country with honour – all save one. Alesio, the youngest. He started out well. Better than I, certainly. He was a good scholar and sang in the church choir, but then, around thirteen or fourteen, he started committing petty crimes. He went to drink and cocaine, and joined a gang of ruffians. His crimes became more serious, and eventually he was sent to prison. I believe the shame of it hastened my parents' deaths. I was now the head of the family, and as such, it was my duty to visit him in that terrible place.

"I could scarcely believe that the piece of human wreckage I saw before me was my own flesh and blood.

"I was bitterly angry with him. 'How did you come to this'? I yelled at him. 'How could you sully the family name? You were a better scholar than me! You were a choirboy . . . .'"

"Tears rolled down his cheeks. 'Yes, a choirboy,' he said. 'That's where it began.' I asked him what he meant, and he told me a horrible story. If I hadn't been there – if I had not seen the sorrow in his eyes, and heard the pain in his voice, perhaps I would not have believed him. He had loved his choirmaster like a second father, and when the man singled him out, he believed that he loved him like a son. But then the choirmaster began . . . *interfering* with him. He forced him to commit obscene acts. Alesio felt that this was wrong, but the choirmaster was an adult, and a respected priest of the Church. Who could he tell? Who would believe him? Was it his fault? Had he invited it without knowing? What would his life be? These thoughts rolled around and around his head until all he wanted was escape from the pain they caused. Alcohol and cocaine numbed him. They also led him to crime. I thought that telling me of his pain might exorcise it. Instead, it brought it closer to the surface. He suffered. A week later he took his own life.

"The choirmaster left Basle. He had friends high up in the Church who helped him rise. You know his name, and what he became. Now do you see?"

"I see that if your brother told the truth, Schwerzinger was guilty of a heinous crime. Why did you not report it?" asked Holmes.

"I could not prove it! Who would believe me? Who would even consider it possible? Now I have caused the death of an innocent man, a good man, even if he had his disagreements with the Holy Father. For that I must die."

273

* * * * *

"Well," said Cardinal Lombino, "the killer wasn't a priest. That's a relief. No scandal on that score. Now he has confessed, it will not be necessary to inform His Holiness of what Bisch claims was his motivation."

"Perhaps not," said Holmes, "but you might do well to investigate any other claims against Schwerzinger."

"Well, that is something for the Swiss Police. Now, the Pope is very appreciative. He would like you to stay another week, as the Church's guests. I'm sure you would like to see the Sistine Chapel, the Castel Sant Angelo, and the rest of the marvels of the Eternal City."

Holmes and I exchanged glances.

"Convey our greatest respects to the Pontiff, but I think we have had enough of Rome for the time being," said Holmes. "Perhaps you would arrange for a carriage to take us from the Emilio to the Stazione Termini."

Shortly after our return to Baker Street, Holmes received a telegram from Cardinal Lombino informing him that due to a severe reaction to one of the curative drugs that had been prescribed to him, Bishop Michael Schwerzinger had died in hospital of a massive heart attack.

I hadn't even considered the idea of turning our experiences in Italy into one of my accounts of my doings with Holmes, but the death of Leo XIII brought it back to my mind. It was a sordid tale, and yet, Holmes's intellect and deductive powers were well on display. I record it here, and will place this narrative in my old tin dispatch box, with instructions that it be published something past seventy-five years after my death.

The Weird Adventure of the Particular Phantom
by Will Murray

"An apparition, you say?"

The speaker was my good friend, Mr. Sherlock Holmes. The occasion was a visit from Inspector Lestrade of Scotland Yard to our Baker Street flat. My notes remind me that these events took place in the early autumn of the year 1895.

"I don't otherwise know what to call it," returned Lestrade in a resigned voice.

"Do you mean a ghost?" asked Holmes.

"I don't know what I mean, since I'm merely the recipient of several reports on the creature."

"Oh, so it's a 'creature' now, is it?"

Lestrade's unhappy expression then became quite miserable. I could see that the man was acutely embarrassed to bring the matter to Holmes's attention. He stood on the hearth-rug in our sitting room, restless and refusing to take a chair.

"The apparition has been described as having some odd features of a creature," explained the inspector, "although it walked upright and is apparently manlike in its general configurations."

"Pray continue, Lestrade," invited Holmes while leaning back in his velvet-lined chair and puffing ruminatively on his black clay pipe. I thought from his expression that Holmes found the matter to be quite amusing.

For my own part, I thought it repugnant. As Lestrade continued speaking, the matter became even more so.

"The first reports came to us after the fog of the night of 7 September. You may recall that it was quite thick."

Holmes nodded as he released a plume of fragrant tobacco smoke.

"Several persons accosted my constables with reports of a man-shaped apparition striding through the fog, blending with it in such a way that its progress smacked of the supernatural."

"What do you mean?"

"As I stated previously," returned the official in an exasperated tone, "I don't know what I mean. I'm only reporting what I have been told. The creature was indistinct, although it walked with a definite clumsy gait, for it wore boots. One witness insisted that its awkward stride suggested a man with a clubbed foot. Otherwise, it was silent, except for an occasional hissing."

"Do you mean a hissing as of a cat?" Holmes asked. "Or a serpent?"

"My reports only describe a hissing," stated Lestrade. "They don't otherwise characterize it."

"Very well. We will leave it at that. Is there more?"

"Several persons were frightened by its approach, but it didn't attack or otherwise molest anyone. It merely strode about in the vicinity of Piccadilly Circus in a seemingly aimless manner with a fixed and glassy stare.

With the stem of his pipe, Holmes pointed toward the short stack of papers on Lestrade's lap, for he had finally succumbed to the comforts of an empty chair.

"Kindly recite for me the essential data from your reports," he stated

Lestrade continued. "A cabman passing through Cambridge Circus was forced to pull back sharply as the thing crossed the way before him. He insisted that he couldn't see it until the penultimate moment. It didn't shy from the horse's approach but merely clumped on, unperturbed. The driver claimed that he could barely make it out in the fog, and that it seemed to melt into the haze as it progressed – although its clumping continued to be heard for some time."

Lestrade looked up from his notes.

Holmes considered all that he had heard. "Remarkable, if somewhat preposterous. Did anyone clearly see the creature's face?"

"Only one person: The cab driver. He said that the monster didn't turn his head, even though it was nearly run over. But that he could make out the face in profile. It was unnaturally round, hairless, hatless, with the features indefinite. Where an ear should have been, there was only a patch of pale skin. But he insisted that the nose stood out in a gruesome way."

"Ah!" said Holmes. "Here we may have a clue. Was the nose aquiline or blunt?"

"Sharply blunt," replied Lestrade.

"I'm afraid that I don't follow," frowned Holmes. "Kindly elaborate."

"The driver insisted that the man owned a nose like a pig's snout. It was blunt, but sharply edged."

Here, I couldn't help but cry out. "Good Lord! Could such a creature exist?

"I rather doubt it," said Holmes dryly, "but since we have these reports from diverse witnesses, we must take them seriously."

Laying aside his notes, Lestrade produced a second set from his coat pocket and proceeded to review them. "Four nights ago, you will recall that there was another fog, one of the pea-soup variety."

"A beastly one," acknowledged Holmes

"The apparition was seen again, this time around Berkeley Square in Mayfair. Here he was less distinct than before, perhaps owing to the smothering fog. But he was more active. He came up upon a man from behind and relieved him of his hat.

"His hat? What type of hat?

"A bowler," supplied Lestrade. "Another man also lost a hat, a brown bowler, but later he found it again, in the gutter. He didn't see who or what had taken the hat, only that something moved through the fog that he sensed more than saw. There again the awkward clumping of booted feet was heard.

"Furthermore, a woman in Golden Square complained of a towering figure that stepped out of the fog and tugged at various ribbons adorning her dress, but made no other advances. She had been hurrying from a carriage to her home and was unaccompanied. Her shriek aroused her husband, who came to the door to see what was what. He saw nothing, but heard only the clumping of the apparition departing.

"Not far from this location, a shop girl complained that she had stepped from her millinery shop and walked a short distance before being accosted by a man-shaped figure that emerged from the fog, yet seemed to be part of it, for she couldn't discern where his outline ended and the fog commenced."

"Remarkable," murmured Holmes.

"She further claimed that the marauder had inhuman amber eyes that possessed a smoky quality that frightened her. But the worst of it was that his nose reminded her of an old sow. Quite naturally, she was brought up short and shrieked in horror at the sight, whereupon the thing drove forward, snatched up her purse, and vanished into the swirl and haze."

The inspector lay down his notes. "This was reported to us as a crime. What do you make of it, Mr. Holmes?"

Holmes removed his black clay pipe from between clenched jaws and observed, "It appears that the mysterious apparition is becoming increasingly emboldened. Unless there is an unreported encounter, and there may well be, the creature has progressed from simply striding about in an unnerving manner to snatching hats, and now a woman's purse. I fear that it will repeat its dastardly machinations at the next fog."

"I hold with the same fear," said Lestrade. "This is why I've come to you. We know of no man living in London who possesses a club foot and a pig's snout in place of a nose."

"The smoky eyes intrigue me more," murmured Holmes.

"How so?" asked Lestrade.

"I would rather not say at this time," replied Holmes.

"I would think that the piggish snout would be of greater interest."

"Yes, that is a remarkable feature," allowed Holmes. "And there may be a way to account for it. But in order to see through the dense fog, one must possess unobstructed vision. Smoky eyes are suggestive of something otherwise."

Inspector Lestrade asked, "Mr. Holmes, are you willing to look into the matter?"

"Are your officers not sufficient?"

Lestrade frowned unhappily. "They are all on guard and on watch, but cannot be everywhere. The pattern that has begun to show itself is that the creature only emerges from its den during a fog. We must await the next fog and hope that our heightened awareness of this damnable haunter of the haze results in a capture."

Holmes considered all this, then spoke up.

"Outwardly all of these details suggest an adult, possibly possessing the mind of a child or perhaps that of a low grade of criminal. However, I don't think sufficient data has been collected to advance this impression as a theory of work. I believe I'll make it a point to ride round London during the next fog in the hope that I can encounter this queer apparition of yours."

Lestrade stood up and said, "It is no apparition of mine! But the abominable problem is my responsibility, of course. And I'm pleased that you intend to make it your business as well."

"It is an intriguing puzzle," agreed Holmes. "And I look forward to parting the fog that conceals the truth behind this hairless man-monster boasting the nose of a pig. Be good enough to lend me your official reports. I'll of course return them in due time."

The inspector laid his papers on the table. "I must hold you responsible for any loss," he warned.

"There will be none," assured Holmes.

With that, Lestrade put on his hat and left us.

After the door closed behind him, I turned to Holmes and said, "It is scientifically impossible for a man to possess the nose of a pig."

Holmes drew on his pipe thoughtfully before responding. "I'm sure you are familiar with Mary Shelley's *Frankenstein*," he said. "If only by reputation."

"Of course I have read it."

"You may recall that the nameless entity that was reanimated was sewn together from disparate parts taken from diverse graveyards.

278

Although the operation was successful, it produced a gruesome monster. This apparition of the fog reminds me of Doctor Frankenstein's haphazard creation."

"Nonsense!" I snapped. "It isn't possible to sew together assorted scraps of graveyard remains and produce a viable organism."

"Science continues its relentless advance, Watson," reminded Holmes. "Things that were considered impossible generations ago are now commonplace. The steam locomotive, for example. There was a time when an Englishman relied upon his sword, but now he carries a pistol, if he carries anything at all. I need not cite further examples. You know them as well as I."

"I'll believe it when I behold such an unholy miracle," I retorted.

"As will I," murmured Holmes contemplatively.

"So we are in agreement then."

"Without more data, I refuse to rule in or rule out any possibility. As you know, the low art of grave robbing, while it may have been suppressed, hasn't entirely been extinguished."

"Grave robbers customarily confine their activities to collecting medical cadavers for sale," I pointed out.

"Innovation may be the watchword of the nineteenth century," stated Holmes without emotion. "Even among the lower class of criminals."

Here, I had reached my limit. "This is a gruesome and grisly trend for conversation, and I have had quite enough of it, thank you."

I fetched my coat and went out for a brisk walk in order to clear my mind. Altogether too-vivid memories of the dissection table troubled me.

When I returned to Baker Street a few hours later, Holmes wasn't in evidence. I imagined that he had already embarked upon his investigation. No doubt it involved the tedious business of interviewing the authors of the many complaints regarding the foggy wraith.

While I often accompanied Holmes on his investigations, I was glad that this was one instance where he left me behind. I didn't care to hear any more about the strange stalker of the London fogs.

Although I had cleared my head regarding the more gruesome aspects of the inspector's reports, I failed to shake the unnerving images that entered my mind regarding the club-footed creature with the snout of a pig. It gave me the shivers to think about it – and I am not one to shudder easily, having attended many dissections during my days as a medical student, and having encountered all manner of gruesome sights while serving in the British Army in India and Afghanistan, and after that, in private practice.

I had believed I was inured from revulsion under extraordinary circumstances. But the stalker in the fog smacked of unclean things. I didn't know what to make of him, or it. I just knew I didn't care to hear any more about the subject

Of course, living in such close proximity to Holmes, I understood that it couldn't be avoided forever.

Upon his return that night, I made it clear to him that I wasn't particularly interested in the unsavory subject.

As he lit up his evening pipe, Holmes remarked, "It is just as well. I've made very little progress, other than to verify several points that stood out from Lestrade's police reports."

I was quietly pleased to hear this. Alas, my peace of mind was destined to be rather short-lived.

Inevitably, a fresh frog rolled over London. This wasn't a particularly soupy one. But it smothered the buildings, byways, and chimney pots just the same.

Peering from the window overlooking Baker Street, I saw its milky tendrils slip over the cobbles like an incoming tide. Before long, all was a misty miasma, and I could only make out the urchin link-lighters, dutifully leading half-blinded Londoners to their destinations by torch light.

Holmes was bundling himself up in a waterproof. He said to me, "I would be glad for the company, but I shall not press the point."

"I thank you, but the air appears to be getting rather clammy. I think I would prefer the comfort of the hearth fire."

"Very well then. I must be off."

With that, Holmes vanished into the night. I attempted to watch him cross Baker Street and seek out a hansom cab from the rank that stood further down the street, but other than his shifting form, which soon melted into the pale murk, I couldn't follow his progress.

The clattering departure of a cab told me that he had gone in search of the fog-shrouded wraith. Inwardly, I wished him luck. But I hoped that if luck should favor him, he didn't come to any harm.

Sherlock Holmes returned rather late that night. He entered the sitting room, removed his waterproof and hat, then took his familiar hearth-side chair

As he absorbed the comfort of the blazing fire, Holmes took out his pipe and methodically charged it with black shag tobacco. Plucking a coal from the fire with a pair of tongs, he ignited the bowl's contents, then commenced puffing away thoughtfully.

Other than to acknowledge me with a curt nod, he said nothing.

I watched him, but I couldn't read his expression. That is, it did not tell me if he had made any headway in his investigation.

At length, I couldn't resist my mounting curiosity and I cleared my throat. "I cannot tell from your expression whether you have made progress," I remarked, "but I would be interested to know if you did."

Holmes released a flood of pungent tobacco fumes in the direction of the ceiling. Then he lowered his head and regarded me steadily

"I fear that I have not. Of course, I was on something of a blind hunt. I made a circuit of Soho, but also prowled other adjacent parts of Westminster. Having no clarity as to where this fog phantom might stalk, I failed to encounter him."

"I imagine you will have to wait for the next fog then," I remarked.

"Actually, I'll wait for the next reports from Lestrade. For if the phantom has been abroad this night, no doubt Scotland Yard will receive complaints regarding his peregrinations."

"You are undoubtedly correct," I allowed.

With that, the subject was quietly closed, and I returned to my evening newspaper with a decided sense of relief.

The next morning, Inspector Lestrade once again paid us a visit.

Holmes was, of course, not surprised to see him, for he was expected.

"Ah, Lestrade," he greeted, "what have you for me this fine morning?

"Two reports, Mr. Holmes. I imagine more might follow, but I thought the two at hand justified paying you a visit."

"Let me have them," requested Holmes.

Lestrade handed over the sheets, then took a seat and waited patiently.

Holmes read them over carefully, before adding the pair to the pile of the previous visit.

"Your apparition appears to have formed habits consistent with becoming a pocket-picker," Holmes offered.

"Indeed," returned Lestrade grimly. "A man and a woman complained of losing their coin purses, as you have just read."

"This phantom is turning increasingly bold."

"I don't understand how he can be so elusive. One of the victims gave out a shriek, and a police officer was at her side within minutes. After hearing her complaint, he blew his whistle and summoned other officers. As much as they fanned out, they failed to locate the foul phantasm."

"This was in Leicester Square, I see," remarked Holmes.

"It is a very troubling development," Lestrade confessed. "The creature has graduated from pranks such as stealing hats to robbing the unwary. I don't doubt that the newspapers will shortly get wind of this latest rash of thefts and make a large noise about this fog-dwelling wraith. This will not help our investigation.

"Perhaps not," admitted Holmes, "but it is certain to educate the public to be wary if they are out and about on a foggy evening."

"There is that," allowed Lestrade, "but I would like to catch this sinister misadventurer, whatever he is."

"As would I," said Holmes.

"Have you any fresh thoughts on the matter?"

"It is intriguing that this gauzy ghost is able to navigate fogs of different thicknesses and colorations."

"I don't think that is significant," muttered Lestrade.

"I quite disagree," returned Holmes. "While very thick fogs offer substantial concealment, thinner fogs are less likely to provide cover for criminality. This individual appears able to take advantage of any fog that happens to roll in. I note from these reports that the thief was capable of slipping up on his victim without being seen until the ultimate moment. And even then he wasn't seen distinctly, but as an apparition of the fog, almost as if he were part of it."

"It gives me a superstitious shiver to think about it," admitted Lestrade. "And I'm not a superstitious soul."

"Oh, I am inclined to think the rotter is human, at least in part."

"I hope so. But I would be interested in your reasoning."

"I don't think a creature such as Doctor Frankenstein's monster would possess the necessary mentality or the clarity of mind to seek out coin purses," averred Holmes. "Someone with a defective brain might find amusement in snatching the hats and ribbons from unwary persons, but now it is showing a clear and criminal intelligence. This clarifies certain aspects of the case."

"I'll take your word for it." Rising to go, the inspector added, "No doubt further reports will be received, and I will tender them to you. I wish that we had apprehended the apparition last night, but luck wasn't with us."

"There will be future fogs," reminded Holmes reassuringly.

"Yes, future fogs. But what will they bring?"

"Opportunity," replied Holmes confidently. "They will bring us opportunity. Every time a fresh haze rolls in, the monster steps out of his lair. We will capture him in a fog, if we capture him at all."

Making a disagreeable sound in his throat, Inspector Lestrade left us.

I then addressed Holmes, saying, "I'm relieved to hear you speak of this creature as human."

"I've never doubted it. But that doesn't make the man any less of a monster. It remains to be seen what he is, and what motivates him."

Once more, the subject was abandoned, to my general relief.

Over the course of the next fortnight, no fogs troubled the city of London.

Holmes wasn't idle. He was often out and about, and while he didn't often divulge his activities to me, I imagine that he was interviewing victims of what Fleet Street called "The Phantom of the Fog".

I read only a few of those newspaper accounts, as they were quite fanciful. Some insisted that this stalker of the mists stood nearly seven-feet tall, but none of the police reports remotely suggested such a fantastic towering figure.

Once, Holmes favored me with an account of his doings.

"I've been 'round to see various tailors in Soho and Mayfair," he chanced to remark late one afternoon.

"Are you in need of a new winter coat?" I wondered.

"It is possible that I am, but that isn't my chief concern at the moment. Rather, I've been inquiring about various weaves and fabrics."

"To what end?" I inquired.

"To no good end," said Holmes rather dejectedly. He was making up his pipe, and I saw that it was the briar this time. That meant his mood one of discouragement. Since he didn't offer anything more by way of explanation, and I could tell from his attitude that he didn't wish to go too deeply into the stubborn matter, I changed the subject to something less disagreeable.

I placed no great store in Holmes's interest in tailors, for I couldn't imagine what connection it might have to the striding spectre.

When next a fog rolled around, it was a dreadful one. Almost the entirety of London was swallowed by the soupy condensation.

Holmes was only too eager to plunge into it, of course. He was absent the greater part of the afternoon, and well into the evening.

I did not accompany him. I saw no point in it. Aside from that, I detested attempting to navigate the more difficult conditions, for the clammy sort of sea fog was odious to me. I had my hearth fire and my newspaper. I needed no more on such a beastly day.

Holmes returned quite late that night. He took off his waterproof and flung himself into his chair. There was something about the cast of his face and its tense expression that rather unnerved me.

"Has something transpired?" I inquired.

"I have just come from Scotland Yard. There has been an attempted murder."

"Do tell!"

283

"Yes," said Holmes gravely. "The Phantom has been abroad again. Only this time, he waylaid a man and attempted to take his wallet. The man resisted with his fists. For his pains, he was stabbed. He managed to retain his wallet, but he has been conveyed to Charing Cross Hospital, where he now lies."

"Is he seriously wounded?" I asked.

"Seriously enough that I'm not permitted to speak with him. But Lestrade assures me that if he pulls through the night, I'll be permitted to attend an official interview at his bedside."

"This phantom is becoming more of a growing menace."

"Indeed, my dear Watson. He has progressed from a mere nuisance to a threat to the general public. He must be apprehended as soon as practicable."

"Where did this stabbing take place?"

"Soho Square," replied Holmes. Turning, he fixed me with his penetrating stare and said, "I would like you to come with me in the morning. Your insight might be of inestimable value."

"Well, if he has a proper doctor, I rather doubt it," I said dryly, "but I'm willing to satisfy your request."

"Very good." Holmes began making up his pipe. He smoked thoughtfully yet furiously for the remainder of the evening.

The next morning, we were conveyed by cab to Charing Cross Hospital, where we were met by Lestrade, whose troubled countenance suggested a thunder cloud.

The victim was a man named Oscar Simpson. We found the poor fellow propped up on his pillows and looking rather anemic. Loss of blood, no doubt.

"I am Inspector Lestrade," he said before introducing us. "And this is Sherlock Holmes. With him is Dr. Watson."

Simpson nodded his head silently. "I imagine that you're here to interview me about the dreadful attack," he said wearily.

"Yes. Let us begin. Now, can you describe the person who stabbed you?"

"He was quite tall, perhaps two inches taller than me, but the entirety of his form was indistinct. He seemed to swell out of the fog before me and block my way. In a voice that was more like the growl of an animal than a human utterance, he demanded my wallet. I naturally refused. Then a remarkable thing happened."

"What is that?"

"The bloke made his demand with his arms hanging down by his sides. He didn't raise a hand or a fist to me. And as I said, I couldn't make

284

him out perfectly. The fog was too thick. Beyond that condition, there was an unreal quality about him. It was as if he was made of wisps of fog."

"Can you describe his face?" asked Holmes.

The man shook his head. "It is indescribable. Overall, its countenance was as pale of the rest of him. The eyes were dark, large, like those of a horse, but of a clouded amber hue. His nose was flat and the nostrils exposed. It was a queer sort of round nose. I didn't notice a bridge. Nor any mouth. Yet it spoke in a hollow manner."

Holmes interjected, "By chance did the nose remind you of that of a pig?"

"A pig! Now that you mention it, I suppose that it did. But what would a pig's flat snout be doing on an Englishman's face?"

"We're trying to get to the bottom of that," muttered Lestrade darkly. "Please continue."

"As the robber stood before me," Simpson said, "a hand emerged from the fog and struck me in the abdomen with the knife. After it had withdrawn, one of the other arms – I believe it was the left one – attempted to relieve me of my wallet. I let out a yell of shock that I am ashamed to say was more of a shriek, and the monster faded back into the fog. Don't judge me for what I'm about to say: It seemed to melt away like a misty ghost that had been exposed to sunlight. I heard its heavy footfalls for a time, but those too soon retreated from my hearing.

"Did you notice anything else?" asked Lestrade

"Yes. The monster's right arm swung rather freely, as if not under control, while the left moved hardly at all."

Holmes asked pointedly, "You say there was a third arm?"

"Yes."

"From where did it emerge?"

"I couldn't tell exactly, but my recollection says that it struck me full on.

"And you say that you were facing your assailant when you were struck?" asked Holmes.

"We stood all but toe to toe."

"Then I must conclude that the arm emerged from the torso of the terrible one," Holmes asserted.

"Great Heavens!" I exclaimed. Beside me, Lestrade began muttering to himself.

"I've been reluctant to put it that way, for fear of being thought a madman," admitted Simpson, "but I cannot refute what you say."

"Is it your opinion," asked Holmes, "that your assailant is possessed of three arms?"

"Since there was only my attacker and myself in the immediate vicinity, I'm forced to admit that that is the most likely explanation. I realize that it doesn't seem possible."

"No, it does not," agreed Lestrade, "but if that is your testimony, we are stuck with it."

There was a little more to the interview, but nothing more of substance. I was permitted to examine the unfortunate fellow's wound and pronounced him to be on the mend. It didn't appear that the blade had penetrated very deeply.

Thanking the patient, we were on the verge of departing when Holmes observed a fragment of cloth on the small table beside the hospital bed

Picking this up, he scrutinized it, then asked, "What is this?

"Oh, yes," said Simpson. "I all but forgot about it. During the scuffle, I tore that piece of rough cloth from my assailant's garment. I didn't know what to make of it."

"It is *crash*," pronounced Holmes. "A type of linen. I see that attached to it is a gauze of white cotton, as if a cotton ball was picked apart and glued in place."

"What does this mean to you, Mr. Holmes?" Lestrade asked pointedly.

"It means that our quarry has a very unusual tailor, to say the least of it."

Lestrade plucked the cloth from Holmes's fingers and studied it for himself.

"It looks like a common rag that had been discarded."

"If you'll notice, the weave is quite coarse, and the dye employed is a soiled white that verges on being grey."

"This means nothing to me," said Lestrade with an unhappy grunt.

"Yet it means a great deal to me," returned Holmes. "I begin to understand how this marauder moved about the fog in such a manner that the human eye was fooled, and rendered unable to distinguish his body from that of the surrounding condensation. This cloth is cleverly woven to blend into a typical London fog. More remarkably, it matches the hue of last night's fog to an uncanny degree."

Lestrade considered this for a few moments. Then he spoke up.

"I can see that, Mr. Holmes, but some of our recent fogs are far dirtier than this piece of fabric. It wouldn't have worked in some of them.

"No, I quite agree," murmured Holmes. "I imagine that our phantom might have more than one such cloak."

Exiting the hospital for the street, Lestrade turned to Holmes and exclaimed, "I grow increasingly concerned about this menace. This pig-nosed man with a third arm – I don't know what to make of it."

"Make of it what you will, Lestrade. I'm certain that this apparition of yours will be proven to be largely, if not entirely, human."

"The trend of incidents suggests otherwise. Must we wait for another fog before we can hope to capture him?"

"You may wait," declared Holmes. "I'll pursue such clues as I may glean from your reports."

"Well, good luck to you then. And better luck to Scotland Yard. I've given up reading the morning newspapers because they grow alarmingly fantastic. If they get wind of this third arm, there is no telling what theories they may concoct and what nonsense we'll have to deal with in terms of the public's fears."

"Good day to you, Lestrade. We shall keep in touch."

On the ride back to Baker Street, Holmes remarked, "An additional arm is a remarkable new feature of this creature. I'm once again reminded of Dr. Frankenstein's conglomerate creation."

"Which I trust you take no stock in as a reality."

"I'll admit that my imagination is fired, but the logical part of my brain remains grounded in the very cobblestones over which we ride. Once deceased and interred, the dead do not rise from their graves. Not by themselves, nor with the assistance of rogue medical experimenters. If such persons exist, inspired by Mary Shelley's novel, I rather doubt that they would get far. The spark of life, once extinguished, cannot be blown back into life. What would be the means?"

"I cannot imagine," I agreed. "It is contrary to science, as well as common sense. The deceased are dead, and invariably remain so. The sole exception is known only to the faithful."

Holmes didn't respond to that. He was evidently lost in his own thoughts, which I readily confess were an enigma to me.

One evening, while Holmes and I were relaxing by the comfort of the hearth fire, my friend surprised me with a question.

"I imagine you have tended to a number of abdominal stab wounds in your practice?"

"A number, yes, but not a very great number."

"It's sufficient that you may be able to answer this question authoritatively. Now, is it your professional opinion that the person who stabbed Mr. Simpson was right or left-handed?"

I thought back to the wound I had examined.

"The wound was on the right side of the man's abdomen. Despite what Mr. Simpson said, that the hand struck him directly, the blade came in at an unusual angle and failed to penetrate very far. The angle suggests a right-handed man, but a clumsy one."

"Yet The Phantom used his left hand in an attempt to purloin Simpson's wallet.

"That is because the right hand clutched his knife.

"Irrespective of that fact, I believe he is left-handed.

"I do not follow your reasoning."

"It is unproven," declared Holmes, puffing on his pipe. "For now, it is my considered opinion that the ghostly assailant was left-handed. Furthermore, I judge him to stand no taller than five-feet-six-inches in height."

"According to Simpson, he was much taller."

Holmes made a dismissive sound. "His height was an illusion. I imagine the soles of his boots were built up artificially to increase his stature. Moreover, other embellishments caused him to appear taller than he had any right to be."

"I see. What else do you glean of this person?"

"That he is a seamster of low morals, or conceivably is a tailor."

"That is quite a leap, I must say."

"Not so large as you imagine," stayed Holmes. "The Phantom wears apparel rather cleverly tailored to render him all but invisible in a typical London fog. One does not find such clothing in a tailor's shop, so it must have been sewn for the express purpose of moving about under hazy conditions, entirely unseen."

"That portion of your argument is quite logical," I allowed.

"Thank you."

"How do you propose to find the tailor who is manufacturing these outfits?"

"I would rather find The Phantom first, and learn about the tailor from him."

"Could they be the same person?"

"Conceivably they could. That thought has intruded upon my thinking. But I am of two minds whether I'm interested in one man, or two distinct individuals."

"If you find one, you will find the other."

"No doubt," said Holmes, lapsing back into deep thought again.

I found this conversation quite illuminating as to Holmes's mental processes. As for an explanation for The Phantom of the Fog, I might as well have been smothered by a London pea-souper of the old, dirty days. I could get nowhere in regard to the man or his motives.

There followed a period of some three weeks in which London wasn't troubled by fogs or mists or any similar precipitation. This was unusual for the time of year.

During this interregnum, The Phantom of the Fog naturally made no public appearances. The newspapers ceased to speculate as to his identity and motives. The public, once aroused in a mingling of curiosity and fear, subsided, and turned its fickle attention to other concerns.

Faced with this meteorological interruption, Holmes continued to bend his attention to other matters.

On two occasions, Lestrade stopped by and inquired as to Holmes's progress, but my good friend offered nothing new.

"I have only the odds and ends of theories," Holmes told him, "but I've been unable to sew these scraps into suitable garments."

"If you can get nowhere," said Lestrade glumly, "then it's up to Scotland Yard."

"You're at an impasse then?" I asked after Lestrade had departed for the second time in sullen disappointment.

"So it would seem," replied Holmes. And I thought that his response was vague in a calculated way. It made me suspect that gears and wheels continued to silently turn in his finely-honed brain. Whether they were productive or not was beyond me to reckon.

Inevitably, the foggy drought abated. My notes remind me that it was on Sunday, October 27th of that year when a foul-looking blanket of brown smother overwhelmed the city of London.

This was one of those noisome fogs that are to this day called a "London Particular". It was as thick as the proverbial pea soup, but far more nasty. By the time it moved on, a dark residue of grime obscured every window pane, confounding all efforts to wipe them clean.

Staring out the window overlooking Baker Street, I remarked to Holmes, "I rather doubt that you would want to venture out into this brown pall. I doubt one could see one's own fingers if held out before one's face to the furthest extension of one's arm."

"On the contrary," replied Holmes, who was donning a waterproof.

Turning, I noticed that he gripped a hawthorn walking stick adorned with a stout head of walnut, carved in the likeness of an owl's head.

"Do you imagine to cudgel the elusive beggar with that?" I asked.

"This will enable me to make my way through this abominable yet delightful fog in the careful fashion of the blind," returned Holmes. "Should I need use it as a cudgel, I will not hesitate."

I expressed my doubts as to the wisdom of Holmes's intentions with only a facial expression of disapproval, but kept my tongue still. I knew that speech would accomplish nothing. The determination written upon Holmes's narrow features told me that I could have placed my revolver muzzle against his temple with the hammer cocked and it wouldn't dissuade him one whit.

With a curt wave of farewell, Holmes departed.

Sighing, I turned my attention back to the window and heard rather than saw him cross Baker Street, the tapping of the cane mingling with his brisk steps. This was followed by the familiar sound of a hansom cab pulling away. Judging from the complaining noises made by its springs, it was of the older type some Londoners call a "bonesetter".

I didn't envy Holmes his ride. It wasn't yet so late that the crawling brown fog wasn't illuminated, but I knew that darkness would soon descend upon the city. I feared for Holmes's safety. It was no time to be out and about.

Impatiently, I waited, consuming many cigarettes in the process.

Holmes returned at a trifle past nine o'clock that evening and burst into our shared quarters triumphantly.

"Watson!" he exulted. "I've made tremendous progress."

"Did you get your man?"

"No, but I found him. Or rather, it might be better stated that *he* found *me.*"

Holmes carried in a bundle of what appeared to be a jointed length of wood and deposited this on our dining table, along with his hawthorn stick.

Taking his customary chair, he expounded energetically. "I went to Piccadilly Circus and stood on a certain corner. Instead of blundering about, I simply waited. More than two hours passed. Then I heard the clumping of what might have been a heavyset man afflicted by a club foot. Once I heard that, I knew that The Phantom was drawing near. I couldn't see him through the pestilential brown fog, so I waited.

"It seemed that he would soon be upon me, but abruptly he turned, and the footsteps moved in a sharply different direction.

"I couldn't afford to lose my quarry. Using my cane to sweep the impenetrable brown stuff before me and thus avoid obstacles, I hurried to catch up with him, endeavoring not to make any more noise than absolutely necessary.

"When my ears informed me that I was nearly upon him, I spoke up.

"'Hulloa!' I greeted. 'I fear that I'm lost. Would you be good enough to assist me?'

290

"I first heard a violent hissing. It was as if a snake had been aroused in anger. Of course, I could see nothing, but I sensed the fellow turn and face me.

"Standing my ground, I repeated my greeting. Accompanied by the uncertain heavy footsteps, I waited, my walking stick held in readiness.

"A preposterously round face emerged out of the brownish murkiness. It was, in a word, *hideous*! The eyes were what resolved themselves first, for they were much darker than the countenance. They were quite glassy, and lacked any human qualities. No demarcation was observable between pupil, iris, and eyeball, for they comprised one undivided element. Their color was a peculiar smoky amber.

"Then the nose poked out. Or should I say the snout? Yes, it was definitely the snout of a pig. Once again hissing wordlessly, the apparition reached out with his left arm, but I blocked the outreaching hand with my stick.

"This time The Phantom growled like a beast. A gloved fist formed in the fog and the monster attempted to strike a blow. But I expected that. I struck first. This time I used the walnut knob of my stick and I smashed it soundly against the back of his hand.

"A howl leaped from lips I couldn't see. While the brute recoiled, turning to his left, I struck at his right shoulder and was rewarded by a clatter as of kindling falling to the cobblestones.

"It was at that point that the spectre melted back into the peaty atmosphere. I endeavored to follow him, and I succeeded for some time, but he soon enough became wise to my intensions and ceased moving.

"Without his footsteps to guide me, I couldn't locate him. I tried, of course, sweeping the cane before me. But it was of no use. He had withdrawn into a mews, or possibly a doorway, and waited patiently for me to either fall into his clutches or stumble off in the wrong direction.

"Realizing my peril, I retreated. Again using my cane as a guide, I found what had fallen when I struck at his right shoulder. Lifting this up, I bore it away. And there you see it on the table where I have placed it."

Walking over, I examined the curious bundle. It consisted of two lengths of wood, joined together by wire. At one end was a thin-gauged iron hook, whose tip had been broken off. The other end terminated in a knot of rough cloth, like a bundled glove. I noticed that the cloth was brownish in hue, made gauzy by glued bits of cotton, which were also dyed brown.

Removing the glove revealed something extraordinary. It was a hand, but carved from limewood in the shape of a crude fist.

Stepping in, Holmes drew back the sleeve behind the fisted hand and exposed a hollow wooden tube that was one segment of the jointed contrivance. A plug at the back of the carved fist was inserted into this hollow.

"What is this?" I asked.

"It is the right-hand arm of The Phantom," Holmes said dryly. "Except for the wire joint allowing it to swing loosely at the elbow, it is otherwise inert."

I gasped. "This Phantom possesses only one arm?"

"I doubt it. I suspect that he kept his true right arm inside of his coat, from which it could surreptitiously emerge from between coat buttons and catch the unwary by surprise."

"Oh, I see," said I. "This false arm hung by that hook from the shoulder of his coat. It is jointed so that it swung naturally with his gait."

"An arrangement I suspected as a result of Simpson's testimony," supplied Holmes. "One resounding blow of my stick was sufficient to dislodge it, causing the contraption to slide freely down the otherwise-empty coat sleeve."

"This explains the mysterious third hand that stabbed the poor victim, Simpson. And your deduction that the blighter is left-handed. He would naturally conceal his less dominant hand, leaving the other free to act. I say, this connivance also explains why the knife stroke was so clumsy and ineffective."

"No question about it," snapped Holmes, apparently delighted with himself.

"You seem rather pleased for a man who failed to capture his quarry."

Holmes took his customary seat and began searching for his black clay pipe. "It is of small moment," he said. "The Phantom of the Fog is as good as apprehended."

Taking my own seat, I lighted a cigarette and asked, "I do not see how you can say that. The bounder got away from you."

"I struck the fellow a resounding blow on the back of his left hand. This will no doubt handicap him and will leave a bruise that can scarcely be concealed. It is simply a matter of locating a suitable man sporting such a hemorrhage."

"That hardly narrows it down, you know."

"I imagine my phantom to weigh approximately fifteen stone," remarked Holmes."

"Did you see him that clearly?"

"I did not. But if you examine the brown crash enwrapping the false fist, you will note that it is soaked rather thoroughly from being in contact with the moisture inherent to a fog."

"I did notice that it was frightfully wet."

"Imagine wearing a long coat or cloak of the identical material, further encumbered by cotton gauze and wool fragments. One would have to be rather muscular to manage all that accumulated water weight."

"That is a very good point," I remarked. "Yes, he must be a hardy individual."

"And he must stand a certain height. Probably less, because I imagine his boots to be fitted with extra thick soles."

"Could he be a cobbler?" I wondered.

Holmes shook his head. "I've already discarded that theory. A cobbler would have made boots that didn't have such irregular soles that the wearer would clump around as if one foot was deformed. No, I incline once again in the direction of a tailor or a seamster."

"You will be making the rounds of the tailor shops then?"

"Indeed," said Holmes, lighting his pipe. "And I would be grateful if you would accompany me on that errand."

"Surely you don't need my advice or assistance."

"No, but since you abhor The Phantom of the Fog so thoroughly, perhaps you would like to witness his arrest."

For several minutes, I considered that offer. My distaste for the entire affair was soon enough overcome by my interest in seeing it brought to a satisfactory conclusion.

"If you wish my company," I said simply, "I shall not deprive you of it. But I thoroughly hope and trust that this detestable business will cease as expeditiously as possible."

"You may count on it," murmured Holmes confidently.

I couldn't tell whether the satisfaction in his tone derived from the black shag tobacco he was enjoying, or his confidence in anticipated success. I suspected a mixture of elements in combination produced this soothing result.

The next morning, Holmes and I climbed into a cab and were whisked through the West End.

"I have long maintained," said Holmes, as we bounced and rattled along, "that The Phantom must of necessity either live or work in proximate distance from the locations where he has been reported. This perforce must be the West End. He could hardly travel by cab, owing to his repulsive attire."

"Could he not carry his kit with him from a more distant point and don these outrageous garments while being smothered by a fog?"

"If that were the case," Holmes pointed out, "then his operations wouldn't be so strictly confined to the West End. He would logically travel farther in order to confuse the issue. He has not. Therefore, he can be found in the West End, most probably in Soho."

Holmes's logic was of course unassailable. I could see no flaw in it.

"I have had several suspects in mind," he continued, "but since last night's encounter, I've narrowed it down to two. We will go and see if we can't locate a seamster with a bruised left hand."

"I would think a bruised left hand, if you did a good job of caning it, would preclude today being a day of work."

"In that case, the absence of the man will damn him as much as would a visible bruise."

Again, I surrendered the point.

We drew up before a tailor shop in Carnaby Street, whose sign said *Thomas Gaunt and Son.* I was unfamiliar with the establishment.

Alighting, we entered, with Holmes stepping in first.

A thick-faced man I took to be the tailor looked up from his work and came over to the counter, greeting us most effusively.

"How may I help you, gentlemen?"

Looking around him, Holmes said, "I don't see your son, who I presume to be your seamster."

"You are quite correct. But I don't recognize you. Are you a customer?"

"I am not, but I've been in this shop before. I noticed a strapping young man doing the work of a seamster. I took him to be your son."

"Yes, he is. Alvin is his name. What do you want of him?"

"Only to ask him some questions," said Holmes diffidently.

"Any questions having to do with this establishment, I'm quite certain I can answer."

"These questions only young Mr. Gaunt can answer."

At this remark, the tailor's face tightened with concern, causing his mustache to gather noticeably.

"I don't follow you, sir," he said tensely.

"Perhaps this will enlighten you," returned Holmes. "If I were to guess as to why your son is absent from work today, I would postulate that he suffered an injury to his left hand."

An expression of startlement came over the senior Mr. Gaunt's thick features. Now his mustache drooped.

"And you would be correct, sir," he said, "but I don't understand how you came by this knowledge."

"Perhaps it is because I am Sherlock Holmes, of whom you may have heard."

"I *have* heard of you! And I'm quite delighted to meet you. But I am also puzzled. Kindly enlighten me."

294

Holmes hesitated only a few seconds. I gathered he was sizing up the man before embarking upon a line of attack.

"Last night, Mr. Gaunt, I was in Piccadilly Circus and I bumped into a fellow I couldn't make out in the fog. Unfortunately, a scuffle ensued and I was forced to strike him on the back of his left hand with my walking stick. I don't think I broke the hand, but I'm quite certain that an ugly bruise resulted."

"Are you saying that you struck my son – that you attacked him?"

"On the contrary. He attacked me. I was forced to fend him off."

Anger and indignation overtook Mr. Gaunt. "I cannot imagine such a thing. And I do not care that you are Holmes – casting such aspersions on my son, who is an upstanding young man and a hard worker as well! By Gad, sir, I am taken aback beyond words. If you have no further business, I must ask you to leave my shop."

"I'll be happy to do so," replied Holmes in an even tone. "However, it is my duty to inform you that I'll be going straight away to Scotland Yard, where I will reveal to Inspector Lestrade my firm conviction that your son is the man whom the newspapers have dubbed 'The Phantom of the Fog'."

Mr. Gaunt absorbed these words without a change in expression. He simply stared. Soon, however, he pressed his lips together, compressing them to a degree that suggested intense strain.

"I do not believe you!" he burst out.

"You may believe what you wish," replied Holmes, "but you will know The Phantom to be your son by the mark I have stamped upon his left hand. This damns him as a cutpurse and an attacker of innocent Londoners. He must be brought before Old Bailey to answer for these crimes."

Gaunt, whose face had been on the pale side up until now, suddenly flushed. It was a remarkable transformation. It was as if all the blood circulating in his body rushed to his features. His mustache all but bristled.

Without a word, he reached for the hot iron known as a tailor's goose and lifted it upwards in a threatening manner.

"If you don't leave this instant," he declared, "I'm going to hurl this at your skull and the damage will be your responsibility, not mine."

"Now see here!" I exclaimed. "We are doing nothing more than asking questions."

"You are accusing my flesh and blood of being a monster! Now go!"

Prudently, we withdrew from the shop and Holmes led me down the street and around the corner to a stand of hansom cabs.

"We are off to Scotland Yard?" I asked.

"Quickly, let us claim the rearmost cab. I'll decide our course of action after I see what Mr. Gaunt does next, for he can hardly ignore my accusation."

We climbed aboard the cab and waited patiently. The driver was only too happy to let us simply sit there, for he is one who was known to Holmes from past experience, as many cabmen are.

Not long after, Mr. Gaunt came bustling around the corner and selected the first cab in the queue. Off he went. After a suitable interval, Holmes ordered the driver to follow him at an appropriate pace and in doing so keep back a reasonable distance.

We followed the man to a modest home on Shaftesbury Avenue. Disembarking, he entered the front door with a bustling determination. Our driver shortly thereafter pulled up and Holmes took note of the address.

"This must be where young Mr. Gaunt is recuperating," he said quietly.

"Shall we confront the man?" I inquired.

Holmes shook his head, "It wouldn't be wise. We have no quarrel with the senior Mr. Gaunt, and he is in rather a lather. Let us hie to Scotland Yard and lay the matter before Lestrade."

I was quite surprised at this decision, but I understood it.

It wasn't long before we were at the door to Lestrade's modest office. Upon entering, Holmes announced, "Greetings. I have located your foggy phantasm."

"You have! What is his name?"

"Alvin Gaunt, son of Mr. Thomas Gaunt. Mr. Gaunt Senior is a tailor, and his son is a seamster. It is this latter skill that enabled the junior Gaunt to create the various outlandish garments that allowed him to float through the fog all but unseen. But not unheard, I must add."

"Do you have a motive?"

Holmes shook his head firmly. "No. Mr. Gaunt will have to provide that. I suggest we pay the family a call."

"I am with you in that sentiment," said Lestrade, reaching for his hat.

A most curious development followed. We were comfortably ensconced in a growler and on our way to Scotland Yard when, turning a corner hard by Cambridge Circus, a hansom cab came charging by, going in the opposite direction. In the seat were recognizably the senior Mr. Gaunt and a younger blond-haired man who I took to be in his twenties, but whose face was red with something that wasn't exertion. His eyes were wide, and he looked rather frightened.

"Lestrade!" cried Holmes. "Did you notice that hansom cab that just now flew by? It was carrying Mr. Gaunt and his son."

"The very devil!" said Lestrade. He ordered the driver to turn around and follow the fast-traveling cab.

Before long, we were back at the arched entrance to Scotland Yard. We watched in surprise as the senior Mr. Gaunt forcefully pulled his son out of his seat and all but dragged him into the building.

"What do you suppose is going on?" I asked.

"I believe," replied Holmes, "that Mr. Gaunt is turning in his son for the outrageous crimes he committed."

Lestrade pushed ahead of us and caught up with the pair. He introduced himself. At that point young Mr. Gaunt fell to his knees, took hold of his blond hair, and began pulling at it as if he desired to remove his scalp entirely. I could clearly see the blue-black bruise on the back of his left hand.

"Buck up!" remonstrated the father. "Be a man. Face the music – for you wrote it by your deeds."

I will spare the reader what followed, but after introductions had been made and matters sorted out, we all retired to the inspector's office, where under the hectoring of his stern father, young Alvin Gaunt tendered a full confession.

"At first," he said miserably, "it was simply a lark, a bit of sport. I made up a funny outfit that matched a London fog. I learned that I could move through the misty gauze, unseen. It gave me a rather dark thrill."

"This thrill developed into something more brazen during a subsequent outing," reminded Holmes.

Alvin Gaunt nodded. "Yes, yes. I began plucking at people's hats for fun. Then I realized I could earn a few bob relieving them of their purses. I told myself it was all in the spirit of playfulness. But of course, it was not."

"It was nearly murder," reminded Lestrade stiffly

Gaunt hung his head. "I got carried away. I admit it. I wish I could take it all back."

"You're very fortunate," said Holmes in a stern manner, "that the man you stabbed did not expire. Otherwise, this *would* be murder."

"It is yet a serious crime," interjected Lestrade. "And one for which you will have to face the judge."

"He has no choice in the matter," said the senior Mr. Gaunt somberly.

At this point, Alvin Gaunt broke down utterly. Tears ran down his face and he seemed no longer a fully grown man, but perhaps a wayward youth of fifteen or sixteen. I deduced from this unseemly outburst that he was rather immature.

The senior Mr. Gaunt spoke up. "When I confronted Alvin about the matter, the shock on his face told me the truth of Mr. Holmes's accusation.

Not that I required such confirmation. The bruise on the back of his hand was previously known to me. Then he began to confess, attempting to explain what I found to be inexplicable. If you care to, I can show you the various ridiculous outfits he contrived in order to move through the fog. They are outlandish in the extreme. For he made different frock coats and dyed them varying colors in order to blend in with fogs of different colorations and densities. On top of it, he created a wooden helmet of a thing adorned with the nose of a butchered pig, and so presented himself as a freak of nature and not what he truly is, a well-meaning but misguided young man who, I'm afraid, is going to cause me to remove the legend '*and Son*' from my shingle."

Hearing this, Alvin let out a wail and understood that his future had now become exceedingly bleak.

There wasn't much more to the story. In due course, Sherlock Holmes and I had the opportunity to examine the various outfits. Frock coats, adorned with wisps of crash cotton intended to blur the sharpness of their outlines. Trousers were dyed to match each coat, whose shades ran the gamut from dull white to London-particular brown. Of the boots, I will only say that they weren't a true pair, but obviously scavenged from some rubbish dump, bleached, and clumsily resoled. This is what produced the clumping sound suggesting a clubbed foot.

The artificial head was a ghastly sight. The eyes were ovals of smoked amber glass that had been glued into apertures set in the helmet of limewood. The nose was simply a pig snout affixed with glue. It was reminiscent of a sallet helmet, and there was nothing human about it.

Holmes donned this helmet and peered out through the smoked glass eyes.

"As I imagined," he murmured as he removed the hideous contrivance. "The amber glass lenses permitted young Gaunt to see his way through the less dense fogs, and thus have an advantage over his victims. No question but he smoked them to obscure the fact that ordinary human eyes resided behind their glassy and unnerving stare."

Upon examining these atrocious things, I remarked, "The young man is nothing if not industrious."

"I would suggest that he bordered on being demented. No normal person would contrive such oddities."

"The false arm was an interesting development, do you not agree?"

"Further proof of his addled mentality," said Holmes decisively. "It shows a progression from mere sport to criminality. This marks him. It is fortunate that his advancing mental deterioration was halted by his capture. Otherwise, I fear what he would have done next."

298

"I never believed that The Phantom was a modern Frankenstein monster."

"Nor did I. But as a guiding rule, I'm disinclined to believe things. I care only about facts, and they did not point in a sane direction. I hold that the basis of this ugly matter is insanity, not ingenuity."

"I remain unclear on one point."

"Permit me to assume that you are wondering how I came to go to the correct tailor shop at first attempt, when in fact, I had *two* suspects in mind."

"Indeed, you're absolutely correct."

"It was rather elementary. Only two tailor shops were inhabited by men weighing fifteen stone. One was a tailor, and the other a seamster. I reasoned that a seamster was more likely to be the culprit. Indeed, a seamster must be involved in some way, either as the perpetrator or his accomplice. My thinking was that a man who owned a tailor shop was unlikely to be prone to such frivolities that did in time turn criminal. Furthermore, a scheme involving two persons in such a somber profession struck me as improbable. Logic dictated that the most likely marauder was therefore younger, and held a less responsible position. Furthermore, he was of unsound mind. A man running a respectable tailor shop could only be in business if his brain functioned normally."

"Yes, that is imminently sensible. Well done!"

That was almost the last word on The Phantom of the Fog. The newspapers carried the story in full, and it wasn't long before Alvin Gaunt stood before the judge and received his sentence.

It was ten years. But two years into his sentence, young Gaunt crossed over into actual insanity and was removed from Newgate Prison and placed in Hanwell Insane Asylum, where he died ignominiously before his fortieth birthday, which constituted a tragedy after a fashion.

The Violated Grave
by Paula Hammond

It was a cold, breezy December morning. The season had London firmly in its grip, and the usual riot of carriages and hawkers on the street outside had been silenced by the frost. The blinds were still drawn against the boisterous weather, and Holmes and I were settled on either side of the blazing fire, enjoying the lethargy that comes to busy men who suddenly find they have nothing urgent requiring their attention.

I had been flicking, half-heartedly, through the newspaper when a curious headline caught my attention – *Mummy's Curse Strikes Again!*

"Well, well," I chuckled, glancing at Holmes, who lay curled up on the horsehair sofa, pulling contentedly on his pipe.

The article mentioned Dr. Winter, who was something of a legend in the medical fraternity. The venerable gentleman had honed his craft in the days when doctoring was learned via the violated grave. In the last sixty years, his techniques had progressed little beyond bleeding and cutting – Indeed, it was said that he still regarded a stethoscope as some "new-fangled French toy".

During my time at Barts, Winter had become a byword for every type of bunkum and quackery. I'd imagined him long dead, so it was with some surprise that I saw, beneath the improbable headline, the name of the same "Wooden-Head" Winter.

Holmes glanced at me, languidly. "Someone you know making the news?" he asked.

For a reply, I threw him the newspaper.

"Dr. Winter – a body snatcher from the time of the old king," I said in way of explanation. "He was quite notorious when I was a student." I was just about to launch into an account of some of the more outrageous tales attributed to Winter when Holmes gave a strangled cry and sat bolt upright.

"By Jove!" he cried, jabbing his finger at the article in an attitude of intense excitement.

Suddenly, the listlessness occasioned by a cold day and a warm fire vanished. Holmes had an uncanny nose for a mystery.

"Why, whatever is it?" I asked, my nerves tingling to the sudden thrill in Holmes's tone.

"'*Strange Death at the London Polytechnic . . .*'" Holmes began reading. He galloped through the first part of the article which, despite the

300

headline, detailed the events of the previous day in a surprisingly sober tone. "Ah, now, here we are . . . ."

It was as Dr. Winter was undertaking a necropsy of an Egyptian princess that a member of the audience was struck down by a series of violent fits which were to claim his life. Constable Jones of H Division was called to the scene, where he saw the body and pronounced life extinct. This death is not the first to be attributed to the so-called "Cursed Mummy". Indeed, the princess has been linked to numerous uncanny events since she was removed from her resting place in Luxor, Egypt. Constable Jones deposed that the gentleman was between thirty to forty years of age, possibly of Italian origin, and may have been an entertainer. The deceased's likeness is reproduced here. Anyone able to assist with identification is asked to contact the Coroner at the City of London Mortuary.

"I'd warrant," my companion said in an excited whisper, "that the gentleman was discovered to be wearing embellishments of some sort. The police see an entertainer. I see a disguise."

"Recognize the man?"

"It isn't a face I've ever seen, but he bears similarities to someone who has recently been brought to our attention," Holmes replied enigmatically. "It's strange that the article makes no mention of an inquest, but I begin to suspect why."

I knew better than to press Holmes for an explanation before he was ready to share his thoughts. Instead, I asked if he intended to contact the coroner.

"Indeed. I'll telegram ahead. What of your Dr. Winter? Any idea where he might be found?"

"None. Years ago, he was appointed head of the Barts branch of the British Medical Association, but he turned in his notice after the first meeting, if you can believe it. It was all bit too new and fast for him! Still, if he's still in practice, they'll have his details. I'll find out."

Holmes opened up the window and leaned his lean frame out into the frosty morning air. His hawkish eyes scoured the street below. I saw him give the flicker of a smile and wave his hand. A clear high whistle came in reply to the summons and, within minutes, I heard the ring of the street bell, Mrs. Hudson's distinctive sigh, followed by the clatter of youthful feet on the stairs.

Simpson is one of what Holmes calls his "Baker Street Boys".

My colleague employed a seeming menagerie of street urchins to run errands and find the unfindable, for the princely sum of a shilling a day. This particular scrap of mischief was as lean as a greyhound, and twice as keen. His face quite fell when he learned that Holmes merely wished him to send telegrams, rather than track down some errant villain. However, a shiny coin in his pocket quickly brought the smile back to his face.

"Want me to wait fer replies, Mr. 'Olmes?" he chirruped in that cheery Cockney way his breed employed.

"If you would, please."

Simpson vanished, leaving us to make a leisurely breakfast while we waited for the boy to return.

My friend busied himself loading his plate, in a way that showed that an energetic fit had quite superseded the apathetic one. As for myself, I found Holmes's mood contagious and ate with relish, looking forward to what the day would bring.

"So, this Winter chap," Holmes prompted, clearly keen to indulge my desire to share my reminiscences. "An Egyptaphile?"

"Probably just checking up on one of his old patients!" I laughed.

Holmes chuckled appreciatively. "'*Necropsy*' is an interesting choice of terminology," he said.

"Yes, very Winter-ish. If the word *necropsy* was commonly used, he would surely adopt the term '*autopsy*' by preference. This is a man who utterly rejected Germ Theory. As for Natural Selection, it was said he would laugh himself to tears at the very mention of it!"

I was just about to entertain Holmes with the story of Sir John Sirwell's gaul stone when Simpson re-appeared with not two, but three, telegrams clasped in his grubby hand. "I let the girl know I'd wait and take anyfink that came across the wires for you," was his explanation.

I had witnessed Holmes insult royalty to their face, yet he always spoke to the lowliest beggar with the utmost courtesy. It wasn't that he was a political animal, but he had a strong sense of natural justice. He couldn't abide the cruel, arrogant, or inept, but any man or boy who was useful, hardworking, and intelligent was sure to win his approval.

"Excellent, excellent!" Holmes said, offering Simpson an additional coin for "his diligence".

The urchin scampered off, looking mightily pleased with himself as Holmes shuffled through the telegrams.

"You know, Watson, I've often marveled at Brother Mycroft's uncanny ability to know what is *happening* without ever leaving his armchair, but this verges on the supernatural."

He passed over a telegram to me to read, which I reproduce here:

302

To: Mr. Holmes, 221b Baker Street, NW
Received at 10:15 a.m., December 2nd, 1895

Strongly suspect Italian to be French gentleman, last of Campden Mansions, Notting Hill. Friends of England await your report, as do I.

Mycroft

It was only a few weeks earlier that Holmes and I had been engaged in the Cadogan West affair. Surely "the French gentleman" referred to was one of the foreign agents who Mycroft had suspected of involvement in the case?

"The name you're struggling to recall," Holmes said, seeing my furrowed brow, "is Louis La Rothière."

I picked up the newspaper and looked, once again, at the face of the dead man. "What did Mycroft tell you of him?"

"I've no doubt he has extensive files and photographs, but all he gave me were the broadest brushstrokes: Keen sportsman, athletic build, skilled marksman, mid-thirties, brown eyes, dark complexion, aquiline nose, and, most usefully, 'a long scar under the chin, from a knife wound'."

"It's quite impossible to see his chin with that soup-strainer he's wearing," I said, peering at the sketch of the heavily bearded man with renewed interest.

"That in itself is suggestive, given the current fashion for men to be clean-shaven. Still, it doesn't do to speculate before all the facts are known." Holmes glanced through the remaining correspondence before passing the document on to me to peruse. "While Mycroft's involvement will doubtless muddy the waters, the one thing we do now know is why Winter was invited to take part in the *'necropsy'*."

I looked at the address and noted with amusement that, according the Medical Association, Winter lived literally next door to the Polytechnic!

Holmes had also received a reply from the coroner. "Where to first?" I asked.

My companion hummed distractedly, as though weighing up the options. "With weather such as this, we can be fairly certain that, if Winter's still in practice, he won't be too busy. The City Mortuary, however, is always busy, especially this time of year. "

His logic was as sound as ever and, having decided to make Winter our first port of call, we donned our Ulsters, and five minutes later were in a hansom, driving furiously for Regent Street.

In his pomp, Winter must have been an impressive specimen. In his eighth decade, he was still remarkably vigorous. His face was browned from the elements, and his hair was brindled with flashes of pure white, so that he looked more magpie than man.

We were ushered into Winter's neat little consulting room, where he sat, glowering at the world, as though ready to catch malingerers in the act.

"Come, come!" he cawed. "And don't forget to close the door, lest the germs get in!"

"Dr. Winter," I said, "it's very good of you to see us."

"Not at all. Molly mentioned you're here to talk about the chap who died at the necropsy? Terribly bad show. Didn't even get to unwrap the old gal."

Holmes gave an curious, choked cough, "Yes, I see, Doctor. I can imagine that must have been . . . frustrating . . . Perhaps you could talk us through the events of that evening? Any detail – no matter how small – will be of immense assistance."

The doctor rang for Molly to bring brandy and, thus fortified, he settled down to tell his tale.

"This sort of thing was all the rage in my youth," he said, by way of introduction. "People went mad for anything Egyptian – and it was quite fashionable to watch a mummy being unwrapped. Of course, it was done very respectfully. Chap would always give a little talk about the history and what-not, before you got down to the bandages and bones.

"Mind you, people then weren't as squeamish as today's lot. You'd pass around the bandages, fish out any trinkets. Ladies always loved those. And then, of course, there'd be the chance to eat some of the flesh – "

"I'm sorry?" Holmes said, shooting me a look of alarm.

"*Mummia*, you know?" Winter replied, as though eating the corpses of dead Egyptians, in the belief they medicinal properties, was the most natural thing in the world to do.

"Ah!" Holmes nodded. I could see the humor in his eyes, but his face was the very picture of studious attention. "And you've done a number of these 'unwrappings'?"

"Oh, dozens!" Winter said, airily. "But this was the first time I've encountered one with a curse attached to it."

Again Holmes nodded, his face appropriately Sphinx-like. "I rather thought this sort of thing had fallen out of fashion."

"Absolutely. Haven't done one since old Brummell died. But I'm always the first port of call whenever anyone at the Polytechnic needs anything of a medical nature. And when the history fella there was offered the chance to examine the mummy that's been causing everyone so much trouble, he could hardly refuse."

Now it was my turn to express surprise. "Trouble?"

"Accidents, apparitions. To hear people talk, you can't even look at the thing without chinaware flying across the room, or dogs dropping dead."

Rather stumped for anything else to say, I followed Holmes's lead. "Ah! I see," I said. "Please, do continue."

"My thought immediately was that the fella who owned it wanted to offload her. She might be a princess, but there have been too many scare stories. He couldn't sell her now for any amount of money. He'd clearly decided the best way to realize his investment was with a public lecture. "

"If I may ask," Holmes interrupted, "do *you* believe that the mummy's cursed?"

"Not saying I do. Not saying I don't. But if a man lives long enough, he sees *things*."

"You weren't worried about performing the necropsy, then? That it might . . . *precipitate something*?"

"Did I think she'd curse me? *Ppfft*. Let her try. I'm an Englishman!"

"But a man did die."

"Yes, but he was *Italian*. Still, it wasn't a natural death – not at all."

I could see that Holmes wanted to ask Winter what he meant, but the doctor was clearly a man not be rushed when he was spinning a yarn.

"Jenkins had just given his talk on Ancient Egypt, and I could see the audience were already half-asleep. Dull as ditchwater, that Jenkins, so I quickly stepped up.

"Back in my youth, a party wasn't a party without some form of entertainment. Old gypsies would do the rounds telling fortunes, magicians would conjure up lightning in bottles, mediums would spew out ectoplasm. The best trick I ever saw was a spiritualist who sold her whole act with some patter about science. The more she banged on about science, the more people expected something uncanny to happen . . . I've used her exact words at every unwrapping. Works every time!

"'Ladies and gentleman,' I began, 'we're here in the pursuit of *science*. Whatever you see tonight, please remember that science – *and science alone* – has the answers . . . Now, what we have to show you this evening is the body of a young woman who died three-thousand years ago, preserved using arcane methods, long lost to time. Her body was hidden so that she could sleep the sleep of the ages, undisturbed. Alas, that was not to be – for here she is, transported from the tomb of her ancestors to this dusty hall.

305

"'You will all have heard of the curse. You will have heard how those who removed her from her resting place died, their bodies wracked and bloodied. You will have heard that whenever anyone attempted to put her on display, the glass on her case would shatter. You will have heard how moans and sobs have been heard to emanate from her sarcophagus. You may even have heard how, when her photograph was first taken, and when the plate was developed – although the negative hadn't been touched in any way, it was seen that, imposed over the bandaged face, was the image of a living woman, whose eyes stared furiously at the viewer with an expression of singular malevolence!

"'If you believe in spirts – if you believe that the dead have power over the living – then I ask you to leave now, for this is a place of *science*."

As Winter spoke, he'd risen to his feet, quite wrapped in his memories, gesturing to Holmes and me as though we were the audience and the desk between us was the mummy. Then he paused, seemed to recall himself, and sat back down, chuckling.

Winter looked from Holmes to myself, his face creased with silent laughter. Knowing him by reputation, I couldn't help but wonder what he found the more amusing – the sideshow patter he was dishing out, or the appeal to *science*.

"I could hear little thrills run through the audience" he continued, collecting himself, "so I knew they were ready, which is when I asked for volunteers to help me take off the first layers of wrapping.

"Usually I'd expect a couple of young bucks to come forward, looking to prove their courage. But no one did. Like I said, this generation is soft – namby-pambies, the lot of them. Anyway, I was standing there scissors in hand, ready to do the necessary on my own, when this chap bursts in through the side door and plants himself right beside the mummy. *Ho-ho!* I thought. *Here's a man after my own heart after all!*

"Side door?" Holmes asked.

"Yes. The hall has two doors. The one at the top of the tiered auditorium, where the audience usually enters, and one in the stage area, that's used to move equipment from storage, without having to negotiate the steps.

"Well, the chap was followed in quick order by the doorman – apparently he hadn't shown his ticket. Well, I wasn't about to let some silly argument over money steal my thunder, so I told him to leave us be.

"I started clipping at the wrappings and asked my volunteer to hold the scissors. I wasn't sure he had heard me because he just stood there, sort of gulping, over and over, his eyes fairly popping out of his head.

"I guess he wasn't as brave as he imagined, because he was as jumpy as a cat, covered in cold sweat. Then it happened. He put his hand up to

306

wipe his forehead, and suddenly there was blood everywhere. His face, his hands. Someone in the front row screamed – and that was when the ladies started fainting."

"Blood?" Holmes interjected. "Was he cut? Please be as clear as possible, Doctor. This is very important."

"Didn't get a proper look. By then that damned doorman, Brown, was on him, like a dog worrying a bone. He'd grabbed the man by his sleeve and was pulling him away from the mummy. All the time, the chap was jabbering something – sounded like Italian – *Tué! Tué*! There was this awful tug-of-war going on. The man's face was covered in blood, the ladies in the audience were getting more and more distressed, and Brown kept yabbering about '*No ticket!*'

"Then suddenly, someone screamed, and that set off a stampede. There was an almighty rush for the doors, and I had to cling onto the mummy to stop her from being knocked to the ground and trampled. I fear that I may have oversold the curse a little. For a while, all I could see were bodies pushing and shoving. When the crowds cleared, I could see the doorman had finally noticed something was amiss. He was white as a sheet – and I'm not surprised. Our chap was standing there, mouth opening and closing like a fish gasping for air. He had this curious stiffness of posture, face tight, jaws clenched, as though he was already dead. You see that sort of thing often enough, you know what's coming. And sure enough, he dropped like a stone. By the time I could get to him, the poor fellow was on the floor, convulsing so badly I thought he'd break his back."

"What did you do?" I asked.

"All I could do was try and hold him down, to stop him injuring himself. But the fits came in waves, one after another, and within in fifteen minutes he was gone."

"Did you call for help?"

"I sent the doorman to find a constable."

Having already formed my own conclusions, I asked Winter what he thought had caused the man's death.

"An aneurysm. Given how he gawped at the mummy, I wouldn't be surprised if the chap had scared himself to death."

"When you made your examination, were you able to discern where the blood had come from?"

"With an aneurysm, a nosebleed would be most likely."

"But you said, you didn't see any blood until he wiped his forehead?"

Winter shrugged his huge shoulders. He could easily have smeared the blood from his nose across his face."

"And how close to the mummy was he? Could anything on the corpse have affected him?" Holmes asked.

"No, there was no decay to speak of. No strong miasmas at all."

"Mould?"

"None."

I thanked Winter for his time, feeling, I confess, a little nonplussed at the man's lack of rigor. "Well," I sighed as we walked towards the street door, "at least the miasmas didn't kill him."

"Indeed," Holmes barked out a laugh. "They haven't killed anyone for a couple of decades now."

Being so close to the Polytechnic, we took the opportunity to speak to the doorman who, after the bootless errand at Doctor Winter's, proved refreshingly helpful.

The man could have been Simpson grown to adulthood. Wiry, with keen eyes, he fairly jumped to attention when Holmes asked him about the "Italian gentleman".

"Lord, it's murder then?" he said, eyes widening. "I thought as much. He came in here, all red-faced and panting. At first I thought he was just another student running late – they always are, you know? But then, when I saw that blood in the lecture hall, I knew someone had done fer him."

"You saw him come in?" Holmes asked, regarding the man with his steady grey eyes.

"Not exactly. I heard the bell over back door. Lots of students use the tradesman's entrance, see. I'm a cyclist myself, and I let them leave their bicycles in storage for safekeeping. I walked through to see who it was, but he was already heading for the lecture hall – ran right past me. He'd left the back door ajar and I could see his bicycle outside, so brought it in. Then I realized I hadn't seen his ticket and, this being a public lecture, I couldn't let that pass."

"When you went outside, did you see anyone?"

"Wasn't looking. But if anyone was running after the gent – if that's what you're suggesting – I'd have heard them. These backstreets echo so."

"Where did you find the bicycle, exactly?"

"Just beside the door, but if you're wondering where he was coming from, then there are only two routes that are any good for city bicycling that lead here – traveling east from Cavendish Square, or west from Smithfields.

Holmes asked to see the bicycle. It was resting amongst an assorted jumble of boxes and scientific equipment, and it was some time before it could be untangled and brought out into the light.

I'd lost count of the number of times I'd see Holmes stretched out on the floor, magnifier in hand, in order to better examine some vital piece of evidence. Yet the spectacle never failed to interest. As I watched him examining first the pedals and then the wheels of the bicycle – sniffing at this and that – I wondered what clues he would uncover.

"No grass," he said eventually "but lots of mud and slurry. Smithfield Market, I'd warrant. And, see here, blood on the handlebars. Our man was attacked and pursued, of that I've no doubt. But why did he come here?"

"Well, Mr. 'Olmes," the doorman said thoughtfully, "south from Smithfield, you can ride hard and fast, following the Thames, as far as you like. But if I was being followed, I'd want to go north – lose myself in the mess of the city . . . and these backstreets are right warren, and no mistake."

"That's an excellent hypothesis, Mr. Brown. Just one more question: Did you hear the gentleman *say* anything?"

"Lord he was jabbering, but I don't have the lingo. Let me think. '*Metuee*', sounded like."

"Wonderful! Absolutely wonderful!" Holmes grasped the doorman by the hand, and pumped it so effusively I feared it would fall off. "Thank you, Mr. Brown. You've no idea how helpful you've been."

Provision for the dead, in a city of five-and-a-half million, has long been a subject of debate. Thirty years earlier, it wouldn't be unusual for the poorest families – often living in one room – to be compelled to spend weeks with the corpse of a deceased loved one before he or she could be interred. It was fear of disease that finally forced the hand of the authorities.

One could still find taverns co-opted into use as Coroner's Courts, and tiny backstreet hovels used as makeshift charnel houses, but the City of London Mortuary was a veritable palace of the dead. With *post-mortem* rooms, a disinfecting chamber, ambulance station, and Coroner's Court, it represented the very best in modern medical and criminal practices.

We were quickly introduced to Mr. Ellis Thompson, Surgeon, who, despite looking quite knocked up, greeted us warmly.

He explained that the season, foul weather, and general illness had caused something of a backlog – to wit, no autopsy or inquest had yet been carried out on our questionable Italian.

I was surprised. An inquest would normally be called almost immediately. And, it was usual, if death occurred with a medical practitioner present, for the doctor to be asked to carry out the *post-mortem*, unless he was implicated in the death. "Dr. Winter wasn't asked to perform the examination?" I asked.

Thompson shrugged his shoulders, flicking through the paperwork with an attitude of confusion. "You are Dr. *Watson*?" he finally asked.

"Yes . . . ."

"Well, don't ask me how or why, but it seems that *you* are to undertake the autopsy."

"But we only telegrammed a few hours ago."

"I'm aware of that, Doctor. But see – here's your name on the order." Holmes shot me a knowing look.

"Mycroft?" I asked in amazement.

"It would appear so," Holmes replied, his eyes sparkling. "Do lead on, Mr. Thompson. At least we'll be able to reduce your backlog by one."

If one is accustomed to it, there's no mistaking the smell of death. But the *look* of death – that's something that's unique to each individual. I've seen women eaten by cancer who, on their deathbed, appear decades younger, as though, in those final moments, they had somehow shed the suffering they'd endured. I've seen stillborn babies whose faces bore such a look that one might imagine they'd stared into Hell itself. Murder victims are no different. While a body can carry the most appalling wounds, the face may look as peaceful as if the dead person was asleep.

This is why poison is such a popular method of murder. For while the effect of poison on the living body may be savage upon death, it's often only possible to prove wrongdoing by a thorough *post-mortem* examination.

This wasn't the case with body we were tasked with identifying. Such had been the strength of the spasms and choking that preceded death that the evidence of it was writ large on the face – and body – of the man who lay on the cold marble of the mortuary table.

Neither Holmes nor I needed to open the body to know the cause of such a violent death. Only one poison made its victims convulse, and eventually asphyxiate in such a way: *Strychnine*.

We approached the dead man in the usual way. First we looked to the posture. The back was twisted and the hands and jaw clenched, which was consistent with our supposition of strychnine poisoning. The room was so cold that there were thankfully no unpleasant odors, other than those that the body had gained in the last hours of life.

"Almond oil and rose water" Holmes noted. "Likely cold cream." He took another deep breath, his nose hovering only inches away from the body. "Chalk and bergamot – that will be face powder. There's a hint of orris root, too, which is used in rouge. So, our victim has indeed used embellishments to change his appearance. Ah – interesting. Orange notes and – Ah, ah – petitgrain. Our man favors Orloff's Special Cologne – a Russian perfume. It would seem that our man has recently been to Russia.

310

"There's one more scent too: *Sweat*. Given what we know, that shouldn't be so surprising. In the final hour of his life, he exerted himself enough to perspire freely."

"What about the strychnine? " I asked, pointing to the signs of dried liquid around the deceased's mouth. "Ingested?"

"Possible, but I think not," Holmes replied, pointing to the rows of angry cuts on the back of the man's hands. "Defensive wounds. Very deep. And here, too purple welts on the calves of each leg. Interesting and – Ho! What's here?"

The man's right hand seemed to be clasped around something small, so that we had the terrible task of breaking the fingers in order to see what it was he was still guarding, so carefully, in death.

The object in question turned out to be a silver key, which Holmes examined before putting it to one side.

The body had already been stripped, and the key now joined the rest of the man's possessions.

There was only one more thing that was needed to confirm the victim's identity – which Holmes was able to do by feeling for the long white scar that ran just beneath his beard.

I glanced at Holmes whose eager eyes told me everything I needed to know.

"Louis La Rothière?"

"Yes," Holmes, said, "and his story is almost complete. Now, let us fill in the gaps. What else do we have here? A small coin purse, a leather wallet with gilt mounts, a Hunter pocket-watch – he was a sportsman – a silk handkerchief, and a platform ticket from Liverpool Street Station. The clothes are clearly of French design. There are no labels, but the cut is very distinctive. And, here, in the pockets of his jacket – gloves. The color – tan – is unusual. You wouldn't choose these for daywear. They're kid leather – very thin and soft – presumably for bicycling.

"So now we have it: The final, sad moments of Louis La Rothière, spy, murderer, and *agent provocateur*. It begins, I believe, at the station – He meets someone on the platform. The key is of a type used in private deposit boxes. Martin's Bank is on Lombard Steet. Let us say that our man collects *something* from a fellow agent at the station, then deposits it at the nearby bank.

"At some point, he is attacked – suddenly and viciously. He has no time, or is too injured, to put on his gloves. He flees the scene, using a bicycle to affect a speedy escape. Let us imagine his pursuer manages to follow him, for why else would La Rothière work so hard at losing himself in the City's backstreets? How long, Watson, do you think it would take for strychnine to begin to have its effect?"

311

"It would depend on the dose, but at least fifteen to twenty minutes."

"Yes! Yes!" Holmes exclaimed, "the timing works. He cycles furiously for fifteen to twenty minutes. He reaches Regent's Street, already beginning to slow, to feel the effects of the poison that's entered his system through the cuts on his hands. He's beginning to get clumsy, uncoordinated. Remember the bruises on his calves – from where his feet have repeatedly slipped off the pedals. They continue to spin, hitting him on the leg.

"Lord, he must have been as strong as a horse to have made it so far. If Mr. Brown was correct, by now he's lost his pursuers, but the game isn't over. It isn't unreasonable for him to think that whoever is pursuing him wants what he's collected. Spotting the backdoor of the Polytechnic, he makes one last, Herculean effort. The key is in his hand – He's looking, perhaps, for a safe place to hide it. Somewhere no one would ever think of looking. Maybe in the innards of a New Kingdom princess? We'll never know for sure, for it's there that he exits this world, exclaiming not '*tué*' or '*metuee*', but '*Il m'a tué*' – '*He has killed me*.'"

"But that's horrible!" I cried. La Rothière may have been a foreign agent, but it was hard not to be shocked as Holmes outlined the moments of a man's life in such pitiful detail.

"It is horrible. And the use of poison on the blade suggests a deliberate assassination. Whoever did this wasn't interested in retrieving what was taken, for with La Rothière dead, whatever was hidden would stay hidden. No, nether England not 'England's friends' are to blame here. If I had to point the finger, it would be to Russia. Remember the cologne? And France's growing influence over the Tzar isn't approved of by everyone. But I'm sure my brother will be better informed of these things than I am, and able to take the appropriate action."

There was little left for Holmes and me to do, save make our report to Mycroft – by way of a detour to Martin's Bank, where we retrieved a large bundle of papers that, we were assured, "England's friends will be delighted to know are safe."

Soon we were digesting the day's events back in the comfort of Baker Street.

Once more, the drapes were drawn, the fire was lit, and with our pipes well-packed, it felt as though all was well with the world once again.

My friend looked especially thoughtful in the flickering half light. "What are you thinking?" I asked, companionably.

"I think," Holmes said, throwing me a wry smile, "that I'm very happy that Egyptians don't come over to England to dig up our royalty and banquet on their remains."

NOTES

- ☐ Watson's editor, Sir Arthur Conan Doyle, was a medical doctor, and appeared to have also been familiar with Dr. Winter. The gentleman appears in one of Conan Doyle's narratives, "Behind the Times".
- ☐ The violated grave refers to the practice of grave robbing, which was used to supply medical students with bodies for dissection. After the Anatomy Act of 1832, unclaimed bodies were made available for medical use, effectively putting the grave robbers out of work. However, the Act was hugely controversial as it particularly impacted the poor. Many Victorians, who believed in the literal resurrection of the body, feared that their relatives would be denied salvation because they would not be buried whole.
- ☐ The stethoscope was invented in France in 1816.
- ☐ Louis Pasteur published his *Germ Theory* in 1861. This was a turning point in modern medicine. Pasteur argued that microbes in the air caused decay, and not the air itself, as was commonly believed.
- ☐ Although photographs began to appear in newspapers in the mid-1800's, they were barely legible until the development of the half-tone reproduction process in the 1890's. Many papers therefore still used etchings, where illustrations were required.
- ☐ In the Victorian era, "cosmetics" referred to anything medicinal that was applied to the skin. Embellishments were pastes, powders, and paints, which were used to alter the appearance.
- ☐ Although *autopsy* is the term used today, there was a great deal of disagreement in the Victorian era about exactly what word should be used to describe the process. "*Autopsia*" (autopsy), *post-mortem*, "*sectio cadaveris*" (dissection of a dead body), *necropsia*, and *necroscopy* were variously used, until autopsy was finally adopted. It should be noted that the term *necropsy* is now used exclusively for animal *post-mortems*, but the word did not have that meaning in Watson's time.
- ☐ While Watson doesn't finish the story of Sir John Sirwell's gaul stone, Conan Doyle does. In "Behind the Times", he describes how Winter, having witnessed a young doctor cut into Sir John, only to find no gaul stone, provided one from his own pocket: "*It's always well to bring one in your waistcoat pocket," said he with a chuckle, "but I suppose you youngsters are above all that.*"
- ☐ Egyptomania did indeed include public "unwrapping parties". However unsavory and disrespectful this may seem, the term "party" is slightly misleading. These events were more like public lectures, and neither especially wild nor, indeed, party-ish. The best-known mummy unroller was a surgeon and antiquary, Thomas Pettigrew, whose lectures and public unwrappings were very popular and highly regarded by the scientific community.
- ☐ Alarming as it may seem, *mummia* was taken and prescribed regularly until the 1700's, and was still available as a medicine until 1924. Mummia

originally referred to a type of bituminous resin, used in the embalming process, which has antiseptic properties. This resin was used throughout the ancient world. When supplies began to run short in the 1800's, mummia slowly morphed from the resin used to embalm mummies to whole or powdered mummy flesh. After Egypt banned the gruesome trade, European apothecaries began using the corpses of criminals, whose bodies were left to dry in the sun, after execution, before ground into powder.

☐ Brummell refers to the royal fashionista, Beau Brummell, who died in 1840.

☐ The term *namby-pamby*, meaning weak, ineffective, and maudlin, was coined by the poet Henry Carey (1687-1743), who used it as a mocking nickname for fellow poet Ambrose Philips.

☐ The incidents that Winter ascribes to the cursed mummy closely match stories told about the so-called "*Unlucky Mummy*". The mummy's strikingly beautiful wooden sarcophagus can currently be seen in the British Museum. Interestingly, the whereabouts of the mummy that the sarcophagus once contained are unknown.

☐ In 1876, Robert Koch proved that a bacterium caused anthrax. This brought an end to the miasma theory.

☐ The Orloff Special Cologne was created in 1890 for Russia's Prince Orloff. When the fragrance was re-launched by British perfumers, Floris, they renamed it *Special 127* after the page in their "Specials" formula book. Special 127 was Winston Churchill's favourite cologne.

☐ The *Okhrana* were the Russian secret police, whose activities included infiltration and assassination.

☐ In the 1880's, relations between France and Imperial Russia were strained by the competing colonial aspirations of both nations. However, relations gradually improved, as France began to see Russia as the only ally who could stand up against Britain. At the start of the 1890's, Russia received a number of large loans from France which brought the allies even closer. However, the loans shifted the balance of power, and some believed that the Tzar was then too reliant on France.

The Mystery of the Major's Music Box
by Margaret Walsh

It was a warm spring afternoon when Mrs. Cordelia Portgrove, the widow of Major Reginald Portgrove, came to 221b Baker Street.

The lady was dressed in full widow's weeds: A gown of black crepe with a black veil that fell from the black widow's cap on her head to down below her knees. It was clear that her widowhood was fairly recent. Such an ensemble was only dictated for the first year and a day after the death. After that time, half-mourning was permissible, adding white, grey, and mauve to the sombre black palette.

She was accompanied by a young servant girl who was carrying a parcel. The lass was comely, with deep doe-like brown eyes, and a wealth of black hair that was arranged in a simple chignon. Like her mistress, she was dressed in mourning, though her dress appeared to be practical bombazine rather than the less-practical crepe. She wore no veil, but kept her eyes downcast.

The lady took the offered seat and, casting her veil back over her head, looked Holmes squarely in the eyes. "I am Cordelia Portgrove, Mr. Holmes. I wish to consult you on the matter of my husband's death. He was Major Reginald Portgrove. He was retired from the army, though he had served in India."

"Rather like my friend here," Holmes commented. "How did your husband die?

"He was killed by this." Mrs. Portgrove indicated the parcel the girl was carrying.

"And what would this be?" Holmes asked.

"A music box," Mrs. Portgrove replied.

"Interesting," Holmes murmured. "Tell me the sequence of events."

"There really isn't much to tell," the lady said. "One morning, my husband didn't come to breakfast. His valet said he had risen at his normal time and gone to his study. I thought that maybe he had lost track of time, so I went to the study to chide him, and escort him to breakfast. When I entered the room . . . ." Mrs. Portgrove stopped, her voice choking on tears. Silently, the servant girl withdrew a black-edged silk handkerchief from her pocket and handed it to the lady. Mrs. Portgrove dabbed at her eyes for a moment before handing the slip of cloth back to the girl.

315

Mrs. Portgrove took a deep breath. "When I entered the room, I found my husband sitting, slumped in his chair in front of his desk. On the desk was this music box."

"Was this box familiar?" Holmes asked.

Mrs. Portgrove shook her head. "I had never seen it before. I would be prepared to swear that until that morning, it hadn't been in the house. At least, not to my knowledge."

Holmes looked at the girl seated quietly beside her mistress. "That is the mysterious music box, I presume?"

Mrs. Portgrove nodded. "It is."

"May I see it?"

"Certainly." She turned to the serving girl. "Regina, give Mr. Holmes the parcel."

The girl, rather reluctantly I thought, handed the package to Holmes. The box that was revealed when he unwrapped it was made of highly polished rosewood, trimmed with ebony. On the lid was a fanciful picture etched in gold of cherubs playing musical instruments. The box was a simple one, playing, according to the listing on the inside of the lid, only four tunes. Some, naturally more expensive boxes, could play as many as twelve. Holmes carefully wound it up and soon tinkling notes of *The Sailor's Hornpipe* filled the air.

Holmes examined the box carefully. "A charming example of the type, but at first glance I can see nothing that could cause a man's death. May I be permitted to keep the box?"

Mrs. Portgrove nodded. "You may. I never want to see the thing again."

Holmes nodded. "What do the police say of your husband's death?"

"Nothing. They weren't involved. Our doctor said that my husband died of heart failure, and that there was nothing suspicious about his death."

"But you think otherwise?"

"Mr. Holmes, one day my husband was hale and hearty. The next he was dead in his study with that box in front of him. Is that not suspicious?"

"Indeed," Holmes murmured. "We shall need to speak to your doctor."

"You have my permission to do so. We were attended by Dr. Moore Agar. He has premises in Harley Street." On that note, the lady got to her feet and bid us a good day. Then, trailed by her servant, she swept out of our rooms.

Holmes chuckled dryly. "Quite a departure. Well, what do you make of the good widow's tale?"

"It is quite the fantastic one. How on earth could a music box cause someone's death?"

"That, my dear Watson, is something we need to find out. Care to accompany me on a visit to Harley Street?"

"Of course."

Our rooms weren't far from Harley Street, and it was a pleasant day, so we elected to walk the distance. Holmes often chose to walk around London, taking note of the various changes around him. A new shop here or a new office there. A family moved into a house, and another moved out – all the small things that make up the beating heart of a thriving city.

When we arrived at Dr. Agar's surgery, the gentleman was having a break between patients. He listened to Holmes's request and then ushered us into his office.

When we were seated comfortably, each with a cup of excellent coffee from the elegant silver pot which sat upon his desk, Dr. Agar commented, "I really cannot get through the day without coffee."

Holmes concurred. He regularly began the day with coffee. While my preference was for tea, the bitter, inky beverage had grown on me over the years, and it was a capital drink.

Dr. Agar settled back into his seat and took a sip. "Reginald Portgrove died of heart failure. There is no surprise about his death."

"His widow thinks otherwise," I observed.

Agar inclined his head. "The musical box."

"You say there is no surprise about his death," Holmes said. "Why so?"

"You know that Portgrove was in the army?"

We nodded.

"A major, we were told," Holmes said, "and that he served in India."

"The last part is the problem."

I understood immediately. "Enteric fever," I said. Enteric fever, more properly known as *typhoid fever*, is the scourge of places like India. It had left me a wrung-out shadow of my former self, but I was lucky and recovered.

Agar nodded. "Exactly. Portgrove was invalided out of the army and returned home when his heart became damaged after contracting enteric fever. He was deeply distressed about being sent back to Britain, and consulted doctor after doctor, trying to get them to say he was healthy enough to return to India."

"But he wasn't healthy?" Holmes queried.

"He was healthy enough for day-to-day life, as long as he took it quietly with little excitement. To be blunt, he had cardiac insufficiency.

317

Sooner or later, it was going to kill him. He wasn't an old man when he died. Portgrove was only forty-five."

"You are saying any sort of shock or surprise could have killed him?"

"Yes, Mr. Holmes, I am."

"Interesting. Thank you for your time, Dr. Agar, and for your information and your coffee, both of which were excellent. Come along, Watson."

Holmes fairly hurried from the room, leaving me to make more polite goodbyes to the the doctor and join Holmes outside. He was pacing impatiently as he waited. "That is an excellent physician, Watson. I shall keep him in mind in case I should ever need a doctor, apart from your good self."

"Where to now?" I asked.

"We need to find exactly where in India, and with which regiment, the late Major Portgrove served."

"That will be time consuming," I noted. "Without a definitive place to start, we'll be at this for weeks, if not months."

Holmes chuckled dryly. "I think not. I do have two excellent resources at my fingertips."

I thought for a moment. "Langdale Pike, and your brother, Mycroft."

"Exactly. Langdale will be able to tell us if any scandal is attached to the late Major Portgrove, and Mycroft will be able to point us in the direction of officers who served with Portgrove. Mycroft takes a keen interest in Britain's military affairs, after all."

"If only to stop our military from having to fight wars," I observed.

"True. Mycroft views war as the losing move in the great game of international politics."

Holmes succeeded in flagging down a cab. "Where to first?" I asked as we climbed in.

"Langdale Pike," Holmes replied. He tapped on the ceiling of the cab. "St James's Street, Cabbie".

The cabman's voice floated down to us, "Right yew are, Guv'nor."

Langdale Pike, the noted gossip columnist and university acquaintance, if not friend, of Sherlock Holmes, spent almost all his time at his club. It was situated in St. James's Street, and I will not name it. During the hours of daylight, Langdale Pike could be seen sitting in one of the elegant bow windows, hard at work. The great and the good, and those that worked for and against them, flocked to Langdale with the latest titbit of gossip. For the subjects of his columns, there was a certain cachet to being the centrepiece – the star of the show, if you like. For many that sold him information, it was bread-and-butter on the table, with the luxury

318

of a little jam added. I profess that I didn't particularly like the man, but I do admit that he had been useful to Holmes on more than one occasion.

Pike was pleased to see us when one of the club's footmen showed us to his table. "Sherlock! And Dr. Watson! What can I do for you today?"

Taking seats, we turned down offers of tea, but waited until the footman brought Pike a cup.

"What do you know of the late Major Reginald Portgrove?" Holmes asked.

Pike thought for a moment. "Not a blessed thing. What has he done, apart from die? You did say the *late* Major Portgrove, did you not?"

"I did. It is less the fact that he is dead that I am interested in, and more the manner of his death."

"And that was?" Pike asked curiously.

"He was found dead in his study with an unknown music box sitting on the desk in front of him."

"That is a little different. How exactly did he die?"

"Heart failure," I said. "And not unexpected, according to his doctor."

"Who was?" Pike asked.

"Dr. Moore Agar of Harley Street."

"Ah yes, I know of Agar. Grumpy exterior concealing a heart of gold. Charges the aristocracy like a wounded bull, but his rates for the working-class patients he sees are low. He also donates his time to the Foundling Hospital. A good man," Pike pronounced. "I shall ask around, Sherlock, about your Major Portgrove. If I hear anything, I will let you know."

Holmes got to his feet, and I followed. "Thank you, Langdale. I am particularly interested in where he served in India and with whom."

I saw Pike make a note of that in one of his notebooks that littered the table in front of him.

Holmes and I took our leave and headed outside. Holmes consulted his pocket-watch. "It's four-forty, Watson. If we gently stroll down to Pall Mall we should reach the Diogenes Club at around the same time that my brother does. Shall we?"

I nodded my agreement and we set off along St. James's Street at a leisurely pace.

Mycroft Holmes didn't appear to be discommoded by our appearance at the Diogenes Club shortly after his own arrival. We were escorted to the Stranger's Room, the only location in the club where conversation was permitted, and Mycroft joined us shortly afterwards.

A uniformed usher poured us each a brandy before withdrawing gracefully.

Mycroft settled himself comfortably into one of the expensive leather upholstered chairs and gazed at his brother expectantly. "What new little problem brings you to me, Sherlock?"

Once again, Holmes recounted the tale of the dead major and the mysterious music box. He also told Mycroft what Dr. Agar had said.

Mycroft nodded thoughtfully. "Agar is very sound. If he says that Portgrove had a weak heart, then that is exactly what he had, and that is exactly what killed him. It hardly seems like a case of murder."

"That rather depends on what the motive was for placing the music box where Portgrove would see it," his brother replied.

"A very good point," Mycroft agreed. "And, after all, it is the puzzle that interests you, not any crime that has been committed."

Holmes took a sip of his brandy and did not comment.

"You want to know Portgrove's military background." It was a statement, not a question.

"I do," Holmes replied.

"I shall see what I can obtain for you. Now, will you and Dr. Watson be joining me for dinner?"

Holmes shook his head. "Thank you for the offer, Mycroft, but Mrs. Hudson was hard at work this morning baking a rhubarb tart for pudding, and my good Watson doesn't want to miss that."

I snorted. "No more than you do. That last time she made rhubarb tart, you waxed lyrical about it for days."

Mycroft raised an eyebrow. "My brother waxed lyrical about food?"

"I said it was a pleasant enough dish," Holmes replied.

"That is waxing lyrical, for you," I said.

Mycroft suppressed a smile. "I am sure there is more on offer than that."

"Mutton chops with asparagus and beans," I replied, having overheard Mrs. Hudson's conversations with both the butcher's boy and the grocer's boy that morning.

"An excellent repast," Mycroft agreed. "I shall bid you gentlemen a good night. Sherlock, I will be in touch when I have any information for you." With that he got to his feet and left the room.

A moment later, an usher appeared to escort us from the club.

We returned to Baker Street to Mrs. Hudson's excellent cooking. After dining, Holmes began to contemplate the music box, turning it this way and that in his hands and examining every inch of it with his magnifying glass. Seeing that there would be no conversation that night, I went up to my room to fetch a book to read. I was enjoying the exciting African adventures contained within Sir Henry Rider Haggard's excellent book, *She: A History of Adventure*. I read for about three hours before heading to bed, leaving Holmes still studying the music box. A grunt was his only response to my wishing him a good night.

It was a different scene when I got up the next morning. Holmes was already seated at the table when I arrived. He waved a piece of toast at me. "Hurry up, Watson. Mrs. Hudson will be up shortly with plates of her excellent bacon and eggs."

I took my seat and buttered a slice of toast. "You are in a better mood this morning. Did the music box reveal its secrets?"

"I'm not sure it has any," Holmes said frankly. "But if it does, I have thought of the perfect person to reveal them. And if the box doesn't contain secrets, then the same person may be able to at least tell me where the box came from."

I took a bite of my toast and chewed thoughtfully before asking, "Who is this person?"

"His name is Matthias Compton. He makes music boxes – not on the scale of Nicole Freres in Switzerland, but his boxes are well thought of, and well sought after."

"I look forward to meeting him," I replied.

All thoughts of music boxes and their makers was put aside as Mrs. Hudson brought in the bacon and eggs, as well as more toast and a pot of coffee. We ate in companionable silence.

After breakfast we made our way to Knightsbridge, where Matthias Compton had his shop, tucked away on Basil Street within the shadow of Harrods.

Matthias Compton turned out to be a genial, portly gentleman of some forty-five years. He beamed delightedly when he saw Holmes. "A pleasure to see you! It has been too long."

"I am afraid I have been busy, Compton," Holmes replied.

Compton chuckled. "I am aware. I read Dr. Watson's enthralling stories in *The Strand*."

He turned to me and shook my hand. "A genuine pleasure to meet you, Doctor."

"And to meet you, Mr. Compton," I replied with a smile. It was hard not to like this jovial man.

Releasing my hand, Compton turned to Holmes. "What brings you to my shop?"

"A case involving a music box."

Compton gestured to the rear of the building. "Then let us go out the back and you can tell me exactly why you are here – though I do not need to be a detective to know that you must need my expertise in this area."

Matthias Compton led us out the back into what was obviously an area that was quite clearly not open to the public. Half-formed boxes in a plethora of woods sat strewn along a long table. A second, only slightly smaller, table held what I took to be the inner workings of music boxes. Odd little metal combs, polished cylinders with strange snub-like protrusions, and a few coils, springs, and screws. Compton noticed my interest. "Hard to believe that they produce pretty tunes, is it not?"

"It is, rather," I agreed.

"I do not have an ear for music, so I purchase my barrels, rather than make them, and also purchase pre-tuned combs. The tunes are produced by the combs striking the barrel's pins as it rotates in the box." He smiled somewhat self-deprecatingly. "I am better at making the boxes."

"Don't let him fool you, Watson," Holmes said with a slight smile. "Compton's boxes are quite popular. I am told a certain gracious lady of high rank was given one of them and was quite charmed by it – so much so, that owning a genuine Compton is now something of a cachet amongst certain people."

Compton's face went slightly pink. His work must be brilliant indeed to have so delighted Her Majesty. I didn't doubt Holmes's word. He had no use for flattery, either for himself or for others. Where Compton's work was concerned, Holmes spoke the simple truth. That became apparent when Compton showed us a recently completed music box. It was quite a large sample. The box was made of carved and polished English oak with a lid inlaid with mother-of-pearl. When wound up, the box played several patriotic airs including "Rule, Britannia!" Compton wouldn't say for whom it had been commissioned, but merely that it was a gift. It wasn't hard to imagine exactly for whom the box was intended.

Compton carefully wrapped the box up and put it away. Turning back to us he said, "Now, Holmes, tell me exactly why you are here."

Holmes produced the music box that had been left with us. He handed the box to Compton, who unwrapped it carefully. As Compton looked for the box, Holmes quickly told him what we knew of the death of Major Portgrove.

Compton's examination of the box was as thorough as Holmes's had been. He selected an item from his tools on the table that I recognised: A loupe, or jeweller's glass, for close examination. This was a highly compact magnifying lense designed to get closer to an object than a glass like the one Holmes used. They had come to prominence in 1876, when a German surgeon pioneered using them to see clearly when doing delicate surgical work.

"There is nothing special about the box, Holmes, but I can tell you where and by whom it was made."

"You can?" I asked, somewhat started. "How?"

Compton held out the loupe to me. "See for yourself."

322

He directed me to look just under the base of one of the box's legs. Carved into the wood was a delicate lotus. I handed the box to Holmes, along with the loupe. He peered closely at the carving, nodded to himself, and handed the loupe back to Compton.

"This carving tells you where it was made?" Holmes asked.

Compton nodded. "It is a maker's mark, you could say. There is a gentleman in Lucknow who makes music boxes. This is his mark. He carves a lotus onto every one he makes. That box was made in India."

"Are his boxes exported at all?" Holmes asked.

Compton shook his head. "No. Like myself, he is a one-man enterprise. If his boxes go outside of India, it is because someone has purchased one and brought it out."

Holmes carefully wrapped the box up again. "Thank you, Compton. You've been most helpful."

"My pleasure, Holmes."

Compton showed us to the door and stood there smiling as we hailed a cab.

As we drove away, I asked, "Was that at all helpful?"

Holmes nodded. "We knew Portgrove served in India. The box came from India. This case stretches from London to Lucknow. I have an inkling of what happened, but I need to find out what regiment Portgrove was serving with when he contracted enteric fever. It all comes back to Portgrove's illness."

I looked at Holmes in some bewilderment, but I knew better than to ask questions. He simply would not tell me. I resigned myself to waiting until he had all of the pieces that he needed to solve the puzzle.

When we reached Baker Street I got out of the cab, by Holmes didn't follow. I looked up at him enquiringly.

"I have some people I need to talk with, and it will be a little dull for you." With that, Holmes called out to the driver, and the cab pulled away from the kerb. I watched it go with a sigh and turned and trudged upstairs.

I stood in our sitting room and looked around. There was really nothing I had to do. A glare from Mrs. Hudson, who was trying to clean the room, sent me upstairs into the sanctuary of my bedroom. In there, my eyes fell on one of my old dispatch boxes where I kept my writing. I realised that I also had papers in one of them that covered my time in India. With a little more enthusiasm than I had possessed a few minutes ago, I dragged out the boxes and began sorting through them.

One thing of which I had kept meticulous records was incidences of illness. Any illness could spread like fire through a garrison, so not only had I detailed information about what I'd treated, but I had also recorded outbreaks elsewhere. My personal records went up until the day before a Jezail bullet had ended my military career.

I sat down and began to reread my notes carefully, looking mostly for instances of enteric fever. There were a lot outbreaks of various diseases, including cholera, malaria, and plague, as well as the usual ones acquired by soldiers everywhere: Syphilis and gonorrhoea. After an hour's reading, I thought I might have pinpointed where Portgrove had served and with whom.

I returned to the sitting room and paced, waiting for Holmes to return.

My friend was amused by my impatience when he arrived. "I perceive that you have some news for me."

"I have. I believe I have found with whom Major Portgrove served."

"The 17th ----shire Regiment of Foot?" Holmes asked with a smile.

I deflated instantly. "Dash it all, Holmes! Do you know everything?"

"My apologies, I didn't mean to upset you. I see that you came by the information a lot more easily than I did. I have spent the day poring over the army roles, courtesy of Mycroft, as well as visiting several elderly clergymen. I'm curious as to how and where you found the information."

"From my own notes, which I kept on disease outbreaks – just in case. There was an outbreak of enteric fever in the Lucknow garrison. The timing was right for it to be the one where Portgrove took so ill."

"I wish I had consulted you first. It would have saved a lot of time."

"To be honest," I confessed, "if Mrs. Hudson hadn't driven me from the sitting room with her desire to clean, I doubt it would have occurred to me to go through my boxes."

"Then we must thank Mrs. Hudson for her desire to clean. And also ask her to prepare some comestibles for our guests."

"We are having guests?"

"We are."

"You have solved the case, then?"

"I have." Holmes walked to the window and stood staring down at the street, though I could tell he wasn't really seeing anything the passed before him.

"Who is coming?" I asked.

"Mrs. Portgrove and her maid, Regina." Holmes turned back from the window. "Also, a former comrade of Portgrove's – Colonel James Newling. That gentleman should be arriving first." Holmes gave me a sombre look. "I think it might be best if you had some treatment for shock close at hand. This isn't going to be pleasant."

I stared at Holmes for a long moment, then I nodded and went to my room to fetch my bag.

I had just returned to the sitting room when Mrs. Hudson showed Colonel Newling in. The man may have been handsome once, but his face was bloated, and his nose decorated with red lines. This was a man who hadn't been near a battle for years, but had been keeping a bottle as a constant companion instead. Privately, I thought gout was likely as well, given the way that he slightly limped.

Holmes greeting was slightly cool as he directed the man toward a chair. "We shall start properly when our other guests arrive. We are expecting Mrs. Portgrove shortly."

If Newling could have jumped to his feet, he would have. Instead, he hauled himself upright and glared at Holmes. "I shall not stay then." He turned to leave.

Holmes's voice cracked like a whip. "Sit down! It is time, Newling, for you to face what you have done. To see the four lives you and your comrades destroyed. I say again: *Sit down!*"

Newling slunk back into the chair and placed his head in his hands. The man was shaking. I started forward. Holmes grasped my shoulder. "Leave him to his misery, Watson. He does not deserve your pity."

I looked at Holmesin shock. The grey eyes were cold and hard as they looked at the man that I suspected was weeping. Whatever it was the Newling had done, he had angered Holmes beyond all compassion. And that was something that I had rarely seen.

The doorbell ringing downstairs told us that Mrs. Portgrove and her maid had arrived. I hastened to meet them and guided them to the sofa. Both women gave the distraught Newling curious looks before turning their attention to Holmes.

Mrs. Hudson brought in tea and biscuits. I poured tea for everyone, but no one touched it. All eyes were on Holmes, including those of the ashen Colonel Newling.

"You have solved the mystery of my husband's death, Mr. Holmes?" Mrs. Portgrove asked.

"I have," Holmes responded gravely. "It is a sad and sorry tale that begins in India. It is also a tale that you will not like."

Mrs. Portgrove indicated that he should continue regardless.

Holmes went and stood by the fireplace, and turned towards us. "Reginald Portgrove served in the 17th ----shire Regiment of Foot which was, for a time, stationed near the city of Lucknow. While there he met a local girl. Nothing unusual in that. What was unusual was that instead of making her his mistress, he married her."

Mrs. Portgrove gave a slight gasp of astonishment.

"Portgrove's fellow officers did not approve – especially as he married her with the full rites of the Anglican Church in Lucknow. I spoke today with an elderly churchman who was serving at Christ Church in Lucknow at the time. He told me it was quite a scandal, and that several of Portgrove's colleagues tried to protest the marriage. I understand that, on the instructions of the clergyman performing the service, these men were thrown out on their collective ears."

Newling went rather red. I gathered that he was one of the men thrown from the church.

"The Portgroves hadn't been married long," Holmes continued, "when enteric fever swept through the area. Portgrove became seriously ill. His life was despaired of. His despicable comrades took the opportunity presented."

"What do you mean?" I asked.

"These men, led by Newling here, told Portgrove's wife that he was dead and bundled her out of the garrison and away without care or compassion. When Portgrove was well enough, they told him his wife was dead. The still-ill and now-grieving man was discharged from the military and promptly placed on a ship back to England."

I stared at Holmes in shock. I turned to look at Newling, hoping he would deny it. Instead, it was patently obvious that every word Holmes had said was true. Newling was looking at his shoes, the very picture of shame and dejection."

"Portgrove's insistence on trying to get back to India wasn't due to his desire to continue serving his country, but his need to discover what had truly happened to his wife. I think, at some level, he knew that his former comrades had lied to him."

"What about the music box?" I asked.

"It was a gift from Portgrove to his wife. The sight of it on his desk was too much for his weakened heart."

"But who put it there?" I asked.

"That would be his daughter," Holmes replied.

"Daughter!" The word was gasped out in unison by Mrs. Portgrove and Colonel Newling.

"His daughter," Holmes said again. "Newling and his fellows neither knew nor cared that the recently married Mrs. Portgrove was with child when they treated her so abominably."

Holmes walked to his desk and picked up the music box. Crossing the room, he placed the box into the hands of Mrs. Portgrove's maid. "Your music box, Miss Portgrove."

She looked up at him and spoke for the first time. "How did you know?" Her voice was low and musical.

"It had to be someone in the household who placed the box on the Major's desk. Once I learned that the box was made in Lucknow and that your father had married over there, it all became obvious."

The girl stroked the box. "The box was a gift from my father to my mother when they were courting."

"What happened to your mother?" Holmes asked softly.

"As you said, she was carrying me when she was so dreadfully treated by my father's so-called friends. She returned to her family to grieve. All this I only know through what my grandfather told me. Not long before my birth, a friend of my grandfather's came to visit in a state of great agitation. He had been in Lucknow and had seen my father getting into the carriage along with a great deal of luggage. It was obvious that my father was alive, and was leaving both India and my mother."

The girl stroked the music box gently. "My mother was in great anguish at the betrayal. Several days after I was born, she instructed my *ayah* to take me to my grandfather. When the nurse returned, she discovered that my mother had hanged herself. My grandfather swore vengeance. He raised me to honour my mother and, if possible, to track down and confront my father. When grandfather died two years ago, my uncles helped me to find my father and sent me here to England. I stayed with another uncle and his wife here in London. This uncle had tracked down my father several years earlier and learned that he had married again. It was easy enough to get me into the household as a maid. I . . . ." The girl stopped.

Holmes continued gently. "You hoped that, somehow, he would realise that you were his daughter?"

She nodded. "It was foolish, I know, but I hoped. I decided that if he didn't know me, then he would know the music box, so I slipped downstairs and left it on his desk." The girl looked up at Holmes. "I didn't mean to kill him. This I swear!"

"You didn't know about his weakened heart?"

"Even I did not," Mrs. Portgrove interjected. "If he didn't tell me, why would he tell . . . ." Her voice trailed off.

Holmes turned back to the girl. "Miss Portgrove, may I ask how old you are?"

The girl looked at him in bewilderment. "I am sixteen, Mr. Holmes."

Holmes turned to Mrs. Portgrove. "When did you and Major Portgrove marry?"

To my horror I realised where Holmes was going with this. Mrs. Portgrove may not have been Mrs. Portgrove at all!

Mrs. Portgrove looked at him, slightly puzzled. "We were married only twelve years ago." Her eyes widened and she drew in a sharp breath.

Holmes turned to Newling. "That is something, I suppose. That you weren't also responsible for causing a case of bigamy and bringing shame to this good lady." He looked at Newling in contempt. "Your bigotry and callousness, along with that of your comrades, has caused misery and distress to many and ruined four lives. Get out of my sight!"

Newling got to his feet and slunk out of the door. He didn't even attempt to apologise to the ladies. Somehow, I thought that such an apology wouldn't have been accepted by either one of them.

Mrs. Portgrove had turned to look at the girl, who sat there staring at the music box in her lap. "Come, Regina. It is time to go home."

The girl lifted her head and stared at the woman. "You wish me to return with you, knowing now what you know? What I am?"

Mrs. Portgrove got to her feet. "Of course I do. Where else is my stepdaughter to live, but with me?"

"Stepdaughter?"

"I am your father's second wife, after all. Come, my dear. Let us go home and get you settled into a room more fitting your estate. I was thinking the green bedroom next to mine, what do you think?" Mrs. Portgrove turned to Holmes. "Thank you, Mr. Holmes. You have not only solved the mystery of my husband's death, but you have given me something that I had always wanted: A daughter."

The ladies took their leave, and I watched them go in some bemusement. Holmes was equally bemused. "There, my friend, are two exceptional women."

"They are indeed," I replied. "How did you know that the girl was actually the Major's daughter?"

"Once I found out what had happened in Lucknow, it became obvious. Someone from his first wife's family had to be involved. The backgrounds of the Portgrove's servants were easily traced, except for the girl, who only arrived two years ago. Then there was her name."

"Her name?" I asked.

"*Regina*. It is Latin for *Queen*, but it is often used as the feminine equivalent of *Reginald*. The lass was named for her father."

The Adventure of the
Unexpected Corpse
by Tracy J. Revels

"This, Watson, may be the oddest case of my career," Sherlock Holmes said, brandishing a letter that had just arrived and which he had been reading while emitting a series of low chuckles. "I have been asked to clear up a small matter for Lord Vincent Hollister."

"My congratulations," I said, thinking of how well-regarded the nobleman was in society. "What type of problem is he presenting?"

"A murder."

"Indeed!"

"Yes, and in the family."

"Why, I have seen nothing of it," I commented, shuffling through the messy pile of newspapers on the rug. It was a cold winter's morning, and I had done little except warm my feet by the fire and acquaint myself with the doings of more energetic men, as chronicled by the London press. "Surely such a thing would have caused a scandal."

"It did. A scandal and an outcry – over a hundred years ago."

Holmes smiled at my look of astonishment. He settled into his chair and lit his pipe.

"In 1790, Lady Elinor Hollister was betrothed to the Marquis of Edgewater, a near neighbor in the countryside, a man of considerable wealth and formidable temper. The young miss had been quite the local belle, and on the eve of the wedding, her disappointed suitors gathered at The Swan Public House, where intemperate consumption of strong spirits soon generated a foolish scheme. They vowed to descend upon the Hollister seat, Hollyreed, as a body, lay siege to its walls, and abduct the bride. Naturally, the drunken louts were met by both the irate father and the furious groom-elect, who gave them a sound thrashing. Meanwhile, the frightened girl ran upstairs and locked herself in her chamber. Once the ruffians were put to flight, the Marquis ascended the stairs and knocked on the door, assuring his intended that all was well. But there was no answer, and the parties became alarmed. The door was eventually broken down, and the lass was found within, cold and dead."

"My word!"

"At first, it was feared Lady Elinor had swallowed poison, choosing self-destruction over the potential of dishonor. None of the usual signs of poison were visible, however, and her coiffure and costume were disordered, hinting at violence. The distraught father and the highly placed groom refused to permit the body to be examined and cowed a coroner's jury into issuing a verdict of death due to 'fear and nervous collapse'. You will agree this was an unlikely explanation for the demise of a healthy young woman." Holmes rose and placed the letter on the mantel, impaling it with his jack-knife. "The funeral and burial were held privately, and the matter was forgotten for decades."

"This is certainly an interesting bit of English folklore," I said. "But what exactly does Lord Hollister expect of you in regard to it?"

"He wishes me to read the witness statements and review other forms of evidence. The lady's room has also been preserved as it was on the night of the murder."

"But even if you named the culprit – "

"That individual has long since faced a higher judgement. However, Lord Hollister has revealed in his letter that Elinor's brother Harold, the third son of the family, was privately blamed for her death. The Hollisters of the Regency Era made him a pariah. He later took to drink and died in an insane asylum. His guilt has taken on the nature of a legend in the Hollister line, though why brother would slay sister has never been satisfactorily addressed."

I considered my words carefully. "Holmes, if you will pardon me for saying so, this seems rather a waste of your talents."

My friend nodded. "Perhaps someday when the forensic sciences have advanced far beyond my meager contributions to the field, even the reported crime of Cain against Abel may be discovered to be a miscarriage of justice. Until that time, I can offer no more than my professional opinion. Fortunately, an educated hypothesis is all Lord Hollister requires. I have stated my fee, and he is willing to meet it." Holmes gave a sharp puff on his pipe. "It is a day's work, and the compensation will permit me to discharge a troublesome debt. May I count upon your assistance?"

"Of course, though I hardly see how I can help."

"You will be invaluable," Holmes said. "Especially as Lord Hollister wishes my examination of the case to begin with an exhumation."

We arose early the next morning and, just as the sun was clearing away the mist, we found ourselves at Hollyreed, a manor which displayed its medieval ancestry in its turrets and gray stone walls. The Hollister family had, fifty years previously, abandoned the old manse for a new home on another property of their substantial estate, leaving Hollyreed to fall into picturesque disrepair. A page boy met us at the door and led us through grim, clammy corridors to the great hall, where moth-eaten tapestries remained as relics of more dramatic days. Lord Vincent Hollister rose from an antique chair and provided a warm welcome. He was a tall, slender, elegant man of some forty years, strikingly handsome, with dark hair, bright blue eyes, and an affable nature. I felt I already knew him well from his many appearances in the society columns, where he was praised as a generous patron of the arts and a frequent contributor to worthy charities, and proclaimed one of the nation's most admirable nobles.

"May I ask, Lord Hollister, why it is so important to you to have this old mystery solved now?" I inquired. "Has some new evidence recently emerged that my friend might make use of?"

The nobleman gave a light laugh. "No, not at all, but our vicar is pleading with me not to allow Hollyreed to crumble, but to put it to good use, perhaps as a hospital or a home for the aged. I am not averse to seeing it transformed for the betterment of the parish, but I should lay the family ghost to rest before doing so." He leaned closer, speaking softly to prevent the young boy from hearing. "Over the last year, rumors have spread in the village that the specter of Lady Elinor walks these halls. When I announce that the great detective Sherlock Holmes has examined the business, surely even the most superstitious shall be satisfied there is no specter in Hollyreed."

"See what comes of published stories and sensational fame," Holmes muttered to me. I could tell Holmes was vexed by this turn. It had been one thing to satisfy a noble descendant's curiosity about a family crime, another to be publicly portrayed as a dispeller of ghosts.

"Let us begin in the crypt," Lord Hollister said. "It lies beneath the chapel."

We followed our host to a substantial private sanctuary in one corner of the manor. Ancient banners with coats of arms hung from aged timbers, and a miniature rose window bathed the small room in jewel-toned light. Lord Hollister led us to an opening behind a lovely pink marble altar.

"The entrance is here," he said. "Be careful upon the ladder."

We descended, one by one, into a frigid chamber, its inkiness repelled by a pair of lanterns held by two burly men. They snatched off their caps as Lord Hollister climbed down.

"Begging your pardon, Guv'nor," the larger of the two said, "but there's been someone here before us. The mortar was all broken up."

Lord Hollister scowled. "Broken?"

Holmes stepped forward, pulling out his lens and motioning for a light to be brought close to the large sarcophagus the men indicated was damaged. I noted the elaborate inscription on the top panel which provided the birth and death dates of Lady Elinor.

"This is recent work," Holmes said, as his fingers traced the damage. "Clumsy as well. Note the scarring of the tomb around the shattered seal."

Lord Hollister shook his head, sputtering in disbelief.

"But no one has been here since Harold Hollister was buried within, more than eighty years ago. The door to the chapel is kept locked, and there is no other entrance to the crypt."

"A locked door is no deterrent to the determined," Holmes said. He took up the lantern and made a quick circuit of the small, grim room. There was nothing within except another pair of tombs, and a half-dozen wooden coffins on shelves. All of them had deteriorated to various degrees, revealing the lead lined caskets within their hulls. "No treasure was stored in this chamber, I presume?"

"Nothing lies here except the bones of my ancestors. Unless – " Lord Hollister drew a sharp breath. "Family legend states the girl was buried in her wedding finery, including her jewels. Perhaps a thief came for them, and we shall find her tomb plundered."

I could tell, by the set of my friend's brow and the firm compression of his lips, that he disagreed with this theory.

"Let us investigate," Holmes said. "If some villain has already disturbed the lady's rest, we can do no further harm."

The workmen took up the task of sliding aside the heavy panel. They moved it off the tomb and gently laid it on the ground. Holmes lifted his lantern above the dark interior of the sarcophagus.

"Lord Hollister," he said softly, "I fear we have a far more recent mystery to solve."

"Who is the unfortunate lady?" Holmes asked. We had retired to the chapel, sending the workmen and the page boy off to fetch the local authorities. Holmes had made a more thorough inspection of the crypt, but none of the other burials had been disturbed, and no convenient clues were scattered on the floor.

"I . . . I do not know," our host murmured. Holmes whirled on him with impatience.

"Come, come. I cannot aid you if you dissemble. It was obvious from your reaction when you leaned forward to look that you knew the deceased. You even whispered a name."

Lord Hollister dipped his head. The sight of the corpse, hideous in the grey-green hue of death, but spared the disgust of purification by the extreme cold of the crypt, was enough to unnerve any man, much less one who had known the woman in life. Her long black hair and elegant figure, revealed in an ornate white lace and satin nightdress, hinted at her former beauty. Reluctantly, the nobleman spoke.

"She is . . . was . . . Sally Hale."

"The dancer," I said.

"Yes. A glorious performer, an unearthly beauty, a goddess of the footlights. And, for almost a year . . . my mistress," Lord Hollister confessed. He raked his hands through his hair, his eyes suddenly wild with horror. "My God, this is a disaster! It will turn into a public scandal. I shall be ruined in society. The police will think *I* killed her!"

Holmes folded his arms. "Make a clean breast of it now. It will do you no good to keep secrets from the one man who can help you."

Lord Hollister exhaled raggedly. "You know who she was and how her fame was acquired?"

We both nodded. It would be a rare man in London who did not know of Miss Sally Hale, and how she began her career in a ballet chorus, but soon eclipsed her fellow ballerinas. Her solo dances were untraditional and exotic, set to music from across the Empire. At times she slithered and twisted like a cobra as Indian flutes wailed. At others she leapt like a gazelle to the beat of African drums. Her costumes were likewise inspired by foreign attire, and often so diaphanous her exquisite form might be readily admired. The critics dubbed her the "nymph of the modern", and her performances were inevitably sold out.

"I met her last winter," Lord Hollister said. "I was in London for my nephew's nuptials, and he treated the gentlemen of his wedding party to her show. I was enthralled, entranced, spellbound by her grace and beauty. We went backstage afterward to present our compliments, along with a legion of other admirers, all of them wealthy, titled men. Sally's dressing room was awash in roses, I can still feel myself drowning in their scent. I plucked the simple white carnation from my lapel and presented it to her. Perhaps it was that gesture, so different from the rest, which gathered her attention, for the very next day I received a note from the lady, inviting me to call upon her at her residence."

"After which, an affair commenced," Holmes said brusquely, clearly unconcerned about the romantic details. Lord Hollister nodded, shamefaced.

"Until that day, I had always been faithful to my wife. Hester – Lady Hollister – was the sweetheart of my youth, but our love was in ashes. Eddie, our infant son and only child, died of diphtheria only a few weeks before I met Sally. Instead of bringing us closer, our grief for our boy drove us apart. I needed consolation, and some respite from Hester's incessant wailing."

Holmes showed no sign of emotion. "And how long did the affair with Miss Hale continue?"

"Until two months ago. I had a suite of rooms fixed for her convenience here at Hollyreed. I even renovated one of the galleries, so she could rehearse her dances. She was firm with me that she didn't plan to retire from the stage, swearing if I ever pressured her to do so, she would leave me. All I asked of her in return was that she take no other lover."

"Yet she did."

"No! No, she . . . My God, it is my fault! My fault!"

Lord Hollister began to weep. Holmes allowed his hysterics for only a few moments before reminding him that the authorities were probably already on their way from the village, and that notice of the corpse's discovery would have flown to an inspector in London as well. Lord Hollister coughed and resumed speaking.

"Sally began to whine about headaches and blurred vision, nothing more than any woman experiences with the cycles of the moon, though she complained excessively and annoyingly, as was her dramatic nature. I arrived one morning to watch Sally practice, as I often did, but she wasn't herself on that day. She was clumsy. She staggered, fell to the boards, complained of vertigo. I thought I would tease her and lighten her mood, so I told her she was growing too stout to jump so high, too aged for her acrobatics. I playfully suggested she should renounce her art and retire.

"She turned on me like a fury. She had a temperamental soul – she was a passionate creature – but this was beyond anything I had seen or experienced. She sprang up from the floor and clawed at me like a cat, then ordered me out. I told her it was my estate, and I would leave when it pleased me. When she continued in her rage, telling me to go, I firmly reminded her of my title and reputation, and how one word from me could destroy her."

"'You cannot bring me low!' she cried. 'I am immortal! The world will remember me when you are dust!'"

"I had no time for such crazed, foolish talk. I left her behind. I had business to attend to in London, and the next day I received a summons to France, where I also have interests. The travel gave me time to muse upon the situation. I had grown tired of Sally's hypochondria. One hysterical female in my life was enough! I sent Sally a letter breaking off our relationship and ordering her from my property. When I returned a fortnight ago, all her belongings were gone from Hollyreed."

"And you heard no more from her?"

"No, but shortly after my return, I received a note from Mr. Raymond Alberton, Sally's theatrical manager. He hadn't seen her for over a month."

"Yet he didn't alert the authorities to her disappearance?"

"No, because he knew her temperamental ways. He had also received a letter from her a few days previously, telling him not to worry, that she was ill but was being cared for. The message was written on my stationery – that was why he contacted me, to find out what might be amiss with her. I can only presume she purloined some of my paper, but I had no idea why she would wish to give the impression that I was her nurse."

"Had the lady made any threats to expose you?"

"No."

"And your wife was never aware of your relationship with Miss Hale?"

"No, I am certain of it. We have lived separate lives since Eddie died." Lord Hollister covered his face with his hands. His words were a humiliated whisper. "Just a week ago, I tried to make amends with Hester. I begged her to be a wife to me again. After all, there is the need for an heir, for I don't wish my title and estate to pass to my younger brother, who is a great wastrel. She wouldn't permit me so much as a chaste kiss, but her coldness to me is due to the loss of our child, not to her knowledge of my affair."

"You are certain?"

The nobleman lifted his head and gave my friend a hard look. "Of course I am. I took great precautions in my affair. No one knew of it." He groaned, leaning forward, and tugging at his neckpiece. "And now, it shall come out and I am destroyed."

Holmes rose and walked into the light of the rose window. He stood for a moment, his arms folded and his hand stroking his chin.

"Did your wife know of your willingness to give Hollyreed to the parish, for charitable use?"

"I mentioned it to her. I also told her last week that I was seeking your services to put the rumors of a ghost to rest. She showed no interest in the information. Hester is an entirely domestic woman and remains morbidly obsessed with mourning our child."

"Even so, it is essential that I interview her."

Lord Hollister appeared shocked, but after a moment he assented. "Very well. Only allow me to bring this terrible news to her first. I wouldn't wish her to hear it from a stranger, or from the police."

"A private interview, this evening?"

"I shall arrange it."

"Excellent. Watson, let us retire from the scene for a few hours. Lord Hollister, we shall be at your residence at six."

"We are fortunate to be so close to London," Holmes said, as we settled into our seats on the train. "I have no doubt that Lestrade or

Gregson will be sent out to handle matters, which will insure cooperation with our agency." My friend turned his head, glaring at the scenery as we picked up speed. "The nerve of his Lordship to try to play me for a fool – to make me his investigator of the supernatural when he knew the 'ghost' was nothing more than his mistress walking about the property! I am of a mind to double my fee!"

"Why are we returning to the city?" I asked, thinking sadly of the wonderful smells wafting from a local pie shop near the station, which Holmes had hurried past in the rush to catch the express back to Paddington.

"Because I wish to speak with Miss Hale's manager before the police arrive, and likely bungle the business." Holmes scowled. "They will no doubt start by arresting the girl's lover, though perhaps his elevated status might dissuade them for a time."

"I don't understand," I said. "If Lord Hollister murdered Sally Hale, why would he have placed her in the very tomb he hired you to open?"

"An excellent question, one which our friends in the official forces will probably forget to ask themselves. However," Holmes added, "it isn't beyond the realm of imagination that Lord Hollister did away with the lady and disposed of her body in a different place, only to have an enemy reinter her in the vault where she would be found. But let us collect more data before we theorize on unexpected corpses."

An hour later, we arrived at the Alberton Theatrical Agency. The outer chamber was filled with individuals seeking representation, all of them prepared to audition for the agent. Two winsome girls in short, fluffy skirts chatted with a red-robed magician in a peaked hat, who entertained them by pulling scarves and roses from his belled sleeves. A contortionist in a spotted leotard limbered up by placing his left heel behind his head. A flush-faced fellow and a sad looking hound sat in a corner. A placard beside the man's bag read *Felix the Talking Dog*. Clearly, Alberton catered to the lower rung of the entertainment ladder, the music and beer halls where any novelty act would please an intoxicated crowd.

A young woman crowned with garish orange hair sat at a desk before an inner door. She was certainly Alberton's gatekeeper. She squinted up at us through heavy spectacles.

"What's your trick?" she snapped.

"Prophecy," Holmes replied solemnly. "I predict your employer will be in a most distressed state to learn that Miss Sally Hale has been murdered."

The woman gasped and raced inside her employer's private chamber without knocking. A moment later, a juggler and a clown were evicted, and we were summoned within.

Mr. Alberton was a small man with a pock-marked face and greasy brown hair parted in the middle. His heavily waxed mustaches thrust from beneath his bulbous nose like two daggers. He wrung his chubby hands as Holmes told him of the discovery in the crypt.

"How horrible! It is just as I feared. I knew some evil fate would claim her!"

"You have been her agent for her entire career?"

"Yes, ever since Sally was an ingenue of sixteen. I know what you must be thinking – How could I, a man who provides diversions for the lower orders, have represented such a gifted artist, an inspired terpsichorean who performed for titled gentlemen? It is simple – I gave her a chance when she was very young, when other agents laughed at her because she danced to Oriental tunes. She proved loyal to a fault. She never threw me over, even when far more prestigious agents came to call."

"You knew her well, then."

"Like a father."

"Had she other family?"

"No, she is an orphan."

"And you were aware of her affair with Lord Hollister?"

The little man hesitated. Holmes raised an eyebrow.

"Yes," Albertson sighed. "I knew of it from the start, and I advised her against it. 'He will never leave his wife for you,' I warned her. 'He will cast you out when you no longer amuse him.' But she claimed she loved him and wouldn't listen, and now he has slain her!"

"There is no proof of such."

"Did you not just tell me she was found amid his tombs? What else could it be? Please tell me the poor child wasn't buried alive. It is too awful to consider."

"Why do you think Lord Hollister would have killed her?" I asked the man.

"Blackmail," Holmes stated with a dismissive wave. "She threatened to expose him. Lord Hollister is quite sensitive about his reputation."

"No!" Alberton shouted, slamming a fist to his desk. "Sally would never do such a thing! She was tempestuous, I admit, but she wasn't immoral. If anything, it might have been to hide . . . ."

Holmes nodded for him to continue. The agent mopped his brow.

"For the last three months before she vanished, Sally was pale and ill, she couldn't eat without distress. I insisted she consult a doctor, for I feared . . . ."

The unspoken words hung between us. At last, Holmes gave them voice.

"That she carried Lord Hollister's child."

"Yes. She spoke with a doctor, and afterward told me she dared not dance. What else could it have been?"

"If your speculation is correct, the autopsy will reveal it," Holmes said. "But for now, time is of the essence. Do you still have the letter Miss Hale sent to you? The one written on Lord Hollister's stationery?"

The agent shook his head. "It pained me to read it, for the writing wasn't like Sally's usual bold script. The letters wavered and quivered. The ink was blotted. I threw it in the fire."

"A pity," Holmes said. "Might we gain access to Miss Hale's lodgings in London? I presume as her manager, you have some sway with her landlady."

"Once again, we are fortunate to have a few hours' start on the police," Holmes said, after the bitter old woman, whose only response to learning of her tenant's death was to complain that the rent was in arrears, admitted us to the dancer's chambers. "Let us not be as careless as they will be when they inevitably arrive."

Miss Hale's dwelling was a small suite of rooms only short walk from our own in Baker Street. For a performer of such renown, she led a surprisingly spartan life. Her furnishings were simple, her wardrobe small. Her bedchamber was decorated with theatrical posters and pictures of famous dancers, along with many foreign curiosities such as African masks, Indian shawls, and Chinese paper lanterns. A notebook contained jotted thoughts on music, as well as sketches for costumes, but a careful inspection of the suite uncovered no diaries or private papers. Holmes found only one note in a drawer – a single, undated line was written on creamy, expensive stationery with the Hollister crest:

> You must go. I do not love you. Be removed from your rooms
> at Hollyreed when I return, or actions will be taken and you
> will suffer.
>
> H

"This does not bode well for his Lordship," Holmes said, returning the paper to its hiding place. "Perhaps Mr. Alberton's theory is correct."

"Or – "

"Yes, Watson?"

Something was amiss. A vague, nagging thought had chewed at my brain since Hollister's confession in the chapel, yet I couldn't make it take coherent form. I returned to the washroom adjourning the bedchamber, looking more closely at the handful of bottles on a shelf, and a doctor's

338

note tucked beside them, providing instruction for dosage. An electric pulse suddenly surged through me. All the pieces that had been scattered snapped into place. I gave a startled cry.

"Holmes – *I know the answer!*"

After taking our belated lunch and a brief respite in our rooms, we returned to the Hollister estate at six for our interview. The Hollister butler was a surprisingly young fellow, a tall and broad-shouldered man, perhaps a former prize-fighter based on his barrel chest, thick fingers, and crooked nose. He escorted us directly to a formal parlor, where our client's wife rose to greet us.

Lady Hollister – *nèe* Hester Rathvern – was thin-faced and pinch-lipped, with small, restless eyes and prematurely graying hair. She was dressed in dark gray mourning, which had the unfortunate effect of making her skin yellow and sickly. She regarded us coolly, then spoke with regal stiffness.

"You are too late for glory, Mr. Holmes. Inspector Tobias Gregson of Scotland Yard was here a few hours ago. He found my husband's answers to his questions unsatisfactory and took Vincent away in a police carriage. He did, however, have the remarkable courtesy not to slap my spouse in irons in my presence."

"I am sorry to hear Lord Hollister was arrested."

"Sorry to hear that justice will be done, and that he shall hang for the murder of his mistress?" the lady posed. "If so, then you aren't in real life as you are portrayed in your friend's stories."

"I am far from certain that detaining Lord Hollister is justice," Holmes replied, taking a seat even though none had been offered. "But you seem to be."

The lady sniffed as she settled onto a divan.

"I was aware of the little dancer, of course. Men choose to believe they fool their wives, but a woman always knows when she is being betrayed. I saw the bills for the wine, the late suppers, the excursions when he claimed to be away on 'business'. I discovered he had a suite of rooms fixed for her at Hollyreed, a hideaway for their trysts. I knew of it all."

"And never objected?"

"What good would it have done? Men hold power in the world. Women were created only to suffer."

"Including Miss Hale, it seems. Did you know she was ill?"

"What of it?"

"I wonder if you knew the exact nature of her condition – it was a most *interesting* one," Holmes said, with a biting edge to his tone. "One that promised great joy in a matter of nine months."

339

The lady jumped to her feet. Her pale eyes blazed with anger.

"I will thank you to leave my house – immediately!"

Holmes shook his head. "I have a few more questions, Madam. Surely you wish me to aid your husband."

"Not if he is guilty."

"And if he is innocent?"

She snorted. "That is beyond belief."

"It seems possible, Lady Hollister, that you had more motive to do away with your husband's paramour than he did."

The lady refused to be cowed. "And if so, then how, pray tell, would I have managed to murder her?"

Holmes shrugged. "Perhaps you visited her in her suite at Hollyreed, drugged her, and sealed her alive inside the tomb."

At this, Lady Hollister wavered. One hand flew to her face. "You are mad?" she hissed.

Holmes shot a quick glance in my direction before turning back to the lady. "Allow us to inspect your bedchamber."

"Certainly not!"

"Then we shall go to Scotland Yard with our suspicions, and return with Inspector Gregson and a warrant," Holmes said, rising with a weary sigh. "Good evening, Lady Hollister."

"No – wait!" she ordered, almost grabbing my friend's arm. She seemed to recall her dignity, and stepped backward at the last moment, giving her hair a needless pat. "I have nothing to hide. What you ask is an indignity, but better you than that miserable policeman." She seized a bell and rang for her butler. "Jefferies, escort these gentlemen to my bedchamber, but watch them. I wouldn't want any of my jewels pilfered."

Holmes offered a short bow. The butler led us up a set of stairs and down a long hallway. Holmes coughed, then spoke loudly.

"Watson, do you recall Charles Downing?"

I had never heard the name, but a quick glance at Holmes's expression alerted me that we were playing a game. "Yes, I do."

"Butler to a noble family – you resemble him greatly, Jefferies. Same build, same hair, young and able, rapidly rising through the ranks of the household, clearly the favorite of the matriarch. How long have you held your position, Jefferies?"

"About six months, sir."

"Remarkable. Well, let us hope you don't share Downing's fate."

The butler halted with his hand upon a doorknob. "And what was that, sir?"

"He was hanged last year for being an accessory to murder. Ah, thank you."

We stepped past the startled servant, making our way into a sizeable boudoir. The bed was high and canopied, clearly Georgian in design. Lady Hollister possessed several chests of drawers and a delicate marble-topped vanity littered with silver combs and brushes. Devotional pictures in the Renaissance style hung upon the walls. I moved into the adjoining washroom and noted nothing except the expected toiletries. Holmes opened a large mahogany armoire despite a warning rumble from Jefferies, who stood near the bedroom door. I noticed Jefferies had left it ajar.

"I am not here to steal," Holmes assured the butler, "but dear me, someone has indeed pilfered the lady's things. Why, what a lovely white satin robe, with such ornate lace. Would it not have a matching nightdress? Miss Hale was discovered in just such a gown. Surely that could not be a coincidence." As Holmes spoke, I noted Jefferies' face was awash in perspiration, and his body had begun to tremble. Holmes ignored him, walking to the marble vanity and picking up a brush. "My word, how strange! Come, Watson, and look at this. Stray tresses, locks of fallen hair, and they are raven black, while Lady Hollister's hair is – "

A frightful scream came from the hallway, followed by the thud of a fallen body. Jefferies threw up his fists, but I drew my revolver, grateful that Holmes had insisted I slip it into my pocket during our late luncheon at Baker Street. At the sight of my firearm, all the fight went out of Jefferies. He collapsed against the wall, barely able to stand on quivering legs.

"Oh, please sir, you must believe me! I only helped Lady Hollister with the girl, and I carried her body over to Hollyreed, to give her a decent burial. I never laid a hand on Miss Hale – I had nothing to do with her death! I don't want to hang! Please, please believe me!"

"I do believe you," Holmes said gently, "but now go and collect your mistress. We have much to discuss with her."

"Sally Hale was dying," I said. We were seated in the parlor, with Lady Hollister stretched upon the divan, brought around by smelling salts and a swallow of brandy. Holmes had sent Jefferies away to summon Gregson back from London. "Her condition wasn't impending motherhood, but a tumor in the brain. It would explain her sudden, vicious headaches, her extreme nausea, her loss of co-ordination, and her inability to dance. Such tragic cases aren't unknown, even in the young and seemingly healthy. In her room I found the strongest medications for dulling pain, and notes from a physician of my acquaintance who specializes in cancers. He knew there was nothing to be done for her, other than to try to ease her agony."

The lady did not speak, but tears formed in her eyes. Holmes took up the story.

"About two months ago, Lord Hollister mocked Miss Hale for being ill. She hadn't yet revealed to him the exact nature of her condition, and he callously wounded her passionate pride. Shortly thereafter, he broke faith with her in a letter. I believe it was then that she came to you."

Slowly, Lady Hollister sat up. She nodded, pushing back her long hair, which had escaped its tight chignon and now hung in tangles about her pale face.

"Little Sally came to me some five weeks ago. She simply appeared on my doorstep while Vincent was away in France. My first inclination was to have Jefferies cast her onto the common road, but then she fell to her knees, clutched my skirts, and begged my forgiveness for what she had done. She fainted at the conclusion of her confession, and I had Jefferies carry her to my bedchamber.

"When she revived, she told me of the cancer the doctor said was killing her. She spoke of her life, and repented of her casual, irregular love affairs, but never of her desire to dance and inspire her audience. Despite everything, I found myself strangely drawn to her, and I realized how cruel Vincent had been to both of us. As I held her hand, I imagined myself tending to a dying daughter, and was reminded of my love for my own dear infant, so recently gone to Heaven. I swore Jefferies to secrecy, and together we managed to hide Sally from the household, claiming it was I who was inconsolable from melancholy. I administered laudanum and other palliatives, so that when Sally died, it was with the gentleness of a lamb. That was three days ago. Vincent never knew his cast-off lover slipped away under his own roof."

Lady Hollister hesitated. Holmes whispered for her to continue.

"At midnight following Sally's death, Jefferies and I carried her back to Hollyreed, and laid her in the crypt of Lady Elinor. It seemed a fitting resting place for such a tragic beauty. I dressed her in my best nightgown, combed her hair, and folded her hands. No disrespect was shown to her body. I did nothing wrong."

Holmes frowned. "I cannot absolve you so easily, Lady Hollister. You knew your husband was considering gifting the property to the parish and had asked me to investigate rumors of a ghost. Those negotiations were made before Miss Hale's passing. You wanted her to be found." My friend leaned forward, holding his hands open. "We have only your word, and Jefferies's, that you didn't purposefully hasten the girl's death, to achieve the goal of implicating your husband."

342

The lady asked if she might have another sip of brandy. I poured some into a teacup, and she sipped it slowly. When she spoke again, all her defiance had vanished.

"You are indeed as the stories portray you, Mr. Holmes. You are exceedingly clever."

My friend shook his head. "I mustn't take credit for accolades I don't deserve. It was Watson who noted the nature of the medications, and accurately surmised the young woman's fatal condition. He pointed out how a letter could have come from this house, on his Lordship's stationery, and how Miss Hale's handwriting would have been altered because of her illness."

Lady Hollister nodded. "Sally didn't wish her agent to worry about her. She told me Mr. Alberton knew of her affair, so I thought nothing of the paper we used."

"Thus, it was easy to make the connections to you as the involved party, providing Lord Hollister had been honest in his statements. We had only to put you to the test, as we did." Holmes folded his arms. "It is a great benefit to a detective to have a medical man as a companion. The honor for the solution of this case must go to my good friend."

I felt my cheeks flush. Such praise from Holmes was rare indeed.

"Then please," Lady Hollister whispered, "you must believe me when I say I never harmed Sally, and she died when it pleased God to take her. Yes, I hoped Vincent would be suspected in her death, but I wouldn't have allowed my husband to hang. There would be a scandal, of course, but that is no more than he deserves."

I saw Holmes's eyes narrow. When he spoke, it wasn't without sympathy.

"You are hardly the first woman to lose her husband's affection to a mistress."

The lady's eyes widened. Her voice rose into the tenor of righteous anger.

"That isn't the reason I wished vengeance. All men are weak, I could forgive Vincent for dallying with a beautiful girl. No – I hate him because he is *cruel*! He blamed *me* for Eddie's death! He claimed I was careless and exposed our baby to disease. For weeks after the funeral, he wouldn't speak to me except to berate me for our child's passing – to call me a failure as a mother. Summon the other servants if you think I lie. They can tell you of his abuse, piled atop my boundless grief. And now when he speaks to me of our union, it isn't for love or comfort, but merely because he requires another heir." Lady Hollister drew back, her face crimson. "Yes, I wanted him punished, but I swear to you upon my soul that I wouldn't have allowed him to continue in jail beyond an evening at most.

343

I would have told the truth, once his vaunted reputation was in tatters, and the world aware of his hypocrisy and meanness." When neither of us responded to this remarkable revelation, she shook her head. "It would do me no good to have Vincent hanged. His brother, Reggie, is a drunkard and a wastrel, who would throw me to the wolves if he inherited the title."

"Hiding a death, even a natural one, is no trifling matter," Holmes warned. "But it isn't for us to judge you – We shall leave that to the courts." He pulled out his watch and scowled. "I wonder what is taking Gregson so long? He is normally quite punctual when summoned."

Holmes snapped his watch closed. We waited in silence for another half-hour. Lady Hollister nervously picked up some embroidery, and Holmes perused the books upon the shelves. I was about to offer to walk to the village, to see if there was some mishap – for I feared Jefferies might have fled instead of performing his duty – when a maid opened the door and announced the inspector.

Tobias Gregson stepped inside. I had known him since the first time I accompanied Holmes on an investigation. I saw at once that something was amiss in the drooping nature of his shoulders and the troubled expression in his eyes.

"I fear I am the bearer of bad news," he said. "The telegram, Mr. Holmes, implied the case was solved and Lord Hollister should be freed. However . . . I fear it is too late. Forgive me, Lady Hollister, but your husband is dead."

For a terrible moment we all stood frozen. The lady's fingers flew to her lips.

"Dead? But how?" Holmes demanded.

"He tried to intimidate us with his title, but when it was clear we meant to charge him, he became distraught and incoherent in his speech. We thought an hour alone in a felon's cell might be to his benefit, to calm him and make him more forthcoming. We never suspected he was suicidal, or we would have taken his braces."

Lady Hollister screamed and dropped senseless to the floor.

Careful readers of the sensational press will recall the death of Lord Hollister and the scandal that followed, which tarnished the legacy of the previously well-esteemed nobleman. These same readers may also recall how the sad figure of Lady Hollister succumbed to a fever not six months later, after being confined to a lunatic asylum by her brother-in-law, who claimed grief had stolen her sanity.

Meanwhile, Holmes pointed out something I had missed on the dramatic morning when the body of Miss Sarah Hale was discovered. No older human remains of any kind had been found inside the tomb, nor had any bones or grave goods been misplaced inside the crypt. Had the lady's final resting place been pilfered in the years since her death? That question plagued Holmes, until he spent almost a week at the British Library, reviewing antique newspapers and periodicals, as well as revisiting the scene and pouring over parish records. At last, he returned with the flush of victory in his cheeks.

"I found her, Watson! It seems the family legend, as told by the late Lord Hollister, omitted some key details. Lady Elinor was being forced to marry the Marquis, who offered to pay her father's substantial debts as a wedding gift. She, however, was in love with a certain Mr. Peter Jones, one of the 'drunken suitors' who staged the raid. She eloped with him."

"But the lady's room was locked from within."

"No – that was the story, along with a false funeral and private burial, devised by Lord Hollister and the Marquis of Edgewater, to save face. The Marquis did not wish to admit his espoused had run away with a younger and more charming man. The infuriated and nearly penniless Lord Hollister wished to make certain his errant daughter could never return to the family fold. I found evidence – in a spritely little memoir, privately published, something of a collector's item – that Lady Elinor and her groom fled to Gretna Green, married quietly, and lived a long and loving life together."

"Remarkable. At least that mystery resolved with a happy ending." I shook my head in wry amusement. "Too bad your fee will never be paid."

The Case of the
Benevolent Professor
by Naching T. Kassa

"It appears we have a client, Watson," Sherlock Holmes said as our cab drew to a halt before 221b. He indicated the middle-aged gentleman who stood waiting outside our door. The fellow possessed a head of graying hair and a dark mustache. He wore tweed and favored his right hand. Holmes quickly alighted from the cab and, after paying the driver, I followed suit.

"This gentleman is in need of your assistance," Holmes said when I joined him. "Come, Professor Dixon. Our rooms are just up the stairs."

He led the gentleman up and within seconds, entered our rooms. The professor's hand had been wrapped rather hastily in a torn and bloodied bandage. Upon removing the wrappings, I discovered that he had sustained a terrible bite. I began work at once.

"Your mission must be an urgent one," Holmes remarked, taking the chair opposite the fellow. "The journey from Cambridge couldn't have been easy."

Dixon showed no sign of astonishment. "You haven't given me your name, sir, but I think I know it. Only one man could recognize me on our first meeting. That man is Sherlock Holmes. How did you do it? Have you spoken with Cyril Overton? Or have you deduced it from my person?"

"The latter," Holmes said with a smile. "Your name, Emerson Dixon, your profession, and your address are inscribed upon the correspondence in the top pocket of your coat. As to Overton: We have had dealings with him in the past, but I haven't spoken to him since."

"Then . . . you are unaware of the circumstances surrounding my nephew, Jeremy Dixon?"

"The owner of the wondrous draghound, Pompey?" said I.

"The same. Though I am unsure of how wondrous he is. The wretched creature fastened himself to my hand only this morning."

"Pompey did this?" I cried. "That is quite unlike him. He was a most even-tempered dog, and quite useful in discovering the whereabouts of the three-quarter, Godfrey Staunton."

"He is hardly even-tempered now. My nephew has gone missing, and the dog is the only one who might track him. Unfortunately, the little beast has become snappish and strange ever since Jeremy disappeared. He

346

refuses to leave the boy's room, and when I tried to remove him, he bit me.

"Jeremy said you were the only other man who could employ the dog's talents as a draghound, Mr. Holmes, and I fear you are the only one who can control him. Will you come to Farrington Hall and find my nephew?"

Holmes rose and plucked the black and oily clay from the pipe rack. "What are the particulars of your nephew's disappearance? Spare no detail. What you may find trivial will not be so to me."

The professor pursed his thin lips and furrowed his brows. "He went missing Tuesday last."

"Three days ago?"

"Yes."

"And was the constabulary informed?"

"Yes. But they have found nothing." He shifted in his chair. "I am afraid they aren't as invested in the search as I."

"Why?"

The professor rose to his feet and paced the floor. He peered out the window as he did so, and then turned back to Holmes.

"This isn't the first time Jeremy has disappeared," he said at last. "He was willful, even as a child. He'd often run off into the woods and stay there for hours. My brother spoiled him terribly, you see, and when he died, it was up to me to bring order to the household. When Jeremy reached the age of seventeen, I left him in the wood to fend for himself. He soon came home with his tail between his legs. Never did it again. Until now."

Holmes took a draw on his pipe. "How old is the young Dixon?"

"Nineteen."

Holmes raised a brow.

"I have tried to impress upon him the responsibilities of manhood – his mother sent him to university with the hopes that he might change, but it seems his experiences in higher education have done little to improve him. He is still as prone to childish fits as ever."

"And what would upset him so? What would send him into such a fit of willfulness?"

Dixon tugged at his collar and cleared his throat. "When his father – my brother and Lord of Farrington Hall – passed away, my sister-in-law, Lady Clara Dixon inherited. She was much aggrieved at first, but in the two years she has known me, the bond between us has grown. The Lady and I are to be married next month."

"And when did you inform Jeremy of these nuptials?"

Dixon lowered his gaze. "On Tuesday. He returned home to have supper with us and, when we shared the news, he caused quite a scene. He ran off soon after."

"Into the woods."

"Yes."

"And he didn't return to the house?"

Dixon shook his head. He glanced up, his blue eyes welling with tears. "He has never been gone this long, Mr. Holmes. Never more than two days. We have telegraphed his friends from university and visited those who reside in the village – no one has seen him and no one knows where he has gone. His mother is beside herself with worry. She hasn't slept or eaten in more than a day. To see her so affected – Well, it is more than I can bear."

He covered his face with both hands and shook with emotion. I brought him a glass of brandy and, with some cajoling, convinced him to sip some of the liquid. When he had composed himself, he turned, red-faced, to Holmes.

"Will you help us? I am not a rich man, but I will give all I have to see that boy safely in his mother's arms once again."

Holmes rose to his feet. "I will look into this matter, Professor, and discover the whereabouts of your nephew."

"Thank Heavens! If there is anything I can do to aid you in your investigation, you only have to ask."

A knock sounded on the door and Mrs. Hudson entered, a telegram in hand. Upon seeing it, the professor leapt to his feet and snatched it from her.

"That is for Mr. Holmes!" our landlady cried.

"It is from Lady Dixon," the professor said. "I asked her to telegraph me here should there be any developments."

"But it is addressed to Mr. Holmes!"

"It is quite all right, Mrs. Hudson," Holmes replied. "You may go."

Mrs. Hudson turned on her heel and took her leave.

"Why, this is wonderful news!" Professor Dixon cried. "Jeremy has been found! He returned soon after I left. It seems I will not need your services after all, Mr. Holmes."

"It seems so," Holmes replied.

The professor crumpled the telegram and tossed it among the dying embers in the fireplace, where flames licked it's edges. After glancing at it a moment, Dixon said, "I am most grateful, gentlemen. Would you dine with me? I should like to celebrate this turn of events, and lunch at the Savoy would be very much in order."

"I am afraid we cannot," Holmes said. "There are one or two matters which still require our attention."

"Then I shall take my leave and trouble you no more. Good afternoon."

"Good afternoon."

When Dixon had gone, Holmes sprang to the fireplace, snatching the crumpled and singed paper from among the ashes. He carefully read it, and then for his hat and coat.

"Come, Watson," said he, "We haven't a moment to lose. We must make for Cambridge and thence to Barrington immediately."

"To Cambridge?" I cried. "Whatever for?"

"We must find Jeremy Dixon before his uncle gets there to hinder our search."

"Hinder it? You don't trust him?"

Holmes handed the wrinkled telegram to me. It had come from Barrington, and the words chilled me to the marrow.

Claudius has come to murder Hamlet.
The general knows.

Lady Clara Dixon

"Lady Clara?" I cried. "The boy's mother?"

"Yes."

"And Claudius was the uncle of Hamlet," I continued. "Does this mean – ?"

"The message of the telegram is clear," Holmes replied. "The professor means to kill young Dixon."

"Kill him? Surely not."

"It isn't the first time we've encountered a villain in the realms of academia. Look at the facts. I have often remarked on what one may learn about a family from their treatment of children and animals. Professor Dixon's opinions on the subject of both are quite clear. I am not well-acquainted with the younger Dixon, but I do know Pompey, and I find it unlikely that he should inflict such a grievous wound without reason.

"There is also the matter of the professor's visit. The moment he arrived, his manner was one of a nervous man, pacing the floor as though he expected the imminent arrival of something or someone. When he snatched the telegram from Mrs. Hudson, I knew he had come to intercept it."

"If he feared it so, why did he toss it in the fireplace where you might find it?"

349

"He fancies himself a clever man and such fancies lead to arrogance. He thought he had outwitted us when he saw it start to catch fire." Holmes opened the door. "Have you your revolver? I think we may have need of it."

I removed the gun from the desk drawer. "Are you armed?"

Holmes reached for his trusty hunting crop and a ten-penny whistle. "If you have your revolver, these and a dark lantern is all I shall need."

Holmes led me out into the street where we hailed a cab. Soon, we were on our way to King's Cross Station.

"One thing puzzles me," I said, as the cab rolled along. "In the second part of the telegram, Lady Dixon mentions a 'general'. Who could such a person be? Is it a clue to whom we might speak to next?"

Holmes smiled. "There is a Shakespearean thread running through her missive. One need only look to *Antony and Cleopatra* for the answer. Surely, you know of whom he speaks."

The answer, once obscure, became clear. "*Pompey!*" I cried. "The Roman General."

"And namesake of our canine friend. Come, Watson. Here's the station. We must be quick if we are to find young Dixon."

The sun had begun its slow descent from the sky when we arrived in Cambridge, and it was dark by the time we had secured transport from the village of Barrington to Farrington Hall. Before we left the more populated environs, Holmes ushered me into the telegraph office, where we faced a rather grim-looking man with a balding pate.

"What do you want?" the fellow said, glancing up at Holmes and myself, his expression one of suspicion.

"I wonder if you can be of service," Holmes said. "I received a telegram this morning – "

"You sure it's from us? There's more than one telegraph office in Cambridge."

Holmes delved into his pocket and removed the telegram. He handed it to the telegrapher.

"Yeah, this is one of ours."

"Can you tell me who sent it?"

"Who do you think I am? Bleedin' Sherlock Holmes? I don't remember every Tom, Dick and . . . ." He trailed off, his eyes widening. "Wait. This here telegram is *for* Sherlock Holmes. Are you – ?"

"I am."

The transformation which overcame our new acquaintance was so swift and complete that I thought another man must've taken his place.

Gone was the ill-tempered expression and manner. A welcoming smile and gentle tone replaced them.

"My word. If my Susan knew I had you in the office, she'd burst with pride. We've both been admirers of you, sir. And your friend and colleague Dr. Watson, of course. Is this him? I mean, *he*? Blimey, I thought you'd be taller."

"We are in somewhat of a hurry, Mr. – ?"

"Smith. Gerald Smith. How can I be of service?"

"Do you know who sent this telegram?"

The telegrapher peered at the sheet once more. "I do. All dressed in black and wearing a veil, she was, but I knew her well enough. It was Lady Dixon of Farrington Hall. "

"You're certain?"

"I've known her since her husband died, God rest his soul. And like you, Mr. Holmes, I don't see, I *observe*. Lady Dixon possesses a *pince-nez*, one she wears on a chain. When she lifted her veil to place them on her nose, I glimpsed her face. It was her all right. She was pale and trembling, and kept looking toward the door as though she expected someone to come through it. A moment later, someone did."

"Professor Dixon," Holmes said.

"You know him?"

"We have had the dubious pleasure."

"Well, he asked her who she had telegraphed. Asked if it was Jeremy and she wouldn't answer. Professor Dixon is known to be a kind man, the type that would never hurt anyone, but Lady Dixon acted as though she were deathly afraid of him. He seemed saddened by her manner and asked her to wait for him in the carriage. She turned to me, her eyes pleading-like, and then she took her leave. The professor apologized. Said that Jeremy and he had had a row, and that Lady Dixon had taken his side in the matter. He was quite embarrassed by it all. He even promised me a sovereign if I didn't send the telegram. If I simply tore it up. I told him I couldn't do that, I'd already sent the telegram. He asked who it was sent to. I told him it's against the rules to tell him. So what does he do? He reaches into his pocket and pulls out a five-pound note. Says he'll give it to me if I break the rules this once.

"This all seemed too strange to me, so I call for my supervisor in the back. When I turned back 'round, the professor had gone. I rushed to the door, and when I looked out, I saw him gettin' into the carriage. He and the Lady were headed for Farrington Hall. Suppose he was taking her home, before returning to his."

"I expect that will change soon enough, when they're married."

351

Smith cocked his head to one side. "They ain't gettin' married. Mrs. Cornelius – that's Lady Dixon's housekeeper – says she hasn't spoken to him for three days, and she's instructed Mrs. Cornelius not to allow him in the house."

Holmes nodded. "Odd – If he is as kind as you say he is."

"Well, I may be telling tales out of school, but there's some that say he's more interested in the Lady's *fortune* than in her *heart*. She inherited Farrington Hall from her husband, you see. And some say it should have gone to the professor, him being the second-born son and all."

"A rather dramatic circumstance," Holmes said with a sigh. "I am most grateful for your help, Mr. Smith."

"I am glad to be of service, Mr. Holmes. If you ever need it again, you only have to ask."

"Then I will ask it," Holmes said. "May I have a form and a pencil, please?"

Holmes scrawled a message on the form and handed it to Smith. "I will need no answer, but if one is given, we will be at Farrington Hall."

"I have many agents throughout London," Holmes said, once we had taken our leave, "and, aside from the Irregulars, I find telegraphers to be among the most indispensable. They come in contact with a great deal of information and can sometimes be quite astute. Mr. Smith is one such fellow. I believe I shall offer him employment when this matter is concluded."

"Mr. Holmes?" a voice called out. "Mr. Sherlock Holmes?"

Two men approached us from the west side of the street. The first was a small man with an even smaller mustache, and the second a large fellow who towered above Holmes. The giant stared at us with contempt, while the first fellow smiled like a Cheshire Cat. Both men were dressed in brown tweed and bowler hats.

"I am he," Holmes replied.

"Constables Markham and Dawes," the fellow said by way of introduction. "What brings you to our little village."

"A friend," Holmes said with an easy smile. "And though I am flattered by the attentions I have gained from the Barrington Constabulary, I am, unfortunately, otherwise engaged."

"Have you come to see a woman?" the giant growled. "Lady Dixon for instance?"

"Why yes," my friend said, amiably. "Do you know her?"

Markham glanced at Dawes, his grin broadening. "She has her quirks. A bit . . . funny in the head. She's the vengeful sort, you see. Whenever she's thwarted or suffers an offense, she complains to the constabulary in an attempt to place a black mark on the more reputable people in the village."

"People like Professor Dixon?" Holmes asked, his expression one of complete innocence.

Both men frowned.

"You do know the professor?" Holmes continued.

"I think you should return to London, Mr. Holmes," Markham said. "Barrington isn't a safe place for you."

"And if I refuse?"

Markham's smile returned. "Then Dawes will see you to the train and wait with you until it arrives."

"Regretfully, I must refuse."

Dawes reached for my friend and I went for the revolver in my pocket, smashing him across the face with the butt. He fell back, clutching at his nose.

"He broke it!" Dawes cried. "He broke my nose!"

"Your friend should see a physician," Holmes remarked. "I would loan you mine, but I have need of him. Oh, and gentlemen, should the professor inquire after me, you may inform him that I am on my way to Farrington Hall. If you wish to continue this particular conversation, you will find me there."

Holmes and I hurried to the dogcart we had procured, and the driver who sat waiting for us.

"Quick, man!" Holmes called to the driver. "A gold sovereign if you can reach Farrington Hall within the next ten minutes."

The dogcart lurched forward and away.

"I wonder," Holmes said, raising his voice above the din, "if the Professor took the early train as we did."

"We didn't see him."

"He may have taken pains to see that we did not. And his cronies, Markham and Dawes, may have delayed us so that he might escape to the Hall unnoticed. Time is the key. And I believe it is running out."

Minutes later, we sighted Farrington Hall. The once-proud Tudor loomed before us in the darkness, its mysterious form filling me with dread. Perhaps it was the time of day or the nature of our visit which curdled my blood and caused a chill to climb my spine. Or, perhaps, I feared what we might find inside.

Holmes instructed the driver to stop and we alighted upon the road. Here, he left us.

Without a word, Holmes rushed down the drive. He moved quickly, much quicker than I, forcing me to run in order to keep pace with him. By the time I reached the Hall, my leg had begun to ache.

353

The Tudor, though aged, seemed strong and sturdy. The only exception to this was a section of the eastern wall. A great oak had fallen against it, and it had caved beneath the weight. Stone lay crumbled on the lawn nearby.

This part of the house seemed unoccupied. A small and lonely light flickered at the opposite end.

"Are you quite all right?" Holmes whispered. I nodded, though the pain in my leg said otherwise.

"Come then." He carried the dark lantern aloft, and together we crept toward the small beacon glowing in the darkness.

We couldn't have been more than thirty feet away when the sound of horse's hooves drifted toward us from the road. Holmes glanced toward it, and then urged me back into the shadows. Several seconds passed as the horse drew closer, and I held my breath as the creak of wooden wheels also became audible.

For a moment, I thought the cart had entered the drive, but the sound continued on and quickly faded away. When it had gone, Holmes led me back toward the light.

"Did you see them?"

I shook my head.

"There was a big fellow driving that cart – too big to be anyone other than Dawes."

"Then we must make haste," I said.

We approached the door and found it flung open on its hinges. A howl of anguish sounded from inside.

"Quickly!" Holmes cried.

We rushed into the house and followed the voice down a passage on the left. There we found a small parlor and hurried inside.

An elderly woman, clad in black, her hair askew, knelt beside the unconscious form of another woman and sobbed. When she saw us, she started and threw herself over the prone woman.

"You'll not touch her!" the woman cried. "He's harmed her enough!"

"My name is Sherlock Holmes," my friend replied. "This is Dr. Watson – "

"Mr. Holmes! Dr. Watson! Thank Heavens you've come!" she cried, as I hurried to aid the woman upon the floor. "You must help her. Please!"

I examined the unconscious woman, noting the ugly, purpling bruise which had begun to form on the right side of her face.

"She will recover," I said. "Have you some brandy that we might revive her?"

The elderly woman nodded and struggled to her feet. She rushed to the tantalus on the opposite side of the room and soon returned with a glass of brandy. I lifted Lady Dixon, while the elderly woman – who proved to be the housekeeper, Mrs. Cornelius – poured a few drops between her lips.

"My poor mistress!" Mrs. Cornelius said. "What could two women do against such a brute as that? That professor – he has never forced his way inside before. But tonight, he was like a madman!"

"He came for Pompey?" Holmes asked, turning from the mantelpiece and the fractured mirror above it. He glanced across the room at the curtained window.

Mrs. Cornelius nodded. "He came to fetch him so he might find Jeremy, but my mistress wouldn't hear of it. She set the dog free before he broke into the house. When she told the professor so, he knocked her to the floor."

The Lady's eyes fluttered open. She glanced about, fear gleaming in them as she looked upon us.

"Shh, now!" Mrs. Cornelius said. "It's all right. They aren't with the professor. It's Sherlock Holmes and Dr. Watson. The Devil himself couldn't keep them away."

"Mr. Holmes?" Lady Dixon whispered. "Are you Mr. Holmes?"

"At your service," Holmes said. "Time grows short, Lady Dixon. If you know where your son is, you must tell me at once."

The woman shook her head, her blonde hair falling about her shoulders.

"I don't know! Only Pompey could find him now. And if the professor gets the dog . . . ." She shuddered. "My son is lost."

Holmes took her hand and stared into her eyes. "Where is Pompey?"

"The dining room. I took him through the dining room."

"Down the hall, to the left," Mrs. Cornelius directed. "The French doors."

"Do you have anything of Jeremy's?" Holmes asked.

The two women looked at one another.

"For the scent. For the dog."

"There is a coat near the door." Mrs. Cornelius said. "Jeremy wears it in the winter."

"Thank you. Now, if you'll be so good as to lock the door when we have gone, we shall find Lady Dixon's son."

Holmes and I dashed out of the parlor and into the corridor. Holmes collected the coat while I retrieved a leather lead I found hanging beside it. We retraced our steps and, following Mrs. Cornelius's instructions, found a large dining room on our first left. A mahogany table at its center. The French doors lay beyond – opened.

"How will we find him in the dark," I asked, "without alerting the professor?"

Holmes reached into his pocket and withdrew the whistle. He placed it to his lips and appeared to blow two short blasts. The instrument made no sound.

We waited for several moments, with nothing but the wind among the trees to greet us.

And then, across the lawn, something rustled among the brush. A blur of white streaked toward us.

The dog, his tan-and-white body wiggling every which way, hurried to Holmes. My friend dropped to one knee, and Pompey whimpered as Holmes scratched just behind his lop-ears.

"There now, Pompey. You look no worse for wear. Watson, the lead."

I placed it over the dog's head and handed the other end to Holmes. With Pompey now safely in tow, we slipped out into the night.

"There is a moon," Holmes said. "It will be at its zenith in a few moments."

"A boon and a curse," I said softly. "We shall see our quarry, but he'll also see us."

Holmes held the coat out for Pompey's inspection. "The professor didn't come out the French doors."

"How do you know?"

"Come now. You have only to observe."

I glanced about the dirt path which led toward the wood and the green lawn.

"There are no footprints."

"Bravo! And it seems Jeremy hasn't come this way either. Pompey hasn't yet caught his scent."

I expected Holmes to lead Pompey toward the wood, but he did not. Instead, he kept near the house, leading Pompey toward the eastern wing. With precious moments slipping away, I felt I must intervene.

"Holmes, shouldn't we make for the wood?"

"Whatever for?" Holmes asked.

"The professor said we should seek Jeremy in the wood."

"And you believe him?"

"I –"

"You'll be happy to know that Pompey isn't the vicious beast that the professor described. The dog didn't attack the villain in Jeremy's room. He attacked him in the parlor. The blood from the wound Pompey inflicted had stained the rug near the chair and the hearth. And the cloth on the table had been torn. It corresponded with the bandages Professor Dixon used upon his hand."

"Another lie," I said, shaking my head. "It seems the professor is wholly unacquainted with the truth."

356

"And that is precisely the reason we shouldn't consider anything he says as fact." He chuckled. "I must congratulate him on his acting skills. The ability to bring forth tears upon command is a skill I find most enviable."

"Well, then, if we cannot consider what the professor says as fact, we should search in the opposite direction. Perhaps Jeremy is near the house."

"That is what we must discover."

Pompey suddenly lurched forward, panting with excitement.

"It seems he has found the scent," Holmes said.

We had rounded the house and found ourselves near the Hall's entrance. Pompey strained at the lead, pulling Holmes toward the fallen tree against the wall. The dog whimpered as he sniffed about the rubble.

"He is here," Holmes whispered. "Pompey has found him. But where . . . *Ah!*"

Pompey dived forward and into a small space beneath the tree, vanishing into a crevice which had gone unnoticed. My friend dropped to his knees and crawled after him.

I wish that I could say that I too pursued the dog, but my old wound would not allow it. I couldn't bend down, let alone crawl upon my knees.

"Watson!" Holmes cried from the crevice, his voice hushed.

"Holmes, I can't – !"

"Stay there. I shall return shortly." Within moments he had gone, taking the dark lantern with him.

Silence deafened me as I secreted myself against what remained of the wall, the branches of the tree hiding me from view. The revolver felt cold and heavy in my hand, but it comforted me.

I stood vigil for some time, waiting for Holmes and the dog to reemerge.

As the moon rose higher in the sky, it revealed the drive and the lawn before me in its glow. I shifted my feet as my leg throbbed, and I might have abandoned my hiding place had I not heard the return of the cart upon the road. This time, it swung into the drive and a figure that I hadn't noticed broke away from the shadows near the fallen tree behind which I hid.

"You fools!" the professor cried. "Where have you been?"

"It's Holmes," Markham replied. "He's here. Dawes might have seen him near the house, so we passed by. We thought we'd come back when he wasn't expectin' us."

"And capture him," Dawes said.

"You imbeciles. He's probably gone into the woods. There is no help for it now. For all we know, Holmes may have found the blasted hound.

357

We must get another dog. Go to the village. Find the best you can – steal it if you must, but bring it back without delay."

"What will you do, Professor?"

"I will do my best to bring the little coward forward."

The cart turned and rolled back down the drive.

The professor strode back toward the house. I heard a door open and then shut.

A sudden fear coursed through me. Lady Dixon and Mrs. Cornelius, though locked behind the parlor doors, might find themselves in grave danger.

The longer I stayed hidden, the worse my trepidation became. At last, I stepped from my hiding place and slipped out toward the tree.

The sharp explosion of a revolver shot rang out, startling me. It had come from inside the house.

Without a thought for my leg, I rushed to the door and slipped inside.

A deathly silence filled the hall. Then voices emanated from the parlor and I slowed that I might creep up upon it. The chime of a grandfather clock, striking the midnight hour, hid the sound of my footsteps as I approached the doorway.

From my vantage point outside, I viewed Professor Dixon standing before me, his revolver aimed at the Lady. The woman stood, her face grim, a hint of steel in her eyes, Mrs. Cornelius at her side.

"You cannot force me to marry you now, Emerson," said she. "The fortune is no longer mine."

"Then there is no longer a reason to keep you alive, Clara," he replied. "Not even the Good Doctor can save you now."

His reflection in the broken mantelpiece mirror smiled. He turned on me and fired.

The bullet whizzed by me like an angry bee, and my own shot went wild. Lady Dixon grasped hold of his arm, but he shook her off and she fell against Mrs. Cornelius.

"Where is your friend, Doctor?" he asked. "I know he must be here. Has he found the boy? If he has, he must turn him over to me immediately, or I will shoot the Lady where she lies."

A snarl filled the air and something rushed through the door. It sank its teeth into the professor's ankle and he screamed in pain.

"You vicious beast!" he cried, training the revolver on Pompey.

Before he could discharge it, Holmes was upon him. He struck the professor's hand with his hunting crop, forcing him to drop the revolver. I stepped forward and kicked it away.

"Damn you!" the professor roared, all trace of his former civility vanishing like a wisp of smoke. "Damn you all!"

358

"No, Professor," a voice said from the doorway. "Damn *you!*"

Pompey rushed to the young man who could only be Jeremy Dixon. He stood before us, his clothes thick with dust and his face dirty, holding that same steely resolve I had seen in his mother but moments earlier.

"It is midnight, Professor, and I must insist you leave this house."

"Wretched boy!" the professor sneered. "Sniveling coward, hiding behind your mother's skirts! What right have you to eject me from this house?"

"I am Lord Dixon, the master of Farrington Hall, as my father before me. You are unworthy of the title and shall never possess it."

"We shall see about that! I believe the local magistrate will see things quite differently. I will tell him of how you and your friends assaulted *me* – how you set your dog upon me. How the local constabulary was forced to subdue you. I will shame you from this title and it will be stripped away."

Holmes pulled a pair of bracelets from his pocket and clapped them on the professor's wrists. "And I suppose no one will believe the five witnesses who stand before you?"

"I will ruin you, Holmes!" the professor snarled.

Holmes lowered his gaze and nodded. "And what of Inspector Lestrade of Scotland Yard? Will you ruin him as well?"

The sight of the inspector entering the room from behind the door, astonished me almost as much as it did the professor. Lestrade tipped his hat. "I received your telegram, Mr. Holmes," said he. "And I believe I've heard quite enough."

Professor Dixon's eyes widened as Lestrade took hold of him and led him to the door.

"Inspector," I called out.

"Yes, Doctor?"

"There are two constables in the village attempting to steal a dog. You may wish to take them into custody as well."

"We cannot thank you enough, Mr. Holmes," Lady Dixon said. She sat beside her son, her hand clutching his arm, as though fearing he might vanish once again. "For three days, we haven't had a moment's peace from that blackguard."

"We have heard the professor's false story, Lady Dixon. Will you now relate yours? It would be refreshing to hear the truth of the matter."

"Then I would be glad to, Mr. Holmes," the Lady replied. "I suppose it all began after my husband died long ago. There had been a falling out between Emerson and James, and so neither I nor Jeremy had made the professor's acquaintance. James had never revealed the reason for the row

359

between them and I hadn't thought to ask. It seemed so tragic that they could never resolve their differences before James' death.

"I am ashamed to say that Emerson began wooing me at once – as soon as he introduced himself at the funeral. My husband had been buried but two months before he revealed his feelings for me. I was flattered, I suppose, and Emerson seemed so sincere. Ah, but I was brokenhearted and foolish. That was two years ago, and only recently did I discover his true nature.

"A fortnight ago, when Emerson again came to visit. I imprudently revealed the exact terms of my husband's will and Jeremy's trust. I told him how Jeremy would inherit all on his twentieth birthday, just two weeks hence.

"Emerson accepted the news well, I thought. We dined and then, in a manner quite unusual to him, he took his leave.

"Jeremy and I remained in the parlor, and when the clock struck nine, he wished me good night. He had risen to his feet when there was a shot. It shattered the window glass."

"And the bullet struck the mirror instead of your son," Holmes said.

"Yes, it missed him by mere inches. We were shaken by the events, but Jeremy recovered quickly. Against my counsel, he rushed into the dining room and out the French doors. He returned moments later with a handkerchief, one which I had given Emerson only a few months before. White silk with his monogram upon it.

"The next day, when Emerson returned, I confronted him with the handkerchief. He said he'd lost it while walking, and suggested we report the matter to the local constabulary. They were, as you have no doubt noticed, rather unconcerned. They refused to investigate, as it was their opinion that someone had been out poaching at night and fired into the house by mistake. I made the error of believing them, for I didn't wish to think that Emerson capable of something so heinous.

"And then, that following Tuesday, something occurred which made me believe.

"Jeremy had gone out riding that morning, in preparation for the hunt which would take place the following week. While he was gone, Emerson came to see me. He had grave news to relate – about Jeremy.

"For twenty minutes or more, he shared an outrageous story of how Jeremy had engineered the attempt on his own life and how he had tried to implicate Emerson for it. He said Jeremy was a jealous and spoiled boy, and that it was his aim to ruin our relationship and part us forever.

"The story, though spoken with the greatest of sincerity, was so excessive that I actually laughed outright. My mirth soon turned to anger, however, and I ordered him from the house.

360

"And that was when he showed his true colors. He shouted at me, saying he would sooner see my son dead than master of Farrington Hall. Then he stormed out.

"Jeremy didn't return home for some time. I couldn't rest until he did, so fearful was I of the professor's words. The moment he entered the house, I told him what had happened and how we must go to the police. It was a terrible mistake. When I tried to alert them to the professor's threats, they simply nodded, as though I were mad. That constable, Markham, simply sat there, grinning at me. He promised to look into the matter, but I knew he wouldn't. There was nothing more to do.

"Upon returning to the Hall, I devised a plan. Only a few days remained until Jeremy's birthday. If he could hide where not even I could find him, he might remerge on his birthday as the master of Farrington Hall.

"I didn't agree with the plan," Jeremy said. "I wanted to face the villain. It was my intention that we see you, Mr. Holmes. But mother thought you might be swayed as the constables were."

"And for that, I am heartily sorry," Lady Dixon said. "I didn't know you wouldn't believe that scoundrel. It was Jeremy's idea to send you the telegram if matters grew dire. Unfortunately, after Jeremy vanished, they did.

"Emerson returned the following day and when Mrs. Cornelius refused him entry, he went mad. He demanded to speak to me and I did so, through the shut door. I told him Jeremy had vanished and that I was unaware of his whereabouts. This seemed to send him into an even greater rage, and he pounded on the door, shouting that he would return the next day.

"That is when I decided to do as Jeremy wished and send you a telegram. I worried that Emerson might discover me, and I was right to do so. That is why I phrased the telegram with terms associated with Shakespeare. Emerson hates the Bard and has never read him. I knew he wouldn't understand."

"It seems the telegrapher would not disclose the name to him, for when he discovered me and forced me to return to the Hall with him, he questioned me endlessly on who I had sent the message to. When I wouldn't answer, he threatened to strike me. That was when Pompey rushed into the room." She glanced at the dog who slept near Jeremy's feet on the floor. "Brave, wonderful Pompey. He attacked Emerson before he could harm me. Emerson snatched up the poker and would've beaten him to death, had I not at last divulged your name to him. I saw the look in his eyes, Mr. Holmes. Your name frightened him.

"He fled then, and I wondered if he might have gone to London to keep you from coming to Farrington Hall. The answer came later when he returned this evening and forced his way past Mrs. Cornelius.

"I thought him a gentleman, incapable of such things," Mrs. Cornelius said, her gaze upon the floor. "I didn't think to lock the door against him."

"I feared for Pompey, and so I sent him out the French doors. Emerson caught me in the corridor, after I had freed him, and dragged me back to the parlor. He struck me down when I wouldn't tell him where Pompey had gone. I remember very little after that."

"I should never have left you, Mother," Jeremy said. "I should never have listened."

"If you had not, you would be dead," Holmes responded. "And the professor would have triumphed. His influence over the local magistrate and constabulary would have guaranteed your mother's expulsion from the house."

"I suppose so, Mr. Holmes – though I will say that I would have appreciated several moments alone with the blackguard, and a pistol of his choosing. He is no great shot, that is for certain."

"We have Pompey to thank," Holmes said, as we boarded the train bound for London. "It was he who discovered Jeremy's hiding place, and an ingenious one at that. No one would think to look for him within the crevice which led to the Priest's Hole beneath the fallen wall."

"He is fortunate," said I, "that the wall didn't come crashing down upon him."

"If I hadn't had the dog, it might have come crashing down on me. Jeremy had laid a trap inside should anyone discover his hiding spot. He could escape from either of the two entrances, the original entrance to the Priest's Hole or the one created by the fallen tree. I was a fool, Watson. The Tudor-style of Farrington Hall should have alerted me at once to the possibility of such a hiding place."

"Apparently, the professor didn't consider the possibility either," I said. "What subject did he teach?"

"I am told it was history."

"Ah, then, that is the problem. He failed to heed it, for if he had, he would know that no professor with evil intent can best Sherlock Holmes."

Inspector Gregson at Bay
by Susan Knight

"Mr. Holmes, I am being blackmailed."

These were the stark words that greeted me as I joined Holmes for breakfast. Even more astonishing was the identity of the speaker, for I soon recognised the familiar fair-haired figure of Inspector Gregson of Scotland Yard, one of the most upright of men, and one who surely would have no sufficient blot on his character to render him vulnerable to such threats.

"Come in, Watson," Holmes said. "I'm sure the Inspector will not mind having you privy to his account."

Gregson nodded.

"Of course, Mr. Holmes," he replied. "I know that the doctor is trustworthy. I shall be happy for him to hear of the unfortunate circumstances that have brought me to this pass."

I took my seat at the table laden with all the usual breakfast fare, including some juicy-looking kippers. But, although I was hungry, I decided it would hardly be appropriate even to start buttering a slice of toast. Since Holmes and Gregson already held cups of tea, however, I poured one for myself while the inspector started to explain.

"Over the past few months, gentlemen, I've noticed a change in my son, Philip. He is no longer the open cheerful young lad my wife and I have heretofore known and loved. He has become secretive and troubled. At first, I put this down to the natural restlessness of youth."

"What age is he?" Holmes asked.

"He is but seventeen years old, apprenticed to a printer and, up until recently, doing well. However, it seems now that he has been missing work, and providing all manner of unlikely excuses. Finally, Mr. Clarke, the printer, contacted me to ask if I was recovered from my illness, and when he might expect Philip to return to work . . . Mr. Holmes, I was shocked. I haven't had a day's sickness since I was a boy with the measles."

"So what did Philip say when you confronted him?"

"He mumbled some excuse about his mistreatment at the hands of his employer and fellow apprentices, and that he feared to go back – something I very much doubted. Mr. Clarke is a gentle, kindly man and, in the past, Philip had nothing but good to say of him. As for the other lads, they all seemed to be good friends."

"You mentioned blackmail. Where does that come in?"

Inspector Gregson buried his head in his hands, overcome. At last, he pulled himself together and continued.

"Where did we go wrong, Mr. Holmes? My wife and I consider that we have been neither too strict nor too lax with the boy, yet didn't notice that he had fallen into bad company. Only yesterday . . . ."

His voice broke.

"Take your time, my friend." Holmes's tone was unusually gentle.

Again, Gregson got a grip on himself.

"Philip failed to return home last night. Instead, we received this missive."

He pulled an envelope from his inside pocket and gave it to Holmes, who extracted the note within. He read it, frowning, then passed it to me. In a shaky hand, it said:

Father,

Forgive me. I have fallen prey to some bad men and owe them a considerable sum – gambling losses. They are holding me until the debt is settled and threaten that if it is not, then I shall pay with my life.

"Good Heavens! How abominable!" I exclaimed. "But can you not just pay it, man, however much it is?"

"I suspect that it isn't as simple as that," Holmes said. "Am I right, Gregson?"

"Indeed. My first thought on reading this was indeed to pay whatever the villains asked, somehow or other, retrieve my poor son, and then try and hunt them down."

"But the man who brought the letter to you had other ideas."

Gregson looked astonished.

"How did you know that?"

"The envelope bears no stamp, so it was hand-delivered. There is a greasy thumbprint on the front of it, and similar fingerprints on the back, which suggests it was waved in front of you before you snatched it away, as this torn edge indicates. Additionally, your son makes no mention of the sum involved. If money were the object of the plan – or rather *your* money – then you would need to know how much to pay. I assume some rascal gained entry to your home and threatened you there."

"Indeed, Mr. Holmes, and with a pistol. Luckily, my wife and daughter were occupied in the kitchen, for, were they present, I cannot imagine the effect of the news upon them." He shook his head at the memory. "I offered to pay whatever was asked, but the villain replied that nothing would be enough. Instead, he told me that I could be of immense assistance to the gang – he didn't call them that, of course. He said 'to me and my friends' – in a trivial matter that would cause me no bother. And that thereafter Philip would be returned safe and sound."

"The nature of this trivial matter? Some crime, I suppose."

"You have it, Mr. Holmes," he replied. "They plan a robbery. So far, I know no more than that. Once they are convinced that they can trust me, they will provide further details. My role, as outlined by this miscreant, will be to clear the way for the robbers, keeping the Metropolitan Police occupied elsewhere on the night in question, and thereafter taking over the subsequent investigation, muddying the waters to the extent that the perpetrators remain undiscovered. I told the fellow that it wouldn't be up to me, and that I could not guarantee that I should be called on to investigate."

"What did he say to that?" asked Holmes.

"'You had better be!' was the grim reply. He told me that if I betrayed them, I might expect to see my son again – only as a cold corpse."

"The monsters!" I exclaimed. "But why come here?" I continued. "Why not tell your colleagues at Scotland Yard?"

Gregson raised a despairing face to mine.

"If you had children of your own, Dr. Watson, you wouldn't ask such a question. If I consulted Lestrade or Hopkins, do you think those villains would hesitate to carry out their threat and kill my son."

I felt remorseful. He was right. How could I know how a father felt? I was sad, as well. Mary and I had hoped so much to start a family before her untimely death.

"I am sorry," I said. "It was a thoughtless remark."

He nodded in acceptance of my apology. "It even occurred to me," he continued, "to comply with their demands. But a moment's thought set me to rights again. Even if they released Philip, I should be their creature thereafter. They would hold what I had done over me. If I confessed to my superiors, my career would be over. I can imagine how much Lestrade would crow over that."

It was well known that the two men were rivals, sometimes bitter ones.

"You did well to come to me," Holmes said. "It is quite true that once you have compromised yourself with these people, even if your son is returned safe and well, you will henceforth be in their power."

"Exactly." Gregson shook his head. "You are my only hope, Mr. Holmes. Please say you will help me."

The poor man looked abjectly at my friend who sat back in his chair, closed his eyes, and made a steeple of his fingers. After a few silent seconds, he leapt to his feet,

"When are you to hear further from these people?" he asked.

"I cannot say. Soon, I'm sure."

"Of course. I only hope that you weren't followed here. You must know that they are likely to be watching you."

"I took precautions and left my house in the early hours by the back entrance. I'm sure no one came after me."

Holmes moved to the window and peered out.

"Nothing out of the ordinary there. All the same, do nothing further to arouse their suspicion, and don't return here until you hear from me that it is safe to do so. We can communicate by telegram. Let me know when they contact you again, recounting exactly what they tell you to do. You must of course agree to everything they ask of you."

Gregson started.

"I cannot," he exclaimed.

"Don't worry. I promise that you will not have to do anything against your conscience. Your agreement is only to buy time and ensure that Philip remains alive and unharmed. I suggest, too, that you demand he write a short message to you to that effect on a page of each day's newspaper. Meanwhile, I shall be doing my very best to hunt these animals down."

"How will you accomplish that?"

"Ways and means, dear Gregson, ways and means . . . First of all, you must tell me as much as you can about your visitor, and about Philip's habits and friends. And let us move away from the table, so that Watson may at last satisfy his appetite and eat his kippers before they get too cold. He has been eying them this long while."

Gregson cast a glance my way, as if reproaching me for my animal needs at such a time. My excuse is that I think less clearly when hungry, unlike Holmes, whose senses seem sharpened by lack of food.

"What do you make of that?" Holmes asked when at last our guest had departed.

"A nasty business," I replied. "You made great promises to the poor fellow, but how ever will you track these men down, with so little information?"

"On the contrary, I consider that I already have plenty to go on . . . But perhaps you could ask Mrs. Hudson for some more toast. This has gone quite hard. Oh, and another kipper wouldn't go amiss."

I was surprised. Given the urgency of the situation, was he not planning to rush off at once? It seemed not. It was only after a leisurely

366

breakfast that he at last readied himself to go out. I admit that I was rather disappointed that he didn't request that I join him.

"Better you stay here and await communications from Gregson," he said.

A long dull day ensued, with no developments. I perused so many learned articles from old copies of *The Lancet* and *The Times of London* that my head was become quite fog-bound. It was only in the late afternoon that a telegram at last arrived, addressed to Holmes. Since I was privy to the matter, I considered it fitting that I should open it. The telegram consisted of nine words: *Day after tomorrow. Caledon and Dunedin Bank. London Wall.*

I gasped. The Caledon and Dunedin was a well-established merchant bank, known to possess, as well as the usual sums of ready cash necessary for everyday purposes, a store of safety deposit boxes whose owners were rumoured to be among the richest men in Europe. A robbery there would shake the financial and political foundation of many states. But at the same time, I wondered at the choice: The bank was well guarded, its vaults said to be impregnable, thus posing a mighty challenge for thieves.

Soon thereafter, Holmes arrived back in that state of extreme exhilaration I recognised only too well. Like a bloodhound, he had picked up a scent and was tugging at the leash to race off after it. He hardly looked at Gregson's telegram before disappearing into his room, only to emerge a while later transformed into one of those disreputable individuals that hang around low bars or places of ill fame.

"Don't wait up for me, Watson!" he yelled as he ran out. "I have no notion how long I shall be."

It was all most unsatisfactory. Was I supposed to stay behind and simply hope for further messages from Gregson? Even if such arrived, I myself shouldn't be able to act upon them or pass them on to Holmes. I decided, therefore, to go out, at least to clear my head.

Light was fading as I strolled towards Regent's Park. Already summer was giving way to autumn, the leaves of the elm, beech, and chestnut trees changing from green to motley shades of red, brown, yellow, and gold, and soon to fall. A light mist hung over the lake, where swans and mallards glided sedately. Distant voices of children filled the air as nursemaids walked their charges. Old folk sat on benches absorbing the peaceful scene. It was hard to believe in the villainy of man in such a setting.

I went back to Baker Street in the hope that Holmes would have returned in the meantime. However, there was no sign of him, and I ate my supper in solitude. Reluctant to go to bed, I lingered over a glass of brandy-and-water. It must have been the second glass that lulled me asleep where I sat, for I woke with a start in the middle of the night, though I could find no cause for it. The house was as still as ever. I couldn't help but worry for my friend. Holmes was forever placing himself in situations of danger, convinced that he could extract himself safely if necessary. But surely the day would come when this wasn't the case. Already he had escaped by the skin of his teeth at the Reichenbach Falls. If a cat has nine lives, how many does a consulting detective have? I sat in darkness, for who knew how many hours, brooding over this, watching eerie shadows dancing on the walls.

Eventually the sky outside started to lighten, and the nocturnal silence of the street was broken by the comforting noises of early morning: The clanking urns of the milkman, the trundling of the breadman's wagon, the postman whistling. I crossed to the window to look out, but there was still no sign of Holmes. Downstairs, I heard Mrs. Hudson and the maids bustling about. Then a sudden shriek of alarm. I raced down to find what was the matter and discovered the maids cowering in the passageway, and our landlady in the kitchen eyeing what appeared to be a most disreputable-looking individual lying, apparently out cold, across the table. After a moment or two, the fellow raised his head, bleary-eyed, and grinned.

"Mr. Holmes," said our landlady severely, "you'll be the death of me one of these days. And you have scared the life out of poor Phoebe."

This being the scullery maid, a young person of limited intelligence and capabilities, whom Mrs. Hudson must employ out of the goodness of her heart, for the girl had no redeeming features that I could see.

"My sincere apologies," Holmes said. "I returned in the early hours with a terrible thirst on me, and must have fallen asleep here."

Mrs. Hudson sniffed the air. "It seems to me that it was more than water that was drunk."

In truth, a powerful odour of strong liquor, as well as tobacco smoke, permeated the room.

Holmes laughed.

"Not much escapes you, Mrs. Hudson. I admit I had occasion to take a glass or two of rum last night with some unsavoury types, solely in the line of duty, you understand. However, I can assure you that only the purest water has passed my lips since I came home. And now a strong pot of coffee wouldn't go amiss, if you can manage it. I'm sure Watson would concur. He looks to have been up half the night himself."

I nodded. Relieved to find Holmes none the worse for his adventure, I was anxious to return upstairs and learn what he had discovered.

"Well, gentlemen," Mrs. Hudson said, somewhat appeased, "I suppose that can be managed."

The maids were still in the passageway when Holmes and I proceeded back to our rooms. While in general Holmes has little time for Phoebe – unless to complain about her – on this occasion he actually apologised for scaring her, an attention which, I rather suspected, terrified the poor child even more.

Despite my impatience to learn of his discoveries, Holmes insisted on cleaning himself up before all else, and so it was only when we were seated at the breakfast table with the aforementioned pot of coffee, boiled eggs, and toast in front of us, that my friend allowed himself to describe his adventure of the previous night.

"Gregson having furnished me with precise details of his unwelcome visitor," he began, "I applied to one of my informants, who directed me to one of low gambling haunts of Limehouse, a so-called 'copper hell' which a person of that description was known to frequent. I soon recognised my quarry and settled myself down to observe the play for a while. A crowd of foolish youths were being cheated so cleverly, they never suspected a thing, which, I suppose, is how they netted young Gregson. Once I understood the set-up, I myself joined them for a hand of cards."

He smiled in satisfaction. I knew well the reason, for I had played against him myself and never got to the bottom of the fact that he invariably won, even in a seeming game of chance.

"My successes caused quite a stir," he continued. "Of course, one has to be careful and not antagonise men who might be inclined to take revenge, especially in a place like that. I won against those same poor young fools, addicted to the vain hope that sooner or later they would come out on top."

"So did you find the men who have abducted Philip?"

Holmes cut the top of his egg and regarded the contents with satisfaction.

"Mrs. Hudson is learning. She has cooked this to perfection. A five-minute-fifteen-second egg, Watson. Near enough." He dipped a soldier of toast into the soft centre and ate it with relish. "What did you ask?" he said at last. "Whether I had tracked down the men holding young Philip. As to that, Watson: You are looking at the newest member of the gang."

"What!"

"After I collected my winnings, I could tell that I was being watched closely and suspiciously by certain villainous-looking denizens of the place, including one that exactly matched the description of Gregson's unwelcome visitor, so I treated them all to a round of rum punch. Without asking me directly, they clearly wanted to know how I had pulled off such a coup. I replied that I was just lucky, winking at the same time, so that they knew I had a trick or two up my sleeve."

369

"Quite literally," I remarked.

"No! I should never resort to such a low dodge,"

"Hmm." I had often suspected it of him whenever we played together. His face, of course, remained a mask of innocence. "So what then?"

"I let it be known," he continued, "that I was but newly arrived in London, intimating that I had recently been detained up north at Her Majesty's pleasure – I pride myself on mimicking a Lancashire accent with accuracy – and was now looking to make my fortune in the big city, far from where I was known. When the scoundrels ascertained, from various hints and remarks I dropped, that I was a man with no scruples whatsoever, and after I had plied them with more rum punch, they let on that they were looking for such a one as me to help out in a forthcoming enterprise. If I performed to their satisfaction, they said, they might even consider recruiting me to their exclusive club."

"Good Heavens! Who are these men?"

"The leader of the band is one Dudgeon, a dwarfish greasy man built like a brick privy and quite as filthy, nicknamed 'Bulldog' for his unfortunate facial resemblance to that beast. Then there is his deputy in devilry, Rogers, a long, skinny, slippery sort of fellow, never at rest. And, finally, Crick, our friend who visited Gregson: A hefty, wall-eyed individual. You never know if he is watching you or if his attention is quite elsewhere. It is most disconcerting. A lucky affliction for us, though, for it was the description of him that was recognised by my informant, and enabled me to track the gang down with such little difficulty."

"So what now?"

"I've employed the latest scion of the Tribe of Wiggins, along with the rest of the Irregulars, to follow my new friends, trusting that one or the other will lead us to where Philip is confined. For my part – or that of 'Jeremiah Cotter', the name I gave to the gang – I'm to meet them in the same copper hell tonight, presumably in order to proceed to rob the Caledon and Dunedin Bank."

"Then there's no time to be lost," I said.

Holmes nodded. "Unless we have some luck, the outlook is certainly grim. If the men are arrested in the course of the robbery, Philip is doomed. Or if Gregson does what the villains demand, and distracts his men away from the scene, then he will be disgraced and most probably imprisoned himself."

"It's a pity he doesn't feel able to confide in his fellow officers. Would they not assist him under the circumstances?"

"Rightly or wrongly, he feels not. You yourself know well how he and Lestrade dislike each other – how jealous they are of each other's success, how happy with each other's failure."

I shook my head. "It's a sorry state of affairs when men in their position succumb to such petty rivalries."

Holmes smiled. "I think you will find, my innocent friend, that the self-same petty rivalries occur in all walks of life, even in the medical profession."

I nodded then, recalling a sorry instance concerning two colleagues at Barts that had recently come to my notice. "Especially in the medical profession," I said.

At that moment, a violent hammering could be heard on the front door below, followed by a loud altercation between the housemaid, Clara, and a child's insistent voice, after which heavy steps pounded up the stairs to our room. It was Wiggins himself who burst in, a raggedy boy of twelve, bearing such an extraordinary resemblance to the elder brother who had first assisted Holmes in his investigations, that I was quite transported back several years. The boots the lad was wearing were clearly several sizes too big for him, which accounted for the excessive noise they made. He was followed in by a ratty little fellow of about eight, his bare feet blackened by city filth. These same extremities seemed to fascinate the boy, for he stared down at them without raising his head.

"Mister 'Olmes, sir! We found 'im!" Wiggins shouted. "We found 'im!"

Holmes leapt up.

"Are you sure?" he asked.

"One-hunnerd-per-cent, sir. Down by the river in one o' them shacks on the wharf. It were Jimsy, 'ere, what follwered the skinny feller, what found 'im. Weren't it, Jimsy? 'E peeped through a crack in the wood and seed 'im, all tied up. Din'cher, Jimsy?"

"Yurs." The child's voice was surprisingly deep and hoarse. He continued to stare at his feet.

"So tell Mr. 'Olmes 'ow it was, Jimsy."

Reluctantly the little fellow looked up. He apparently didn't care for what he saw, so looked down again.

"Go on," Holmes barked. "Has the cat got your tongue, young fellow?"

Jimsy lowered his head even further, while Wiggins cumbersomely hopped from one foot to the other.

"The boys look cold," I ventured, "Perhaps a nice hot cup of tea with some of Mrs. Hudson's drop scones might not go amiss."

Holmes looked at me impatiently, but the two lads clearly approved of the suggestion, and I rang down instantly to place the order.

Perhaps Mrs. Hudson had anticipated such a demand, for the comestibles arrived in record time, and soon the two lads, perched on the

371

very edge of the couch as if fearful of soiling it, were munching and slurping away.

"Milk *and* sugar," Wiggins commented approvingly. "Yer Mrs. 'Udson's a real treasure, ain't she, gents, even if she 'as a sharp tongue on 'er."

Holmes made no reply, pacing restlessly, his frown deepening every time one of the lads reached for another buttery scone.

"So now, Jimsy," I said at last, considering that sufficient refreshments had been availed of, "please tell us exactly what you saw."

The boy stared up at me, his eyes green as bottle glass. Perhaps it was my softer tone, compared to Holmes's testy one, but he seemed readier to confide in me.

"Yurs," he said, his mouth still full of pastry. "I follered 'im to the river, I did. 'E wuz a-lookin' back all the time, to see if 'e were follered, but din pay no 'eed to me. Soon enough, we gets to this broken old shack in one o' them wharves and in 'e goes . . . So I creeps up . . ." By now, Jimsy had relaxed into his account and was enjoying himself tremendously. An' don't I find a broken plank where I can see in. An' what d'yer think? There's this young feller, all tied up, and a big stout, red-faced woman standin' over 'im. 'Ow's our guest, Molly?' sez the skinny cove. 'Behavin 'isself, is 'e?' She mutters some complaint about 'ow much longer she 'as to stay with 'im. 'Not much longer. Molly,' sez 'e. 'One way or t'other,' sez 'e. 'Untie 'is 'ands, will yer.' Then 'e pulls a newspaper from out 'is pocket and tells the lad to write on it. The booby starts to blubber. Then and the woman 'its 'im. Weren't nice ter watch, sir."

"No, indeed," I replied, "but you did well, Jimsy. Didn't he, Holmes?"

Holmes nodded.

"But there's more," said Wiggins. "Ain't there, Jimsy?"

"Yurs." Since, by now, the little chap had stuffed another scone into his mouth, we had to wait a minute or two before he was able to proceed.

Holmes drummed his fingers on the table, but it wasn't until after Jimsy had washed the crumbs down his throat with a slurp of tea that he looked up at us again.

"The fat woman follered the skinny feller out. They din see me, but I could peep round at 'em and 'ear 'em well enough, even though they was whisperin'."

"Jimsy's got sharp ears," Wiggins put in proudly. "'Aven't yer, Jimsy?"

"Yurs," came the reply. "I 'ave."

"Yes, yes. Very good," said Holmes. "What did you hear?"

372

"So Fattie asks, 'You ain't reely goin' ter let 'im go, are yer, Bill? Not when 'e knows our names and faces.' Skinny feller laughs. 'Doncha worry about that, Molly girl,' sez 'e. And then 'e done this."

With an unfortunate degree of relish, Jimsy drew a dirty finger across his throat.

"No honour among thieves," I remarked with a shudder.

"Well, Jimsy," Holmes said, "I reckon you have saved the day. Well done, lad."

The boy regarded him with astonishment. I doubted he was much used to praise.

"Tell me," Holmes continued, "was this Molly the only guard you could see?"

"Yurs," Jimsy replied. "Only she's a big 'un, Mister."

"All the same," Holmes said, "I suppose she'd hardly pose a threat to Watson here, armed with his pistol."

Jimsy looked dubious. "She's a big 'un, she is," he repeated.

Now, I pride myself that I am not by nature a coward. and yet I see no good reason to place myself at an unnecessary risk.

"Can we not call in the regular police at this stage?" I suggested. "After all, it's a clear case of abduction."

Holmes shook his head. "In order not to alert the gang, and, as well, to allow Gregson the honour of catching them in the act of robbery, I deem it better not to involve Scotland Yard at this point."

"Doc an' us'll manage," Wiggins said, pushing out his chest in a manly way. "Doncha worry about that, Mr. 'Olmes, sir."

"That's the spirit," my friend replied, "because I myself need to be elsewhere. We must turn the tables on these villains and put them out of action forever. In the meantime, I must send a telegram to Gregson, explaining what's happening."

To make sure that none of the gang members were hanging around the wharf, we decided to leave our expedition to release Philip until late afternoon, when Holmes was to join the rest of the gang at Limehouse.

Thus it was that twilight was already setting in when Wiggins, Jimsy, and I made our cautious way to the banks of the Thames, to those miserable reaches of broken-down warehouses where flitting shadows signal the presence of individuals bent on activities of a dubious nature. I was glad of the reassuring presence of my pistol, and not just for the undertaking ahead of us.

At last we arrived, Jimsy silently pointing at our goal. Of all the run-down edifices in the vicinity, this had to be one of the worst: A construction of rough planks set in a puddle of mud and stagnant water. Wiggins and I stayed in the shadow of an upturned fishing boat while

Jimsy crept up to the hovel and peered through one of the many cracks in the walls. He then beckoned us forwards, whereupon I put my eye to the crack. I found it hard to see. The space was dark, and it took a moment or two for my eyes to adjust. Finally, I managed to make out a large woman dozing on a chair, a bottle in her hand. A shape on the ground, presumably the wretched Philip, lay stretched out beside her. This should be easy, I thought, especially if the woman was, as it seemed, drunk on liquor. We moved round as silently as we could to the door.

My notion was a straightforward one: To enter, pistol at the ready, subdue the woman, and, with the help of the two lads, free poor Philip. Alas, for the best laid plans . . . .

As I entered, there echoed an unearthly screech which almost caused me to drop my pistol. It was nothing supernatural, however, but came from a caged parrot rearing up on its perch, and fluttering its wings in excitement. The woman, awakened, jumped up.

"'Oo are you?" she growled. "Wha' d'yer want?"

Jimsy had not exaggerated his description. This was a big woman indeed: As tall as myself, wide as a barrel, with the thick arms of a stevedore, and a ruddy complexion to match.

"I have come to free the boy!" I said. "Stand back, if you know what's good for you."

She might be big, but wasn't encumbered by her flesh, for "Oh no yer don't!" she uttered, flinging the bottle at me with so much force and so true an aim that it hit me on the side of the head, sending me reeling sideways. Taking advantage of my momentary confusion, she leapt forward and tried to grab my gun. We grappled and I felt her strength. She twisted my arm and I dropped the pistol. Laughing, she kicked it out of the way.

"Free the boy, is it? Not while Molly's in charge, Mister."

She knocked me to the floor with her huge fist and set her boot upon my chest, pressing down so hard that I gasped for breath. All the while the parrot continued to screech frenziedly.

I have to admit that, at that moment, I feared for my life. The woman was crushing my ribs, squeezing the breath out of me. Suddenly, however, it was she who was screeching. She lurched away from me as if electrocuted, screaming vile abuse. Raising myself up with some difficulty, I perceived an extraordinary sight: Somehow, Jimsy had managed to leap on to the woman's shoulders, his skinny knees gripping her head, and was pulling at her hair while she spun around trying to grab him.

"That's enough, Jimsy," a calm voice said. "Get down." Wiggins had retrieved my pistol and was jabbing it into the woman's side. "Now ma'am," he continued after Jimsy had released her from his iron grip. "I don't want to kill yer, but will if necess'ry. Be quiet, now, there's a good woman. Sit down."

I suppose she realised she was outnumbered, even if it was by one rather ineffectual adult man and two children. She sat back down in her chair, mumbling curses.

Rather ungracefully, I pulled myself up off the floor and crossed over to where Philip was lying. I took off his gag and loosened his bonds.

"'Ere, doc," Wiggins said. "Give them ropes ter Jimsy. We can use them to tie up Madam, 'ere."

"Who are you?" Philip asked, in shrill tones. "Are you going to kill me?"

The poor lad's eyes were wide with terror. I tried to reassure him, but days spent awaiting his fate at the hands of the gang had clearly affected his mind, for he shuddered away from me.

Wiggins had no patience for this behaviour.

"Be grateful we 'ave come ter save yer," he said. "At great risk and danger to ourselles."

The woman Molly, now trussed up like a chicken, gave a harsh laugh.

"Wait 'til my men come a-looking for yer," she scoffed. "Ye'll be right sorry for this night's work then, my laddies."

"I think not," I said, sounding more confident than I felt. "Inspector Gregson will have arrested the three of them by now."

"Oh, yurs. Where's that then?"

"Robbing the Caledon and Dunedin Bank. Your men won't see the light of day for many years. No more will you."

"Is that so, Mister?" The confident mockery in her voice gave me pause. Perhaps we were wrong, after all.

"Shut 'er up, Jimsy," Wiggins said. "I'm sick of the sound of 'er 'orrible voice."

The woman shook her head violently from side to side.

"Don't gag me, Dearie," she said, apparently suddenly cowed. "I'd be afeared I can't breathe. I 'ave a weak chest, I 'ave . . . I promise to be quiet. Promise."

Jimsy looked at Wiggins for instruction.

"Do it," the latter said coldly. "Did she ever show mercy to this feller?" indicating Philip, sitting up now, tears rolling down his cheeks, rubbing his chafed wrists and ankles.

To get the gag on the woman was a mighty struggle, in which Wiggins and I had to hold her still, while Jimsy tied it tight round her mouth.

"And shut up that bleedin' parrot, too, Jimsy," for the bird continued to screech. "'E'd waken the dead, 'e would."

In case neck-wringing was in prospect, I hastily threw a moth-eaten blanket over the cage, silencing the parrot in an instant.

By now, Philip was assured that we were there not to harm but to help him. However, the lad was so weakened by his ordeal that there was no way he could depart the shack on his own steam. In any case, I was unwilling to leave Molly alone. Like Samson in the temple of the Philistines, weak chest or no, she seemed strong enough, once left to herself, to break out of her bonds, so I penned a note for Jimsy to deliver to the nearest police station, reckoning that, under the circumstances, it was permissible to enlist the support of the local constabulary. To this, I added a cryptic message, to be conveyed, with all possible haste, to Inspector Gregson, informing him that our endeavour had been successfully concluded, the inference thereby being that the arrest of the rest of the gang would no longer pose a threat to his son. The messenger, admittedly, wasn't of the sort to inspire confidence, but I hoped that my missive would overcome the lad's visible deficiencies.

Thus it turned out, for, in a short space of time, a couple of bemused constables arrived with a wagon in which to transport Philip, accompanied by myself, to hospital, and Molly, cursing and scratching, to prison.

I was, of course, agog to learn if Holmes's enterprise had reached an equally happy conclusion, while only too aware that my part in the lad's liberation was hardly distinguished. Nevertheless, Philip was free, and, even as I left him in the hospital, awaiting the arrival of his mother.

Back at Baker Street, there was as yet no sign of my friend and colleague. No word, as Mrs. Hudson averred, had reached her, but, shocked by my dishevelled and bruised appearance, the good woman started to fuss rather overmuch. I was sporting the beginnings of a formidable black eye, thanks to Molly's well-aimed bottle. Nothing would satisfy my landlady, even though I assured her that all was well, but that I would sit by the fire with a blanket over my knees sipping a scalding brew of beef tea. It was in vain to suggest that I should much prefer to pace up and down with a stiff brandy in my hand, for I was restless and, as time passed, was growing more and more concerned about the fate of my friend.

Mrs. Hudson was having none of it.

"Mr. Holmes will come back in his own good time, as he always does. Meanwhile, you stay quiet, Doctor, and finish your tea."

I promised to do so. Luckily, she was far too busy to stand over me and make sure I did as I was told.

It was after midnight and into the early hours before I at last heard the front door open and steps on the stairs – halting steps, however, not the firm tread I associated with my friend. Nevertheless, it was he, or rather Jeremiah Cotter, who fell into the room. To my chagrin, he burst out laughing at the sight of me, but my vexation soon turned to concern, as I saw how he winced.

"Are you all right?" I asked.

"I'm afraid the two of us might have bitten off more than we could chew this time," he remarked ruefully. "I rather underestimated the cunning and strength of our adversaries."

He sank into his chair. I reheated some beef tea on the Bunsen burner that he habitually used for his chemical experiments and gave it to him.

"What the devil is this?" he asked, sniffing at it.

"Mrs. Hudson's patent restorative," I replied. "It did wonders for me – especially with the addition of a splash of brandy."

While he was partaking of the broth, I recounted my adventure.

"Without Wiggins and Jimsy," I said, "the outcome might have been very different. They were the heroes of the night."

"They shall be rewarded handsomely."

He then described his own experiences. He had gone to the gambling den, as arranged, to meet with the three villains.

"Huddled around a table, and already well-oiled with rum, they informed me that the plan that night was to rob a certain diamond merchants in the City."

"Not the Caledon and Dunedin Bank, then!" I exclaimed.

"Apparently not. They hadn't trusted Gregson with the truth, and now I realised – noticing they were watching me very closely as they told me of the plan – that they didn't trust me either. I don't know what had raised their suspicions. Or maybe they were just generally cautious. However, I think my blank look dispelled, for the moment anyway, their mistrust. But now, since there was no way I could get word to Gregson, I realised I would have to thwart their enterprise on my own."

In fact, as it turned out, the establishment in question backed on to the Caledon and Dunedin Bank, so that the orders to Gregson to distract the police from the area would still serve the men's purposes. However, the rest of the inspector's plan, to install constables secretly inside the bank, would now prove fruitless.

"Our destination was a back alley behind the diamond merchants," Holmes related. "On the way, the men joked how useful it was to have powerful friends. In addition to Gregson, whom they supposed to be obeying their orders, it turned out that they had another creature inside the merchant's establishment, another blackmail victim. This wretched man had provided them with keys and the combinations of the safe. The robbery would be, as Dudgeon laughed, like taking sweetmeats from an infant."

Holmes shook his head. "When we arrived, I was left with wall-eyed Crick to keep watch outside, while Dudgeon and Rogers went within. Crick was wary, but surprise was on my side and I was able to floor him with some baritsu moves. I then followed the other gang members inside and found them about to raid the safe. Telling them that the place was surrounded by constables who had already overpowered Crick, I urged them to flee. Rogers panicked, but Dudgeon, frowning at me, said that Gregson would never have put his son's life at risk. He sent Rogers to look outside, to check if I was telling the truth, while I was to stay behind with him. I tried the same moves on him as on Crick, but he was ready for me, and the struggle was tougher, he being as strong as the bulldog he so much resembled. Rogers returned in the midst of all, shouting that Crick was laid low and that there was no sign of any constables. Now it was two against one and I feared that I would come off the worst and fail in my attempt, especially when Rogers drew a knife from his belt and thrust it into my thigh . . . ."

"Holmes!" I cried. "Let me see."

"A glancing blow, nothing more."

But now I saw a darker patch on his trouser leg. He waved me away.

"I've patched it up. It will surely keep until I finish my account." But noticing now how he was grey with pain, I urged him to let me tend to the wound. He was stubborn. I had no choice but to let him continue.

"Luckily," he related, "I was able to grab the weapon and turn it on my assailants. Rogers at least will long bear the scars on his face and arms. However, my advantage was slight. Bulldog Dudgeon was coming for me again with a roar, and all looked to be lost when suddenly the door burst open and two hefty constables appeared. They had given up on the bank raid and were returning to their beat when they heard the fracas, and come to investigate. At first, they handled me roughly, taking me for one of the gang, and imagining we had fallen out over the loot. However, after I mentioned Gregson's name and my own, they took better stock of the situation, and left me be, handcuffing the two crooks . . . ."

Holmes looked downcast.

"I very nearly failed, Watson," he said, after a pause.

I felt for my friend, who liked to be in control of the situation at all times. At least, I mused, for once he couldn't chide me for my own shortcomings. On this occasion, both Holmes and I had been saved by others.

"I gained some satisfaction, however," he continued. "As Dudgeon was being led away, he sneered at me. 'A hollow victory, Sherlock,' he whispered. "When news of our arrest goes abroad, it will be all up with you-know-who. My friend will make sure his father never sees him alive again.' Well, you can imagine how delighted I was to be able to inform him that Philip was safe and that his "friend" had been arrested also."

"But you didn't know that," I said.

"I have the greatest faith in you, Watson," he replied, much to my gratification. But then he added, "Admittedly, Wiggins had dropped by the gambling den before we set off, to give me a discreet thumbs up."

No doubt to Lestrade's dismay, Gregson and his men were crowned in glory at the apprehension of such a notorious and dangerous gang, while our own involvement remaining unrecorded, as Holmes wished it to be. The inspector himself, however, visiting us subsequently with his son in tow, was effusive in his thanks, and most concerned regarding the injuries we had sustained, minor though they turned out to be.

"How can I ever reward you sufficiently?" he said, reaching for his wallet.

Holmes waved it away.

"No reward necessary for a friend and colleague," he remarked magnanimously, adding, "I'm sure at some time or other there will be a *quid pro quo*."

The inspector looked somewhat puzzled at this, but smiled his gratitude.

Philip, much restored since I had last seen him, assured us that he had learned his lesson, that the horrors of his confinement had brought him to his senses, and that he would never again cross the threshold of a "copper hell". It seems that he has kept his word, for the last we heard, he was back working for Mr. Clarke, the printer, acquitting himself well and leading a quiet life.

Wiggins and Jimsy were amply rewarded out of the inspector's pocket, which was only right. I myself purchased two pairs of boots for the lads, though the last time I saw them, Wiggins was still wearing the overlarge ones and Jimsy was still barefoot, so I suppose they had pawned the good new ones. Ah well!

The Case of the
Spitalfields Man
by Stephen Herczeg

A result of his eternal quest to assist in solving as many crimes as possible saw Sherlock Holmes make quite a large number of acquaintances and form relationships with a vast number of people. Some he kept in regular contact, strengthening those bonds over time, while others were merely treated like ships passing in the night – a name, and possibly some tid-bit of information, to be stored away for future reference if the need ever arose.

One chap who entered into Holmes's orbit on several occasions was Inspector Stanley Hopkins. When we first met, he was new to Scotland Yard, and as those instances multiplied, I noticed Holmes take a strong interest in Hopkins's career and abilities, to the point that he could speak quite at length about the man's disposition and skills.

"He has his head on straight," I caught Holmes saying one night. "If Hopkins maintains a persistent level of achievement, he will climb the ranks through the Yard with relative ease. And I would say that they could do with someone of his talents, rather than the run-of-the-mill inspectors they allow to take on higher managerial positions . . . ."

It was with some delight that I intercepted a telegram courier upon returning to 221b Baker Street one late afternoon. Luckily, it was addressed to both of us, so I had no hesitation in opening it.

The contents were an invitation to lunch at Inspector Stanley Hopkins' residence. There wasn't enough detail to ascertain what the occasion was, but it was signed Stanley and Madelyn. It was with wide eyes that I read the second name. I had never realised that Hopkins was married.

Climbing the steps to our shared rooms, I found Holmes crouched over some esoteric papers, reading the fine print by a very dull candlelight. A short *Harrumph!* from me had him straighten up, much to my relief. I often worried what effect these activities would have upon his normally ramrod-straight back, and feared that his dedication to such undertakings would take him into his dotage as a crook-backed old man.

"Why, Watson!" said Holmes, his eyes dropping to the telegram. "What have you there?"

He took the paper, unfolded it, and read it to himself. A slight smile came to his lips. "I do believe that young Hopkins is about to take a wife and wishes for us to meet her."

"Well, I wasn't sure if he was married, but the name Madelyn made me feel he was."

"Oh, I know for sure he isn't yet encumbered by a wife. I wouldn't think it would be his sister, so I can only assume that signing off the telegram with the woman's name means he intends for them to become a single item."

"Are you free on Sunday? I don't have any patients to see, and I think this would be a wonderful respite from our daily duties."

"Of course. I have nothing planned. Simply a day to undertake my studies and diversions."

Checking the mantel, I noticed that it wasn't quite four o'clock. "Then I shall send a reply." Holmes merely nodded as I made my way to the door, snatching up my coat and hat to fend off the autumn chill outside.

The following Sunday was dull and overcast, with the unrelenting chill that heralded the onset of winter. However, I made sure to set aside any thoughts of the weather to ensure that our invitation to Hopkins' house was met with the best of intentions and mindsets.

The hansom dropped us before a modest little terraced residence in Bermondsey. It looked just the place to be occupied by a young member of Britain's law enforcement making his way up through the ranks.

Standing before the house, I remarked, "Hopkins appears to be doing well."

"And so he should. The man is quite bright, and one of the highlights of Scotland Yard." And it was true. Hopkins had assisted in a few of Holmes's adventures over the last few years, and from what I had heard from my colleague, he held the young inspector in the highest regard. "Shall we?" Holmes asked, before moving up to the front door.

Within a moment of ringing the bell, the door was opened by Hopkins' beaming face. "Gentlemen! I was so thrilled to receive your telegram in the affirmative." Stepping aside, he ushered us in. "Come, come, it's far too cold outside. Welcome to my home. We've warmed the place to make it as comfortable as possible."

Indeed, as we stripped off our coats and hung them on nearby hooks, I was delighted at the heat emanating from within.

"What a wonderful place you have," I said as I scanned the furnishings of the little parlour into which the inspector led us.

"Yes. I cannot attest to affording the property on my own. I had help from some money bequeathed to me by my late father."

"He was from the Yard as well, was he not?" asked Holmes.

"Yes, indeed, he was. Spent his entire career in the Force, and worked his way up to Detective Superintendent before retiring to the country. Sadly, he passed away only last year. Never one to splurge on any frivolities, my father bought this little place when he lived in London, and also held a large parcel of land near Chichester when he died."

Just as we sat and became comfortable, a beautiful young woman entered holding a tray with cups, saucers, and a teapot. Holmes and I stood, as we hadn't expected a servant girl of any form, and assumed this was the mysterious Madelyn.

"Sit, gentlemen," she said, bringing a smile to my face. "No need to put on airs for me, but I thought a spot of tea before lunch might be called for to warm what ills." With that simple statement, I realised this woman didn't hold with formalities. She quickly distributed the crockery, asking each of us – by name no less, and without hesitation – how we would like our tea before disappearing once more and returning with a small tray of *petit fours* and cakes.

"I do believe my fiancé has technically introduced herself, but I'll do the formal honours. This is Madelyn Brackley, my soon-to-be wife – though we haven't set a date as yet, which is why the two of you haven't received invitations, though I would be delighted for you to attend."

"And I prefer Maddie if it's all the same," said the wonderfully forthright girl.

"Pleased to make your acquaintance, Maddie," I said, holding out my hand and lightly shaking hers. Holmes repeated the action, mirroring my statement.

Over the next few minutes, we exchanged small talk about how Hopkins and Maddie met. She was a teacher at the nearby Bermondsey Grammar School, and most impressively how she had read Literature at London University, concentrating mostly on ancient texts. At that point, Holmes commented on the contents of the bookcase that nestled in one corner of the parlour.

"I can now only presume that the texts in that bookcase are indeed yours. I've been puzzling over them since we arrived. When Hopkins stated that he inherited this house from his father, I presumed they were his, but now, I believe they must be yours."

We all turned towards the bookcase. It was filled to overflowing with many thick leather-bound books. I noticed such titles as *The Iliad*, *The Odyssey*, and *La Morte D'Arthur*, among others.

"Yes," said Maddie, "As Stanley and I will be married soon, and we intend to move in here, I wanted those wonderful books to be displayed." She shook her head a little sadly. "I'm currently living in a bedsit across

382

the way in Rotherhithe, and many of those books were gifted by relatives who supported me during my studies, but have since been sitting in boxes."

"A remarkable collection," Holmes added, before delving a little deeper. "You never looked to undertaking further studies?"

"No." That sad little shake of the head again. "No. I passed my exams, but there are very few positions available in the Literature Faculty, and the prospects of a woman seeking tenure at the University are low. When I finished my studies, it was all I could do to find a teaching position, and even with that I have already had to seek out permission to continue once I'm married."

"Yes." It was Holmes's turn to shake his head. "Our society has much to learn. There is such a wealth of knowledge and ability that we simply let disappear from view with these arcane traditions of sending married women to the kitchen instead of allowing them to continue in their chosen fields of endeavour. We can only hope that the approaching new century leads to enlightenment for all of us."

"Why thank you, Mr. Holmes. That is very forward-thinking of you."

"And that brings us to another matter altogether," said Hopkins. "With our approaching nuptials, we have also decided to quit London altogether and settle at my deceased father's Chichester farm. We have hopes of raising livestock as well as a family."

"But what about your position at the Yard?" I asked.

"I have applied for a transfer to the Chichester Station. They are quite a bit larger than other country areas and have inspectors on staff. I may have to take a slight cut to my pay, but the costs of living in that area will be far less."

"I think that would be a great loss for Scotland Yard," said Holmes, "but we must all pursue what makes us happy."

It was then I caught a look of sadness cross Maddie's face. Her eyes locked with mine momentarily, widening at the realisation, before darting away. In that flash of emotion, I realised that the Chichester dream was possibly Hopkins' alone.

The small silence that descended upon us on the back of Hopkins' announcement was interrupted before it could become uncomfortable by the doorbell ringing, followed by a slightly frantic banging.

"What in the blazes could that be about?" asked Hopkins, standing and striding from the room without seeking an answer.

It was then that Maddie took it upon herself to plead for our help.

Placing a hand lightly upon Holmes's forearm, she laid out her fears. "Oh, Mr. Holmes, please help me!"

"What is it my dear?" he replied placing his hand upon hers. "You seem utterly despondent."

"Oh, as much as I love Stanley, and wish to share in all his wants and dreams, I'm afraid that I simply don't wish to follow him to Chichester. I'm a London girl, born and bred, and I set up a life here even before I met Stanley. I have a job, which, as I mentioned, I will be allowed to pursue even once married. I have a wide circle of friends. My family is here, which would be so much help when we do expand our little family. And I still have my own dreams of furthering my studies." She waved towards the bookcase. "This collection is in its infancy. There are so many tomes that I wish to read, and my heart is set on documenting them with the intention of releasing papers to that effect." A drop of the head and a sad slow nodding followed. "I just don't think the life of a country farmer's wife would allow any of that to continue."

Holmes patted the young girl's hand. "My dear, if you feel this way, simply tell Hopkins. I'm sure once he knows, he'll be fine to stay in London."

"No. No, he won't. It's all he has talked about since his father's passing. He wants for the life of a country laird – a man of the land, who can mix with the local gentry."

Holmes chuckled, suppressing a wider laugh. "Oh, that would be very interesting to see. But I can tell that you are almost horrified at the thought. We'll do what I can to convince him to stay. As I mentioned, he would be a great loss to Scotland Yard, one they can ill afford."

The two conspirators broke apart just as Hopkins appeared in the doorway of the parlour. His face was a little flushed, and I noticed he had donned a thick coat in readiness to leave.

"Gentlemen, if I could call upon your patience. Something very interesting has just been delivered to me, and I feel that the two of you would prove a great asset in unveiling the solution."

"What is this puzzle that needs solving?" asked Holmes, with an air of concealed excitement.

Hopkins' face was a mask of seriousness. "We have a body."

"Well, he's dead, and that's for certain," I said, touching the man's neck to find it cold, clammy, and very still. "I make him to be about thirty-five years old, perhaps older." Stepping back, I mentally calculated his height and possible weight. "Five-feet-ten in height, give or take a couple of inches. Possibly, around one-seventy to one-eighty pounds." I leaned forward and touched his upper arm, feeling the muscle tone and size. Regardless of the length of time he had been dead, he was extraordinarily

384

powerfully built. "Hmm. I might have to revise my weight estimate. This man was exceedingly strong."

Turning I stared towards Holmes and Hopkins.

"Can I move his hands?" When they both nodded, I gently picked up the hands which sat folded in the man's lap and turned them over. The arms resisted slightly, indicating a high level of *rigor mortis* remained in the outer extremities. "Ah," I said, as I examined the darkened skin of the palms. "He has a history of manual labour. He has very pronounced callouses on the proximal pads of the palm. They may be from swinging a sledge or pushing a heavily laden barrow. And this – " I pointed at the dark areas. " – indicates a build-up of blood from having been sitting here for quite some time."

"Any idea how long?" asked Hopkins, taking notes on a little pad.

"With the *rigor*, the blood pooling, and the lividity of the skin, I would say between ten and twelve hours. It's been cold, so more likely twelve hours."

Holmes waited until Hopkins had finished his notetaking before adding his findings. "From what I've seen, and this is a very cursory observation, as the area has been devastated by some of your colleagues, Hopkins – " I noticed a slight sheepish look flash across the inspector's face. " – this man has all the look of a dock worker or builder, but the manner of his appearance places him far from that occupation."

Holmes was right, and it was something I had first noticed. The dead man was impeccably dressed in a morning suit, with a neatly pressed shirt, neat tie, new or recently polished shoes, and a clean bowler hat pressed onto his head. "Anyone would have believed this man to be waiting to hurry off to his employ in an office in the business district, but instead he is dead and sitting on a bench here." Holmes swept an arm in a semi-circle, taking in the object of his attention across the street.

The police wagon had parked nearby on Spital Square, and the bobby that had intruded on Hopkins' impending luncheon had led us to the dead man. He sat on a small bench, nestled amongst the greenery of Eldritch Park as if he was simply admiring the goings-on across the way in the Spitalfields Market.

"From his physique, it is more likely that he was under the employ of one of the stallholders that his dead eyes have been viewing."

"What do you make of it then?" asked Hopkins.

"I'm interested in your view, Inspector, and also what you intend to do next."

"I'm thinking the first thing is to get this fellow to the morgue. I think there's something missing, and we need to inspect him and his clothing for clues. I sent Jones off to bring the coroner back. As to his identity, I have the constables doing the rounds of the stalls, so hopefully we'll find someone who knows him, or at least has seen him. This is a pretty rough area at night, and if the Good Doctor is correct, he died sometime late last evening. Given there's no blood on him, or anywhere, it seems to have been natural causes, so it might be completely innocent."

"True. As you well stated, we need more clues." Holmes looked up as one of the constables returned. "And this may provide some."

"Ah, Franklin," asked Hopkins. "What do you have?"

The young constable stopped, pulled out a small pad of paper, and started to read. "I talked to all the nearest stall holders. Only one noticed this man, and that was when he was taking a break about ten o'clock. He simply presumed the fellow was doing the same. Nothing more. They are a busy lot, and not much time for taking in the sights, so to speak."

"Coroner it is then," said Hopkins, his face dropping slightly at the delay.

As annoying as it seemed to me, Holmes was undeterred by the hour we lost waiting for the coroner to arrive and he examined the area thoroughly before the coroner removed the body and returned to the morgue with it. It was a Sunday afternoon after all, so the man on coronial duty only worked part-time, spending the rest of his working life as a doctor at a nearby attached hospital.

We had been lucky enough for him to have recognised Holmes's name, and he allowed us to accompany him. While he worked away, Holmes, Hopkins, and I stood nearby studiously watching his every move.

"Well, as you would be aware," the coroner said, loud enough for us to hear, and also his assistant standing in the opposite corner, "this man is perhaps in his mid- to late-thirties. There are no obvious marks or wounds on the visible areas of his body. The lividity of the exposed skin, and the pooling of blood in the hands and feet, suggest a time of death near ten o'clock last night." He glanced at me momentarily, having taken my advice upon arrival at Spitalfields. As he began to undress the man, I moved over to assist in moving the body and taking the clothes away. It was as he unbuttoned the shirt and exposed the chest that I gasped in horror. The dead man's chest and sides were a patchwork of mottled bruises and contusions.

"Intriguing," I heard Holmes mutter over my shoulder.

"Hmm. This man has been beaten severely. The wounds appear to have come from some form of blunt weapon."

"I would posit that they were made by a fist, Dr. Everett."

The coroner turned towards Holmes and gave him a look that questioned whether my associate was mad, before seeing the serious expression on his face and turning back to take a closer look at the wounds. "Good Lord, you may be right."

"How so?" asked Hopkins, having stayed quiet for most of the time.

It was the coroner that took the lead, pointing one gloved finger at the arrangement of some of the bruises. "These wounds appear in groups of four, arranged in almost perfect lines – as if from knuckles. There are so many of them that they could well be from someone punching this poor fellow."

"Given the ferocity and the broken skin, here and here – " Holmes pointed to several points on the body. " – I would think these were probably delivered with some form of knuckle covering. Probably a simple pair of iron knuckles."

To test out a theory, the coroner pressed against several of the contusions and nodded to himself. "Hmm. I would need to examine the interior, but some of the wounds on the ribcage appear to have produced breakages in the bones."

"Do you think that's what killed him?"

"Unsure at this stage," he replied. The coroner gave me a glance and nodded. I lifted the man's torso, and Dr. Everett pulled the shirt completely off, sliding the sleeves off the arms. It was then I caught sight of the dead man's back and gasped. It was riddled with more bruises and wounds, and the one that I spied partway down the back convinced me of how the dead man perished.

"Ah, this is horrid," remarked the coroner. He pointed at the bruising up and down the back, and then at the inch-wide puncture mark between the second and third rib on the left-hand side of the man's back. "This poor fellow underwent a horrible amount of damage before someone decided to finish him off."

"I think he was tortured," said Holmes.

We all stared at him in disbelief.

"Why so?" asked the coroner.

Holmes pointed at the dead man's wrists, which had been covered by the sleeve cuffs of his neatly pressed shirt. The skin on the wrists was torn and raw, with some of the meat beneath exposed.

"These wounds are probably from rope burns. Given the bruising to both front and back, I would think that he was tied up in a standing position while someone worked him over."

"Not just a simple beating?" asked Hopkins.

"There are no marks on his face or the back of his head. If the attack had been indiscriminate, then there should be wounds there. That's the first place an assailant would target. Much easier to cause pain. A man can succumb to much damage to the ribcage – it's designed to protect the internal organs, after all. And this – " Holmes pointed at the single puncture wound. " – would appear to be the *coup de grace*. The assailant, having finished, decided to end the man's life with a single thrust up through the ribcage and into the heart. I can only assume that when you open him up, you'll find the evidence."

"But why?" asked Hopkins. "It appears he was robbed. There was nothing in his pockets. No purse or wallet. No money. Nothing at all."

"Yes. There are two questions: Why was this done at all? And why was he left in the way that we found him? It's obvious that he was moved after he died. If the clothing we found him in was his, then it was removed prior to his beating, and the wound had closed up, and cleaned of any blood before he was once again dressed."

"Torture?"

"Oh, naturally. This represents all the hallmarks of someone undergoing some form of torture. Why? I don't know. Did he give up the sought information finally and he was dispatched, or did he keep quiet for so long that the torturer became frustrated and simply finished the job?"

"But who would do such a thing?" I asked. I had grown just as confused as I was horrified by what had happened to this poor man.

"Oh, I can think of dozens of men who would do such a thing," answered Hopkins.

"I believe you would have that information at your disposal," said Holmes, "As have I. It just comes down to which miscreant would have the audacity to then publicly display the results in the way we found this man."

"Hmm," said Hopkins, his hand beneath his chin with one finger extended up his cheek. It was a pose I had seen on many occasions displayed by my colleague. "He was found in Spitalfields, and we are after a nasty sort of villain that would be both happy to do this to someone, and then show them off to the world. It's almost as if he was a message to someone."

"Yes," said Holmes, a small smile on his face as he watched Hopkins think.

"Could it be a bit of a dust-up between gangs? This fellow doesn't appear to be the sort to associate with gangs."

"Hmm," said Holmes, "No, he doesn't, does he? Far too refined looking it would seem. Perhaps he crossed paths with the wrong person, or became indebted to one or another?" Stepping closer to the body, Holmes pointed to a puckered round mark on the man's upper thigh. "This is interesting though," he added, "What do you make of it?"

Examining the scar, I said, "An old bullet wound? Was he a villain?"

"Possibly, or maybe this man was in the services. Perhaps wounded in the line of duty and pensioned off."

"That would explain his physique. A life in the Army, perhaps. A hard-working trooper could develop such muscles. And if he received a hefty payout due to some injury in the field, it may explain his manner of dress."

It was that statement which drew Holmes's attention to the pile of clothing which lay discarded to one side. He moved across and began to reassemble the man's suit, shirt, tie, pants, and shoes as if they were adorning a ghost of the man. Stepping back to admire his handiwork, he stood arms crossed, his chin resting on his hand, and stared at the clothing. I was torn between watching Dr. Everett work and Holmes ponder.

Once the Y-cut was finished and the doctor had removed internal organs, I asked about the heart. "Ah," said Dr. Everette, "Yes, just as we suspected. There is a small puncture. Death would have been immediate, and the blood loss would have been minimal. Without this to pump, the wound would have simply seeped a small amount of blood as the body's internal pressure lessened."

With the final cause of death established, I moved away while Dr. Everett finished off the formal part of the autopsy and joined Holmes, hoping for some more information. I found him in the middle of a hands-on examination of the clothing. With his glass in hand, he searched every square inch, analysing stray threads, visible fibres, and other detritus. Except for the odd *Umm* or *Ah*, he said nothing until he felt down the interior seam of the jacket. A slight noise made him stand up.

"You heard that?"

"I did. Sounded like paper. That's very strange."

"It is, but not when you consider this." He held the jacket open and pointed at the seam. I wasn't much of a seamstress, but even I could tell that it had been roughly picked apart, leaving a small pocket into which some paper had been slipped. "Could you find me a spare scalpel or pair of scissors, please."

I did as asked, returning quickly with a scalpel. He slid it under the exposed thread and sliced easily through, pulling at the cotton and creating a wider opening in the seam. From within his pocket came a small pair of tweezers which he pushed into the gap and extracted a folded sheet.

Carrying the page to a nearby empty bench, Holmes placed it down and read out handwritten words on the outer part of the page. "*Tamam shud.*"

"Sounds Indian, or even Arabic?"

Holmes repeated the words. "I have heard that phrase, but I can't place it."

Hopkins, who had been watching Holmes for a while, but grown bored and moved across to observe the coroner, walked over and said, "What was that, you just said?"

"*Tamam shud*," repeated Holmes.

"I've heard that phrase before," Hopkins said, his face changing into an expression of deep confusion.

Turning the page over, Holmes confirmed that nothing further was written on the outside. Placing it down, he used the blunt side of the scalpel to hold it still while manipulating the folded page with the tweezers. Once open, it showed a decidedly strange jumble of numbers, words, and letters. It read, in very fine print:

BB
RM
57 – 1 – 2
36 – 4 – 4

17 – 4 – 2
12 – 1 – 7
20 – 2 – 2
20 – 3 – 5

79 – 1 – 7
3 – 3 – 8
6 – 3 – 1
19 – 1 – 4

60 – 4 – 5
64 – 1 – 2
69 – 2 – 3
45 – 3 – 10

Tamam Shud

10 – 1 – 2
Josie
13 – 4 – 9

"There's that phrase again," I said. "*Tamam Shud*. And a name – *Josie*. What do you think the *BB* and *RM* relate to?"

"I can only guess that it is a code of some form. It's no simple transform cypher, as the numbers are too large to represent letters. *BB* may

390

be the addressee, and I'm unsure about the *RM*, but I believe these are words. I've seen something similar before. The first number is a page, the second a paragraph or sentence, and the third represents the word within."

"Which book?"

"Yes, indeed. And more precisely, which *edition* of which book – or perhaps a magazine or newspaper? As you know, there can be multiple copies of the same work."

Hopkins, who had remained deep in thought but kept an ear open to our conversation, spoke up. "I don't know which book, but I believe I know someone who might be able to narrow it down further."

We both turned to face the inspector. "Who?"

He smiled. "My future bride."

"'*Tamam shud*'?" said Maddie as she studied the cypher from the Spitalfields man's pocket. We had kept the details of his demise from her and simply stated that he had been found, and that the message was all that was upon his person. "I remember reading that same phrase not long ago. I think it means, *It is done*, or something like that."

Turning towards her bookcase, she stared at the books before walking forward and running a finger along several of their spines. I noticed additional titles that impressed me even more. *The Epic of Gilgamesh* was there, nestled next to *Beowulf* and an English translation of *A Hundred-and-One Arabian Nights*.

"This really is simply a remarkable collection," I said, bringing a short sharp *Shhh!* from Holmes. I realised he meant that I should not break Maddie's concentration, so I went silent, stepping back to give her more room to think.

"A-ha!" she cried, pulling out a rather thin volume and stepping across to a small reading table. Maddie laid the book down and I saw the title was *The Rubaiyat of Omar Khayyam*. The cover stated that the work was translated by Edward FitzGerald. I had heard of the book, but wasn't familiar with it.

I thought it a strange choice and remained bemused until Maddie opened the book to the last page which displayed several small paragraphs of verse. The very last line read *Tamam shud* in a larger font, with the smaller English translation below that stated, "*It is done*."

"Oh, that works perfectly," said Holmes bringing the opened paper to the side of the manuscript. It was then I saw what he meant. The book consisted of ninety-six verses, each of four lines. Pointing at the first code, Holmes added, "If you would kindly turn to verse fifty-seven." Maddie did as Holmes had asked. "There. Verse fifty-seven, line one, second word: *Is*. *RM is*. Can you turn to verse thirty-six?" A few pages were

391

flipped back. "Verse thirty-six. line four, word four. *Dead. RM is dead.*" I gasped a little. The cypher appeared to be working. Within a few minutes, Holmes had the entire message written out.

It read: *RM is dead. Buried beneath rose garden. Close to Red Lion. Gold is with him.* Tamam Shud. *Let Josie go.*

I stared at the three faces around me. Hopkins was perplexed, Maddie was slightly aghast, and Holmes had a sly grin on his face. "What can it mean?" I asked.

"If we are to take the message at face value, then I can only assume that our man has observed or participated in dispatching this *RM*, who was then interred beneath a rose garden somewhere near a Red Lion."

"What 'Red Lion'?" asked Hopkins. "That could be a statue, or a pub, or even a flag."

"Most statues of lions, such as in Trafalgar Square, are either black or white. There would be far too many flags bearing the three red lions of England to make it worthwhile creating a coded message. But we have another clue: A rose garden. Perhaps you're right, Inspector. Are there any Red Lion pubs in the vicinity with a rose garden nearby?"

Silence descended for a moment before Hopkins broke it with a thought. "There's a Red Lion pub in Finsbury, up the road from the Finsbury Circus Garden."

"I read somewhere that they recently installed a small rose garden to commemorate the Queen's Diamond Jubilee," I added, hoping to be useful.

"Splendid!" said Holmes, looking from face to face. "The four of us appear to be quite the team."

"There's the rose garden," said Hopkins, pointing at the newly cleared patch of dirt which had been carved from an area of lawn in one corner of the garden. As we hiked towards the spot, I glanced around, impressed to find such a little sanctuary of green in amongst the Georgian terraces that circled it. Other members of the public also appeared to be enjoying the park, even if the temperature was a little lower than was comfortable at that time of early evening. Couples strode through the gardens, arm in arm, all around them ignored as they dwelt only within their own little worlds. Some families strolled along as well, the children running between the adults, and receiving harsh shouts as they strayed onto the grass.

It was idyllic – something that I knew was about to be broken if Holmes's insight was correct.

As we came within a few yards of the rose garden, it was clear that the ground was newly tilled, with dozens of rose bushes, mature yet bare of leaves and flowers, planted in a random but organised way.

"Any idea where this supposed *RM* was deposited?" I asked Holmes.

He stood at the edge of the garden and simply surveyed the area. He then strolled along the little gravel path which had been laid to assist others who wanted to view the garden, rubbing his chin for inspiration before stopping. Without any indication, Holmes broke protocol and strode across between two rows of bushes. I was a bit surprised, but understood that this was more important than complying with the unwritten rules regarding parklands in London.

"Hope the gardener doesn't see us," said Hopkins, striding along in Holmes's wake, with me in tow.

Finally, Holmes stopped before a small mound. Even with the roughness of the surrounding area, this stuck out as more of a heap of dirt than any of the other piles and furrows left by the gardeners. The soil was of a darker colour, which indicated that it hadn't dried as much as that at the base of the newly planted bushes and must have been drawn from beneath the ground.

"This looks like somewhere that might be hiding a body, or some other buried treasure," said Holmes, now glancing around for some other clue. And again he was off, not waiting for a response from either Hopkins or me. I watched him head towards a small shed, nestled amongst a copse of trees, before returning moments later, armed with three shovels. He handed one to each of us before adding, "Shall we?"

Hopkins stared at his shovel for a moment before shrugging and getting to work. Holmes had already begun and had moved a small pile of dirt aside. Resigning myself, I found an empty spot and began to dig as well.

It didn't take long before Hopkins cried out. "I've hit something." Carefully, he scooped more dirt from the hole he'd dug and fulfilled our quest. "Shoes. I've got shoes. Looks like you were right, Mr. Holmes."

We spent the next twenty minutes gently dragging the dirt away from yet another body. Holmes knelt down and used his hands, uncovering the person's face. Then we heard from behind us, "Oi! What do you think you three are playing at?"

Turning, we were greeted by a red-faced policeman, waving his arms and shouting orders and near obscenities at us. Hopkins stood, holding up one hand. "It's all right, Constable. I am Inspector Hopkins of the Yard."

The young policeman stopped, suspiciously eyeing up his superior before his eyes fell upon the body. "My word!" he cried, the whistle at his lips before we could calm him down. Within minutes, four more blue-coated bobbies had appeared beside the shallow grave. Questions and accusations rained down upon us, while Hopkins called for calm.

Finally, the five young constables became quiet and allowed Hopkins to explain the situation. While he directed them to fetch the coroner and a wagon to take the body to the morgue, Holmes unearthed more of the poor unfortunate fellow and the greatest treasure of all, a small box containing several gold ingots.

Standing, he brushed dirt from his hands and said, "This gets curiouser and curiouser."

"The three of you are back, I see," said Dr. Everett as he walked into the morgue, followed by his assistant, the newly discovered body lying on the autopsy table. "If you keep this up on a Sunday, I won't get any respite all week."

"Admittedly, we are simply responsible for finding the bodies, not creating them," I said, a little miffed at my medical colleague's attitude.

"Never mind," Holmes said. "I can fully appreciate the doctor's apprehension. There are enough deaths in this city without the addition of mystery surrounding them." He stepped up to the latest body and stated, "This poor gent was found in a shallow grave in Finchley. We believe he is intertwined with the Spitalfields man that was brought in earlier."

"In what way?" asked Everett.

"The note we found in the other man's coat lining led us straight to him."

"Incredible. This truly is a mystery." Everett stood looking over the newly discovered body and took in as much as he could. "Hmm. Similar age – about mid-thirties. Similar height and weight." He pressed the skin on the man's cheeks and tested them for lividity. "He's probably been dead twelve hours longer than your Spitalfields man." Examining the man's head, he added, "A contusion to the rear of the head, probably from a blunt object. It may have been the cause of death, but I'll need to complete my examination first."

I donned a pair of gloves and assisted Everett with undressing the man. Holmes took the clothes away and laid them on another gurney.

"Well, this fellow didn't suffer the same treatment as your friend. He's remarkably unmarked. No contusions. No obvious wounds." Rolling the body onto its side, Everett brought a magnifying glass on a small stand across to the gurney and examined the back of the dead man's head, pulling the hair aside to reveal a nasty, deep gash. "Hmm. Yes. This was the cause of death after all." Pushing at the wound, I noticed a slight movement. "The skull has been fractured, the bone possibly piercing the brain. He was hit with some force."

394

"As if by someone exhibiting extreme anger or fear?"

Nodding, Everett answered Holmes's question. "Yes, possibly." Staring closer, the coroner stopped and reached for a pair of tweezers, removing a sliver of material from the bloody wound. "Ah, yes," he said, placing the shard into a small metal bowl. "A splinter of wood. Looks like he was hit with a piece of lumber or some such."

Holmes regarded the dead body for a while, before replying, "Not the type of weapon generally associated with a professional. Rather, more someone acting in self-defence or on a whim. Possibly grabbed at random and swung at the victim by someone with great strength." He went back to study the victim's clothing while Everett continued his examination.

After several minutes, the coroner concluded his external examination, stating that there was no further evidence of any attacks on the body, and that the likely cause was indeed the blow to the head. This theory was strengthened after wiping some of the dirt and grime away, and finding a small bruise on the victim's forehead. He stated that the man must have been struck from behind before he fell face-first to the ground. The bruise was indicative of such an event.

"Anything else, Mr. Holmes?" asked Hopkins. "There's nothing in his pants or shoes. Just simple scuffing from normal wear, and the ever-present dirt from his grave."

"No. The only clues we have are held in that box, and all it contains are the gold ingots. One can only assume that once the Spitalfields man knocked this fellow to the ground, he tossed anything held in the man's pockets away, or the man simply had nothing in them to begin with."

"Do you think this is *RM*? The possible person from the message?"

"Most likely."

It was at that moment that a constable entered the morgue. His eyes shot towards the corpse, just then being cut open by the coroner. Those eyes opened wider than any I'd seen in a while, and the blood drained from the young man's face. Hopkins noticed, and a small grin appeared on his face. To break the constable's trance, he spoke loudly. "What is it Adcock?"

The policeman's eyes broke from the autopsy and swivelled towards Hopkins' voice. "Inspector. Sorry. I, umm . . . ."

"Out with it man."

"We combed the rest of the Finchley Garden. Nothing. The three shovels you found were the only ones in the area, and there were no other weapons of any kind about."

"Did you find a barrow or small truck of any kind in the vicinity?"

The young constable's head gave an inadvertent nod and he looked at Holmes. "Why, yes. How – ?"

"The body is far too heavy for a single man to move, especially if our Spitalfields man was the culprit. More likely this poor unfortunate was moved in such a way."

Adcock's eyes traced slowly back to the corpse as the coroner worked away.

"You can leave if you like, Adcock," said Hopkins. "No need to keep staring at that. I know it's a little breathtaking if you aren't used to it."

"Umm. Sorry, Sir, yes, I'd like to leave, but something just came to me." He walked across to the gurney, grasping Everett's attention for a moment before the coroner dismissed him and went back to work. Adcock stared down at the corpse's face for a while before his eyes opened wide once more. "I knew it. I knew I'd seen him before."

"Who?"

"This dead fella. That's Reggie. Umm . . . Reggie Marlston."

"Marlston?" asked Hopkins, his eyes drifting off as he searched his memories. "I know that name as well. Runs with the Bow Lane Gang. Small time criminals. Rumours have it they've been trying to push south and expand their territory."

"What of this Marlston fellow?" asked Holmes.

"Bit of a rough. Spent some time in Wentworth a couple of years ago for burglary."

"Hmm," said Holmes, relaxing into his thinking pose and growing silent for a moment.

I waited for a moment, before prompting him. "Connections?"

"There are threads – only loose ends – that need to be tied together. But this Reggie Marlston, or *RM* as the note suggests, appears to have been the object of a despicable act played out by our Spitalfields man." He waved nonchalantly across the room towards another gurney with a body covered by a sheet. I realised that was the earlier victim, who now appeared to be the perpetrator. Turning towards the young constable he asked, "Adcock, this Bow Lane gang?"

"Yes, sir."

"Do they have any roughs amongst them, especially men that have a reputation on the streets for violence?"

The young constable thought for a moment, then nodded. "Ye, sir. Tommy Winston. Nasty fella. They call him 'Knuckles' because he likes to beat people up with a set of iron studs over his knuckles. The strange thing is, he never hits anyone in the face. Good thing, too. He'd kill someone if he did."

Hopkins blurted it out before we could. "That's our man. Adcock, take two with you and bring this villain into the Yard. I reckon I can sweat something out of him."

Once the constable had removed himself, I piped up and asked a question that had been burning in the back of my mind. "And Josie? Any idea who that might be?"

"Ah, that's the real question," said Holmes. "I've been searching my recent memory, and I believe that I've recalled something that could prove very useful. In all the rush to examine these bodies, I simply put the snippet of information away for safekeeping and have only now re-examined it."

"Well, out with it."

"Two days ago, Inspector Bell dropped by. A young woman, from a reputable family – Miss Margaret Middleton – disappeared. There was nothing to investigate. She had simply vanished during a shopping trip. A quick chat with family members unearthed the fact that she had a suitor, a man called Alfred Somerton, an ex-soldier who had been retired from service due to being wounded in the line of duty.

"At the time, I didn't think there was any purpose in tracking down Somerton, as there was no indication that there was anything untoward. The couple may have simply scurried off for a liaison somewhere – not something I had any reason to pursue. I told Bell that until further evidence, such as a ransom note, were to arrive there wasn't much I could do."

He turned and walked across to the Spitalfields man and drew the sheet away, revealing his face. "Now that I think on it again, I remember that her full name was Miss Margaret Josephine Middleton. Perhaps her beau knew her as 'Josie'? And if this is indeed Alfred Somerton, I'm struggling to understand why he now lays dead on this gurney."

Hopkins slammed the wicked-looking set of iron knuckles, with a small three-inch blade extending out of the thumb side, down on the table hard enough to rattle the door in its frame. I almost had to cover my ears to block out the thundering echo inside the small, cramped interrogation room.

"What did you think you were going to do with this horrible little thing?"

The stocky man, whom we knew to be Tommy Winston, also known as Knuckles, took one look at the weapon and then glanced up at Hopkins, a sneer on his lips that held back any word with a level of defiance that only a committed villain could maintain.

"Isn't mine, is it?" he almost spat at the inspector.

Hopkins stared into those black pits for what seemed like an hour, before whispering with a hint of vitriolic menace that I found incredibly disconcerting. "You attacked my men with this knife. I have three witnesses to that fact. We only wanted to have a word with you, but you've

397

given yourself a life term already. You are mine to do with as I wish, and one way or another, you will talk."

"You don't scare me, Copper."

"I don't have to scare you. That's the Judge's job."

Winston went silent. He simply stared at Hopkins with that sardonic sneer fixed on his face.

"If I might, Inspector," said Holmes, "I think perhaps that Mr. Winston here requires a gentler approach."

After another thirty-second stare into those menacing eyes, Hopkins said, "Fine, Mr. Holmes. He's all yours."

"Holmes?" asked Winston, a widening of the eyes, giving the first hint at any fear in the man.

"Yes, Mr. Winston. I am Sherlock Holmes. By your question, I assume that you know of me, for I cannot place ever having met you myself."

Winston's eyes stared up into my colleague's aquiline face for a moment before dropping to stare at the table before him.

"Now, Mr. Winston – or do you prefer *Knuckles*?" Silence, not even a small movement of his head. "You are a member of the Bow Lane Gang." That statement received a grunt as if of affirmation. "Your role is one of . . . *troubleshooter*, as the Americans say. You resolve any problems that confront the other members." Another grunt. "Now, as I understand it, one of your members goes by the name Reggie. Ah, Reggie Marlston." Nothing. "Reggie is a bit of a cracksman. Used from time to time to bolster the finances of the gang, is that correct?" Again nothing. "Do you know that Reggie is dead?" A slight flicker of the eyes, but more from anger than surprise. "We believe he was killed by a man called Alfred Somerton."

"Don't know no Somerton." Again, reading the man's face there was no indication of surprise or ignorance.

"I think you do. I think you knew that Somerton had killed Reggie, and you used your nasty weapon to extract information out of him."

A shake of the head, with no hint of shock or surprise. This man was either cold-hearted or completely innocent. "Nuh! Haven't used my knuckles for ages. They's only to make people scared."

"Is that so?" Holmes pulled out his glass and donned his kid gloves before picking up the iron knuckles. Stepping towards a gas light in the corner of the room, he examined the weapon with an exaggerated level of intent. "I would think that a with thorough examination of this item, a competent coroner would find traces of skin on the knuckles themselves, and some residue of blood at the base of the blade." Turning towards me, with his back to the criminal, Holmes asked, emphasising my title, "Now, Dr. John Watson, would you agree that our coroner would be able to match

398

the skin and blood to the poor unfortunate Alfred Somerton?" Holmes grinned at me, and I knew I what I had to do, even though no such test existed.

"Oh, yes, the procedure is very simple. It would take a coroner mere moments to confirm your suspicions." As I spoke, I watched Knuckles carefully. The first hint of fear showed in his eyes.

Turning back, Holmes continued. "We can quickly confirm that your iron knuckles, the ones you used to assault the police constables, were also used to murder Alfred Somerton. The question I have for you is . . . *Why?*"

"I done nothing."

Holmes stood, examining the face of the gang member for quite some time, before he almost whispered, "Where is Josie?"

Knuckles's face broke into an expression of complete surprise. His eyes went wide in confusion, and his mouth dropped slightly open from the misdirection of the question. "Who in blazes is Josie? Never heard of her."

"And I finally believe some of the words from your mouth. Your expression is all I needed. The rest has been pure fabrication and a web of lies. I put it to you Mr. Winston that you knew Reggie was dead. You knew who killed him. You had that man captured, and you tortured him for hours, but he didn't say anything did he? He was an ex-soldier, trained to resist torturing."

Knuckles's stern face dropped into a look of resignation.

"And then you killed him. That's the part I don't understand. You killed him, but then didn't act on the information he gave you, if any." Holmes reached into his pocket, withdrew the little wooden box we had found with Reggie's corpse, opened the lid, and spilt the gold ingots onto the table. "This was found with your colleague's body."

Winston stared at the pile of gold, his face unmoving, until his eyes slowly rose and stared at Holmes. "He never said nothin'. Stupid pillock just took the beating and then . . . ." His face dropped again. "It was an accident. I got careless and swung at him the wrong way."

I gasped at the thought. Here was a brute of a man who had no compunction in beating another man senseless with a horrid weapon, and who then accidentally killed him. Studying his face, I couldn't determine whether he was upset at the fact he'd killed him, or the fact he hadn't gotten the information he needed before killing him. It was with horror that I realised it was the latter case.

"And the gold?"

The man dropped his eyes back to the gold. "We'd heard that Benny Bottin had pulled in a debt from a well-heeled client. Just the sort of thing that would help us gain a foothold further south, so we sent Reggie to nick

399

it. Next, I here's some plonker's asking around for Reggie. He was meant to come straight back, but I got concerned, so's I put the word out to find Reggie or the fella looking for him. When the boys brought the plonker back, I started asking him questions, but he wouldn't talk no matter what, and when I . . . when he stopped, there was no way of finding Reggie or that gold."

As he slowly scooped up the gold and placed it in the box, Holmes added, "I can only assume that your men positioned the poor unfortunate Mr. Somerton on a bench near Eldritch Park as a warning to the Spitalfields Mob.

At this, a smile cracked across Winston's sour face. "Yeah, that was a bit of fun on our part. Hope it worked. Those blighters shouldn't be messing with us."

"Indeed."

As Holmes handed the box to Hopkins, the inspector asked, "What now, Mr. Holmes?"

"I think it's time to talk with this Bennie Bottin fellow."

"To what do I owe this pleasure?"

It was almost as if we were speaking to Knuckles Winston once more. Bottin was another thick-necked rough who had risen through the ranks of his little gang of thieves and bandits through brute force rather than any other abilities.

"Do you know the name Alfred Somerton?"

A twitch of a grin at the corner of Bottin's mouth told me he knew him all right. "Yeah, the toffy blighter owes me a lot of money. He likes a bit of a game, does Mr. Somerton. Could you pass him a message for me?"

"We could," said Hopkins, "but I'm afraid he's dead. Killed by some rivals of yours, after he had killed one of theirs. It seems it was payback for a bit of thievery on their part." Hopkins threw the box of gold onto the table. "Know anything about this?"

Bottin's eyes glanced down at the box and grew wide for several moments while the rest of him stayed still. Hopkins reached forward and lifted the lid. A gleam of gold shone out, reflecting the strong gas lights ablaze behind Bottin's desk. Without breaking, he said, "Ooh, now that's pretty, isn't it? Is that for me?"

"You tell us? Rumour has it that this gold was payment to you from a client that found himself in trouble – probably Alfred Somerton."

"What rumours?"

"A member of the Bow Lane Gang supposedly stole this box from you, but Alfred Somerton was sent to get it back. Is that right?"

"Alfred Somerton? Why would he do that?"

400

Holmes stepped forward and said, "It may have something to do with the kidnapping of his potential fiancé, Miss Margaret Josephine Middleton."

"Never heard of her."

"Oh, I think you would know her as 'Josie'." A flash appeared in Bottin's eyes, followed by a sly grin on Holmes's face. Stepping back, he asked in a quiet voice. "Do you know the phrase, *Tamam shud*?" Bottin's eyes grew wide and darted down to his left, hovering for a second, before returning to stare at Holmes. Over his shoulder, Holmes said, "Inspector, could you be so kind as to examine the contents of the top left drawer of Mr. Bottin's desk."

As Hopkins stepped around, Bottin threw a hand to keep the drawer closed. "Shouldn't you have a warrant or somefin'?"

"Only if you have something to hide," said Hopkins before slapping the hand away and snatching the drawer open. "Well, that looks familiar." He pulled a thin book from the drawer and tossed it on the desk, where it slid across to Holmes. "Ah, another fan of Omar Khayyam." He picked the slim volume up and flipped to the back page. It was missing, torn from the book, leaving only the final three passages and the phrase *Tamam shud*. Beneath the last phrase was written in the same handwriting as the note: "*I think they know. If I don't return, find me. Check my coat lining.*"

"Not your book, I presume?" asked Holmes.

Bottin's face had that look that the game was up. He simply shook his head.

"A young street urchin dropped it by around noon?" A nod.

"What do you make of it, Mr. Holmes?" asked Hopkins.

"Well, let me state what I believe happened, and let Mr. Bottin here confirm." Holmes said. "I assume that Somerton had a large gambling debt with you?" Bottin nodded in agreement. "He paid you with some pure gold ingots. Where he got them is immaterial." Another nod. "The gold was stolen by Reggie Marlston." A nod. "Rather than send one of your men after it, you kidnapped Miss Middleton, and then used her to convince Somerton to retrieve it."

A sneer came to Bottin's lips. "Prove it."

"I think Mr. Somerton has already done that." Holmes brought a small envelope from his pocket, opened it, and lay the slip of paper with the cryptic message on the desk. He pointed to the two letters at the very top. "'*BB*'. Benny Bottin, if I'm not mistaken. The fact that he sent you his copy of the *Rubaiyat* – not a very common book, and not one that I would have expected you to own, I might say – and that he wrote that message inside telling that he knew he might be in trouble, showed that he wanted to make sure that his heart's desire was safe, even in the face of possible death."

"Is she safe, or are you going down for even more than just kidnapping and coercion to commit murder?" asked Hopkins, stepping closer to the desk and staring down at the gang leader.

Bottin glanced up at the policeman once, then nodded. "I let her go when I received that. The girl's no good to me now. The gold was somewhere. We just had to find it."

"Good," said Holmes. "Well, I think our job here is done, Inspector."

Hopkins simply nodded.

"What an eventful afternoon," said Madelyn as she poured us each a brandy.

We had returned to Hopkins' house, as we hadn't finished our luncheon, or said our goodbyes. Madelyn immediately sent us to the parlour to rest up and prepared a delightful meal.

As we dined, we filled her in on everything that had happened that afternoon.

"And as it was," said Holmes, "we couldn't have solved the case without both your input and Hopkins' here. I may have solved it given enough time, but that helped quicken things."

"I'm so glad we could help," replied Maddie. "I never thought that my interest in exotic books would ever be of any practical use."

"And your knowledge of the local criminal population was invaluable as well, Hopkins. It would seem that in one fell swoop, you helped to not only solve two deaths, but broke the back of two fledgling but growing criminal gangs in London. I'm sure that a little word in the right ear at the Yard will result in a large boost to your reputation, and would do no end of good to your possible prospects in the future."

"But none of that matters. Once we move to Chichester, I won't care anymore."

Even I could see that there was a hesitation in Hopkins' voice and a slight look of confusion in his eyes.

"That may be," said Holmes, "but I believe that your value has never been truly appreciated in this fine metropolis. With the conclusion of this little adventure, I don't think that will be the case from now on."

Hopkins remained silent for quite some time before nodding and saying, "I think you're right. Maybe my place is indeed here." He looked from person to person, before his eyes settled on Maddie. He reached out and took her hands in his. "But you so want to go to the country. I'm not sure that I could do that to you."

"Oh, don't worry about that." Maddie's show of mock regret was one for the West End stage. "We have all the time in the world, my darling. I'm sure that a few more years in London would see us become far more prosperous, and give us a far easier future when the time is right."

Hopkins nodded and patted her hand before letting it go and saying, "You are such a treasure. I'm the luckiest man in the world."

Later, as we boarded the hansom that Holmes flagged down outside, Maddie leaned into the carriage and whispered, "Thank you so much! I don't know how to repay you. I'm sure he'll be so busy that thoughts of moving to the country won't reoccur for years. Please expect invitations to the wedding, and no excuses for not attending."

We smiled at the last order and waved them out of the cold as we were taken away in the hansom.

The Unpaid Bills
by Chris Chan

"Watson, when was the last time you received payment for your medical work?"

I reflected for a moment, trying to recall when the post had delivered my compensation for services rendered. "I must say, I can't remember."

"When was the last time you went to the bank to make a deposit? If you don't mind, would you please take a look at your check book?" Holmes reached into his pocket, extracted the key to the drawer where he kept the aforementioned item at my request, and tossed it to me. After retrieving my banking materials, I checked the ledger and realized that I hadn't deposited any money into my account in nearly three weeks.

"That's odd," I said. "Normally I stop by my bank at least once a week, sometimes twice depending on how many of my patients pay promptly." A moment's reflection led me to realize that the last few weeks had not been exactly typical. I had been attending a conference in Glasgow recently and had been away for a week, and on my way home, I had caught a cold and been bedridden for several days. I was still nursing myself back to full fitness with hot soups and tea, and my bookkeeping had fallen down several places on my list of priorities. I rifled through the stack of letters that had arrived over the last several days, found no payments anywhere, and informed Holmes of this fact.

"Hmm . . . ." Holmes tented his fingertips. "That matches my experiences. It has been exactly eighteen days since I last received a paid bill in the mail. And the stream of clients visiting 221b hasn't been slow. It hasn't been up to record-breaking levels, but my bank account should be quite healthy. Instead, it's dwindling. I have enough to cover my personal expenses for the next couple of weeks, and then I shall have exhausted my cash resources. Are your own finances in a similar state?"

After a few quick calculations, I shamefacedly admitted that my own funds would be utterly depleted in just over a week's time. "I shall have to start economizing."

"And yet, you haven't seen a significant decrease in clients, have you?"

I had not, and suddenly the downturn in my finances started to take on a more sinister aspect. "Holmes, the fact that both of us haven't received our fees cannot be a coincidence."

"I agree. I first became suspicious a couple of weeks ago, when I realized that I hadn't received any payments in the post for a few days. For a little while longer, I decided to wait and see if there was simply some fluke delaying the paid bills, but midway through last week I decided that coincidence was not an acceptable explanation for the missing money. I have been making inquiries, but it wasn't until several minutes ago that I thought to ask if you might be suffering from the same situation. That was most remiss of me. I'm very disappointed in myself. You never thought it odd that you hadn't received your fees?"

Aware that I was blushing, I admitted that my mind had been on matters other than my finances. I am a slapdash bookkeeper at the best of times, and as I had been distracted lately due to my health, some difficult medical cases, and some personal challenges of no concern to anybody but myself, the weeks had slipped by without my realizing the state of my bank balance.

"Of course, several clients pay in person," Holmes mused, "so we're not completely destitute, but the lion's share of our income is received through the post."

"Just what sort of inquiries have you been making?" I asked.

"One or two clients failing to pay their bills is to be expected. Even the clients who profess the most gratitude for my services often are neglectful of handling their financial matters. But even if many satisfied clients forget to pay, there are always a significant number of individuals who settle their accounts promptly and in full. Even if ninety percent of my clients from the last few weeks defaulted on their payments for whatever reason, I should still receive a few pounds, especially from clients I have worked with in the past. The same applies to you."

"Could there be some sort of mass movement against us?" I wondered. "Have we done something that could have alienated our clients and patients and caused them to close their wallets to us?"

"I wondered that myself, but over the last few days I have made some inquiries and found that not to be the case. After visiting over a dozen individuals who have sought my services over the past two weeks, the vast majority of them claimed that they sent me payment in full days ago, and that they were completely satisfied with my services. A few admitted they were behind in paying their bills, and gave me my fee in cash then and there, so you needn't worry about our reputations. But the vast majority claimed that they'd already sent me my fee. What does that tell you?"

"Organization? That for whatever reason, many of your clients banded together to deny you your fees and then lied about having paid you?"

"No, no, no, my dear fellow, that explanation won't do. When I spoke to them, they all seemed surprised and a little uneasy at the thought of their bills being unpaid. A couple of them worried if their other payments to tradesmen and the like might not have been received, and they stated that they'd get in touch with those merchants as soon as I left. Indeed, there was nothing unusual about any of their manners. All seemed to think there was no reason why their payment didn't arrive in the post. That means that there are only two possibilities as to why I haven't received my fees. The first is that the envelopes containing payment were intercepted when they reached 221b, which would mean that Mrs. Hudson is responsible for our losses. This theory, I am sure you agree, doesn't warrant further scrutiny."

"Quite right," I concurred. "Which means that the envelopes with our money were pilfered *before* they came to our homes, which leads to the possibility that a *postman* took the letters."

"Bravo, Watson! It gives me deep and sincere pleasure to hear you come to that conclusion. Yes, a member of the Post Office must be involved, possibly more than one. Take a look at these envelopes. These arrived this morning, and are as yet unopened by me."

I studied the envelopes for a few moments before admitting that I could see nothing of note.

"Tut, tut! Examine the wax seals. These appear to be intact and unbroken, but if you examine the right-hand side of each wax seal, you can see a couple of little scratches on the side. This is an inevitable result when one attempts to open a sealed envelope without breaking the wax. A thin-bladed knife is heated to a high temperature, which, with a bit of dexterity, is then placed at the base of the seal and teased until the entire blade can be passed underneath the seal, freeing it from the paper, and allowing the knife-wielder to lift up the flap of the envelope and examine the contents inside. Once the miscreant has studied whatever is inside the envelope and possibly extracted or added something, the flat of the reheated knife blade is pressed against the wax seal until it becomes sticky again, and the flap of the envelope is then carefully lowered back into place and allowed to cool. When the intended recipient of the letter receives it, the average individual is unlikely to detect any sign that their correspondence has been subject to tampering."

A silent moment passed, as I wondered to myself if some of my letters had been opened and read without my knowledge over the years. Holmes interrupted my ruminations by explaining, "So you see, we have a general idea of what we have to look for here. A postman, quite possibly the one assigned to delivering to 221b. I rather doubt that a postman would have the time to examine our letters and still keep up with his deliveries, so I think it more likely that the postman in question handed over our letters to some other person, who took a hot knife to each seal and searched each envelope for our financial remunerations, keeping any envelopes that contained money, and re-sealing the rest and returning them to the postman for delivery."

"But could be is the purpose of this? Is this simply a case of robbery?"

"Possible, but unlikely. I have met with a fair degree of popularity of late, with a rather significant number of clients visiting me over the past month. However, even when I am particularly blessed with fees coming in my direction, the profits are certainly adequate, though not particularly lucrative. As for yourself, your work provides you with enough to make a decent living, but, if you will excuse me for saying so, should someone go to such lengths to gain control over the post, then a savvy criminal would focus on an individual with a much larger income. I trust you will not take any offense to that observation."

I am not sensitive about the fact that my income isn't nearly so large as that of several of my peers, and I assured my friend that my pride was in no way harmed by his comment.

"Very well then. Another salient point is that not *all* of our correspondence has been taken from us, only those envelopes that contained money in one form or another. I still receive armloads of letters from people asking me questions on all sort of inane issues. Just this morning I was asked by a duke to help him find his pet mastiff's favorite toy. I am not, I hope afflicted with an overinflated sense of my own importance, but there are some matters where even the humblest man can draw the line and refuse a commission that is far below his talents."

"Then if not all of our post is being intercepted, perhaps there is one piece of mail that someone wishes to keep out of our hands," I theorized. "Perhaps some person intends to send us some sort of potentially inflammatory information. What if there is some, say, terminally ill person who has some document that they is set to be mailed to your after that person's death? A confession to a crime, perhaps, that implicates someone else? And that person will go to any lengths to avoid prison and public humiliation. So that person hired somebody to intercept the mail for the article in question, and while that person waits for the particular envelope he needs, he's been helping himself to as much cash money as he can get his hands upon as his own little bonus."

I was rather pleased with that theory, but when I saw the corners of Holmes's mouth twitch upward, I knew at once that he was about to shatter it to pieces. "A clever idea," he said, showing obvious amusement, "but not quite in keeping with what we know. The theft of our money has been going on for a couple of weeks. If someone knew that a potentially dangerous letter might be sent to us after someone's death, then the window for our receiving that letter would be rather narrower – perhaps a few days at most. In any event, it would be counterproductive to steal the money, because the result is to draw attention to the fact that our post is being intercepted. Surely, if a single piece of correspondence were being targeted, the perpetrator would make sure that nothing else was taken."

As usual, Holmes was right. "I agree," I informed him. "But the obviousness of this theft indicates that someone *wants* us to realize that we're being robbed."

"Precisely. This isn't mere infiltration, where a few missing envelopes of payment here and there might be dismissed as wrongly delivered mail or something else innocent along those lines. Arguably, an intelligent thief would take *all* of our letters as a means of disguising the purpose of the threats, and anyway, such a criminal would be hesitant to take the time to sort through the letters, carefully open them, and keep only the ones with money inside them. Why hurriedly open all the letters and make sure the ones that weren't filled with payments were resealed and delivered to us that same day? This is theatre. Not the best-written and directed theatre, but a performance nonetheless, meant to perplex considerably and intimidate slightly. Certainly we are both harmed financially, and inconvenienced as well. The scope of this interference indicates that the perpetrator is playing the long game here. This has gone on too long to be a mere prank, and the person involved must have sufficient funds to pay off the accomplices who no doubt played a critical role in the thefts – though perhaps, on reflection, the bulk of their remuneration comes from keeping any money they find."

"Who do you think is behind this?"

"At present, I must confess myself baffled. I have gone through my records of active criminals, and I can find no one with sufficient animosity towards me – or you, for that matter – to get involved in this farce, and hardly anyone with the imagination to embark upon such an elaborate project."

"Surely you must have some idea which of your enemies would be involved in this."

"Is it an enemy? I wonder. A truly malicious person could do so much more to wreck our financial prosperity. A lawsuit, a smash and grab burglar on 221b, inflicting physical wounds on us that would make it impossible for us to work . . . these are means by which we might be quickly and efficiently bankrupted. But this – this is a direct challenge, an unknown opponent who is testing my wits . . . ."

"Are you certain that I am not the real target? Isn't it possible that some patient of mine might have developed some sort of grudge, and is targeting my finances, and yours as well, simply to deny you the opportunity to tide me over with a loan?'

Holmes sat motionless for a few moments before chuckling. "An excellent point! My vanity led me to the conclusion that I was at the center of this charade, and that you were merely damaged in the attack on me. But perhaps it was the other way around, it's certainly possible. What do you say? Is there some reason why one of your patients might seek revenge by pilfering all of your income?

I was flattered by Holmes's words, but after some reflection, I could come up with no suspects, and admitted as much.

We both sat quietly to think, until Mrs. Hudson knocked upon the door. "Two gentlemen to see you, Mr. Holmes. They say they've lost a lot of money through stolen letters."

After a shared glance between us, Holmes asked Mrs. Hudson to let the gentlemen in, and a moment later two men came in, wearing expensive suits and topcoats, but looking rather bedraggled. Given their extreme similarity, it seemed obvious that the pair were identical twins.

"We're Steven – " began one.

" – And Scott Sobotta," replied the other.

Steven mopped his forehead. "I don't know if you remember us – "

"Yes, of course I remember you," Holmes replied. "You are solicitors who run a very successful small firm. You called on me some time ago in the case of the two-line note. And now you're coming to me because your income has taken a severe blow. Clients have been paying their bills, but the money they've sent hasn't made it to you. Other mail that does not contain payment has arrived. It's only the money you've earned that is missing. I suppose that you've made inquiries, and you're convinced that your clients have tried to settle their debts to you, so you feel uncomfortable asking them to pay their debts again. But you need the money, so you are coming to me to figure out what happened to your hard-earned pounds."

The brothers' mouth sagged open. "How did you – ?" Steven asked.

"Know that?" Scott finished.

"I've sworn off telling people how I make my deductions," Holmes replied. "As Watson can confirm, people have an annoying habit of being less-than-impressed when they find out how I draw conclusions from observations."

The brothers looked at each other and then said in unison, "Can you help us?"

Holmes tented his fingertips and very thin smile passed across his face. "You are most fortunate. I am extremely interested in your case, and I shall start investigating immediately."

The brothers rose to their feet. "We're most – " Scott began.

" – Grateful," Steven continued.

Holmes informed them that he would be in touch with them as soon as he made some progress, and after a round of profuse thanks and handshaking, the twin brothers hurried out of 221b.

Immediately after Holmes shut the door, I crossed the room to him and folded my arms. "Doesn't this entire affair strike you as more than a little coincidental?"

"Coincidence is a word that is often used when people believe that they see a pattern that is unnatural. Certainly it's a bit surprising that very casual acquaintances of mine would be in a similar situation, but a person or organization with sufficient resources to intercept multiple letters in the mail in order to steal our funds ought not to be underestimated. After all, it might be hubris to assume that the miscreants in question are primarily interested in us. It's perfectly logical to wonder if we are only two of many victims of these thefts. It just so happens that two other victims have a previous history with me, so they thought of me when they realized they needed help."

"How many people do you think are being targeted by these thieves?"

Holmes returned to his chair and leaned back. "It's impossible to pose a reliable conjecture based on such scanty evidence. Of course, the nature of our professions makes us susceptible to this form of targeting."

"Our professions? A consulting detective, a doctor, and two solicitors? Why would we be targeted?"

"Simply because our payment for our services is often delivered through the post. Think about it. Many clerks and servants and other working people are paid in cash or by cheque in person. They receive their wages in their hands directly from their employers, or their employer's representative. But we are different. We perform our services, send a bill through the mail, and expect to receive our payment the same way. Tradesmen generally have a middleman between their clients and themselves, and that middleman is the postman."

Holmes lit a pipe, and I waited for him to resume speaking again. From the brightness in his eyes, I could tell that he was thinking. Fortunately, my many years of acquaintance with Holmes had taught me how to prioritize patience over curiosity. Time passed, and my tolerance for Holmes's silence came within a moment of reaching its limit. Perhaps Holmes sensed this, for he knocked out the contents of the pipe into an ashtray and began speaking again.

"It seems to me that if we are ever going to figure out what has happened to our payments, we need to start looking into our local postman. Or postmen, perhaps. I must say that my knowledge of the habits of many

410

of the people who come to 221b is often lacking. Indeed, I've rarely seen our postman, aside from those instances when I stand at the window and make observations about the people walking up and down Baker Street. So if someone were to impersonate our regular postman, it's unlikely that I would be aware of this fact. "

"Is that the answer? A false postman"

"I'm not so sure, actually. Consider, Watson: Over the last weeks, dozens of envelopes addressed to us have been intercepted. It's an impossible task to steal our letters right after the senders post them. No, no, the letters must be being taken after the Post Office has sorted the letters, cancelled the stamps, and sent them on their way to their final destinations. Now, the idea of a false postman taking over the normal postman's route is ridiculous. What would they do with the real postman? Tie him up and leave him somewhere? Kill him? Nonsense. A live, detained man would cause unwanted attention when he was eventually freed, and a corpse – or even a missing postman – would cause no shortage of interest on the part of the police, either. Besides, what sort of criminal would want to spend hours finishing off the real postman's route? No, it's far more likely that our postman is being bribed. A few pounds change hands, the postman gives our villain our letters, and after sorting through them and keeping the ones with payments. The postman receives regular payments to keep his mouth closed, and no one is the wiser. Of course, more than one postman must be having his wallet padded. The Sobottas' office is far from Baker Street, so a second postman, possibly more must be being bribed."

"How do you plan to proceed?"

"We wait for the next post, of course. Then we ask our questions directly."

Holmes carried a chair down to the front door and sat and smoked, informing a curious Mrs. Hudson that he wanted to meet our postman.

"He's a friendly fellow. I give him a biscuit now and then," she told us.

Holmes seemed uninterested in the postman's eating habits. He spent an hour smoking in silence, until without warning he leapt to his feet and flung open the door, revealing a startled-looking postman. "Come in, won't you?"

The postman looked absolutely terrified as Holmes pulled him inside and pushed him down into the chair. Shutting the door, Holmes leaned over the postman. "What's your name, sir?"

"Jon Jordan, sir. What's yours?"

"You know what it is, Mr. Jordan. It's on the letters that you're being bribed to hand over to some third party."

411

The postman gasped. "I never took a bribe in my life, sir!"

Holmes started to speak, then changed his mind. A moment later, he began talking again. "For some reason, I believe you. But you have been handing over my letters to someone else, Mr. Jordan. And Dr. Watson's, too."

Jordan turned very pale, but eventually he nodded.

"Why did you do this, Mr. Jordan?" A moment later, Holmes answered his own question. "You didn't take a bribe, but you still participated in this scheme . . . You were threatened, weren't you?"

He sat frozen for a few moments, then Jordan nodded. "Not me, sir. My sister. She was a lady's maid, but she was accused of stealing her mistress's pearls. But she didn't do it, sir. They falsely accused her, and she was convicted and sent to prison. And then this man – he never told me his name – told me that if I didn't hand over your letters to him, he'd see to it that my sister would be beaten – and worse – in prison. I can't let that happen to her, sir."

Patting his shoulder, Holmes said, "I understand. You aren't at fault here. But tell me, please: When and where do you give him my letters?"

"Every post, sir. Of the eight daily deliveries to you, I cover half of them. I suppose something similar's happening with the other fellow or fellows who deliver to you. He waits for me at the pub down the road, and every trip I hand all the letters that are meant for you to him. And then every visit he hands me the letters back – most of them, anyway – so you get your post a bit later than you should. I knew it was wrong, but – "

"You were looking after your sister, Jordan. I cannot fault you."

"I don't know what he did with the letters he kept, sir."

"I have a fair idea, Jordan. Now, I realize that you are worried about your sister, but I can assure you that if you work with me, no harm shall befall her or you or anybody else you care about – you have my word on that. Understood?"

"Yes, Mr. Holmes."

"Good. Now, if you'll allow us to get our coats, you will please be good enough to take us to the pub where you have met this man."

A few moments later, we entered a rather pleasant drinking establishment with gleaming wooden paneling and comfortable seats. Mr. Jordan pointed to a corpulent man who was seated a table in the corner, leaning back in a chair with several newspapers in front of him on the table. "Good. There are still a few more post deliveries left in the day. Continue your habit of handing my mail to him and taking back what he gives you. Try to show no agitation, just continue as normally."

"Very good, sir. I'll do as you ask."

Holmes and I returned to 221b. As we walked, Holmes replied, "There is no need to stay here all day. Our man will wait until Jordan comes by for the last post. We'll be ready for him then."

"Why is that fellow doing this?"

"The man in the pub is a flunky. The person who organized this attempt to impoverish us – and others, I'm quite certain many more people besides the Sobottas were targeted, but I have no idea how many, or why these people were targeted – wouldn't waste his entire day in a pub. He hired someone to do the work, such as it is, for him. In any event, we want this fellow's boss. Tonight, after Jordan hands him the last of today's letters, we'll follow him."

A few hours later, after a quick supper, we hurried back to the pub and waited in the shadows across the street. After about ten minutes, we saw Jordan entering the pub and leaving a minute later. Our unknown target was right behind him.

We trailed him for several streets, staying far enough back to avoid his notice, though the darkening night made it easier to escape detection. After about twenty minutes of walking, we saw him enter a nondescript building on the Thames. "So," Holmes murmured, "our adversary works for the British Government. This building is a headquarters for one of the more secretive branches of Her Majesty's loyal public servants."

"Spies?"

"More accurately, bureaucrats who don't like being accountable to Parliament or the public eye. Let's have a word."

The door was unlocked, which I thought was lax security, though I figured that the man who had gathered up our letters wasn't the sharpest or most conscientious of fellows. so we walked inside the building and noticed our quarry heading down a dark corridor. We followed him to the room at the end of the hall. The man knocked and obeyed the command to "Enter," and the two of us hurried forward and followed him inside. The man from the pub gasped when we barged into the room, but the aristocratic-looking man at the desk didn't flinch.

"Mr. Holmes," he said. "I was wondering when you would find us."

"My apologies for keeping you waiting. I've been busy. You know who we are, but what is your name, sir?"

"You may call me Derrick Belanger." The man turned to his employee. "Give the gentlemen their letters and go." He tossed him a sovereign and the man obeyed.

"I'm a busy man, so we'll make this quick," Belanger snapped. "No doubt you've figured out what I've done. I wanted to drain your resources, and I also wanted to see how soon you could figure out what was happening. I wanted to show my influence. I know how to bend the Post

413

Office to my will – I have over seventy postmen under my thumb – whether by blackmail, bribery, or threats – turning letters over to me whenever I order it."

"And your motives for doing so, sir?"

"I want you to work for me, Holmes. For my department. You're a valuable man. You can do a lot more good putting your skills to the tasks I assign."

"Do you need a doctor as well, Mr. Belanger?"

"Of course not. Watson is immaterial to me aside from as a further encouragement to sway you. I wanted to leave you both desperate for money, and I wanted you to see the level of influence I wield. I wish to make it clear that your days as a consulting detective are over. From now on, you are one of my agents. You'll do what I say when I tell you to do it, and in return, you'll be paid slightly more than you are making now. Watson can continue to see whatever patients he wishes, and he can join you if he likes, but he can't write any accounts of your cases."

"Why did you take the Sobattas' money?" Holmes inquired.

"No concern of yours. They happen to have some valuable information regarding some clients of theirs that I wish to know, and I decided to put some pressure on them. Once their money runs low, I'll stop by, and if they wish to avoid penury they'll give me what I need. Come back tomorrow morning, Holmes, and I'll give you your first assignment."

"You seem to be under the impression that I will agree to become one of your lackeys, Mr. Belanger."

"You've only witnessed one of my methods for impoverishing people. If you cross me, you'll never make a living again. I used one of the least embarrassing methods I know of on you first, but say 'No' and you'll be publicly humiliated. Your business will be ruined, and then you'll have no choice but to work for me. And I'll be offering you much less money when you come crawling to me on your knees."

Holmes glared at him with cool disdain. "Good evening to you, sir."

As he turned and exited, I followed.

"Holmes! Come back!" Belanger barked. We ignored him.

Once we were back on the streets, I asked Holmes, "What are we going to do? That man wasn't joking. He'd easily bankrupt and embarrass us to help us get what he wants."

"Have no fear. This is a case when it is fortunate that we are on the side of the big battalions."

"What do you mean?"

"Belanger is an agent of the British Government. Therefore, we will speak to the British Government."

After a few moments of confusion, I realized what Holmes was saying. We hailed a carriage and soon arrived at the rooms of Holmes's brother Mycroft. We had a brief conversation explaining the situation, and Mycroft grumbled about Belanger.

"I've never cared for the fellow. He thinks that the Empire would fall if he wasn't engaged in his skullduggery. Utter hubris."

"Unlike in your case, dear brother, as you actually *are* indispensable to England's stability."

"Flattery means nothing to me, you know that. But leave this matter to me."

The next morning, Mrs. Hudson struggled up the stairs, carrying a mountain of letters up to our rooms. All of our correspondence had been steamed open and resealed, and in every case the envelopes contained some form of payment.

"I must say, it can at times be handy to have a brother so firmly ensconced in the corridors of power," Holmes commented, extracting a guinea from an envelope.

"I suppose Mycroft informed Belanger that if he didn't return our money, then his department would be shuttered."

"Not just our post, Watson. That of the Sobottas and all of the other people Belanger has targeted, too."

"Do you think we'll cross paths with Belanger again?"

"I expect we will. He was most anxious to gain control over my skills. He may not try to force me into servitude again, but I wouldn't be surprised if he tried different, perhaps more conciliatory ends to obtain my assistance at some point in the future."

The Sobottas were most appreciative when their missing funds were returned to them, and particularly generous when providing remuneration for Holmes's services. Holmes used a portion of this reward to launch an investigation into the pearls that were allegedly stolen by Mr. Jordan's sister. After an hour's work, Holmes discovered them in the owner's rose garden. The clasp had broken, and the necklace had innocently slipped down amongst the bushes. The owner was severely embarrassed, and accused Holmes of planting the jewelry there to set a guilty woman free.

A little judicious pressure from some of the woman's friends, who were Holmes's former clients, and she eventually admitted that her maid was innocent, leading to her release and a modest sum of money as compensation. A crusading journalist found out about the case, wrote a story describing the false accusation and imprisonment, and the woman responsible for sending an innocent woman to prison was so humiliated she retreated to a cottage in a tiny village in Wales in order to escape the opprobrium of her social circle. As of this writing, to my knowledge, she has never returned to London.

The postman, Mr. Jordan, was profuse with his gratitude, and Holmes refused to accept any of his sister's new windfall. As for Mr. Belanger, at the request of the Prime Minister we were eventually forced to work with him on a trio of cases of national importance, but the details of those cases must remain secret for many years to come.

NOTE

Steven and Scott Sobotta, Jon Jordan, and Derrick Belanger all contributed to a recent Kickstarter campaign for my book *The Autistic Sleuth*, and as a reward chose to have their names included as characters in a Sherlock Holmes story. Please note that Derrick Belanger specifically requested to have his name assigned to the villain of the story.

About the Contributors

The following contributors appear in this volume:
The MX Book of New Sherlock Holmes Stories
Part XLVII – Occupants of the Canonical Realm (1890-1898)

Ian Ableson is an ecologist by training and a writer by choice. When not reading or writing, he can reliably be found scowling at a clipboard while ankle-deep in a marsh somewhere in Michigan. His love for the stories of Arthur Conan Doyle started when his grandfather gave him a copy of *The Original Illustrated Sherlock Holmes* when he was in high school, and he's proud to have been able to contribute to the continuation of the tales of Sherlock Holmes and Dr. Watson.

Tim Newton Anderson is a former senior daily newspaper journalist and PR manager who has recently started writing fiction. In the past six months, he has placed fourteen stories in publications including *Parsec Magazine*, *Tales of the Shadowmen*, *SF Writers Guild*, *Zoetic Press*, *Dark Lane Books*, *Dark Horses Magazine*, *Emanations*, and *Planet Bizarro*.

Dan Andriacco BSI, editor of *The Baker Street Journal*, is also a mystery writer. His long-running Sebastian McCabe – Jeff Cody series, starting with *No Police Like Holmes*, features a Sherlockian amateur sleuth and numerous Canonical references. He also wrote the Sherlock pastiche novels *House of the Doomed* and *The Sword of Death*. His scholarly articles have appeared in the *BSJ*, *The Sherlock Holmes Journal*, *Canadian Holmes*, *Sherlock Holmes Mystery Magazine*, and in numerous books. As leader of *The Tankerville Club of Cincinnati* scion society, he holds the title "Most Scandalous Member". He is also "Top Knot" of *His Last Bow*, a BSI scion for bow tie wearers.

"Anon." is a devoted Sherlockian and player of The Game.

Brian Belanger, PSI, is a publisher, illustrator, graphic designer, editor, and author. In 2015, he co-founded Belanger Books publishing company along with his brother, author Derrick Belanger. His illustrations have appeared in *The Essential Sherlock Holmes* and *Sherlock Holmes: A Three-Pipe Christmas*, and in children's books such as *The MacDougall Twins with Sherlock Holmes* series, *Dragonella*, and *Scones and Bones on Baker Street*. Brian has published a number of Sherlock Holmes anthologies and novels through Belanger Books, as well as new editions of August Derleth's classic Solar Pons mysteries. Brian continues to design all of the covers for Belanger Books, and since 2016 he has designed the majority of book covers for MX Publishing. In 2019, Brian received his investiture in the PSI as "Sir Ronald Duveen." More recently, he illustrated a comic book featuring the band The Moonlight Initiative, created the logo for the Arthur Conan Doyle Society and designed *The Great Game of Sherlock Holmes* card game. Find him online at:
www.belangerbooks.com and
www.redbubble.com/people/zhahadun and
zhahadun.wixsite.com/221b

Chris Chan is a writer, educator, and historian. He works as a researcher and "International Goodwill Ambassador" for Agatha Christie Ltd. His true crime articles, reviews, and short fiction have appeared (or will soon appear) in *The Strand*, *The Wisconsin Magazine of History*, *Mystery Weekly*, *Gilbert!*, *Nerd HQ*, Akashic Books' *Mondays are Murder* web series, *The Baker Street Journal*, *The MX Book of New Sherlock Holmes Stories*, *Masthead: The Best New England Crime Stories*, *Sherlock Holmes Mystery Magazine*, and multiple Belanger Books anthologies. He is the creator of the Funderburke mysteries, a series featuring a private investigator who works for a school and helps students during times of crisis. The Funderburke short story "The Six-Year-Old Serial Killer" was nominated for a Derringer Award. His books include *Sherlock & Irene: The Secret Truth Behind "A Scandal in Bohemia"*, *Murder Most Grotesque: The Comedic Crime Fiction of Joyce Porter*, *Sherlock's Secretary*, *Of Course He Pushed Him*, *Nessie's Nemesis*, *Ghosting My Friend*, She *Ruined Our Lives*, and *The Autistic Sleuth.*

Steven Connelly was born in Scotland, and lived for twenty years in London. When first visiting London, his first excited touristic trip was not Buckingham Palace or the Houses of Parliament, but Baker Street. This is his first Sherlock Pastiche but won't be the last.

Alan Dimes was born in Northwest London and graduated from Sussex University with a BA in English Literature. He has spent most of his working life teaching English. Living in the Czech Republic since 2003, he is now semi-retired and divides his time between Prague and his country cottage. He has also written some fifty stories of horror and fantasy and thirty stories about his husband-and-wife detectives, Peter and Deirdre Creighton, set in the 1930's.

Sir Arthur Conan Doyle (1859-1930) *Holmes Chronicler Emeritus.* If not for him, this anthology would not exist. Author, physician, patriot, sportsman, spiritualist, husband and father, and advocate for the oppressed. He is remembered and honored for the purposes of this collection by being the man who introduced Sherlock Holmes to the world. Through fifty-six Holmes short stories, four novels, and additional Apocryphal entries, Doyle revolutionized mystery stories and also greatly influenced and improved police forensic methods and techniques for the betterment of all. *Steel True Blade Straight.*

Steve Emecz's main field is technology, in which he has been working for about twenty-five years. Steve is a regular speaker at trade shows and his tech career has taken him to more than fifty countries – so he's no stranger to planes and airports. In 2008, MX published its first Sherlock Holmes book, and MX has gone on to become the largest specialist Holmes publisher in the world with over 500 books. MX is a social enterprise and supports three main causes. The first is Happy Life, a children's rescue project in Nairobi, Kenya, where he and his wife, Sharon, spend every Christmas at the rescue centre in Kasarani. They have written two editions of a short book about the project, *The Happy Life Story*. The second is Undershaw, Sir Arthur Conan Doyle's former home, which is a school for children with learning disabilities for which Steve is a patron. Steve has been a mentor for the World Food Programme for several years, and was part of the Nobel Peace Prize winning team in 2020.

Mark A. Gagen BSI is co-founder of Wessex Press, sponsor of the popular *From Gillette to Brett* conferences, and publisher of *The Sherlock Holmes Reference Library* and many other fine Sherlockian titles. A life-long Holmes enthusiast, he is a member of *The Baker Street Irregulars* and *The Illustrious Clients of Indianapolis*. A graphic artist by profession, his work is often seen on the covers of *The Baker Street Journal* and various BSI books.

John Atkinson Grimshaw (1836-1893) was born in Leeds, England. His amazing paintings, usually featuring twilight or night scenes illuminated by gas-lamps or moonlight, are easily recognizable, and are often used on the covers of books about The Great

Detective to set the mood, as shadowy figures move in the distance through misty mysterious settings and over rain-slicked streets.

Arthur Hall was born in Aston, Birmingham, UK, in 1944. He discovered his interest in writing during his schooldays, along with a love of fictional adventure and suspense. His first novel, *Sole Contact*, was an espionage story about an ultra-secret government department known as "Sector Three", and was followed, to date, by three sequels. Other works include seven Sherlock Holmes novels, *The Demon of the Dusk, The One Hundred Percent Society, The Secret Assassin, The Phantom Killer, In Pursuit of the Dead, The Justice Master,* and *The Experience Club* as well as three collections of Holmes *Further Little-Known Cases of Sherlock* Holmes, *Tales from the Annals of Sherlock* Holmes, and *The Additional Investigations of Sherlock Holmes.* He has also written other short stories and a modern detective novel. He lives in the West Midlands, United Kingdom.

Paula Hammond has written over sixty fiction and non-fiction books, as well as short stories, comics, poetry, and scripts for educational DVD's. When not glued to the keyboard, she can usually be found prowling round second-hand books shops or hunkered down in a hide, soaking up the joys of the natural world.

Stephen Herczeg is an IT Geek, writer, actor, and film-maker based in Canberra Australia. He has been writing for over twenty years and has completed a couple of dodgy novels, sixteen feature-length screenplays, and numerous short stories and scripts. Stephen was very successful in 2017's International Horror Hotel screenplay competition, with his scripts *TITAN* winning the Sci-Fi category and *Dark are the Woods* placing second in the horror category. His three-volume short story collection, *The Curious Cases of Sherlock Holmes*, will be published in 2021. His work has featured in *Sproutlings – A Compendium of Little Fictions* from Hunter Anthologies, the *Hells Bells* Christmas horror anthology published by the Australasian Horror Writers Association, and the *Below the Stairs, Trickster's Treats, Shades of Santa, Behind the Mask,* and *Beyond the Infinite* anthologies from *OzHorror.Com, The Body Horror Book, Anemone Enemy,* and *Petrified Punks* from Oscillate Wildly Press, and *Sherlock Holmes In the Realms of H.G. Wells* and *Sherlock Holmes: Adventures Beyond the Canon* from Belanger Books.

Roger Johnson, BSI, ASH, PSI, etc, is a member of more Holmesian societies than he can remember, thanks to his (so far) 16 years as editor of *The Sherlock Holmes Journal*, and thirty-two years as editor of *The District Messenger*, the newsletter of *The Sherlock Holmes Society of London*. He collaborated with his wife, Jean Upton, on the well-received book, *The Sherlock Holmes Miscellany.* Roger is resigned to the fact that he will never match the Duke of Holdernesse, whose name was followed by "*half the alphabet*".

Naching T. Kassa is a wife, mother, and writer. She's created short stories, novellas, poems, and co-created three children. She resides in Eastern Washington State with her husband, Dan Kassa. Naching is a member of *The Horror Writers Association, Mystery Writers of America, The Sound of the Baskervilles, The ACD Society, The Crew of the Barque Lone Star,* and *The Sherlock Holmes Society of London.* She works in Talent Relations at Crystal Lake Publishing and was a recipient of the 2022 HWA Diversity Grant. You can find her work on Amazon.
https://www.amazon.com/Naching-T-Kassa/e/B005ZGHTI0

Susan Knight's newest novel, *Death in the Harem*, is forthcoming from MX publishing, is the latest in a series which began with her collection of stories, *Mrs. Hudson Investigates*

(2019), and the novels *Mrs. Hudson goes to Ireland* (2020), *Mrs. Hudson Goes to Paris* (2022) and *Death in the Garden of England* (2023) She has contributed to many recent MX anthologies of new Sherlock Holmes short stories and enjoys writing as Dr. Watson as much as she does Mrs. Hudson. Nine of these stories comprised *The Strange Case of the Pale Boy and Other Mysteries* (2023). Susan is the author of two other non-Sherlockian story collections, as well as three novels, a book of non-fiction, and several plays, and has won several prizes for her writing. Susan lives in Dublin.

David Marcum plays *The Game* with deadly seriousness. He first discovered Sherlock Holmes in 1975 at the age of ten, and since that time, he has collected, read, and chronologicized literally thousands of traditional Holmes pastiches in the form of novels, short stories, radio and television episodes, movies and scripts, comics, fan-fiction, and unpublished manuscripts. He is the author of over one-hundred-thirty Sherlockian pastiches, some published in anthologies and magazines such as *The Best Mystery Stories of the Year 2021* and *The Strand*, and others collected in his own books, *The Papers of Sherlock Holmes, Sherlock Holmes and A Quantity of Debt, Sherlock Holmes – Tangled Skeins, Sherlock Holmes and The Eye of Heka*, and *The Collected Papers of Sherlock Holmes* – six volumes and more to come. He has won back-to-back first place fiction awards from *The Arthur Conan Doyle Society* (2023 and 2024) and the Nero Wolfe *Wolfe Pack*. He has edited over 1,100 Holmes adventures and ninety books, including dozens of traditional Sherlockian anthologies, such as the ongoing series *The MX Book of New Sherlock Holmes Stories*, which he created in 2015 to promote traditional Canonical Holmes. This collection is now at forty-eight volumes, with more in preparation. He was responsible for bringing back August Derleth's Solar Pons for a new generation with his collections of authorized Pons stories, *The Papers of Solar Pons* and *The Further Papers of Solar Pons*. Pons's return was further assisted by his editing of the reissued authorized versions of the original Pons books, and then several volumes of new Pons adventures. He has done the same for the adventures of Dr. Thorndyke, and has plans for similar projects in the future. He has contributed numerous essays to various publications, and is a member of a number of Sherlockian groups and Scions, as well as *The Mystery Writers of America*. His irregular Sherlockian blog, *A Seventeen Step Program*, addresses various topics related to his favorite book friends (as his son used to call them when he was small), and can be found at *http://17stepprogram.blogspot.com/* He is a licensed Civil Engineer, living in Tennessee with his wife and son. Since the age of nineteen, he has worn a deerstalker as his regular-and-only hat. In 2013, he and his deerstalker were finally able make his first trip-of-a-lifetime Holmes Pilgrimage to England, with return Pilgrimages in 2015, 2016, and 2024, where you may have spotted him. Another is planned in mid-2025. If you ever run into him and his deerstalker out and about, feel free to say hello!

Will Murray is the author of some 75 novels, including some 20 posthumous Doc Savage collaborations with Lester Dent, and 40 books in the long-running Destroyer series. Other Murray novels star the Executioner, Tarzan of the Apes, The Spider, Pat Savage and the Mars Attacks characters. His book, *Nick Fury, Agent of S.H.I.E.L.D.: Empyre* (2000) foreshadowed the 9/11 terrorist attacks. Murray has penned more than 45 Sherlock Holmes short stories. Twenty of Murray's Holmes short stories have been collected as *The Wild Adventures of Sherlock Holmes*, Vols 1 and 2. His novelette, "The Adventure of the Vengeful Viscount", in which Tarzan of the Apes, otherwise Lord Greystoke, hires Sherlock Holmes to solve a mystery, was approved by both the Estate of Sir Arthur Conan Doyle and Edgar Rice Burroughs, Inc. Murray is the author of the non-fiction book, *Master of Mystery: The Rise of The Shadow*, which is an exploration of the famous radio and magazine character, and a sequel, *Dark Avenger: The Strange Saga of The Shadow*. The

Wild Adventures of Cthulhu Vols 1 & 2 collect Murray's Lovecraftan short stories. For Marvel Comics, Murray created the Unbeatable Squirrel Girl with legendary artist Steve Ditko. Website:
www.adventuresinbronze.com

Sidney Paget (1860-1908), a few of whose illustrations are used within this anthology, was born in London, and like his two older brothers, became a famed illustrator and painter. He completed over three-hundred-and-fifty drawings for the Sherlock Holmes stories that were first published in *The Strand* magazine, defining Holmes's image forever after in the public mind.

Tracy J. Revels, BSI, a Sherlockian from the age of eleven, is a professor of history at Wofford College in Spartanburg, South Carolina. She is a member of *The Survivors of the Gloria Scott* and *The Studious Scarlets Society*, and is a past recipient of the Beacon Society Award. Almost every semester, she teaches a class that covers The Canon, either to college students or to senior citizens. She is also the author of three supernatural Sherlockian pastiches with MX (*Shadowfall*, *Shadowblood*, and *Shadowwraith*), and most recently, the three-volume pastiche set, *Tales of Light*, *Tales of Shadow*, and *Tales of Darkness*. She is a regular contributor to her scion's newsletter. She also has some notoriety as an author of very silly skits: For proof, see "The Adventure of the Adversarial Adventuress" and "Occupy Baker Street" on YouTube. When not studying Sherlock, she can be found researching the history of her native state, and has written books on Florida in the Civil War and on the development of Florida's tourism industry.

Roger Riccard's family history has Scottish roots, which trace his lineage back to Highland Scotland. This ancestry encouraged his interest in the writings of Sir Arthur Conan Doyle. He has authored the novels, *Sherlock Holmes & The Case of the Poisoned Lilly*, and *Sherlock Holmes & The Case of the Twain Papers,* which was featured at the Museum of London Sherlock Holmes Exhibit in 2015. In addition, he has produced dozens of short stories, and has now joined the Sherlock Holmes 60+ Club, having exceeded Sir Arthur Conan Doyle's number of original Sherlock Holmes stories. All of his books have been published by Baker Street Studios and can be found at his website: *www.sherlockriccard.com* He credits his success to the encouragement of his wife/editor/inspiration and Sherlock Holmes fan, Rosilyn. She passed in 2021, and it is in her memory that he continues to contribute to the legacy of the "*man who never lived and will never die*".

Fifteen of **Brenda Seabrooke**'s Sherlock Holmes pastiches have been anthologized in MX Publishing and Belanger Books, six in *Best Crime Stories of New England*, one in *Destination: Mystery* and *Mystery Tribune*, and twelve in literary reviews such as *Yemassee*, *Confrontation*, and one in *Redbook*. Twenty-two of her books for young readers have been published at Penguin, Clarion, *etc.*, and won awards such as a Notable from the National Council of Social Studies, Junior Literary Guild, Hornbook Honor, an Edgar finalist, *etc.* She received a grant from the National Endowment for the Arts, and The Robie Macauley Award from Emerson College. In 2022, MX published her collection, *Sherlock Holmes: The Persian Slipper and Other Stories.*

DJ Tyrer is the person behind Atlantean Publishing and has had fiction featuring Sherlock Holmes published in volumes from MX Publishing and Belanger Books, and an issue of *Awesome Tales*, and has a forthcoming story in *Sherlock Holmes Mystery Magazine*. DJ's non-Sherlockian mysteries can be found in anthologies such as *Mardi Gras Mysteries*

(Mystery and Horror LLC) and *The Trench Coat Chronicles* (Celestial Echo Press), and on *Mystery Tribune.*
DJ Tyrer's website is at *https://djtyrer.blogspot.co.uk/*
DJ's Facebook page is at *https://www.facebook.com/DJTyrerwriter/*
The Atlantean Publishing website is at *https://atlanteanpublishing.wordpress.com/*

Emma West joined Undershaw in April 2021 as the Director of Education with a brief to ensure that qualifications formed the bedrock of our provision, whilst facilitating a positive balance between academia, pastoral care, and well-being. She quickly took on the role of Acting Headteacher from early summer 2021. Under her leadership, Undershaw has embraced its new name, new vision, and consequently we have seen an exponential increase in demand for places. There is a buzz in the air as we invite prospective students and families through the doors. Emma has overseen a strategic review, re-cemented relationships with Local Authorities, and positioned Undershaw at the helm of SEND education in Surrey and beyond. Undershaw has a wide appeal: Our students present to us with mild to moderate learning needs and therefore may have some very recent memories of poor experiences in their previous schools. Emma's background as a senior leader within the independent school sector has meant she is well-versed in brokering relationships between the key stakeholders, our many interdependences, local businesses, families, and staff, and all this while ensuring Undershaw remains relentlessly child-centric in its approach. Emma's energetic smile and boundless enthusiasm for Undershaw is inspiring.

Margaret Walsh was born Auckland, New Zealand and now lives in Melbourne, Australia. She is the author of *Sherlock Holmes and the Molly-Boy Murders*, *Sherlock Holmes and the Case of the Perplexed Politician*, *Sherlock Holmes and the Case of the London Dock Deaths*, *The Adventure of the Bloody Duck and Other Tales of Sherlock Holmes*, *Sherlock Holmes and the Curse of Neb-Heka-Ra*, and *Sherlock Holmes and the Hellfire Heirs*, all published by MX Publishing. She is currently working on her seventh book, *Sherlock Holmes and the Deathly Clairvoyant.* Margaret has been a devotee of Sherlock Holmes since childhood and has had several Holmesian related essays printed in anthologies, and is a member of the online society *Doyle's Rotary Coffin,* as well as being a member of *Sisters of Crime Australia.* She has an ongoing love affair with the city of London. When she's not working or planning trips to London. Margaret can be found frequenting the many and varied bookshops of Melbourne.

More than forty of **Vicki Weisfeld**'s short stories have appeared in leading mystery magazines and anthologies, most recently in the 2023 Bouchercon anthology (*Killin' Time in San Diego*), *Yellow Mama*, *Sherlock Holmes: A Year of Mystery 1884* and *1885*, and *Alfred Hitchcock Mystery Magazine.* They've won awards from the *Short Mystery Fiction Society* and *Public Safety Writers Association.* Her first mystery novel, *Architect of Courage*, was published June 2022 by Black Opal Books. She blogs regularly at *www.vweisfeld.com* and is a book reviewer for the UK website, *crimefictionlover.com*

Marcia Wilson is a freelance researcher and illustrator who likes to work in a style compatible for the color blind and visually impaired. She is Canon-centric, and her first MX offering, *You Buy Bones*, uses the point-of-view of Scotland Yard to show the unique talents of Dr. Watson. This continued with the publication of *Test of the Professionals: The Adventure of the Flying Blue Pidgeon* and *The Peaceful Night Poisonings.* She can be contacted at: *gravelgirty.deviantart.com*

424

Mike Adamson holds a Doctoral degree from Flinders University of South Australia. After early aspirations in art and writing, Mike secured qualifications in both marine biology and archaeology. Mike has been a university educator since 2006, has worked in the replication of convincing ancient fossils, is a passionate photographer, master-level hobbyist, and journalist for international magazines. Short fiction sales include to *Metastellar*, *Strand Magazine*, *Little Blue Marble*, *Abyss*, and *Apex*, *Daily Science Fiction*, *Compelling Science Fiction*, and *Nature Futures*. Mike has placed some two-hundred stories to date, totaling over a million words. Mike has completed his first Sherlock Holmes novel with Belanger Books, and will be appearing in translation in European magazines. You can catch up with his journey at his blog "The View From the Keyboard"
http://mike-adamson.blogspot.com

Donald I. Baxter has practiced medicine for over forty years. He resides in Erie Pennsylvania with his wife and their dog. His family and his friends are for the most part lawyers who have given him the ability to make stuff up just as they do.

Gustavo Bondoni is a novelist and short story writer with over four-hundred stories published in fifteen countries, in seven languages. He has published six science fiction novels including one trilogy, four monster books, a dark military fantasy and a thriller. His short fiction is collected in *Pale Reflection* (2020), *Off the Beaten Path* (2019), *Tenth Orbit and Other Faraway Places* (2010) and *Virtuoso and Other Stories* (2011). In 2019, Gustavo was awarded second place in The Jim Baen Memorial Contest, and in 2018 he received a Judges Commendation (and second place) in The James White Award. He was also a 2019 finalist in the Writers of the Future Contest. His website is at *www.gustavobondoni.com*

Craig Stephen Copland confesses that he discovered Sherlock Holmes when, sometime in the muddled early 1960's, he pinched his older brother's copy of the immortal stories and was forever afterward thoroughly hooked. He is very grateful to his high school English teachers in Toronto who inculcated in him a love of literature and writing, and even inspired him to be an English major at the University of Toronto. There he was blessed to sit at the feet of both Northrup Frye and Marshall McLuhan, and other great literary professors, who led him to believe that he was called to be a high school English teacher. It was his good fortune to come to his pecuniary senses, abandon that goal, and pursue a varied professional career that took him to over one-hundred countries and endless adventures. He considers himself to have been and to continue to be one of the luckiest men on God's good earth. A few years back he took a step in the direction of Sherlockian studies and joined *The Sherlock Holmes Society of Canada* – also known as *The Toronto Bootmakers*. In May of 2014, this esteemed group of scholars announced a contest for the writing of a new Sherlock Holmes mystery. Although he had never tried his hand at fiction before, Craig entered and was pleasantly surprised to be selected as one of the winners. Having enjoyed the experience, he decided to write more of the same, and he has now written new Sherlock Holmes mysteries related to and inspired by each of the sixty stories in the original Canon, along with a number of others.

Martin Daley was born in Carlisle, Cumbria in 1964. His thirty-year writing career has seen over twenty books and numerous short stories published. Inevitably, Holmes and

Watson remain his favourite literary characters, and they continue to inspire his own detective writing. In 2010, Martin created Inspector Cornelius Armstrong, who carries out his police work against the backdrop of Edwardian Carlisle. With the publication of the first *Inspector Armstrong Casebook* (published by MX Publishing), Martin became a member of the Crime Writers' Association. Most recently, he published *The Selected Cases of Sherlock Holmes.* He lives with his wife Wendy, in Kirkcudbrightshire, in Southwest.

Arthur Hall *also contributed to Part XLVIII*

Paul Hiscock is an author of crime, fantasy, horror, and science fiction tales. His short stories have appeared in a variety of anthologies, and include a seventeenth-century whodunnit, a science fiction western, a clockpunk fairytale, and numerous Sherlock Holmes pastiches. He lives with his family in Kent (England) and spends his days taking care of his two children. You can find out more about Paul's writing at: *www.detectivesanddragons.uk.*

Jeremy Holstein has had a lifelong infatuation with Sherlock Holmes. He is the current Artistic Director for the Post-Meridian Radio Players theater company out of Cambridge, Mass., which has produced Sherlock Holmes dramas on stage every summer for the last decade, most of which Jeremy both wrote and directed. He lives near Boston with his wife and daughter, who both tolerate his obsession with The Great Detective.

Christopher James was born in 1975 in Paisley, Scotland. Educated at Newcastle and UEA, he was a winner of the UK's National Poetry Competition in 2008. He has written three full length Sherlock Holmes novels, *The Adventure of the Ruby Elephant*, *The Jeweller of Florence*, and *The Adventure of the Beer Barons*, all published by MX.

Gordon Linzner is founder and former editor of *Space and Time Magazine*, and author of four published novels and dozens of short stories in *F&SF*, *Twilight Zone*, *Sherlock Holmes Mystery Magazine*, and numerous other magazines and anthologies. He is a full member of the *Horror Writers Association* and a lifetime member of *Science Fiction and Fantasy Writers Association.*

David MacGregor was born in Detroit and is a Resident Artist at The Purple Rose Theatre in Chelsea, Michigan, where he has had ten productions: *The Late Great Henry Boyle*, *Vino Veritas*, *Gravity*, *Consider the Oyster*, *Just Desserts*, *Vino Veritas* (revival), *Sherlock Holmes and the Adventure of the Elusive Ear*, *Sherlock Holmes and the Adventure of the Fallen Soufflé*, *Sherlock Holmes and the Adventure of the Ghost Machine*, and *The Antichrist Cometh*. His holiday comedy, *Scrooge Macbeth*, premiered at Theatre B in Fargo, North Dakota. His plays have been performed from New York to Tasmania, and his work has been published by Dramatic Publishing, Playscripts, Applause, Smith & Kraus, and Heuer Publishing. He adapted his play, *Vino Veritas*, into a feature film featuring Emmy-winner Carrie Preston (who stars in the CBS series *Elsbeth*). His short play, *For Old Time's Sake*, was adapted into a film starring Oscar-nominee John Savage. His screenplay *In the Land of Fire & Ice* is an Athena Award winner (best screenplay featuring a female protagonist), and is currently under option with Emmy-winner Shohreh Aghdashloo attached as the lead. He adapted all three of his Sherlock Holmes plays into novels for MX Publishing in London, and also wrote the two-volume nonfiction book, *Sherlock Holmes: The Hero with a Thousand Faces*. He has been hanged in effigy and has also had his writing publicly burned.

426

Michael Mallory is the author of the "Amelia Watson" and "Dave Beauchamp" mystery series, and the stand-alone novels *The Mural, Death Walks Skid Row*, and *The Ambulance*. His short stories – some 185 to date (including more than fifty in the Sherlockian realm) – have been published everywhere from *Alfred Hitchcock's Mystery Magazine* to *Fox Kids Magazine*. His story "What the Cat Dragged In," first published in *The Strand Magazine*, was selected for inclusion in *The Mysterious Bookshop Presents the Best Mystery Stories of 2023*. In the realm of nonfiction, Mike has authored eleven books on popular culture subjects, including the bestselling *Universal Studios Monsters: A Legacy of Horror*, and hundreds of articles for *Variety, The Los Angeles Times, Animation Magazine, Mystery Scene*, and scores of other publications. A former actor whose credits include the television shows *Mad Men*, V*egas*, *Mob City*, and *Angie Tribeca*, Mike lives in the Greater Los Angeles area.

David Marcum *also has stories in Parts XLVI and XLVIII*

Mark Mower is a long-standing member of the *Crime Writers' Association, The Sherlock Holmes Society of London*, and *The Solar Pons Society of London*. His pastiche collections include *Sherlock Holmes: The Baker Street Case-Files, Sherlock Holmes: The Baker Street Legacy, Sherlock Holmes: The Baker Street Epilogue*, and *Sherlock Holmes: The Baker Street Archive* (all with MX Publishing). His non-fiction works include the bestselling book *Zeppelin Over Suffolk: The Final Raid of the L48* (Pen & Sword Books). Alongside his writing, Mark maintains a sizeable collection of pastiches, and never tires of discovering new stories about Sherlock Holmes and Dr. Watson.

Will Murray *also has stories in Part XLVI*

Ember Pepper was born and raised in San Diego, CA. She has an M.F.A. degree in Creative Fiction Writing. She has been a fan of The Great Detective since she was a pre-teen and her greatest artistic enjoyment is challenging herself to write quality pastiches of Sherlock Holmes and his stalwart biographer and friend, John Watson.

Tracy J. Revels *also contributed stories to Parts XLVI and XLVIII*

Roger Riccard *also contributed to Parts XLVI and XLVIII*

Dan Rowley practiced law for over forty years in private practice and with a large international corporation. He is retired and lives in Erie, Pennsylvania, with his wife Judy, who puts her artistic eye to his transcription of Watson's manuscripts. He inherited his writing ability and creativity from his children, Jim and Katy, and his love of mysteries from his parents, Jim and Ruth.

Jane Rubino is the author of *A Jersey Shore* mystery series, featuring a Jane Austen-loving amateur sleuth and a Sherlock Holmes-quoting detective, *Knight Errant, Lady Vernon and Her Daughter*, (a novel-length adaptation of Jane Austen's novella *Lady Susan*, co-authored with her daughter Caitlen Rubino-Bradway, *What Would Austen Do?*, also co-authored with her daughter, a short story in the anthology *Jane Austen Made Me Do It, The Rucastles' Pawn, The Copper Beeches from Violet Turner's POV*, and, of course, there's the Sherlockian novel *Hidden Fires*. Jane lives on a barrier island at the New Jersey shore.

Brenda Seabrooke *also has a story in Part XLVI*

Peter Shumway is a retired computer professional residing in Pennsylvania with his wife, Patty. They have been married forty-one years and have two daughters and four grandchildren. In the early 1970's, Peter performed magic with Bill Baker's World of Magic, John Bundy's Magic Concert, and traded secrets with David Copperfield when they were teenagers. Peter read the original Sherlock Holmes stories while in college in 1979, and has enjoyed rereading them many times since. He published his pastiche *Sherlock Holmes and The Kiss of Death in* 2005 and *Gullible's Journey* in 2023. When he was offered the opportunity to write a short story for the MX Series, he picked up his pen one more time.

Shane Simmons is the author of the occult detective novels *necropolis* and *Epitaph,* and the crime collection *Raw and Other Stories.* An award-winning screenwriter and graphic novelist, his work has appeared in international film festivals, museums, and lectures about design and structure. He was born in Lachine, a suburb of Montreal best known for being massacred in 1689 and having a joke name. Visit Shane's homepage at *eyestrainproductions.com* for more information.

Elbert Smith is a small-town writer, filmmaker, and illustrator, studying for his M.F.A. in screenwriting at The University Of Georgia. He has won multiple awards for his film *Murder in Black Satin*, and worked for Troma Entertainment as a video editor. When he is not writing or making movies, he can be found creating art for a Doctor Who magazine called *The Celestial Toyroom.* He has done illustration work for *Thunderbirds Are Go!* and *Space 1999* fiftieth anniversary sketch card lines. He also believes that Jeremy Brett is the ultimate Sherlock.

Robert V. Stapleton was born and brought up in Leeds, Yorkshire, England, and studied at Durham University. After working in various parts of the country as an Anglican parish priest, he is now retired and lives with his wife in North Yorkshire. As a member of his local writing group, he now has time to develop his other life as a writer of adventure stories. He has published a number of short stories, and he is hoping to have a couple of completed novels published at some time in the future.

Award winning poet and author **Joseph W. Svec III** enjoys writing, poetry, and stories, and creating new adventures for Holmes and Watson that take them into the worlds of famous literary authors and scientists. His *Missing Authors* trilogy introduced Holmes to Lewis Carroll, Jules Verne, H.G. Wells, and Alfred Lord Tennyson, as well as many of their characters. His transitional story *Sherlock Holmes and the Mystery of the First Unicorn* involved several historical figures, besides a Unicorn or two. He has also written the rhymed and metered Sherlock Holmes Christmas adventure, *The Night Before Christmas in 221b,* sure to be a delight for Sherlock Holmes enthusiasts of all ages. Joseph won the Amador Arts Council 2021 Original Poetry Contest, with his Rhymed and metered story poem, "The Homecoming". Joseph has presented a literary paper on Sherlock Holmes/Alice in Wonderland crossover literature to the Lewis Carroll Society of North America, as well as given several presentations to the Amador County Holmes Hounds, Sherlockian Society. He is currently working on his first book in the Missing Scientist Trilogy, *Sherlock Holmes and the Adventure of the Demonstrative Dinosaur,* in which Sherlock meets Professor George Edward Challenger. Joseph has Masters Degrees in Systems Engineering and Human Organization Management, and has written numerous technical papers on Aerospace Testing. In addition to writing, Joseph enjoys creating miniature dioramas based on music, literature, and history from many different eras. His dioramas have been featured in magazine articles and many different blogs, including the

North American Jules Verne society newsletter. He currently has 57 dioramas set up in his display area, and has written a reference book on toy castles and knights from around the world. An avid tea enthusiast, his tea cabinet contains over 500 different varieties, and he delights in sharing afternoon tea with his childhood sweetheart and wonderful wife, who has inspired and coauthored several books with him.

A Sherlock Holmes fan since reading *The Hound of the Baskervilles* at about age twelve, **Tom Turley** has been writing pastiches since 2006. Most have appeared in previous volumes of *The MX Book of New Sherlock Holmes Stories*. All except the latest two have been collected in two books available from MX Publishing and Amazon. *Sherlock Holmes and the Crowned Heads of Europe* (2021) is a collection of four historical novellas that involve Holmes and Watson in the events leading up to World War I. The four stories are also available individually on Audible. As its title indicates, *Watson's Wives and Other Tales of Sherlock Holmes* (2023) focuses primarily on the Doctor's marriages. It likewise will soon be available on Audible. Currently, Tom is at work on a Sherlockian novel. A retired historian and archivist, he resides with his wife Paula in Montgomery, Alabama.

I.A. Watson's first professional publishing credit was with a Sherlock Holmes story. The tale in this book will be his 50th (counting his novel *Holmes and Houdini*, and one or two short stories in publishers' queues). He is constantly surprised at how many ways there are to tell Sherlock Holmes adventures, which he holds to be a sign of Sir Arthur Conan Doyle's genius in developing so flexible and resilient a format for such a compelling cast of characters. A full list of I.A. Watson's 100+ published works including twenty or so novels is available at:
http://www.chillwater.org.uk/writing/iawatsonhome.htm

The MX Book of New Sherlock Holmes Stories
Edited by David Marcum
(MX Publishing, 2015-   )

"This is the finest volume of Sherlockian fiction I have ever read, and I have read, literally, thousands." – Philip K. Jones

"Beyond Impressive . . . This is a splendid venture for a great cause!"
– Roger Johnson, Editor, *The Sherlock Holmes Journal,*
The Sherlock Holmes Society of London

Part I: 1881-1889; Part II: 1890-1895; Part III: 1896-1929
Part IV: 2016 Annual

Part V: Christmas Adventures

Part VI: 2017 Annual

Eliminate the Impossible
Part VII: (1880-1891); Part VIII: (1892-1905)

2018 Annual
Part IX: (1879-1895); Part X: (1896-1916)

Some Untold Cases
Part XI: (1880-1891); Part XII: (1894-1902)

2019 Annual
Part XIII: (1881-1890); Part XIV: (1891-1897); Part XV: (1898-1917)

Whatever Remains . . . Must be the Truth
Part XVI: (1881-1890); Part XVII: (1891-1898); Part XVIII: (1898-1925)

2020 Annual
Part XIX: (1882-1890); Part XX: (1891-1897); Part XXI: (1898-1923)·

Some More Untold Cases
Part XXII: (1877-1887); Part XXIII: (1888-1894); Part XXIV: (1895-1903)

2021 Annual
Part XXV: (1881-1888); Part XXVI: (1889-1897); Part XXVII: (1898-1928)

More Christmas Adventures
Part XXVIII: (1869-1888); Part XXIX: (1889-1896); Part XXX: (1897-1928)

2022 Annual
Part XXXI: (1875-1887); Part XXXII: (1888-1895); Part XXXIII: (1896-1919)

"However Improbable . . . ."
Part XXXIV: (1878-1888); Part XXXV: (1889-1896); Part XXXVI: (1897-1919)

2023 Annual
Parts XXXVII (1875-1889), XXXVIII (1889-1896), and *XXXIX (1897-1923)*

Further Untold Cases
Part XL: (1879-1886), Part XLI: (1887-1892) and *Part XLII: (1894-1922)*

2024 Annual
Parts XLIII (1874-1888), XLIV (1889-1897), and *XLV (1898-1917)*

Occupants of the Canonical Realm
Parts XLVI (1861-1889), XLVII (1890-1898), and *XLVIII (1899-1924)*

And in Preparation . . . The Final Volumes of
The MX Book of New Sherlock Holmes Stories: Parts XLIX and L

The MX Book of New Sherlock Holmes Stories
Edited by David Marcum
(MX Publishing, 2015-   )

<u>*Publishers Weekly* says:</u>

Part VI: *The traditional pastiche is alive and well . . . .*

Part VII: *Sherlockians eager for faithful-to-the-canon plots and characters will be delighted.*

Part VIII: *The imagination of the contributors in coming up with variations on the volume's theme is matched by their ingenious resolutions.*

Part IX: *The 18 stories . . . will satisfy fans of Conan Doyle's originals. Sherlockians will rejoice that more volumes are on the way.*

Part X: *. . . new Sherlock Holmes adventures of consistently high quality.*

Part XI: *. . . an essential volume for Sherlock Holmes fans.*

Part XII: *. . . continues to amaze with the number of high-quality pastiches.*

Part XIII: *. . . Amazingly, Marcum has found 22 superb pastiches . . . his is more catnip for fans of stories faithful to Conan Doyle's original*

Part XIV: *. . . this standout anthology of 21 short stories written in the spirit of Conan Doyle's originals.*

Part XV: *Stories pitting Sherlock Holmes against seemingly supernatural phenomena highlight Marcum's 15th anthology of superior short pastiches.*

Part XVI: *Marcum has once again done fans of Conan Doyle's originals a service.*

Part XVII: *This is yet another impressive array of new but traditional Holmes stories.*

Part XVIII: *Sherlockians will again be grateful to Marcum and MX for high-quality new Holmes tales.*

Part XIX: *Inventive plots and intriguing explorations of aspects of Dr. Watson's life and beliefs lift the 24 pastiches in Marcum's impressive 19th Sherlock Holmes anthology*

Part XX: *Marcum's reserve of high-quality new Holmes exploits seems endless.*

Part XXI: *This is another must-have for Sherlockians.*

Part XXII: *Marcum's superlative 22nd Sherlock Holmes pastiche anthology features 21 short stories that successfully emulate the spirit of Conan Doyle's originals while expanding on the canon's tantalizing references to mysteries Dr. Watson never got around to chronicling.*

Part XXIII: *Marcum's well of talented authors able to mimic the feel of The Canon seems bottomless.*

Part XXIV: *Marcum's expertise at selecting high-quality pastiches remains impressive.*

Part XXVIII: *All entries adhere to the spirit, language, and characterizations of Conan Doyle's originals, evincing the deep pool of talent Marcum has access to. Against the odds, this series remains strong, hundreds of stories in.*

Part XXXI: *. . . yet another stellar anthology of 21 short pastiches that effectively mimic the originals . . . Marcum's diligent searches for high-quality stories has again paid off for Sherlockians.*

Part XXXIV: *Mind-bending puzzles are the highlight of Marcum's fully satisfying 34th anthology, which again demonstrates that multiple authors are capable of giving Sherlock Holmes and Watson innovative mysteries to tackle while staying in character. Marcum's inventory of canonical pastiches shows no signs of being exhausted any time soon.*

The MX Book of New Sherlock Holmes Stories
Edited by David Marcum
(MX Publishing, 2015-   )

An Investees' Anthology
Edited by David Marcum
(MX Publishing, 2022)

Selected Contributions to
The MX Book of New Sherlock Holmes Stories
by Members of
The Baker Street Irregulars

*All royalties from this collection are being donated
for the benefit of the preservation of Undershaw,
a school for special needs students located at
one of the former homes of Sir Arthur Conan Doyle*

Stories, Forewords, and Poems in this volume
have previously appeared in Parts I – XXXVI of
The MX Book of New Sherlock Holmes Stories

Featuring Contributions by:

Mark Alberstat, Marino C. Alvarez, Peter Calamai, Catherine Cooke, Carla Coupe, David Stuart Davies, John Farrell, Lyndsay Faye, Sonia Fetherston, Jayantika Ganguly, Jeffrey Hatcher, Roger Johnson, Leslie S. Klinger, Ann Margaret Lewis, Bonnie MacBird, Stephen Mason, Julie McKuras Nicholas Meyer, Jacquelynn Morris, Otto Penzler, Christopher Redmond, Tracy J. Revels, Steven Rothman, Nancy Holder, Mark Levy (and Arlene Mantin Levy), Nicholas Utechin, and Sean M. Wright (and DeForeest B. Wright, III)

MX Publishing

MX Publishing is the world's largest specialist Sherlock Holmes publisher, with over six-hundred titles and over two-hundred authors creating the latest in Sherlock Holmes fiction and non-fiction

The catalogue includes several award winning books, and over four-hundred-and-fifty have been converted into audio.

MX Publishing also has one of the largest communities of Holmes fans on Facebook, with regular contributions from dozens of authors.

www.mxpublishing.com

@mxpublishing on Facebook, Twitter, and Instagram